Omnibus of
SCIENCE FICTION

Omnibus of
SCIENCE
FICTION

EDITED WITH AN INTRODUCTION BY

GROFF CONKLIN

WITH A NEW FOREWORD BY

R. SCOTT LATHAM

BONANZA BOOKS, NEW YORK

COPYRIGHT ACKNOWLEDGMENTS

Robert Abernathy, HERITAGE. Copyright, 1942, by Street and Smith Publications, Inc. Reprinted by permission of the author from *Astounding Science Fiction,* June, 1942.

Isaac Asimov, HOMO SOL. Copyright, 1940, by Street and Smith Publications, Inc. Reprinted by permission of Frederik Pohl from *Astounding Science Fiction,* September, 1940.

James Blish, THE BOX. Copyright, 1949, by Standard Magazines, Inc. Reprinted by permission of Frederik Pohl from *Thrilling Wonder Stories,* April, 1949.

Anthony Boucher, THE STAR DUMMY. Copyright, 1952, by Ziff-Davis Publishing Co. Reprinted by permission of Willis Kingsley Wing from *Fantastic,* Fall, 1952.

Ray Bradbury, KALEIDOSCOPE. Copyright, 1949, by Standard Magazines, Inc. Reprinted by permission of Harold Matson from *Thrilling Wonder Stories,* October, 1949.

Fredric Brown, THE WEAPON. Copyright, 1951, by Street and Smith Publications, Inc. Reprinted by permission of Harry Altshuler from *Astounding Science Fiction,* April, 1951.

Arthur C. Clarke, HISTORY LESSON. Copyright, 1949, by Standard Magazines, Inc. Reprinted by permission of Scott Meredith from *Startling Stories,* May, 1949.

Mark Clifton, THE CONQUEROR. Copyright, 1952, by Street and Smith Publications, Inc. Reprinted by permission of Forrest J. Ackerman from *Astounding Science Fiction,* August, 1952.

L. Sprague de Camp, HYPERPILOSITY. Copyright, 1938, by Street and Smith Publications, Inc. Reprinted by permission of the author from *Astounding Science Fiction,* April, 1938. Copyright, 1949, by L. Sprague de Camp and reprinted by permission of Shasta Publishers from "The Wheels of If, and Other Science Fiction."

Lester del Rey, INSTINCT. Copyright, 1952, by Street and Smith Publications, Inc. Reprinted by permission of Scott Meredith from *Astounding Science Fiction,* January, 1952.

A. J. Deutsch, A SUBWAY NAMED MOBIUS. Copyright, 1950, by Street and Smith Publications, Inc. Reprinted by permission of Street and Smith Publications, Inc., from *Astounding Science Fiction,* December, 1950.

Paul Ernst, "NOTHING HAPPENS ON THE MOON." Copyright, 1939, by Street and Smith Publications, Inc. Reprinted by permission of the author from *Astounding Science Fiction,* February, 1939.

H. B. Fyfe, MANNERS OF THE AGE. Copyright, 1952, by Galaxy Publishing Corporation. Reprinted by permission of the author from *Galaxy Science Fiction,* March, 1952.

v

Library of Congress Cataloging in Publication Data

Conklin, Groff, 1904-1968, ed.
  Omnibus of science fiction.

  Reprint of the ed. published by Crown Publishers, New York.
  1. Science fiction.   I. Title.
PZ1.C760940m 1980 [PN6120.95.S33] 823'.0876'08
ISBN 0-517-32097-5   80-15314

FOREWORD

To see a favorite book, long unavailable, restored to print is very much like greeting an old friend who has been away on a long journey. Many things have happened since you last met and yet the memories are as vivid as ever. This book is my own personal old friend, the one that introduced me to the world of science fiction, and I'd like to introduce it.

Groff Conklin's first three pioneering anthologies concentrated on the early days of science fiction, with a look at the changes which began to occur in the period around World War II. *The Omnibus of Science Fiction*, while recapitulating many of the themes and styles of the earlier collections, is markedly different, in that it contains a new element—the beginnings of the 50s science fiction boom. America in the postwar, post-Hiroshima years was fascinated by technology. So many breakthroughs had come about so quickly during the war that we began to see fast-paced, radical change as a fact of life. We eagerly anticipated, and sometimes feared, the world of tomorrow. We were intrigued by the seemingly limitless possibilities of technological progress and felt that the vistas opening before us were endless; we wanted to dream the dreams of the fabulous things to come. And science fiction gave shape and substance to the dreams.

Thus, in the late forties and early fifties, the field of science fiction expanded at an astounding rate. New magazines were born virtually every month, book publishing boomed (particularly the new paperback editions), fan clubs sprang up nationwide, conventions were organized. What had been dismissed by some as a minor form of juvenile escapist trivia became an industry, and, more significantly, a vital force in people's imaginations. We came to science fiction, not to escape what we were, but to explore what we might become. Some of the dreams were nightmarish, and some visions of utopia, but they all shared the qualities of wonder and excitement.

This collection—with its careful selection of early works which give balance and perspective to the newer innovations—conveys the sheer excitement of that time. The growth of the field liberated reader, writer, and publisher, and all things became possible. No concept was taboo, no style too experimental, no notion too perilous to explore. It was a heady, exhilarating time, and that is why I welcome back these tales. And if this excitement can be passed on to newer readers of science fiction, I hope that they, too, can share in the pure wonder of these dreams.

R. Scott Latham
New York, 1980

vii

INTRODUCTION

In the nearly seven years that have passed since the first of my four Crown collections, *The Best of Science Fiction*, appeared in April, 1946,* at least *fifty* other anthologies in the science fiction field have been published. This is an average of six collections a year, in a highly specialized branch of the short story—something of a record, I am sure.

Not all of these books merited publication. Not all have sold well, either —although it is interesting to note that, to my knowledge, none of them has yet been relegated to the remainder shelves, that last resting-place of unsuccessful books. But as a general thing these anthologies, plus the nearly two hundred novels and collections of an author's short stories that have been published under the identifying label of science fiction during the same period, are signs of healthy growth for the newest permanent addition to types of creative writing.

Let us admit it: fantasies based upon extrapolation of scientific or quasi-scientific ideas are definitely with us, at least for as long as our society is based upon a complex technology. There may soon be a falling-off in the high rate of publication that has characterized the past few years, if only because the amount of good new material is insufficient to maintain such an output of books. Even so, the genre will continue to grow sturdily with the growth of interest in, and understanding of, scientific and technological matters.

The more difficult question of whether the quality of science fiction has improved during this frantic period of growth can be answered only equivocally. Truly great science fiction tales are little more frequent today than they were a decade or more ago. Greatness in anything is very rare, and science fiction is no exception to the rule. But sterling-quality science fiction stories, the kind that constitute the major attraction for the mature reader, have increased very greatly in number, as the market has expanded and the rewards for the writers have increased.

Ten years ago the mature-appeal science fiction story had only one major outlet—Street and Smith's *Astounding Science Fiction,* under the creative editorship of John W. Campbell, Jr. Today *Astounding* has very severe competition from three sources, the oldest of which was started as recently as the fall of 1949. This is *The Magazine of Fantasy and Science Fiction*, edited by Anthony Boucher and J. Francis McComas. For some time the Boucher-McComas magazine was a bi-monthly concentrating primarily on fantasy and the supernatural; but by the middle of 1952 it had

* The second was *The Treasury of Science Fiction* (April, 1948); the third, *The Big Book of Science Fiction* (September, 1950).

become a monthly and was more evenly divided between excellent science fiction and equally first-rate fantastic stories.

Second in the group of competitors for *Astounding's* quality record, in point of time, was *Galaxy Science Fiction*, which started off on a monthly schedule in October, 1950. From the start, H. L. Gold, the editor, set out to take over the lead in the science fiction field, and in the opinion of many readers he has achieved his goal. Emphasizing the sociological and psychological aspects of good science fantasy, and occasionally opening his pages to first-rate satirical stories, Gold has done much to help upgrade science fiction from the gadget-crazy space opera "pulps" to the mature and quasi-literary tales of the present. It is a pointed commentary that there are in this book eighteen stories from sixteen years of *Astounding* (1936-1952), and seven from less than two years of *Galaxy*.

Third and newest of *Astounding's* competitors is Ziff-Davis' *Fantastic*, edited by Howard Browne. Only three issues of this magazine had appeared as this book went to press, but already it has made a remarkable impression. A bi-monthly at present, it is far and away the most handsomely printed of the science fiction magazines. It is also the most sensational and perhaps the most uneven in its contents. Browne, who also edits one of the most financially successful (and one of the most juvenile) science fiction pulps, *Amazing Stories,* has yet to prove that his new magazine can make an enduring place for itself in the field, but he has made a first-rate, though somewhat jumpy, start.

Aside from these four, the current magazine output in the field of science fiction is not particularly healthy. It has been estimated that there were on the newsstands in the fall of 1952 over twenty-four monthlies, bi-monthlies, quarterlies and annuals, *not* including science fiction comic books. Most of these were shaky newcomers, with life expectancies of no more than a handful of issues. A few were well-established operations, catering to various levels of education, intelligence and prejudice, but none could claim the designation of a quality magazine.

Sometimes, it is true, even the poorest fly-by-night pulp will publish a first-rate story, for one of the astonishing things about the typical science fiction author is his loyalty to his friends, even when they become editors of *terrible* magazines! Both author and editor probably were nurtured in the frenetic atmosphere of some science fiction fan club, and such ties are hard to break. In addition, of course, a great many top-grade science fiction writers are completely unable to operate themselves efficiently from the business point of view; they will sometimes turn over their best work to the first comer, avid for a sale and constantly remembering those dreadful years when there were so very few outlets for science fiction of any kind.

This helplessness on the part of the writer, this inability to deal with the economic world with any degree of instinct for survival, has brought about another special, though minor, phenomenon in the publishing field —the agent specializing in science fiction and fantasy. As recently as five years ago only one or at most two literary agents could be said to have made science fiction a specialty; and they were not doing too well. Today there are five or six, some of them with astonishingly long lists of clients. Of the forty-four authors represented in this volume, only nine or ten are still operating without agents, and some of them are beginning to wonder whether or not they are being smart.

Obviously, then, from every point of view the science fiction field has been expanding with almost unbelievable rapidity during the past few years. One of the most exciting aspects of this almost explosive growth in what was only recently an almost non-existent field for the writer is the way in which it has brought forth a host of new talent, young people who are swiftly exploring new horizons in science fiction ideas, and forcing the oldsters to look to their laurels. Of the science fiction writers represented in this book, only thirteen had published anything in the science fiction magazines prior to 1938, according to Donald B. Day's invaluable *Index to Science Fiction Magazines, 1926-1950.* Twenty-one were first published between 1938 and 1950, and eight in 1950 and 1951.

This not only means that the new writers are taking over, as they should. It also means that the thin vein of early high-quality science fiction, that which appeared before the advent of John Campbell to the editorship of *Astounding* in the latter part of 1937, is just about exhausted. In my first Crown anthology, twenty-nine out of the thirty-six authors represented appeared in the science fiction magazines before 1938, twenty-two of them before 1933. Thus the present book represents a complete reversal of trend when compared with my first.

It would be unwise to say that there are not still some excellent stories from the twenties and thirties awaiting future anthologists. There are, a few—but most are too long for modern anthologies. Much of the best early science fiction is found in novelettes or serials whose length afforded more scope to the authors for the establishment of such completely unfamiliar backgrounds and subject matters as are used in this imaginative branch of writing. At any rate, the pioneers in science fiction were rarely very deft in handling the short story.

Today, however, the short story form is being excellently practiced by the newer crop of writers. Their growing success with tales running from 2,000 to 6,000 words is indicated by the difference in the contents of the present book and of my *Best of Science Fiction.* The *Omnibus,* which you now are reading, has forty-three stories in 560-odd pages—250 *fewer* pages than were needed for the forty stories and 814 pages of *The Best.* And this without trickery or special attempt to select short items, too, although one or two extremely long novelettes were reluctantly omitted, simply because they were nearer novel-length than short-story, and therefore seemed unsuited for anthologizing.*

Whether these particular stories are *better* than those published seven years ago is hard to say. The editor believes that they are, but then he is somewhat prejudiced. And prejudice is an intellectual weakness that has

* Even so, it should be noted that the longest novelette ever to appear in a Conklin anthology is published in this volume—A. E. van Vogt's "Recruiting Station," which runs to about 35,000 words.

dogged the footsteps of science fiction for years, though a somewhat different type of prejudice than that claimed by the editor.

For example, the prejudiced uninitiated assume that science fiction is exemplified by flying saucer manias, low-grade television and radio space opera, and an occasional slick magazine fantasy with a "scientific" background. As far as this individual goes, he is right—but he does not go far enough. There *is* quality science fiction, as this book proves.

But let me be the first to admit that even top-grade science fiction is primarily entertainment. Science fiction is not really an Educational Force. I am not even sure that it is particularly Elevating, although I think I could prove that it is more intellectually exciting and more elastically imaginative than most of the historical, problem and "character" novels that constitute the best-seller literature of the day.

What we do claim, we confirmed science fiction lovers, is that this type of fiction, when well done, is particularly attractive because it is so gay with the Idea. Profundity of character analysis, depth of observation and sharpness of social insight are not *necessarily* the major qualities for which science fiction is famous; I for one object to the analyses of those who try to apply to science fiction the same standards they would apply to James Joyce or Thomas Mann or William Faulkner. But if one reads it for sheer intellectual-imaginative fun, for often very sharp satiric comment, for a kind of mind-stretching flight above the humdrum, the crass, the workaday —in other words, for escape from the dullness and boredom of life—science fiction is just about what the doctor ordered.

As for the actual stories you are about to read in this book, they are put before you without individual comment or critique, and even without special notes here in the Introduction. Some are light and for fun; others are ponderous with meaning; still others are out-and-out adventures, seasoned with a bit of sharp comment. All are, in the editor's opinion, Good Reading. They stand on their own two feet; they do not need the inflation of an editor's puff beforehand.

About the book's arrangement, I have only one remark to make. Sometimes you may cavil at the placing of certain tales in certain sections. It has not always been easy to decide what is the dominant characteristic, subjectwise, of a given story. One so complex as Ross Rocklynne's "Backfire" (merely to use an example) could have safely been included in any one of three sections—time travel, tales of tomorrow, or dangerous inventions. I chose the latter in this instance mainly because of the oddly brilliant way in which the author has pointed out the relativity of "dangerous" inventions: in this story immortality, an explosively dangerous invention in itself, is made nearly impossible by another, much less tangible, much more dangerous invention, in a world of the not-too-distant future.

Similar choices have had to be made in a number of instances. You may be sure that the editor always had a good reason for placing the stories where they are, even though it may not be obvious upon first glance. And in any event, it is the stories—not their arrangement—that count in this book. Skip the section headings, if you wish, and you will avoid all argument and just have a fine time reading good tales!

An exhaustive effort has been made to locate all persons having any rights or interests in the stories appearing in this book, and to clear reprint permissions with them. If any required acknowledgments have been omitted, or any rights overlooked, it is by inadvertence, and forgiveness is requested therefor.

As suggested earlier, the last stages of the preparation of this book were made measurably easier by Donald B. Day's *Index to Science Fiction Magazines, 1926-1950.* From now on, the student of science fiction will be able to turn to one of the most useful research tools ever forged for the benefit of a particular literary form. Sincerest thanks to Mr. Day for having devoted so many arduous months to the compilation of this essential reference work.

In addition, I would like to express my thanks for special favors and good advice received from the following friends and business associates: Forrest J. Ackerman, Harry Altshuler, Jerome Bixby, Anthony Boucher Howard Browne, Matthew Cammen, Don Congdon, Mildred Constantine, L. Sprague de Camp, Grace Delaney, August Derleth, Oscar J. Friend, Horace L. Gold, Robert Guinn, Damon Knight, Bertha Krantz, Arthur P. Lawler, Willy (and Olga) Ley, Scott Meredith, Samuel Mines, Frederik Pohl, Fletcher Pratt, Dero Saunders, Robert Simon, Theodore Sturgeon— And Lucy.

GROFF CONKLIN

New York, New York
October, 1952

CONTENTS

PART I

Wonders of Earth and of Man

John Leimert

JOHN THOMAS'S CUBE

John Thomas Thompson, aged eight years and nine months, lived in a house with an old, warped, but extremely large and fruitful apple tree in the back yard. Beneath this tree, leaning with his back against the trunk, or in it, wedged between forking limbs, John Thomas often took refuge. Here he came to escape the turmoil of his expanding world and to dream the dreams and think the thoughts important to a boy aged eight years and nine months.

John Thomas went out to visit this tree at seven-thirty o'clock of the morning of September 30. He didn't even wait for his breakfast. He just tumbled out of bed, threw his clothes on, and dashed out. He wasn't much more than past the door when he set up a clamor for his mother to come and see what he had found. His mother, however, was busy making toast, and frying bacon, and pouring John's father's coffee. She called to him to hurry back into the house and eat his breakfast, and to be sure his hands and face were clean, or else he would be late for school.

John Thomas ordinarily was an obedient boy, but on this morning he ignored his mother's summons. "But, Mother," he said, "it's the queerest thing I've found. A little block of metal so heavy I can't lift it. Come and see. Please, Mother."

"You might just as well," John Thomas's father said.

When his mother came to where John Thomas was standing under the apple tree, she at first could see nothing. But the boy pointed to a bare spot and there on the ground was a perfect cube about one inch each way.

"It appears to be made of highly polished steel," Mrs. Thompson said, and stooped to pick it up. To her surprise, she could not lift it. "That's the strangest thing I ever saw," she said as her fingers slipped on the gleaming surfaces.

By this time Mr. Thompson had come out to see what was going on, and he, too, tried to lift the cube, without success. "John Thomas," he said, "did you bury a steel rod in the ground just to see what would happen?"

"No, Father," the boy said, "I didn't. Honest. I found it that way."

"Why don't you get a shovel and see whether it's buried?" Mrs. Thompson asked reasonably.

"I believe I will," Mr. Thompson said. He got a garden spade from the garage and shoved it into the ground at an angle under the metal cube. The spade cut easily into the soft earth without striking an obstruction.

"You see," Mrs. Thompson said, "it isn't buried."

Mr. Thompson grasped the spade firmly and tried to lift the dirt with the cube resting on top. He couldn't do it. He then shifted both hands to the end of the spade handle and tried to pry with it. The handle bent slightly with his effort, but the metal cube remained immovable.

Mr. Thompson now pulled the spade out of the ground, bringing a quantity of loose dirt from beneath the cube as he did so. John Thomas squatted to inspect the cube more narrowly. "Look, Father," he said. "The block isn't even touching the ground."

"That," Mr. Thompson said, "is impossible." Nevertheless, he stooped to look, and after looking returned to his spade. He began to dig a hole around the cube, and before long he was able to take a spadeful from directly beneath it. The weight of the small cube had been astonishing enough, but what now occurred dumfounded them.

When the supporting column of earth was removed, the cube, contrary to all the laws with which the Thompsons were familiar, remained suspended a good two inches in the air. As they stared at the perverse, shiny object, a few grains of dirt fell from its under surface, as though to demonstrate that for dirt, at least, the law of gravitational attraction still held firm.

"Perhaps the hole isn't deep enough to make it fall," Mrs. Thompson said, and her husband, anxious for an explanation, excavated another six inches of dirt from beneath the cube. Nothing happened.

Mr. Thompson now thought of another force. "Stand back," he said to his wife and son. "I'll fix this thing's clock for it." He raised the spade above his head, took careful aim, and then swung down at the cube with all his strength. He was rewarded with a terrific clang. The spade bounced into the air again, almost wrenching itself out of his hands, but the cube continued serenely to occupy the precise sections of time and space as before.

Five minutes later, when the city editor of the largest daily heard an excited account of these events from Mr. Thompson, he was understandably skeptical. Nevertheless, he sent a reporter out to have a look. The reporter, who was a cynical and degraded person, cynical without conviction and degraded without villainy, because his station in life required it of him, also was skeptical. He stopped along the way for two or three quick ones and when he finally arrived, looking bored and smelling of strong liquor, he found not only the Thompsons but most of their near neighbors impatiently awaiting him.

The hole had been enlarged by succeeding workers, who had the same idea as John Thomas's father, to a diameter of four feet and a depth of two. The reporter surveyed the hole, the block of metal suspended above it, and a branch of the apple tree directly above the cube. Then he said knowingly, "Which is the kid who found it?"

"I am," John Thomas said.

"Quite a magician, ain't you?" the reporter said, and taking off his hat, he swung it vigorously above the cube. The hat met nothing more resistant than air, and therewith the reporter became the first of a series of professional gentlemen who came to scoff and stayed to wonder.

The news spread rapidly and the mayor was among the earliest of the dignitaries to arrive. He was followed by a committee of inquiry from the university, consisting of its president, the head of the physics department, the head of the chemistry department, an associate professor who was an expert metallurgist, the professor of astronomy, and their respective assistants bearing scientific instruments of all kinds.

"Here, gentlemen," the mayor greeted them, "is an incredible situation. This block of metal arrived in the Thompsons' yard, no one knows precisely when nor from where. There it remains, suspended in mid-air. Where did it come from? Why doesn't it fall? Will there be more like it? When will it go?"

"One question at a time, if you please, Mr. Mayor," the president of the university said. "Let us first have the facts so far known, and then proceed with an orderly inquiry. Mr. Thompson, would you mind telling us whatever you know about this cube?"

John Thomas's father obliged with a recital of the events of the morning, suppressing, however, the episode of hitting the cube with the spade. He did not want these people to know that he could lose his temper at an inanimate object.

When Mr. Thompson had finished, the president of the university went on. "I have formed a hypothesis that I am confident will explain all the puzzling questions that here confront us. There was a shower of meteors last night, a fact that my astronomical colleague will confirm, and this object arrived in the place it now is, in the form it now has, from the limitless distances of outer space.

"Why does it neither fall nor fly away again? We all know that there are two opposite but unequal forces that act upon every body at the earth's surface. One of these is the centrifugal force that results from the spinning of the earth upon its axis, a force that tends to hurl objects away. The other and stronger force is that of gravity, tending to pull objects towards the earth's center.

"This particular object, moving freely at tremendous velocity through space, entered into the gravitational field of the earth and was pulled from its course. As it hurtled through the atmosphere that envelops us, it became increasingly hot from friction, with the result that its molecular activity was distorted in such a way as to set up within the structure of the cube itself a force that neutralizes the force of gravity.

"The result we all see. The cube is at rest in a perfect state of equilibrium. Centrifugal force plus the gravity-resistant force within the material itself exactly equals the force of gravity. In a moment I shall prove my contention by lifting upward against the cube, thus giving it an impetus that will destroy its perfect balance and send it flying back into the void from whence it came. Before I do so, does anyone question the accuracy of my hypothesis?"

The various scientists present remained silent, but John Thomas said, "I don't think it will fly away."

"Well, well," the president of the university said. "And why not, my little man?"

"Because my father hit it with a spade and it didn't budge."

The president reversed his field with a mental agility that no doubt had contributed to his reputation as an administrator. "Exactly," he said. "What this boy has said exactly proves the point I was trying to make. When confronted with the unknown, it is idle to speculate, however rationally, without having first erected a sound foundation of fact. I shall now retire in favor of my colleagues of the physics and chemistry departments. When they have examined this object from every scientific aspect, we shall consult together and, in the light of known mathematical formulae, arrive at the correct description."

The chemists and physicists now came forward with acids and bases, with agents and reagents, with spectroscopes and microscopes, with cyclotrons and atom smashers, with electric furnaces and vacuum machines— in fact with every known instrument by means of which man projects his senses into the infinite. The results were disappointing.

Viewed under the most powerful microscope, the surface of the cube looked no different than when viewed with the naked eye. No slightest fissure was revealed, no clue obtained as to the structure of the block. After finishing this part of the examination, the metallurgist said, "All I can say is that the surface is absolutely smooth, so that no part of it reflects more or less light than any other part. It is amazing."

The use of various chemicals proved equally ineffective. The block was impervious to every test and shed the most vitriolic concoctions like water off a duck's back. When it was exposed to intense heat, it not only remained cool, but it refused to expand or contract. No matter what they did to it, its dimensions remained constant.

It proved to be a nonconductor of electricity and had neither a positive nor a negative pole; yet when someone touched the base of an electric light bulb to it, the bulb lit. When this phenomenon occurred, the scientists retired to a corner of the yard for consultation.

Their places were taken by a delegation from the principal churches of the town headed by the president of the local theological seminary. "Mr. Mayor," this gentleman said, "we believe that further scientific inquiry into the nature of this object will prove fruitless. It belongs not to man but to God. What we witness is a veritable and unquestioned miracle.

"No material description of this block is possible, since it is not material, but spiritual. Science, in its search for a purely mechanistic explanation of reality, sooner or later comes up against an irreducible minimum which remains as unfathomable and mysterious as the larger conglomerate it was intended to explain.

"What we now have before us is a corporeal representation of this irreducible minimum. God in His wisdom has chosen to send us a reminder made manifest that, though men can tinker with the building blocks of nature, they cannot explain them."

At this stage of the proceedings a Mr. Heartly, chief engineer for a firm of tool and die makers in the town, stepped forward and asked to be heard. "I am neither a pure scientist," he said, "nor am I trained in theology and metaphysics, and therefore I am unqualified to make any statements concerning the nature of this block. But I am a toolmaker, and if I cannot account for the unusual behavior of this cube of metal, at least I can name it.

"In our business we use similar cubes machined with nearly perfect precision so that each face forms exactly a 90-degree angle with every adjacent face, and so smooth that when two blocks are placed together, the pressure of the surrounding atmosphere holds them firmly in place. Gentlemen, this mysterious object is a Johanssen Block, and with your permission I will now prove it."

With these words Mr. Heartly took a second block of metal from his pocket exactly like the suspended cube in every respect except that it was larger, and placed two faces of the cubes together. He then stepped back for all to see that they firmly adhered—so firmly that he was forced to strike his own cube a sharp blow to release it. "Only Johanssen Blocks," he said, "are machined perfectly enough to hold together in this fashion."

It would be pleasant to report that Mr. Heartly's solution proved satisfactory to all concerned. The scientists, however, while they thanked Mr. Heartly for identifying the object and demonstrating some of its properties, felt that to name a thing is not necessarily to have it. They advanced the proposition that no Johanssen Block could be expected to remain suspended in mid-air, equally resisting all forces exerted upon it, and to this Mr. Heartly agreed.

They stated that since the metal cube had been shown in certain respects to possess perfectly natural qualities and quantities, it must be assumed that its apparently unnatural qualities were capable of a natural and materialistic explanation. All that was needed was a patient application of the scientific method until the truth was made known.

To this the churchmen dissented. They did not deny that the block was a Johanssen Block if Mr. Heartly said it was, nor that it possessed some of the attributes of a Johanssen Block. But it did not possess all of those attributes, and the Divine purpose was to make the basic contradiction more clear. The shiny cube was sent to demonstrate that the fundamental mystery can never be discovered with man-made measuring sticks, not even that incorporeal measuring stick, the higher mathematics.

By now it was past noon and John Thomas suddenly realized that he was hungry. Not only that, but most of the discussions he had been hearing were totally without meaning for him. He recognized a word here and there, but that was all. It is true that the general feeling of excitement and wonder had communicated itself to him and he had enjoyed being the center, directly and indirectly, of so much attention. But at last he was bored and wanted his lunch.

His mother took him into the house and made him a peanut butter and jelly sandwich and gave him a glass of milk. While he was eating, he said to her, "Mother, do you like having that funny block in our back yard and all those queer people?"

"No," she said, "I don't. I'll never get any work done, and all that talk makes my head swim. I don't know who's right and who's wrong, but I do know that your father will want to stay around to superintend things, and the people he works for won't like that. I wish that block would take itself off to whatever place it came from."

"So do I," John Thomas said. "I'm tired of it."

At that precise moment there was a shout from the yard. "It's gone. The block has gone."

So it had. The mayor noted this fact with relief, since he believed that once the object that had caused so much discord and disquiet no longer existed, the problems it had raised were no longer of any importance. He stated this point of view and found that the majority of those present agreed with him, which, of course, is why he had been elected mayor.

The crowd dispersed at his direction, peaceably, except for the scientists and the churchmen, who could be seen contending for their respective positions as they walked off down the street.

As for John Thomas, he heard no more of the affair until that night at supper, but what he didn't know was that his father and mother had been holding a conference about him. His father approached the problem obliquely, as is the custom with parents.

"John Thomas," he said, "your mother tells me that the moment you said you were tired of the block, it disappeared. Is that right?"

"What block, Father?" John Thomas said.

"You know very well what block. The block in our back yard that caused all the trouble and excitement this morning."

Actually, being only eight years old, John Thomas had forgotten about the block. "Oh," he said, "that block."

"Yes, that block," his father said. "I know you had something to do with its being there. You were the first to see it, and when you said you were tired of it, it was gone. Did you have some reason why you didn't want to go to school today? Did you play during study hour yesterday and fail to prepare your lessons?"

When confronted with this partly right guess, John Thomas supposed that everything was known and that the best thing was to confess his crime in detail.

"It wasn't my fault," he said. "Billy Dixon kept whispering to me and writing notes and I couldn't get my work done. When I woke up this morning, I thought wouldn't it be swell if I didn't have to go to school. And then I thought that if there was a shiny little cube in the back yard that nobody could lift or move, maybe everyone would get so interested that I wouldn't have to go. Then I got to thinking there was such a cube, and when I went out to see, it was there."

The next morning John Thomas's father and mother took him to Dr. Emanuel Klein, the famous psychiatrist with offices in the Rookery Building. Like nearly everyone else in town, Dr. Klein was familiar with the facts in the case, and indeed had spent the previous evening discussing it with members of the committee of inquiry from the university. However, he was devoted to his profession and conscientious in the practice of it, and therefore first listened to a detailed account of the events as described by the Thompsons, and then proceeded with a careful examination of the boy.

John Thomas spent nearly an hour having his reflexes tested, starting at sudden noises, arranging blocks, sorting colors, identifying qualities of tone, and finding his way through labyrinths with pencil on paper. He then answered questions as politely and accurately as he could about the food he ate, how he liked his school, what his favorite games were, and the content of any dreams he could remember. When the examination at last was finished, Dr. Klein with great solemnity pronounced the opinion he had formed the night before.

In every respect save one, he said, John Thomas was perfectly normal for a boy of his age. He was above average in intelligence, had an excellent emotional balance, and was on the whole happy and content with his life. For this his parents were to be congratulated.

Nevertheless, he did have an unusually vivid imagination and was subject to hallucinations, auditory, visual, tactual. Further, through the operation of a kind of mass hypnosis, he had the rare faculty of making the creation of his imagination as real to others as to himself. Hallucinations, however, are likely to become antisocial, as witness the perverse characteristics of John Thomas's cube, and dangerous, therefore, to the subject and his family. For this reason, Dr. Klein recommended a series of treatments designed to teach John Thomas to distinguish between the fabrications of his subconscious mind and the hearty, solid world outside of him.

Mr. and Mrs. Thompson, relieved that it was no worse, agreed to this program. They took the boy home confident that he soon would be able to tell the false from the true, the imagined from the real, as easily as the next one. As for John Thomas, he determined never again to admit adults to his own special world. The fuss they stirred up, he decided, wasn't worth it.

HYPERPILOSITY

I FIRST KNEW J. Román Oliveira when I was a mere student at the Medical Center and he was a professor of virology. The J in his name stands for Haysoos, spelled J-e-s-u-s, which is a perfectly good Mexican name. But he'd been so much kidded about it in the States that he preferred to go by Román.

You remember that the Great Change—which is what this story has to do with—started in the winter of 1971, with that awful flu epidemic. Oliveira came down with it. I went around to see him to get an assignment, and found him perched on a pile of pillows and wearing the awfullest pink and green pajamas. His wife was reading to him in Spanish.

"Leesten, Pat," he said when I came in, "I know you're a worthy student, but I weesh you and the whole damn virology class were roasting on the hottest greedle in Hell. Tell me what you want, and then go away and let me die in peace."

I got my information, and was just going, when his doctor came in—old Fogarty, who used to lecture on sinuses. He'd given up G. P. long before, but he was so scared of losing a good virologist that he was handling Oliveira's case himself.

"Stick around, sonny," he said to me when I started to follow Mrs. Oliveira out, "and learn a little practical medicine. I've always thought it a mistake that we haven't a class to train doctors in bedside manners. Now observe how I do it. I smile at Oliveira here, but I don't act so damned cheerful that he'd find death a welcome relief from my company. That's a mistake some young doctors make. Notice that I walk up briskly, and not as if I were afraid my patient was liable to fall in pieces at the slightest jar—" and so on.

The fun came when he put the end of his stethoscope on Oliveira's chest.

"Can't hear a damn thing," he snorted, "or rather, you've got so much hair that all I can hear is the ends of it scraping on the diaphragm. May have to shave it. But say, isn't that rather unusual for a Mexican?"

"You're jolly well right she ees," retorted the sufferer. "Like most natives of my beautiful Mehheeco, I am of mostly Eendian descent, and Eendians are of Mongoloid race, and so have little body hair. It's all come out in the last week."

"That's funny—" Fogarty said.

I spoke up: "Say, Dr. Fogarty, it's more than that. I had my flu a month ago, and the same thing's been happening to me. I've always felt

The original opening of this story has been eliminated, with the permission of the author, since it seemed to weaken its impact somewhat. G. C.

like a sissy because of not having any hair on my torso to speak of. Now I've got a crop that's almost long enough to braid. I didn't think anything especial about it—"

I don't remember what was said next, because we all talked at once. But when we got calmed down there didn't seem to be anything we could do without some systematic investigation, and I promised Fogarty to come around to his place so he could look me over.

I did, the next day, but he didn't find anything except a lot of hair. He took samples of everything he could think of, of course. I'd given up wearing underwear because it itched, and anyway the hair was warm enough to make it unnecessary, even in a New York January.

The next thing I heard was a week later, when Oliveira returned to his classes, and told me that Fogarty had caught the flu. Oliveira had been making observations on the old boy's thorax, and found that he, too, had begun to grow body hair at an unprecedented rate.

Then my girl friend—not the present missus; I hadn't met her yet—overcame her embarrassment enough to ask me whether I could explain how it was that *she* was getting hairy. I could see that the poor girl was pretty badly cut up about it, because obviously her chances of catching a good man would be reduced by her growing a pelt like a bear or a gorilla. I wasn't able to enlighten her, but told her that, if it was any comfort, a lot of other people were suffering from the same thing.

Then we heard that Fogarty had died. He was a good egg and we were sorry, but he'd led a pretty full life, and you couldn't say that he was cut off in his prime.

Oliveira called me to his office. "Pat," he said, "you were looking for a chob last fall, ees it not? Well, I need an asseestant. We're going to find out about this hair beezness. Are you on?" I was.

We started by examining all the clinical cases. Everybody who had, or had had, the flu was growing hair. And it was a severe winter, and it looked as though everybody were going to have the flu sooner or later.

Just about that time I had a bright idea. I looked up all the cosmetic companies that made depilatories, and soaked what little money I had into their stock. I was sorry later, but I'll come to that.

Roman Oliveira was a glutton for work, and with the hours he made me keep I began to have uneasy visions of flunking out. But the fact that my girl friend had become so self-conscious about her hair that she wouldn't go out any more saved me some time.

We worked and worked over our guinea-pigs and rats, but didn't get anywhere. Oliveira got a bunch of hairless Chihuahua dogs and tried assorted gunks on them, but nothing happened. He even got a pair of East African sand rats—*Heterocephalus*—hideous-looking hairless things —but that was a blank, too.

Then the business got into the papers. I noticed a little article in the New York *Times*, on an inside page. A week later there was a full-column story on page 1 of the second part. Then it was on the front page. It was mostly "Dr. So-and-so says he thinks this nation-wide attack of hyper-pilosity" (swell word, huh? Wish I could remember the name of the doc who invented it) "is due to this, that, or the other thing."

Our usual February dance had to be called off because almost none of the students could get their girls to go. Attendance at the movie houses had fallen off pretty badly for much the same reason. It was a cinch to get a good seat, even if you arrived around 8:00 P. M. I noticed one funny little item in the paper, to the effect that the filming of "Tarzan and the Octopus-Men" had been called off because the actors were supposed to go running around in G-strings. The company had found that they had to clip and shave the whole cast all over every few days if they didn't want the actors and the gorillas confused.

It was fun to ride on a bus about then and watch the people, who were pretty well bundled up. Most of them scratched, and those who were too well-bred to scratch just squirmed and looked unhappy.

Next I read that application for marriage licenses had fallen off so that three clerks were able to handle the entire business for Greater New York, including Yonkers, which had just been incorporated into the Bronx.

I was gratified to see that my cosmetic stocks were going up nicely. I tried to get my roommate, Bert Kafket, to get in on them too. But he just smiled mysteriously, and said he had other plans.

Bert was a kind of professional pessimist. "Pat," he said, "maybe you and Oliveira will lick this business, and maybe not. I'm betting that you won't. If I win, the stocks that I've bought will be doing famously long after your depilatories are forgotten."

As you know, people were pretty excited about the plague. But when the weather began to get warm, the fun really started. First the four big underwear companies ceased operations, one after another. Two of them were placed in receivership, another liquidated completely, and the fourth was able to pull through by switching to the manufacturing of table-cloths and American flags. The bottom dropped completely out of the cotton market, as this alleged "hair-growing flu" had spread all over the world by now. Congress had been planning to go home early, and was, as usual, being urged to do so by the conservative newspapers. But now Washington was jammed with cotton-planters demanding that the Government Do Something, and they didn't dare. The Government was willing enough to Do Something, but unfortunately didn't have the foggiest idea of how to go about it.

All this time Oliveira, more or less assisted by me, was working night and day on the problem, but we didn't seem to have any better luck than the Government.

You couldn't hear anything on the radio in the building where I lived, because of the interference from the big, powerful electric clippers that everybody had installed and kept going all the time.

It's an ill wind, as the prophet saith, and Bert Kafket got some good out of it. His girl, whom he had been pursuing for some years, had been making a good salary as a model at Josephine Lyon's exclusive dress establishment on Fifth Avenue, and she had been leading Bert a dance. But now all of a sudden the Lyon place folded up, as nobody seemed to be buying any clothes, and the girl was only too glad to take Bert as her lawful wedded husband. Not much hair was grown on the women's faces, fortunately for them or God knows what would have become of the race. Bert and I flipped a coin to see which of us should move, and I won.

Congress finally passed a bill setting up a reward of a million dollars for whoever should find a permanent cure for hyperpilosity, and then adjourned, having, as usual, left a flock of important bills not acted upon.

When the weather became really hot in June, all the men quit wearing shirts, as their pelts covered them quite as effectively. The police force kicked so about having to wear their regular uniforms, that they were allowed to go around in dark blue polo shirts and shorts. But pretty soon they were rolling up their shirts and sticking them in the pockets of their shorts. It wasn't long before the rest of the male population of the United States was doing likewise. In growing hair the human race hadn't lost any of its capacity to sweat, and you'd pass out with the heat if you tried to walk anywhere on a hot day with any amount of clothes on. I can still remember holding onto a hydrant at Third Avenue and Sixtieth Street and trying not to faint, with the sweat pouring out the ankles of my pants and the buildings going 'round and 'round. After that I was sensible and stripped down to shorts like everyone else.

In July Natasha, the gorilla in the Bronx Zoo, escaped from her cage and wandered around the park for hours before anyone noticed her. The zoo visitors all thought she was merely an unusually ugly member of their own species.

If the hair played hob with the textile and clothing business generally, the market for silk simply disappeared. Stockings were just quaint things that our ancestors had worn. Like cocked hats and periwigs. One result was that the economy of the Japanese Empire, always a pretty shaky proposition, went completely to pot, which is how they had a revolution and are now a Socialist Soviet Republic.

Neither Oliveira nor I took any vacation that summer, as we were working like fury on the hair problem. Román promised me a cut of the reward when and if he won it.

But we didn't get anywhere at all during the summer. When classes started we had to slow down a bit on the research, as I was in my last year, and Oliveira had to teach. But we kept at it as best we could.

It was funny to read the editorials in the papers. The Chicago *Tribune* even suspected a Red Plot. You can imagine the time that the cartoonists for the *New Yorker* and *Esquire* had.

With the drop in the price of cotton, the South was really flat on its back this time. I remember when the Harwick bill was introduced in Congress, to require every citizen over the age of five to be clipped at least once a week. A bunch of Southerners were back of it, of course.

When that was defeated, largely on the argument of unconstitutionality, the you-alls put forward one requiring every person to be clipped before he'd be allowed to cross a state line. The theory was that human hair is a commodity—which it is sometimes—and that crossing a state line with a coat of the stuff, whether your own or someone else's, constituted interstate commerce, and brought you under control of the Federal Government. It looked for a while as though it would pass, but the Southerners finally accepted a substitute bill requiring all Federal employees, and cadets at the military and naval academies, to be clipped.

The destitution in the South intensified the ever-present race problem, and led eventually to the Negro revolt in Alabama and Mississippi, which was put down only after some pretty savage fighting. Under the agreement that ended that little civil war the Negroes were given the present Pale, a sort of reservation with considerable local autonomy. They haven't done as well as they claimed they were going to under that arrangement, but they've done better than the Southern whites said they would. Which I suppose is about what you'd expect. But, boy, just let a white man visiting their territory get uppity, and see what happens to him! They won't take any lip.

About this time—in the autumn of 1971—the cotton and textile interests got out a big advertising campaign to promote clipping. They had slogans, such as "Don't be a Hairy Ape!" and pictures of a couple of male swimmers, one with hair and the other without, and a pretty girl turning in disgust from the hirsute swimmer and fairly pouncing on the clipped one.

I don't know how much good their campaign would have done, but they overplayed their hand. They, and all the clothing outfits, tried to insist on boiled shirts, not only for evening wear, but for daytime wear as well. I never thought a long-suffering people would really revolt against the tyrant Style, but we did. The thing that really tore it was the inauguration of President Passavant. There was an unusually warm January thaw that year, and the president, the v-p, and all the justices of the Supreme Court appeared without a stitch on above the waist, and damn little below.

We became a nation of confirmed near-nudists, just as did everybody else sooner or later. The one drawback to real nudism was the fact that, unlike the marsupials, man hasn't any natural pockets. So we compromised between the hair, the need for something to hold fountain-pens, money, and so forth, and our traditional ideas of modesty by adopting an up-to-date version of the Scottish sporran.

The winter was a bad one for flu, and everybody who hadn't caught it the preceding winter got it now. Soon a hairless person became such a rarity that one wondered if the poor fellow had the mange.

In May of 1972 we finally began to get somewhere. Oliveira had the bright idea—which both of us ought to have thought of sooner—of examining ectogenic babies. Up to now, nobody had noticed that they began to develop hair a little later than babies born the normal way. You remember that human ectogenesis was just beginning to be worked about then. Test tube babies aren't yet practical for large-scale production by a long shot, but we'll get there some day.

Well, Oliveira found that if the ectogens were subjected to a really rigid quarantine, they never developed hair at all—at least not in more than the normal quantities. By really rigid quarantine, I mean that the air they breathed was heated to 800° C., then liquefied, run through a battery of cyclones, and washed with a dozen disinfectants. Their food was treated in a comparable manner. I don't quite see how the poor little fellows survived such unholy sanitation, but they did, and didn't grow hair—until they were brought in contact with other human beings, or were injected with sera from the blood of hairy babies.

Oliveira figured out that the cause of the hyperpilosity was what he'd suspected all along—another of these damned self-perpetuating protein molecules. As you know, you can't see a protein molecule, and you can't do much with it chemically because, if you do, it forthwith ceases to be a protein molecule. We have their structure worked out pretty well now, but it's been a slow process with lots of inferences from inadequate data. Sometimes the inferences were right and sometimes they weren't.

But to do much in the way of detailed analysis of the things, you need a respectable quantity of them, and these that we were after didn't exist in even a disrespectable amount. Then Oliveira worked out his method of counting them. The reputation he made from that method is about the only permanent thing he got out of all his work.

When we applied the method, we found something decidedly screwy— an ectogen's virus count after catching hyperpil was the same as it had been before. That didn't seem right. We knew that he had been injected with hyperpil molecules, and had come out with a fine mattress as a result.

Then one morning I found Oliveira at his desk looking like a medieval monk who had just seen a vision after a forty-day fast. (Incidentally, you try fasting that long and you'll see visions too, lots of 'em.) He said, "Pat, don't buy a yacht with your share of that meelion. They cost too much to upkeep."

"Huh?" was the brightest remark I could think of.

"Look here," he said, going to the blackboard. It was covered with chalk diagrams of protein molecules. "We have three proteins, alpha, beta, and gamma. No alphas have exeested for thousands of years. Now, you will note that the only deefference between the alpha and the beta is that these nitrogens"—he pointed—"are hooked onto *thees* chain instead of that one. You will also observe, from the energy relations wreeten down here, that if one beta is eentroduced eento a set of alphas, all the alphas will presently turn into betas.

"Now, we know now that all sorts of protein molecules are being assembled inside us all the time. Most of them are unstable and break up again, or are inert and harmless, or lack the power of self-production—anyway, nothing happens because of them. But, because they are so beeg and complicated, the possible forms they take are very many, and it is possible that once in a long time some new kind of protein appears with self-reproducing qualities; in other words, a virus. Probably that's how the various disease viruses got started, all because something choggled an ordinary protein molecule that was chust being feenished and got the nitrogens hooked on the wrong chains.

"My idea is thees: The alpha protein, which I have reconstructed from what we know about its descendants beta and gamma, once exeested as a harmless and inert protein molecule in the human body. Then one day somebody heecupped as one of them was being formed, and presto! We had a beta. But the beta is not harmless. It reproduces itself fast, and it inheebits the growth of hair on most of our bodies. So presently all our species—wheech at the time was pretty apish—catch this virus, and lose their hair. Moreover, it is one of the viruses that is transmeeted to the embryo, so the new babies don't have hair, either.

"Well, our ancestors sheever a while, and then learn to cover themselves with animal skeens to keep warm, and also to keep fire. And so, the march of ceevilizations it is commence! Chust theenk—except for that one original beta protein molecule, we should probably today all be merely a kind of goreela or cheempanzee. Anyway, an ordinary anthropoid ape.

"Now, I feegure that what has happened is that another change in the form of the molecule has taken place, changing it from beta to gamma—and gamma is a harmless and inert leetle fellow, like alpha. So we are back where we started.

"Our problem, yours and mine, is to find how to turn the gammas, with wheech we are all swarming, back into betas. In other words, now that we have become all of a sudden cured of the disease that was endemic in the whole race for thousands of years, we want our disease back again. And I theenk I see how it can be done."

I couldn't get much more out of him; we went to work harder than ever. After several weeks he announced that he was ready to experiment on himself; his method consisted of a combination of a number of drugs—one of them was the standard cure for glanders in horses, as I recall—and a high-frequency electromagnetic fever.

I wasn't very keen about it, because I'd gotten to like the fellow, and that awful dose he was going to give himself looked enough to kill a regiment. But he went right ahead.

Well, it nearly did kill him. But after three days he was more or less back to normal, and was whooping at the discovery that the hair on his limbs and body was rapidly falling out. In a couple of weeks he had no more hair than you'd expect a Mexican professor of virology to have.

But then our real surprise came, and it wasn't a pleasant one!

We expected to be more or less swamped by publicity, and had made our preparations accordingly. I remember staring into Oliveira's face for a full minute and then reassuring him that he had trimmed his mustache to exact symmetry, and getting him to straighten my new necktie.

Our epoch-making announcement dug up two personal calls from bored reporters, a couple of 'phone interviews from science editors, and not one photographer! We did make the science section of the New York *Times*, but with only about twelve lines of type—the paper merely stated that Professor Oliveira and his assistant—not named—had found the cause and cure of hyperpilosity. Not a word about the possible effects of the discovery.

Our contracts with the Medical Center prohibited us from exploiting our discovery commercially, but we expected that plenty of other people would be quick to do so as soon as the method was made public. But it didn't happen. In fact, we might have discovered a correlation between temperature and the pitch of the bullfrog's croak for all the splash we made.

A week later Oliveira and I talked to the department head, Wheelock, about the discovery. Oliveira wanted him to use his influence to get a dehairing clinic set up. But Wheelock couldn't see it.

"We've had a couple of inquiries," he admitted, "but nothing to get excited about. Remember the rush there was when the Zimmerman cancer-treatment came out? Well, there's been nothing like that. In fact, I—ah—doubt whether I personally should care to undergo your treatment, sure-fire though it may be, Dr. Oliveira. I'm not in the least disparaging the remarkable piece of work you've done. But"—here he ran his fingers through the hair on his chest, which was over six inches long, thick, and a beautiful silky white—"you know, I've gotten rather fond of the old pelt, and I'd feel slightly indecent back in my bare skin. Also, it's a lot more economical than a suit of clothes. And—ah—if I may say so with due modesty—I don't think it's bad-looking. My family has always ridden me about my sloppy clothes, but now the laugh's on them. Not one of them can show a coat of fur like mine!"

Oliveira and I left, sagging in the breeches a bit. We inquired of people we knew, and wrote letters to a number of them, asking what they thought of the idea of undergoing the Oliveira treatment. A few said they might if enough others did, but most of them responded in much the same vein that Doc Wheelock had. They'd gotten used to their hair, and saw no good reason for going back to their former glabrous state.

"So, Pat," said Oliveira to me, "it lukes as though we don't get much fame out of our discovery. But we may essteel salvage a leetle fortune. You remember that meelion-dollar reward? I sent in my application as soon as I recovered from my treatment, and we should hear from the government any day."

We did. I was up at his apartment, and we were talking about nothing in particular, when Mrs. O. rushed in with the letter, squeaking, "Open eet! Open eet, Román!"

He opened it without hurry, spread the sheet of paper out, and read it.

Then he frowned and read it again. Then he laid it down, very carefully took out and lit the wrong end of a cork-tipped cigarette, and said in his levellest voice, "I have been esstupid again, Pat. I never thought that there might be a time-leemit on that reward offer. Now it seems that some crafty *sanamagoon* in Congress poot one een, so that the offer expired on May first. You remember, I mailed the claim on the nineteenth, and they got it on the twenty-first. Three weeks too late!"

I looked at Oliveira, and he looked at me and then at his wife. And she looked at him and then went without a word to the cabinet and got out two large bottles of *tequila* and three tumblers.

Oliveira pulled up three chairs around a little table, and settled with a sigh in one of them. "Pat," he said, "I may not have a meelion dollars, but I have something more valuable by far—a wooman who knows what is needed at a time like thees!"

And that's the inside story of the Great Change—or at least of one aspect thereof. That's how it happens that, when we today speak of a platinum-blonde movie-star, we aren't referring to her scalp-hair alone, but the beautiful silvery pelt that covers her from crown to ankle.

There was just one more incident. Bert Kafket had me up to his place to dinner a few nights later. After I had told him and his wife about Oliveira's and my troubles, he asked how I had made out on that depilatory-manufacturer stock I'd bought.

"I notice those stocks are back about where they started from before the Change," he added.

"Didn't make anything to speak of," I told him. "About the time they started to slide down from their peak, I was too busy working for Román to pay much attention to them. When I finally did look them up I was just able to unload with a few cents profit per share. How did you do on those stocks you were so mysterious about last year?"

"Maybe you noticed my new car as you came in?" asked Bert with a grin. "That's them. Or rather, it; there was only one—Jones and Galloway Company."

"What do Jones and Galloway make? I never heard of them?"

"They make"—here Bert's grin looked as if it were going to run around his head and meet behind—"currycombs!"

FLETCHER PRATT *and* B. F. RUBY

THE THING IN THE WOODS

The opening paragraphs of this story have been rewritten by Fletcher Pratt especially for this collection. Thanks are due him for this extra labor, which has markedly improved the tale. *G. C.*

RALPH PARKER RUBBED his fingers across goggled eyes. It looked as though it had moved. He bent more closely over the fungus bed and twisted his head to cut out the annoying refractions. The thing was certainly out of alignment with the other four mutants.

From the other side of the room Barkeley said, "What is it now? Another case of *Agaricus giganteus?*"

Parker gave an inarticulate gurk. The reference was to one of the less successful experiments he had made in the vaults beneath the Central Packing Company's building. Instead of the expected giant mushrooms, they got a collection of tiny purple pinpricks, almost as impalpable as dust, which sailed sporelike through the air of the laboratory to settle on everything and there reproduce themselves. After that experience they had to close the laboratory for a month and kill every living thing in it to get rid of the pin-point plague.

"No," he said. "It's too big. And growing. Ought to be useful for something, but it looked as though it wiggled."

Barkeley set down the tube he was working with, and came over to look. Just as he glanced down it happened again. The little grey-brown ball turned over, at first tentatively, as though trying its paces; then more rapidly. It rolled to the side of the fungus bed and swung back, as though seeking a way to surmount the wooden rim of the box.

"Mobile," said Barkeley solemnly. "Ralph, we've got something unknown to the history of botany."

Parker turned and shook him by the hand. "I don't think Central Packing will pin any medals on us for it," he observed. "I doubt if the thing's edible, and that's all they're interested in upstairs there. But it's certainly going to make a piece of reputation for a couple of guys named Parker and Barkeley. Watch it while I get some magnifying goggles. I want to see the external features."

Coming through the door on his return, he was arrested by a shout from his assistant. "Hey! This damn thing has visual sense!"

"How do you know?" demanded Parker.

"Why, it was rolling and I stuck this cardboard in front of it, and it turned away. I've tried it three times now."

"Let's see," said Parker, peering at the bed. "Oh—that's all right. It's only slightly photo-sensitive. Likes light and rolled away from the shadow cast by your cardboard."

"Yeah?" said Barkeley. "Well, how about this? Watch, now."

He held the cardboard in front of the pea-like object at a slight angle so that the overhead light was fully reflected on it, and approached it to the fungus. The thing turned over and moved away before it was touched.

"Well, I'll be damned," said Parker. "Almost as though it had senses. There's a kind of tiny green fan at one side that I'll bet contains chlorophyll, so it can probably convert atmospheric carbon dioxide into carbohydrates."

"But what will it do for nitrogen? See any sign of roots?"

"No-o-o; unless . . . There's a tiny green line around its middle, almost as though it really were a pea. May be an atrophied or vestigial root. I hope it isn't a fatal mutation."

"So do I," said Barkeley devoutly. "If this thing lives, it's going to be worth observing. Say, I have an idea. It seems to go for light, and your little green plume would indicate that it can use it. Why not build a special pen for it on the roof, where it can get sunlight?"

That was the small beginning of a major problem. Left to sunlight and its own devices, the tiny fungoid prospered. It basked in the sunlight of the roof, rolling here and there, and seeming more definitely than ever to be provided with senses, for when placed in shadow it always rolled toward the nearest spot of light. By the third day it had attained the size of a grape; the line around its equator was more and more pronounced, but it still showed not the slightest sign of rooting. By the fourth the median line had split along and formed what was apparently a kind of pouch, whose purpose was completely obscure. But it was on the eighth day when Barkeley came dashing into the underground laboratory, visibly excited.

"Come on up to the roof and see what our little friend is up to now!" he invited, visibly excited.

"Our little friend," Ralph said slowly, looking up from the slide rule, "is going to be exactly as tall as the Central Packing building in one month, if it keeps on growing at the present rate."

"Yeah, if!" laughed Barkeley. "So would you if you had kept on growing as fast as you did when you were a baby."

"Why didn't I?" Parker insisted seriously.

"I suppose there's something that stops growth, isn't there?"

"Exactly. At least it's supposed there's a growth-arresting hormone. But suppose the fungus—or, well we won't worry about that! What do you think you've discovered now, Columbus?"

"Wait till we get up to the roof and I show you," Barkeley promised, mysteriously

When they arrived at the roof, Barkeley began snatching handfuls of empty air with all the appearance of a man suddenly gone crazy. At last he approached the fungus with his hand tightly closed, then with his other hand he extracted a wriggling fly and presented it to the thing.

"Well, I'll be dumb-jiggered!" Ralph exclaimed as he saw the fungus shoot out a tentacle from its middle and sweep the fly into its equatorial pouch. "It's insectivorous!"

After that Ralph realized that its nitrogen supply was acquired in this way and he kept Barkeley busy supplying the fungus with insects and caterpillars. It seemed to have an insatiable appetite for them and it now began to have an odor of strongly ammoniacal character. From this fact Ralph concluded that it probably could not digest proteins like an animal; they were evidently merely split up by putrefaction in the pouch and the thing just soaked up the ammonia and other soluble compounds produced, just as a plant would.

Every day Ralph measured its growth and, so far, he could see no reason to revise his startling prediction. It was now as big as the fruit of an egg plant and while its actual size was not alarming, its *rate* of growth was astonishing. And those central tentacles—

"Well!" Ralph said to himself. "If that thing were as big as I and it snatched at me with one of those tentacles, I'd say my prayers!"

Routine work had piled up in the laboratory while Parker and his assistant had been playing with the fungoid mutant of which their lord and master, the General Manager of the Central Packing Company, knew exactly nothing. Fascinating though it was, they were obliged to confine themselves for a while to necessary lab work. But each evening they went up to observe it before going home.

Then one night, as they watched in the dusk, they heard a squeal and hastened closer just in time to see the fungus chasing something. It was a mouse. Somehow, the poor thing had strayed into the bed and it didn't have a chance against the hungry fungus. This way and that, the fungus rolled swiftly after the desperately squealing mouse. And finally, after chasing it across the bed, the fungus, now the size of a watermelon, steam-rollered the frantic rodent to death and swept it into its digestive pouch.

"Well," remarked Barkeley, "that solves the feeding problem anyway. If it'll eat a mouse, we can feed it chunks of meat."

"Yeah," replied Parker. "But what worries me is that it's increasing in size so rapidly. It might get dangerous!"

They had to enlarge and strengthen the pen and provide a trough into which scraps of meat could be thrown. Ralph was glad he had completed this job when he received, one Thursday, an invitation from the boss to spend the week-end at his summer home. Barkeley was invited too and both knew it was a royal command which could not be refused. So they had to leave their interesting fungus until the following Monday.

Before starting on Thursday, however, they loaded up the trough with meat scraps. Not merely a few handfuls, but a large wooden pail full to the brim.

"Can't understand why it has such an appetite for nitrogenous food," Barkeley commented. "Its tissues are cellulose, aren't they? And it gets the carbon from the CO_2 in the air."

"Not all cellulose. All plant forms need some nitrogen. And while this thing probably doesn't need much, its digestive apparatus is so crude, it has to eat enormous quantities of meat to get the little it requires."

This was Ralph's explanation. But he wasn't at all sure it was right. There were so many things about this carnivorous fungus he didn't as yet understand. It was mysterious. Yes, and a little alarming.

The manager was a perfect host and ordinarily Ralph and Barkeley would have had a gloriously hectic time. But all the time while they were taking a dip, or playing tennis, or sipping iced tea on the cool terrace, they were thinking of the strange thing back there on the roof.

"Will it never end?" Ralph thought wearily, as he and Barkeley endured the pleasures provided for them. They held out nobly until Sunday night. Then, after several hands of bridge, Ralph yawned and suggested that they had better turn in, as it was essential they get to the lab early next morning. He looked significantly at Barkeley, who took the hint and seconded the suggestion strongly.

At three o'clock, Ralph rapped softly on Barkeley's door.

"Hey, dopey, get up," he whispered. "Let's scram and apologize later. I just thought of something about that thing. Not worrying exactly, but—"

They dressed, let themselves out noiselessly and in a few minutes were burning up the road toward town. Barkeley, who had a bad case of accelerator-foot anyway, was making the big car do eighty or better. But Ralph, normally nervous at high speeds, hardly noticed. He was thinking of something and the more he thought about it the more anxious he got.

"I'll bet I know what's worrying you," Barkeley spoke for the first time as they crossed the town line and he reduced the speed to legal (?) limits. "I just thought of it, myself."

"What?"

"The growth factor!"

"That's it," admitted Ralph. "Why, the damn thing must be seven feet high by now, because it was three feet Thursday night!"

"Cripes! Supposed it busted out of the pen and fell off the roof?"

"That's what I'm afraid of. If it fell on anybody—"

He did not finish his sentence because at this moment they pulled up in front of the plant. Ralph started to get out of the car to unlock the gate to the shipping yard so they could drive into the employees' garage, when he noticed the gate was ajar. Like a flash he was out of the car to examine the lock. He saw that the lock was intact but the wooden picket to which it was affixed had been splintered.

"Either a truck has backed into it," he started to say to Barkeley, "or else—"

But Barkeley was headed on a run for the shipping platform.

"Holy fried cakes!" he yelled. "Look at this window!"

Following him, Ralph sprinted to the platform and surveyed the ruin of one metal-frame, wired glass window. Shattered, its metal mullions torn loose and bent, it looked as if a freight car had plunged through it. And clinging to its sharp edges of metal and glass were bits of brownish-white, vegetable tissue!

Both knew well enough what that meant and they mounted the stairs quickly in silence. And when they reached the stair-shaft penthouse on the roof, the open door, which was a swinging, metal-clad fire door, confirmed their suspicions.

"Well, it's gone all right!" Barkeley exclaimed.

"Yeah, of course," replied Ralph, as he surveyed the wreck of the pen.

"But how did it get the penthouse door open? And where in hell is the watchman?"

"Shhh—! What was that?" Barkeley whispered.

As he spoke there was audible a faint groan. Listening in silence they heard it again and it seemed to come from the front parapet overlooking the street. Hastening to the front they discerned in the dimness the limp figure of the watchman lying across the tile coping of the parapet wall. His flashlight and revolver lay on the gravel roof beside him.

"Jake!" Ralph cried, running to him and pulling him back. "What's the matter? Are you hurt?"

There was a frightened look in the man's face and he was obviously relieved to see Ralph's familiar countenance.

"I don't know exactly what did happen, Mr. Parker," he said slowly, speaking with difficulty as he was evidently in pain. "I came up to the roof about four-thirty to punch the watchman station, when I heard a racket in that pen where you had that big fungus. I'd just started toward it when the whole pen seemed to rise right up and that thing was coming toward the penthouse. If I'd only dodged back and slammed the door it would have been all right. But I was rattled and pulled out my gun."

"Did you fire?" Ralph inquired.

"Emptied my gun at it. But say, it had no more effect than a pea-shooter. It just came toward the door, rolling like, and when I tried to get between it and the door, it reached out and grabbed me 'round the waist. Must have broke a rib from the way it hurts. But I was so scared I didn't hardly notice. It was awful, Mr. Parker, being pulled up against that thing—like a corpse it was, so cold, and it smelled something awful."

"But you got away evidently."

"I pulled and struggled like a madman. And then, all of a sudden its hand, or whatever you call it, broke right off. I must'a sprawled in a heap and was knocked dizzy. Because when I came to, the thing was gone."

"How'd you come to be up in front?"

"Why, I guess my leg was broke when I sprawled and I dragged myself up there to try to get help. But nobody came along until you fellows came."

Meanwhile, Barkeley had been searching the roof with the flashlight and returned now with a slimy object about a foot long.

"The tentacle segment, eh? Good! We're going to need that, I think," Ralph approved. "Take it down to the lab and I'll phone for the ambulance. Then we'll have to notify the police."

When Barkeley came up from the lab, Ralph met him at the ground floor, watch in hand.

"You jump in the car, Bark, and drive to the police station, while I wait for the ambulance. You've got a good chance of catching it if you sort of spiral out from the building—if this all happened at 4:30 it can't be far away. And don't tell the cop it's a wild mushroom that's escaped, because they'll put you in a padded cell."

At the police station Barkeley found a sleepy desk-sergeant who wanted to write things on a large white sheet of paper, names, addresses and other "red tape."

"My God, man!" Barkeley cried explosively. "Do you realize that thing's loose on the street now? It may be crushing women and children to death right this minute!"

Galvanized into action by Barkeley's angry burst, he jabbed a bell summoning two cops with sawed-off shot guns, and briskly ordered them to take Barkeley with them in the scout car and round up the thing. One of the cops drove, while Barkeley and the other cop sat with riot guns in hand ready to leap out when they spied the beast. It was still too early for there to be many people on the street, but what few were out stared curiously after the scout car as they circled in swiftly widening circles about the Central Packing building.

"We could easy miss it this way," one of the coppers growled when they were five or six blocks from the building. "The Sarge ought to have waited for an alarm."

"Yeah?" said Barkeley. "And have it kill half a dozen people first?"

"Phooey," the cop sneered. "It ain't no worse'n a lion, is it? And I remember when old Leo got out of the Zoo he didn't do nothin' at all—just hid in a corner like a scared kitten, till they come an' got him."

"What in hell is it, anyway?" the other asked.

"Giant agaricus," said Barkeley, suppressing a grin as he wondered what they'd say if he told them it was a mushroom. "It's seven feet high and it'll mind these riot guns about as much as an air rifle."

"What are we goin' to do when we find it then? And how in hell are we going to locate it?" was the somewhat less assured response.

"Run it down with the car if we can. And as to finding it, if you notice a rotten smell, we are probably near it," was Barkeley's reply.

They were on the outskirts of the town before Barkeley's nostrils detected the tell-tale emanation of the fungus. Even in this small town the circling process had taken nearly half an hour and it was now broad daylight. The view was less obstructed here, city buildings having given place to scattered farmhouses and green pastures on the gentle hillside that led to a thinly wooded strip.

The circling process could not be continued any longer and Barkeley had to be guided by his nose. Observing that the odor was getting fainter he directed the driver to turn around and was gratified to notice that after going a quarter of a mile it grew perceptibly stronger. As they came to a fork in the road, Barkeley directed the driver to turn. He wasn't sure, but he thought he saw a commotion in the pasture near a farmhouse.

He strained his eyes and the next moment shouted to the driver:

"Step on it! I see it in that pasture and it's after some animal!"

The little car bounced over the rough road as it shot ahead when the driver jammed his foot down on the gas. Leaning out the side, Barkeley was ready to jump when they got near enough.

"Here!" Barkeley shouted. "Stop her here!"

He leapt from the car and all three stood petrified for a moment by the ghastly spectacle they witnessed.

An awkward brown calf, terror in its appealing eyes, was being chased this way and that by the huge rolling fungus. Bleating wildly, the helpless animal dashed madly to and fro, but the huge brownish-white ball rolled rapidly in pursuit no matter which way it went. Steadily the pursuer gained on the calf, despite the victim's frantic efforts to escape; the animal's agonized bleats became like the wail of a terror-stricken child. Then it stumbled . . .

In an instant the great bulk of the spherical fungus rolled upon its hind-quarters. Inexorably the heavy ball rolled forward toward the calf's head and the sound of the crushing bones could be heard even where Barkeley and the cops stood. The cries of the helpless beast were terrible, like a gasping scream, as the thing rolled slowly forward, squeezing the animal flat.

Seemingly the fungus knew its victim was dead, for now it rolled off and waved its outspread fan-head in a gloating madness of blood thirst. The great thing, seven feet in diameter, despite its grotesque spherical shape, seemed like a blood-crazed cannibal; a thing of cellulose, yet strangely like some colossal savage ancestor of man. It was grasping the mangled calf with its powerful tentacles now, lifting it toward the equatorial pouch—

But Barkeley was tugging frantically at the wooden rails of the fence, pulling it apart, while he yelled to the men to get the car headed for the opening he was making. Obeying him, one of them got into the car, faced the car toward the opening and started forward. Barkeley had the fence down but the car lacked sufficient impetus to plough through the ditch. The engine died.

"Damn it, man!" Barkeley swore. "Why didn't you get a start? Try and back her up and—"

As he spoke, he heard a gun go off with a terrific bang. He looked up to see the other man, who had approached the fungus with his riot gun and fired from a distance of a few feet. As he looked the unfortunate fellow was snatched up by the swift, powerful tentacle and drawn against the nauseous pouch. Before Barkeley could utter a cry of warning, the other policeman leapt out, riot gun in hand, and ran to his companion's aid. He was right on top of the fungus when he fired but the heavy charge seemed to do no more than tear off a little fleshy bark.

Another tentacle shot out! And he too was dangled in the air while the fungoid monster waved his fan head in a perfect fury.

It had dropped the mangled calf and it seemed trying to decide which of its three victims to engulf.

Would it hurl them to the ground and crunch out their lives too?

Barkeley did not wait to see—

Leaping into the scout car, he threw it into reverse and backed up to get a start. Then, putting it into first gear, he jammed down the accelerator and let the clutch in. For one sickening instant as the car plunged forward, the front wheels dug into the mud of the ditch and the rear wheels began to spin. The fungus still dangled the helpless policemen in the air but any minute it might dash them to the ground and roll them to death.

Then the rear wheels began to take hold again. The car jerked forward up the banks of the ditch and through the fence opening—

Would the thing retreat? he wondered as he bumped across the pasture toward the flesh-maddened monster which thrashed its victims about in the air with its powerful, slimy tentacles. It was the only chance. He remembered how it had fled from the cardboard in the laboratory pen. Maybe it would flee from the approaching car.

Reaching smoother ground, the car gained speed and bore down on the fungus with increased effect. Closer and closer. But still the agaric didn't budge! At last, when the car was hardly ten feet away, the thing dropped its squirming victims, folded its fan-head, and rolled swiftly away—

Swerving abruptly to avoid running over the men, Barkeley continued pursuit. But it was useless. On smooth ground he might have been able to run it down. But on this bumpy field, the odds were all in favor of the fungus. Gradually gaining distance, it reached the opposite side of the pasture where Barkeley saw it crash through the fence and disappear in the woods.

Returning, Barkeley found the two policemen ruefully brushing off their clothes, unhurt except for minor bruises where the tentacles of the fungus had encircled their bodies.

"Back to the station," Barkeley cried. "And step on it! That thing will come back and the citizens have got to be warned to stay indoors until it's caught."

But on the way back, Barkeley noticed that the streets were deserted. Although it was the hour when the citizens would normally be on their way to shops and offices, not a soul was to be seen.

At the police station he found Ralph waiting for him.

Barkeley and the policemen told their exciting story while police reporters interrupted with curt demands for answers to questions, jotting down notes on scraps of paper, and then scampered to telephones.

"We ought to have a radio-warning broadcast, Ralph," Barkeley advised in an anxious voice.

"It has already been done," Parker told him. "Didn't you notice that nobody's on the streets?"

"Oh yes, I did," Barkeley admitted. "But can't we get out the reserves and corner the thing?"

"No good!" exclaimed Ralph. "You ought to know from your experience policemen and guns are no good against that thing. We've got to wait for it to return and when it does I'm ready for it!"

His remark was overheard by Chief of Police, Harry Parsons, who had listened with a fishy eye to Barkeley's and the policemen's tale. Ralph had gone over the Chief's head in asking the Mayor to send the radio-warning and Harry Parsons was plenty sore. It was plain he thought the whole thing much ado about nothing.

"Listen, Parker," he said, with an undisguised sneer. "When the police department needs your help I'll ask for it. Now get out of here and stay out or I'll lock you up."

"Okay," said Ralph cheerfully. "I was going anyway."

"Where to now?" inquired Barkeley as they issued from the police station.

"Not far," Ralph said, smiling. "Just around the corner, in fact."

To Barkeley's surprise, Ralph led him to Fire Headquarters where he flopped into an easy chair near the switchboard and offered Barkeley a cigarette.

"See that apparatus?" Ralph said, pointing to the motor-pumper engine which stood in front. "And the tank truck?"

"Yeah, but what—?"

"That's what we fight the thing with, when it comes back for lunch."

Barkeley knit his brows. He was accustomed to Ralph's mystifying ways but this was a little too much.

"What's in the tank truck?" he inquired, completely baffled.

"Nothing," replied Ralph, succinctly. "But there will be in a minute. See that Standard Chemical Co. truck backing up there? Watch and see."

As Barkeley watched, several men began to shovel into the manhole of the tank truck some black crystalline substance. And then they hoisted several steel drums up on the tank truck and ran their contents, water-white and slightly fuming, into the tank.

Barkeley's quick wits began to get the idea.

"I see," he said, thoughtfully. "You did a little experimenting with that tentacle segment, I guess."

"Right," said Parker. "And I also anticipated that Chief Parsons would countermand that radio-warning. See the people on the streets?"

"The damned fool!" Barkeley ejaculated. "Why it's murder to let people out on the street, while that thing's loose. Think of it. Children will be on their way to school—"

"I know," Ralph replied, shaking his head. "The *Times* police reporter will phone the switchboard here if anything breaks. And we can only pray that we'll get there in time to prevent loss of life."

"I think I know what is in the tank truck now," Barkeley hazarded. "Will you tell me if I'm right?"

He scribbled a chemical formula on a piece of paper and passed it over to Ralph. The latter glanced at it and nodded.

"Good guess," he commented. "Of course it's an ordinary chemical known as a solvent for cellulose. But I was really amazed the way it ate up scraps of that tentacle segment. Is was like magic."

As he finished speaking, the man at the switchboard looked up.

"McNamara just phoned," he informed Ralph. "The Chief's got **men** out with riot guns, going through the woods."

In view of the fact that the woods referred to consisted of a thin strip of grove dividing the farm lands from a newly developed residential section to the north of the town, this seemed particularly idiotic to Ralph.

"Bright idea," he remarked. "If the thing succeeds in squeezing through the woods, it'll probably roll right down Union Road."

Barkeley looked at his watch.

"That'd be bad. It's just about time—"

He was interrupted by the staccato voice of the man at the board.

"The thing's reported seen near 22 school. Cruiser No. 4 phoned from Union and Beverly Road."

As he spoke he sounded the alarm and by the time Parker and Barkeley were seated in the Battalion Chief's car the firemen were already at their places on the pumper and tank truck.

Word must have spread that the thing was loose again for they had little need of their siren in the nearly deserted streets. It took less than three minutes to arrive at the point from which the cruiser had phoned.

The sound of a shot, followed by several more, told Ralph the location of the fungoid.

"The school!" he shouted.

The Battalion Chief whirled his car around the corner, followed more slowly by the heavy apparatus. As they approached, Ralph saw to his relief that there were no children in the street or yard. Evidently they had been able to escape. But the sound of another shot made him leap from the car and motion to the firemen to follow.

Dashing to the back of the school he saw the monster waving the fan-like protuberance at the top of its huge spherical body and trying to climb the steps of a rear entrance. At the top, vainly trying to open the heavy door and shrinking in deadly terror from the tentacles reached out for her, was a little girl.

"Why don't they open that door and get her in?" he heard someone shout.

"They can't," a patrolman answered as he withdrew a shell from his smoking riot gun and inserted another. "They don't use it and it's rusted shut or something."

The little group of police were hysterically firing as rapidly as they could into the monster's bulk. But they might as well have been firing at a lumber pile.

"If they only get that hose here in time," Ralph prayed silently.

As the long tentacles stretched out toward the little girl, Ralph heard the hoarse warnings that were shouted, and heard the sound of hammers inside trying to break open the door. And then two firemen dragged the hose around the corner and held the nozzle while the hose swelled and jerked and then began to spurt a dark fluid.

"Aim at the head," he called to the firemen. "That fan-like thing."

Amazement was written on the faces of the policemen as they saw the stream of blue-black fluid hit the fan-like head.

Before their eyes, they saw it melt, dissolving in the dark liquid. And as it did so, the tentacles suddenly ceased their movement. The direction of the powerful stream was altered now at Ralph's direction, attacking its middle, and gradually the whole thing melted like a lump of ice cream on a hot day, dwindling until there was nothing left but a pile of nauseous jelly.

"That ain't water," Ralph heard the voice of Harry Parsons exclaim. "What is it?"

"Ammoniacal cupric oxide," Ralph announced briefly. "The thing was a cellulose beast and the only way to kill it was to dissolve it."

"Listen, you!" the Chief warned him. "If you got any more baby Silly Looses up there on your roof, yuh better kill 'em off right now."

"Don't worry," Ralph replied. "I'm all through fooling with cute baby fungoids!"

KATHERINE MACLEAN

AND BE MERRY...

> The tusks that clashed in mighty brawls
> Of mastodons are billiard balls.
>
> The sword of Charlemagne the Just
> Is ferric oxide, known as rust.
>
> The grizzly bear whose potent hug
> Was feared by all, is now a rug.
>
> Great Caesar's bust is on the shelf
> And I don't feel so well myself!
>
> Arthur Guiterman

IT WAS AFTERNOON. The walls of the room glared back the white sunlight, their smooth plaster coating concealing the rickety bones of the building. Through the barred window drifted miasmic vapors, laden with microscopic living things that could turn food to poison while one ate, bacteria that could find root in lungs or skin, and multiply, swarming through the blood.

And yet it seemed to be a nice day. A smoky hint of burning leaves blurred the other odors into a pleasant autumn tang, and sunlight streaming in the windows reflected brightly from the white walls. The surface appearance of things was harmless enough. The knack of staying calm was to think only of the surface, never of the meaning, to try to ignore what could not be helped. After all, one cannot refuse to eat, one cannot refuse to breathe. There was nothing to be done.

One of her feet had gone to sleep. She shifted her elbow to the other knee and leaned her chin in her hand again, feeling the blood prickling back into her toes. It was not good to sit on the edge of the bed too long without moving. It was not good to think too long. Thinking opened the gates to fear. She looked at her fingernails. They were pale, cyanotic. She had been breathing reluctantly, almost holding her breath. Fear is impractical. One cannot refuse to breathe.

And yet, to solve the problems of safety it was necessary to look at the danger clearly, to weigh it, to sum it up and consider it as a whole. But each time she tried to face it her imagination would flinch away. Always her thinking trailed off in a blind impulse to turn to Alec for rescue.

When someone tapped her shoulder she made sure that her face was calm and blank before raising it from her hands. A man in a white coat stood before her, proffering a pill and a cup of water. He spoke tonelessly. "Swallow."

There was no use fighting back. There was no use provoking them to force. Putting aside the frantic futile images of escape she took the pill, her hands almost steady.

She scarcely felt the prick of the needle.

It was afternoon.

Alexander Berent stood in the middle of the laboratory kitchen, looking around vaguely. He had no hope of seeing her.

His wife was missing.

She was not singing in the living room, or cooking at the stove, or washing dishes at the sink. Helen was not in the apartment.

She was not visiting any of her friends' houses. The hospitals had no one of her description in their accident wards. The police had not found her body on any slab of the city morgue.

Helen Berent was missing.

In the corner cages the guinea pigs whistled and chirred for food, and the rabbits snuffled and tried to shove their pink noses through the grille. They looked gaunt. He fed them and refilled their water bottles automatically.

There was something different about the laboratory. It was not the way he had left it. Naturally after five months of the stupendous deserts and mountains of Tibet any room seemed small and cramped and artificial, but there were other changes. The cot had been dragged away from the wall, towards the icebox. Beside the cot was a wastebasket and a small table that used to be in the living room. On top of the table were the telephone and the dictation recorder surrounded by hypodermics, small bottles cryptically labeled with a red pencil scrawl, and an alcohol jar with its swab of cotton still in it. Alec touched the cotton. It was dusty to his fingers, and completely dry.

The dictation recorder and the telephone had been oddly linked into one circuit with a timer clock, but the connections were open, and when he picked up the receiver the telephone buzzed as it should.

Alec replaced the receiver and somberly considered the number of things that could be reached by a woman lying down. She could easily spend days there. Even the lower drawers of the filing cabinet were within reach.

He found what he was looking for in the lowest drawer of the filing cabinet, filed under "A", a special folder marked "ALEC". In it were a letter and two voice records dated and filed in order.

The letter was dated the day he had left, four months ago. He held it in his hand a minute before beginning to read.

Dear Alec,

You never guessed how silly I felt with my foot in that idiotic bandage. You were so considerate I didn't know whether to laugh or to cry. After you got on board I heard the plane officials paging a tardy passenger. I knew his place was empty, and it took all my will power to keep from running up the walk into the plane. If I had yielded to the temptation, I would be on the plane with you now, sitting in that vacant seat, looking down at the cool blue Atlantic, and in a month hiking across those windy horizons to the diggings.

But I can't give up all my lovely plans, so I sublimated the impulse to confess by promising myself to write this letter, and then made myself watch the plane take off with the proper attitude of sad resignation, like a dutiful wife with a hurt foot.

This is the confession. The bandage was a fake. My foot is all right. I just pretended to be too lame to hike to have an excuse to stay home this summer. Nothing else would have made you leave without me.

New York seems twice as hot and sticky now that the plane has taken you away. Honestly, I love you and my vacations too much to abandon the expedition to the unsanitary horrors of native cooking for just laziness. Remember, Alec, once when I was swearing at the gnats along the Whangpo, you quoth, "I could not love you so, my dear, loved I not science more." I put salt in your coffee for that, but you were right. I am the wife of an archeologist. Whither thou goest I must go, your worries are my worries, your job, my job.

What you forget is that besides being your wife, I am an endocrinologist, and an expert. If you can cheerfully expose me to cliffs, swamps, man-eating tigers and malarial mosquitoes, all in the name of Archeology, I have an even better right to stick hypodermics in myself in the name of Endocrinology.

You know my experiments in cell metabolism. Well naturally the next step in the investigation is to try something on myself to see how it works. But for ten years, ever since you caught me with that hypodermic and threw such a fit, I have given up the personal guinea pig habit so as to save you worry. Mosquitoes can beat hypos any day, but there is no use trying to argue with a husband.

So I pretended to have broken one of the small phalanges of my foot instead. Much simpler.

I am writing this letter in the upstairs lobby of the Paramount, whither I escaped from the heat. I will write other letters every so often to help you keep up with the experiment, but right now I am going in to see this movie and have a fine time weeping over Joan Crawford's phony troubles, then home and to work.

G'by, darling. Remember your airsick tablets, and don't fall out.

Yours always,
Helen

P.S. Don't eat anything the cook doesn't eat first. And have a good time.

After the letter there were just two voice records in envelopes. The oldest was dated July 24th. Alec put it on the turntable and switched on the play-back arm. For a moment the machine made no sound but the faint scratching of the needle, and then Helen spoke, sounding close to the microphone, her voice warm and lazy.

"Hello, Alec. The day after writing that first letter, while I was looking for a stamp, I suddenly decided not to mail it. There is no use worrying you with my experiment until it is finished. I resolved to write daily letters and save them for you to read all together when you get home.

"Of course, after making that good resolution I didn't write anything for a month but the bare clinical record of symptoms, injections and re- actions.

"I concede you that any report has to include the human detail to be readable, but honestly, the minute I stray off the straight and narrow track of formulas, my reports get so chatty they read like a gossip column. It's hopeless.

"When you get back you can write in the explanatory material yourself, from what I tell you on this disk. You write better anyhow. Here goes:

"It's hard to organize my words. I'm not used to talking at a faceless dictaphone. A typewriter is more my style, but I can't type lying down, and every time I try writing with a pen, I guess I get excited, and clutch too hard, and my finger bones start bending, and I have to stop and straighten them out. Bending one's finger bones is no fun. The rubbery feel of them bothers me, and if I get scared enough, the adrenaline will upset my whole endocrine balance and set me back a week's work.

"Let's see: Introduction. Official purpose of experiment—to investigate the condition of old age. Aging is a progressive failure of anabolism. Old age is a disease. No one has ever liked growing old, so when you write this into beautiful prose you can call it—'The Age-Old Old-Age problem.'

"Nowadays there is no evolutionary reason why we should be built to get old. Since we are learning animals, longevity is a survival factor. It should be an easy conquest, considering that each cell is equipped to duplicate itself and leave a couple of young successor cells to carry on the good work. The trouble is, some of them just *don't*. Some tissues brace themselves to hang on fifty years, and you have to get along with the same deteriorating cells until death do you part.

"From Nature's point of view that is reasonable. The human race evolved in an environment consisting mainly of plagues, famines, blizzards, and saber-toothed tigers. Any man's chances of staying unkilled for fifty years were pretty thin. Longevity was not worth much those days. What good is longevity to a corpse?

"We have eliminated plagues, famines, and saber-toothed tigers, but old age is still with us. One was meant to go with the other, but evolution hasn't had time to adjust us to that change.

"That Russian scientist started me on this idea. He gave oldsters a little of their lost elasticity by injections of an antibody that attacked and dissolved some of their old connective tissue and forced a partial replacement.

"I just want to go him one better, and see if I can coax a replacement for every creaking cell in the body.

"You can see how it would be a drastic process—halfway between being born again and being run through a washing machine. There is nobody I dare try it on except myself, for I'll have to feel my way, working out each step from the reactions to the last step, like making up a new recipe by adding and tasting.

"Item: The best way to test your theories is to try them on yourself. Emergency is the mother of exertion.

"Thirty-eight is just old enough to make me a good guinea pig. I am not so old and fragile that I would break down under the first strain, but I am not so young that a little added youth won't show.

"One question is—just how many tissues of any kind dare I destroy at once. The more I clear away at once, the more complete the replacement, but it is rather like replacing parts in a running motor. You wonder just how many bolts you can take out before the flywheel comes off its shaft and flies away. Speed should help. A quick regrowth can replace dissolved tissue before the gap is felt. The human machine is tough and elastic. It can run along on its own momentum when it should be stopped.

"This winter I bred a special strain of mold from some hints I had found in the wartime research reports on the penicillia. The mold makes an art of carrying on most of the processes of life outside of itself. Digestion and even most of the resynthesis of assimilation is finished before the food touches the plant. Its roots secrete enzymes that attack protein, dismantle it neatly down to small soluble molecules, and leave them linked to catalytic hooks, ready to be reassembled like the parts of a prefabricated house.

"The food below the mold becomes a pool. The mold plants draw the liquid up through their roots, give it the last touch that converts it to protoplasm, provide it with nucleus and throw it up in a high waving fur of sporangia.

"But that liquid is magic. It could become the protoplasm of any creature with the same ease and speed. It could be put into the bloodstream and be as harmless as the normal rough aminos, and yet provide for an almost instantaneous regrowth of missing flesh, a regrowth complete enough, I hope, to allow the drastic destruction and replacement I need.

"That may provide the necessary regeneration, but to have the old cells missing at the proper time and place, in the proper controlled amounts, is another problem entirely. The Russians used the antibody technique on horses to get a selectively destructive serum. That is all right for them, but it sounds too slow and troublesome for me. The idea of innoculating a horse with some of my connective tissue doesn't appeal to me somehow. How am I supposed to get this connective tissue? Besides I don't have a horse. The serum farms charge high.

"After watching a particularly healthy colony of mold melting down a tough piece of raw beef I decided there are other destructives than antibodies.

"I forced alternate generations of the mold to live on the toughest fresh meat I could find, and then on the dead mold mats of its own species. To feed without suicide it had to learn a fine selectivity, attacking only flesh that had passed the thin line between death and life. Twice, variants went past the line and dissolved themselves back to puddles, but the other strains learned to produce what was needed.

"Then I took some of the enzyme juice from under a mat, and shot the deadly stuff into a rabbit—the brown bunny with the white spot. Nothing happened to Bunny, she just grew very hungry and gained an ounce. I cut myself, and swabbed the juice on the cut. It skinned the callus from my fingertips, but nothing happened to the cut. So then I sent a sample over to the hospital for a test, with a note to Williams that this was a trial sample of a fine selective between dead and live tissue, to be used cautiously in cleaning out ragged infected wounds and small local gangrene.

"Williams is the same irresponsible old goat he always was. There was an ancient patient dying of everything in the book, including a gangrenous leg. Williams shot the whole tube of juice into the leg at once, just to see what would happen. Of course it made a sloppy mess that he had to clean up himself. It served him right. He said that the surprise simply turned his stomach, but the stuff fixed the gangrene all right, just as I said it would. It was as close and clean as a surgical amputation. Nevertheless he came back with what was left of the sample and was glad to be rid of it. He guessed it to be a super catalyst, somehow trained to be selective, and he wanted to get rid of it before it forgot its training.

"When I asked about the old patient later, they said that he woke up very hungry, and demanded a steak, so they satisfied him with intravenous amino acids, and he lived five days longer than expected.

"That was not a conclusive check, but it was enough. I labeled the juice 'H' for the acid ion. 'H' seemed a good name somehow.

"The first treatment on schedule was bone replacement. Middle age brings a sort of acromegaly. People ossify, their bones thicken, their gristle turns to bone and their arteries cake and stiffen. My framework needs a polishing down.

"For weeks I had cut my calcium intake down to almost nothing. Now I brought the calcium level in my blood down below the safe limit. The blood tried to stay normal by dissolving the treated bone. For safety, I had to play with parathyroid shots, depressants, and even a little calcium lactate on an hour-to-hour observation basis, to keep from crossing the spasm level of muscle irritability.

"But the hullabaloo must have upset my own endocrines, for they started behaving erratically, and yesterday suddenly they threw me into a fit before I could reach the depressant. I didn't break any bones, but I came out of the fit with one of my ulna uncomfortably bent. The sight of it almost gave me another fit.

"When one's bones start bending it is time to stop. I must have overdone the treatment a bit. There seems to be almost no mineral left in the smaller bones, just stiff healthy gristle. I am now lying flat on the cot drinking milk, eggnogs, and cod liver oil. I dreamed of chop suey last night, but until I ossify properly, I refuse to get up and go out for a meal. The icebox is within easy reach. Maybe my large bones are still hard, and maybe not, but I'll take no chances on bow legs and flat feet just for an oriental dinner.

"Darling, I'm having a wonderful time, and I wish you were here to look over my shoulder and make sarcastic remarks. Every step is a guess based on the wildest deductions, and almost every guess checks and has to be written down as right. At this rate, when I get through I'll be way ahead of the field. I'll be one of the best cockeyed endocrinologists practicing.

"I hope you are having a good time too, and finding hundreds of broken vases and old teeth.

"I've got to switch back to the notes and hours record now and take down my pulse rate, irritability level, PH and so on. The time is now seven ten, I'll give you another record soon.

"G'by, Hon—"

Her voice stopped and the needle ran onto the label and scratched with a heavy tearing noise. Alec turned the record over. The label on the other side was dated one week later.

Helen said cheerfully:

"Hello, Alec. This is a week later. I took a chance today and walked. Flat on my back again now, just a bit winded, but unbowed.

"Remember the time the obelisk fell on me? They set my arm badly, and it healed crooked with a big bump in the bones where the broken ends knitted. That bump made a good test to check the amount of chromosome control in this replacement business. If it approaches true regeneration, the bump should be noticeably reduced, and the knitting truer, to conform better to the gene blueprint of how an arm should be.

"The minute I thought of that test I had to try it. Risking flattened arches I got up and took the elevator down to the second floor office of Dr. Stanton, and walked right through an anteroom of waiting patients to the consulting room, where I promptly lay down on his examination table.

"He was inspecting a little boy's tonsils and said irritably:

" 'I really *must* ask you to wait your turn— Oh, it's Dr. Berent. Really Dr. Berent, you shouldn't take advantage of your professional position to— Do you feel faint?'

" 'Oh I feel fine,' I told him charmingly, 'I just want to borrow your fluoroscope a minute to look at an old break in the right humerus.'

" 'Oh, yes, I understand,' he says, blinking. 'But why are you lying down?'

"Well, Alec, you remember how that young man is—rather innocent, and trying to be dignified and stuffy to make up for it. The last time we spoke to him, and you made those wonderful cracks, I could see him thinking that we were somewhat odd, if not completely off our rockers. If I tried to tell him now that I was afraid my legs would bend, he would have called for a padded wagon to come and take me away.

"I said, 'I am afraid that I have upset my parathyroids. They are on a rampage. Just a momentary condition, but I have to stay relaxed for a while. You should see my irritability index! A little higher and . . . ah . . . I feel rather twitchy. Do you happen to have any curare around?'

"He looked at me as if I had just stabbed him with a hatpin, and then pulled out the fluoroscope so fast it almost ran over him, screened my arm bones and hustled me out of there before I could even say aha. Apparently the idea of my throwing a fit right there didn't arouse his professional ardor one bit.

"Alec, when I saw those bone shadows it was as much as I could do to keep from frightening the poor boy with war whoops. I put both arms under together, and I couldn't see any bumps at all. *They were exactly the same.*

"This means that cells retain wider gene blueprints than they need. And they just need a little encouragement to rebuild injuries according to specifications. Regeneration must be an unused potential of the body. I don't see why. We can't evolve *unused* abilities. Natural selection only works in life and death trials—probably evolution had no part in this. It is just a lucky break from being fetal apes, a hang-over bit of arrested development.

"I wonder how wide a blueprint each cell retains. Can a hand sprout new fingers, a wrist a new hand, a shoulder a new arm? Where does the control stop?

"The problem is a natural for the data I am getting now. Next winter when I am through with this silly rejuvenation business I'll get down to some solid work on regeneration, and try sprouting new arms on amputees. Maybe we can pry a grant from the Government, through that military bureau for the design of artificial limbs. After all, new legs would be the artificial limbs to end all artificial limbs.

"But that is all for next year. Right now all I can use it for is to speed up replacement. If I can kid my cells into moving up onto embryo level activity—they would regrow fast enough to keep the inside works ticking after a really stiff jolt of that bottled dissolution. I'd have to follow it fast with the liquid protein— No, if they regrew that fast they would be using the material from the dissolved old cells. It could telescope treatment down to a few hours. And the nucleus control so active that it rebuilds according to its ideal.

"Demolition and Reconstruction going on simultaneously. Business as Usual.

"Next step is the replacement of various soft tissues. If I were not in such a hurry, I would do it in two long slow simple Ghandi-like fasts, with practically no scientific mumbo jumbo. The way a sea squirt does it I mean—though I'd like to see someone starve himself down to a foot high.

"I have to start working now. The record is running out anyhow, so good-by until the next record, whenever that is.

"Having wonderful time.

"Wish you were here."

He took the record off hurriedly and put on the next one. It was recorded on only one face, and dated September 17th about fifty days later, seven weeks.

Helen started speaking without any introduction, her voice clearer and more distant as if she were speaking a few feet from the microphone.

"I'm rather upset, Alec. Something rather astonishing has happened. Have to get up to date first.

"The fasting treatment went fine. Of course I had to stay indoors and keep out of sight until I was fit to be seen. I'm almost back to normal now, gaining about a pound a day. The embryo status treatment stimulated my cells to really get to work. They seem to be rebuilding from an adult blueprint and not a fetal one, so I am getting flesh again in proper proportion and not like an overgrown baby.

"If I am talking disjointedly it is because I am trying hard not to get to the point. The point is too big to be said easily.

"Of course you know that I started this experimenting just to check my theoretical understanding of cell metabolism. Even the best available theory is sketchy, and my own guesses are doubtful and tentative. I never could be sure whether a patient recovered because of my treatment, in spite of my treatment—or just reacted psychosomatically to the size of my consultant fee.

"The best way to correct faulty theory is to carry it to its logical absurdity, and then to use the silliness as a clue to the initial fault.

"Recipe: To test theories of some process take one neutral subject— that's me—and try to induce a specific stage of that process by artificial means dictated by the theories. The point of failure will be the clue to the revision of the theories.

"I expected to spend the second half of my vacation in the hospital, checking over records of the experiment, and happily writing an article on the meaning of its failure.

"To be ready for the emergency I had hitched one of the electric timer clocks to the dictaphone and the telephone. If I didn't punch it at five-hour intervals, the alarm would knock off the telephone receiver, and the dictaphone would yell for an ambulance.

"Pinned to a big sign just inside the door was an explanation and full instructions for the proper emergency treatment. At every step in the experiment I would rewrite the instructions to match. 'Be Prepared' was the motto. 'Plan for every contingency.' No matter when the experiment decided to blow up in my face, I would be ready for it.

"There was only one contingency I did not plan for.

"Alec, I was just looking in the mirror. The only mirror that is any good is the big one in the front bedroom, but I had put off looking into it. For a week I lounged around reading and sleeping on the lab cot and the chair beside the window. I suppose I was still waiting for something to go wrong, but nothing did, and the skin of my hands was obviously different—no scars, no calluses, no tan, just smooth pink translucent skin—so I finally went and looked.

"Then I checked it with a medical exam. You'll find that data in with the other medical notes. Alec, I'm eighteen years old. That is as young as an adult can *get*.

"I wonder how Aladdin felt after rubbing a rusty lamp just to polish it up a bit.

"Surprised I suppose. The most noticeable feature of this new face so far is its surprised expression. It looks surprised from every angle, and sometimes it looks pale, and alarmed.

"Alarmed. Einstein was not alarmed when he discovered relativity, but they made a bomb out of it anyhow. I don't see how they could make a bomb out of this, but people are a wild, unpredictable lot. How will they react to being ageless? I can't guess, but I'm not reckless enough to hand out another Pandora's box to the world. The only safe way is to keep the secret until you get back, and then call a quiet council of experts for advice.

"But meanwhile, what if one of our friends happens to see me on the street looking like eighteen years old? What am I supposed to say?

"It is hard to be practical, darling. My imagination keeps galloping off in all directions. Did you know your hair is getting thin in back? Another two years with that crew cut and you would have begun to look like a monk.

"I know, I know, you'll tell me it is not fair for you to be a juvenile when every one else is gray, but what is fair? To be fair at all everyone will have to have the treatment available free, for *nothing*. And I mean *everyone*. We can leave it to an economist to worry out how. Meanwhile we will have to change our names and move to California. You don't want people to recognize you, and wonder who I am, do you? You don't want to go around looking twice as old as your wife and having people calling you a cradle snatcher, now do you?

"Wheedling aside, it is fair enough. The process is still dangerous. You can call yourself Guinea Pig Number Two. That's fair. We can sign hotel registers G. Igpay and wife. Pardon me, Alec, I digress. It *is* hard to be practical, darling.

"If the treatment gets safely out of the lab and into circulation—rejuvenation worked down to a sort of official vaccination against old age—it would be good for the race I think. It may even help evolution. Regeneration would remove environmental handicaps, old scars of bad raising, and give every man a body as good as his genes. A world full of the age proof would be a sort of sound-mind, sound-body health marathon, with the longest breeding period won by the people with the best chromosomes and the healthiest family tradition.

"Thank heavens I can strike a blow for evolution at last. Usually I find myself on the opposite side, fighting to preserve the life of some case whose descendants will give doctors a headache.

"And look at cultural evolution! For the first time we humans will be able to use our one talent, learning, the way it should be used, the way it was meant to be used from the beginning, an unstoppable growth of skill and humor and understanding, experience adding layer on layer like the bark of a California Redwood.

"And we need thinkers with time to boil the huge accumulation of science down to some reasonable size. It is an emergency job—and not just for geniuses, the rest of us will have to help look for common denominators, too. Even ordinary specialists will have time to learn more, do some integrating of their own, join hands with specialists of related fields.

"Take us, a good sample of disjointed specialties. You could learn neurology, and I could learn anthropology and psychology, and then we could talk the same language and still be like Jack Spratt and his wife, covering the field of human behavior between us. We would be close enough to collaborate—without *many* gaps of absolute ignorance—to write the most wonderful books. We could even . . . ah— We *can* even—"

(There was a silence, and then a shaky laugh.)

"I forgot. I said, 'Take us for example,' as if we weren't examples already. Research is supposed to be for other people. This is for us. It *is* a shock. Funny—funny how it keeps taking me by surprise.

"It shouldn't make that much difference. After all one lifetime is like another. We'll be the same people on the same job—with more time. Time enough to see the sequoias grow, and watch the ripening of the race. A long time.

"But the outside of the condemned cell is not very different from the inside. It is the same world full of the same harebrained human beings. And yet here I am, as shaky as if I've just missed being run over by a truck."

(There was another uncertain laugh.)

"I can't talk just now, Alec. I have to think."

For some minutes after the record stopped Alec stared out of the window, his hands locked behind his back, the knuckles working and whitening with tension. It was the last record, the only clue he had. The quaver in her voice, her choice of words, had emphatically filled his mind with the nameless emotion that had held her. It was almost a thought, a concept half felt, half seen, lying on the borderline of logic.

Before his eyes persistently there grew a vision of the great pyramid of Cheops, half completed, with slaves toiling and dying on its slopes. He stared blindly out over the rooftops of the city, waiting, not daring to force the explanation. Presently the vision began to slip away, and his mind wandered to other thoughts. Somewhere down in that maze of buildings was Helen. Where?

It was no use. Unclenching his stiffening fingers Alec jotted down a small triangle on the envelope of the record, to remind himself that a pyramid held some sort of clue. As he did it, suddenly he remembered that Helen, when she was puzzled, liked to jot the problem down on paper as she thought.

On the bedroom vanity table there was a tablet of white paper, and beside it an ashtray holding a few cigarette stubs. The tablet was blank, but he found two crumpled sheets of paper in the wastebasket and smoothed them carefully out on the table.

It began "Dear Alec" and then there were words crossed and blotted out. "Dear Alec" was written again halfway down the sheet, and the letters absently embroidered into elaborate script. Under it were a few doodles, and then a clear surrealistic sketch of a wisdom tooth marked with neat dental work, lying on its side in the foreground of a desert. Subscribed was the title "TIME", and beside it was written critically, "Derivative: The lone and level sands stretch far away." Doodles and vague figures and faces covered the bottom of the page and extended over the next page. In the midst of them was written the single stark thought "There is something wrong."

That was all. Numbly Alec folded the two sheets and put them into the envelope of the record. A tooth and a triangle. It should have been funny, but he could not laugh. He took the record out and considered it.

There was another concentric ribbon of sound on the face of the disk. Helen had used it again, but the needle had balked at a narrow blank line where she had restarted the recorder and placed the stylus a little too far in.

He put the record back on the turntable and placed the needle by hand.

"Alec darling, I wish you were here. You aren't as good a parlor psychologist as any woman, but you do know human nature in a broad way, and can always explain its odder tricks. I thought I was clever at interpreting other people's behavior, but tonight I can't even interpret my own. Nothing startling has happened. It is just that I have been acting unlike myself all day and I feel that it is a symptom of something unpleasant.

"I walked downtown to stretch my legs and see the crowds and bright lights again. I was looking at the movie stills in a theater front when I saw Lucy Hughes hurrying by with a package under one arm. I didn't turn around, but she recognized me and hurried over.

"'Why Helen Berent! I thought you were in Tibet.'

"I turned around and looked at her. Lucy, with her baby ways and feminine intuition. It would be easy to confide in her but she was not the kind to keep a secret. I didn't say anything. I suppose I just looked at her with that blank expression you say I wear when I am thinking.

"She looked back, and her eyes widened slowly.

"'Why you're too young. You're not—Heavens! I'm awfully sorry. I thought you were someone else. Silly of me, but you look just like a friend of mine—when she was younger I mean. It's almost uncanny!'

"I put on a slight western drawl, and answered politely, as a stranger should, and she went away shaking her head. Poor Lucy!

"I went in to see the movie. Alec, what happened next worries me. I stayed in that movie eight hours. It was an obnoxious movie, a hard-boiled detective story full of blood and violence and slaughter. I saw it three and a half times. You used to make critical remarks on the mental state of a public that battens on that sort of thud and blunder—something about Roman circuses. I wish I could remember how you explained it, because I need that explanation. When the movie house closed for the night I went home in a taxi. It drove too fast but I got home all right. There was some meat stew contaminated with botulus in the icebox, but I tasted the difference and threw it out. I have to be very critical. People are too careless. I never realized it before, but they are.

"I had better go to bed now and see if I can get some sleep."

Automatically Alec took the record off and slid it back into its envelope. The penciled triangle caught his eye, and his hands slowed and stopped. For a long time he looked at it without moving—the pyramids, the tombs of kings. An ancient religion that taught that one of a man's souls lived on in his mummy, a ghostly spark that vanished if the human form was lost. A whisper of immortality on earth. Cheops, spending the piled treasures of his kingdom and the helpless lives of slaves merely for a tomb to shield his corpse, building a pitiful mountain of rock to mock his name down the centuries. Hope—and fear.

There are wells of madness in us never tapped.

Alec put away the record and stepped to the window. The brown towers of Columbia Medical Center showed in the distance. Cornell Medical was downtown, Bellevue—"Hope" said Alec. "When there is life there is hope," said Alec, and laughed harshly at the pun. He knew now what he had to do. He turned away from the window, and picking up a classified telephone directory, turned to "Hospitals."

It was evening. The psychiatric resident doctor escorted him down the hall talking companionably.

"She wouldn't give her name. Part of the complex. A symptom for us, but pretty hard on you. It would have helped you to find her if she had some identifying marks I suppose, like scars I mean. It is unusual to find anyone without any—"

"What's her trouble?" asked Alec. "Anxiety? Afraid of things, germs, falls—?"

"She's afraid all right. Even afraid of me! Says I have germs. Says I'm incompetent. It's all a symptom of some other fear of course. These things are not what she is really afraid of. Once we find the single repressed fear and explain it to her—" He checked Alec's objection. "It's not rational to be afraid of little things. Those little dangers are not what she is really afraid of anyhow. Now suppression—"

Alec interrupted with a slight edge to his voice.

"Are you afraid of death?"

"Not much. There is nothing you can do about it, after all, so normal people must manage to get used to the idea. Now she—"

"You have a religion?"

"Vedanta. What of it? Now her attitude in this case is—"

"Even a mouse can have a nervous breakdown!" Alec snapped. "Where is the repression there? Vedanta you said? Trouble is, Helen is just too rational!" They had stopped. "Is this the room?"

"Yeah," said the doctor sullenly, making no move to open the door. "She is probably still asleep." He looked at his watch. "No, she would be coming out of it now."

"Drugs," said Alec coldly. "I suppose you have been psychoanalyzing her, trying to trace her trouble back to some time when her mother slapped her with a lollypop, eh? Or shock treatment perhaps, burning out the powers of imagination, eh?"

The young psychiatrist let his annoyance show. "We know our jobs, sir. Sedatives and analysis, without them she would be screaming the roof off. She's too suspicious to consciously confide her warp to us, but under scopolamine she seems to think she is a middle-aged woman. How rational is *that*?" With an effort he regained his professional blandness. "She has not said much so far, but we expect to learn more after the next treatment. Of course being told her family history will help us immeasurably. We would like to meet her father and mother."

"I'll do everything in my power to help," Alec replied. "Where there is life there is hope." He laughed harshly, on a note that drew a keen professional glance from the doctor. The young man put his hand to the knob, his face bland.

"You may go in and identify her now. Remember, be very careful not to frighten her." He opened the door and stood aside, then followed Alec in.

Helen lay on the bed asleep, her dark hair lying across one cheek. She looked like a tired kid of nineteen, but to Alec there seemed to be no change. She had always looked this way. It was Helen.

The doctor called gently. "Miss . . . ah . . . Berent. Miss Berent."

Helen's body stiffened, but she did not open her eyes. "Go away," she said in a small flat voice. "Please!"

"It is just Dr. Marro," the young man said soothingly.

"How do I know you are a doctor?" she said without stirring. "You'd say that anyway. Maybe you escaped and disguised yourself as a doctor. Maybe you are a paranoiac."

"I'm just myself," said the resident, shrugging. "Just Dr. Marro. How can I prove it to you if you don't look at me?"

The small voice sounded like a child reciting. It said: "If you are a doctor, you will see that having you here upsets me. You won't want to upset me, so you will go away." She smiled secretly at the wall. "Go away please."

Then, abruptly terrified, she was sitting up, staring, "You called me Miss Berent. Oh, Alec!" Her eyes dilated like dark pools in a chalk face, and then Helen crumpled up and rolled to face the wall, gasping in dry sobs. "Please, please—"

"You are exciting her, Mr. Berent," said the resident. "I'm sorry, but I'm afraid you'll have to leave."

It had to be done. Alec swallowed with a dry mouth, and then said in a loud clear voice, enunciating every syllable:

"Helen, honey, you are dying."

For a moment there was a strange silence. The doctor was looking at him with a shocked white face; then he moved, fumbling for an arm lock, fumbling with his voice for the proper cheerful tone. "Come, Mr. Berent, you . . . we must be going now."

Alec swung his clenched fist into the babbling white face. The jolt on his knuckles felt right. He did not bother to watch the doctor fall. It only meant that he would have a short time without interruption. Helen was cowering in the far corner of the bed, muttering "No-no-no-no—" in a meaningless voice. The limp weight of the psychiatrist leaned against his leg and then slipped down and pressed across the toes of his shoes.

"Helen," Alec called clearly, "Helen, you are dying. You have cancer."

She answered only with a wordless animal whimper. Alec looked away. The gleaming white walls began to lean at crazy angles. He shut his eyes and thought of darkness and silence. Presently the whimpering stopped. A voice faltered: "No, I am never going to d— No, I am not."

"Yes," he said firmly, "you are." The darkness ebbed. Alec opened his eyes. Helen had turned around and was watching him, a line of puzzlement on her forehead. "Really?" she asked childishly.

His face was damp, but he did not move to wipe it. "Yes," he stated, "absolutely certain. Cancer, incurable cancer."

"Cancer," she murmured wonderingly. "Where?"

He had that answer ready. He had picked it from an atlas of anatomy as an inaccessible spot, hard to confirm or deny, impossible to operate for. He told her.

She considered for a second, a vague puzzlement wrinkling her face. "Then . . . I can't do anything about it. It would happen just the same. It's there now." She looked up absently, rubbing a hand across her forehead. "The deadline?"

"It's very small and encysted." Casually he waved a hand. "Maybe even ten-twenty years."

Thinking, she got out of bed and stood looking out the window, her lips pursed as if she were whistling.

Alec turned to watch her, a polite smile fixed on his lips. He could feel the doctor's weight shifting as his head cleared.

"Cells." Helen murmured, once, then exclaimed suddenly to herself. "Of course not!" She chuckled, and chuckling spoke in her own warm voice, the thin note of fear gone. "Alec, you'll never guess what I have been doing. Wait until you hear the records!" She laughed delightedly. "A wild goose chase! I'm ashamed to face you. And I didn't see it until this minute."

"Didn't see what, honey?"

The doctor got to his knees and softly crawled away.

Helen swung around gayly. "Didn't see that all cells are mutable, not just germ cells, but all cells. If they keep on multiplying—each cell with the same probability of mutation—and some viable mutations would be cancerous, then everybody— Work it out on a slide rule for me, Hon, with so many million cells in the body, with—"

She had been looking past him at the new idea, but now her gaze focused and softened. "Alec, you look so tired. You shouldn't be pale after all your tramping around in—" The mists of thought cleared. She saw him. "Alec, you're back."

And now there was no space or time separating them and she was warm and alive in his arms, nuzzling his cheek, whispering a chuckle in his ear. "And I was standing there lecturing you about cells! I must have been crazy."

He could hear the doctor padding up the hall with a squad of husky attendants, but he didn't care. Helen was back.

From too much love of living
From hope and fear set free
We thank with brief thanksgiving
Whatever gods may be
That no life lives for ever;
That dead men rise up never;
That even the weariest river
Winds somewhere safe to sea.
                              Swinburne

————————

Will H. Gray

THE BEES FROM BORNEO

Silas Donaghy was by far the best beekeeper and queen breeder in the United States; not because of the amount of honey he produced but because he had bred a strain of bees that produced records. Those two hundred hives consistently averaged three hundred pounds of honey each. Naturally enough, everyone who had read about his results in the different bee journals wanted queens from his yard, and his yearly production of two thousand queens was always bought up ahead of time at two dollars each, which is just double the usual price.

Silas was a keen student of biology besides an expert beekeeper. He had tried all the usual experiments with different races of bees before falling back on Italian stock, bred for many generations in the United States for honey-gathering qualities, gentleness, and color.

Although he had achieved commercial success, he still found the ex-perimental side most fascinating, especially with regard to artificial fertili-zation of drone eggs—a comparatively simple matter, only requiring a little care. His greatest ambition was to cross-breed different species and even different genera. From his studies he found out that the freaks exhibited in side shows were not crosses between dog and rabbit or cat and dog, as advertised, such things being impossible, owing, it is thought, to chemical differences in the life germs.

Every beekeeper knows that the queen bee lays fertile or unfertile eggs at will. One mating is sufficient for life, and after it the queen can lay a million or more fertile eggs at the rate of as many as two thousand a day in summer. The fertile eggs become females, either workers or queens, depending on how they are fed, while the unfertile eggs hatch out into drones, which are the big, clumsy, stingless males. For the most part they are useless, for they require the labor of five workers to keep them fed, and only a very few ever perform the services for which they were created.

Nature is very bounteous when it comes to reproduction, but seems to desert her children once they are safely ushered into this wicked world.

All might have gone well if someone had not sent Silas Donaghy a queen bee from the wilds of Borneo. After careful examination, he introduced it to one of his hives which he had just deprived of its own queen. In a month's time the new brood had hatched and were on the wing; pretty bees they were with a red tuft on the abdomen and long, graceful bodies with strong wings. Soon the honey began to come in and pile up on that hive, which was mounted on a weighing scale. Up and up crept the weight until Silas saw that he had something as far beyond his own strain as his own were above the ordinary black bee. In his enthusiasm for these new and beautiful creatures, he overlooked the source of their honey. Not alone did they gather from the flowers but from every plant that had sweet juice in its stems or leaves, and they did not hesitate to enter other hives and rob them of their stores. In fact, wherever there was a sign of sugar, they seemed to find it and carry it off. When that hive had piled up a thousand pounds of honey, Silas took eggs from it and put them in every hive he had. Risking everything, he bought extra hives and equipment and raised five thousand of the new queens, which he sold for five dollars each. Soon his mail was flooded with letters of two kinds: one lot praising his queens as the most wonderful honey gatherers in the world, the other abusing him for scattering a race of robbers that were ruining crops and cleaning out all other hives within a radius of five miles.

Things might have righted themselves if it had not been for a California senator who owned two thousand hives and had them completely robbed out by another beekeeper who had only five hundred, all mothered by the new Borneo strain.

By means of influence at Washington, and without consulting the Bureau of Entomology, this senator had the mails closed to Silas Donaghy's queens. It was a dreadful shock to Silas because he had already begun refunding people their money and replacing the queens free of charge. Now he could no longer make amends, but the letters of abuse continued to come in by the hundred. He said nothing, but devoted himself more and more to his experiments.

It was with an ordinary wasp or yellow jacket that he succeeded in producing a creature that soon turned the continent upside down.

Under his super-microscope he was looking at an unfertile egg of a Borneo queen. Something buzzed into the room and flew around the microscope, making a breeze that threatened to blow away the delicate egg from its glass slide. Impatiently he put out his hand and to his surprise caught something between his fingers. It was a drone wasp and he had partly crushed it. An idea suddenly struck him; he took a fine camel's-hair brush and touched it to the fluid containing the microscopic spermatazoa or life germs exuding from the dead wasp. With infinite care he applied the brush to the large end of the tiny, cucumber-shaped egg on the stage of the microscope. Presently he saw several minute, eel-like creatures burrowing into the egg. One outswam the others; its long tail was replaced by protoplasmic radiations and it united with the female pronucleus. With a tense look, the experimenter sat on with his eye rigidly glued to the microscope.

Had he succeeded? Would cleavage take place? He was called to lunch, but the call went unheeded. At last the pronucleus elongated, became narrow in the middle and finally split into two.

Wonderful! Extraordinary! It would seem that he had accomplished that which no other man had ever done.

Carefully he transferred the wonderful egg to a queen cup and covered it with royal jelly, that special food that in quantity would make it a queen.

Now he must trust it to the tender mercies of the bees, for no man knows the exact constituents of the food fed to the larvæ day by day. Then there is always the chance that the bees will reject the egg thus offered to them; they show their disapproval by licking up the royal jelly and devouring the delicate egg.

Silas went through agonies in those three days that it takes the egg to hatch. Everything went as it should, and in fourteen days he had a perfect queen resembling a wasp except for a few reddish hairs on the abdomen. His anxieties were not yet over, for a week after hatching the queen goes on her wedding flight. High up into the air she soars with all the drones after her in a flock. To the strong goes the victory, but his joy is short lived, for after one embrace he falls to the ground, dead, his vitals torn from him and attached to the queen. Such is the queen's first flight and after it she returns to the hive to lay countless thousands of eggs. Had he wished to, Silas could have fertilized the queen by the Sladen method, almost amounting to an operation, but he thought it wiser to let nature take her course.

On the seventh day the young queen came out of the hive, ran about the alighting board nervously for a minute, then took a short flight to get her bearings and finally shot into the air and out of sight while the drones followed in desperate haste.

Silas waited and watched, but she did not return. Days passed and his spirits fell to zero, for the chance of a lifetime had slipped from his grasp.

It was a month or so later that young Silas came running into his father's study one morning with the news:

"Oh, Father! Come quick and bring the cyanide. There's a wasp's nest bigger than a pumpkin down on a tree in the wood lot."

"Now, Silas, I've often told you not to exaggerate. You know it isn't that size."

"Well, Father, it's enormous, anyway."

When Silas, senior, went down to investigate he found his son's description not in the least exaggerated. If anything, the size was underestimated. There, to his astonishment, hung the largest wasp's nest he had ever seen or heard about. The insects going in and out seemed different from the ordinary yellow jackets. Walking over to investigate, he received a sting that temporarily knocked him out. He was well inoculated to bee stings and they hardly affected him, but this was something quite different. Some way or other he reached the house and collapsed on the doorstep.

It was three days before he was about again, feeling very shaky on his legs. He did not lack courage, for he took a butterfly net and veil and went down to see how the new insects were getting along. The nest was bigger still and the numbers of bees coming in and out had greatly increased. He managed to capture one before he was chased home, and a sting on the hand, though very painful, did not incapacitate him so badly as the first had done.

To his astonishment the captured insect had the red tip to its abdomen. Here was a great discovery. His escaped queen had settled down on her own account and started a paper-pulp nest like ordinary wasps instead of returning to her own hive. Interest in the new species overcame everything else in his mind, even the severity of the sting.

Putting the captured specimen in a queen mailing cage, he posted it to the professor of entomology at the State University, who had been friendly to him through all his late troubles. Alas for the regulations which he had quite forgotten in his excitement. The Post Office people returned his specimen with a prosecution notice. He was summoned to court and heavily fined.

While he was away from home, little Silas was stung by one of the bees and died the same evening.

Something gave way in the poor man's mind and he hated the whole world with a deadly hatred.

Making himself a perfectly bee-tight costume, he sat near the great nest for hours at a time, capturing young queens as they emerged. Next he bought a gross of little rubber balloons and some cylinders of compressed hydrogen. Making small paper cages, he attached an inflated balloon to each, put in a young queen and started them off wherever the wind would take them. When the queen got tired of her paper prison, she chewed her way out to freedom and, single-handed, started a new colony.

It was getting late in the season and the new strain of insects did not make much headway before the cold weather set in.

Early the next spring the country papers began to complain of the prevalence of deaths from bee or wasp stings. Every year some people die of stings, but now the number was greatly increased. Animals also were frequently found dead without apparent reason. Many people got stung and recovered after a week in bed.

In the cities these constant accounts from the country became a sort of joke. The words "stung," "sting" and "stings" were used on every occasion, in season and out. When a man was away from work without permission, instead of saying he was burying his grandmother he said he had been laid up with a bee sting.

At last official notice was taken of the new menace and they were recognized as being descended from the famous Borneo queens. The bees from Borneo were now discussed in every state in the Union. The cities were still joking, but the country people were getting desperate. Many had sold out for what they could get and had moved to parts not yet infested with the new pest. Those that remained wore special clothes, had all doors and windows carefully screened, and took every precaution not to let the insects into the house. It was soon discovered that even the chimneys had to be covered when fires were not burning. The new insects had to have sugar as well as insect or flesh diet, but they preferred to get their sweets in any other way rather than from the flowers. All beehives were quickly robbed and the bees killed off. Soon it was realized that there would be no fruit crop in many districts, for even if pickers could be found who would run the risk of being stung, the insects were always ahead of them devouring the fruit as soon as ripe.

The cities began to wake up when the new insects found that open fruit stalls and candy stores were theirs for the taking. They built their nests from waste paper or old wood or any fibrous material that they could find. The nests were built high up under cornices and gables where it was very difficult to find them and still more difficult to destroy them. The death toll was now greater, for the city people were not inoculated as many of the country folk were. One in every four died from the stings. The conversation became more serious, the papers had a special column for deaths from stings. A fellow worker would not turn up at the office; his friends looked at each other gravely and cast lots to see who should ring up to find out the sad news. If he did come back after being in a hospital he was hailed with enthusiasm.

All the leading scientists and doctors were working hard to devise a serum or antitoxin. Some brave men were undergoing a series of injections with formic acid to see if it would immunize them. Every newspaper had a list of so-called cures sent in by people who professed to have cured themselves or others. It was hard to judge these things, for it was impossible to know if the sting were really of a Borneo queen and not of some other hymenopterous insect. Panic alone killed many, so great was the fright of those stung by any insect. Those who recovered from a sting practically never died when stung again; this fact was of great use when recruiting began later on in the year.

A dreadful catastrophe raised the menace of the bees to an importance exceeding everything else.

A trainload of molasses was entering a suburb of a great city where the bees had obtained quite a foothold. The engineer was stung in the face and staggered back into the arms of the fireman. A lurch and both fell out on the track. On rushed the heavy train with throttle open. Soon it entered the yards at great speed, jumped the switches and collided with an outgoing passenger train. Sounds of rending steel and splintering wood filled the air. Roaring, hissing steam drowned the cries of the injured. Over track and wreckage spread a turgid mass of strong-smelling molasses.

Before the work of rescue was half completed the air was swarming with millions of buzzing insects. Doctors, nurses, railway workers, policemen and ambulance drivers were stung into insensibility and death. To complete the awful drama some well-intentioned persons bravely started smudge fires, hoping to smoke away the bees. Now fire was added and the flames licked through the seething, treacly mass, converting it into a holocaust such as had not been witnessed since the days of the Great War. Five hundred persons lost their lives through accident, fire and stings. Thirty or forty casualties, at the most, would have been the total if it had not been for the bees.

The nation was awake now. Complete destruction of this new pest was demanded in all the great newspapers. Expense could not be spared in such an emergency. There must be no half-hearted measures, for the very life of the country was being strangled by the creation of a madman.

Volunteers were organized all over the country. They were equipped with extension ladders and strong sacks, which they put over the suspended nest, drew tight the running string, and transferred the whole thing to a woven wire burner, where it was sprayed with gasoline and burnt. At first they seemed to make some headway, but a fine spell of weather and millions of emerging young queens gave the bees fresh impetus and the newly started nests could not be found so easily as the large old ones.

The national capital proved a specially happy hunting ground for the bees. The public buildings provided thousands of nooks and corners where the nests were not discovered until they were as large as barrels. Sometimes the weight would break them down. If they fell in a street, there were sure to be many deaths before traffic could be diverted, and men protected to the last degree destroyed the insects with flaming sprays and poison gas. At last things became so bad that the seat of government was moved to a town in Arizona which had not yet been invaded by bees.

Many new industries sprang into being, for anything advertised to combat the pests found a ready sale. Traps of every size, shape and description were sold; many of them more ingenious to look at than practical in use. Poison baits were sold and used by the ton, many harmless animals and not a few children fell victims to their use.

In spite of everything the pests went on increasing in numbers until the country seemed on the verge of bankruptcy. When farm mortgages, considered so safe, fell due, it was not worth while foreclosing them, for the land was useless. The new insects did not pollinate the fruit, but they destroyed the insects that did. Farm produce rose to unheard-of prices. Passenger traffic was reduced to a minimum, for nobody traveled who could possibly avoid it. Excursions and pleasure trips seemed to be a thing of the past. Even free insurance against stings did not stimulate travel, for no one seemed keen on being stung, however big the compensation to their heirs!

When fruit reached a certain price, large syndicates bought up fertile stretches for almost nothing and screened them in at enormous cost. In these enclosures the most intensive culture known was practiced with very profitable results. Not alone were there gardeners, but numerous guards patrolled the high framework with shotguns charged with salt ready to shoot any bee that should find its way in. Common bees had to be introduced from great distances for pollination purposes.

Silas Donaghy gibbered and raved in the state asylum; when he saw anyone stung he was convulsed with mirth. From morning to night he played tricks on the attendants, doctors and other patients. They never could tell when he might have a bee concealed about his clothing or wrapped in his handkerchief. It was most disturbing to the officials to get suddenly chased by a man who held sudden death in his hand. They put him in the padded cell, but it did not disturb him in the least. When his food was brought, he imitated the buzzing of a bee so skilfully that the attendant dropped the food and ran, followed by Silas' unearthly shrieks of merriment. At times he appeared quite sane and would skilfully catch and kill every bee that accidentally got let in. When he got stung himself, which was very rarely, he would wince with the pain and fall to his knees and grope about half blinded for support while the poison coursed through his veins. Getting to his feet again, he would stagger about with the tears of agony running down his cheeks, the while laughing at himself and cursing his weakness. Those who saw him marveled, for most people collapsed in a writhing heap and mercifully became unconscious.

In his sane moments he begged for his beloved microscope and experimental equipment. At last, to humor him and incidentally save themselves unlimited trouble, they gave him a little hut in the grounds where he could do as he liked so long as he did not annoy anyone. The first thing he did was to tear off all the screen wire and let the bees have free access to his living and sleeping rooms. He even let them share his meals and they sat in rows on the edge of his plate. It wasn't long before there was a nest right above his bed; it remained there undisturbed, for no one went near his little abode. The official bee swatters kept clear of Silas, for they had their dignity to uphold and Silas made fun of their bee-tight costumes and elaborate equipment. He could kill more bees in a day, if he wanted to, than they could in a week.

The Government was still busy working out methods to control the plague. One that seemed to promise some success was the introduction of a large fly belonging to the hawk-like family that prey on honey bees, catching them on the wing and tearing them asunder to feed on the sweet juices within. These flies were bred in great numbers and distributed over the country. Spiders and bee-eating birds were also extensively tried out.

With the first days of autumn the nation breathed more freely, for the Borneo bees were even more sensitive to cold than the ordinary hive bees. So great was the relief that all the activities of summer began to take place in the winter. People went visiting and the railways ran excursions. Such is the spirit of the people that they quickly forget their troubles and trust that the past will bury its past. But the entomologists of the country knew and trembled at the thought of spring when the fine weather would entice from their wintering places thousands and millions of queens that would quickly construct nests and raise broods that would far exceed anything that had yet gone before. A bounty of ten cents a queen was offered and thousands of people collected the dormant insects from their hiding places. Special instructors visited all the schools, telling of the dangers that awaited them if the queens were not destroyed now.

The fine weather came and with it the queens came out of their hiding places in countless millions. Those gathered were as a drop in the bucket, compared to those left undisturbed. For a few short weeks things got steadily worse and worse. All the devices of the previous year were used and a lot of new ones. Single screen doors were no longer of any use. Double doors were better, but the most reliable system proved to be a cold passage kept at a very low temperature. In this passage the insects became chilled and could be swept up and destroyed.

Every day now seemed closer to the time when things would end. A heat wave came along and the overstrained public services collapsed. The dead lay in the streets. The frantic telephone calls went unanswered. Even the water pipes were choked with the dead insects and the water tainted with the acrid poison that also filled the air.

Those who had the means and were able fled to other parts where the breakdown had not yet occurred. The military forces of the country were fully organized for relief purposes and those who remained were rescued from the cities of the dead.

The State Lunatic Asylum collapsed with all the rest of society and patients wandered out and were soon stung to death.

Silas was undecided what to do at first. Then he thought it would be a good plan to put the screen wire back on his shack. The bees objected to the hammering, so he waited until night and did it then. He was rather disappointed at having to destroy the nest inside, but it could not be helped. Several visits to the storeroom of the asylum yielded all the food he needed. For a few days he remained in solitude, then he packed his beloved microscope, put on a light bee veil and started home over the deserted roads. He was careful not to annoy the insects in any way. He never batted at them or made quick, jerky movements and he avoided going near their nests. He took it very easy so that he would not perspire, for bees hate the smell of sweat.

Sad sights met his gaze as he trudged along. The whitened bones of cows and horses and smaller animals littered the fields, for the insects picked their victims clean, requiring as they did a partly animal diet like ordinary wasps. A disabled truck stood by the roadside and sitting in the driver's seat was a grim skeleton. Further on a cheap touring car lay on its side and four skeletons, two large and two small, told the sad tale of a family wiped out in a few minutes. These sights did not seem to affect Silas at all; he was more interested in the nests that hung from every tree and telegraph pole and from the gables and eaves of houses and barns. Once he was overtaken by an armored and screened military ambulance. He refused their aid and they hurried on, the wheels crushing a bee at every turn. A crushed bee is smelled by the other bees and they are immediately on the warpath, so Silas had to leave the road and take to the fields.

When he reached home he found his wife alone in the well-screened house. She had been ostracized by all the neighbors long before they had left, and but for Silas' letters of instruction, she could not have carried on single-handed. Somehow she had expected Silas. He entered by the cellar steps and slipped through so dexterously that only seven bees got in with him. They flew to a window, where he quickly killed them, for Mrs. Donaghy, strange to say, had never been stung. He took off his outer-clothing and found five more. Disposing of these, he went upstairs and carried his microscope to the study, where he carefully unpacked it and put a glass cover over it. He fussed about the study in an absent-minded way until Mrs. Donaghy called him to supper. Sitting down, he looked at the place where little Silas used to sit.

"Where's the boy?" he questioned. "You know I like him to be on time to his meals."

A pained look came over the poor lady's face.

"Silas, you know he's gone."

"Gone where? What do you mean?"

She looked up flushing and for the first time in her married life spoke with heat:

"Dead, you know he's dead; stung to death by one of your accursed bees."

Silas collapsed on the table. Covering his face with his hands, great sobs wracked his body. "My God, my God, what have I done?" he moaned.

Presently he was in his study again, looking at everything with a new light in his eyes. He was alert and methodical now, and there was a set appearance about his jaw that had not been there for a long, long while.

Taking the plug out of the keyhole, he waited till a bee came in and dexterously catching it by the wings, brought it to his study. His tired eyes were bright now and he appeared to be looking at something he had never seen before. Frequently he came to the living-room to ask his wife questions about what had happened in the last year or so. He seemed appalled, but a glance from any window verified all she said.

That night he visited a deep bee cellar constructed underground where he used to winter some of his colonies. He found that it had been used as an ice house while he had been away. Seeing an old hive in the corner, he went over and lifted the lid. To his utter astonishment a faint buzz greeted him that was quite different from the high note of the all-pervading pest outside. Here was the remnant of a colony of honey bees that had been forgotten. How could they have survived all this time? He didn't know, unless it was the ice making a continuous winter for two years. Shouldering the hive, he carried it out and placed it in a little screened chicken yard where Mrs. Donaghy had endeavored to raise a few vegetables. Next morning the survivors were buzzing about getting their bearings, though there wasn't much fear of their straying very far in the little enclosure.

For the next week Silas hardly slept or took time to eat. If he wasn't at the microscope he was in the small yard where the last honey bees in North America flew about and licked up the honey given them. Little they knew that the fate of a continent depended on them.

At last he produced a drone that seemed to fill the requirements. It must be able to outfly the drones of the vicious half-breeds all around. It must be able to produce grandsons, for by the laws of parthenogenesis a drone cannot have sons that would also be swift and amorous. It must produce daughters and granddaughters resembling honey bees and incapable of surviving the winter alone.

Most scientists would have waited to test out these qualities before scattering the new product broadcast. Silas, however, was always impetuous, as the sale of his first Borneo queens had shown him to be. He realized now that the situation might be better but could not be worse.

Setting to work in his little enclosure, he bred drones in large numbers and liberated them. If only he had some way of distributing them quickly! Balloons and hydrogen? Alas, he had neither. He wandered about, thinking hard. There in the basement stood the little lighting plant with its neat row of batteries and a large jar of acid in the corner. Ha! There was hydrogen, either by electrolysis or more quickly still with strips of zinc or nails and the acid. Paper bags would do for the balloons.

In a day or so he was sending the drones off on the wind by the dozen together, hoping that they would seek out the young queens wherever they went and father a new race of harmless bees that would die out entirely in the winter.

In a month he noticed young queens without the familiar red tuft on their tails. Capturing a few, he put them in his enclosure and fed them carefully, even opening a precious tin of meat to help them along; but they did not respond and some died. They were incapable of living alone. However, those put into nests flourished and outdid their vicious half-sister. It was a treat to see the new drones on the wing rushing about in their wild search for virgin queens. The workers of the new breed had barbed stings and died on using them. It was not very painful either.

Every day now Silas was in his garden getting things to rights, planting and harvesting. He smiled now at the millions of bees, for they were all different from the old race that was quickly dying off.

He often wondered if there was anyone else alive. Making a trip to the deserted village, he was rummaging around looking for canned goods when he was astonished to hear a telephone ring. It was a long distance call searching for anyone alive.

"The bees have played themselves out," he was told. "The breed did not hold true. Nature righted herself automatically."

Silas went home smiling. He knew that he had started and ended the awful plague.

DAVID GRINNELL

THE RAG THING

IT WOULD HAVE been all right if spring had never come. During the winter nothing had happened and nothing was likely to happen as long as the weather remained cold and Mrs. Larch kept the radiators going. In a way, though, it is quite possible to hold Mrs. Larch to blame for everything that happened. Not that she had what people would call malicious intentions, but just that she was two things practically every boarding-house landlady is—thrifty and not too clean.

She shouldn't have been in such a hurry to turn the heat off so early in March. March is a tricky month and she should have known that the first warm day is usually an isolated phenomenon. But then you could always claim that she shouldn't have been so sloppy in her cleaning last November. She shouldn't have dropped that rag behind the radiator in the third floor front room.

As a matter of fact, one could well wonder what she was doing using such a rag anyway. Polishing furniture doesn't require a clean rag to start with, certainly not the rag you stick into the furniture polish, that's going to be greasy anyway—but she didn't have to use that particular rag. The one that had so much dried blood on it from the meat that had been lying on it in the kitchen.

On top of that, it is probable that she had spit into the filthy thing, too. Mrs. Larch was no prize package. Gross, dull, unkempt, widowed and careless, she fitted into the house—one of innumerable other brownstone fronts in the lower sixties of New York. Houses that in former days, fifty or sixty years ago, were considered the height of fashion and the residences of the well-to-do, now reduced to dingy rooming places for all manner of itinerants, lonely people with no hope in life other than dreary jobs, or an occasional young and confused person from the hinterland seeking fame and fortune in a city which rarely grants it.

So it was not particularly odd that when she accidentally dropped the filthy old rag behind the radiator in the room on the third floor front late in November, she had simply left it there and forgotten to pick it up.

It gathered dust all winter, unnoticed. Skelty, who had the room, might have cleaned it out himself save that he was always too tired for that. He worked at some indefinite factory all day and when he came home he was always too tired to do much more than read the sports and comics pages of the newspapers and then maybe stare at the streaky brown walls a bit before dragging himself into bed to sleep the dreamless sleep of the weary.

The radiator, a steam one oddly enough (for most of these houses used the older hot-air circulation), was in none too good condition. Installed many many years ago by the house's last Victorian owner, it was given to knocks, leaks, and cantankerous action. Along in December it developed a slow drip, and drops of hot water would fall to seep slowly into the floor and leave the rag lying on a moist hot surface. Steam was constantly escaping from a bad valve that Mrs. Larch would have repaired if it had blown off completely but, because the radiator always managed to be hot, never did.

Because Mrs. Larch feared drafts, the windows were rarely open in the winter and the room would become oppressively hot at times when Skelty was away.

It is hard to say what is the cause of chemical reactions. Some hold that all things are mechanical in nature, others that life has a psychic side which cannot be duplicated in laboratories. The problem is one for metaphysicians; everyone knows that some chemicals are attracted to heat, others to light, and they may not necessarily be alive at all. Tropisms is the scientific term used, and if you want to believe that living matter is stuff with a great number of tropisms and dead matter is stuff with little or no tropisms, that's one way of looking at it. Heat and moisture and greasy chemical compounds were the sole ingredients of the birth of life in some ancient unremembered swamp.

Which is why it probably would have been all right if spring had never come. Because Mrs. Larch turned the radiators off one day early in March. The warm hours were but few. It grew cold with the darkness and by night it was back in the chill of February again. But Mrs. Larch had turned the heat off and, being lazy, decided not to turn it on again till the next morning, provided of course that it stayed cold the next day (which it did).

Anyway Skelty was found dead in bed the next morning. Mrs. Larch knocked on his door when he failed to come down to breakfast and when he hadn't answered, she turned the knob and went in. He was lying in bed, blue and cold, and he had been smothered in his sleep.

There was quite a to-do about the whole business but nothing came of it. A few stupid detectives blundered around the room, asked silly questions, made a few notes, and then left the matter to the coroner and the morgue. Skelty was a nobody, no one cared whether he lived or died, he had no enemies and no friends, there were no suspicious visitors, and he had probably smothered accidentally in the blankets. Of course the body was unusually cold when Mrs. Larch found it, as if the heat had been sucked out of him, but who notices a thing like that? They also discounted the grease smudge on the top sheet, the grease stains on the floor, and the slime on his face. Probably some grease he might have been using for some imagined skin trouble, though Mrs. Larch had not heard of his doing so. In any case, no one really cared.

Mrs. Larch wore black for a day and then advertised in the papers. She made a perfunctory job of cleaning the room. Skelty's possessions were taken away by a drab sister-in-law from Brooklyn who didn't seem to care much either, and Mrs. Larch was all ready to rent the room to someone else.

The weather remained cold for the next ten days and the heat was kept up in the pipes.

The new occupant of the room was a nervous young man from up-state who was trying to get a job in New York. He was a high-strung young man who entertained any number of illusions about life and society. He thought that people did things for the love of it and he wanted to find a job where he could work for that motivation rather than the sort of things he might have done back home. He thought New York was different, which was a mistake.

He smoked like fury which was something Mrs. Larch did not like because it meant ashes on the floor and burned spots on her furniture (not that there weren't plenty already), but there was nothing Mrs. Larch would do about it because it would have meant exertion.

After four days in New York, this young man, Gorman by name, was more nervous than ever. He would lie in bed nights smoking cigarette after cigarette thinking and thinking and getting nowhere. Over and over he was facing the problem of resigning himself to a life of gray drab. It was a thought he had tried not to face and now that it was thrusting itself upon him, it was becoming intolerable.

The next time a warm day came, Mrs. Larch left the radiators on because she was not going to be fooled twice. As a result, when the weather stayed warm, the rooms became insufferably hot because she was still keeping the windows down. So that when she turned the heat off finally, the afternoon of the second day, it was pretty tropic in the rooms.

When the March weather turned about suddenly again and became chilly about nine at night, Mrs. Larch was going to bed and figured that no one would complain that it would be warm again the next day. Which may or may not be true, it does not matter.

Gorman got home about ten, opened the window, got undressed, moved a pack of cigarettes and an ash tray next to his bed on the floor, got into bed, turned out the light and started to smoke.

He stared at the ceiling, blowing smoke upwards into the darkened room trying to see its outlines in the dim light coming in from the street. When he finished one cigarette, he let his hand dangle out the side of the bed and picked up another cigarette from the pack on the floor, lit it from the butt in his mouth, and dropped the butt into the ash tray on the floor.

The rag under the radiator was getting cold, the room was getting cold, there was one source of heat radiation in the room. That was the man in the bed. Skelty had proven a source of heat supply once. Heat attraction was chemical force that could not be denied. Strange forces began to accumulate in the long-transformed fibers of the rag.

Gorman thought he heard something flap in the room but he paid it no attention. Things were always creaking in the house. Gorman heard a swishing noise and ascribed it to the mice.

Gorman reached down for a cigarette, fumbled for it, found the pack, deftly extracted a smoke in the one-handed manner chain smokers become accustomed to, lifted it to his mouth, lit it from the burning butt in his mouth, and reached down with the butt to crush it out against the tray.

He pressed the butt into something wet like a used handkerchief, there was a sudden hiss, something coiled and whipped about his wrist; Gorman gasped and drew his hand back fast. A flaming horror, twisting and writhing, was curled around it. Before Gorman could shriek, it had whipped itself from his hand and fastened over his face, over the warm, heat-radiating skin and the glowing flame of the cigarette.

Mrs. Larch was awakened by the clang of fire engines. When the fire was put out, most of the third floor had been gutted. Gorman was an unrecognizable charred mass.

The fire department put the blaze down to Gorman's habit of smoking in bed. Mrs. Larch collected on the fire insurance and bought a new house, selling the old one to a widow who wanted to start a boarding house.

Mark Clifton

THE CONQUEROR

FACTS ON THE CULTURE OF DAHLIAS:
1. The dahlia does not breed true from seed. Every seedling is a mutant.
2. A favorable mutant is propagated by tuber division, and as such remains reasonably fast.
3. It is possible to average ten plants from one each year. In twelve years one could have a hundred billion plants from one mutation.

4. Every gardener who grows dahlias throws away bushels of unwanted tubers. He has speculated numerous times on what a bountiful food supply they would make if they were only edible.
5. The dahlia is not too fussy about its soil, and with proper selection and care it may be matured from the equator to the arctic.
6. The dahlia grows wild in Guatemala, and through the centuries has self-seeded into endless mutations. It is reasonable to assume that one of these mutations might have peculiar properties—most peculiar indeed.

PADRE TOMÁS CHRISTENED him Juan Rafael de la Medina Torres, and so of naturally he was called Pepe. By the time he was of five years his body had begun to lose its infant roundness and his Indian cheekbones already showed their promise. Under his tangled black hair and behind his snapping black eyes there were dreams.

For one who knew only the path leading down the side of the volcano to the village at its foot, where also stood the mission; on the path leading up the side of the mountain to his papa's precarious corn and bean patches; or the path leading around the side of the volcano and down to the coffee finca; these were dreams indeed.

His papa would shake his head in slow bewilderment and remind Pepe, without too much affection or harshness either, that instead of conquering the world he would better think more about gathering of the grass to dry for his mama's weaving, or to thatch the roof, or for sleep upon the dirt floor of their hut.

Sometimes Pepe was to be a powerful brujo, even more respected than the wizard of the village—yes, much more than such a one who was old and without teeth and did not use his magic powers to make people do things. When he became so powerful, then would he torture and shame his sister for her taunts and jibes. Of naturally, he would not hurt her too much, for that would make Padre Tomás angry with him. So, after he had caused her enough suffering then would he forgive her and dress her as rich as the señora Norte Americana he saw one day in the village market place.

But most of the time he dreamed much grander dreams than that. He dreamed of being even as el Presidente de Guatemala. Pepe had never seen el Presidente who lived in a fine palace in Guatemala City, but he suspected that such a one might be almost as grand as Padre Tomás himself.

Then there would be plenty of tortillas and beans always. Everyone could pack his belly so tight it would glisten like a shining gourd in the sun. No, that was not too much for such a powerful politico as he would be. To all the world he would become even as a father. It would be necessary for him first to conquer the world, and perhaps he would have to punish people a little to make them respect him, but then he would give it of all these things.

Such were the dreams of Pepe, christened Juan Rafael de la Medina Torres.

So it was until one day.

Of naturally, Pepe knew the wild dahlia roots were not fit to eat. All the world knows that much, even that ignorant señora Norte Americana who knew nothing else, no nothing never at all. The silly questions she asked about every little thing. Still, the dahlia tubers were so succulent to look upon, almost like the yam, each time he dug them up he would taste them a little, just perhaps.

One day when he was supposed to be gathering grass he accidentally tugged and strained and finally pulled up one dahlia. It was a fine one with a big stalk and many tubers. Tentatively, he broke one of the tubers and tasted of it. A look of bliss came over his face, for it was indeed good to eat.

His sister, ever loud in the mouth, was hiding in a grevile tree, spying on him. She scrambled to the ground and ran tattling to her mama that Pepe was eating of the dirt again. Mama wearily lay down her weaving of the grass mats and stood to her feet. Ordinarily Pepe would have run away to hide when he saw her coming, shouting imprecations at him, but this time he sat and handed his mamacita a piece of the tuber when she came up to him.

His unusual conduct so startled her that instead of cuffing at him, she stopped and sniffed at the root suspiciously. The same rapture spread over her face when she tasted. She carefully gathered up the tightly packed bunch of tubers, containing the crown where the next year's plant buds lay dormant and waiting.

Marguerita, the sister, watched them both with wide eyes and with her bucktoothed mouth closed for once. Wiping her nose with her finger, she came closer, but not so close that Pepe could strike out and hit her. She stretched out her hand for a taste. Her slanting eyes stretched wider still and her mouth hung open in surprise when Pepe as well as her mama freely offered her bits of the tuber. The little wild one tasted also of the root.

No one looked on in surprise when she threw her arms about her little brother and called him "Pepito." Even this unheard of action did not ruffle his serenity.

Now with care the three of them uprooted all the other dahlias in the glade beside the path, but these were harsh and bitter. Only this one plant was good of the taste.

Mama handled her machete as skillfully as a surgeon's scalpel when she split the crown again and again, so that each bud had one tuber hanging below it for stored food to grow upon. While Pepe and his sister stood by and watched, she planted the ten tubers in the rich volcanic earth close by the doorway of their hut. There she could watch and care for them tenderly.

Papa would think she had gone sick in the head if he knew she was growing the dahlia, so she cut a small bit from the end of one of the tubers and saved it for him.

All through the rest of the day, she and her children worked peacefully and industriously together. So long as he could return frequently to look upon the place where the tubers had been planted, Pepe was happy. He gathered more grass to weave than ever before.

Marguerita, too, for the first time, bent herself willingly to the task of learning to weave of the petates. She stopped her work only to get up occasionally and look upon the moist soft earth where the dahlias had been planted. Mama did not scold her for this, for mama also found that she must look upon the spot a little time more or less.

The sun was down and the cold wet clouds were swirling around the mountain when papa came back from his day of work in the coffee finca. His black eyes glittered with sudden anger and his face became as the thunder of Fuego when he saw no smoke filtering through the grass thatch of their roof, and smelled no odor of beans cooking for his supper. But the unusual sight of his wife and children weaving industriously in the dusk stopped his outburst.

When mama saw his shadow darken the doorway, she sprang to her feet like a light and active girl again. She held out a piece of the tuber as he came through the doorway. He took it, looked at it, and back at her.

"Eat of it," she said.

With bewilderment and perhaps a little fear replacing his anger, he bit tentatively at the edge of the fragment. With the one taste his face took on the same rapture which his family had known all through the afternoon.

It was the middle of the next day before any of them knew hunger again.

In several more days the bliss faded from their faces as the narcotic value of the tuber wore away. Pepe and his sister fought like wild animals again, while mama cuffed and shouted at them as ever. Papa was alternately harsh and silent as usual.

Still, all the family carefully watched the patch where the dahlias had been planted. Even in their most angry scuffling, Pepe and Marguerita never failed to keep clear of the dahlia bed.

The pale and succulent shoots came to the surface of the ground and grew with great rapidity. Daily, and almost hourly, the family watched the ten plants to see that no worm or bug damaged the shoots, to see that the bony wild chickens did not pick off the tender buds, to see that the yellow dog did not make a bed among them where it could ease its rickety bones.

In two months the dahlias began to bloom, and the Torres family knew that under the cover of the soil new clusters of tubers were forming. The leaves, the petals of the flower, these were not good of the taste, but when the blossoms opened there was a delicate perfume which wafted through the doorway of the hut and around the yard.

Again, in the fragrance, the Torres family became peaceful and good.

Now there was no harsh word spoken. Now papa was no longer to be found lying in the perfume of the suquinay tree drinking of his chica where one minute he would threaten his friends with the machete and the next he would weep with remorse. Marguerita no longer teased Pepe but spent her days crooning monotonously at her weaving. No longer did Pepe fashion of the traps to catch and torture the parrots.

No longer were there the many and many sins to confess to Padre Tomás.

Finally Padre Tomás could bear it no longer. Well he knew his Indians, and he knew there must be something most wrong at the house of Torres. No Indians could possibly be as good as these pretended in the confessional. He began to fear for their very souls.

So it was in his rounds he came upon the Torres hut one day when they were digging the plants of the dahlia. He looked with great surprise upon their careful handling of this wild plant, and even greater surprise upon the serenity and rapture of their faces.

When Mama Torres saw him coming, she broke off a bit of tuber and handed it to the good Padre, indicating that he should eat it. For the sake of his work and his success among his children, the Padre Tomás had endured many things. He showed no hesitancy of eating this acrid and bitter root if that was needed to regain their confidence.

Standing there with the black earth torn up about his feet, at the doorway of the hut, suddenly Padre Tomás felt as though the choir of Heaven itself burst into rapture in his head.

This time there was more than a hundred plants. Padre Tomás stayed and helped until the last was safely back in the good earth.

When he found that he also wished no more food until the following day, he came back to the house of Torres and instructed them, "Guard them with care, my children."

They had saved a few loose tubers and they gave him a share. He took them back to the mission and planted them.

When Pepe was of the years eight, there were a thousand plants. By the time he was nine there were ten thousand plants spread over all the village. Now there was peace and prosperity in the village. No man's hand was raised against his brother. Even the chickens, the pigs and the dogs received good care.

Long since, Padre Tomás had sent tubers of the plant to other villages and missions. Before very long all of Guatemala was eating regularly of the dahlia.

It had been well known to everyone that the military was carefully plotting the overthrow of el Presidente, mañana, and some day they might even be moved to do so. So well along was the plot that another plot back of that was formed to overthrow that dictatorship in its turn.

Now one by one the leaders of the revolution, and the second revolution, found they preferred to cultivate their gardens of the dahlia. They found they preferred to spend long hours and many successful conferences with one another in determining new ways by which they could save money for the taxed, even to send the soldiers to help the citizens in peaceful pursuits.

The politicos stopped robbing the treasury and sending monies to banks in foreign lands to live in luxury after the revolutions they engineered to give them excuse to leave the country had succeeded. They began to build of the schools and roads for the people instead.

In all Guatemala there was no unhappiness, no laziness, no evil. Every day was as fiesta, for fiesta was most of all the time for enjoyment. What greater enjoyment could there be than that of growing the dahlia? Each day the market place must be piled high with the tubers so that every city dweller might receive his share of the miracle food.

And the market place was constantly filled with tourists as from all the world who bought of the plant to send to their homes and friends for the growing there.

As everywhere, at the embassies at Guatemala City there had been the endless game of spying and counterspying. No Norte Americano business man made a move but what a counter move was made by the English counterpart. Every Hindu watched a Moslem, and every Moslem watched a Hindu. Even Wun Sing Low, laundryman for twenty years, was now known to be a Red spy, sending out his messages by marks upon the shirts of business men. All were enemies to the Soviet, and that embassy chose to see a world threat in the blink of every peon's eyes.

The governments of the world were accustomed to the voluminous reports, and they sifted through them with yawns of boredom. A man's diplomatic worth was judged by the poundage of his reports and the frequency of the crises he might uncover. Even so, it took some time before the governments became aware of the cessation of such reports from Guatemala.

Peace and prosperity and good will permeated all the reports from all the spy headquarters. No man could believe ill of his neighbor, for no man could partake of evil, or evil thought, where the dahlia was to be eaten.

Moscow, ever wary in its inferiority complex, and never ceasing to jockey for position, was the first of the capitals to summon its embassy's return. It demanded an account of these un-Marxian reports of serenity and peace in a capitalistic country. It wished to know why if there was no indigenous trouble some had not been manufactured.

The embassy took with it a plentiful supply of the tubers of the dahlia and ate heavily of them. It had been learned that the human body could store the food value of the dahlia for months and they were taking no chances. Throughout the routine of their torture, they maintained their rapture. Finally their inquisitors had no course left but to taste of the dahlia itself to check these fantastic tales and so give the lie to the diplomats.

Then the inquisitors in turn must endure the torture, for they no longer wished to carry forth their duties, and in turn their questioners ate. It became that there were none left but the Politbureau itself to carry on the torture since there were none others to be trusted to carry out the true democratic blessings upon their fellow men.

So it came about that one by one the members of the Politbureau tasted of the dahlia, even to the leader himself.

All of this took much time, and meanwhile the heads of other nations who were not so suspicious of every shadow, and not so inaccessible, were eating regularly of the dahlia.

When finally the sincere word of peace and good will came ringing from Moscow to all the world, it was echoed back with all sincerity.

By the end of twelve years over all the world the dahlia grew and thrived and was eaten. The Bering Strait Eskimo, the Congo Pigmy, the Australian Bushman, the Tibetan yak herder, each had his carefully bred offshoot of the dahlia. For the first time within written history the wretched masses of India and the famine-accustomed Chinese knew the full belly and peace and progress.

So it became in the world. There was but good will and happiness for all.

Pepe was now seventeen, and well beyond the age to marry. But there was not the economic urgency there once had been and children were permitted to remain without so much responsibility a little longer.

But today he was seventeen and today was his wedding day. Today was a most important day and he would not be called Pepe. He would be called for this one day by his true name of Juan Rafael de la Medina Torres. Now he was a grown man and his village was prosperous and everyone was happy.

Dimly he was aware that there was a world beyond his own village. But like all his forebears it had no reality for him. In truth he still knew only the path leading down the side of the volcano to the village; or the path up the mountain to where they once had grown corn and beans and now grew dahlias; or the path around the volcano and down to the coffee finca.

Barefoot still, but with his finest knee britches striped like peppermint candy, with his red cummerbund wrapped around his slender wrist, he trotted down the path toward the mission where Maria waited and where the good Padre Tomás would make them as one person. This was his world.

Half waking, half running in eagerness, the sight of the particular glade where he had first found the dahlia recalled his memory of himself as a little boy.

He laughed joyously and threw his shoulders back and breathed the mountain air of the morning in ecstasy. "What a one I was," he called aloud and shouted again with laughter. "I remember I was so fierce in those days. Why, I was going to conquer all the world!"

PART II

Inventions, Dangerous and Otherwise

THEODORE STURGEON

NEVER UNDERESTIMATE...

"SHE WAS BRAZEN, of course," said Lucinda, passing the marmalade, "but the brass was beautifully polished. The whole thing made me quite angry, though at the same time I was delighted."

Meticulously Dr. Lefferts closed the newly-arrived *Journal of the Microbiological Institute*, placed it on the copy of *Strength of Materials in Various Radioisotopic Alloys* which lay beside his plate, and carefully removed his pince-nez. "You begin in mid-sequence," he said, picking up a butter-knife. "Your thought is a predicate without a stated subject. Finally, your description of your reactions contains parts which appear mutually exclusive." He attacked the marmalade. "Will you elucidate?"

Lucinda laughed good-naturedly. "Of course, darling. Where would you like me to begin?"

"Oh . . ." Dr. Lefferts made a vague gesture. "Practically anywhere. Anywhere at all. Simply supply more relative data in order that I may extrapolate the entire episode and thereby dispose of it. Otherwise I shall certainly keep returning to it all day long. Lucinda, why do you continually do this to me?"

"Do what, dear?"

"Present me with colorful trivialities in just such amounts as will make me demand to hear you out. I have a trained mind, Lucinda; a fine-honed, logical mind. It must think things through. You know that. Why do you continually *do* this to me?"

"Because," said Lucinda placidly, "if I started at the beginning and went right through to the end, you wouldn't listen."

"I most certainly . . . eh. Perhaps you're right." He laid marmalade on to an English muffin in three parallel bands, and began smoothing them together at right angles to their original lay. "You are right, my dear. That must be rather difficult for you from time to time . . . yes?"

"No indeed," said Lucinda, and smiled. "Not as long as I can get your full attention when I want it. And I can."

Dr. Lefferts chewed her statement with his muffin. At last he said, "I admit that in your inimitable—uh—I think one calls it *female* way, you can. At least in regard to small issues. Now do me the kindness to explain to me what stimuli could cause you to"—his voice supplied the punctuation—"feel 'quite angry' and 'delighted' simultaneously."

Lucinda leaned forward to pour fresh coffee into his cooling cup. She was an ample woman, with an almost tailored combination of sveltness and relaxation. Her voice was like sofa-pillows and her eyes like blued steel. "It was on the Boulevard," she said. "I was waiting to cross when this girl drove through a red light right under the nose of a policeman. It was like watching a magazine illustration come to life—the bright-yellow convertible and the blazing blonde in the bright-yellow dress . . . darling, I do think you should call in this year's bra manufacturers for consultation in your Anti-Gravity Research Division. They achieve the most baffling effects . . . anyway, there she was and there by the car was the traffic-cop, as red-faced and Hibernian a piece of type-casting as you could wish. He came blustering over to her demanding to know begorry—I think he actually did say begorry—was she color-blind, now, or did she perhaps not give a care this marnin'?"

"In albinos," said Dr. Lefferts, "color perception is—"

Lucinda raised her smooth voice just sufficiently to override him without a break in continuity. "Now, here was an arrant violation of the law, flagrantly committed under the eyes of an enforcement officer. I don't have to tell you what should have happened. What *did* happen was that the girl kept her head turned away from him until his hands were on the car door. In the sun that hair of hers was positively dazzling. When he was close enough—within range, that is—she tossed her hair back and was face to face with him. You could see that great lump of bog-peat turn to putty. And she said to him (and if I'd had a musical notebook with me I could have jotted down her voice in sharp and flats)—she said, 'Why, officer, I did it on purpose just so I could see you up close.'"

Dr. Lefferts made a slight, disgusted sound. "He arrested her."

"He did not," said Lucinda. "He shook a big thick forefinger at her as if she were a naughty but beloved child, and the push-button blarney that oozed out of him was as easy to see as the wink he gave her. That's what made me mad."

"And well it should." He folded his napkin. "Violations of the law should be immediately pun—"

"The law had little to do with it," Lucinda said warmly. "I was angry because I know what would have happened to you or to me in that same situation. We're just not equipped."

"I begin to see." He put his pince-nez back on and peered at her. "And what was it that delighted you?"

She stretched easily and half-closed her eyes. "The—what you have called the *femaleness* of it. It's good to be a woman, darling, and to watch another woman be female skillfully."

"I quarrel with your use of the term 'skillfully,'" he said, folding his napkin. "Her 'skill' is analogous to an odor of musk or other such exudation in the lower animals."

"It is *not*," she said flatly. "With the lower animals, bait of that kind means one thing and one thing only, complete and final. With a woman, it means nothing of the kind. Never mind what it *might* mean; consider what it *does* mean. Do you think for a moment that the blonde in the convertible was making herself available to the policeman?"

"She was hypothesizing a situation in which—"

"She was hypothesizing nothing of the kind. She was blatantly and brazenly getting out of paying a traffic fine, and that was absolutely all. And you can carry it one step further; do you think that for one split second the policeman actually believed that she was inviting him? Of course he didn't! And yet that situation is one that has obtained through the ages. Women have always been able to get what they wanted from men by pretending to promise a thing which they know men want but will not or cannot take. Mind you, I'm not talking about situations where this yielding is the main issue. I'm talking about the infinitely greater number of occasions where yielding has nothing to do with it. Like weaseling out of traffic tickets."

"Or skillfully gaining your husband's reluctant attention over the breakfast table."

Her sudden laughter was like a shower of sparks. "You'd better get down to the Institute," she said. "You'll be late."

He arose, picked up his book and pamphlet, and walked slowly to the door. Lucinda came with him, hooking her arm through his. Suddenly he stopped, and without looking at her, asked quietly, "That policeman was a manipulated, undignified fool, wasn't he?"

"Of course he was, darling, and it made a man of him."

He nodded as if accepting a statistic, and, kissing her, walked out of the house.

Darling, she thought, *dear sweet chrome-plated, fine-drawn, high-polished blue-print . . . I think I've found where you keep your vanity.* She watched him walk with his even, efficient, unhurried stride to the gate. There he paused and looked back.

"This has been going on too long," he called. "I shall alter it."

Lucinda stopped smiling.

"May I come in?"

"Jenny, of course," Lucinda went to the kitchen door and unhooked it. "Come in, come in. My, you're prettier than ever this morning."

"I brought you violets," said Jenny breathlessly. "Just scads of 'em in the woods behind my place. You took your red curtains down. Is that a new apron? My! you had Canadian bacon for breakfast."

She darted in past Lucinda, a small, wiry, vibrant girl with sunlit hair and moonlit eyes. "Can I help with the dishes?"

"Thank you, you doll." Lucinda took down a shallow glass bowl for the violets.

Jenny busily ran hot water into the sink. "I couldn't help seeing," she said. "Your big picture window . . . Lucinda, you *never* leave the breakfast dishes. I keep telling Bob, some day I'll have the routines you have, everything always so neat, never running out of anything, never in a hurry, never surprised . . . anyway, all the way over I could see you just sitting by the table there, and the dishes not done and all . . . is everything all right? I mean, don't tell me if I shouldn't ask, but I couldn't help . . ." Her voice trailed off into an ardent and respectful mumble.

"You're such a sweetheart," Lucinda said mistily. She came over to the sink carrying clean dishtowels and stood holding them, staring out past Jenny's head to the level lawns of the village. "Actually, I did have something on my mind . . . something . . ."

She related the whole conversation over breakfast that morning, from her abrupt and partial mentioning of the anecdote about the blonde and the policeman, to her husband's extraordinary and unequivocal statement about women's power over men: *This has been going on too long. I shall alter it.*

"Is that all?" Jenny asked when she had finished.

"Mm. It's all that was said."

"Oh, I don't think you should worry about that." She crinkled up her eyes, and Lucinda understood that she was putting herself and her young husband in the place of Lucinda and Dr. Lefferts, and trying to empathize a solution. "I think you might have hurt his feelings a little, maybe," Jenny said at length. "I mean, you admitted that you handled him in much the same way as that blonde handled the policeman, and then you said the policeman was a fool."

Lucinda smiled. "Very shrewd. And what's your guess about that parting shot?"

Jenny turned to face her. "You're not teasing me, asking my opinion, Lucinda? I never thought I'd see the day! Not you—you're so wise!"

Lucinda patted her shoulder. "The older I get, the more I feel that among women there is a lowest common denominator of wisdom, and that the chief difference between them is a random scattering of blind spots. No, honey, I'm not teasing you. You may be able to see just where I can't. Now tell me: what do you think he meant by that?"

"'*I shall alter it,*'" Jenny quoted thoughtfully. "Oh, I don't think he meant anything much. You showed him how you could make him do things, and he didn't like it. He's decided not to let you do it any more, but—but . . ."

"But what?"

"Well, it's like with Bob. When he gets masterful and lays down the law I just agree with him. He forgets about it soon enough. If you agree with men all the time they can't get stubborn about anything."

Lucinda laughed aloud. "There's the wisdom!" she cried. Sobering, she shook her head. "You don't know the doctor the way I do. He's a great man—a truly great one, with a great mind. It's great in a way no other mind has ever been. He's—different. Jenny, I know how people talk, and what a lot of them say. People wonder why I married him, why I've stayed with him all these years. They say he's stuffy and didactic and that he has no sense of humor. Well, to them he may be; but to me he is a continual challenge. The rules-of-thumb that keep most men in line don't apply to him.

"And if he says he can do something, he can. If he says he will do something, he will."

Jenny dried her hands and sat down slowly. "He meant," she said positively, "that he would alter your ability to make him do things. Because the only other thing he could have meant was that he was going to alter the thing that makes it possible for any woman to handle any man. And that just couldn't be. How could he change human nature?"

"How? How? He's the scientist. I'm not. I simply eliminate that 'how' from my thinking. The worrisome thing about it is that he doesn't think in small ways about small issues. I'm afraid that's just what he meant— that he was going to change some factor in humanity that is responsible for this power we have over men."

"Oh . . . really," said Jenny. She looked up at Lucinda, moved her hands uneasily. "Lucinda, I know how great the doctor is, and how much you think of him, but—but no one man could do such a thing! Not outside of his own home." She grinned fleetingly. "Probably not inside of it, for very long . . . I never understood just what sort of a scientist he is. Can you tell me, I mean, aside from any secret projects he might be on? Like Bob, now; Bob's a high-temperature metallurgist. What is the doctor, exactly?"

"That's the right question to ask," Lucinda said, and her voice was shadowed. "Dr. Lefferts is a—well, the closest you could get to it would be to call him a specializing non-specialist. You see, science has reached the point where each branch of it continually branches into specialties, and each specialty has its own crop of experts. Most experts live in the confines of their own work. The doctor was saying just the other day that he'd discovered a fluorine-boron step-reaction in mineralogy that had been known for so long that the mineralogists had forgotten about it— yet it was unknown to metallurgy. Just as I said a moment ago, his mind is great, and—different. His job is to draw together the chemists and the biologists, the pure mathematicians and the practical physicists, the clinical psychologists and the engineers and all the other -ists and -ologies. His specialty is scientific thought as applied to all the sciences. He has no assignments except to survey all the fields and transfer needed information from one to the other. There has never been such a position in the Institute before, nor a man to fill it. And there is no other institute like this one on earth.

"He has entree into every shop and lab and library in this Institute. He can do anything or get anything done in any of them.

"And when he said 'I shall alter it' he meant what he said!"

"I never knew that's what he did," breathed Jenny. "I never knew that's what . . . *who* he is."

"That's who he is."

"But what can he change?" Jenny burst out. "What can he change in us, in all men, in all women? What is the power he's talking about, and where does it come from, and what would . . . will . . . happen if it's changed?"

"I don't know," Lucinda said thoughtfully, "I—do—not—know. The blonde in the convertible . . . that sort of thing is just one of the things a woman naturally does, because she is a woman, without thinking of it."

Unexpectedly, Jenny giggled. "You don't plan those things. You just do them. It's nice when it works. A better roast from the butcher. A reminder from one of the men at the bank that a check's overdrawn, in time to cover it."

"I know," smiled Lucinda, "I know. It's easy and inaccurate to say that all those men are on the prowl—or all those women either. A few are, but most are not. The willingness of men to do things for women has survived even equal opportunities and equal pay for women. The ability of women to get what they want from men lies completely in their knowledge of that willingness. So the thing my husband wants to alter—*will* alter—lies in that department."

"Lucinda, why don't you just ask him?"

"I shall. But I don't know if I'll get an answer. If he regards it as a security matter, nothing will get it out of him."

"You'll tell me, won't you?"

"Jenny, my sweet, if he tells me nothing, I can't tell you. If he tells me and asks me to keep his confidence, I won't tell you. If he tells me and puts no restrictions on it, I'll tell you everything."

"But—"

"I know, dear. You're thinking that it's a bigger thing than just what it might mean to the two of us. Well, you're right. But down deep I'm confident. I'd pit few women against most men and expect them to win out. But anytime all womankind is against all mankind, the men don't stand a chance. Think hard about it, anyway. At least we should be able to figure out where the attack is coming from."

"At least you admit it's an attack."

"You bet your sweet life it's an attack. There's been a woman behind most thrones all through history. The few times that hasn't been true, it's taken a woman to clean up the mess afterward. We won't give up easily, darling!"

" 'The North wind doth blow, and we shall have snow', and so on," said Lucinda as she lit the fire. "I'm going to need a new coat."

"Very well," said Dr. Lefferts.

"A fur coat this time."

"Fur coats," pronounced the doctor, "are impractical. Get one with the fur inside. You'll keep warmer with less to carry."

"I want a fur coat with the fur outside, where it shows."

"I understand and at times admire the decorative compulsions," said the doctor, rising from the adjusted cube he used for an easy chair, "but not when they are unhealthy, uneconomical, and inefficient. My dear, vanity does not become you."

"A thing that has always fascinated me," said Lucinda in a dangerously quiet voice, "in rabbits, weasels, skunks, pumas, pandas, and mink, and all other known mammals and marsupials, is their huge vanity. They *all* wear their fur outside."

He put on his pince-nez to stare at her. "Your logic limits its factors. I find such sequences remarkable because of the end results one may obtain. However, I shall not follow this one."

"If you're so preoccupied with efficiency and function," she snapped, "why do you insist on wearing those pince-nez instead of getting corneal lenses?"

"Functional living is a pattern which includes all predictable phenomena," he said reasonably. "One of these is habit. I recognize that I shall continue to like pince-nez as much as I shall continue to dislike rice pudding. My functionalism therefore includes these glasses and excludes that particular comestible. If you had the fur-coat habit, the possibility of a fur coat would be calculable. Since you have never had such a coat, we can consider the matter disposed of."

"I think some factors were selected for that sequence," said Lucinda between her teeth, "but I can't seem to put my finger on the missing ones."

"I beg your pardon?"

"I said," appended Lucinda distinctly, "that speaking of factors, I wonder how you're coming with your adjustments of human nature to eliminate the deadliness of the female."

"Oh, that. I expect results momentarily."

"Why bother?" she said bitterly. "My powers don't seem to be good enough for a fur coat as it is."

"Oh," he said mildly, "were you using them?"

Because she was Lucinda, she laughed. "No, darling, I wasn't." She went to him and pressed him back into the big cubical chair and sat on the arm. "I was demanding, cynical, and unpleasant. These things in a woman represent the scorched earth retreat rather than the looting advance."

"An excellent analogy," he said. "Excellent. It has been a long and bitter war, hasn't it? And now it's coming to an end. It is an extraordinary thing that in our difficult progress toward the elimination of wars, we have until now ignored the greatest and most pernicious conflict of all—the one between the sexes."

"Why so pernicious?" she chuckled. "There are times when it's rather fun."

He said solemnly, "There are moments of exhilaration, even of glory, in every great conflict. But such conflicts tear down so much more than they build."

"What's been so damaging about the war between the sexes?"

"Though it has been the women who made men, it has been largely men who have made the world as we know it. However, they have had to do so against a truly terrible obstacle: the emotional climate created by women. Only by becoming an ascetic can a man avoid the oscillations between intoxication and distrust instilled into him by women. And ascetics usually are already insane or rapidly become so."

"I think you're overstating a natural state of affairs."

"I am overstating," he admitted, "for clarity's sake, and off the record. However, this great war is by no means natural. On the contrary, it is a most unnatural state of affairs. You see, *homo sapiens* is, in one small but important respect, an atypical mammal."

"Do tell."

He raised his eyebrows, but continued. "In virtually all species but ours, the female has a rigidly fixed cycle of conjugal acceptability."

"But the human female has a—"

"I am not referring to that lunar cycle, unmentionable everywhere except in blatant magazine advertisements," he said shortly, "but a cycle of desire. Of rut."

"A pretty word." Her eyes began to glitter.

"Mahomet taught that it occurred every eight days, Zoroaster nine days, Socrates and Solomon agreed on ten. Everyone else, as far as I can discover, seems to disagree with these pundits, or to ignore the matter. Actually there are such cycles, but they are subtle at best, and differ in the individual from time to time, with age, physical experience, geography, and even emotional state. These cycles are vestigial; the original, *natural* cycle disappeared early in the history of the species, and has been trembling on the verge ever since. It will be a simple matter to bring it back."

"May I ask how?"

"You may not. It is a security matter."

"May I then ask what effect you expect this development to have?"

"Obvious, isn't it? The source of woman's persistent and effective control over man, the thing that makes him subject to all her intolerances, whims, and bewildering coyness, is the simple fact of her perennial availability. She has no regular and predictable cycle of desire. The lower animals have. During the brief time that a female mouse, a marten, or a mare is approachable, every male of her species in the vicinity will know of it and seek her out; will, in effect, drop everything to answer a basic call. But unless and until that call occurs, the male is free to think of other things. With the human female, on the other hand, the call is mildly present at all times, and the male is *never* completely free to think of other things. It is natural for this drive to be strong. It is unnatural indeed for it to be constant. In this respect Freud was quite correct; nearly every neurosis has a sexual basis. We are a race of neurotics, and the great wonder is that we have retained any of the elements of sanity at all. I shall liberate humanity from this curse. I shall restore the natural alternations of drive and rest. I shall free men to think and women to take their rightful places as thinking individuals beside them, rather than be the forced-draft furnaces of sexual heat they have become."

"Are you telling me," said Lucinda in a small, shocked voice, "that you have found a way to—to neuterize women except for a few hours a month?"

"I am and I have," said Dr. Lefferts. "And incidentally, I must say I am grateful to you for having turned me to this problem." He looked up sharply. "Where are you going, my dear?"

"I've got to th-think," said Lucinda, and ran from the room. If she had stayed there for another fifteen seconds, she knew she would have crushed his skull in with the poker.

"Who—Oh, Lucinda! How nice. Come in . . . why, what's the matter?"

"Jenny, I've got to talk to you. Is Bob home?"

"No. He's got night duty at the high temperature lab this week. Whatever is wrong?"

"It's the end of the world," said Lucinda in real anguish. She sank down on the sofa and looked up at the younger woman. "My husband is putting a—a chastity belt on every woman on earth."

"A *what?*"

"A chastity belt." She began to laugh hysterically. "With a timelock on it."

Jenny sat beside her. "Don't," she said. "Don't laugh like that. You're frightening me."

Lucinda lay back, gasping. "You should be frightened. . . . Listen to me, Jenny. Listen carefully, because this is the biggest thing that has happened since the deluge." She began to talk.

Five minutes later Jenny asked dazedly, "You mean—if this crazy thing happens Bob won't . . . won't *want* me most of the time?"

"It's you who won't do any wanting. And when you don't, he won't want either. . . . It isn't that that bothers me so much, Jenny, now that I've had a chance to think about it. I'm worried about the revolution."

"What revolution?"

"Why, this is going to cause the greatest upheaval of all time! Once these cycles become recognized for what they are, there will be fireworks. Look at the way we dress, the way we use cosmetics. Why do we do it? Basically, to appear to be available to men. Practically all perfumes have a musk or musk-like base for that very reason. But how long do you think women will keep up the hypocrisy of lipstick and plunging necklines when men *know* better—*know* that they couldn't possibly be approachable all the time? How many men will let their women appear in public looking as if they were?"

"They'll tie us up in the house the way I do Mitzi-poodle," said Jenny in an awed tone.

"They'll leave us smugly alone with easy minds for three weeks out of four," said Lucinda, "and stand guard over us like bull elks the rest of the time, to keep other men away."

"Lucinda!" Jenny squeaked and covered her face in horror. "What about other women? How can we compete with another woman when she's— she's—and we're not?"

"Especially when men are conditioned the way they are. Women will want to stick to one man, more likely than not. But men—men, building up pressures for weeks on end . . ."

"There'll be harems again," said Jenny.

"This is the absolute, final, bitter end of any power we ever had over the beasts, Jenny—do you see that? All the old tricks—the arch half-promise, the come-on, the manipulations of jealousy—they'll be utterly meaningless! The whole arsenal of womankind is based on her ability to yield or not to yield. And my husband is going to take the choice away from us. He's going to make it absolutely certain that at one time we can't yield, and at another we must!"

"And they'll never have to be nice to us at either time," added Jenny miserably.

"Women," said Lucinda bitterly, "are going to have to work for a living."

"But we do!"

"Oh, you know what I mean, Jenny! The lit-tul wife in the lit-tul home . . . that whole concept is based on women's perpetual availability. We're not going to be able to be home-makers, in that sense, at monthly intervals."

Jenny jumped up. Her face was chalky. "He hasn't stopped any war," she ground out. Lucinda had never seen her like this. "He's started one, and it's a beaut. Lucinda, he's got to be stopped, even if you—we have to . . ."

"Come on."

They started for Dr. Lefferts' house, striding along like a couple of avenging angels.

"Ah," said Dr. Lefferts, rising politely. "You brought Jenny. Good evening, Jenny."

Lucinda planted herself in front of him and put her hands on her hips. "You listen to me," she growled. "You've got to stop that nonsense about changing women."

"It is not nonsense and I shall do nothing of the kind."

"Dr. Lefferts," said Jenny in a quaking voice, "can you really do this— this awful thing?"

"Of course," said the doctor. "It was quite simple, once the principles were worked out."

"It *was* quite simple? You mean you've already—"

Dr. Lefferts looked at his watch. "At two o'clock this afternoon. Seven hours ago."

"I think," said Lucinda quietly, "that you had better tell us just exactly what you did, and what we can expect."

"I told you it is a security matter."

"What has my libido to do with national defense?"

"That," said the doctor, in a tone which referred to *that* as the merest trifle, "is a side issue. I coincided it with a much more serious project."

"What could be more serious than . . ."

"There's only one thing *that* serious, from a security standpoint," said Lucinda. She turned to the doctor. "I know better than to ask you any direct questions. But if I assume that this horrible thing was done in conjunction with a super-bomb test—just a guess, you understand—is there any way for an H-blast to bring about a change in women such as you describe?"

He clasped both hands around one knee and looked up at her in genuine admiration. "Brilliant," he said. "And most skillfully phrased. Speaking hypothetically—hypothetically, you understand," he interjected, waving a warning finger, "a hydrogen bomb has an immense power of diffusion. A jet of energy of that size, at that temperature, for even three or four microseconds, is capable of penetrating the upper reaches of stratosphere. But the effect does not end there. The upward displacement causes great volumes of air to rush in toward the rushing column from all sides. This in turn is carried upward and replaced, a process which continues for a considerable time. One of the results must be the imbalance of any distinct high or low pressure areas within several thousand miles, and for a day or two freak weather developments can be observed. In other words, these primary and secondary effects are capable of diffusing a—ah—substance placed in the bomb throughout the upper atmosphere, where, in a matter of days, it will be diffused throughout the entire envelope."

Lucinda clasped her hands in a slow, controlled way, as if one of them planned to immobolize the other and thereby keep both occupied.

"And is there any substance . . . I'm still asking hypothetical questions, you understand—is there anything which could be added to the hydrogen fusion reaction which might bring about these—these new cycles in women?"

"They are not new cycles," said the doctor flatly. "They are as old as the development of warm-blooded animals. The lack of them is, in biological terms, a very recent development in an atypical mammal; so recent and so small that it is subject to adjustment. As to your hypothetical question"—he smiled—"I should judge that such an effect is perfectly possible. Within the extremes of temperature, pressure, and radiation which takes place in a fusion reaction, many things are possible. A minute quantity of certain alloys, for example, introduced into the shell of the bomb itself, or perhaps in the structure of a supporting tower or even a nearby temporary shed, might key a number of phenomenal reaction chains. Such a chain might go through several phases and result in certain subtle isotopic alterations in one of the atmosphere's otherwise inert gases, say xenon. And this isotope, acting upon the adrenal cortex and the parathyroid, which are instrumental in controlling certain cycles in the human body, might very readily bring about the effect we are discussing in an atypical species."

Lucinda threw up her hands and turned to Jenny. "Then that's it," she said wearily.

"What's 'it'? What? I don't understand," whimpered Jenny. "What's he done, Lucinda?"

"In his nasty, cold-blooded hypothetical way," said Lucinda, "he has put something in or near an H-bomb which was tested today, which is going to have some effect on the air we breathe, which is going to do what we were discussing at your house."

"Dr. Lefferts," said Jenny piteously. She went to him, stood looking down at him as he sat primly in his big easy chair. "Why—why? Just to annoy us? Just to keep us from having a little, petty influence over you?"

"By no means," said the doctor. "I will admit that I might have turned my ambition to the matter for such reasons. But some concentrated thought brought up a number of extra-polations which are by no means petty."

He rose and stood by the mantel, pince-nez in hand, the perfect picture of the Pedant At Home. "Consider," he said. "Homo sapiens, in terms of comparative anatomy, should mature physically at 35 and emotionally between 30 and 40. He should have a life expectancy of between 150 and 200 years. And he unquestionably should be able to live a life uncluttered by such insistent trifles as clothing conventions, unfunctional chivalries, psychic turmoils and dangerous mental and physical escapes into what the psychologists call romances. Women should phase their sexual cycles with those of the seasons, gestate their young longer, and eliminate the unpredictable nature of their psycho-sexual appetites—the very basis of all their insecurity and therefore that of most men. Women will not be chained to these cycles, Jenny, and become breeding machines, if that's what you fear. You will begin to live in and with these cycles as you live with a well-made and serviced automatic machine. You will be liberated from the constant control and direction of your somatic existence as you have been liberated from shifting gears in your car."

"But . . . we're not conditioned for such a change!" blazed Lucinda. "And what of the fashion industry . . . cosmetics . . . the entertainment world . . . what's going to become of these and the millions of people employed by them, and the people dependent on all those people, if you do a thing like this?"

"The thing is done. As for these people . . ." He paused. "Yes, there will be some disturbance. A considerable one. But in over-all historical terms, it will be slight and it will be brief. I like to think that the television service man is one who was liberated by the cotton gin and the power loom."

"It's . . . hard to think in historical terms just now," said Lucinda. "Jenny, come on."

"Where are you going."

She faced him, her blued-steel eyes blazing. "Away from you. And I—
I think I have a warning to give to the women."

"I wouldn't do that," he said dryly. "They'll find out in time. All you'll
succeed in doing is to alert many women to the fact that they will be
unattractive to their husbands at times when other women may seem more
desirable. Women will not unite with one another, my dear, even to unite
against men."

There was a tense pause. Then Jenny quavered, "How long did you
say this—this thing will take?"

"I did not say. I would judge between thirty-six and forty-eight hours."

"I've got to get home."

"May I come with you?" asked Lucinda.

Jenny looked at her, her full face, her ample, controlled body. A surprising series of emotions chased themselves across her young face. She
said, "I don't think . . . I mean . . . no, not tonight; I have to—to—good-
night, Lucinda."

When she had gone, the doctor uttered one of his rare chuckles. "She
has absorbed perhaps a tenth of this whole concept," he said, "but until
she's sure of herself she's not going to let you or any woman near her
husband."

"You . . . you complacent *pig!*" said Lucinda whitely. She stormed
upstairs.

"Hello . . . hello—Jenny?"

"Lucinda! I'm—glad you called."

Something cold and tense deep inside Lucinda relaxed. She sat down
slowly on the couch, leaned back comfortably with the telephone cradled
between her cheek and her wide soft shoulder. "I'm glad you're glad,
Jenny darling. It's been six weeks . . . how are you?"

"I'm . . . all right now. It was pretty awful, for a while, not knowing
how it would be, waiting for it to happen. And when it did happen, it
was hard to get used to. But it hasn't changed things *too* much. How
about you?"

"Oh, I'm fine," said Lucinda. She smiled slowly, touched her tongue to
her full lower lip. "Jenny, have you told anyone?"

"Not a soul. Not even Bob. I think he's a little bewildered. He thinks
I'm being very . . . understanding. Lucinda, is it wrong for me to let
him think that?"

"It's never wrong for a woman to keep her knowledge to herself if it
makes her more attractive," said Lucinda, and smiled again.

"How's Dr. Lefferts?"

"He's bewildered too. I suppose I've been a little . . . understanding
too." She chuckled.

Over the phone she heard Jenny's answering laughter. "The poor
things," she said. "The poor, poor things. Lucinda—"

"Yes, honey."

"I know how to handle this, now. But I don't really understand it. Do you?"

"Yes, I think I do."

"How can it be, then? How can this change in us affect men that way? I thought *we* would be the ones who would be turned off and on like a neon sign."

"*What?* Now wait a minute, Jenny! You mean you don't realize what's happened?"

"That's just what I said. How could such a change in women do such a thing to the men?"

"Jenny, I think you're wonderful, wonderful, wonderful," breathed Lucinda. "As a matter of fact, I think women are wonderful. I suddenly realized that you haven't the foggiest notion of what's happened, yet you've taken it in stride and used it *exactly* right!"

"Whatever do you mean?"

"Jenny, do you feel any difference in yourself?"

"Why, no. All the difference is in Bob. That's what I—"

"Honey, there *isn't* any difference in you, nor in me, nor in any other woman. For the very first time in his scientific life, the great man made an error in his calculations."

There was a silence for a time, and then the telephone uttered a soft, delighted, long-drawn-out "Oh-h-h-h-h . . ."

Lucinda said, "He's sure that in the long run it will have all the benefits he described—the longer life expectancy, the subduing of insecurities, the streamlining of our manners and customs."

"You mean that all men from now on will . . ."

"I mean that for about twelve days in every two weeks, men can't do anything with us, which is restful. And for forty-eight hours they can't do anything without us, which is"—she laughed—"useful. It would seem that *homo sapiens* is still an atypical mammal."

Jenny's voice was awed. "And I thought we were going to lose the battle of the sexes. Bob brings me little presents every single day, Lucinda!"

"He'd better. Jenny, put down that phone and come over here. I want to hug you. And"—she glanced over at the hall closet, where hung the symbol of her triumph—"I want to show you my new fur coat."

DAVID H. KELLER

THE DOORBELL

Two MEN STOOD on the suspension bridge that hung over the trackage of the largest steel works in America. They were watching the crane and an electro-magnet load scrap-iron from the ground to small freight cars. The crane swung the magnet over the hill of scrap; several tons of iron moved up to meet the magnet; then the crane carried the magnet and the mass of attracted metal to a position above a car, where the load of iron fell.

"Rather clever!" exclaimed one of the men. "I see it every day but never fail to think it clever. Man throws a switch and the magnet starts pulling, throws another switch and it stops pulling. Does the work of twenty men and does it better. I own this place and am extremely busy, but almost every day I walk out on this bridge and watch the thing work. It's been a big help to me."

"I wish it would help me," sighed the other. "There ought to be a story in it, but I can't identify it. That's the tough part of being an author; you could write lots of things if you just had lots of things to write about."

"There *is* a story in it," replied the steel man. "I owe you something and I think I ought to pay you with a story. How about spending the week end with me up at my shack in Canada?"

The author blushed.

"Sorry. I can't. I've no money to pay the fare; nor the right clothes for the kind of guests you'll have. Thanks for the invitation, but the answer is no."

"Come on," urged the rich man. "There'll be only one other guest—but he stays by himself all the time. Here's the program. Be at the front door of my office at three, Friday afternoon. One of my men will be waiting for you in a Rolls-Royce. Tell him who you are and he'll drive you up. He's a fast driver and makes the trip in six hours. He'll leave you at the front door. Push the electric button on the side of the porch and my man will admit you. I'll wait supper for you and return to New York with you early Monday morning. You'll find the visit interesting—and I promise you a real story, though whether you'll be able to sell it, I don't know. What must a story have to be saleable?"

"Originality—the sound of truth—human interest."

"Then you'll never sell it because no one will believe it—but come anyway. Sorry your wife can't come along but this is the kind of party I can't invite her to. Just tell her that it's a business trip—that I want you to write a book about me. Tell her I paid you five hundred in advance. Show her the money. Here it is in hundred dollar bills."

"I can't do that," protested the writer. "I admit that I'm broke but I can't take the money for nothing."

"Sure you can. I owe you more than that. Be at the office Friday at three. I'll see you at supper."

Even Mrs. Hubler admitted Jacob Hubler had done Henry Cecil a genuine service, though she raised her eyebrows when her husband explained that it was to be a stag party for two. At any rate, the appointment was kept.

The trip through New York and into Canada was long and tiresome.

Hubler lost all sense of direction. The chauffeur was a better driver than a conversationalist and most of the time simply grunted. Hubler tired of the grunted answers and stopped asking questions. The last fifteen minutes, they drove through a forest of heavy pine. At last they arrived at the house.

"There's the door," announced the chauffeur. "I go back to town."

There was nothing for Hubler to do but to walk up the pathway and ring the doorbell. There was a light over the front door—otherwise, the house was dark. The night was as black as pitch. It was impossible to tell anything about the house, its size, or its architecture. The author could see only the front door. He could hear only the constantly diminishing sound of the automobile returning to New York.

Stepping onto the porch he at once found the electric push-button which served as a doorbell. There was nothing peculiar about it—just a circular piece of polished brass with a small white button in the middle. He looked at it and thought that in some way it was incongruous with the doorway and the house and the dark silent night. A brass door-knocker, a pull bell that would tinkle merrily, some kind of announcer that could be heard by the visitor would have been more friendly, more sympathetic to his lonely mood. He hesitated, and his hesitation was born of the haunting fear that if he pushed the button, he would not hear the bell within; he would not know whether it rang within the house or, if it rang, whether there was anyone to hear it. He wished he had a horn to blow and then laughed bitterly, realizing that he had never blown one, and even if he knew how and did blow it lustily, how could anyone hear him if there were no one in the house? He realized the neurasthenic quality of his fear, the almost psychopathic tendency of his imagination. Perhaps Cecil had done this on purpose to furnish him the thread of a story—a six-hour ride ending on the porch of an empty house, and the nearest dwelling God knew where. Already there was a sort of story, and it might become a really good one before he returned to New York. He looked moodily at the doorbell. It was just a plain, ordinary, everyday electric push-button.

Cursing himself for an imaginative fool, he pressed the button; he rang the doorbell.

Suddenly, the silence was broken by the sobbing shriek of a thing in pain, the terrible howling of a tortured animal. The menacing noise rose into the night, carrying with it the terror of deadly agony, only to die away in throaty sobbings as he withdrew his finger from the white button.

Hubler wanted suddenly to escape, to run down the dark road, to plunge into the friendly, silent darkness.

Then the door was flung open, lights blazed in all the windows of the house. A stately butler bade him enter. Cecil came to meet him—Cecil the steel man, in evening clothes, with a friendly smile, and a warm greeting.

"You are five minutes late," he scolded laughingly. "You were due at nine. Hurry to your room and clean up. Then join me as soon as you can. Supper's ready and I'm sure you're hungry."

Everything seemed different. Hubler wondered if he had been the victim of auditory hallucinosis. Here were light, warmth, good fellowship, and the cheer of a fireplace. Supper was served before the glowing fire instead of in a formal dining room—a supper of roast duck in front of the cheery fireplace. Henry Cecil made a charming host; the butler was everything a butler should be; there was a quiet charm in the atmosphere of the room. Gradually, Hubler relaxed; by the time the meal was over, he was silently laughing at his former fears. The table was removed, the butler withdrew, and then the author asked the steel millionaire the question that had been bothering him for several days.

"You promised me a story, Mr. Cecil."

"So I did. In fact, as I remember it, that was your real reason for making the trip."

"Exactly."

"Not being an author, I hardly know how to even start a story."

"You start with a title. Every story has to have a name."

"I understand that. You can call the story what you wish. If I were going to write it, I would call it *The Doorbell*, but perhaps that wouldn't sound interesting enough to you." He spoke softly, with a smile.

Hubler stared at him. Doorbell? Suddenly a memory which he had almost thrust into the subconscious returned. He answered sharply:

"That will do for the name of the story. Go on, please."

"For a proper understanding I'll have to begin with a bit of family history," said the steel man. "Originally I came from the western part of South Carolina. Perhaps we were related to the Cecils on the eastern shore of Maryland, or the Cecils of Louisiana. I've read their family histories, but I was never satisfied that my father was of either branch of the family. In fact, I never saw my father, for he died when I was a little fellow. My mother was Amy Worth from Atlanta, Georgia. She was related to the Fannings and the Stills. They were proud people, but poor. After father died, she tried to support the three of us. You see, I had a brother who was much older than I, but not yet a man.

"We lived in a house in the country that formerly had been the home of a rich man. Beside the front door was a doorbell. It was the old-fashioned pull-bell kind. A wire ran from the door to the kitchen, and when the knob was pulled, the bell *tingled-tangled* in the kitchen. Mother kept it in repair, saying it was a symbol of former greatness and something for us boys to try to grow up to. She wanted us to become real men. The bell was seldom rung because we had few visitors and mostly they, being neighbors, just came around the back way, like neighbors would.

"Father had enemies. There were four brothers who claimed they owned our farm, but Mother declared that she had a clear title to it. One day I was away hunting, like any shaver will do, and when I came home toward dusk, I noticed that the front door was open. Brother was dead and Mother was almost dead, but she managed to gasp out what had happened. From the way she was shot, I don't see how she lived as long as she did, but she had Fanning blood in her and the Fannings die hard. Anyway, I sat down on the floor and put her head in my lap and wiped the blood from her lips while she told me what had happened. Perhaps this is not interesting you, Mr. Hubler?"

"On the contrary, I find it more than interesting. Please go on with it."

"All right. Anytime you tire, tell me to stop.

"Mother said that she and Brother were in the kitchen when the doorbell rang. It was such an unusual thing that they were sure something was going to happen, but they went to the front door and opened it because they were in their own house and were not afraid. There stood the four brothers. They had come to the front door and rung the doorbell instead of going around to the back door as friendly neighbors would have done. Without saying a word they just started to shoot, and when they left, they told Mother they were coming back after dusk and finish me off. I wanted to stay, but Mother made me promise to leave. She said there was work a-plenty for me but that I'd have to wait until I got to be a man for it wasn't work for a boy to undertake. She died in a while —after she had told me what there was to tell. So I took my rifle and left that part of the country. The neighbors found Mother and Brother and buried them. Many years later, I went back and put a stone over their graves. That is the end of the story."

"Not much of an ending," Hubler insisted, disappointedly. "It's not the ending that would interest the average editor. The story just couldn't stop there. There must be something more."

"Perhaps," replied Henry Cecil, "but so far it is all true. And there's the rifle I took with me from the Carolina mountains. When I bought this land and built this house, I brought it up here and hung it over the fireplace. End the story yourself."

"I can't do it. A thousand endings have already been written to the story you've just told me. You should have taken the rifle and hunted down the four brothers. You should have shot them one at a time. But things like that have been written before—nothing new to it. Instead, you came north, learned the steel business, became a rich man, built a palace in Canada, and hung the gun above the fireplace. That's interesting, but it is not a story. Why didn't you use the gun?"

Cecil smiled.

"There would have been no originality in it. A thousand mountain boys would have done that, but as far as I know, I am the only mountain boy who become interested in steel and electricity. I had to be different in every way. You see, I was just a lad when Mother died with her head on my lap, and when I wasn't looking at her face, I kept looking at the doorbell. She always said that the doorbell was a symbol; that rich people had doorbells, that the Worths and Fannings and Stills in Georgia always had doorbells and if Brother and I kept that in mind, we would grow up to live with doorbells, have servants in the kitchen and everything that went with doorbells. But instead of bringing joy and happiness and prosperity into her life, it had been the signal of death to Brother and her.

"So I have never been able to forget the doorbell."

"You mean?"

"Something like that. I'm trying to explain why the rifle was never used. Now a doorbell would be something different. You can see that for yourself."

"There certainly is a difference—so much so, that there's no resemblance," agreed the puzzled author.

"At least, Mother's ambitions for me have been satisfied. I've become rich, well known, and somewhat important to the financial life of the nation. In fact, some of the Maryland Cecils have recently been trying to prove they are related to the Carolina branch. I have a home in the country and a doorbell at the front door. I have servants who can be trusted. My butler is a man of breeding and well educated. Being an ex-convict, in fact an escaped convict, he realizes and appreciates that this place is a city of refuge for him. His wife is the cook. My chauffeur also has certain things for which to be grateful to me and, in addition, knows how to drive and keep his mouth shut."

"He certainly is no conversationalist."

"No. He doesn't talk. Then there is the doctor. I just had to have a doctor. I have guests occasionally, and if they become sick, it's so much better to have a physician in the house instead of having to send to Montreal. This man is a good fellow; he drinks though and can't return to the States. But he's a wonderful nurse too, and takes very good care of my ill guests. It was a long time before I found a doctor who answered my purpose. Different doctors, you realize, have different ideas concerning the administration of drugs. Some give powders, others liquids or hypodermics, and only rarely do you find one who thinks that the *only* way to administer any and all medicine is in the form of capsules. This man I have is what you might call a 'capsule doctor.' He's mighty clever. He has some capsules that dissolve in the stomach and some that don't dissolve till they enter certain sections of the intestines. That's my doctor and family up here. Sometimes I meet a man and become interested in him and invite him up for the week end. If he gets sick, he's well cared for—very well cared for. Well, it's late and you're tired from the drive. Suppose we go to bed now."

"That suits me," said Hubler. "And is that all there is to the story?"

"All for tonight, and it's enough for you to work on as you drift into the land of dreams. Will you go with me? Often before I go to bed, I go out to the front door. It makes me think of Mother and the brother who died so unnecessarily in his early manhood. Come."

It was a command rather than an invitation. Opening the door, Henry Cecil turned a switch and the house darkened—all except the light over the front door. The two men stood on the landing out in the night air. The darkness was like velvet silence.

"Often we hear a great horned owl, and occasionally a wildcat. Did you ever hear a wildcat, Hubler? At times they sound like a child crying—and again—"

Hubler shook his head. "I never heard a wildcat," he answered. "Do you hear them often?"

"Now and then," Cecil answered casually. "Now and then." Turning, he pressed strong and hard with his right index finger against the door-bell.

Suddenly the stillness was rent with a sobbing, shuddering shriek, a cry that rose in intensity, that carried with it the terror of a soul torn to bits and cast into the flames of hell. Cecil removed his finger, and slowly the yelling died to sobbing and the sobbing to moaning and the moaning to silence.

"That's what a wildcat sounds like," explained Cecil. "Come. Let's go to bed. Tomorrow is another day."

He turned the lights on and personally took his guest to his room. Hubler went to sleep slowly, telling himself that here he'd found a wonderful story—but that somehow there wasn't any sequence. It did not make sense.

Next morning the butler served his breakfast in his room. Hubler tried to question him, but the man was everything a loyal servant should be. All he would say was that the master was busy and would see him at two for dinner and that he would find interesting books in the library, or the butler would be glad to bring him some. Or if the gentleman cared to play pool, the butler would be pleased to play with him. So Hubler called for a typewriter and spent the morning writing the story in a dozen different ways and tearing it up as fast as he wrote, because he realized that all the versions were poor and far from the truth.

Disgusted with himself, he rang for the butler and spent the rest of the time playing pool. He found the man an excellent opponent.

At two, as Cecil entered the billiard room, the butler left silently. Commonplace remarks were exchanged, and then the steel man led the way to dinner. A third man awaited them and was introduced as Doctor Murdock. The meal was served with some formality and a complete lack of conversation. Finally, Cecil asked the doctor, "How is your patient?"

"Rested fairly well today but had two severe attacks last night."

"Your medicine does not relieve him?"

"No. He is going like the other three."

"Have you made a diagnosis?"

"No. Nothing seems typical of any condition I am familiar with. I really would like a consultation. My professional pride—"

The rich man interrupted him.

"Tut, tut! You have nothing to worry about. You're doing as well as any other doctor could. Let me make the situation clear to you, Mr. Hubler. I have recently had four guests, one at a time. They came at my invitation to enjoy my hospitality and fatten their purses on my bounty. Each became mysteriously ill, went into a stupor which, of course, may have been caused by drinking too much. They were taken to our little hospital room, and Doctor Murdock took charge of them. Each patient's symptoms were the same, occasional pains of a terrifying nature at irregular intervals accompanied by a progressive anemia. Three of my guests died, and the doctor now states that the last one is going rapidly. He's a good physician and I have the greatest confidence in him. There's no occasion for him to worry. Everything is perfectly regular and each man has had a legal death certificate and a simple, but satisfactory, burial. Of course, it is to be greatly regretted. It may make other guests, like yourself, feel ill at ease, but I don't think there'll be any more such cases. Are you still giving the capsules, Doctor?"

"Yes. It's a favorite prescription of mine and one that should be good for cholera."

"I had your prescription filled by the best druggist in New York."

"I know. You said that before. An autopsy might help with a diagnosis."

"No, Doctor Murdock—But come, let's finish the meal. I want to show Mr. Hubler the place."

For several hours, the two men rode slowly on horseback through the woods. Hubler expressed continual astonishment at the large number of birds and animals and their obvious tameness.

"It's nothing to wonder at," explained his host. "I don't hunt myself and I let no one else hunt on my property. As a result, even the deer have become tame. It seems cruel to kill just for the sake of killing. Of course, they kill each other. The birds eat insects and the weasels eat the birds, and, now and then, one of the big wildcats catches a rabbit or a very young fawn, but that's just a natural course of events. I used to hunt when I was a boy, but after my mother died in my arms, I've never been able to pull a trigger."

Through the dying day they rode, and at last, almost in the darkness, returned to the house. An Irishman was waiting for them on a third horse, to take the horses back to the stable, some miles from the house.

Inside the house again, Cecil became proud and boastfully expansive. He delighted in showing Hubler through the different rooms, the library, the picture gallery, and a small, but complete, laboratory for electrical experimentation. At last, they came to a little room. It was empty except for a large mass of wire and iron in the center of the room, reaching from floor to ceiling.

"That's something of which I'm especially proud," said Cecil. "It's an electromagnet—probably as large and powerful a magnet as there is in the world. If it could touch iron, it would probably be able to attract a load of four tons. It can attract iron particles at a distance of twenty feet. In fact, I had to have this part of the house built without iron nails; otherwise it would have pulled the place apart. It's very simple in construction and most of the time is inert, dead. But if a button is pressed at a distant part of the house and the electric current turned on, it becomes instantly alive and functions perfectly. It's very similar to the electromagnet I have at the mills, but this one is much more powerful. I thought you might like to see it. Perhaps it may help you with the story you came up here to write. Have you started it yet?"

"Yes—a dozen times this morning, but I tell you frankly—I can't write it. It doesn't make sense; none of it. I feel there's a story here but it doesn't click as yet."

"Perhaps it will later. Suppose we go down to see our patient. The hospital room is directly below. We'll take off our shoes and put on carpet slippers. Nails in the shoes, you know, and all that sort of thing. You must be careful when you're near a magnet such as this. Come along."

As the butler approached down the hall Cecil asked him, "What time have you?"

"Eight-thirty-five, sir."

"I have the same. At exactly nine o'clock will you ring the doorbell? Remember—exactly at nine."

"I will, sir."

"A faithful and obedient servant," commented Cecil.

"Before we go to the hospital, I should tell you about the furnishings. Since it's directly under the electromagnet, there's no iron or steel there. The bed is of wood throughout, but very comfortable. A series of hour-glasses mark the time. All instruments and hypodermics are of hardened gold. At my request the doctor wears slippers. He thinks I'm sort of queer, but as I employ him, he puts up with what he considers my eccentricities. Should the electromagnet start working while we're there, for example at nine, when the doorbell is pushed, you need have no fear for your personal safety. The last thing in the world I desire is to see you harmed in any way. Come on."

They entered the room. Sharp shadows were thrown by a burning candle in a glass holder. Doctor Murdock rose to meet them.

"He's had a quiet day, Mr. Cecil," he whispered. "It's been the sleep of exhaustion, but there has been no recurrence of the colic."

"Have you used any of the sedative?"

"Yes. He has had his capsules every hour."

"Good. That's all that can be done for him. Doctor Murdock is a great believer in capsules, Mr. Hubler. He's not a pharmacist, so I have his prescription capsules filled in New York. What time have you, Doctor?"

"According to the hour-glasses, it should soon be nine."

"We'll wait till then. We left our watches upstairs. Will you tell us when it's nearly nine?"

They sat down and waited. The doctor went over, looked at the hour-glasses steadily pouring their golden sands.

"Only a few second now. The hour-glass is nearly empty," he soon said.

The sleeping patient moved restlessly. Hubler watched him closely. The author was trying to think, to coördinate his thinking so that it would make sense. Suddenly, the man sat up in bed shrieking and pulling at his abdomen. His cry was a mixture of curses and utter despair. It so completely filled Hubler's soul with terror that instinctively he covered his ears with his hands to try to shut out the horror of it. For he recognized it; it was what he had heard the night he pressed the doorbell, and once heard could not ever be forgotten. Doctor Murdock bent over the man trying to calm him. Cecil looked on with detached interest. Suddenly, the unearthly cries ceased as the man dropped backwards.

"He's dead!" cried Doctor Murdock.

"No wonder," sighed Cecil. "No one can stand pain like that forever. He's better off dead. You know how to proceed, Doctor. Come with me, Mr. Hubler. It may be that a glass of brandy will help you. That was not a pleasant sight."

They were back in the living room in front of the fireplace. Hubler had taken three fingers of liquor, shuddered and felt better.

"And now for the story." The steel man sighed. "I realize that you must get this story settled in your mind or you won't sleep tonight, and tomorrow we'll leave early for the city, so you'd better have your rest. You've seen the electromagnet. Now I'll tell you that the four men who have died in our little hospital room were the four brothers who murdered my mother and brother. And as there was a doorbell in our home in Carolina, it seemed best to have a doorbell here. Of course, I *had* to have a doorbell. Every house, especially a house of wealth, has a doorbell, and you remember that my mother thought it a very important symbol. Of course, it's important for you to know that the doorbell was connected with the electromagnet. When it was pressed, the magnet started to work. Now the first brother who came was drunk; he just would not stop drinking, so we put him in the hospital. Then I had the second one come here and he pressed the doorbell a number of times. You see, I was giving him a lot of money and he wanted to please me. Later he became ill and took his brother's place. Then the third brother came, and did the same thing. Finally the last brother, who was the man you saw die tonight, came. Of course, when he became sick, there was no one to press the button but the butler and myself and so I asked you to come up so you could have a hand in it. And now, since the last of the four brothers has died from this strange disease, I won't use the electromagnet any more but will connect the push-button with a sweet, musical bell which will welcome guests with the true sound of hospitality. Now you can write the story about the doorbell."

Hubler protested. "There's still something left out. What had the magnet to do with it? Doctor Murdock took care of all these men, and he did not die. Evidently he didn't have even a bit of pain. You're leaving something out! What it is? I *have to know*. It's not fair to tell me so much and still tell me so little."

"Perhaps you're right," answered Cecil. "But even after I tell you, you won't be able to sell the story, because no one will believe you. It was the capsules that did the trick."

"But you told me Doctor Murdock wrote the prescriptions and they were prepared by the best drug house in New York!"

"That's true. But I forgot to tell you one thing. After I got the capsules, I opened them and into each one I put a small fishhook. Murdock gave a good many capsules to each of his patients. Now write the story."

A. J. DEUTSCH

A SUBWAY NAMED MOBIUS

IN A COMPLEX and ingenious pattern, the subway had spread out from a focus at Park Street. A shunt connected the Lechmere line with the Ashmont for trains southbound, and with the Forest Hills line for those northbound. Harvard and Brookline had been linked with a tunnel that passed through Kenmore Under, and during rush hours every other train was switched through the Kenmore Branch back to Egleston. The Kenmore Branch joined the Maverick Tunnel near Fields Corner. It climbed a hundred feet in two blocks to connect Copley Over with Scollay Square; then it dipped down again to join the Cambridge line at Boylston. The Boylston shuttle had finally tied together the seven principal lines on four different levels. It went into service, you remember, on March 3rd. After that, a train could travel from any one station to any other station in the whole system.

There were two hundred twenty-seven trains running the subways every weekday, and they carried about a million and a half passengers. The Cambridge-Dorchester train that disappeared on March 4th was Number 86. Nobody missed it at first. During the evening rush, the traffic was a little heavier than usual on that line. But a crowd is a crowd. The ad posters at the Forest Hills yards looked for 86 about 7:30, but neither of them mentioned its absence until three days later. The controller at the Milk Street Cross-Over called the Harvard checker for an extra train after the hockey game that night, and the Harvard checker relayed the call to the yards. The dispatcher there sent out 87, which had been put to bed at ten o'clock, as usual. He didn't notice that 86 was missing.

It was near the peak of the rush the next morning that Jack O'Brien, at the Park Street Control, called Warren Sweeney at the Forest Hills yards and told him to put another train on the Cambridge run. Sweeney was short, so he went to the board and scanned it for a spare train and crew. Then, for the first time, he noticed that Gallagher had not checked out the night before. He put the tag up and left a note. Gallagher was due on at ten. At ten-thirty, Sweeney was down looking at the board again, and he noticed Gallagher's tag still up, and the note where he had left it. He groused to the checker and asked if Gallagher had come in late. The checker said he hadn't seen Gallagher at all that morning. Then Sweeney wanted to know who was running 86? A few minutes later he found that Dorkin's card was still up, although it was Dorkin's day off. It was 11:30 before he finally realized that he had lost a train.

Sweeney spent the next hour and a half on the phone, and he quizzed every dispatcher, controller, and checker on the whole system. When he finished his lunch at 1:30, he covered the whole net again. At 4:40, just before he left for the day, he reported the matter, with some indignation, to Central Traffic. The phones buzzed through the tunnels and shops until nearly midnight before the general manager was finally notified at his home.

It was the engineer on the main switchbank who, late in the morning of the 6th, first associated the missing train with the newspaper stories about the sudden rash of missing persons. He tipped off the *Transcript,* and by the end of the lunch hour three papers had Extras on the streets. That was the way the story got out.

Kelvin Whyte, the General Manager, spent a good part of that afternoon with the police. They checked Gallagher's wife, and Dorkin's. The motorman and the conductor had not been home since the morning of the 4th. By mid-afternoon, it was clear to the police that three hundred and fifty Bostonians, more or less, had been lost with the train. The System buzzed, and Whyte nearly expired with simple exasperation. But the train was not found.

Roger Tupelo, the Harvard mathematician, stepped into the picture the evening of the 6th. He reached Whyte by phone, late, at his home, and told him he had some ideas about the missing train. Then he taxied to Whyte's home in Newton and had the first of many talks with Whyte about Number 86.

Whyte was an intelligent man, a good organizer, and not without imagination. "But I don't know what you're talking about!" he expostulated.

Tupelo was resolved to be patient. "This is a very hard thing for *anybody* to understand, Mr. Whyte," he said. "I can see why you are puzzled. But it's the only explanation. The train has vanished, and the people on it. But the System is closed. Trains are conserved. It's somewhere on the System!"

Whyte's voice grew louder again. "And I tell you, Dr. Tupelo, that train is *not* on the System! It is *not!* You can't overlook a seven-car train carrying four hundred passengers. The System has been combed. Do you think I'm trying to *hide* the train?"

"Of course not. Now look, let's be reasonable. We know the train was en route to Cambridge at 8:40 a.m. on the 4th. At least twenty of the missing people probably boarded the train a few minutes earlier at Washington, and forty more at Park Street Under. A few got off at both stations. And that's the last. The ones who were going to Kendall, to Central, to Harvard—they never got there. The train did not get to Cambridge."

"I know that, Dr. Tupelo," Whyte said savagely. "In the tunnel under the River, the train turned into a boat. It left the tunnel and sailed for Africa."

"No, Mr. Whyte. I'm trying to tell you. It hit a node."

Whyte was livid. "What is a node!" he exploded. "The System keeps the tracks clear. Nothing on the tracks but trains, no nodes left lying around—"

"You still don't understand. A node is not an obstruction. It's a singularity. A pole of high order."

Tupelo's explanations that night did not greatly clarify the situation for Kelvin Whyte. But at two in the morning, the general manager conceded to Tupelo the privilege of examining the master maps of the System. He put in a call first to the police, who could not assist him with his first attempt to master topology, and then, finally, to Central Traffic. Tupelo taxied down there alone, and pored over the maps till morning. He had coffee and a snail, and then went to Whyte's office.

He found the general manager on the telephone. There was a conversation having to do with another, more elaborate inspection of the Dorchester-Cambridge tunnel under the Charles River. When the conversation ended, Whyte slammed the telephone into its cradle and glared at Tupelo. The mathematician spoke first.

"I think probably it's the new shuttle that did this," he said.

Whyte gripped the edge of his desk and prowled silently through his vocabulary until he had located some civil words. "Dr. Tupelo," he said, "I have been awake all night going over your theory. I don't understand it all. I don't know what the Boylston shuttle has to do with this."

"Remember what I was saying last night about the connective properties of networks?" Tupelo asked quietly. "Remember the Möbius band we made—the surface with one face and one edge? Remember this—?" and he removed a little glass Klein bottle from his pocket and placed it on the desk.

Whyte sat back in his chair and stared wordlessly at the mathematician. Three emotions marched across his face in quick succession—anger, bewilderment, and utter dejection. Tupelo went on.

"Mr. Whyte, the System is a network of amazing topological complexity. It was already complex before the Boylston shuttle was installed, and of a high order of connectivity. But this shuttle makes the network absolutely unique. I don't fully understand it, but the situation seems to be something like this: the shuttle has made the connectivity of the whole System of an order so high that I don't know how to calculate it. I suspect the connectivity has become infinite."

The general manager listened as though in a daze. He kept his eyes glued to the little Klein bottle.

"The Möbius band," Tupelo said, "has unusual properties because it has a singularity. The Klein bottle, with two singularities, manages to be inside of itself. The topologists know surfaces with as many as a thousand singularities, and they have properties that make the Möbius band and the Klein bottle both look simple. But a network with infinite connectivity must have an infinite number of singularities. Can you imagine what the properties of that network could be?"

After a long pause, Tupelo added: "I can't either. To tell the truth, the structure of the System, with the Boylston shuttle, is completely beyond me. I can only guess."

Whyte swiveled his eyes up from the desk at a moment when anger was the dominant feeling within him. "And you call yourself a mathematician, Professor Tupelo!" he said.

Tupelo almost laughed aloud. The incongruous, the absolute foolishness of the situation, all but overwhelmed him. He smiled thinly, and said: "I'm no topologist. Really, Mr. Whyte, I'm a tyro in the field—not much better acquainted with it than you are. Mathematics is a big pasture. I happen to be an algebraist."

His candor softened Whyte a little. "Well, then," he ventured, "if you don't understand it, maybe we should call in a topologist. Are there any in Boston?"

"Yes and no," Tupelo answered. "The best in the world is at Tech."

Whyte reached for the telephone. "What's his name?" he asked. "I'll call him."

"Merritt Turnbull. He can't be reached. I've tried for three days."

"Is he out of town?" Whyte asked. "We'll send for him—emergency."

"I don't know. Professor Turnbull is a bachelor. He lives alone at the Brattle Club. He has not been seen since the morning of the 4th."

Whyte was uncommonly perceptive. "Was he on the train?" he asked tensely.

"I don't know," the mathematician replied. "What do you think?"

There was a long silence. Whyte looked alternately at Tupelo and at the glass object on the desk. "I don't understand it," he said finally. "We've looked everywhere on the System. There was no way for the train to get out."

"The train didn't get out. It's still on the System," Tupelo said.

"Where?"

Tupelo shrugged. "The train has no real 'where.' The whole System is without real 'whereness.' It's double-valued, or worse."

"How can we find it?"

"I don't think we can," Tupelo said.

There was another long silence. Whyte broke it with a loud exclamation. He rose suddenly, and sent the Klein bottle flying across the room. "You are crazy, professor!" he shouted. Between midnight tonight and 6:00 a.m. tomorrow, we'll get every train out of the tunnels. I'll send in three hundred men, to comb every inch of the tracks—every inch of the one hundred eighty-three miles. We'll find the train! Now, please excuse me." He glared at Tupelo.

Tupelo left the office. He felt tired, completely exhausted. Mechanically, he walked along Washington Street toward the Essex Station. Halfway down the stairs, he stopped abruptly, looked around him slowly. Then he ascended again to the street and hailed a taxi. At home, he helped himself to a double shot. He fell into bed.

At 3:30 that afternoon he met his class in "Algebra of Fields and Rings." After a quick supper at the Crimson Spa, he went to his apartment and spent the evening in a second attempt to analyze the connective properties of the System. The attempt was vain, but the mathematician came to a few important conclusions. At eleven o'clock he telephoned Whyte at Central Traffic.

"I think you might want to consult me during tonight's search," he said. "May I come down?"

The general manager was none too gracious about Tupelo's offer of help. He indicated that the System would solve this little problem without any help from harebrained professors who thought that whole subway trains could jump off into the fourth dimension. Tupelo submitted to Whyte's unkindness, then went to bed. At about 4:00 a.m. the telephone awakened him. His caller was a contrite Kelvin Whyte.

"Perhaps I was a bit hasty last night, professor," he stammered. "You may be able to help us after all. Could you come down to the Milk Street Cross-Over?"

Tupelo agreed readily. He felt none of the satisfaction he had anticipated. He called a taxi, and in less than half an hour was at the prescribed station. At the foot of the stairs, on the upper level, he saw that the tunnel was brightly lighted, as during normal operation of the System. But the platforms were deserted except for a tight little knot of seven men near the far end. As he walked towards the group, he noticed that two were policemen. He observed a one-car train on the track beside the platform. The forward door was open, the car brightly lit, and empty. Whyte heard his footsteps and greeted him sheepishly.

"Thanks for coming down, professor," he said, extending his hand. "Gentlemen, Dr. Roger Tupelo, of Harvard. Dr. Tupelo, Mr. Kennedy, our chief engineer; Mr. Wilson, representing the Mayor; Dr. Gannot, of Mercy Hospital." Whyte did not bother to introduce the motorman and the two policemen.

"How do you do," said Tupelo. "Any results, Mr. Whyte?"

The general manager exchanged embarrassed glances with his companions. "Well . . . yes, Dr. Tupelo," he finally answered. "I think we do have some results, of a kind."

"Has the train been seen?"

"Yes," said Whyte. "That is, practically seen. At least, we know it's somewhere in the tunnels." The six others nodded their agreement.

Tupelo was not surprised to learn that the train was still on the System. After all, the System was closed. "Would you mind telling me just what happened?" Tupelo insisted.

"I hit a red signal," the motorman volunteered. "Just outside the Copley junction."

"The tracks have been completely cleared of all trains," Whyte explained, "except for this one. We've been riding it, all over the System, for four hours now. When Edmunds, here, hit a red light at the Copley junction, he stopped, of course. I thought the light must be defective, and told him to go ahead. But then we heard another train pass the junction."

"Did you see it?" Tupelo asked.

"We couldn't see it. The light is placed just behind a curve. But we all heard it. There's no doubt the train went through the junction. And it must be Number 86, because our car was the only other one on the tracks."

"What happened then?"

"Well, then the light changed to yellow, and Edmunds went ahead."

"Did he follow the other train?"

"No. We couldn't be sure which way it was going. We must have guessed wrong."

"How long ago did this happen?"

"At 1:38, the first time—"

"Oh," said Tupelo, "then it happened again later?"

"Yes. But not at the same spot, of course. We hit another red signal near South Station at 2:15. And then at 3:28—"

Tupelo interrupted the general manager. "Did you see the train at 2:15?"

"We didn't even hear it, that time. Edmunds tried to catch it, but it must have turned off onto the Boylston shuttle."

"What happened at 3:28?"

"Another red light. Near Park Street. We heard it up ahead of us."

"But you didn't see it?"

"No. There is a little slope beyond the light. But we all heard it. The only thing I don't understand, Dr. Tupelo, is how that train could run the tracks for nearly five days without anybody seeing—"

Whyte's words trailed off into silence, and his right hand went up in a peremptory gesture for quiet. In the distance, the low metallic thunder of a fast-rolling train swelled up suddenly into a sharp, shrill roar of wheels below. The platform vibrated perceptibly as the train passed.

"Now we've got it!" Whyte exclaimed. "Right past the men on the platform below!" He broke into a run towards the stairs to the lower level. All the others followed him, except Tupelo. He thought he knew what was going to happen. It did. Before Whyte reached the stairs, a policeman bounded up to the top.

"Did you see it, now?" he shouted.

Whyte stopped in his tracks, and the others with him.

"Did you see that train?" the policeman from the lower level asked again, as two more men came running up the stairs.

"What happened?" Wilson wanted to know.

"Didn't *you* see it?" snapped Kennedy.

"Sure not," the policeman replied. "It passed through up here."

"It did *not*," roared Whyte. "Down there!"

The six men with Whyte glowered at the three from the lower level. Tupelo walked to Whyte's elbow. "The train can't be seen, Mr. Whyte," he said quietly.

Whyte looked down at him in utter disbelief. "You heard it yourself. It passed right below—"

"Can we go to the car, Mr. Whyte?" Tupelo asked. "I think we ought to talk a little."

Whyte nodded dumbly, then turned to the policeman and the others who had been watching at the lower level. "You really didn't see it?" he begged them.

"We heard it," the policeman answered. "It passed up here, going that way, I think," and he gestured with his thumb.

"Get back downstairs, Maloney," one of the policemen with Whyte commanded. Maloney scratched his head, turned, and disappeared below. The two other men followed him. Tupelo led the original group to the car beside the station platform. They went in and took seats, silently. Then they all watched the mathematician and waited.

"You didn't call me down here tonight just to tell me you'd found the missing train," Tupelo began, looking at Whyte. "Has this sort of thing happened before?"

Whyte squirmed in his seat and exchanged glances with the chief engineer. "Not exactly like this," he said, evasively, "but there have been some funny things."

"Like what?" Tupelo snapped.

"Well, like the red lights. The watchers near Kendall found a red light at the same time we hit the one near South Station."

"Go on."

"Mr. Sweeney called me from Forest Hills at Park Street Under. He heard the train there just two minutes after we heard it at the Copley junction. Twenty-eight track miles away."

"As a matter of fact, Dr. Tupelo," Wilson broke in, "several dozen men have seen lights go red, or have heard the train, or both, inside of the last four hours. The thing acts as though it can be in several places at once."

"It can," Tupelo said.

"We keep getting reports of watchers seeing the thing," the engineer added. "Well, not exactly seeing it, either, but everything except that. Sometimes at two or even three places, far apart, at the same time. It's sure to be on the tracks. Maybe the cars are uncoupled."

"Are you really sure it's on the tracks, Mr. Kennedy?" Tupelo asked.

"Positive," the engineer said. "The dynamometers at the power house show that it's drawing power. It's been drawing power all night. So at 3:30 we broke the circuits. Cut the power."

"What happened?"

"Nothing," Whyte answered. "Nothing at all. The power was off for twenty minutes. During that time, not one of the two hundred fifty men in the tunnels saw a red light or heard a train. But the power wasn't on for five minutes before we had two reports again—one from Arlington, the other from Egleston."

There was a long silence after Whyte finished speaking. In the tunnel below, one man could be heard calling something to another. Tupelo looked at his watch. The time was 5:20.

"In short, Dr. Tupelo," the general manager finally said, "we are compelled to admit that there may be something in your theory." The others nodded agreement.

"Thank you, gentlemen," Tupelo said.

The physician cleared his throat. "Now about the passengers," he began. "Have you any idea what—?"

"None," Tupelo interrupted.

"What should we do, Dr. Tupelo?" the mayor's representative asked.

"I don't know. What can you do?"

"As I understand it from Mr. Whyte," Wilson continued, "the train has . . . well, it has jumped into another dimension. It isn't really on the System at all. It's just gone. Is that right?"

"In a manner of speaking."

"And this . . . er . . . peculiar behavior has resulted from certain mathematical properties associated with the new Boylston shuttle?"

"Correct."

"And there is nothing we can do to bring the train back to . . . uh . . . this dimension?"

"I know of nothing."

Wilson took the bit in his teeth. "In this case, gentlemen," he said, "our course is clear. First, we must close off the new shuttle, so this fantastic thing can never happen again. Then, since the missing train is really gone, in spite of all these red lights and noises, we can resume normal operation of the System. At least there will be no danger of collision— which has worried you so much, Whyte. As for the missing train and the people on it—" He gestured them into infinity. "Do you agree, Dr. Tupelo?" he asked the mathematician.

Tupelo shook his head slowly. "Not entirely, Mr. Wilson," he responded. "Now, please keep in mind that I don't fully comprehend what has happened. It's unfortunate that you won't find anybody who can give a good explanation. The one man who might have done so is Professor Turnbull, of Tech, and he was on the train. But in any case, you will want to check my conclusions against those of some competent topologists. I can put you in touch with several.

"Now, with regard to the recovery of the missing train, I can say that I think this is not hopeless. There is a finite probability, as I see it, that the train will eventually pass from the nonspatial part of the network, which it now occupies, back to the spatial part. Since the nonspatial part is wholly inaccessible, there is unfortunately nothing we can do to bring about this transition, or even to predict when or how it will occur. But the possibility of the transition will vanish if the Boylston shuttle is taken out. It is just this section of the track that gives the network its essential singularities. If the singularities are removed, the train can never reappear. Is this clear?"

It was not clear, of course, but the seven listening men nodded agreement. Tupelo continued.

"As for the continued operation of the System while the missing train is in the nonspatial part of the network, I can only give you the facts as I see them and leave to your judgment the difficult decision to be drawn from them. The transition back to the spatial part is unpredictable, as I have already told you. There is no way to know when it will occur, or where. In particular, there is a fifty percent probability that, if and when the train reappears, it will be running on the wrong track. Then there will be a collision, of course."

The engineer asked: "To rule out this possibility, Dr. Tupelo, couldn't we leave the Boylston shuttle open, but send no trains through it? Then, when the missing train reappears on the shuttle, it cannot meet another train."

"That precaution would be ineffective, Mr. Kennedy," Tupelo answered. "You see, the train can reappear anywhere on the System. It is true that the System owes its topological complexity to the new shuttle. But, with the shuttle in the System, it is now the whole System that possesses infinite connectivity. In other words, the relevant topological property is a property *derived* from the shuttle, but *belonging to* the whole System. Remember that the train made its first transition at a point between Park and Kendall, more than three miles away from the shuttle.

"There is one question more you will want answered. If you decide to go on operating the System, with the Boylston shuttle left in until the train reappears, can this happen again, to another train? I am not certain of the answer, but I think it is: No. I believe an exclusion principle operates here, such that only one train at a time can occupy the nonspatial network."

The physician rose from his seat. "Dr. Tupelo," he began, timorously, "when the train does reappear, will the passengers—?"

"I don't know about the people on the train," Tupelo cut in. "The topological theory does not consider such matters." He looked quickly at each of the seven tired, querulous faces before him. "I am sorry, gentlemen," he added, somewhat more gently. "I simply do not know." To Whyte, he added: "I think I can be of no more help tonight. You know where to reach me." And, turning on his heel, he left the car and climbed the stairs. He found dawn spilling over the street, dissolving the shadows of night.

That impromptu conference in a lonely subway car was never reported in the papers. Nor were the full results of the night-long vigil over the dark and twisted tunnels. During the week that followed, Tupelo participated in four more formal conferences with Kelvin Whyte and certain city officials. At two of these, other topologists were present. Ornstein was imported to Boston from Philadelphia, Kashta from Chicago, and Michaelis from Los Angeles. The mathematicians were unable to reach a concensus. None of the three would fully endorse Tupelo's conclusions, although Kashta indicated that there *might* be something to them. Ornstein averred that a finite network could not possess infinite connectivity, although he could not prove this proposition and could not actually calculate the connectivity of the System. Michaelis expressed his opinion that the affair was a hoax and had nothing whatever to do with the topology of the System. He insisted that if the train could not be found on the System then the System must be open, or at least must once have been open.

But the more deeply Tupelo analyzed the problem, the more fully he was convinced of the essential correctness of his first analysis. From the point of view of topology, the System soon suggested whole families of multiple-valued networks, each with an infinite number of infinite discontinuities. But a definitive discussion of these new spatio-hyperspatial networks somehow eluded him. He gave the subject his full attention for only a week. Then his other duties compelled him to lay the analysis aside. He resolved to go back to the problem later in the spring, after courses were over.

Meanwhile, the System was operated as though nothing untoward had happened. The general manager and the mayor's representative had somehow managed to forget the night of the search, or at least to reinterpret what they had seen and not seen. The newspapers and the public at large speculated wildly, and they kept continuing pressure on Whyte. A number of suits were filed against the System on behalf of persons who had lost a relative. The State stepped into the affair and prepared its own thorough investigation. Recriminations were sounded in the halls of Congress. A garbled version of Tupelo's theory eventually found its way into the press. He ignored it, and it was soon forgotten.

The weeks passed, and then a month. The State's investigation was

completed. The newspaper stories moved from the first page to the
second; to the twenty-third; and then stopped. The missing persons did
not return. In the large, they were no longer missed.

One day in mid-April, Tupelo traveled by subway again, from Charles
Street to Harvard. He sat stiffly in the front of the first car, and watched
the tracks and gray tunnel walls hurl themselves at the train. Twice the
train stopped for a red light, and Tupelo found himself wondering
whether the other train was really just ahead, or just beyond space. He
half-hoped, out of curiosity, that his exclusion principle was wrong, that
the train might make the transition. But he arrived at Harvard on time.
Only he among the passengers had found the trip exciting.

The next week he made another trip by subway, and again the next.
As experiments, they were unsuccessful, and much less tense than the
first ride in mid-April. Tupelo began to doubt his own analysis. Sometime in May, he reverted to the practice of commuting by subway between his Beacon Hill apartment and his office at Harvard. His mind
stopped racing down the knotted gray caverns ahead of the train. He
read the morning newspaper, or the abstracts in *Reviews of Modern
Mathematics*.

Then there was one morning when he looked up from the newspaper
and sensed something. He pushed panic back on its stiff, quivering spring,
and looked quickly out the window at his right. The lights of the car
showed the black and gray lines of wall-spots streaking by. The tracks
ground out their familiar steely dissonance. The train rounded a curve
and crossed a junction that he remembered. Swiftly, he recalled boarding
the train at Charles, noting the girl on the ice-carnival poster at Kendall,
meeting the southbound train going into Central.

He looked at the man sitting beside him, with a lunch pail on his lap.
The other seats were filled, and there were a dozen or so straphangers. A
mealy-faced youth near the front door smoked a cigarette, in violation of
the rules. Two girls behind him across the aisle were discussing a club
meeting. In the seat ahead, a young woman was scolding her little son.
The man on the aisle, in the seat ahead of that, was reading the paper.
The Transit-Ad above him extolled Florida oranges.

He looked again at the man two seats ahead and fought down the terror
within. He studied that man. What was it? Brunet, graying hair; a round-
ish head; wan complexion; rather flat features; a thick neck, with the hair-
line a little low, a little ragged; a gray, pin-stripe suit. While Tupelo
watched, the man waved a fly away from his left ear. He swayed a little
with the train. His newspaper was folded vertically down the middle. His
newspaper! It was last March's!

Tupelo's eyes swiveled to the man beside him. Below his lunch pail was
a paper. Today's. He turned in his seat and looked behind him. A young
man held the *Transcript* open to the sports pages. The date was March
4th. Tupelo's eyes raced up and down the aisle. There were a dozen passengers carrying papers ten weeks old.

Tupelo lunged out of his seat. The man on the aisle muttered a curse as the mathematician crowded in front of him. He crossed the aisle in a bound and pulled the cord above the windows. The brakes sawed and screeched at the tracks, and the train ground to a stop. The startled passengers eyed Tupelo with hostility. At the rear of the car, the door flew open and a tall, thin man in a blue uniform burst in. Tupelo spoke first.

"Mr. Dorkin?" he called, vehemently.

The conductor stopped short and groped for words.

"There's been a serious accident, Dorkin," Tupelo said, loudly, to carry over the rising swell of protest from the passengers. "Get Gallagher back here right away!"

Dorkin reached up and pulled the cord four times. "What happened?" he asked.

Tupelo ignored the question, and asked one of his own. "Where have you been, Dorkin?"

The conductor's face was blank. "In the next car, but—"

Tupelo cut him off. He glanced at his watch, then shouted at the passengers. "It's ten minutes to nine on May 17th!"

The announcement stilled the rising clamor for a moment. The passengers exchanged bewildered glances.

"Look at your newspapers!" Tupelo shouted. "Your newspapers!"

The passengers began to buzz. As they discovered each other's papers, the voices rose. Tupelo took Dorkin's arm and led him to the rear of the car. "What time is it?" he asked.

"8:21," Dorkin said, looking at his watch.

"Open the door," said Tupelo, motioning ahead. "Let me out. Where's the phone?"

Dorkin followed Tupelo's directions. He pointed to a niche in the tunnel wall a hundred yards ahead. Tupelo vaulted to the ground and raced down the narrow lane between the cars and the wall. "Central Traffic!" he barked at the operator. He waited a few seconds, and saw that a train had stopped at the red signal behind his train. Flashlights were advancing down the tunnel. He saw Gallagher's legs running down the tunnel on the other side of 86. "Get me Whyte!" he commanded, when Central Traffic answered. "Emergency!"

There was a delay. He heard voices rising from the train beside him. The sound was mixed—anger, fear, hysteria.

"Hello!" he shouted. "Hello! Emergency! Get me Whyte!"

"I'll take it," a man's voice said at the other end of the line. "Whyte's busy!"

"Number 86 is back," Tupelo called. "Between Central and Harvard now. Don't know when it made the jump. I caught it at Charles ten minutes ago, and didn't notice it till a minute ago."

The man at the other end gulped hard enough to carry over the telephone. "The passengers?" he croaked.

"All right, the ones that are left," Tupelo said. "Some must have got off already at Kendall and Central."

"Where have they been?"

Tupelo dropped the receiver from his ear and stared at it, his mouth wide open. Then he slammed the receiver onto the hook and ran back to the open door.

Eventually, order was restored, and within a half hour the train proceeded to Harvard. At the station, the police took all passengers into protective custody. Whyte himself arrived at Harvard before the train did. Tupelo found him on the platform.

Whyte motioned weakly towards the passengers. "They're really all right?" he asked.

"Perfectly," said Tupelo. "Don't know they've been gone."

"Any sign of Professor Turnbull?" asked the general manager.

"I didn't see him. He probably got off at Kendall, as usual."

"Too bad," said Whyte. "I'd like to see him!"

"So would I!" Tupelo answered. "By the way, now is the time to close the Boylston shuttle."

"Now is too late," Whyte said. "Train 143 vanished twenty-five minutes ago between Egleston and Dorchester."

Tupelo stared past Whyte, and down and down the tracks.

"We've got to find Turnbull," Whyte said.

Tupelo looked at Whyte and smiled thinly.

"Do you really think Turnbull got off this train at Kendall?" he asked.

"Of course!" answered Whyte. "Where else?"

Ross Rocklynne

BACKFIRE

BRUCE PAUSED ON his way through the gate onto the runway that led to the towering spaceship. He had heard his name called. He turned, and Jan Tomaz, training under Bruce as an Administrator of Physico-Stasis Application Bureau, pushed his way through the moving crowd toward him.

"You'll have to call off your trip, Bruce."

Bruce smiled. "By whose authority, Jan?"

"By the authority of the people."

"I don't follow you."

"By the authority," said the other patiently, "of one Thomas Q. Greeley. You're the only one in full possession of the facts of the case. He knows the law. He knows he can demand a hearing any time he wants it. He's over eighteen and he says that he's eligible for immediate decision. He wants his immortality. He says he's been here six weeks, under observation like a guinea pig. He's been wearing the hypnobioscope every night and he's learned the language. He says he's going to have a hearing or else. What the 'or else' means I don't know. Does that sound like a threat to you?"

Jan said it simply, without alarm. In all the twenty-one years of his life, he had never had cause for alarm. Nor had Bruce. Both, although Bruce had been born five hundred thirteen years ago, were cut to a pattern, black of hair and brow, straight-nosed; beneath smooth skin glowed the subtle radiance of immortality. They were dressed loosely, in heavy, patterned silks. This was the year 3555 A.D. and Kearney Field was but one of the many spaceports outside New York State City.

Bruce considered the information. He answered finally, "A bluff, Jan. Look the word up in the *World Encyclopedia* of the twentieth century. Its ingredients are a loud voice and an aggressive manner designed to intimidate another person into an action which does not conform with his desires or beliefs." He fell silent, then shrugged his shoulders and turned. Shortly he was ensconced beside Jan in Jan's *Bullet-nose*, and the ship was lifting soundlessly over the city. He thoughtfully watched the low, dimly lighted skyline, the shimmer of ocean.

He said at length, "Greeley knows the law. He has a quick mind. In his own era, he made his living with his wits, in various guises. He started off as a sideshow barker, and a shyster lawyer was impressed with his voice and his manner and his unusual show of language, and tutored him in the fine art of shystering. A politician in turn heard him in a courtroom, and Greeley took another step upward. Somewhere along the line he was a labor organizer."

"His mind must be very complex," said Jan.

"Not unusually so for his era—which may be," Bruce said thoughtfully, "not so good for us. I wish we could send him back to the twentieth century where he came from."

Jan reached forward and touched certain controls. The ship slanted, hovered, and landed on the roof of the Justice Building. They got out and by elevator descended to Greeley's quarters.

A big man with tousled hair was sitting on the edge of a couch when they came into the room. He had a finely patterned robe wrapped around his body. Items of his clothing littered the floor. A cigar stuck at an acute angle from the corner of his lips, which were sensuously thick. Smoke was drifting away in layers to be swallowed by the ventilator. When he saw the two men, he put two heavily ringed, beefy hands on the edge of the couch and shoved himself energetically erect and came forward with long, pounding strides.

His eyes flickered over Bruce. "You're the guy that's been studying me, eh? Here. Have a cigar. Sit down," he said when Bruce shook his head. He threw items of clothing off the chair. "Sit down. Damn! Is it true that tobacco's gone out? What will I do *now*? My record's a cigar every two hours." He grinned suddenly, as suddenly stopped grinning. A mocking expression changed his face subtly. "Sorry I interrupted your joy jaunt. Sit down."

Bruce and Jan sat down without saying anything, and Greeley paced back and forth, exuding smoke, turning his head with quick, birdlike glances, keeping his shrewd, small eyes on Bruce. Bruce crossed his legs, and let his personality dwindle away to a shadow as Greeley, alive with an inductive animal magnetism which showed in every gesture, every tone, every subtle change of expression, went on talking.

"I'm sorry, see?" said Greeley, jutting his head at Bruce impatiently. He flicked ashes in a calcium cloud. "I know you guys got to have your fun same as anybody else. But not at my expense. I can't take it, see? I've got different stuff in me. I feel like I'm in stir. I don't mean behind bars, real bars, I'm talking about this body of mine. I'm imprisoned in mortality. Every second that passes I feel the noose drawing tighter—the Grim Reaper scything along. See what I mean? *You* fellows don't feel that. You never will. Neither will anybody else in this civilization. You'll never die except by accident, but you don't have any accidents; no disease, either. Death! Ugh!"

A very real shudder shook him. Suddenly he sat down, leaning forward, his elbows on his knees. His eyes narrowed on Bruce, grew ugly with fury.

"What's your decision?"

Bruce crossed his legs. He said quietly, "There are several things you don't understand about our civilization, Greeley. Very important things. Maybe you *can't* understand them. I don't know. I've studied the twentieth century in many of its phases, but I confess that I don't completely understand the motives that drove humanity then. Look at our world. I think we've changed human nature. It's taken a long time, but here we are, without disease, either physical or mental. We move quietly and with a contentment which may be incredible to you. Immortality has helped. We have no death fears.

"But look at our immortality. What good would it be with *fear* in the background? Fear of each other. Of superstition. Fear based on unfounded beliefs. We have eradicated fear—we've cut it away like a tumor." Bruce made an incisive motion with his finger. "So we can appreciate our immortality, because we are not afraid to live. Now a new factor, a twentieth-century being, comes to the thirty-sixth century. The mixture is not good. Such a person, we feel, could not by any stretch of the imagination add to the general welfare of our race; much less add to his own welfare. I operate according to that code of office."

Greeley slid to the very edge of the couch, eyes squinted up against the smoke from the cigar. "What's your decision?" he ground out.

Bruce said, "No."

The big man rose with an oath and threw his cigar violently against the wall. "I thought so," he shouted, his face turning slowly red. "I thought so when you began stalling me three or four weeks ago. All that bunk about studying me. You decided then that I didn't 'fit' into your namby-pamby silk civilization where everybody falls into a mold and too bad for them if they don't.

"You're all eighteen years old, and polite and noble and gentle. You work every other year for four hours a day. The rest of the time, you para-sitize off of machines. You're so damned superior you stink. You haven't got an ounce of charity in you. You can't appreciate a man from the twentieth century, born in an age when you had to work your guts out to get any place. When you had to harden up like steel and knock the other guy down before he took you over the ropes. So now I don't 'fit' and you won't give me immortality."

He burst into a wild, incredulous laugh which abruptly stopped as he fastened his intense, feral eyes on Bruce.

"Why, I'm so superior in real, animal aliveness to you birds," he bit out, "that I wouldn't trade my body or my outlook for a dozen of yours. Noble! Gentle! Courteous! Weak, sniveling, snobbish degenerates, you mean. O. K., O. K. You asked for it. And believe you me, you're going to regret it. You're going to be glad to give me immortality before I'm through with you. It's a promise! Now get out. I know my rights. These are my quarters until I choose to move, and what the hell do you mean walking in without knocking? *Get out!*"

Bruce stood up, face slightly pale. "Come on," he told Jan quietly.

Greeley slammed the door after them.

Bruce hesitated with his well-manicured finger hovering an inch from the elevator button. He turned to Jan, lips flickering with a curious smile. "So that's what they were like," he said slowly. He gave a convulsive shudder.

Bruce Cort, Administrator of the Terrestrial Physico-Stasis Application Bureau, walked the decks of the Alpha Centauri passenger liner. It was his third day out. He had forgotten Greeley entirely, for the problem he presented had been solved. Greeley had received the only death sentence that was possible, and after he had lived his span of years, civilization would go on as it had before; indeed, its even pulse would be not one whit disturbed by Greeley's presence. Bruce Cort walked briskly, five hundred years of life behind him. To all appearance, he was eighteen years of age.

He was vaguely surprised that the decks were empty. Ordinarily, young-sters, both in the changed and unchanged classification, would have been scattered along the transparency of the observation ports goggling at the pure blackness behind and the blackness in front; and stumbling with the difficult explanation of the rainbow ring perpendicular to the ship's course, and of which the ship was ever the center. The ship was traveling at several times the speed of light.

There was no one on deck. Bruce started toward the lower deck, and ran into the captain.

"Hi there, Bruce. Did you hear him?"

"Hear who?"

"Greeley. They've got him tuned in on the Public Wave." Captain Iowa Lasser grinned. "A rather funny chap. Of course, it's ridiculous, but he's got an audience, and they're laughing as they never laughed before. Salon's packed."

Bruce frowned at him and said, "Think I'll go down and listen to that."

"I'll go with you."

As they neared the salon, Bruce heard a wave of laughter that quickly died away. He and Lasser stepped into the salon. From the grating above the orchestra stand Greeley's voice was coming. It was a pleasant voice, powerful, unctuous, rhythmic, modulated as if the speaker were following a scale.

"And them were the days, fellows, believe you me. Thirteen hundred years ago. Standing here on the Square, looking into your beaming, intelligent faces, still I got to admit that compared to the real he-men of my time, all of you are jackasses."

The crowd roared. Captain Iowa Lasser giggled a high-pitched sound. He turned to Bruce. "What are jackasses, Bruce?" he gasped.

Bruce stared at him uncomprehendingly. Finally he shrugged. "Look it up in the *Encyclopedia*." His expression hovered between a frown and an uncertain smile.

"Everything and everybody in *them* days," said Greeley, "was stronger and better built. Them were the men that built your present civilization. Immortality! I have to laugh. If they'd suspected for one minute that *their* civilization was going to give way to one like *this*, they would have cut their throats. They believed in liberty and freedom and justice for all, they believed in the hallowed tenets that their forefathers laid down. Washington, Lincoln, Roosevelt—their names went ringing down the corridors of time! Why? Because they died, and nobody gave a damn for 'em while they were alive."

The crowd was silent. Lasser's eyes moistened at bit. "He's got a nice choice of phrases, eh?" he asked of Bruce.

Bruce wrinkled his nose.

Lasser, eyes still moist, said, his eyes fastened on the annunciator, "He's got a good point, anyway."

Bruce said patiently, "Just what, captain, is he talking about?"

Greeley was talking again, however. "Civilization! Putrefaction, you mean. Why even the canaries of *my* time was hardier, and believe you me, I got in mind two particular canaries."

The crowd was quiet, tense, as he told a long story of a canary that became involved in a badminton game.

Lasser opened his mouth and bellowed. Bruce hardly heard him above a similarly loud indication of amusement from the crowd. There were tears running down Lasser's cheeks. "A riot, isn't he?" Lasser choked. "What's badminton, anyway?"

"Why," asked Bruce, "are you laughing if you don't know that?"

Lasser gurgled between spasms of laughter, "It's . . . just . . . something in his voice."

Greeley signed off a few minutes later. "So long, folks. Don't forget to tune in on the Public Wave tomorrow at this same time. One hour of fun, riot, and some common sense. This is yours truly, Thomas Q. Greeley, signing off."

Lasser wiped his eyes as the crowd, humming with laughter and talk, disbanded.

"You don't care for him, eh, Bruce?"

Bruce had a faraway, hard look in his eyes. He said slowly, "What do you think about his talk on immortality?"

Lasser's hovering grin faded. "It's good common sense," he said seriously. "Immortality has made us soft. At eighteen years of age we apply for physico-stasis, and physically we never develop beyond eighteen years of age, though mentally it's a different story."

Bruce said, "But in our civilization, with disease wiped out, we don't need anything more than eighteen-year-old bodies, do we?"

"W-well. I guess not. Still"—Lasser shook his head uneasily—"it just makes you wonder, Bruce." He partly changed the subject, looking at Bruce, curiously. "What's the story about Greeley, anyway?"

"He appeared out of thin air on the streets one day, talking a different language. I identified his clothing as twentieth century. They put him under a hypnobioscope and taught him the language. His general explanation was that somebody back in the twentieth century wanted to get rid of him, and sent him on a one-way trip with a time machine. Political enemies."

"He doesn't sound like the type to have enemies, Bruce."

Bruce smiled crookedly and told him the rest of the story.

"No! You don't mean to say he *wanted* immortality?" Lasser was plainly shocked.

"He wanted it all right."

"But . . . but from the way he talked—" Lasser began falteringly.

"You believe everything you hear?"

"Why shouldn't I?"

Bruce thought that over. "No reason," he said slowly. "Not in our civilization. But when two civilizations like his and ours gets mixed up—" He broke off thoughtfully.

Lasser looked at his watch. "Hard to believe he wants immortality," he muttered, chewing at his upper lip. Then suddenly, "Well, I have to be getting back to the bridge. We're due in at Centauri I in seven hours. Be seeing you." He went clicking away briskly, head down.

Bruce Cort had a ranch on Centauri I. He stayed there three days, but his mind wasn't on his thoroughbred *centaurs*, which weren't really centaurs at all, but six-legged, high-spirited animals indigenous to Centauri I. He found himself tuning in on Greeley's Hour. The man's voice came from Earth at almost infinite velocity, carried through light rays the way electrons are transmitted through a copper wire. He discovered that everybody else on the ranch was listening, too.

Bruce tried to listen without prejudice, which meant that by autohypnosis he had to rid his mind of memory associations of Greeley. He succeeded partly. Greeley's voice was a song, plucking at the emotional centers of his brain. There was no logic in what he said, but it didn't matter. Greeley's was a voice which commanded humor and pathos. He damned civilization and aroused no rancor.

"Our civilization," said Greeley, "was built on the word *mother*. Mother! I wish you could have seen mine, fellows. I sure wish you could—and I'd hate to have *you* point out *your* mothers. I'd sicken at the sight of them. Now my mother. She was old. She didn't have a silky face, and curving legs and hips and a sexy smile. She was the way the great Creator meant her to be. She was my *mother*! She had the respect that was due her, and she had a sweet smile, and there were silver hairs amongst the gold. I shudder for this civilization. Where will you find a crowning glory such as that? Silver hairs among the gold!"

("Nice choice of phrases," Lasser had said, his eyes moist. Probably he was crying now.)

"She died, yes. But was there anything terrible about death? As I sat at her bedside, and clasped her dear old hand in mine, there was no fright in her eyes. She knew she was going to a happier land. She knew that the arms of her Creator were outstretched to gather her to His bosom, and she passed away with a gentle smile on her lips, and her last words were, 'We will see each other again soon, son.' And then she was no more. And I strode away feeling as if I had seen a great truth—for it was then that I saw the real immortality; not an immortality in life, which is but a mockery of the real thing, but an immortality beyond death. I was a happier man for that, fellows, believe you me, when I saw my mother pass into the great beyond."

(Such new thoughts, such beautiful thoughts, such great truths, Lasser was thinking.)

After the broadcast, Bruce decided to go back home. He took a last stroll around his grounds. At the tables were some youths who next year would have their immortality. They were bedding down the *centaurs*, but they stopped at their job and looked at Bruce curiously. With the blunt forthrightness of the race one spoke the thought of all: "You're over a half millennium, aren't you, Bruce?"

Bruce stopped in midstride. The question was strange, since age was of little moment. He smiled quickly. "Five hundred and thirteen. Fourteen next June."

"How many children?"

Bruce thought, "Good heavens!" Out loud, he said, "I've really lost track."

He escaped them with a curiously unsettled state of mind. "They're looking at my hair," he thought in astonishment. He found the stable keeper, and jerked his head.

"What goes on in their heads?"

"Oh." The stable keeper added quickly, "They asked you too, eh? They've been listening to Greeley." He scowled, tentatively touched at his hair. He said uncertainly, "I don't see anything wrong with good healthy black hair, do you? I almost feel ashamed of myself. They ought to squeeze him off the air."

"He's got his prerogative," Bruce reminded him. "Until the demand for the Public Wave doesn't leave him any time he's allowed one hour in twenty-four. I think he'll keep it."

Why he went back to Earth ahead of schedule, Bruce could not have said. But he suspected that he was alarmed. Alarm! Wasn't that a neurotic symptom, to be dealt with quickly at Psychiatry? It was as bad as dreams. And yet, on the three-day trip, the outlawed emotion grew, for a strange thing was happening to this thirty-sixth century civilization. It was in the air, evident in a glance, or whispers; evident in the crowds who gathered to listen to one Thomas Q. Greeley, late of the twentieth century, where life was lived as it should have been lived, where men were he-men, and women were she-women, and mothers were *mothers*, and fathers were *fathers*, where human beings lived the lives their God intended them to live. Immortality! Luciferian device designed to trap men forever in their mortal bodies, to strip them of purposes; to rob them of the incomparable rewards of aging bodies.

Gone was Greeley the humorist. But people listened to him more greedily, and it seemed to Bruce that they were growing mightily ashamed of their smooth faces and their ugly, unsilvered hair.

Bruce came into his office in the Justice Building, stripping his plasticoat from his shoulders, and grinning as Jan Tomaz looked up from behind the big desk, surprise on his face.

Bruce clapped him on the shoulders. "Been keeping the job down?" he questioned, eyes straying to the litter of papers on the desk. "What's this?"

Jan accompanied him awkwardly to the desk. "Rejections," he said nervously.

Bruce shot him a quick glance. "You mean you've been rejecting applicants?"

"No; they've been rejecting their mailed application forms, with letters accompanying."

There was something sharp and stabbing in Bruce's brain. He snatched up half a dozen letters, passed his eyes over them. He made a sound in his throat, and dropped the letters with a little tnrust of his hand. "Humph."

He sat down behind the desk, leaned back and crossed his legs, fondling slowly at his chin. A slow, crooked, bitter smile grew on his lips. He nodded his head toward the near wall, where a radio and television utility was built in.

"Greeley comes on in one minute. Put him on." And, as Jan made the necessary adjustments and the screen lighted, "You've been listening to Greeley?"

Jan sat down, with a peculiar hesitation. Bruce noted now that there were peculiar haggard lines around his eyes. A case for Psychiatry. Bruce in that moment diagnosed Jan's case completely and accurately.

"I've been listening to him," said Jan thickly.

"What's your reaction?"

Jan opened his lips to speak, but no words would come forth.

Bruce leaned farther back and put his hands behind his head. "I want you to listen to me, Jan—and I don't want you to listen to Greeley any more." He got up and turned off the radio and televisor. "At least not for a while," he amended. He sat down again.

"I know the way your mind is working," he continued quietly. "You've been in a doubly exposed position, and I only wish you'd have wired me. I'd have come back before I did. Listening to Greeley, *and*, on top of that, reading letters from his supporters, and, still worse, knowing that the man is giving off false opinions, haven't been too good for you.

"Keep in mind, Jan, that Greeley wants the very thing he's condemning."

Jan's head shot up. "That's just it," he said tinnily. "I don't understand it. I'm not a neurotic. At least I wasn't when you left."

"I wish," Bruce said, "you'd have been bulwarked the way I was, Jan. I know twentieth-century history. More, I realize in some small way the outlook they had. They weren't all like Greeley, far from it. But they were hard, and they were immune to jingoism to some degree.

"Greeley, admittedly, doesn't talk sense. Nor does he talk lies. He talks what are ostensibly opinions. Therein, he shows his knowledge of our law. If it could be proven that he talks lies, he would be barred from the ether. As it is, we can't prove that he talks false opinions.

"Greeley doesn't have to talk sense. He has qualities which have never been necessary in our civilization. He's got a voice, for one thing, which reacts solely on the thalamus. In the twentieth century, nothing else was needed. It is notorious fact, and would be true today if anyone wanted to make use of it, that logic, carefully presented facts, does not appeal to the human brain. There's no bridge across which logic can travel to make an actual contact between one person's brain and another.

"Logic is appreciated; but it does not make for action. Men act only through emotion. Greeley's got virgin territory. That's the reason for these letters of rejection we've received. We'll receive more before this thing is over."

Jan sat stone still, face pale and drawn.

"Before it's over?" he jerked out. "When?"

Bruce riffled his hand absently through stacks of letters. "I don't know —yet. I do know that we'll need—a serum."

He laughed quietly. "Not a real serum. Figurative. Picture the twentieth century, Jan. A riot of speeches, and newspapers, and counterspeeches, and emotional jamborees, and 'my dear old mother, silver hair amongst the gold.' Prophets and fortunetellers and astrologers. Baby-kissing politicians with golden voices and big stomachs. 'My country, right or wrong.' And other nonsense wherein one did not die, one 'passed away.' Churches and faiths all with the same God, only different.

"In this morass, the people lived. They were very hard, or they learned to be hard. They were eternally on their guard, and many of them fought to peer beneath the razzle dazzle of jingoism for the solid cloth of truth. Of course, it was impossible to succeed very much, but they realized the presence of the enemy. To great degree, the civilization was diseased, but there was the fight for immunity.

"Now, out of the madhouse comes one Thomas Q. Greeley, one of the disease germs, and lands in the body—our thirty-sixth century. Thomas Q. Greeley is a very potent disease germ, Jan, and he has not only diseased the body, but the body does not realize the presence of the enemy.

"To cure the body, one needs a serum that will make the body strong enough to throw off its disease.

"Peculiarly, Jan, you're in the position of realizing the disease, but, by certain factors, are suppressed from fighting it, and therefore diseased yourself. Not a pretty picture, is it? But an accurate one, I think. You've got two opposing beliefs fixed in your mind, and it's a mind that's not accustomed to such a problem. And therefore, you're somewhat neurotic. Everybody in the twentieth century had a neurosis in one form or another, and it was the accepted thing, but it caused all the troubles in the world: the futile fight between the conscious and the unconscious, the soldiers being sordid untruths against mathematically precise realism."

Jan drew a long breath. "I feel a little bit better," he admitted.

"We'll have to send you to Psychiatry, anyway, Jan—after it's over. They'll shock your thalamus—all I can do is talk to the prefrontal lobes. In the meantime, go to your quarters and stay there a couple of days, and try not to talk to anybody, particularly about Greeley. Then you might drop back here and maybe I'll have the ingredients of a serum."

After Jan had gone, Bruce sat still, frowning, his lips hovering over the word "maybe."

But presently, he moved, and switched in the televisor, leaving the radio off. The screen lighted, swirled, and the pieces of the picture fell into place. It was seven minutes after three. Greeley was talking.

The pickup took in the Square at the heart of the city. Low buildings bounded it. The square was jam-packed, and Greeley stood on the platform at the center, facing a microphone and the scanning apparatus. Greeley was talking, throwing his head to the left in little emphatic movements, now and then using his hands, his expression changing subtly and astonishingly with every word. He was a big man, with a little extra fat, and a broad face bisected with a great blade of a nose. He was thirty-two years of age.

Bruce figured there must be twenty or twenty-five thousand of the Unchanged listening. There were probably some five thousand of the Changed, these latter all being under twenty-five. Bruce diagnosed the situation. Men as old as himself, or in the same magnitude of age, would listen, but they would be resentful. They might even feel shame. Captain Iowa Lasser was two hundred years. The stable keeper was about that. It was likely that the majority of men in that age group felt as they did. Changed and Unchanged they would be affected. Diseased.

But Bruce knew that he was immune.

Was he the only one that was immune, from here to the farthest inhabited planet of the Universe? That was not likely. There would be a few others—those who understood the twentieth century. Among these would be psychiatrists, almost certainly. But even they would not have Bruce's resistance, because only Bruce understood the game Greeley was playing.

Bruce's breath came short. Good heavens! From here to the farthest inhabited planet!

What could he do? Tell them Greeley wanted immortality? No. Logic again. Lasser had preferred not to believe him.

Bruce turned the radio on, and as Greeley's voice swelled, cut down for volume. Then he sat down again.

"—cut to a pattern. That's what immortality has done for you, fellows. One color hair and good-looking noses and slim, eighteen-year-old bodies. I sure wish you could have been born in the twentieth century. Look at me!" Greeley slapped his swelling chest. "I'm different. I'm the most distinguished man in this civilization right now. Oh, I'm not conceited. It's a *fact!* I'm *different*. Why are you listening to me instead of to one of your own kind? Because I stand out. I'm older. I show my *age!* I don't hide behind a silk body, skulking, while my mind grows older. I'm not ashamed, see? That's what all of you are. Ashamed. Ashamed of yourselves, and hiding from the benevolent eye of the Creator.

"I wish you could have been born in the twentieth century, fellows. Everybody was different. Everybody stood out. Everybody was looked up to by *somebody*. I don't care who he was. But who looks up to you when you're all at the same level and there's no basis for comparison? Who calls you 'mister'? Why, the youngest brat amongst you calls the oldest by his first name, and there's no respect."

After this broadcast, Bruce sat still, waiting. The waiting was not long. The girl in the outer office stuck her head in the door. She was stuttering, a phenomenon which Bruce had heard of, but not heard. She announced one Thomas Q. Greeley.

Greeley came pounding into the office with long strides, shoving the door shut behind him without a break in his motion. There was a glitter deep beneath his eyes.

"Hello, Cort," he said jovially. "Man, did I panic 'em today? I've got 'em groveling. They worship me." His hand plunged into his pocket and came out with a cigar as he sat down, stretching long legs out before him. He held the cigar up, a grieved expression on his broad face.

"My last one!" he exclaimed. "I'm not smoking it. I'm thinking maybe we can grow some more tobacco the way they grew that chicken heart back in my time."

"That might be possible," Bruce nodded.

"I'll have every last man in this civilization with a cigarette in his mouth before I'm through!" Greeley charged, his eyes cunning with delight as he watched Bruce's reaction.

"Smoking is a delayed manifestation of the suckling instinct," Bruce informed him.

Greeley stared at him. He gave a short laugh. "You birds give me a pain. You've got every human emotion catalogued and under control. It's a damned shame, that's what it is. Why, back in my time—"

Bruce said, "Careful. Now you're beginning to believe your own arguments against immortality."

Greeley's face fell. He hunched forward. "You may be right at that," he said seriously. Then he jumped up, walking furiously back and forth. He stopped and looked at Bruce through beetling brows.

"That's just a sample!" he stated, jerking his thumb in the direction of the Square. "I've got billions of people listening to me. I'm insulting them and they're loving every word of it. This is revolution, Cort—revolution! Can you get that through your head? The civilization of the immortals is about to fall. I'm telling you it will. I'll arouse them to fever pitch. I'll have them charging the Radiogen Hospitals all over the Universe. And I'll get away with it and nobody'll stop me!"

Bruce's eyes lidded. He swung one foot slowly back and forth. "What makes you so sure you can keep on?"

"Because I know the law." Greeley's massive head jutted forward. "You can't stop me, nobody can. I'm not telling lies. I'm giving off good, sound opinions. And I'll have the Square every day because that's what the Square is for. Only nobody has ever used it lately because everybody's got the same opinions as everybody else, and who wants to listen to somebody spout off their own thoughts?

"I've got *new* thoughts, Cort. New for this day and age, anyway." He leered. "More, I know mob psychology. I'll whip them to fever heat. All over the Universe. Nobody listens to the regular broadcasts any more when they can tune in on Greeley's Hour. It's something new. It's wild and rugged and shocking and it's the truth. So help me, it's the truth. And they know it. Everybody knows it. Everywhere, the Unchanged are sending in rejection letters, saying they don't want immortality. That's only the beginning—if you let me go on. Physico-Stasis Administrators will be affected, too. They don't want their children growing up to become Immortal. Laws will be made banishing immortality.

"Think I can't do it, Cort?"

"Of course you can."

Greeley smashed his hand on the desk, his eyes hot. "Then give me immortality! I'll stop it. I'll wean 'em back the other way, and everything will die down!"

Bruce said, "Perhaps you know that if I gave you immortality, I'd violate my code of office?"

Greeley sneered. "Look who's talking. Instead you prefer to betray humanity. Why, by Heaven, I'll make a one-man conquest of the Universe. I've got the sheer vocal power to do it. I'll break civilization if necessary. Can't you get it through your head that this is the blow-up, the big push? I'm a bull in a china shop!"

"I thought of a better metaphor," said Bruce.

Greeley panted, "And you let a damned code of office stand in your way. Grow up! Back in my time, nobody would have thought twice about violating his code of office to save his own life, or to make an extra thousand bucks. Grow up, Cort. Break a law for a change. I'd have some respect for you if you did!"

Bruce stared at him silently, his eyes curiously expressionless. He said at last, "Come back in two days from now, after the broadcast."

Greeley tried to read his expression. "You'll give me a definite 'yes' or 'no' answer then?"

"That's it."

The muscles of Greeley's face slowly relaxed. He turned and flung open the door. His eyes narrowed. "O. K. I'll be back. But in the meantime, I don't figure on calling off my big guns. I'll go on the air and say what I intended to say, according to plan. 'By!"

The door slammed.

Bruce sat quite still after Greeley's departure, leg swinging idly back and forth.

"Break a law for a change," he whispered at length. A peculiar convulsion crossed his face. His hand was trembling when he worked the radiophone strapped around his wrist.

Seryn Channing, Chief Administrator of the Psychiatry Department of the Radiogen Building, answered.

"Bruce," said Bruce. He moistened his lips. "You've listened to Greeley?"

Seryn hesitated a long moment. At length he said dangerously, "If you mean do I believe that pap of his, no."

Bruce's face showed his relief. He launched into an account of his connection with Greeley.

"Our peculiar system of law—peculiar from the standpoint of the twentieth century, that is—will let him get away with it, as long as he wants to carry on. We can't stop him, not by direct action. But he has to be stopped."

Seryn said dryly, "You admit the man has us in a trap we can't escape from. In the same breath, you say we have to escape. Where's the logic?"

Bruce was patient. "In all my four hundred years taking care of the Bureau in the City, Greeley is the first I've ever refused immortality. But now—" He stopped, and went on with difficulty, his face whitening imperceptibly. He talked for several minutes, while the other man listened.

A silence followed. Seryn said slowly, "You can't do that, Bruce."

"Can't I?" Bruce laughed unsteadily. "I've made up my mind. If I fail in my plan, I've broken the law most drastically, and doubtless will be given my punishment.

"If I succeed, I will have adhered to the letter of the law. I want you to keep this under your hat, and I want you to take care of it when we get there. I'll take the blame. In the meantime, the more rabid he gets his followers, the better it'll be. For us."

Greeley showed up on the dot, half an hour after the broadcast. He was wiping his heavy face. "I've got 'em yelling now, 'Down with immortality.' Sometimes I scare myself. I made a labor chain out of five thousand department stores in the States—back in my time—but that took some talking and pamphlets and banners. All you got to do here is talk; say anything. You're a bunch of dopes. I got trouble holding them in now."

He sat down heavily. "Tomorrow they'll bust loose if I give 'em the word, Cort. Unless I do something about it. What is it about my voice that gets 'em? Must be the same thing that Hitler had. Hitler was a dictator," he explained, but Bruce nodded. "He was going strong when I was spirited away." He scowled in memory. "Whatever happened to him, anyway?"

"He supposedly committed suicide," said Bruce. "He was defeated in the spring of 1945."

Greeley sighed. "He was a good organizer, too." His eyes wandered restlessly about the room, and finally centered on Bruce's impassive face. "Well," he scowled, "I'm waiting. You told me to come back in two days. Here I am."

Bruce said, "We're due at the Radiogen Laboratories at four o'clock."

"I thought so," Greeley said, heaving himself to his feet. "You're getting smart, eh?"

"I've simply decided you're worthy of immortality."

Greeley looked at him admiringly. "I'll be damned if I don't think you would have made a good politician. You're smart. It don't pay to buck the current, Cort," he said in satisfaction. "Let's go."

"It's a simple process," Bruce explained to Greeley's avid, yet somewhat apprehensive questions as they sped along comfortably high above the city. "At the core of body cells there are what are known as radiogens— the real life principle. Only they're also inverted with the properties of death. Sooner or later they deteriorate. A new cell has been developed by biologists. They remove the deteriorating elements, then remake an old body out of them. You'll live seven years in the radiogen chamber, and quite literally you'll come out a new body. A complete new body. It'll really take only a couple hours, but you won't know anything from the minute you go in to the minute you come out."

"You've got a good civilization here," said Greeley, nodding his heavy head in satisfaction.

Bruce smiled tightly. He looked sidewise at the big man. "You don't mistrust me?"

Greeley grinned mockingly. "Hell, no, I don't. You fellows can't tell a lie. You believe in the good things of life. You couldn't commit a crime. I know psychology. You go at things fair and square."

He added hastily, "Not that I don't appreciate it. Believe you me, I do. Tomorrow, with some long centuries ahead of me, I'll start my little game of backtracking with the mob, like I promised. You've got the word of Mrs. Greeley's little boy!"

Bruce guided the foolproof craft to a landing, thinking his own unexpressed thoughts. *What will you do after you've been given your immortality, Mrs. Greeley's son? Where will you find a substitute for the rotten, jangling excitement of the twentieth century that your nerves demand? What will you do to our civilization when you begin to get restless for the sounds and smells of corruption that aren't here?* So Bruce's thoughts ran.

Seryn Channing met them, and himself gave Greeley the anæsthetic. Bruce saw Greeley wheeled into the radiogen chamber, saw the door close, saw the interior of the chamber grow foggy. Bruce tried to control his nerves, and recognized it as a neurotic symptom. He found himself dwelling with peculiar introspect on the intricacies of a mind which could commit a crime, or otherwise break a law, either in a moral or legal sense. But at the end of two hours, Greeley came out of the chamber a new man, and, strangely silent, returned with Bruce to his quarters in the Justice Building. Greeley's skin shone with the almost undetectable inner radiance of immortality.

Bruce went back to his office, and sat in the dark, trying to untangle his thoughts. It seemed to him, then, as if the greatest danger was not to civilization, but to himself. He might lose his respect for himself. Back in the twentieth century, however, such loss of integrity must have been very common.

The luxury of integrity! Tomorrow, if he failed, he would have loosed upon humanity an incurable malady in the person of one Thomas Q. Greeley.

Half an hour before Greeley was due on the air, Bruce called Jan Tomaz. The recently Changed man came into the office slowly, hesitantly, as if in shame for his partial breakdown. The lines of strain were somewhat gone from his face. Bruce was almost jovial when he spoke, but it was evident to him that that was a symptom of hysteria.

He said, watching Jan narrowly, "I've purposely put off telling you this to the last minute, because I saw nothing to be gained by giving you time to think. There's no one else for the job, though. I'll have to send you to the infected area, Jan."

A pathetic despair tugged suddenly at Jan's face. Bruce winced. He said patiently, "I mean that I want you to use your prerogative on the Square."

He rapidly told Jan what he wanted him to do. He concluded, "If you use words with emotional connotations, the chances of success are increased. *But*—don't let Greeley get the microphone afterward."

Jan looked at Bruce as if Bruce had subtly betrayed him. He stuttered, "B-but if it doesn't work?"

"It has to work, Jan."

Bruce held Jan's eyes, and walked forward until he was a few inches separated from the younger man.

He shouted full into Jan's face: "Go ahead!"

Jan had no defense against such a highly emotional command. He left the room on a run.

Bruce turned on the televisor and auditory unit, and immediately heard the subway rumble of the mob. A twentieth-century mob, flaming with infected passions, dangerous, furious, solidly packed on the Square around the dais, waiting for Greeley to come up through the trapdoor in the floor of the dais, eager to drink in his voice, his expressions, his logic. They were a mob that only Greeley could handle. But what species of logic was he intending to use that would turn off the flame beneath their steaming hatred of immortality?

Bruce stood quite still, waiting for Greeley to appear. Each heartbeat was a second. Bruce marveled. Had this alarm, these uncertain stabs of agony, these shortenings of the breath, been a regular part of twentieth-century life? Yet man had lived through it. There were the wars, for instance. And other pestilences. These things were gone by the turn of the thirty-first century. Then, in the thirty-sixth century, along had come one Thomas Q. Greeley—

At one minute of three o'clock, Greeley came up onto the dais from stairs connected with the underground tunnel. The mob gave him their ovation. They were thunder and lightning, Bruce thought, but the lightning was submerged. They were standing on tiptoe.

Greeley was looking at his watch, waiting.

Bruce saw Jan in the fore of the mob now. He was working his way toward one of the two broad stairs that led to the top of the dais. He made the dais, and to Bruce he looked very small compared to Greeley. Jan was small in other ways, too, he saw with sinking heart. When Jan grabbed the microphone and spoke, his voice was high, without volume, without compulsion. Furthermore, it was muted, overridden by the voice of the mob. Jan was demanding the prerogative of the Public Wave. The seconds ticked away, and the cheering died down in some measure.

Jan's desperate voice blasted out. "Citizens! Behind you stands the man who has showed you the truth about immortality."

There were some half-hearted cheers of agreement. Bruce slowly, help-lessly, shook his head back and forth.

"He has showed you the *sins* of immortality!"

This elicited a greater response. The building surrounding the Square threw back thundering echoes. Greeley was standing stone still, wary of face, looking at Jan with his heavy brows drawn suddenly down. He started forward suddenly, his jaw hanging open in an amazed, blistering curse.

Jan saw him coming. He dramatically pointed his arm at Greeley and yelled, "Examine his skin! Yesterday he was made immortal, at his own request."

An invisible switch was thrown and there was no sound. Nor was there motion, save that of Greeley. Greeley came up on Jan's left and his big arm went up and shoved Jim against the railing. Greeley made a furious grab for the microphone. His voice bit out, "Fellows—" But it was a voice filled with scalding panic, for Greeley must have seen the youths who suddenly urged themselves up the stairs. He turned with a flurry of panic contorting his face. By that time, the youths were on him. They grabbed at his arms and held him. Then Greeley went down, submerged in a tangle of human beings. The microphone went down, too.

"Fellows," came Greeley's voice, but it was a high-pitched scream of protest. A roar rippled over the crowd, spreading outward from the dais. A stream of human beings came surging up onto the dais.

Bruce vainly tried to pick Jan from the sickening carnival of motion and sound. But he couldn't keep his fascinated eyes from Greeley. The man was suddenly held aloft. His clothing had been stripped from his body. Red furrows were on his skin. His neck was hanging at an unnatural angle. Bruce guessed that he was dead. They had examined Greeley's skin.

He turned away from the scene, and sat down, holding his sick head in his hands. By the time Jan showed up twenty minutes later, he had ra-tionalized and was calmer. Jan's clothing was in shreds, and his hair was mussed.

"It was sickening," he choked. He buried his head in his hands, and then raised his eyes and stared at Bruce as if in a fascination of horror. "How could you have plotted a thing like that, Bruce! It wasn't even human!"

Bruce felt an inner convulsion. He had broken no law, not a legal law. Greeley had served the best interests of humanity by being made im-mortal. Proof: he was dead. But what about other laws, moral laws?

"We're both patients for the Psychiatry Department, Jan," he said grimly. "Looked at that way, my actions are justified. We found a serum and administered it. The corpuscles in the area of infection received the strength they needed to overthrow the disease. The wound will, therefore, heal and the body will eventually rid itself of the toxic substances the dis-ease left behind.

"Greeley, I think, realized he was a disease, even if he didn't think of that exact metaphor. What he overlooked was the fact that he might disease *me*. He did. When one wishes to discommode, or otherwise render one's enemies impotent, one stoops to a trick. So Greeley taught me, not realizing that since I'm considered an authority on the twentieth century, I was extremely susceptible to contamination from his brand of ethics, and, therefore, no longer incapable of deceit. I applied the principal of trickery to Greeley, administering a body blow below the belt. Place the blame on him, Jan, not me. He backfired on himself!"

JAMES BLISH

THE BOX

WHEN MEISTER GOT out of bed that Tuesday morning, he thought that it was before dawn. He rarely needed an alarm clock these days—a little light in his eyes was enough to awaken him and sometimes his dreams brought him upright long before the sun came up.

It had seemed a reasonably dreamless night, but probably he had just forgotten the dreams. Anyhow, here he was, awake early. He padded over to the window, shut it, pulled up the shade and looked out.

The street lights were not off yet, but the sky was already a smooth, dark gray. Meister had never before seen such a sky. Even the dullest overcast before a snowfall shows some variation in brightness. The sky here—what he could see of it between the apartment house—was like the inside of a lead helmet.

He shrugged and turned away, picking the clock up from the table to turn off the alarm. Some day, he promised himself, he would sleep long enough to hear it ring. That would be a good day; it would mean that the dreams were gone. In Concentration Camp Dora, one had awakened the moment the tunnel lights were put on; otherwise, one might be beaten awake, or dead. Meister was deaf in the left ear on that account. For the first three days at Dora he had had to be awakened.

He became aware suddenly that he was staring fixedly at the face of the clock, his subconscious ringing alarm bells of its own. *Nine o'clock!* No, it was not possible. It was obviously close to sunrise. He shook the clock stupidly, although it was ticking and had been since he first noticed it. Tentatively he touched the keys at the back.

The alarm had run down.

This was obviously ridiculous. The clock was wrong. He put it back on the table and turned on the little radio. After a moment it responded with a terrific thrumming, as if a vacuum cleaner were imprisoned in its workings.

"B-flat," Meister thought automatically. He had only one good ear, but he still had perfect pitch—a necessity for a resonance engineer. He shifted the setting. The hum got louder. Hastily he reversed the dial. Around 830 Kc, where WNYC came in, the hum was almost gone, but of course it was too early yet for the city station to be on the air—

". . . in your homes," a voice struck in clearly above the humming. "We are awaiting a report from Army headquarters. In the meantime, any crowding at the boundaries of the barrier will interrupt the work of the Mayor's inquiry commission. . . . Here's a word just in from the Port Authority: all ferry service has been suspended until further notice. Subways and tubes are running outbound trains only; however, local service remains about normal so far."

Barrier? Meister went to the window again and looked out. The radio voice continued:

"NBC at Radio City disclaims all knowledge of the persistent signal which has blotted out radio programs from nine hundred kilocycles on up since midnight last night. This completes the roster of broadcasting stations in the city proper. It is believed that the tone is associated with the current wall around Manhattan and most of the other boroughs. Some outside stations are still getting through, but at less than a fiftieth of their normal input." The voice went on:

"At Columbia University, the dean of the Physics Department estimates that about the same proportion of sunlight is also getting through. We do not yet have any report about the passage of air through the barrier. The flow of water in the portions of the East and Hudson Rivers which lie under the screen is said to be normal, and no abnormalities are evident at the Whitehall Street tidal station."

There was a pause; the humming went on unabated. Then there was a sharp *beep!* and the voice said, "At the signal—nine A.M., Eastern Summer Time."

Meister left the radio on while he dressed. The alarming pronouncements kept on, but he was not yet thoroughly disturbed, except for Ellen. She might be frightened; but probably nothing more serious would happen. Right now, he should be at the labs. If the Team had put this thing up overnight, they would tease him unmercifully for sleeping through the great event.

The radio voice continued to reel off special notices, warnings, new bulletins. The announcer sounded as if he were on the thin edge of hysteria; evidently he had not yet been told what it was all about. Meister was tying his left shoe when he realized that the reports were beginning to sound much worse.

"From LaGuardia Field we have just been notified that an experimental plane had been flown through the barrier at a point over the jammed Triboro Bridge. It has not appeared over the city and is presumed lost. On the *Miss New York* disaster early this morning we still have no complete report. Authorities on Staten Island say the ferry ordinarily carried less than two hundred passengers at that hour, but thus far only eleven have been picked up. One of these survivors was brought in to a Manhattan slip by the tug *Marjorie Q;* he is still in a state of extreme shock and Bellevue Hospital says no statement can be expected from him until tomorrow. It appears, however, that he swam *under* the barrier."

His voice carried the tension he evidently felt. "Outside the screen a heavy fog still prevails—the same fog which hid the barrier from the ferry captain until his ship was destroyed almost to the midpoint. The Police Department has again requested that all New Yorkers stay—"

Alarmed at last, Meister switched off the machine and left the apartment, locking it carefully. Unless those idiots turned off their screen, there would be panic and looting before the day was out.

Downstairs, in the little grocery, there was a mob arguing in low, terrified voices, their faces as gray as the ominous sky. He pushed through them to the phone.

The grocer was sitting in back of it. "Phone service is tied up, Mr. Meister," he said hoarsely.

"I can get through, I think. What has happened?"

"Some foreign enemy, is *my* guess. There's a big dome of somethin' all around the city. Nobody can get in or out. You stick your hand in, you draw back a bloody stump. Stuff put through on the other side don't come through." He picked up the phone with a trembling hand and passed it over. "Good luck!"

Meister dialed Ellen first; he needed to know if she were badly frightened, and to reassure her if she were. Nothing happened for a while; then an operator said, "I'm sorry, sir, but there will be no private calls for the duration of the emergency, unless you have a priority."

"Give me emergency code B-Nineteen, then," Meister said.

"Your group, sir?"

"Screen Team."

There was a faint sound at the other end of the line, as if the girl had taken a quick breath. "Yes, sir," she said. "Right away." There was an angry crackle, and then the droning when the number was being rung.

"Screen Team," a voice said.

"Resonance section, please," Meister said, and when he was connected and had identified himself, a voice growled:

"Hello, Jake, this is Frank Schafer. Where the deuce are you? I sent you a telegram—but I suppose you didn't get it, the boards are jammed. Get on down here, quick!"

"No, I haven't any telegram," Meister said. "Whom do I congratulate?"

"Nobody, you fool! *We* didn't do this. We don't even know how it's been done!"

Meister felt the hairs on the back of his neck stirring; it was as if he were back in the tunnels of Concentration Camp Dora again. He swallowed and said, "But it is the antibomb screen?"

"The very thing," Schafer's tinny voice said bitterly. "Only somebody else has beat us to it—and we're trapped under it."

"It's really bombproof—you're sure of that?"

"It's anything-proof! Nothing can pass it! *And we can't get out of it, either!*"

It took quite a while to get the story straight. Project B-19, the meaningless label borne by the top-secret, billion-dollar Atomic Defense Project, was in turmoil. Much of its laboratory staff had been in the field or in Washington when the thing had happened, and the jam in phone service had made it difficult to get the men who were still in the city back to the central offices.

"It's like this," Frank Schafer said, kneading a chunk of art gum rapidly. "This dome went up last night. It lets in a little light, and a few of the strongest outside radio stations near by. But that's all—or anyhow, all that we've been able to establish so far. It's a perfect dome, over the whole island and parts of the other boroughs and New Jersey. It doesn't penetrate the ground or the water, but the only really big water frontage is way out in the harbor—so that lets out much chance of everybody swimming under it like that man from the *Miss New York.*"

"The subways are running, I heard," Meister said.

"Sure; we can evacuate the city if we have to, but not fast enough." The mobile fingers crumbed bits off the sides of the art gum. "It won't take long to breathe up the air here, and if any fires start it'll be worse. Also there's a layer of ozone about twenty feet deep all along the inside of the barrier—but don't ask me why! Even if we don't have any big blazes, we're losing oxygen at a terrific rate by ozone-fixing and surface oxidization of the ionized area."

"Ionized?" Meister frowned. "Is there much?"

"Plenty!" Schafer said. "We haven't let it out, but in another twenty hours you won't be able to hear anything on the radio but a noise like a tractor climbing a pile of cornflakes. There's been an increase already. Whatever we're using for ether these days is building up tension fast."

A runner came in from the private wires and dropped a flimsy paper on Frank's desk. The physicist looked at it quickly, then passed it to Meister.

"That's what I figured. You can see the spot we're in."

The message reported that oxygen was diffusing inward through the barrier at about the same rate as might be accounted for by osmosis. The figures on loss of CO_2 were less easy to establish, but it appeared that the rate here was also of an osmotic order of magnitude. It was signed by a topnotch university chemist.

"Impossible!" Meister said.

"No, it's so. And New York is entirely too big a cell to live, Jake. If we're getting oxygen only osmotically, we'll be suffocated in a week. And did you ever hear of a semipermeable membrane passing a lump of coal, or a tomato? Air, heat, food—all cut off."

"What does the Army say?"

"What they usually say: 'Do something, on the double!' We're lucky we're civilians, or we'd be court-martialed for dying!" Schafer laughed angrily and pitched the art gum away. "It's a very pretty problem, in a way," he said. "We have our antibomb screen. Now we have to find how to make ourselves *vulnerable* to the bomb—or cash in our chips. And in six days—"

The phone jangled and Schafer snatched at it. "Yeah, this is Dr. Schafer. . . . I'm sorry, Colonel, but we have every available man called in now except those on the Mayor's commission . . . No, I don't know. Nobody knows, yet. We're tracing that radio signal now. If it has anything to do with the barrier, we'll be able to locate the generator and destroy it."

The physicist slammed the phone into its cradle and glared at Meister. "I've been taking this phone stuff all morning! I wish you'd showed up earlier. Here's the picture, briefly: The city is dying. Telephone and telegraph lines give us some communication with the outside, and we will be able to use radio inside the dome for a little while longer. There are teams outside trying to crack the barrier, but all the significant phenomena are taking place inside. Out there it just looks like a big black dome—no radiation effects, no ionization, no radio tone, no nothin'!

"We are evacuating now," he went on, "but if the dome stays up, over three-quarters of the trapped people will die. If there's any fire or violence, almost all of us will die."

"You talk," Meister said, "as if you want me to kill the screen all by myself."

Schafer grinned nastily. "Sure, Jake! This barrier obviously doesn't act specifically on nuclear reactions; it stops almost everything. Almost everyone here is a nuclear man, as useless for this problem as a set of cooky-cutters. Every fact we've gotten so far shows this thing to be an immense and infinitely complicated form of cavity-resonance—and you're the only resonance engineer inside it."

The grin disappeared, and Schafer said, "We can give you all the electronics technicians you need, plenty of official backing, and general theoretical help. It's not much but it's all we've got. We estimate about eleven million people inside this box—eleven million corpses unless you can get the lid off it."

Meister nodded. Somehow, the problem did not weigh as heavily upon him as it might have. He was remembering Dora, the wasted bodies jammed under the stairs, in storerooms, fed into the bake-oven five at a time. One could survive almost anything if one had had practice in surviving. There was only Ellen—

Ellen was probably in "The Box"—the current dome. That meant something, where eleven million was only a number.

"*Entdecken*," he murmured.

Schafer looked up at him, his blue eyes snapping sparks. Schafer certainly didn't look like one of the world's best nuclear physicists: Schafer was a sandy-haired runt—with the bomb hung over his head by a horsehair.

"What's that?" he said.

"A German word," Meister answered. "It means, to discover—literally, to take the roof off. That is the first step, it seems. To take the roof off, we must discover that transmitter."

"I've got men out with loop antennas. The geometrical center of the dome is right at the tip of the Empire State Building, but WNBT says there's nothing up there but their television transmitters."

"What they mean," Meister said, "is that there was nothing else up there two weeks ago. There *must* be a radiator at a radiant-point, no matter how well it is disguised."

"I'll send a team." Schafer got up, fumbling for the art gum he had thrown away. "I'll go myself, I guess. I'm jittery here."

"With your teeth? I would not advise it. You would die slain, as the Italians say!"

"Teeth?" Schafer said. He giggled nervously. "What's that got to—"

"You have metal in your mouth. If the mast is actually radiating this effect, your jawbones might be burnt out of your head. Get a group with perfect teeth, or porcelain fillings at best. And wear nothing with metal in it, not even shoes."

"Oh," Schafer said. "I knew we needed you, Jake." He rubbed the back of his hand over his forehead and reached into his shirt pocket for a cigarette.

Meister struck it out of his hand. "Six days' oxygen remaining," he said.

Schafer lunged up out of his chair, aimed a punch at Meister's head, and fainted across the desk.

The dim city stank of ozone. The street lights were still on, and despite the radioed warnings to stay indoors surging mobs struggled senselessly toward the barrier. Counterwaves surged back, coughing, from the unbreathable stuff pouring out from it. More piled up in subway stations; people screamed and trampled each other. Curiously, the city's "take" that day was enormous—not even disaster could break the deeply-entrenched habit of putting a dime in the turnstile.

The New York Central and Long Island Railroads, whose tracks were above ground where the screen cut across them, were shut down, as were the underground lines which came to the surface inside The Box. Special trains were running every three minutes from Pennsylvania Station, with passengers jamming the aisles and platforms.

In the Hudson Tubes the situation was worse. So great was the crush of fleeing humans there, they could hardly operate at all. The screen drew a lethal line between Hoboken and Newark, so that the Tube trains had to make the longer of the two trips to get their passengers out of The Box. A brief power interruption stopped one train in complete darkness for ten minutes beneath the Hudson River, and terror and madness swept through it.

Queens and Brooklyn subways siphoned off a little pressure from the others, but only a little. In a major disaster the normal human impulse is to go north, on the map-fostered myth that north is "up." Navy launches were readied to ferry as many as cared to make the try out to where The Box lay over the harbor and the rivers but thus far there were no such swimmers. Very few people can swim twenty feet under water, and coming up for air short of that twenty feet would be disastrous.

That would be as fatal as coming up in the barrier itself; ozone is lung-rot in high concentrations. That alone kept most of the foolhardy from trying to run through the wall—that and the gas-masked police cordon. From Governor's Island, about half of which was in The Box, the little Army ferries shipped over several cases of small-arms, which were distributed to subway and railroad guards. Two detachments of infantry also came along, relieving a little of the strain on the police.

Meister, hovering with two technicians and the helicopter pilot over a building on the edge of the screen, peered downward in puzzlement. It was hard to make any sense of the geometry of shadows below him.

"Give me the phone," he said.

The senior technician passed him the mike. A comparatively long-wave channel had been cleared by a major station for the emergency teams and the prowl-cars, since nothing could be heard in the short waves above that eternal humming.

"Frank, are you on?" Meister called. "Any word from Ellen yet?"

"No, but her landlady says she went to Jersey to visit yesterday," came over the air waves. There was an unspoken understanding between them that the hysterical attack of an hour ago would not be mentioned. "You'll have to crack The Box to get more news, I guess, Jake. See anything yet?"

"Nothing but more trouble. Have you thought yet about heat conservation? I am reminded that it is summer; we will soon have an oven here."

"I thought of that, but it isn't so," Frank Schafer's voice said. "It seems hotter only because there's no wind. Actually, the Weather Bureau says we're *losing* heat pretty rapidly; they expect the drop to level at fifteen to twenty above."

Meister whistled. "So low! Yet there is a steady supply of calories in the water—"

"Water's a poor conductor. What worries me is this accursed ozone. It's diffusing through the city—already smells like the inside of a transformer around here!"

"What about the Empire State Building?"

"Not a thing. We ran soap bubbles along the power leads, to see if something was tapping some of WNBT's power, but there isn't a break in them anywhere. Maybe you'd better go over there when you're through at the barrier. There's some things we can't make sense of."

"I shall," Meister said. "I will leave here as soon as I start a fire."

Schafer began to sputter. Meister smiled gently and handled the phone back to the technician.

"Break out the masks," he said. "We can go down now."

A rooftop beside the barrier was like some hell dreamed up in the violent ward of a hospital. Every movement accumulated a small static charge on the surface of the body, which discharged stingingly and repeatedly from the finger tips and even the tip of the nose if it approached a grounded object too closely.

Only a few yards away was the unguessable wall itself, smooth, deep-gray, featureless, and yet somehow quivering with a pseudo-life of its own—a shimmering haze just too dense to penetrate. It had no definite boundary; instead, the tarpaper over which it lay here began to dim, and within a foot had faded into the general mystery.

Meister looked at the barrier. The absence of anything upon which the eye could fasten was dizzying. The mind made up patterns and flashes of livid color and projected them into the grayness, and sometimes it seemed that the fog extended for miles. A masked policeman stepped over from the inside parapet and touched him on the elbow.

"Wouldn't look at her too long, sir," he said. "We've had ambulances below, carting away sightseers who forgot to look away. Pretty soon your eyes sort of get fixed."

Meister nodded. The thing was hypnotic, all right. And yet the eye was drawn to it because it was the only source of light here. The ionization was so intense that it bled off power from the lines, so that the street lamps were off all around the edge. From the helicopter, the city had looked as if its rim had been inked out in a vast ring. Meister could feel the individual hairs all over his body stirring; it made him feel infested. Well, there'd been no shortage of lice at Dora!

Behind him the technicians were unloading the apparatus from the 'copter. Meister beckoned. "Get a reading on field strength first of all," he said gloomily. "Whoever is doing this has plenty of power. Ionized gas, a difficult achievement—"

He stopped suddenly. Not so difficult. The city was enclosed; it was, in effect, a giant Geissler tube. Of course the concentration of rare gases was not high enough to produce a visible glow, but—

"Plenty high," the technician with the loop said. "Between forty-five thousand and fifty thousand. Seems to be rising a little, too."

"Between—" Meister stepped quickly over to the instrument. Sure enough, the black needle was wavering, so rapidly as to be only a fan-shaped blur between the two figures. "This is ridiculous! Is that instrument reliable?"

"I just took the underwriters' seal off it," the technician said. "Did you figure this much ozone could be fixed out without any alternation?"

"Yes, I had presupposed the equivalent of UV bombardment. This changes things. No wonder there is light leaking through that screen! Sergeant—"

"Yessir?" the policeman mumbled through his mask.

"How much of the area below can you clear?"

"As much as you need."

"Good." Meister reached into his jacket pocket and produced the map of the city the pilot had given him. "We are here, yes? Make a cordon, then, from here to here." His soft pencil point scrawled a black line around four buildings. "Then get as much fire-fighting equipment outside the line as you can muster."

"You're expecting a bad fire?"

"No, a *good* one. But hurry!"

The cop scratched his head puzzledly, but he went below. Meister smiled. Members of the Screen Team were the "Mister Bigs" in this city now—and twenty hours ago nobody'd ever heard of the Screen Team.

The technician, working with nervous quickness, was tying an oscilloscope into the loop circuit. Meister nodded approvingly. If there was a pulse to this phenomenon, it would be just as well to know what its form was. He snapped his fingers.

"What's wrong, doctor?"

"My memory. I have put my head on backwards when I got up this morning, I think. We will have to photograph the waveform; it will be too complex to analyze here."

"How do you know?" the technician asked.

"By that radio tone," Meister said. "You Americans work by sight— there are almost no resonance electronics men in this country. But in Germany we worked as much by ear as by eye. Where you convert a wave into a visible pattern, we turned it into an audible one. We had a saying that resonance engineers were disappointed musicians."

The face of the tube suddenly produced a green wiggle. It was the kind of wiggle a crazy man might make. The technician looked at it in dismay. "That," he said, "doesn't exist. I won't work in a science where it *could* exist!"

Meister grinned. "That is what I meant. The radio sound was a fundamental B-flat, but with hundreds of harmonics and overtones. You don't have it all in the field yet."

"I don't?" And he looked. "So I don't! But when I reduce it that much, you can't see the shape of the modulations."

"We will have to photograph it by sections."

Bringing over the camera, the other man set it up. They worked rapidly, oppressed by the unnatural pearly glimmer, the masks, the stink of ozone which crept in at the sides of the treated cloth, the electrical prickling— above all by the silent terror of any trapped animal.

While they worked, the cop came back and stood silently by, watching. The gas mask gave no indication of his expression, but Meister could feel the pressure of faith radiating from the man. Doubtless these bits of equipment were meaningless to him—but bits of equipment like these had put up The Box, beyond the powers of policemen or presidents to take it down again. Men who knew about such things were as good as gods, now.

Unless they failed.

"That does it," the technician said.

The cop stepped forward. "I've got the area you marked roped off," he said diffidently. "We've searched these apartments and there's nobody in them. If there's any fire here, we'll be able to control it."

"Excellent!" Meister said. "Remember that this gas will feed the flames, however. You will need every possible man."

"Yessir. Anything else?"

"Just get out of the district yourself."

Meister climbed into the plane and stood by the open hatch, looking at his wrist watch. He gave the cop ten minutes to leave the tenement and get out to the fire lines. Then he struck a match and pitched it out onto the roof.

"Up!" he shouted.

The rotors roared. The pitch on the roof began to smolder. A tongue of flame shot up. Three seconds later the whole side of the roof nearest the gray screen was blazing.

The helicopter lurched and clawed for altitude.

Behind the plane was a brilliant and terrifying yellow glare. Meister didn't bother to watch it. He squatted with his back to the fire and waved pieces of paper over the neck of a bottle.

The ammonia fumes were invisible and couldn't be smelled through the masks, but on the dry-plates wiggly lines were appearing. Meister studied them, nibbling gently at his lower lip. With luck, the lines would answer one question, at least: they would tell what The Box was. With luck, they might even tell how it was produced.

They would *not* tell where it came from.

The motion of the 'copter changed suddenly, and Meister's stomach stirred uneasily under his belt. He stowed the plates and looked up. The foreshortened spire of the Empire State Building pointed up at him through the transparent deck; another 'copter hovered at its tip. The television antennas were hidden now in what seemed to be a globe of some dark substance.

Meister picked up the radio-phone. "Schafer?" he called—this to the Empire State Building.

"No, this is Talliafero," came back in answer. "Schafer's back at the labs. We're about ready to leave. Need any help?"

"I don't think so," Meister said. "Is that foil you have around the tower mast?"

"Yes, but it's only a precaution. The whole tower's radiating. The foil radiates, too, now that we've got it up. See you later."

The other 'copter stirred and swooped away.

Meister twisted the dial up into the shortwave region. The humming surged in; he valved down the volume and listened intently. The sound was different, somehow. After a moment his mind placed it. The fundamental B-flat was still there, but some of the overtones were gone; that meant that hundreds of them, which the little amplifier could not reproduce, were also gone. The set upon which he was listening was FM; his little table set at the apartment was AM—so the wave was modulated along both axes, and probably pulse-modulated as well. But why should it simplify as one approached its source?

Resonance, of course. The upper harmonics were echoes. Yet a simple primary tone in a well-known frequency range couldn't produce The Box by itself; it was the harmonics that made the difference—and the harmonics couldn't appear without the existence of some chamber like The Box. Along this line of reasoning, The Box was a pre-condition of its own existence. Meister felt his head swimming.

"Hey," the pilot said. "It's starting to snow!"

Meister turned off the set and looked out. "All right, let's go home now."

Despite its depleted staff, the Screen Team was quiet with the intense hush of concentration which was its equivalent of roaring activity. Frank Schafer's door was closed, but Meister didn't bother to knock. He was on the edges of an idea, and there was no time to be consumed in formalities.

There were a number of uniformed men in the office with Frank. There was also a big man in expensive clothes, and a smaller man who looked as if he needed sleep. The smaller man had dark circles under his eyes, but despite his haggardness Meister knew him: the mayor. The big man did not look familiar—nor pleasant.

As for the high brass, nothing in a uniform looked pleasant to Meister. He pushed forward and put the dry-plates down on Schafer's desk. "The resonance products," he said. "If we can duplicate the fundamental in the lab—"

There was a roar from the big man. "Dr. Schafer, is this the man we've been waiting for?"

Schafer made a tired gesture. "Jake, this is Roland Dean," he said. "You know the mayor, I think. These others are Security officers. They seem to think you made The Box."

Meister stiffened. "I? That's idiotic!"

"Any noncitizen is automatically under suspicion," one of the Army men said. "However, Dr. Schafer exaggerates. We just want to ask a few questions."

The mayor coughed. He was obviously tired, and the taint of ozone did not make breathing very comfortable.

"I'm afraid there's more to it than that, Dr. Meister," he added. "Mr. Dean here has insisted upon an arrest. I'd like to say for myself that I think it all quite stupid."

"Thank you," Meister said. "What is Mr. Dean's interest in this?"

"Mr. Dean," Schafer growled, "is the owner of that block of tenements you're burning out up north. The fire's spreading, by the way. When I told him I didn't know why you lit it, he blew his top."

"Why not?" Dean said, glaring at Meister. "I fail to see why this emergency should be made an excuse for irresponsible destruction of property. Have you any reason for burning my buildings, Meister?"

"Are you having any trouble breathing, Mr. Dean?" Meister asked easily.

"Certainly! Who isn't? Do you think you can make it easier for us by filling The Box with smoke?"

Meister nodded. "I gather that you have no knowledge of elementary chemistry, Mr. Dean. The Box is rapidly converting our oxygen into an unbreathable form. A good hot fire will consume some of it, but it will also break up the ozone molecules. The ratio is about two atoms of oxygen consumed for every one set free—out of three which in the form of ozone could not have been breathed at all."

Schafer sighed gustily. "I should have guessed. A neat scheme, Jake— but what about the ratio between reduction of ozone and over-all oxygen consumption?"

"Large enough to maintain five of the six days' grace with which we started. Had we let the ozone-fixing process continue unabated, we should not have lasted forty hours longer."

"Mumbo jumbo!" Dean said stonily, turning to Schafer. "A halfway measure. The problem is to get us out of this mess, not to stretch our sufferings out by three days by invading property rights. This man is a German, probably a Nazi! By your own admission, he's been the only man in your whole section who's seemed to know what to do. And nothing he's done so far has shown any result, except to destroy some of my buildings!"

"Dr. Meister, just what *has* been accomplished thus far?" a colonel of Intelligence said.

"Only a few tentative observations," Meister said. "We have most of the secondary phenomena charted."

"Charts!" Dean snorted.

"Can you offer any assurance that The Box will be down in time?" the colonel asked.

"That," Meister said, "would be very foolish of me. The possibility exists; that is all. Certainly it will take time—we have barely scratched the surface."

"In that case, I'm afraid you'll have to consider yourself under arrest—"

"See here, Colonel!" Schafer surged to his feet, his face flushed. "Don't you know that he's the only man in The Box who can crack it?

That fire was good common sense. If you arrest my men for *not* doing anything, we'll never get anything done!"

"I am not exactly stupid, Dr. Schafer," the colonel said harshly. "I have no interest in Mr. Dean's tenements, and if the mayor is forced to jail Dr. Meister we will spring him at once. All I'm interested in is the chance that Dr. Meister may be *maintaining* The Box instead of trying to *crack it.*"

"Explain, please," Meister said mildly.

Pulling himself up to military straightness, the colonel cleared his throat and said:

"You're inside The Box. If you put it up, you have a way out of it, and know where the generator is. You may go where you please, but from now on we'll have a guard with you . . . Satisfied, Dr. Schafer?"

"It doesn't satisfy me!" Dean rumbled. "What about my property? Are you going to let this madman burn buildings with a guard to help?"

The colonel looked at the landlord. "Mr. Dean," he said quietly, "you seem to think The Box was created to annoy you personally. The Army hasn't the technical knowledge to destroy it, but it has sense enough to realize that more than just New York is under attack here. The enemy, whoever he may be, thinks his screen uncrackable, otherwise he wouldn't have given us this chance to work on it by boxing in one city alone. If The Box is not down in, say, eight days, he'll know that New York failed and died—and every city in the country will be bombed to slag the next morning."

Schafer sat down again, looking surly. "Why?" he asked the army man. "Why would they waste the bombs when they could just box in the cities?"

"Inefficient. America's too big to occupy except slowly, piecemeal. They'd have no reason to care if large parts of it were uninhabitable for a while. The important thing is to knock us out as a military force, as a power in world affairs."

"If they boxed in all the cities at once—"

The colonel shook his head. "We have rocket emplacements of our own, and they *aren't* in large cities. Neither Box nor bomb would catch more than a few of them. No—they have to know that The Box is uncrackable —so they can screen their own cities against our bombs until our whole country is knocked out. With The Box, that would take more than a week, and their cities would suffer along with ours. With bombs, a day would be enough—so they've allowed us this test. If New York comes out of this, there'll be no attack, at least until they've gotten a better screen. The Box seems good enough so far!"

"Politics," Schafer said, shaking his head disgustedly, "is much too devious for me! Doesn't The Box constitute an attack?"

"Certainly—but who's doing the attacking?" the colonel demanded. "We can guess, but we don't know. And I doubt very much that the enemy has left any traces."

Meister stiffened suddenly, a thrill of astonishment shooting up his backbone. Schafer stared at him.

"Traces!" Meister said. "Of course! That is what has been stopping us all along. Naturally there would be no traces; we have been wasting time looking for them. Frank, the generator is not in the Empire State Building. *It is not even in The Box!*"

"But Jake, it's got to be," Schafer said. "It's physically impossible for it to be outside!"

"A trick," Dean rumbled.

Meister waved his hands excitedly. "No, no! This is the reasoning which has made our work so fruitless. Observe: As the colonel says, the enemy would not dare leave traces. Now, workmanship is traceable, particularly if the device is revolutionary, as this one is. Find that generator, and you know at once which country has made it. You observe the principle, and you say to yourself, 'Ah, yes, there were reports, rumors, whispers of shadows of rumors of such a principle, but I discounted them as fantasy; they came out of Country X.' Do you follow?"

"Yes, but—"

"But no country would leave such a fingerprint where it could be found. This we can count upon—whereas, we know as yet next to nothing about the physics of The Box. Therefore, if it is physically impossible for the generator to be outside The Box, this does not mean that we must continue to search for it inside. It means that we must find a physical principle which makes it possible to be outside!"

Frank Schafer threw up his hands. "Revise basic physics in a week! Well, let's try it. I suppose Meister's allowed lab work, Colonel?"

"Certainly, as long as my guards aren't barred from the laboratory."

Thirty hours later the snow had stopped falling, leaving a layer a little over three inches deep. The battling mobs were no longer on the streets. Hopeless masses were jammed body to body in railroad stations and subways. The advancing ozone had driven the trapped people in upon themselves, and into the houses and basements where rooms could be sealed against the searing stench.

Thousands had already died along the periphery; the New Jersey and Brooklyn shores were charnel heaps, where men had fought to get back across the river to Manhattan and cleaner air. The tenements along the West Side of the island still blazed, twenty linear blocks of them, but the fire had failed to jump Ninth Avenue and was dying for want of fuel. Elsewhere, it was very cold; the city was dying.

Over it, The Box was invisible. It was the third night.

And in the big lab at the Team Office, Meister, Schafer and the two technicians suddenly disappeared under a little Box of their own, leaving behind four frantic soldiers. Meister sighed gustily and looked at the black screen a few feet away from his head.

"Now we know," he said. "Frank, you can turn on the light now."

The desk lamp clicked on. In the shaded glow, Meister saw that tears were trickling down Schafer's cheeks.

"No, no, don't weep yet, the job is not quite done!" Meister cried. "But see—so simple, so beautiful!" He gestured at the lump of metal in the exact center of the Boxed area. "Here we are—four men, a bit of metallic trash, an empty desk, a lamp, a cup of foil. Where is the screen generator? Outside!"

Schafer swallowed. "But it isn't," he said hoarsely. "Oh, you were right, Jake—the key projector *is* outside. But it doesn't generate the screen; it just excites the iron, there, and that does the job." He looked at the scattered graphs on the desk top. "I'd never have dreamed such a jam of fields was possible! Look at those waves—catching each other, heterodyning, showing each other up as the tension increases. No wonder the whole structure of space gives way when they finally get in phase!"

One of the technicians looked nervously at the little Box and cleared his throat. "I still don't see why it should leak light, oxygen, and so forth, even the little that it does. The jam has to be radiated away, and the screen should be the subspatial equivalent of a perfect radiator, a black body. But it's gray."

"No, it's black," Schafer said. "But it isn't on all the time. If it were, the catalyst radiation couldn't get through. It's a perfect electromagnetic push-me-pull-you. The apparatus outside projects the catalyst fields in. The lump of iron—in this case, the Empire State Building—is excited and throws off the screen fields; the screen goes up; the screen cuts off the catalyst radiation; the screen goes down; in comes the primary beam again —and so on. The kicker is that without the off-again-on-again, you wouldn't get anything—the screen couldn't exist because the intermittence supplies some of the necessary harmonics."

He grinned ruefully. "Here I am explaining it as if I understood it. You're a good teacher, Jake!"

"Once one realizes that the screen has to *be* up before it can *go* up," Meister said, grinning back, "one has the rest—or most of it. Introducing a rhythmic interruption of the very first pulses is a simple trick. The hardest thing about it is timing—to know just when the screen goes up for the first time, so that the blinker can be cut out at precisely that moment."

"So how do we get out?"

"Feedback," Meister said. "There must be an enormous back EMF in the incoming beam. And whether it is converted and put back into the system again at the source, or just efficiently wasted, we can burn it out." He consulted a chalk line which ran along the floor from the edge of the little Box to the lump of iron, and then picked up the cup of foil and pointed it along the mark away from the lump. "The trick," he said soberly, "is not to nullify, but to amplify—"

The glare of the overheads burst in upon them. The lab was jammed with soldiers, all with rifles at the ready and all the rifles pointing in at them. The smell of burned insulation curled from an apparatus at the other end of the chalkline.

"Oh," said Schafer. "We forgot the most important thing! Which way does our chalk line run from the Empire State, I wonder?"

"It could be anywhere above the horizon," Meister said. "Try pointing your reflector straight up, first."

Schafer swore. "Any time you want a diploma for unscrewing the inscrutable, Jake," he said, "I'll write you one with my nose!"

It was cold and quiet now in the city. The fires on the West Side, where one of the country's worst slums had been burnt out, smoldered and flickered.

The air was a slow, cumulative poison. It was very dark.

On top of the Empire State Building, a great, shining bowl swung in a certain direction, stopped, waited. Fifty miles above it, in a region where neither "cold" nor "air" have any human meaning, a clumsy torpedo began to warm slightly. Inside it, delicate things glowed, fused—melted. There was no other difference; the torpedo kept on, traveled at its assigned twenty-one and eight-tenth miles per minute. It would always do so.

The Box vanished. The morning sunlight glared in. There was a torrent of rain as cold air hit hot July. Within minutes the city was as gray as ever, but with roiling thunderheads. People poured out of the buildings into the downpour, hysterical faces turned to the free air, shouting amid the thunder, embracing each other, dancing in the lightning flares.

The storm passed almost at once, but the dancing went on quite a while.

"Traces!" Meister said to Frank Schafer. "Where else could you hide them? An orbital missile was the only answer."

"That sunlight," Schafer said, "sure looks good! You'd better go home to bed, Jake, before the official hero-worshippers catch up with you."

But Meister was already dreamlessly asleep.

———————

ANN GRIFFITH

ZERITSKY'S LAW

SOMEBODY SOMEDAY WILL make a study of the influence of animals on history. Although not as famous as Mrs. O'Leary's cow, Mrs. Graham's cat should certainly be included in any such study. It has now been definitely established that the experiences of this cat led to the idea of quick-frozen people, which, in turn, led to the passage of Zeritsky's Law.

We must go back to the files of the Los Angeles newspapers for 1950 to find the story. In brief, a Mrs. Fred C. Graham missed her pet cat on the same day that she put a good deal of food down in her home deep-freeze unit. She suspected no connection between the two events. The cat was not to be found until six days later, when its owner went to fetch something from the deep-freeze. Much as she loved her pet, we may imagine that she was more horror- than grief-stricken at her discovery. She lifted the little ice-encased body out of the deep-freeze and set it on the floor. Then she managed to run as far as the next door neighbor's house before fainting.

Mrs. Graham became hysterical after she was revived, and it was several hours before she could be quieted enough to persuade anybody that she hadn't made up the whole thing. She prevailed upon her neighbor to go back to the house with her. In front of the deep-freeze they found a small pool of water, and a wet cat, busily licking itself. The neighbor subsequently told reporters that the cat was concentrating its licking on one of its hind legs, where some ice still remained, so that she, for one, believed the story.

A follow-up dispatch, published a week later, reported that the cat was unharmed by the adventure. Further, Mrs. Graham was quoted as saying that the cat had had a large meal just before its disappearance; that as soon after its rescue as it had dried itself off, it took a long nap, precisely as it always did after a meal; and that it was not hungry again until evening. It was clear from the accounts that the life processes had been stopped dead in their tracks, and had, after defrosting, resumed at exactly the point where they left off.

Perhaps it is unfair to put all the responsibility on one luckless cat. Had such a thing happened anywhere else in the country, it would have been talked about, believed by a few, disbelieved by most, and forgotten. But as the historic kick of Mrs. O'Leary's cow achieved significance because of the time and place that it was delivered, so the falling of Mrs. Graham's cat into the deep-freeze became significant because it occurred in Los Angeles. There, and probably only there, the event was anything but forgotten; the principles it revealed became the basis of a hugely successful business.

How shall we regard the Zeritsky Brothers? As archvillains or pioneers? In support of the latter view, it must be admitted that the spirit of inquiry and the willingness to risk the unknown were indisputably theirs. However, their pioneering—if we agree to call it that—was, equally indisputably, bound up with the quest for a fast buck.

Some of their first clients paid as high as $15,000 for the initial freezing, and the exorbitant rate of $1,000 per year as a storage charge. The Zeritsky Brothers owned and managed one of the largest quick-freezing plants in the world, and it was their claim that converting the freezing equipment and storage facilities to accommodate humans was extremely expensive, hence the high rates.

When the early clients who paid these rates were defrosted years later, and found other clients receiving the same services for as little as $3,000, they threatened a row and the Zeritskys made substantial refunds. By that time they could easily afford it, and since any publicity about their enterprise was unwelcome to them, all refunds were made without a whimper. $3,000 became the standard rate, with $100 per year the storage charge, and no charge for defrosting.

The Zeritskys were businessmen, first and last. Anyone who had the fee could put himself away for whatever period of time he wished, and no questions asked. The ironclad rule that full payment must be made in advance was broken only once, as far as the records show.

A certain young man had a very wealthy uncle, residing in Milwaukee, whose heir he was, but the uncle was not getting along in years fast enough. The young man, then 18 years old, did not wish to waste the "best years of his life" as a poor boy. He wanted the money while he was young, but his uncle was as healthy as he was wealthy. The Zeritskys were the obvious answer to his problem.

The agreement between them has been preserved. They undertook to service the youth without advance payment. They further undertook to watch the Milwaukee papers until the demise of the uncle should be reported, whereupon they would defrost the boy. In exchange for this, the youth, thinking of course that money would be no object when he came out, agreed to pay double.

The uncle lived 17 years longer, during which time he seems to have forgotten his nephew and to have become deeply interested in a mystic society, to which he left his entire fortune. The Zeritskys duly defrosted the boy, and whether they or he were the more disappointed is impossible to imagine. They never forgot the lesson, and never made another exception to their rule.

He, poor fellow, spent the rest of his life, including the best years, paying off his debt which, at $3,000 plus 17 years at $100 per year, and the whole doubled, amounted to $9,400. The books record his slow but regular payments over the next 43 years, and indicate that he had only $250 left to pay when he died. We may, I think, assume that various underworld characters who were grateful ex-clients of the Zeritskys were instrumental in persuading the boy to keep up his payments.

Criminals were the first to apply for quick-freezing, and formed the mainstay of the Zeritskys' business through the years. What more easy than to rob, hide the loot (except for that all-important advance payment), present yourself to the Zeritskys and remain in their admirable chambers for five or ten years, emerge to find the hue and cry long since died down and the crime forgotten, recover your haul and live out your life in luxury?

Due to the shady character of most of their patrons, the Zeritskys kept all records by a system of numbers. Names never appeared on the books, and anonymity was guaranteed.

Law enforcement agents, looking for fugitives from justice, found no way to break down this system, nor any law which they could interpret as making it illegal to quick-freeze. Perhaps the truth is that they did not search too diligently for a law that could be made to apply. As long as the Zeritskys kept things quiet and did not advertise or attract public attention, they could safely continue their bizarre business.

City officials of Los Angeles, and particularly members of the police force, enjoyed a period of unparalleled prosperity. Lawyers and other experts who thought they were on the track of legal means by which to liquidate the Zeritsky empire found themselves suddenly able to buy a ranch or a yacht or both, and retire forever from the arduous task of earning a living.

Even with a goodly part of the population of Los Angeles as permanent pensioners, the Zeritsky fortune grew to incredible proportions. By the time the Zeritsky Brothers died and left the business to their sons, it was a gold mine, and an inexhaustible one at that.

During these later years, the enterprise began to attract a somewhat better class of people. Murderers and other criminals continued to furnish the bulk of the business, but as word of this amazing service seeped through the country, others began to see in it an easy way of solving their problems. They were encouraged, too, by the fact that the process was painless, and the firm completely reliable. There were no risks, no accidents, no fatalities. One could, in short, have confidence in the Zeritskys.

Soon after Monahan's great exposure rocked the nation, however, many of these better-type clients leaped into print to tell their experiences.

One of the most poignant stories came from the daughter of a Zeritsky client. Her father was still, at the age of one hundred and two, passionately interested in politics, but the chances of his lasting until the next election were not good. The daughter herself suggested the deep freeze, and he welcomed the idea. He decided on a twenty year stay because, in his own words, "If the Republicans can't get into the White House in twenty years, I give up." Upon his return, he found that his condition had not been fulfilled. His daughter described him as utterly baffled by the new world. He lived in it just a week before he left it, this time for good. She states his last words were, "How do you people stand it?"

Some professional people patronized the Zeritskys, chiefly movie stars. After the expose, fan magazines were filled with accounts of how the stars had kept youthful. The more zealous ones had prolonged their screen lives for years by the simple expedient of storing themselves away between pictures. We may imagine the feelings of their public upon discovering that the seemingly eternal youth of their favorites was due to the Zeritskys and not, as they had been led to believe, to expensive creams, lotions, diet and exercise. There was a distinctly unfavorable reaction, and the letter columns of the fan magazines bristled with angry charges of cheating.

But next to criminals, the majority of people who applied for quick-freezing seems to have been husbands or wives caught in insupportable marital situations. Their experiences were subsequently written up in the confession magazines. It was usually the husband who fled to Los Angeles and incarcerated himself for an appropriate number of years, at the end of which time his unamiable spouse would have died or made other arrangements. If we can believe the magazines, this scheme worked out very well in most cases.

There was, inevitably, one spiteful wife who divined her husband's intentions. By shrewd reasoning, she figured approximately the number of years he had chosen to be absent, and put herself away for a like period. In a TV dramatization rather pessimistically entitled *You Can't Get Away*, the husband described his sensations upon being defrosted after 15 years, only to find his wife waiting for him, right there in the reception room of the Zeritsky plant.

"She was as perfectly preserved as I was," he said. "Every irritating habit that had made my life unbearable with her was absolutely intact."

The sins of the fathers may be visited on the sons, but how often we see repeated the old familiar pattern of the sons destroying the lifework of the fathers! The Zeritsky Brothers were fanatically meticulous. They supervised every detail of their operations, and kept their records with an elaborate system of checks and doublechecks. They were shrewd enough to realize that complete dependability was essential to their business. A satisfied Zeritsky client was a silent client. One dissatisfied client would be enough to blow the business apart.

The sons, in their greed, over-expanded to the point where they could not, even among the four of them, personally supervise each and every detail. A fatal mistake was bound to occur sooner or later. When it did, the victim broadcast his grievance to the world.

The story appeared in a national magazine, every copy of which was sold an hour after it appeared on the stands. Under the title *They Put the Freeze on Me!* John A. Monahan told his tragic tale. At the age of 37, he had fallen desperately in love with a girl of 16. She was immature and frivolous and wanted to "play around" a little more before she settled down.

"She told me," he wrote, "to come back in five years, and that started me thinking. In five years I'd be 42, and what would a girl of 21 want with a man twice as old as her?"

John Monahan moved in circles where the work of the Zeritskys was well known. Not only did he see an opportunity of being still only 35 when his darling reached 21, but he foresaw a painless way of passing the years which he must endure without her. Accordingly, he presented himself for the deep-freeze, paid his $3,000 and the $500 storage charge in advance, and left, he claimed, "written instructions to let me out in five years, so there'd be no mistakes."

Nobody knows how the slip happened, but somehow John A. Monahan, or rather the number assigned to him, was entered on the books for 25 years instead of five years. Upon being defrosted, and discovering that a quarter of a century had elapsed, his rage was awesome. Along with everything else, his love for his sweetheart had been perfectly preserved, but she had given up waiting for him and was a happy mother of two boys and six girls.

Monahan's accusation that the Zeritskys had "ruined his life" may be taken with a grain of salt. He was still a young man, and the rumor that he got a hundred thousand for the magazine rights to his story was true.

As most readers are aware, what has come to be known as "Zeritsky's Law" was passed by Congress and signed by the President three days after Monahan's story broke.

Seventy-five years after Mrs. Graham's cat fell into the freezer, it became the law of the land that the mandatory penalty for anyone applying quick-freezing methods to any living thing, human or animal, was death. Also, all quick-frozen people were to be defrosted immediately.

Los Angeles papers reported that beginning on the day Monahan's story appeared, men by the thousands poured into the city. They continued to come, choking every available means of transport, for the next two days— until, that is, Zeritsky's Law went through.

When we consider the date, and remember that due to the gravity of the international situation, a bill had just been passed drafting all men from 16 to 60, we realize why Congress had to act.

The Zeritskys, of course, were among the first to be taken. Because of their experience, they were put in charge of a military warehouse for dehydrated foods, and warned not to get any ideas for a new business.

R. R. WINTERBOTHAM

THE FOURTH DYNASTY

THIS MANUSCRIPT was found in a tomb of unbelievable antiquity in the year 2,678,203, near the excavations in the Panhandle strata at Dustorium. Archæologists date the narrative at circa 1,500,000 A. D. from citations in the text and from certain implements found with prehistoric remains in the tomb.

There are certain inconsistencies in the remains. Even the great antiquarian, Jone Smeet, who championed the authenticity of the document, admits the skeletons found were fossilized remains of the true homo sapiens, a type which did not exist later than 50,445 A. D. Besides, the manuscript is written in the dead language, English, which is still translatable by some of the great scholars of our time, and which was the scientific language of the world until nearly 100,000 years ago, but in the dialect form as written in the manuscript is known only in a few fragments, now preserved in the Continental Museum of Antiquity, dating back to the Golden Age of homo sapiens—the Twentieth Century.

But Dr. Smeet pointed out that these inconsistencies are adequately explained in the narrative itself, and science is rapidly discarding the theory that it is a hoax, perpetrated by a practical joker. It is believed to be a key to secrets of the past. The story of two bewildered primitive beings in a modern world is set forth in the text. As folklore of the 1500th millennium it is probably unequaled. But science is beginning to realize that it is probably much more than a myth.

DURING HIS LIFE among us, Victor Hansen spoke often of his Viking ancestors. They explored the seas, Victor declared, while he explored the ages. His words, doubted by some, were the only clue to his race. The Academy of Koro Instinct, in compiling what we know of Victor Hansen, does not seek to enter into the controversy which raged throughout Hansen's lifetime with us and which probably will rage long after we are dead. We will set out only what Hansen disclosed of himself in his valiant career and what was learned from that mysterious being, Georgiana, who appeared at his side on the battlefield of Xubra fifty years ago.

Victor Hansen said he was born on the tenth of July, 1910, in the city of St. Paul, Minnesota, wherever that can be. He died in the year 1,500,-051, giving him a life span of 1,498,141 years. This must be accepted on its face value, because his glands lacked development enough to be tested for veracity by our machines.

He was 27 years old, he said, when he undertook the experiment that brought him out of the dim prehistoric past into our modern times. He was an embalmer, a profession which had to do with preparing the dead for burial. In his experiments to perfect a new type of fluid, he discovered a preservative that prevented not only the decay of tissues, but preserved life itself. It gave the human body a hardness of diamond, which could withstand even the erosive action of wind and water. It was his belief that life could be sustained for thousands, even millions of years by this method.

Assisting Victor in his work was a female *homo sapiens*, Georgiana Jonson, also of Viking ancestry. We may suppose that these primitive creatures had a certain lack of the emotional balance that is the characteristic of the Koro race, and between the two developed a type of mania which Victor termed love. The word appears frequently in old manuscripts which have been recovered from ruins, but a true definition has never been given to us by scientists of our time. Victor, when he was informed of this, said that no true definition had been given in his time, either.

The mental state may be described as a mania for a creature of the opposite sex. The scientific mating of our own age has made such a mania obsolete.

In Victor's age, however, the mania was prevalent, and he was seized with a severe case. He became restless. His natural psychology was disturbed. The disease even affected Victor's appetite. From the symptoms, some of our modern physicians diagnosed the case as a sort of mental paresis, affecting Victor after a fashion that certain lower-type Korans are afflicted when exposed too long to the sun's rays in the stratosphere. It can be cured by several known drugs.

Victor apparently had no desire for a cure. He nursed his sickness with determination, and he became obsessed with a monomania for Georgiana.

She spurned him. Although they were often together in their work in conducting the ancient, barbaric funeral rites, the disease apparently was not contagious, or if so, it was slow to develop after an exposure.

Victor believed she was immune to the disease. He explained that his social status was such that she was slow in contracting the affliction from him. He received such a small compensation for his work that marriage, or the quarantine devised by the tribe for persons ill with love, probably would be distasteful to Georgiana, since it would entail much hardship. Georgiana sought quarantine with a more wealthy invalid.

Despite Victor's resignation to the loss of Georgiana, the disease gnawed at his vitals. Complications set in and he was beset with a desire for self-destruction.

Even in that age, however, the social instincts had made their appearance. Victor, in resolving to die, decided to do so in a fashion that would benefit his fellow creatures. He prepared a potion of his fluid that preserved life as well as cells. He wrote out his formula and that of the antidote which must be administered to restore life. He prepared a dose heavy enough to counteract any amount of the antidote for one hundred years.

He lifted the vial to his lips and drank deeply of the preservative.

Meanwhile, Georgiana had contracted the love disease from Victor. Unbeknownst to the young embalmer, she had decided to abandon her resolve to seek a wealthy mate. She came to Victor's laboratory to accept his offer to go into quarantine together. Instead of finding her lover, she saw his preserved body on the floor.

"Alas! There was nothing left for me to do but join him," Georgiana declared.

But she did not do so at once. First she read the message he left behind. Learning that Victor was not dead, but preserved for one hundred years or more, she resolved to join him.

She used her savings to build a ventilated tomb in a cavern in some rocky mountains. A mineral spring was diverted into the tomb to work a mechanism cleverly devised by the young woman. Small deposits of the mineral would be left behind as the water flowed across the floor of the tomb. Georgiana arranged that when the deposits reached a certain amount, they would trip a lever which would plunge a hypodermic into Victor's shoulder. At Victor's side she placed a glass tube, containing food and an additional supply of antidote. A note in the tube confessed her love and pleaded with Victor to awaken her so that they could enter quarantine together.

Near the close of the hundred years in which Victor and Georgiana slept in the mountain, the geological forces that caused the lowering of the entire range in that vicinity, which is a short distance west of the Panhandle region, began working. The spring ceased to flow. Victor and Georgiana, forgotten by the world, slept on.

As they slept, the Third Dynasty of the world came to an end. Man was the Third Dynasty. Before man was an age of reptiles; huge dinosaurs roamed the Earth and ruled the Earth. Before the reptiles there was an age of fishes. Each dynasty was radically different from the preceding one.

The psychology of fish, as near as our scientists have been able to discover, is one of living and reproducing. Fish have no other aims in life.

Reptiles, while living and reproducing, have a desire for power. They are stubborn fighters. They live, reproduce, and fight to conquer.

Man, the Third Dynasty, acquired a desire to *know*. Man lived, reproduced, fought and thought. But the thinking was not pure thought. Man was as anxious to learn a falsehood as he was to learn the truth. Sophist philosophy was accorded as respectable a place in man's system of knowledge as the great underlying truths of the universe. So many false concepts crept into man's lore that it was often difficult to distinguish what was true and what was false. Like the two dynasties before man, the Third Dynasty fell because it did not progress far enough.

After man came the Fourth Dynasty, the dynasty of the Koro race. While we live and reproduce, those things are not important. While we fight and think, they are not the motives of our civilization. The true Koran seeks truth. He achieves symmetry in thought, appearance and in his deeds.

Victor and Georgiana slept through the close of the Third Dynasty. The Fourth Dynasty struggled to be born. This struggle is known to every school child. In a million books the story is told of how our early types fought hideous, deformed, specialized descendants of the Third Dynasty. The specialized races outnumbered us, but they could not grasp the underlying truths of the universe. Their weakness caused their doom, although even at the battle Xubra, fifty years ago, our future hung in the balance.

Just before Xubra was fought, an earthquake shook the region. In some manner the hypodermic needle was thrust into the skin of Victor Hansen. Enough of the fluid entered his veins to cause him to awaken.

He found the sealed container left at his side by Georgiana and he discovered her sleeping body. Who could describe that reunion? They broke their fast with the food preserved at their side for thousands of centuries and stepped forth into a new and vastly changed world.

Instead of mountains, they found a vast plain outside their tomb. Above even the stars had changed. New stars had appeared. Old stars had faded. Constellations had lost their shape. Even the Moon seemed farther away. They knew that their sleep had not been a short one. It had lasted more than a million years.

As these two humans stood bewildered on the Xubran plain they heard the sounds of the two armies assembling for battle. Victor heard the low, musical cries of our race. The pitch rose, terrifying, yet beautiful to this primitive creature. It was the screaming of a million maniacs, the honking of a vast flock of geese, the howling of a pack of numberless coyotes; yet it was musical, a symphony of terror.

In the distance he heard the faint roar of the advancing Xubrans. More human in sound, the cries also possessed an unearthly chant. Gripped with chilling fear, these two human beings crouched behind a rock and watched the two armies advance on the field of battle.

The flying Xubrans sailed into the air and hovered above our forces. Their psychological blasts threw our ranks in terror. Hundreds of our men were slain before our great thinkers could get into action and bring down the fliers.

Victor and Georgiana were mystified at this first brush of the battle. They heard no sound of weapons, yet men died. It was hard for them to realize that mental power was being used. The men of the two armies were thinking each other to death. Vast beams of fatal thoughts streamed across the field, to drive soldiers into madness and death. Each thought impulse was magnified a thousand times by means of small transmitters. The Korans, because of their curious physiological make-up, were more sensitive than the specialized races, but our weapons were vastly superior because of our greater mental power.

Since the day when our first ancestors sprang from primitive man, we have known our destiny to become the Fourth Dynasty. Not a man hesitated now on the eve of this decisive battle.

"When the two armies approached near enough for me to see the individuals, I was horrified and frightened beyond my wits," Victor states in his account of the battle. "Georgiana swooned at my side. Men of both armies looked like fiends. The specialized fighters of Xubra, with savage claws, leathery hides and wings, looked like fiends incarnate. The Korans, eyeless, earless and noseless, seeing, hearing and smelling through sensitive skins, looked like nothing I had ever seen before. Both had human resemblances, yet neither race was human. Then when men began to fall on both sides without apparent cause, I knew great forces were at work."

Tulor, a captain of our forces, spotted the rock behind which Victor and Georgiana hid. Realizing its strategical value, he set out with a party of soldiers to capture the place. The withering fire of the Xubrans killed all the men, excepting Tulor himself, who reached the rock badly wounded.

Victor did not know what to expect from this creture who appeared suddenly at his side, raving like a madman. To Victor's surprise, the man spoke in English—the language that has been spoken for untold ages on the Earth.

"Who are you?" asked Victor.

Tulor at first mistook the two human beings for Xubrans, and he turned his thought blast on the two of them. To his surprise, it had no effect on their primitive minds. A ray so powerful that it could have paralyzed the brain of a Xubran in two seconds, left Victor and Georgiana unharmed.

Tulor gasped: "Tell me—are you creatures. of the Earth, or do you come from another plane? Never in my life have I seen anything like you. You resemble pictures I have seen in a museum—pictures of ancient animals that once roamed the Earth!"

"We are a man and a woman," said Victor. "We are creatures of the Earth. How long we have slept, we do not know; but we have no desire to injure you. All we ask is safety."

"Safety! Creature, you are immune to dangers that lie about you. A few moments ago I turned my thought ray upon you. Tell me, did you feel anything?"

Victor shook his head. "I felt nothing."

Tulor turned on another blast of his ray. Victor stood unflinching in its path. Then Tulor swung the ray toward the Xubrans. Men in its path fell like straw. "See? You are able to withstand that."

"Stop!" screamed Georgiana. "That slaughter, it's awful!"

Before either man could stop her, she sprung to her feet and ran across the plain between the two armies.

For minutes men of both armies looked at what they thought was a miracle. In the center of a battlefield, with rays coming from all directions, this woman stood unscathed. She was dressed in clothing that was in tatters; her hair fell down over her shoulders; but she stood erect, beautiful in the moonlight.

The Xubrans thought her a goddess. The men of our armies, better versed in science than the primitive enemy, thought her to be a fossil come to life. The firing on both sides suddenly ceased.

Across the plain ran another figure. It was a man. He stood beside the woman.

"Hold your fire!" ordered Victor, for it was he.

But the Xubrans were demoralized. Throwing down their weapons, they ran screaming from the field. Our armies advanced, cheering, to victory. The tide had turned. Our armies would never be opposed again.

The suicidal mania of a lovesick swain of the Twentieth Century had changed the history of the world in the 1501st millennium.

The two "living fossils" were carried to our capital, Koropolis, in royal state. They were fêted and honored throughout the kingdom. Emperor Chrubo gave them rights of full citizenship, an honor which had never before been conferred upon a lower animal.

Our scientists began their controversy as to the authenticity of the two. Many of them doubted that a man and a woman could survive 1,500,000 years in a state of suspended animation. An inquiry was held. The following is a transcript of the record of the inquisition:

Question: Who are you?

Answer: My name is Victor Hansen. I am a citizen of the United States of America.

Question: On what planet is this located?

Answer: The Earth.

Question: What part of the earth?

Answer: Have you never heard of America? I was born in St. Paul. Surely you've heard of that?

Chrubo, interrupting: I recall a valuable fragment in our museum which carries on it a mystical incantation, "Chicago, Milwaukee & St. Paul." We have always believed it had some religious significance. Get it, will you, and let Victor examine it.

Victor—examining the fragment: It is a railroad time-table, sir.

Chrubo: You see! It is religious. The ancients worshiped time!

During the inquiry our scientists were considerably amused at Victor's primitive mathematics. It was the first genuine proof we have had that the Einstein Fables—which every mother reads at bedtime to her children —were fully believed at one time.

Question: What is the sum of two plus two?

Answer: Four. I know the answer to that one all right.

Question: Two plus two do not equal four. The correct answer is **three**.

Answer: What? Two plus two has always been four!

Question: Let us hear you count.

Answer: One, two, three, four—

Question: How much is one and one?

Answer: Two—I think.

Question: That is correct. The first number doubled equals the second. It is only logical that the second number doubled should equal the third. Three follows two; therefore two doubled equals three. There is no relationship between two and four.

Answer: I suppose you will say that two and three do not equal five.

Question: Of course not. Two and three equal three and one half. Any school child knows that.

Answer: But supposing three men came into the room, and only you and I were there to begin with. Wouldn't there be five of us?

Question: We are discussing figures, not facts. Supposing that you prove that two and three make five?

Answer: I'm afraid I can't; I'm not familiar enough with mathematics.

Question: We can prove that two and three make three and one half.

Each numeral in our system, beginning with two, is double the number preceding it. If two twos are three, three and two would be three twos, or three and a half of three.

Answer: Your numerical system is different than mine. I'll stick to mine.

Question: Why is it different? We use the same figures.

Many other facts were elicited during the investigation. The outcome was that the investigators proved that Victor's mind was enmeshed with Sophist philosophy, which held that facts and figures should always correspond. It was as much as to say that if a man dreamed, he should do as he dreamed; that no fiction should ever be written; that lie and truth are the same.

It is unfortunate that a transcript of the inquisition found its way among the common people. Victor became more than the hero of Xubra. He was the leader of a new philosophical movement. Chrubo did the best he could to stop it, but at length he, too, was converted.

There was danger, of course, in the idea, but the people of Koropolis loved danger. Our mathematical systems were revised; dreams were made facts by law, and lies were judged to be truths wherever spoken.

Victor and Georgiana watched these changes sadly. In vain they tried to stem the tide. They could not stop the changes, however.

One day Victor appeared before the emperor. "I wish to report, your majesty, that Georgiana and I are no longer your subjects. We have returned to our own people," Victor said.

"That is the truth," replied the emperor. By law he could not answer otherwise. Victor had made a statement.

From that day to this, Victor and Georgiana have never been seen in our land. On this day, fifty years since the battle of Xubra, a hunting party discovered this tomb. In it slept bodies recognizable as those of Victor and Georgiana. They were dressed in Xubran costume, indicating that after their departure from Koropolis they had made their home among these savage people. This manuscript is being left at their side, so that their true history may survive to a later age.

But the true history of Victor and Georgiana needs a note for its completion. The manuscript discloses that, beyond a doubt, they were misunderstood by people of the Fourth Dynasty, even the people of Xubra, who were the true dominant types of the dynasty. The Korans and Xubrans, like fish, reptiles and men, had their undoing in sophistry. Fish believed that truth lay in life and reproduction, and they were wrong. Reptiles were wrong even when they added struggle to their aims of life. Mankind, in seeking to correlate facts and figures with all-embracing knowledge, lost its race in domination. The Korans sought to legislate truth into being, when truth can only exist with a lie by its side.

When Victor and Georgiana came to live with the Xubrans, they did not seek life; they did not seek children; they did not want strife; they did not want knowledge, nor did they want truth. They gained all of these things.

Their children married Xubrans, who were not so fearful to look upon as the Korans claimed, but who were only slightly developed beyond the human stage.

The descendants of Victor and Georgiana of the Twentieth Century are known to be the founders of the Fifth Dynasty, which wants nothing and by wanting nothing gains everything. Another million years have passed, and the impulse to self-destruction by an embalmer's assistant in the Twentieth Century remains the luckiest thing that has ever happened to the organic kingdom.

PART III

From Outer Space

H. P. LOVECRAFT

THE COLOR OUT OF SPACE

WEST OF ARKHAM the hills rise wild, and there are valleys with deep woods that no axe has ever cut. There are dark narrow glens where the trees slope fantastically, and where thin brooklets trickle without ever having caught the glint of sunlight. On the gentler slopes there are farms, ancient and rocky, with squat, moss-coated cottages brooding eternally over old New England secrets in the lee of great ledges; but these are all vacant now, the wide chimneys crumbling and the shingled sides bulging perilously beneath low gambrel roofs.

The old folk have gone away, and foreigners do not like to live there. French-Canadians have tried it, Italians have tried it, and the Poles have come and departed. It is not because of anything that can be seen or heard or handled, but because of something that is imagined. The place is not good for imagination, and does not bring restful dreams at night. It must be this which keeps the foreigners away, for old Ammi Pierce has never told them of anything he recalls from the strange days. Ammi, whose head has been a little queer for years, is the only one who still remains, or who ever talks of the strange days; and he dares to do this because his house is so near the open fields and the travelled roads around Arkham.

There was once a road over the hills and through the valleys, that ran straight where the blasted heath is now; but people ceased to use it and a new road was laid curving far toward the south. Traces of the old one can still be found amidst the wheels of a returning wilderness, and some of them will doubtless linger even when half the hollows are flooded for the new reservoir. Then the dark woods will be cut down and the blasted heath will slumber far below blue waters whose surface will mirror the sky and ripple in the sun. And the secrets of the strange days will be one with the deep's secrets; one with the hidden lore of old ocean, and all the mystery of primal earth.

When I went into the hills and vales to survey for the new reservoir they told me the place was evil. They told me this in Arkham, and because that is a very old town full of witch legends I thought the evil must be something which grandmas had whispered to children through centuries. The name "blasted heath" seemed to me very odd and theatrical, and I wondered how it had come into the folklore of a Puritan people. Then I saw that dark westward tangle of glens and slopes for myself, and ceased to wonder at anything besides it own elder mystery. It was morning when I saw it, but shadow lurked always there. The trees grew too thickly, and their trunks were too big for any healthy New England wood. There was too much silence in the dim alleys between them, and the floor was too soft with the dank moss and mattings of infinite years of decay.

In the open spaces, mostly along the line of the old road, there were little hillside farms; sometimes with all the buildings standing, sometimes with only one or two, and sometimes with only a lone chimney or fast-filling cellar. Weeds and briers reigned, and furtive wild things rustled in the undergrowth. Upon everything was a haze of restlessness and oppression; a touch of the unreal and the grotesque, as if some vital element of perspective or chiaroscuro were awry. I did not wonder that the foreigners would not stay, for this was no region to sleep in. It was too much like a landscape of Salvator Rosa; too much like some forbidden woodcut in a tale of terror.

But even all this was not so bad as the blasted heath. I knew it the moment I came upon it at the bottom of a spacious valley; for no other name could fit such thing, or any other thing fit such a name. It was as if the poet had coined the phrase from having seen this one particular region. It must, I thought as I viewed it, be the outcome of a fire; but why had nothing new ever grown over those five acres of grey desolation that sprawled open to the sky like a great spot eaten by acid in the woods and fields? It lay largely to the north of the ancient road line, but encroached a little on the other side. I felt an odd reluctance about approaching, and did so at last only because my business took me through and past it. There was no vegetation of any kind on that broad expanse, but only a fine grey dust or ash which no wind seemed ever to blow about. The trees near it were sickly and stunted, and many dead trunks stood or lay rotting at the rim. As I walked hurriedly by I saw the tumbled bricks and stones of an old chimney and cellar on my right, and the yawning black maw of an abandoned well whose stagnant vapours played strange tricks with the hues of the sunlight. Even the long, dark, woodland climb beyond seemed welcome in contrast, and I marvelled no more at the frightened whispers of Arkham people. There had been no house or ruin near; even in the old days the place must have been lonely and remote. And at twilight, dreading to repass that ominous spot, I walked circuitously back to the town by the curving road on the south. I vaguely wished some clouds would gather, for an odd timidity about the deep skyey voids above had crept into my soul.

In the evening I asked old people in Arkham about the blasted heath, and what was meant by that phrase "strange days" which so many evasively muttered. I could not, however, get any good answers, except that all the mystery was much more recent than I had dreamed. It was not a matter of old legendry at all, but something within the lifetime of those who spoke. It had happened in the 'eighties, and a family had disappeared or was killed. Speakers would not be exact; and because they all told me to pay no attention to old Ammi Pierce's crazy tales, I sought him out the next morning, having heard that he lived alone in the ancient tottering cottage where the trees first begin to get very thick. It was a fearsomely ancient place, and had begun to exude the faint miasmal odour which clings about houses that have stood too long. Only with persistent knocking could I rouse the aged man, and when he shuffled timidly to the door I could tell he was not glad to see me. He was not so feeble as I had expected; but his eyes drooped in a curious way, and his unkempt clothing and white beard made him seem very worn and dismal.

Not knowing just how he could best be launched on his tales, I feigned a matter of business; told him of my surveying, and asked vague questions about the district. He was far brighter and more educated than I had been led to think, and before I knew it had grasped quite as much of the subject as any man I had talked with in Arkham. He was not like other rustics I had known in the sections where reservoirs were to be. From him there were no protests at the miles of old wood and farmland to be blotted out, though perhaps there would have been had not his home lain outside the bounds of the future lake. Relief was all that he showed; relief at the doom of the dark ancient valleys through which he had roamed all his life. They were better under water now—better under water since the strange days. And with this opening his husky voice sank low, while his body leaned forward and his right forefinger began to point shakily and impressively.

It was then that I heard the story, and as the rambling voice scraped and whispered on I shivered again and again despite the summer day. Often I had to recall the speaker from ramblings, piece out scientific points which he knew only by a fading parrot memory of professors' talk, or bridge over gaps, where his sense of logic and continuity broke down. When he was done I did not wonder that his mind had snapped a trifle, or that the folk of Arkham would not speak much of the blasted heath. I hurried back before sunset to my hotel, unwilling to have the stars come out above me in the open; and the next day returned to Boston to give up my position. I could not go into that dim chaos of old forest and slope again, or face another time that grey blasted heath where the black well yawned deep beside the tumbled bricks and stones. The reservoir will soon be built now, and all those elder secrets will lie safe forever under watery fathoms. But even then I do not believe I would like to visit that country by night— at least not when the sinister stars are out; and nothing could bribe me to drink the new city water of Arkham.

It all began, old Ammi said, with the meteorite. Before that time there had been no wild legends at all since the witch trials, and even then these western woods were not feared half so much as the small island in the Miskatonic where the devil held court beside a curious stone altar older than the Indians. These were not haunted woods, and their fantastic dusk was never terrible till the strange days. Then there had come that white noontide cloud, that string of explosions in the air, and that pillar of smoke from the valley far in the wood. And by night all Arkham had heard of the great rock that fell out of the sky and bedded itself in the ground beside the well at the Nahum Gardner place. That was the house which had stood where the blasted heath was to come—the trim white Nahum Gardner house amidst its fertile gardens and orchards.

Nahum had come to town to tell people about the stone, and had dropped in at Ammi Pierce's on the way. Ammi was forty then, and all the queer things were fixed very strongly in his mind. He and his wife had gone with the three professors from Miskatonic University who hastened out the next morning to see the weird visitor from unknown stellar space, and had wondered why Nahum had called it so large the day before. It had shrunk, Nahum said as he pointed out the big brownish mound above the ripped earth and charred grass near the archiac well-sweep in his front yard; but the wise men answered that stones do not shrink. Its heat lingered persistently, and Nahum declared it had glowed faintly in the night. The professors tried it with a geologist's hammer and found it was oddly soft. It was, in truth, so soft as to be almost plastic; and they gouged rather than chipped a specimen to take back to the college for testing. They took it in an old pail borrowed from Nahum's kitchen, for even the small piece refused to grow cool. On the trip back they stopped at Ammi's to rest, and seemed thoughtful when Mrs. Pierce remarked that the fragment was growing smaller and burning the bottom of the pail. Truly, it was not large, but perhaps they had taken less than they thought.

The day after that—all this was in June of '82—the professors had trooped out again in a great excitement. As they passed Ammi's they told him what queer things the specimen had done, and how it had faded wholly away when they put it in a glass beaker. The beaker had gone, too, and the wise men talked of the strange stone's affinity for silicon. It had acted quite unbelievably in that well-ordered laboratory; doing nothing at all and showing no occluded gases when heated on charcoal, being wholly negative in the borax bead, and soon proving itself absolutely non-volatile at any producible temperature, including that of the oxy-hydrogen blow-pipe. On an anvil it appeared highly malleable, and in the dark its luminosity was very marked. Stubbornly refusing to grow cool, it soon had the college in a state of real excitement; and when upon heating before the spectroscope it displayed shining bands unlike any known colours of the normal spectrum there was much breathless talk of new elements, bizarre optical properties, and other things which puzzled men of science are wont to say when faced by the unknown.

Hot as it was, they tested it in a crucible with all the proper reagents. Water did nothing. Hydrochloric acid was the same. Nitric acid and even aqua regia merely hissed and spattered against its torrid invulnerability. Ammi had difficulty in recalling all these things, but recognized some solvents as I mentioned them in the usual order of use. There were ammonia and caustic soda, alcohol and ether, nauseous carbon disulphide and a dozen others; but although the weight grew steadily less as time passed, and the fragment seemed to be slightly cooling, there was no change in the solvents to show that they had attacked the substance at all. It was a metal, though, beyond a doubt. It was magnetic, for one thing; and after its immersion in the acid solvents there seemed to be faint traces of the Widmänstätten figures found on meteoric iron. When the cooling had grown very considerable, the testing was carried on in glass; and it was in a glass beaker that they left all the chips made of the original fragment during the work. The next morning both chips and beaker were gone without trace, and only a charred spot marked the place on the wooden shelf where they had been.

All this the professors told Ammi as they paused at his door, and once more he went with them to see the stony messenger from the stars, though this time his wife did not accompany him. It had now most certainly shrunk, and even the sober professors could not doubt the truth of what they saw. All around the dwindling brown lump near the well was a vacant space, except where the earth had caved in; and whereas it had been a good seven feet across the day before, it was now scarcely five. It was still hot, and the sages studied its surface curiously as they detached another and larger piece with hammer and chisel. They gouged deeply this time, and as they pried away the smaller mass they saw that the core of the thing was not quite homogeneous.

They had uncovered what seemed to be the side of a large coloured globule embedded in the substance. The colour, which resembled some of the bands in the meteor's strange spectrum, was almost impossible to describe; and it was only by analogy that they called it colour at all. Its texture was glossy, and upon tapping it appeared to promise both brittleness and hollowness. One of the professors gave it a smart blow with a hammer, and it burst with a nervous little pop. Nothing was emitted, and all trace of the thing vanished with the puncturing. It left behind a hollow spherical space about three inches across, and all thought it probable that others would be discovered as the enclosing substance wasted away.

Conjecture was vain; so after a futile attempt to find additional globules by drilling, the seekers left again with their new specimen—which proved, however, as baffling in the laboratory as its predecessor. Aside from being almost plastic, having heat, magnetism, and slight luminosity, cooling slightly in powerful acids, possessing an unknown spectrum, wasting away in air, and attacking silicon compounds with mutual destruction as a result, it presented no indentifying features whatsoever; and at the end of the tests the college scientists were forced to own that they could not place it. It was nothing of this earth, but a piece of the great outside; and as such dowered with outside properties and obedient to outside laws.

That night there was a thunderstorm, and when the professors went out to Nahum's the next day they met with a bitter disappointment. The stone, magnetic as it had been, must have had some peculiar electrical property; for it had "drawn the lightning," as Nahum said, with a singular persistence. Six times within an hour the farmer saw the lightning strike the furrow in the front yard, and when the storm was over nothing remained but a ragged pit by the ancient well-sweep, half-choked with caved-in earth. Digging had borne no fruit, and the scientists verified the fact of the utter vanishment. The failure was total; so that nothing was left to do but go back to the laboratory and test again the disappearing fragment left carefully cased in lead. That fragment lasted a week, at the end of which nothing of value had been learned of it. When it had gone, no residue was left behind, and in time the professors felt scarcely sure they had indeed seen with waking eyes that cryptic vestige of the fathomless gulfs outside; that lone, weird message from other universes and other realms of matter, force, and entity.

As was natural, the Arkham papers made much of the incident with its collegiate sponsoring, and sent reporters to talk with Nahum Gardner and his family. At least one Boston daily also sent a scribe, and Nahum quickly became a kind of local celebrity. He was a lean, genial person of about fifty, living with his wife and three sons on the pleasant farmstead in the valley. He and Ammi exchanged visits frequently, as did their wives; and Ammi had nothing but praise for him after all these years. He seemed slightly proud of the notice his place had attracted, and talked often of the meteorite in the succeeding weeks. That July and August were hot; and Nahum worked hard at his haying in the ten-acre pasture across Chapman's Brook; his rattling wain wearing deep ruts in the shadowy lanes between. The labour tired him more than it had in other years, and he felt that age was beginning to tell on him.

Then fell the time of fruit and harvest. The pears and apples slowly ripened, and Nahum vowed that his orchards were prospering as never before. The fruit was growing to phenomenal size and unwonted gloss, and in such abundance that extra barrels were ordered to handle the future crop. But with the ripening came sore disappointment, for of all that gorgeous array of specious lusciousness not one single jot was fit to eat. Into the fine flavour of the pears and apples had crept a stealthy bitterness and sickishness, so that even the smallest of bites induced a lasting disgust. It was the same with the melons and tomatoes, and Nahum sadly saw that his entire crop was lost. Quick to connect events, he declared that the meteorite had poisoned the soil, and thanked Heaven that most of the other crops were in the upland lot along the road.

Winter came early, and was very cold. Ammi saw Nahum less often than usual, and observed that he had begun to look worried. The rest of his family too, seemed to have grown taciturn; and were far from steady in their churchgoing or their attendance at the various social events of the countryside. For this reserve or melancholy no cause could be found, though all the household confessed now and then to poorer health and a feeling of vague disquiet. Nahum himself gave the most definite statement of anyone when he said he was disturbed about certain footprints in the snow. They were the usual winter prints of red squirrels, white rabbits, and foxes, but the brooding farmer professed to see something not quite right about their nature and arrangement. He was never specific, but appeared to think that they were not as characteristic of the anatomy and habits of squirrels and rabbits and foxes as they ought to be. Ammi listened without interest to this talk until one night when he drove past Nahum's house in his sleigh on the way back from Clark's Corners. There had been a moon, and a rabbit had run across the road; and the leaps of that rabbit were longer than either Ammi or his horse liked. The latter, indeed, had almost run away when brought up by a firm rein. Thereafter Ammi gave Nahum's tales more respect, and wondered why the Gardner dogs seemed so cowed and quivering every morning. They had, it developed, nearly lost the spirit to bark.

In February the McGregor boys from Meadow Hill were out shooting woodchucks, and not far from the Gardner place bagged a very peculiar specimen. The proportions of its body seemed slightly altered in a queer way impossible to describe, while its face had taken on an expression which no one ever saw in a woodchuck before. The boys were genuinely frightened, and threw the thing away at once, so that only their grotesque tales of it ever reached the people of the countryside. But the shying of horses near Nahum's house had now become an acknowledged thing, and all the basis for a cycle of whispered legend was fast taking form.

People vowed that the snow melted faster around Nahum's than it did anywhere else, and early in March there was an awed discussion in Potter's general store at Clark's Corners. Stephen Rice had driven past Gardner's in the morning, and had noticed the skunk-cabbages coming up through the mud by the woods across the road. Never were things of such size seen before, and they held strange colours that could not be put into any words. Their shapes were monstrous, and the horse had snorted at an odour which struck Stephen as wholly unprecedented. That afternoon several persons drove past to see the abnormal growth, and all agreed that plants of that kind ought never to sprout in a healthy world. The bad fruit of the fall before was freely mentioned, and it went from mouth to mouth that there was poison in Nahum's ground. Of course it was the meteorite; and remembering how strange the men from the college had found that stone to be, several farmers spoke about the matter to them.

One day they paid Nahum a visit; but having no love of wild tales and folklore were very conservative in what they inferred. The plants were certainly odd, but all skunk-cabbages are more or less odd in shape and hue. Perhaps some mineral element from the stone had entered the soil, but it would soon be washed away. And as for the footprints and frightened horses—of course this was mere country talk which such a phenomenon as the aerolite would be certain to start. There was really nothing for serious men to do in cases of wild gossip, for superstitious rustics will say and believe anything. And so all through the strange days the professors stayed away in contempt. Only one of them, when given two phials of dust for analysis in a police job over a year and a half later, recalled that the queer colour of that skunk-cabbage had been very like one of the anomalous bands of light shown by the meteor fragment in the college spectroscope, and like the brittle globule found imbedded in the stone from the abyss. The samples in this analysis case gave the same odd bands at first, though later they lost the property.

The trees budded prematurely around Nahum's, and at night they swayed ominously in the wind. Nahum's second son Thaddeus, a lad of fifteen, swore that they swayed also when there was no wind; but even the gossips would not credit this. Certainly, however, restlessness was in the air. The entire Gardner family developed the habit of stealthy listening, though not for any sound which they could consciously name. The listening was, indeed, rather a product of moments when consciousness seemed half to slip away. Unfortunately such moments increased week by week, till it became common speech that "something was wrong with all Nahum's folks." When the early saxifrage came out it had another strange colour; not quite like that of the skunk-cabbage, but plainly related and equally unknown to anyone who saw it. Nahum took some blossoms to Arkham and showed them to the editor of the *Gazette*, but that dignitary did no more than write a humorous article about them, in which the dark fears of rustics were held up to polite ridicule. It was a mistake of Nahum's to tell a stolid city man about the way the great, overgrown mourning-cloak butterflies behaved in connection with these saxifrages.

April brought a kind of madness to the country folk, and began that disuse of the road past Nahum's which led to its ultimate abandonment. It was next the vegetation. All the orchard trees blossomed forth in strange colours, and through the stony soil of the yard and adjacent pasturage there sprang up a bizarre growth which only a botanist could connect with the proper flora of the region. No sane wholesome colours were anywhere to be seen except in the green grass and leafage; but everywhere were those hectic and prismatic variants of some diseased, underlying primary tone without a place among the known tints of earth. The "Dutchman's breeches" became a thing of sinister menace, and the bloodroots grew insolent in their chromatic perversion. Ammi and the Gardners thought that most of the colours had a sort of haunting familiarity, and decided that they reminded one of the brittle globule in the meteor. Nahum ploughed and sowed the ten-acre pasture and the upland lot, but did nothing with the land around the house. He knew it would be of no use, and hoped that the summer's strange growths would draw all the poison from the soil. He was prepared for almost anything now, and had grown used to the sense of something near him waiting to be heard. The shunning of his house by neighbours told on him, of course; but it told on his wife more. The boys were better off, being at school each day; but they could not help being frightened by the gossip. Thaddeus, an especially sensitive youth, suffered the most.

In May the insects came, and Nahum's place became a nightmare of buzzing and crawling. Most of the creatures seemed not quite usual in their aspects and motions, and their nocturnal habits contradicted all former experience. The Gardners took to watching at night—watching in all directions at random for something they could not tell what. It was then that they all owned that Thaddeus had been right about the trees. Mrs. Gardner was the next to see it from the window as she watched the swollen boughs of a maple against a moonlit sky. The boughs surely moved, and there was no wind. It must be the sap. Strangeness had come into everything growing now. Yet it was none of Nahum's family at all who made the next discovery. Familiarity had dulled them, and what they could not see was glimpsed by a timid windmill salesman from Bolton who drove by one night in ignorance of the country legends. What he told in Arkham was given a short paragraph in the *Gazette*; and it was there that all the farmers, Nahum included, saw it first. The night had been dark and the buggy-lamps faint, but around a farm in the valley which everyone knew from the account must be Nahum's, the darkness had been less thick. A dim though distinct luminosity seemed to inhere in all the vegetation, grass, leaves, and blossoms alike, while at one moment a detached piece of the phosphorescence appeared to stir furtively in the yard near the barn.

The grass had so far seemed untouched, and the cows were freely pastured in the lot near the house, but toward the end of May the milk began to be bad. Then Nahum had the cows driven to the uplands, after which this trouble ceased. Not long after this the change in grass and leaves became apparent to the eye. All the verdure was going grey, and was developing a highly singular quality of brittleness. Ammi was now the only person who ever visited the place, and his visits were becoming fewer and fewer. When school closed the Gardners were virtually cut off from the world, and sometimes let Ammi do their errands in town. They were failing curiously both physically and mentally, and no one was surprised when the news of Mrs. Gardner's madness stole around.

It happened in June, about the anniversary of the meteor's fall, and the poor woman screamed about things in the air which she could not describe. In her raving there was not a single specific noun, but only verbs and pronouns. Things moved and changed and fluttered, and ears tingled to impulses which were not wholly sounds. Something was taken away— she was being drained of something—something was fastening itself on her that ought not to be—someone must make it keep off—nothing was ever still in the night—the walls and windows shifted. Nahum did not send her to the county asylum, but let her wander about the house as long as she was harmless to herself and others. Even when her expression changed he did nothing. But when the boys grew afraid of her, and Thaddeus nearly fainted at the way she made faces at him, he decided to keep her locked in the attic. By July she had ceased to speak and crawled on all fours, and before that month was over Nahum got the mad notion that she was slightly luminous in the dark, as he now clearly saw was the case with the nearby vegetation.

It was a little before this that the horses had stampeded. Something had aroused them in the night, and their neighing and kicking in their stalls had been terrible. There seemed virtually nothing to do to calm them, and when Nahum opened the stable door they all bolted out like frightened woodland deer. It took a week to track all four, and when found they were seen to be quite useless and unmanageable. Something had snapped in their brains, and each one had to be shot for its own good. Nahum borrowed a horse from Ammi for his haying, but found it would not approach the barn. It shied, balked, and whinnied, and in the end he could do nothing but drive it into the yard while the men used their own strength to get the heavy wagon near enough the hayloft for convenient pitching. And all the while the vegetation was turning grey and brittle. Even the flowers whose hues had been so strange were greying now, and the fruit was coming out grey and dwarfed and tasteless. The asters and goldenrod bloomed grey and distorted, and the roses and zinneas and hollyhocks in the front yard were such blasphemous-looking things that Nahum's oldest boy Zenas cut them down. The strangely puffed insects died about that time, even the bees that had left their hives and taken to the woods.

By September all the vegetation was fast crumbling to a greyish powder, and Nahum feared that the trees would die before the poison was out of the soil. His wife now had spells of terrific screaming, and he and the boys were in a constant state of nervous tension. They shunned people now, and when school opened the boys did not go. But it was Ammi, on one of his rare visits, who first realized that the well water was no longer good. It had an evil taste that was not exactly fetid nor exactly salty, and Ammi advised his friend to dig another well on higher ground to use till the soil was good again. Nahum, however, ignored the warning, for he had by that time become calloused to strange and unpleasant things. He and the boys continued to use the tainted supply, drinking it as listlessly and mechanically as they ate the meagre and ill-cooked meals and did their thankless and monotonous chores through the aimless days. There was something of stolid resignation about them all, as if they walked half in another world between lines of nameless guards to a certain and familiar doom.

Thaddeus went mad in September after a visit to the well. He had gone with a pail and had come back empty-handed, shrieking and waving his arms, and sometimes lapsing into an inane titter or a whisper about "the moving colours down there." Two in one family was pretty bad, but Nahum was very brave about it. He let the boy run about for a week until he began stumbling and hurting himself, and then he shut him in an attic room across the hall from his mother's. The way they screamed at each other from behind their locked doors was very terrible, especially to little Merwin, who fancied they talked in some terrible language that was not of earth. Merwin was getting frightfully imaginative, and his restlessness was worse after the shutting away of the brother who had been his greatest playmate.

Almost at the same time the mortality among the livestock commenced. Poultry turned greyish and died very quickly, their meat being found dry and noisome upon cutting. Hogs grew inordinately fat, then suddenly began to undergo loathsome changes which no one could explain. Their meat was of course useless, and Nahum was at his wit's end. No rural veterinary would approach his place, and the city veterinary from Arkham was openly baffled. The swine began growing grey and brittle and falling to pieces before they died, and their eyes and muscles developed singular alterations. It was very inexplicable, for they had never been fed from the tainted vegetation. Then something struck the cows. Certain areas or sometimes the whole body would be uncannily shrivelled or compressed, and atrocious collapses or disintegrations were common. In the last stages —and death was always the result—there would be a greying and turning brittle like that which beset the hogs. There could be no question of poison, for all the cases occurred in a locked and undisturbed barn. No bites of prowling things could have brought the virus, for what live beast of earth can pass through solid obstacles? It must be only natural disease —yet what disease could wreak such results was beyond any mind's guessing. When the harvest came there was not an animal surviving on the place, for the stock and poultry were dead and the dogs had run away. These dogs, three in number, had all vanished one night and were never heard of again. The five cats had left some time before, but their going was scarcely noticed since there now seemed to be no mice, and only Mrs. Gardner had made pets of the graceful felines.

On the nineteenth of October Nahum staggered into Ammi's house with hideous news. The death had come to poor Thaddeus in his attic room, and it had come in a way which could not be told. Nahum had dug a grave in the railed family plot behind the farm, and had put therein what he found. There could have been nothing from outside, for the small barred window and locked door were intact; but it was much as it had been in the barn. Ammi and his wife consoled the stricken man as best they could, but shuddered as they did so. Stark terror seemed to cling around the Gardners and all they touched, and the very presence of one in the house was a breath from regions unnamed and unnamable. Ammi accompanied Nahum home with the greatest reluctance, and did what he might to calm the hysterical sobbing of little Merwin. Zenas needed no calming. He had come of late to do nothing but stare into space and obey what his father told him; and Ammi thought that his fate was very merciful. Now and then Merwin's screams were answered faintly from the attic, and in response to an inquiring look Nahum said that his wife was getting very feeble. When night approached, Ammi managed to get away; for not even friendship could make him stay in that spot when the faint glow of the vegetation began and the trees may or may not have swayed without wind. It was really lucky for Ammi that he was not more imaginative. Even as things were, his mind was bent ever so slightly; but had he been able to connect and reflect upon all the portents around him he must inevitably have turned a total maniac. In the twilight he hastened home, the screams of the mad woman and the nervous child ringing horrible in his ears.

Three days later Nahum burst into Ammi's kitchen in the early morning, and in the absence of his host stammered out a desperate tale once more, while Mrs. Pierce listened in a clutching fright. It was little Merwin this time. He was gone. He had gone out late at night with a lantern and pail for water, and had never come back. He'd been going to pieces for days, and hardly knew what he was about. Screamed at everything. There had been a frantic shriek from the yard then, but before the father could get to the door the boy was gone. There was no glow from the lantern he had taken, and of the child himself no trace. At the time Nahum thought the lantern and pail were gone too; but when the dawn came, and the man had plodded back from his all-night search of the woods and fields, he had found some very curious things near the well. There was a crushed and apparently somewhat melted mass of iron which had certainly been the lantern; while a bent pail and twisted iron hoops beside it, both half-fused, seemed to hint at the remnant of the pail. That was all. Nahum was past imagining, Mrs. Pierce was blank, and Ammi, when he had reached home and heard the tale, could give no guess. Merwin was gone, and there would be no use in telling the people around, who shunned all Gardners now. No use, either, in telling the city people at Arkham who laughed at everything. Thad was gone, and now Merwin was gone. Something was creeping and creeping and waiting to be seen and heard. Nahum would go soon, and he wanted Ammi to look after his wife and Zenas if they survived him. It must all be a judgment of some sort; though he could not fancy what for, since he had always walked uprightly in the Lord's ways so far as he knew.

For over two weeks Ammi saw nothing of Nahum; and then, worried about what might have happened, he overcame his fears and paid the Gardner place a visit. There was no smoke from the great chimney, and for a moment the visitor was apprehensive of the worst. The aspect of the whole farm was shocking—greyish withered grass and leaves on the ground, vines falling in brittle wreckage from archaic walls and gables, and great bare trees clawing up at the grey November sky with a studied malevolence which Ammi could not but feel had come from some subtle change in the tilt of the branches. But Nahum was alive, after all. He was weak, and lying in a couch in the low-ceiled kitchen, but perfectly conscious and able to give simple orders to Zenas. The room was deadly cold; and as Ammi visibly shivered, the host shouted huskily to Zenas for more wood. Wood, indeed, was sorely needed; since the cavernous fireplace was unlit and empty, with a cloud of soot blowing about in the chill wind that came down the chimney. Presently Nahum asked him if the extra wood had made him any more comfortable, and then Ammi saw what had happened. The stoutest cord had broken at last, and the hapless farmer's mind was proof against more sorrow.

Questioning tactfully, Ammi could get no clear data at all about the missing Zenas. "In the well—he lives in the well—" was all that the clouded father would say. Then there flashed across the visitor's mind a sudden thought of the mad wife, and he changed his line of inquiry. "Nabby? Why, here she is!" was the surprised response of poor Nahum, and Ammi soon saw that he must search for himself. Leaving the harmless babbler on the couch, he took the keys from their nail beside the door and climbed the creaking stairs to the attic. It was very close and noisome up there, and no sound could be heard from any direction. Of the four doors in sight, only one was locked, and on this he tried various keys on the ring he had taken. The third key proved the right one, and after some fumbling Ammi threw open the low white door.

It was quite dark inside, for the window was small and half-obscured by the crude wooden bars; and Ammi could see nothing at all on the wide-planked floor. The stench was beyond enduring, and before proceeding further he had to retreat to another room and return with his lungs filled with breathable air. When he did enter he saw something dark in the corner, and upon seeing it more clearly he screamed outright. While he screamed he thought a momentary cloud eclipsed the window, and a second later he felt himself brushed as if by some hateful current of vapour. Strange colours danced before his eyes; and had not a present horror numbed him he would have thought of the globule in the meteor that the geologist's hammer had shattered, and of the morbid vegetation that had sprouted in the spring. As it was he thought only of the blasphemous monstrosity which confronted him, and which all too clearly had shared the nameless fate of young Thaddeus and the livestock. But the terrible thing about the horror was that it very slowly and perceptibly moved as it continued to crumble.

Ammi would give me no added particulars of this scene, but the shape in the corner does not reappear in his tale as a moving object. There are things which cannot be mentioned, and what is done in common humanity is sometimes cruelly judged by the law. I gathered that no moving thing was left in that attic room, and that to leave anything capable of motion there would have been a deed so monstrous as to damn any accountable being to eternal torment. Anyone but a stolid farmer would have fainted or gone mad, but Ammi walked conscious through that low doorway and locked the accursed secret behind him. There would be Nahum to deal with now; he must be fed and tended, and removed to some place where he could be cared for.

Commencing his descent of the dark stairs, Ammi heard a thud below him. He even thought a scream had been suddenly choked off, and recalled nervously the clammy vapour which had brushed by him in that frightful room above. What presence had his cry and entry started up?

Halted by some vague fear, he heard still further sounds below. Indubitably there was a sort of heavy dragging, and a most detestably sticky noise as of some fiendish and unclean species of suction. With an associative sense goaded to feverish heights, he thought unaccountably of what he had seen upstairs. Good God! What eldritch dream-world was this into which he had blundered? He dared move neither backward nor forward, but stood there trembling at the black curve of the boxed-in staircase. Every trifle of the scene burned itself into his brain. The sounds, the sense of dread expectancy, the darkness, the steepness of the narrow steps—and merciful Heaven!—the faint but unmistakable luminosity of all the woodwork in sight; steps, sides, exposed laths, and beams alike.

Then there burst forth a frantic whinny from Ammi's horse outside, followed at once by a clatter which told of a frenzied runaway. In another moment horse and buggy had gone beyond earshot, leaving the frightened man on the dark stairs to guess what had sent them. But that was not all. There had been another sound out there. A sort of liquid splash—water—it must have been the well. He had left Hero untied near it, and a buggy-wheel must have brushed the coping and knocked in a stone. And still the pale phosphorescence glowed in that detestably ancient woodwork. God! how old the house was! Most of it built before 1700.

A feeble scratching on the floor downstairs now sounded distinctly, and Ammi's grip tightened on a heavy stick he had picked up in the attic for some purpose. Slowly nerving himself, he finished his descent and walked boldly toward the kitchen. But he did not complete the walk, because what he sought was no longer there. It had come to meet him, and it was still alive after a fashion. Whether it had crawled or whether it had been dragged by any external forces, Ammi could not say; but the death had been at it. Everything had happened in the last half-hour, but collapse, greying, and disintegration were already far advanced. There was a horrible brittleness, and dry fragments were scaling off. Ammi could not touch it, but looked horrifiedly into the distorted parody that had been a face. "What was it, Nahum—what was it?" He whispered, and the cleft, bulging lips were just able to crackle out a final answer.

"Nothin' . . . nothin' . . . the colour . . . it burns . . . cold an' wet, but it burns . . . it lived in the well . . . I seen it . . . a kind o' smoke . . . jest like the flowers last spring . . . the well shone at night . . . Thad an' Merwin an' Zenas . . . everything alive . . . suckin' the life out of everything . . . in that stone . . . it must o' come in that stone . . . pizened the whole place . . . dun't know what it wants . . . that round thing them men from the college dug outen the stone . . . they smashed it . . . it was that same colour . . . jest the same, like the flowers an' plants . . . must a' ben more of 'em . . . seeds . . . seeds . . . they growed . . . I seen it the fust time this week . . . must a' got strong on Zenas . . . he was a big boy, full o' life . . . it beats down your mind an' then gits ye . . . burns ye up . . . in the well water . . . you was right about that . . . evil water . . . Zenas never come back from the well . . . can't git away . . . draws ye . . . ye know summ'at's comin', but 'tain't no use . . . I seen it time an' agin Zenas was took . . . whar's Nabby, Ammi? . . . my head's no good . . . dun't know how long sence I fed her . . . it'll git her ef we ain't keerful . . . just a colour . . . her face is gittin' to hev that colour sometimes towards night . . . an' it burns an' sucks . . . it come from some place whar things ain't as they is here . . . one o' them professors said so . . . he was right . . . look out, Ammi, it'll do suthin' more . . . sucks the life out. . . ."

But that was all. That which spoke could speak no more because it had completely caved in. Ammi laid a red checked tablecloth over what was left and reeled out the back door into the fields. He climbed the slope to the ten-acre pasture and stumbled home by the north road and the woods. He could not pass that well from which his horses had run away. He had looked at it through the window, and had seen that no stone was missing from the rim. Then the lurching buggy had not dislodged anything after all—the splash had been something else—something which went into the well after it had done with poor Nahum. . . .

When Ammi reached his house the horses and buggy had arrived before him and thrown his wife into fits of anxiety. Reassuring her without explanations, he set out at once for Arkham and notified the authorities that the Gardner family was no more. He indulged in no details, but merely told of the deaths of Nahum and Nabby, that of Thaddeus being already known, and mentioned that the cause seemed to be the same strange ailment which had killed the livestock. He also stated that Merwin and Zenas had disappeared. There was considerable questioning at the police station, and in the end Ammi was compelled to take three officers to the Gardner farm, together with the coroner, the medical examiner, and the veterinary who had treated the diseased animals. He went much against his will, for the afternoon was advancing and he feared the fall of night over that accursed place, but it was some comfort to have so many people with him.

The six men drove out in a democrat-wagon, following Ammi's buggy, and arrived at the pest-ridden farmhouse about four o'clock. Used as the officers were to gruesome experiences, not one remained unmoved at what was found in the attic and under the red checked tablecloth on the floor below. The whole aspect of the farm with its grey desolation was terrible enough, but those two crumbling objects were beyond all bounds. No one could look long at them, and even the medical examiner admitted that there was very little to examine. Specimens could be analysed, of course, so he busied himself in obtaining them—and here it develops that a very puzzling aftermath occurred at the college laboratory where the two phials of dust were finally taken. Under the spectroscope both samples gave off an unknown spectrum, in which many of the baffling bands were precisely like those which the strange meteor had yielded in the previous year. The property of emitting this spectrum vanished in a month, the dust thereafter consisting mainly of alkaline phosphates and carbonates.

Ammi would not have told the men about the well if he had thought they meant to do anything then and there. It was getting toward sunset, and he was anxious to be away. But he could not help glancing nervously at the stony curb by the great sweep, and when a detective questioned him he admitted that Nahum had feared something down there—so much so that he had never even thought of searching it for Merwin or Zenas. After that nothing would do but that they empty and explore the well immediately, so Ammi had to wait trembling while pail after pail of rank water was hauled up and splashed on the soaking ground outside. The men sniffed in disgust at the fluid, and toward the last held their noses against the foetor they were uncovering. It was not so long a job as they had feared it would be, since the water was phenomenally low. There is no need to speak too exactly of what they found. Merwin and Zenas were both there, in part, though the vestiges were mainly skeletal. There were also a small deer and a large dog in about the same state, and a number of bones of smaller animals. The ooze and slime at the bottom seemed inexplicably porous and bubbling, and a man who descended on hand-holds with a long pole found that he could sink the wooden shaft to any depth in the mud of the floor without meeting any solid obstruction.

Twilight had now fallen, and lanterns were brought from the house. Then, when it was seen that nothing further could be gained from the well, everyone went indoors and conferred in the ancient sitting-room while the intermittent light of a spectral half-moon played wanly on the grey desolation outside. The men were frankly nonplussed by the entire case, and could find no convincing common element to link the strange vegetable conditions, the unknown disease of livestock and humans, and the unaccountable deaths of Merwin and Zenas in the tainted well. They had heard the common country talk, it is true; but could not believe that anything contrary to natural law had occurred. No doubt the meteor had poisoned the soil, but the illness of person and animals who had eaten nothing grown in that soil was another matter. Was it the well water? Very possibly. It might be a good idea to analyse it. But what peculiar madness could have made both boys jump into the well? Their deeds were so similar—and the fragments showed that they had both suffered from the grey brittle death. Why was everything so grey and brittle?

It was the coroner, seated near a window overlooking the yard, who first noticed the glow about the well. Night had fully set in, and all the abhorrent grounds seemed faintly luminous with more than the fitful moonbeams; but this new glow was something definite and distinct, and appeared to shoot up from the black pit like a softened ray from a searchlight, giving dull reflections in the little ground pools where the water had been emptied. It had a very queer colour, and as all the men clustered round the window Ammi gave a violent start. For this strange beam of ghastly miasma was to him of no unfamiliar hue. He had seen that colour before, and feared to think what it might mean. He had seen it in the nasty brittle globule in that aerolite two summers ago, had seen it in the crazy vegetation of the springtime, and had thought he had seen it for an instant that very morning against the small barred window of that terrible attic room where nameless things had happened. It had flashed there a second, and a clammy and hateful current of vapour had brushed past him—and then poor Nahum had been taken by something of that colour. He had said so at the last—said it was like the globule and the plants. After that had come the runaway in the yard and the splash in the well—and now that well was belching forth to the night a pale insidious beam of the same demoniac tint.

It does credit to the alertness of Ammi's mind that he puzzled even at that tense moment over a point which was essentially scientific. He could not but wonder at his gleaning of the same impression from a vapour glimpsed in the daytime, against a window opening in the morning sky, and from a nocturnal exhalation seen as a phosphorescent mist against the black and blasted landscape. It wasn't right—it was against Nature—and he thought of those terrible last words of his stricken friend, "It come from some place whar things ain't as they is here . . . one o' them professors said so. . . ."

All three horses outside, tied to a pair of shrivelled saplings by the road, were now neighing and pawing frantically. The wagon driver started for the door to do something, but Ammi laid a shaky hand on his shoulder. "Dun't go out thar," he whispered. "They's more to this nor what we know. Nahum said somethin' lived in the well that sucks your life out. He said it must be some'at growed from a round ball like one we all seen in the meteor stone that fell a year ago June. Sucks an' burns, he said, an' is jest a cloud of colour like that light out thar now, that ye can hardly see an' can't tell what it is. Nahum thought it feeds on everything livin' an' gits stronger all the time. He said he seen it this last week. It must be somethin' from away off in the sky like the men from the college last year says the meteor stone was. The way it's made an' the way it works ain't like no way o' God's world. It's some'at from beyond."

So the men paused indecisively as the light from the well grew stronger and the hitched horses pawed and whinnied in increasing frenzy. It was truly an awful moment; with terror in that ancient and accursed house itself, four monstrous sets of fragments—two from the house and two from the well—in the woodshed behind, and that shaft of unknown and unholy iridescence from the slimy depths in front. Ammi had restrained the driver on impulse, forgetting how uninjured he himself was after the clammy brushing of that coloured vapour in the attic room, but perhaps it is just as well that he acted as he did. No one will ever know what was abroad that night; and though the blasphemy from beyond had not so far hurt any human of unweakened mind, there is no telling what it might not have done at that last moment, and with its seemingly increased strength and the special signs of purpose it was soon to display beneath the half-clouded moonlit sky.

All at once one of the detectives at the window gave a short, sharp gasp. The others looked at him, and then quickly followed his own gaze upward to the point at which its idle straying had been suddenly arrested. There was no need for words. What had been disputed in country gossip was disputable no longer, and it is because of the thing which every man of that party agreed in whispering later on, that strange days are never talked about in Arkham. It is necessary to premise that there was no wind at that hour of the evening. One did arise not long afterward, but there was absolutely none then. Even the dry tips of the lingering hedge-mustard, grey and blighted, and the fringe on the roof of the standing democrat-wagon were unstirred. And yet amid that tense, godless calm the high bare boughs of all the trees in the yard were moving. They were twitching morbidly and spasmodically, clawing in convulsive and epileptic madness at the moonlit clouds; scratching impotently in the noxious air as if jerked by some allied and bodiless line of linkage with subterrene horrors writhing and struggling below the black roots.

Not a man breathed for several seconds. Then a cloud of darker depth passed over the moon, and the silhouette of clutching branches faded out momentarily. At this there was a general cry; muffled with awe, but husky and almost identical from every throat. For the terror had not faded with the silhouette, and in a fearsome instant of deeper darkness the watchers saw wriggling at the treetop height a thousand tiny points of faint and unhaloed radiance, tipping each bough like the fire of St. Elmo or the flames that come down on the apostles' heads at Pentecost. It was a monstrous constellation of unnatural light, like a glutted swarm of corpse-fed fireflies dancing hellish sarabands over an accursed marsh; and its colour was that same nameless intrusion which Ammi had come to recognise and dread. All the while the shaft of phosphorescence from the well was getting brighter and brighter, bringing to the minds of the huddled men, a sense of doom and abnormality which far outraced any image their conscious minds could form. It was no longer *shining* out; it was *pouring* out; and as the shapeless stream of unplaceable colour left the well it seemed to flow directly into the sky.

The veterinary shivered, and walked to the front door to drop the heavy extra bar across it. Ammi shook no less, and had to tug and point for lack of a controllable voice when he wished to draw notice to the growing luminosity of the trees. The neighing and stamping of the horses had become utterly frightful, but not a soul of that group in the old house would have ventured forth for any earthly reward. With the moments the shining of the trees increased, while their restless branches seemed to strain more and more toward verticality. The wood of the well-sweep was shining now, and presently a policeman dumbly pointed to some wooden sheds and beehives near the stone wall on the west. They were commencing to shine, too, though the tethered vehicles of the visitors seemed so far unaffected. Then there was a wild commotion and clopping in the road, and as Ammi quenched the lamp for better seeing they realized that the span of frantic grays had broken their sapling and run off with the democrat-wagon.

The shock served to loosen several tongues, and embarrassed whispers were exchanged. "It spreads on everything organic that's been around here," muttered the medical examiner. No one replied, but the man who had been in the well gave a hint that his long pole must have stirred up something intangible. "It was awful," he added. "There was no bottom at all. Just ooze and bubbles and the feeling of something lurking under there." Ammi's horse still pawed and screamed deafeningly in the road outside, and nearly drowned its owner's faint quaver as he mumbled his formless reflections. "It come from that stone—it growed down thar—it got everything livin'—it fed itself on 'em, mind and body—Thad an' Merwin, Zenas an' Nabby—Nahum was the last—they all drunk the water—it got strong on 'em—it come from beyond, whar things ain't like they be here—now it's goin' home—"

At this point, as the column of unknown colour flared suddenly stronger and began to weave itself into fantastic suggestions of shape which each spectator later described differently, there came from poor tethered Hero such a sound as no man before or since ever heard from a horse. Every person in that low-pitched sitting room stopped his ears, and Ammi turned away from the window in horror and nausea. Words could not convey it—when Ammi looked out again the hapless beast lay huddled inert on the moonlit ground between the splintered shafts of the buggy. That was the last of Hero till they buried him next day. But the present was no time to mourn, for almost at this instant a detective silently called attention to something terrible in the very room with them. In the absence of the lamplight it was clear that a faint phosphorescence had begun to pervade the entire apartment. It glowed on the broad-planked floor where the rag carpet left it bare, and shimmered over the sashes of the small-paned windows. It ran up and down the exposed corner-posts, coruscated about the shelf and mantel, and infected the very doors and furniture. Each minute saw it strengthen, and at last it was very plain that healthy living things must leave that house.

Ammi showed them the back door and the path up through the fields to the ten-acre pasture. They walked and stumbled as in a dream, and did not dare look back till they were far away on the high ground. They were glad of the path, for they could not have gone the front way, by that well. It was bad enough passing the glowing barn and sheds, and those shining orchard trees with their gnarled, fiendish contours; but thank Heaven the branches did their worst twisting high up. The moon went under some very black clouds as they crossed the rustic bridge over Chapman's Brook, and it was blind groping from there to the open meadows.

When they looked back toward the valley and the distant Gardner place at the bottom they saw a fearsome sight. All the farm was shining with the hideous unknown blend of colour; trees, buildings, and even such grass and herbage as had not been wholly changed to lethal grey brittleness. The boughs were all straining skyward, tipped with tongues of foul flame, and lambent tricklings of the same monstrous fire were creeping about the ridgepoles of the house, barn and sheds. It was a scene from a vision of Fuseli, and over all the rest reigned that riot of luminous amorphousness, that alien and undimensioned rainbow of cryptic poison from the well—seething, feeling, lapping, reaching, scintillating, straining, and malignly bubbling in its cosmic and unrecognizable chromaticism.

Then without warning the hideous thing shot vertically up toward the sky like a rocket or meteor, leaving behind no trail and disappearing through a round and curiously regular hole in the clouds before any man could gasp or cry out. No watcher can ever forget that sight, and Ammi stared blankly at the stars of Cygnus, Deneb twinkling above the others, where the unknown colour had melted into the Milky Way. But his gaze was the next moment called swiftly to earth by the crackling in the valley. It was just that. Only a wooden ripping and crackling, and not an explosion, as so many others of the party vowed. Yet the outcome was the same, for in one feverish kaleidoscopic instant there burst up from that doomed and accursed farm a gleamingly eruptive cataclysm of unnatural sparks and substance; blurring the glance of the few who saw it, and sending forth to the zenith a bombarding cloudburst of such coloured and fantastic fragments as our universe must needs disown. Through quickly re-closing vapours they followed the great morbidity that had vanished, and in another second they had vanished too. Behind and below was only a darkness to which the men dared not return, and all about was a mounting wind which seemed to sweep down in black, frore gusts from interstellar space. It shrieked and howled, and lashed the fields and distorted woods in a mad cosmic frenzy, till soon the trembling party realized it would be no use waiting for the moon to show what was left down there at Nahum's.

Too awed even to hint theories, the seven shaking men trudged back toward Arkham by the north road. Ammi was worse than his fellows, and begged them to see him inside his own kitchen, instead of keeping straight on to town. He did not wish to cross the blighted, wind-whipped woods alone to his home on the main road. For he had had an added shock that the others were spared, and was crushed for ever with a brooding fear he dared not even mention for many years to come. As the rest of the watchers on that tempestuous hill had stolidly set their faces toward the road, Ammi had looked back an instant at the shadowed valley of desolation so lately sheltering his ill-starred friend. And from that stricken, far-away spot he had seen something feebly rise, only to sink down again upon the place from which the great shapeless horror had shot into the sky. It was just a colour—but not any colour of our earth or heavens. And because Ammi recognized that colour, and knew that this last faint remnant must still lurk down there in the well, he has never been quite right since.

Ammi would never go near the place again. It is forty-four years now since the horror happened, but he has never been there, and will be glad when the new reservoir blots it out. I shall be glad, too, for I do not like the way the sunlight changed colour around the mouth of that abandoned well I passed. I hope the water will always be very deep—but even so, I shall never drink it. I do not think I shall visit the Arkham country hereafter. Three of the men who had been with Ammi returned the next morning to see the ruins by daylight, but there were not any real ruins. Only the bricks of the chimney, the stones of the cellar, some mineral and metallic litter here and there, and the rim of that nefandous well. Save for Ammi's dead horse, which they towed away and buried, and the buggy which they shortly returned to him, everything that had ever been living had gone. Five eldritch acres of dusty grey desert remained, nor has anything ever grown there since. To this day it sprawls open to the sky like a great spot eaten by acid in the woods and fields, and the few who have ever dared glimpse it in spite of the rural tales have named it "the blasted heath."

The rural tales are queer. They might be even queerer if city men and college chemists could be interested enough to analyse the water from that disused well, or the grey dust that no wind seems ever to disperse. Botanists, too, ought to study the stunted flora on the borders of that spot, for they might shed light on the country notion that the blight is spreading —little by little, perhaps an inch a year. People say the colour of the neighboring herbage is not quite right in the spring, and that wild things leave queer prints in the light winter snow. Snow never seems quite so heavy on the blasted heath as it is elsewhere. Horses—the few that are left in this motor age—grow skittish in the silent valley; and hunters cannot depend on their dogs too near the splotch of greyish dust.

They say the mental influences are very bad, too; numbers went queer in the years after Nahum's taking, and always they lacked the power to get away. Then the stronger-minded folk all left the region, and only the foreigners tried to live in crumbling old homesteads. They could not stay, though; and one sometimes wonders what insight beyond ours their wild, weird stories of whispered magic have given them. Their dreams at night, they protest, are very horrible in that grotesque country; and surely the very look of the dark realm is enough to stir a morbid fancy. No traveler has ever escaped a sense of strangeness in those deep ravines, and artists shiver as they paint thick woods whose mystery is as much of the spirits as of the eye. I myself am curious about the sensation I derived from my one lone walk before Ammi told me his tale. When twilight came I had vaguely wished some clouds would gather, for odd timidity about the deep skyey voids above had crept into my soul.

Do not ask me for my opinion. I do not know—that is all. There was no one but Ammi to question; for Arkham people will not talk about the strange days, and all three professors who saw the aerolite and its coloured globule are dead. There were other globules—depend upon that. One must have fed itself and escaped, and probably there was another which was too late. No doubt it is still down the well—I know there was something wrong with the sunlight I saw above that miasmal brink. The rustics say the blight creeps an inch a year, so perhaps there is a kind of growth or nourishment even now. But whatever demon hatchling is there, it must be tethered to something or else it would quickly spread. Is it fastened to the roots of those trees that claw the air? One of the current Arkham tales is about fat oaks that shine and move as they ought not to do at night.

What it is, only God knows. In terms of matter I suppose the thing Ammi described would be called a gas, but this gas obeyed laws that are not of our cosmos. This was no fruit of such worlds and suns as shine on the telescopes and photographic plates of our observatories. This was no breath from the skies whose motions and dimensions our astronomers measure or deem too vast to measure. It was just a colour out of space— a frightful messenger from unformed realms of infinity beyond all Nature as we know it; from realms whose mere existence stuns the brain and numbs us with the black extra-cosmic gulfs it throws open before our frenzied eyes.

I doubt very much if Ammi consciously lied to me, and I do not think his tale was all a freak of madness as the townsfolk had forewarned. Something terrible came to the hills and valleys on that meteor, and something terrible—though I know not in what proportion—still remains. I shall be glad to see the water come. Meanwhile I hope nothing will happen to Ammi. He saw so much of the thing—and its influence was so insidious. Why has he never been able to move away? How clearly he recalled those dying words of Nahum's—"can't git away—draws ye—ye know summ'at's comin', but 'tain't no use—" Ammi is such a good old man—when the reservoir gang gets to work I must write the chief engineer to keep a sharp watch on him. I would hate to think of him as the grey, twisted, brittle monstrosity which persists more and more in troubling my sleep.

RALPH WILLIAMS

THE HEAD HUNTERS

THE MAN CROUCHED shuddering in the sparse shelter of the spruce clump, flattening himself into the ground, holding moveless, guarding even the terrified thoughts which flitted through his mind. He was gaunt and un-shaven, and the knife-sharp mountain wind whipped through the tat-tered remnants of his clothing. He drew it closer about him—not for warmth, it was past providing warmth—but so the ragged flutter would not betray him.

In the dry wash below, the thing that hunted him rustled and mut-tered to itself. Once it seemed to come his way, and he froze even stiller, striving to quiet the beating of his heart, desperately blanking his mind. It passed and moved on up the valley, and he relaxed slightly; still fearful, but with hope beginning to grow. Half an hour passed, and the thing did not return, and he stretched and burrowed in the moss, making himself comfortable, but still he did not move from his hiding place. For the rest of the afternoon he remained in the shelter of the spruce clump, not moving, not even thinking, simply waiting.

When it was well dark he ventured out, stealthily and fearfully, al-though he knew the thing he feared moved only in the light. He ran silently from cover to cover, stopping and listening often with open mouth. Gradually, as he put distance between himself and danger, the urgency of his terror faded. Yet still he kept moving. It was dark, the wind was cold, he had not eaten his fill for days; and he stumbled often, tearing his hands and bruising his body; still he kept doggedly on, work-ing out of the mountains, down toward the foothills.

Somewhere down there was the railroad and people like himself and safety. The thought of this drove him along, but actually it was farther than he thought, and he was not approaching it directly, he was bearing off at an angle which would have led him down onto the river flats. If he had not seen the fire, he would certainly have died somewhere in the hills or boggy flats.

When he first saw the fire winking and flaring on the far side of a little mountain lake, his none-too-clear mind did not recognize it, and he might have wandered past. Then as he came opposite he suddenly knew it for what it was, a campfire—he could even make out vague figures moving about it, human figures, and he shouted several times. There was no answer. With weary, dogged determination he began to work his way around the lower end of the lake, wading through boggy spots up to his waist, tripping over stunted, rooty willow clumps, crawling through alder brakes woven like basketry by wind and the weight of winter's snows. It was slow, heartbreaking work—

Neely had been hunting sheep, and he had not been finding them. Or rather, though he had seen sheep, he had seen none with the head he wanted, a head which would put his name well up in the record book. Consequently, he was not in a charitable mood.

He was a short, choleric, self-assured man, carrying forty pounds of suet on a frame which had once been muscular; and he had a short, bristly pepper-and-salt mustache and light-blue, unfriendly eyes. He was accustomed to command, to pay well for service and receive it. In this case, he did not think he was getting what he had paid for, and he made no attempt to conceal his displeasure.

Perhaps he was right. Halvarsen had not shown him the sheep he wanted, and it is a guide's business to satisfy his sport's wants within reason—and this was not an unreasonable want. A man does not pay good money for a trip to Alaska, hire airplanes and outfits and the best sheep hunter in the country, spend perhaps one or two thousand dollars, because he has a taste for wild mutton.

He does things like this for heads, and in the four days they had been here Halvarsen had not shown him the right head, or anything near it. Halvarsen himself did not understand it. Only the month before he had flown over this area with the Game Commission man, making a pre-season check, and there had been plenty of sheep, good heads among them. Something had run them out, and it was beginning to worry him, in two more days the float-plane would return to pick them up, and if a man as important as Neely went back to the States without his sheep, it could be very bad business. Big-game hunting does not depend on mass advertising, its clientele is too restricted and specialized, a man's reputation is made or broken by word-of-mouth endorsement or disparaging rumor among the sports in the big cities Outside.

So now Halvarsen moved morosely about the evening camp chores, and Neely sat grumpily back under the lean-to tent, half-reclining against his rolled-back sleeping bag, and sucked at his pipe.

Suddenly Halvarsen froze and turned slowly in a listening attitude to look out over the lake.

Neely listened too, but his city-dulled ears heard nothing.

"What is it?" he asked irritably. "You hear something?"

Halvarsen shrugged. "Somet'ing hollered," he said. "Sounded funny." He moved out a little toward the water's edge.

The fire was crackling and snapping, and the ripples stirred by the breeze lapped against an old stump in the lake, but the next time Neely heard it too—a faint yodeling yell.

"Loon," he snorted contemptuously.

"Might be," Halvarsen said doubtfully. "Sounded funny, though." He listened a few moments longer and then went back to his pots and pans. He thought Neely might be right, but did not believe it. A man long alone in the woods gets away from logical thinking, he grows to depend on feeling and knowledge which comes without conscious thought. He hears a stick crack back in the woods, and he does not think: That might be a moose. Instead, his memory ties instantaneously back to the seen but unnoticed dung half a mile away, the almost invisible hoof prints on a gravel bar, the clipped willow-tips the corner of his eye telegraphed in and stored as he looked at something else; and he *knows* that *is* a moose, a picture of a bull sneaking around through the trees to get down-wind of him comes into his mind.

The noise Halvarsen had heard brought no such picture into his mind, nor any other picture, it was simply a funny noise. Probably, in the subconscious part of his mind which stored and collated the material out of which these pictures were built, there was also filed under "Unidentifiable" certain unnoticed traces of whatever it was that had driven the sheep away, and the absence of the sheep themselves; and this little store of uncertainty may have made him doubly sensitive to further false notes.

A little later, as he was unrolling the sleeping bags and arranging Neely's pneumatic mattress, he heard a faint splash from the bottom end of the lake. He knew this was not a beaver, nor a moose, nor anything else that should have been there, but he did not mention either the noise or this knowledge to Neely.

He crawled into bed and lay quietly, following the thing's progress around the lake by the occasional splash, crash of brush, or suck of feet in marshy grass. It was moving slowly but without caution, and clumsily, and suddenly he knew what it was, it still left some loose ends, but the picture was in his mind now.

He rose on one elbow and nudged Neely.

"Somebody out there," he said. "Coming this way."

"Nuts," Neely said. "What would anybody be doing here?"

Halvarsen did not answer. The man was close now, stumbling recklessly along, and making hard going. And the picture in Halvarsen's mind began to take on detail and color, picturing someone hurt or long lost in the hills, until it resembled surprisingly the ragged man he had not yet seen.

"I better go help," he said. He pulled on his boots and picked up a flashlight. "HOY!" he shouted. "Hold up! I bring a light!"

By the time he was back with the ragged man over his shoulder, Neely had kicked up the fire. Halvarsen eased the man down on one of the sleeping bags. The stranger was conscious, but played out.

"People," he said dully over and over. "Real people. I made it, I foxed the stinking bugger, he won't get me now. People, real people. I made it."

"Shut up," Neely said. He rummaged in a pack and brought out a bottle of whisky. "Here, take a drink of this."

The stranger opened his mouth apathetically and then, as the whisky stung his throat, grasped the bottle and swallowed avidly. Tears started in his eyes and he gasped and then drank greedily again.

"Hey, cut that out." Halvarsen pulled the bottle away. "You drink too much, way you are, you be drunker than a hoot owl. You wait a minute, I warm up some of this stew."

Neely was studying the man closely, noticing the heavy growth of beard and the tattered clothing; the red-rimmed eyes and gaunt belly.

"What happened?" he asked. "You look like you've had a tough time. Lose your outfit?"

The whisky had brightened the man. He sat up now and crouched closer to the fire. "It was the panda," he said. "I was running away from him. He thought he had me in the cage, but I got away, picked the lock and got away." The stranger giggled. "I foxed him, he killed Joe, but I got away, clear away." He glanced nervously at Halvarsen and Neely. "You fellows won't let him get me, will you? You get me out of here, I'll make it worth your while. Wilson's my name, Steve Wilson. I've got plenty of money. I can pay whatever you think it's worth."

"Panda?" Neely said irritably. "What are you talking about? There're no pandas around here."

The ragged man cringed back. "Well, not a panda exactly," he said defensively. "I called it that, it kind of looked like one. It had this cave and kept me in the cage—"

Back in the cave he had hollowed to shelter himself and the spaceship and his equipment, Snrr grumbled sourly to himself. It was a bad habit he had fallen into from being much away from others of his kind; but it seemed to relieve his feelings, especially when things were not going well. They had gone abominably, today. He had had another of those frightening spells of disorientation, the blank periods when he froze unmoving and unseeing. He knew he was getting too old for these one-man field trips; the increasing frequency of the attacks indicated this might be his last.

Worse yet, he had lost his best specimen, a live mammal showing definite signs of intelligence which he had intended to present to the zoo at Ebrrl as the fitting climax to a lifetime of distinguished fieldwork for the Royal Museum. The manner of its escape argued an even higher degree of cunning than he had supposed it possessed, and this made its loss doubly annoying. The door to its cage had over six hundred possible combinations, not too many for any intelligent creature to solve; but still requiring time and fixity of purpose, together with a systematic approach. He had never seen his captive show the slightest interest in the lock; yet it must have fiddled patiently with the thing at every opportunity over a period of days or weeks, whenever he was absent or his back was turned; to learn and memorize the combination for use when opportunity offered.

And what cleverness to wait for one of his attacks, to trip the door catch and sneak quietly out during his paralysis, switch off the protective field outside the cave entrance, and scamper away! He moaned inwardly, feeling a loss like a vacuum in his belly, at the thought of this engaging animal escaping him, and regretting that he had been too busy to properly evaluate and study it before.

Well, he thought resignedly, what can't be helped must be borne. He went about preparing his evening meal, moving with the puttering fussiness of a very old bachelor. Afterward, he plodded wearily up the ramp to his bed in the ship. His bones ached—he had gone far afield that day, trying to track down the runaway. Ordinarily, he worked deliberately and methodically, husbanding his strength, plotting out the ranges of the specimens he sought, feeling them out with his mind, patiently nudging them toward him with carefully disguised mental impulses, till they came within range of his anaesthetic darts. This scurrying and running after a panicky quarry was not to his taste nor best abilities, and the exertion had taken its toll.

Still, he paused for a moment in the storeroom to gloat over his loot—the carefully cleaned and preserved skins, skeletons, and heads, all neatly packed; the bundles of meticulous notes, sketches, and films; and best of all, on the wrapping bench, still unpacked, the twin to the specimen he had lost. He picked up the head and turned it gently in his tentacles, admiring again the regularity of features; the noble height and breadth of forehead, the wisp of black mustache; the lifelike plastic eyes, with their bold, bright, fierce stare.

Neely and Halvarsen had not done too well at prying information from the fugitive. After being fed, he lapsed into semicoma from which he mumbled disjointed and repetitive responses to their questions, and finally they let him sleep. At intervals during the morning they woke him and fed him and tried again, but his rambling replies continued to be irritatingly vague and senseless. Apparently a reaction to the shock of his captivity and flight had set in which made it difficult for him to speak or think coherently.

What they were able to get did not make sense, at least to Neely.

Halvarsen did not try to make sense of it.

He had listened and watched quietly most of the time, while Neely questioned, and a new picture had begun gradually to form in his mind. This picture was of a large, teddy-bearish creature, furry and black, with white markings, and two sets of short sturdy tentacles branching from its shoulders. Halvarsen had never seen a panda, but his business was big game, he had seen pictures and read of them, and he knew this was not one, though Wilson called it that. This was no common animal, it was something which thought and acted like a man, which used tools and machines, which killed for pleasure rather than food. It tortured and mutilated its prey, penning live captives in cages until their turn came.

The picture was full of holes and blurry, the animal moved jerkily and in ways not clear, its motivation was vague and its origin vaguer; but as far as it went it fitted the absence of game and the other little subconscious observations Halvarsen had made.

He believed it.

Neely had no picture and he did not believe what he had heard, but he had come to think something had followed Wilson, perhaps a wolverine, and he was curious.

"There aren't any sheep here," he said flatly. "They've moved out, there's no use looking any more."

Halvarsen nodded gloomily. "That's right. This panda thing scared them away."

Neely eyed him sharply. "You think that's why they've left?"

"Sure," Halvarsen said. "Sheep, they're pretty particular what comes around them."

Neely shrugged. "Maybe. Anyway, we might as well see if we can find this thing, whatever it is. You think you can backtrack Wilson?"

"Sure," Halvarsen said. "Why not?"

Wilson did not take kindly to the idea of being left alone, but they gave him what was left of the bottle and reassured him they would be gone only a short time, and he grudgingly promised to remain at the camp until they returned. Even Neely could follow his backtrail in most places, but the hunters moved cautiously, not knowing just where they might encounter the thing they sought, nor how wary it might be. They came to the place where Wilson had hidden late in the afternoon, and were almost ready to turn back when Halvarsen froze and grunted, pointing with his chin, and Neely followed the direction of his eyes. Neely saw nothing at first, and then suddenly it moved and he saw it, a patch of starkly black and white fur, moving up a little slope perhaps half a mile away. It might have been anything—a skunk, a magpie, or even a man; except that skunks are not found at that altitude, and it did not move like a man or a magpie.

It had not seen nor sensed them, Neely thought, and he motioned Halvarsen down, crouching himself with a slow, almost imperceptible motion, so as to blend into the hillside, till from a little distance he would have seemed an old, gnarled stump, or perhaps a rock. He dared not use the glasses, lest their flash catch the thing's attention, and with his bare eyes he could make out no details. It was simply an indefinable mass, moving unhurriedly, purposefully along.

Snrr was feeling better today. He had started out on a halfhearted continuation of his search for the lost specimen, and sometime during the afternoon had suddenly become aware that two others of the same species were approaching him. What luck! Fresh, unaware minds, susceptible to suggestion!

He followed their progress avidly, his pleasure mounting as he became aware they were consciously seeking him, out of curiosity stirred by knowledge of the escaped animal. He stimulated this curiosity gently, and showed himself to them at the moment they were almost ready to turn back. Now he squatted in the entrance to his cave, feeling them hidden on the ridge across, studying him in their turn. Their wariness and curiosity made them easy subjects; their high-keyed nervous systems reacting beautifully to the slightest mental touch. He let them stay there for a while, wondering how best to ambush them.

Across the narrow valley, Neely lay flat on his stomach just under the ridge, his glasses now glued to his eyes. The light was fading fast, but Snrr's cave was on the westerly slope, and he showed clearly in the glasses. His huge, benign face was turned ruminatively down the valley, and the white markings like spectacles about his eyes, the white-banded muzzle and lower jaw and belly, did make him look startlingly like a huge toy panda. Only the tentacles, coiled idly along his forelegs, were out of place.

"I can't believe it," Neely whispered. "Here, you look. See what you think."

Halvarsen took the glasses and focused them carefully.

"Yah," he said stolidly. "That's him, all right."

He shifted the glasses slightly, studying the approaches to the cave. "You see that funny yiggle in the air, like heat waves?" he asked. "I bet that's that thing that Wilson feller said you couldn't see, but couldn't get through either, till he turned the switch off. What do you think, huh?"

Neely had not noticed. He took the glasses back. Now his attention had been called to it, he could see a faint shimmer in the air directly in front of the cave.

"It must be," he said. "It just don't make sense, but it's there." He was a matter-of-fact individual, used to seeing things proceed in orderly and methodical fashion, and what he was seeing now offended the deepest core of his logic. Still, he found himself accepting it as true. He did not realize this urge for acceptance proceeded, in part, from Snrr.

It was almost dark now, and Snrr did not function well in the dark. He caught the embryo thought in Neely's mind that it might be better to return to camp and come back in the morning for another look. This fitted well with Snrr's plans, it would give him time to prepare a proper ambush for them. He gently built the thought up into resolution in Neely's mind, and followed the two men back until mental contact faded out with distance.

Back at camp, the two men found the whisky gone, Wilson asleep, and the fire out. Neely broke out a fresh bottle while Halvarsen found wood and started the fire.

For the first time, Neely offered to share his whisky, and Halvarsen accepted gratefully, both for the improvement in relations it betokened and for its own sake.

"You know," Neely said while Halvarsen fried bacon and warmed beans, "that screen in front there, that thing you can't see, makes it kind of awkward. You think it might stop a bullet?"

Halvarsen shrugged. "Might be."

"We could try one and see," Neely said thoughtfully. "But then we might spoof him. No, we've got to either catch him outside or get him to turn it off."

"Well," Halvarsen said, "let's eat now, we can figure on it later." He split the beans and bacon carefully between the two pans, whacked off a huge slice of bread with his knife, buttered it and passed the loaf and the butter to Neely. For a while both were too busy to talk, it had been a long time since lunch, and the whisky had sharpened their appetites.

After dinner, over their third cup of tea, they returned to the subject. It did not take them long to work out the possibilities, the object of this hunt was an unusual one, but the principles remained unchanged.

"Well, that might work," Halvarsen said finally. "But how we going to get that Wilson feller to help? He's pretty scared of that panda thing."

"Here's the convincer, right here," Neely said with a tight grin. He held up the second bottle of whisky, still more than half full. "All that boy wants to do is drink himself to sleep so he can forget what happened. We don't have to tell him where we're going, he'll follow this bottle."

"Yah, I guess so," Halvarsen said doubtfully. Something else was troubling him, but he could not quite put his finger on it. By now his mental picture of the strange beast was almost complete, and there had been something out of character in its actions this afternoon.

"You know," he said suddenly, "that Wilson says this feller can get inside your head, make you think things aren't so. You think he might do that to us?"

Neely looked startled and thoughtful. "Well, I don't know," he said finally. "He wouldn't let us come up on him so easy, if he could do that, would he? Wouldn't he steer us away?"

"No, I don't think so," Halvarsen said slowly. "He caught Wilson and Wilson's buddy, maybe he wants to catch us, too? I think maybe we just better be pretty careful tomorrow, not do anything foolish because it looks easy."

Snrr thought they had better be careful, too. In the mid-morning he waited confidently at the entrance to his cave, the controls to his hidden dart-throwers near at hand. Presently he picked up the feeling of the men approaching, coming warily but confidently along. At first the knowledge that Wilson was with them was disconcerting, but then as they came closer and he picked up clearer thoughts, he smiled to himself. It seemed they were bringing his captive back, perhaps as some sort of peace-offering or bribe. So much the better. He would get all three. There was room for only one live specimen, but he could keep the best alive and have two more heads besides.

At the lower end of the valley the men separated, one going along the ridge they had followed the day before, the other two coming straight up the valley toward his cave. This was fine, Snrr thought, he had prepared for either route, this way he could take them one at a time without alarming them. His former captive, he noted, was one of the two coming up the valley, and was now beginning to show signs of panic, which might not be so good, but probably would not frighten the other two seriously, since they had expected this.

The ragged man had been preoccupied before, following the big blond man without paying particular attention to his surroundings, but now he suddenly began to orient himself, and he did not like it. He hung back and remonstrated, and the big man took his arm and pulled him along, and this frightened him more. The big man pulled him around and shoved him ahead up the valley. He screamed then, in a high piercing voice, and ran a little way, then looked wildly around and ran off to one side, apparently with the intent of ducking past. The big man lifted something to his shoulder, dirt spurted in front of the ragged man, there was a sharp crash, and he paused, then began to run blindly up the valley. The big man stopped and calmly watched him go.

Snrr began to have doubts. He had lost track of the third man, and the running man's horrible fright was blanking out what the big man was thinking, but there was an unmistakable aura of menace in the air which Snrr found confusing—something intent and calculating, quite unlike the usual brainless rage of cornered animals.

He let the running man go past the first ambush, uncertain whether to take him or not. At the second point, he decided a bird in the hand was worth two in the bush, and fired. The anaesthetic darts took immediate effect, but Wilson's fright continued to echo in his mind, crashing like static over the lower-pitched thoughts of the other two. The big man had disappeared at the moment Wilson fell, and Snrr could not immediately locate him, but still he received that heavy overtone of menace, like the faraway roar of a lion. He could not see very well either, the shimmer of the protective field directly in front of him blurred his vision. He was beginning to feel boxed-in and unsure of himself, and he decided to cut the field for a moment and get a clear view of what was happening, orient himself for action against the two remaining. He reached out to the switch which controlled the field.

After leaving Halvarsen and Wilson, Neely moved up the ridge toward a spot opposite the thing's cave. The place where they had been yesterday was too far away, a good seven hundred yards, but there was a small hogback angling down to a knob directly across from the cave. It was this he was aiming for. Halfway along the ridge, he began to feel it might be better to go up the farther ridge first and reconnoiter, but this would have disrupted their carefully laid plans, and he turned off. It did not occur to him that Snrr might wish him to go on up to the booby-trapped area they had been in the previous evening, it was just that he was single-mindedly intent on getting to his assigned position. Perhaps if Snrr's attention had not been distracted, he might have felt differently.

Neely came up the far side of the knob and eased around its base until he had a good view of both the valley and the cave. Carefully, he measured the distance with his eye. Two hundred—no, nearer two fifty. Close enough, even if three hundred yards. His sights were set at two fifty, at two hundred yards the bullet would rise one inch. At three hundred it would drop three inches. Dead on would kill, at either range.

Experimentally, he dropped his eye and sighted, his cheek nestling comfortably against the warm walnut stock, right hand automatically bringing the butt tight against his shoulder. In the thrice magnified field of the scope the beast stood sharp and clear, faced a quarter toward him, intently studying something it held in its tentacles, apparently unaware of either Neely or the other two. The picket point rested like a finger against the forward point of its right shoulder.

But was that right? Where would the vital organs of a beast such as this be? The head, perhaps, since its eyes were in its head, and its ears, as in other animals. But suppose its brain was in its belly, as he vaguely thought he remembered some reptiles' was said to be? In the chest then? What if the heart, or what served for a heart, the lungs and blood vessels, were in the abdomen? It must be the neck, for the neck would logically carry communications between the head and body, must be one of the most vulnerable points. Low down in the neck, where the muscles of chest and shoulder would give something for the bullet to work on, give it a chance to open properly, and two hundred and twenty grains of lead and copper alloy, arriving at its destination with a force of slightly better than two tons, would take care of the rest.

The picket swung gently, seeking out the spot, finding it at different angles as the beast moved about, growing used to it.

Then, with his eye still holding the thing in the scope, he moved his right hand away and waved it gently twice. He did not look to see if Halvarsen saw the signal. That was Halvarsen's job.

Presently, he did not need to look. High and shrill across the distance, he heard a scream of fear and terror, then a shot and more cries. The beast heard it too, and stared nearsightedly down the valley toward Halvarsen and the ragged man. Neely kicked the safety with his thumb and put the first faint breath of pressure on the trigger. The beast was restive now, it picked up something and fiddled indecisively with it, then manipulated it in an obscure fashion, and the screams abruptly choked off. The beast peered across at where Neely lay, then back down at Halvarsen. It stepped uncertainly to one side, raised a tentacle to something on the wall, and suddenly the faint shimmer in the air died. In the same instant, the rifle roared. Neely had the bolt worked and the slack half taken up on the trigger in the instant before the scope swung back onto the cavern.

But there was nothing to shoot at, nothing to see, except one black and white paw which scratched jerkily at a sunlit spot on the cavern floor, and then was still. Neely watched it steadily for perhaps five minutes. It did not move.

He met Halvarsen at the bottom of the hill and they climbed up to the cave together. Halvarsen stared around in awe at the ship, the strange implements and instruments, but Neely had eyes only for Snrr.

He smoothed the soft, woolly fur, noting what a beautiful pelt the thing had, and turned the head so the light struck it. Already he could see it mounted on a pedestal, holding something, perhaps a smaller animal, in its curious tentacles, peering nearsightedly off into the middle distance, exactly as it had appeared in his scope.

And underneath, the plaque: "Contributed by S. W. Neely, from his Alaskan hunt; *ursus*—no, new species; *Neeliana* (better yet) *Martianus*—? *Venusian*—? or simply *extraterrestrialis?*"

Anthony Boucher

THE STAR DUMMY

"... IT'S SOMETHING—OUTSIDE of me," Paul Peters found himself saying. "I've read stories, Father, about . . . losing control. It sounded absurd. But this is real. It . . . he talks to me."

It was close and dark in the booth, but Paul could almost see the slow smile spreading from the Paulist priest. "My son, I know that anonymity is usual in the confessional booth. But since there is only one professional ventriloquist in this parish, it's a little hard to maintain in this case, isn't it? And knowing you as I do outside of the confessional, Paul, does make a difference in advising you. You say that your dummy—"

"Chuck Woodchuck," Paul muttered venomously.

"Chuck talks back to you, says things not in your mind?"

"Yes."

"Not even in your subconscious mind?"

"Can my conscious mind answer that?"

"Question withdrawn. Paul, to certain souls I might say simply fast and pray. To others I might suggest consulting with the Archbishop for permission for a formal exorcism. To you, however, I think I might make a more materialistic recommendation: see an analyst."

Paul groaned in the darkness. "It's more than that. It's something *outside* of me. . . ."

"Occam's razor," the Paulist murmured. "With your fondness for science fiction, you'll appreciate that. See if the simplest answer works. If it doesn't, we can discuss less materialistic causes. See an analyst. And perhaps you needn't offend the good doctor by telling him that I also advise prayer along with his treatment."

"... and I see no reason," the eminent analyst concluded, "why we should not dispel your demon in a relatively brief time. In fact, young man, we'll leave you in better shape than when you started having these hallucinations. Your choice of profession is of course highly symptomatic.

A predilection for ventriloquism clearly indicates a basically schizoid personality, which chooses to externalize one portion of itself."

Paul brought his attention back from the splendid view of the Bay. "And you'll fix that up?"

The analyst deigned to smile. "Easily, I hope."

"I don't know," Paul ventured, "if you've heard of a friend of mine named Joe Henderson? Writes science fiction?"

"That escapist dianetics-spawning rubbish?" the analyst exclaimed, as if each word were spelled with four letters.

"As you say. My friend went to an analyst, and in the course of the first interview mentioned his profession. 'Aha!' said the doctor gleefully. 'We'll soon put a stop to that nonsense!'"

"Sound attitude," the analyst agreed.

"Only it occurred to Joe that then how was he going to pay his bills—including, of course, the doctor's. So somehow Joe never did get himself analyzed. . . ."

Paul got up hesitantly. "I'm a professional ventriloquist, Doctor. I'm a good one. I make good money. At least, I used to when . . ." his voice became a little unsteady for a trained ventriloquist, or even for a normal man . . . "when Chuck was nothing more than an amusingly carved piece of wood. It's the only business I know. If you 'cure' me of it, well—Othello's occupation's gone."

"This Othello." The analyst's eyes sharpened. "Another externalization? Does he speak to you too?"

"Tell you what," said Paul. "I'll send Chuck in to see you. He'll tell you more about me than I can."

Which was perfectly true, Paul thought as he rode down fifteen stories. Could anyone, even the psychiatrist—even the priest—imagine what it was like to sit there awake all night in the dark room with the carved wood telling you all about yourself? All the little indecencies, the degradations of humanity hidden deep under your thoughts. Taunting you with the baseness of your flesh viewed with a cold contempt which only wood could feel. Sitting there listening, listening and feeling the contempt probe ever more deeply, ever more accurately.

Somehow he was on the sidewalk in front of the office building, shaking so violently that he suddenly had to force his hands around the standard of a No-Parking sign to keep himself erect.

Fortunately, this was San Francisco, where no one is ever far from a bar. When he was capable again of freeing one hand from the standard, he made the sign of the cross and moved off. A brief wordless prayer and two wordless straight bourbons later he knew, since he could not return to the room where the wood lay, the best place for him that afternoon.

The zoo is a perfect place for relaxation, for undoing internal knots. Paul had often found it so when baffled by script problems, or by the idiosyncrasies of agencies and sponsors. Here are minds of a different order, a cleaner, freer creation to which you can abandon yourself, oblivious of human complexities.

He knew most of the animals by sight as individuals, and he had even acquired a better-than-nodding acquaintance with many of the attendants. It was one of these who literally bumped into him as he stood in front of the parrot cage, and proceeded to make the afternoon far more distracting than he had ever anticipated.

"Tim!" Paul exclaimed. "Where on earth are you running to? Or from? Lion escaped or what?"

"Mr. Peters!" the attendant gasped. "I been chasing all over the place making phone calls to God knows who all. There's something screwy going on over in the wombats'."

"It couldn't pick a better place," Paul smiled. "Catch your breath a minute and tell me what gives."

"Got a cigarette? Thanks. Well, Mr. Peters, I'll tell you: couple of times lately some of the boys they say they see something funny in one of the cages. Somebody checks up, it's always gone. Only today it's in there with the wombats and everybody's looking at it and nobody knows what—"

Paul Peters had always had a highly developed sense of curiosity. (Schizoid externalization? he reflected. No, cancel that. You're forgetting things. This may be fun.) He was already walking toward the wombats' enclosure as he asked. "This thing. What does it look like?"

"Well, Mr. Peters, it's pretty much like a koala," Tim explained, "except for where it's like an anteater."

Paul was never able to better that description. With the exception, of course, that neither koalas nor anteaters have six-digited forepaws with opposing thumbs. But that factor was not obvious on first glance.

He could see the thing now, and it was in body very much like an outsize koala—that oddly charming Australian eucalyptus-climber after whom the Teddy bear was patterned. It had no visible pouch—but then it might be a male—and its ears were less prominent. Its body was about two feet long. And its face was nothing like the flat and permanently startled visage of the koala, but a hairless expanse sloping from a high forehead, past sharp bright eyes, to a protracted proboscis which did indeed resemble nothing so much as the snout of an anteater.

The buzz through which they pushed their way consisted chiefly of "What *is* that?" and "I don't know," with an occasional treble obligato of "*Why* don't you know, Daddy?"

But it was not what it was so much as what it was doing that fascinated Paul. It concentrated on rubbing its right forepaw in circles on the ground, abruptly looking up from time to time at the nearest wombat, while those stumpy marsupials either stared at it detachedly or backed away with suspicion.

"When the other boys saw it," Paul asked, "what was it doing then?"

"It's funny you ask that, Mr. Peters, on account of that's one of the things that's funny about it. What it was doing, I mean. One time when it was in with the llamas it was doing like this, just playing in the dirt."

"Playing?" Paul wondered softly.

"Only when it was in with the monkeys it was chattering at them something fierce, just like a monkey too, this guy said. And when it was in with the lions, well I'm not asking you to believe this and God knows I didn't yesterday and I don't know as I do now, but this other guy says it gives a roar just like a lion. Only not *just* like, of course, because look at it, but like as if you didn't have your radio turned up quite enough."

"Wombats don't make much noise, do they? Or llamas?" All right, Paul said to himself. You're crazy. This is worse than wood talking; but it's nicer. And there *is* a pattern. "Tim," he said abruptly, "can you let me in the wombat enclosure?"

"Jeez, Mr. Peters, there's bigshots coming from the University and . . . But you did give us that show for free at the pension benefit and . . . And," Tim concluded more firmly as he tucked the five unobtrusively into his pocket, "can do, I guess. O.K., everybody! Let's have a little room here. Got to let Dr. Peters in!"

Paul hesitated at the gate. This was unquestionably either the most momentous or the most ridiculous effort he had made in a reasonably momentous-ridiculous life. "Joe Henderson, thou shouldst be with me at this hour!" he breathed, and went in.

He walked up to where the creature squatted by its circles.

He knelt down beside it and pointed his forefinger, first at the small central circle with the lines sticking out all around it, then up at the sun. Next he tapped his finger insistently on the unmarked ground, then thrust it at the large dot on the third of the bigger concentric circles.

The creature looked up at him, and for the first time in his life Paul understood just what Keats had meant by a *wild surmise*. He saw it on the creature's face, and he felt it thrill through his own being.

An animal who can draw, an animal who can recognize a crude diagram of the solar system, is rational—is not merely a beast like the numbly staring wombats.

Hastily the creature held up a single digit of one forepaw and then drew a straight line in the dirt. Paul did the same, with an amused sudden realization of the fact that the figure *one* is probably a straight line in almost any system.

The creature held up two fingers and made an odd squiggle. Paul held up two fingers and made our own particular odd squiggle which is shaped 2. They almost raced each other through the next three numbers.

At the squiggle shape 5, the creature looked at Paul's five fingers, hesitated, then advanced by a daring step. It held up both its hands, each with its six digits, and made a straight line followed by an S-shaped curve.

Paul thought frantically, and wished that he had majored in mathematics. He held up his ten fingers, then marked down a straight line followed by a circle. The creature paused a moment, as if rapidly calculating. Then it nodded, looked carefully at Paul's 2 squiggle, held up its own twelve fingers again, and wrote down 12.

Paul sank back on his heels. This twelve-fingered being had, as was plausible, a duodecimal system, based on twelve as our decimal system is on ten. And it had almost instantaneously grasped the human ten-system so well as to write down its *twelve* in our method.

"Friend," said Paul softly, pitching his voice too low for the crowds outside the enclosure, "you can't understand my language; but in the name of God and Man, welcome to Earth."

"Oh dear," said the creature, "you communicate only by speech! And otherwise you seem such a highly rational being."

Paul gulped. "That's an accusation I haven't had leveled against me recently."

"I never dreamed," it went on, "that the beings shaped like you were the rational ones. I couldn't get any waves from them. I can from you, though, even enough to pick up the language."

"And you got waves from the other animals," Paul mused. "That's why you chattered like a monkey and roared like a lion-not-turned-up-enough. Only they didn't understand your diagrams, so you knew they weren't high enough for you to deal with."

"But why do you have waves and not the others?"

"I am not," said Paul hastily, "a mutant. We can figure out why later. The trouble right now, if I know anything about the people-without-waves, is that nobody's going to believe a word of this scene. As if indeed I did. But it's nicer than wood. . . ."

The creature shuddered, then apologized. "I'm sorry. Something I touched in there. . . ."

"I know," said Paul, abruptly grave and humble. "Maybe we can help each other. God grant. I'm taking a chance—but I think the first thing is to get you out of here before Tim's 'bigshots from the University' show up and maybe decide to dissect you. Will you trust me?"

The pause was a long one—long enough for Paul to think of all the vile weakness of his humanity and know his infinite unworthiness of trust. He could hear the words pouring forth from the wood—and then the creature said simply, "Yes."

And the wood was silent even in memory.

Never, Paul felt, had he invested twenty dollars more wisely. And never had he discovered such unsuspected inborn acting talent as Tim's. There was something approaching genius, in a pure vein of Stanislavsky realism, in Tim's denunciation of Paul as a publicity-seeker—in his explanation to the crowd that the koala-like object was a highly ingenious mechanical dummy planted here by a venal ventriloquist who had planned to "discover" it as some strange being and trade on the good name of the Zoo itself for his own selfish promotional advancement. Bitter lashings of denunciation followed Paul and the creature as they departed—a matter of minutes, Tim confessed *sotto voce,* before the professors from across the Bay were due.

Now they were parked by the beach in Paul's convertible. Sensibly, he felt he should head for home and privacy; but he still could not quite bring himself to enter that room where Chuck Woodchuck waited.

"First of all, I suppose," he ventured, "comes: what's your name?"

"The nearest, my dear Paul, that your phonetics can come to it is something like *Tarvish.*"

"Glad to meet you. Now—how did you know mine? But of course," he added hastily, "if you can read . . . Well, next: where are you from? Mars?"

Tarvish thought. "Mars . . . Ah, you mean the fourth planet? All that sand . . ." He shuddered as if at a memory of infinite boredom. "No. I'm from a planet called Earth, which revolves around a star called the sun."

"Look!" Paul exclaimed. "Fun's fun, but isn't this a little too much of a muchness? This is Earth. That ball getting low over there is the sun. And you—"

"Don't you understand?" The tip of Tarvish's nose twitched faintly. "Then ask me what kind of a creature I am, what race I belong to."

"All right, Mr. Bones, I'm asking."

"I," said Tarvish, twitching violently, "am a man."

It took Paul a minute to interpret; then his laugh, his first free laugh in days was as loud as Tarvish's twitching was vigorous. "Of course. Everybody has a name for everything in the universe—everything *else.* But there aren't names for your own race or your own planet or your own star. You're *men,* you're *people,* you live on the *earth,* you're warmed by the *sun.* I remember reading that some Indian languages were like that: the name for the tribe meant simply *the people* and the name for their country was just *the land.* We've smiled at that, and interplanetarily we're doing the same damned thing. All right—where is *your* sun?"

"How can I tell you? You don't know our system of spatial coördinates. I don't understand what I find in your mind about 'constellations,' meaningless pictures which look different from any two points in space, or 'lightyears,' because your *year* doesn't convey a time-meaning to me."

"It's three hundred and sixty-five days."

"And what is a *day?*"

"Twenty-four—no, skip it. I can see that this is going to be a lot tougher than Joe Henderson and his friends think. Let's start over again. How did you get here?"

Two minutes later Paul repeated the question.

"I've been thinking," said Tarvish. "Trying to find the words in your mind. But they aren't there. Your words make too sharp a distinction between matter and energy. If I say 'a spaceship,' you will think of a metal structure. If I say 'a force field,' you will picture me traveling in something immaterial. Both are wrong."

"Let's try again. Why did you—" Paul stopped abruptly.

The nose twitched. "No," said Tarvish gently, "I am not the advance guard of an invasion and you are not betraying your race by being human to me. Please forget your science-fiction friends. We men of Earth have no desire to take over any of the planets of this star; ever since our terrible experience with the—" it sounded a little like *Khrj* "—we have made it a firm rule never to land on an inhabited planet."

"Then what are you doing here?"

"Because . . ." Tarvish hesitated. A faint blue colored the root of his nose. "Because my girl is here."

"I'm improving," Paul said. "It took me only five seconds to adjust to that *girl*. You're in love?" Oddly, he didn't even feel like smiling.

"That's why I had to land. You see, she went off by herself in the . . . I think if I invent the word 'space dinghy' it will give you the idea. I warned her that the . . . well, an important part was defective; but we had just had a small quarrel and she insisted on spiting me. She never came back. That's why I had to make contact with intelligent life to learn something of the planet which I have to search."

"Only the intelligent life doesn't have waves. Except me because, God help me, I expect strange things to speak. You need a combination of Sherlock Holmes and Frank Buck, and you're stuck with a possibly not quite sane ventriloquist."

"You will help me? When you see her!" Tarvish was almost rapturous. "The most beautiful girl, I swear, on the whole earth. With," he added reminiscently, "the finest pair of ears in the universe." On the word *ears* his voice sank a little, and the blue tinge deepened at the root of his proboscis.

The universe, Paul smiled to himself, must provide a fascinating variety of significant secondary sexual characteristics. "If I can help you," he said sincerely, "I'll try. I'll do my best. And in the meantime we've the little problem of feeding you. I'll have to take you—" he tensed a little "—home. I suppose, that is, you *do* eat?"

"So far as we have observed," Tarvish pronounced solemnly, "all races of rational beings eat and sleep and . . ." The blue was again intensified.

"And relish a fine pair of ears," Paul concluded for him. "Definition of rationality." He started the car.

By the next morning Paul Peters had learned a number of things.

He had learned that men of Tarvish's race are, as they choose, bipeds or quadrupeds. When they entered the Montgomery Block, that sprawling warren of odd studios where Paul lived, Tarvish had trotted behind him on all fours "because," he said, "it would be less conspicuous," as indeed was true. He was only by a small margin the most unusual of the animal and human companions whom Montgomery Block denizens had brought home, few of whom—including the humans—were at the moment functionally bipedal. But once inside the studio apartment, he seemed to prefer the erect posture.

Between them they had worked out the problem of feeding. The proboscidiferous Tarvish was of course edentate, and accustomed to subsisting on liquids and pap. Milk, raw eggs and tomato juice sufficed him for the time being—a surprisingly simple diet to contain most of the requisite vitamins and proteins. Later Paul planned to lay in a supply of prepared baby foods, and looked forward to the astonishment of the clerk at the nearby chain store who knew him as a resolute bachelor.

Paul had also learned an astonishing amount, considering the relative brevity of the conversation, concerning the planet which was to Tarvish *the earth*—from its socio-economic systems to the fascinating fact that at present fine full, ripe ears were, as any man would prefer, in style, whereas only a generation ago they had been unaccountably minimized and even strapped down. Paul's amused explanation of the analogy on this earth served perhaps as much as anything to establish an easy man-to-man intimacy. Tarvish went so far as to elaborate a plan for introducing gradually inflatable false earlobes on his earth. It was never quite clear to Paul how an edentate being could speak so easily, but he imagined that the power resembled his own professional skill.

All of these strange thoughts coursed through Paul's head as he lay slowly waking up the next morning; and it was only after several minutes of savoring them that he perceived the wonderful background note that served as their ground-bass. Not since the first difficult instant of entering the apartment had he so much as thought of the corner of the main room in which Chuck Woodchuck lay.

"You know, Tarvish," Paul said as they finished breakfast, "I like you. You're easy to be with."

"Thank you, Paul." The root of the proboscis blushed faintly blue. "I like you too. We could spend happy days simply talking, exchanging, learning to know . . . But there *is* Vishta."

"Vishta?"

"My girl. I dreamed about her last night, Paul. . . ." Tarvish gave a little sigh, rose, and began bipedally to pace the room. "Your earth is enormous, even though the figures you tell me convey no meaning to me. Whatever a square mile means, one hundred and ninety-seven million of them must represent quite an area. There must be some way . . ."

"Look," Paul said. "Before we tackle the problem again, let's try restating it. (A), we must find Vishta. But that doesn't necessarily mean literally, physically, Dr. Livingstone-I-presume *find*, does it? She'll be over the lovers' quarrel by now; she'll want to get back to the—you'll pardon the expression—spaceship. If we can let her know where you are, that's enough, isn't it?"

Tarvish rubbed the tip of his large nose. "I should think so."

"All right. Restate the restatement. (A), get word to Vishta. (B), without revealing your interplanetary presence to the world at large. Both because it's against your mores and because I think it'll cause just too damned much trouble. Agreed?"

"Agreed."

The two sat in silence for perhaps five minutes. Paul alternately cudgeled his brains, and addressed brief prayers to the Holy Ghost for assistance in helping this other creature of God. Meanwhile, his eyes drifted around the apartment, and for a moment rested on the noble two-volume Knopf edition of Poe.

"My God in Heaven!" he exclaimed. The most devout could not have considered this a violation of the decalog. "Look, Tarvish. We have in our literature a story called *The Purloined Letter*. Its point is that the most over-obvious display can be the subtlest concealment."

"The point occurs in our folklore as well," said Tarvish. "But I don't—" Suddenly he stopped.

Paul grinned. "Did you get a wave? But let me go on out loud—this race is happier that way. Yes, we had it all solved yesterday and let it slip. The lie we bribed Tim to tell—"

"—that I am your new dummy," Tarvish picked up eagerly.

"The act'll be sensational. Because you can really talk, I can do anything. Eat soda crackers while you're talking—it won't make any difference. And you—I hate like hell to say this to any man, but from an audience viewpoint it's true—you're *cute*. You're damned near cuddly. They'll love you. And we bill you with the precise truth: you're a visitant from outer space. It ties a ventriloquism act into the science-fiction trend in TV. You're THE STAR DUMMY. We'll make a fortune—not that I'm thinking of that—"

"Aren't you?" Tarvish asked dryly.

Paul smiled. "Can anyone be a hypocrite in a telepathic civilization?"

"It's been known to happen."

"Well, anyway, I'm not thinking *primarily* of the fortune. We'll get publicity we couldn't buy. And wherever she is, unless it's in Darkest Africa or behind the Iron Curtain, Vishta'll learn where you are."

"Paul," said Tarvish solemnly, "you're inspired. On that I could use a drink."

"Another custom of all rational races?"

"Nearly all. But just a moment: I find in your mind the concept *alcohol*. I'm afraid that doesn't convey much."

Paul tried to think back to his high-school chemistry. Finally he ventured, "C_2H_5OH. That help any?"

"Ah, yes. More correctly, of course, CH_3CH_2OH. You find that mild fluid stimulating? We use it somewhat in preparing food, but . . . Now, if I might have a little $C_8H_{10}N_4O_2$?"

Paul rubbed his head. "Doesn't mean a thing to me. Sounds like some kind of alkaloid. It's the touch of nitrogen that does it with you people?"

"But indeed you do know it. You were drinking it at breakfast. And I must say I admired the ease with which you put away so much strong liquor so early in the day."

Hastily Paul checked in a dictionary. "*Caffein,*" he groaned. "And what do you use to sober up? A few cups of good straight alcohol, no cream?"

And in copious shots of C_2H_5OH and $C_8H_{10}N_4O_2$ the two men pledged the future of THE STAR DUMMY.

So now you see at last to what this story has been leading. What began in a confessional and passed through an analyst's office to a zoo—all symbolism is read into the sequence at your own peril—is in actuality the backstage story of the genesis of your own favorite television program.

Most of the rest of that genesis you know from a thousand enthusiastic recountings, from John Crosby's in the *Herald Tribune* to Philip Hamburger's in the *New Yorker*: how network producers at first greeted Paul Peters skeptically when he returned to show business, after a mysterious absence, with a brand-new type of act; how THE STAR DUMMY was at first somewhat hesitantly showcased on *San Francisco Presents*; how the deluge of fan mail caused that first showing to be kinnied all over the country, while the next week a live performance shot over the nation on a microwave relay; how the outrageous concept of a cuddlesome dummy from Outer Space managed unbelievably to combine the audiences of Charlie McCarthy and *Space Cadet*; how Star Dummies outgrossed the combined total sales of Sparkle Plenty Dolls and Hopalong Cassidy suits.

But there are a few untold backstage scenes which you should still hear.

Scene: Station KMNX-TV. Time: the morning after the first Star Dummy broadcast. Speaker: a vice-president.

"But my God, M.N., there's all hell popping. That was Hollywood on the phone. They've got the same damned show lined up for show-casing next week. Same format—identical dummy—only maybe theirs has bigger ears. The property owner's flying up here and our lawyers had better be good!"

Scene: Same. Time: that afternoon.

"I think," Paul had said, "that we might be able to reach a settlement out of court." The vice-presidents had filed out eagerly, the lawyers somewhat reluctantly.

Once he had been introduced to Vishta (and so close had he come, in weeks of preparing the show, to Tarvish's ways of thinking that he found her enchantingly lovely), it would have been inconceivably rude and prying to do anything but turn his back on the reunion of the lovers. Which meant that he had to keep his eyes on Marcia Judd, property owner of the Hollywood show.

"I'm not a professional ventriloquist like you, Mr. Peters," she was saying. "I couldn't do a thing without Vishta. But when we talked about it, it seemed the most logical way to let Tarvish know where she was. You know, like *The Purloined Letter.*"

"And you have waves?" Paul marveled. It was about the only thing which she did not obviously have on first glance.

"I guess maybe it's because I write fantasy and s.f. Oh, I don't sell much, but a little. And I'm not too sure that there's *anything* that can't happen. So when I was walking through the San Diego zoo and I saw something in with the koalas that was making diagrams . . . Well, I couldn't help remembering Joe's story about inter-cultural communication—"

"Joe Henderson? You know old Joe?"

"He's helped me a lot. I guess you'd sort of say I'm his protege."

"So long," Paul smiled, "as he isn't your protector. But tell me, does Joe still . . ."

And one half of the room was as happy in the perfect chatter of a first meeting as was the other half in the perfect silence of a long-delayed reunion.

Truth had shifted again, and THE STAR DUMMY was in fact a dummy— a brilliantly constructed piece of mechanism which had eaten up the profits of the three shows on which Tarvish himself had appeared. But the show was set now, and Paul's own professional skill could carry it from this point on. And the highly telegenic presence of Marcia Judd did no harm.

Paul's car stopped by a lonely stretch of beach south of the city.

"We can find what you like to call the spaceship from here," said Tarvish. "I'd sooner you didn't see it. I think it would only confuse you."

"We love you both," said Vishta gently. "God bless you."

"God!" Marcia exclaimed. "Don't tell me people with a science like yours believe in God!"

Paul sighed. "I hope you don't mind too much that I'm such a barbarian."

"It's your conditioning," said Marcia. "But with them . . .!"

"And *your* conditioning, Marcia," Tarvish observed, "has driven you the other way? Yes, I do believe in God in a way—if less devoutly than Paul, or at least than Paul being devout. Many do on our earth; not all, but many. There was once a man, or possibly more than a man. We argue about that. His name was Hraz, and some call him the Oiled One." Marcia smiled and Tarvish added, "It refers to a ceremony of honor. I am not quite a follower of Hraz, and yet when I pray—as I did, Paul, shortly before you found me—it is in words that Hraz taught us."

"Which are?"

"We'll say them together," said Vishta. "It makes a good good-bye."

And the lovers recited:

Lifegiver over us, there is blessing in the word that means you. We pray that in time we will live here under your rule as others now live with you there; but in the meantime feed our bodies, for we need that here and now. We are in debt to you for everything, but your love will not hold us accountable for this debt; and so we too should deal with others, holding no man to strict balances of account. Do not let us meet temptations stronger than we can bear; but let us prevail and be free of evil.

Then they were gone, off down the beach.

Marcia sniffled away a tear. "It is *not* the prayer," she protested indignantly. "But they were so *nice*. . . ."

"Yes," said the Paulist at Old St. Mary's, "you may tell your fiancée to come in next Thursday at three to start her pre-marital instruction."

"You'll find her a tartar, Father," Paul grinned.

"Atheism can be the most fanatical of religions. Thank Heaven my duty is only to inform, not to convert her. I'm glad you're getting married, Paul. I don't think anything inside or outside of you will denounce the flesh so violently again. Did the analysis help you?"

"Somehow I never got around to it. Things started happening."

"Now this . . . ah . . . document," the Paulist went on. "Really extraordinary. *Lifegiver over us* . . . Terribly free, of course, but still an unusually stimulating, fresh translation of the *Pater Noster*. I've shown it to Father Massini—he was on the Bishops' Committee for the revised translation of the New Testament—and he was delighted. Where on earth did you get it?"

"Father, you wouldn't believe me if I told you."

"No?" asked the priest.

Damon Knight

CATCH THAT MARTIAN

The first person who got on the Martian's nerves, according to a survey I made just recently, was a Mrs. Frances Economy, about forty-two, five foot three, heavy-set, with prominent mole on left cheek, formerly of 302 West 46th Street, Manhattan. Mrs. Economy went to a neighborhood movie on the night of September 5th, and halfway through the first feature, just as she was scrambling for the last of her popcorn, zip—she wasn't there any more.

That is, she was only half there. She could still see the screen, but it was like a television with the sound off. The way she realized something had happened to her, she started stomping her feet, like you do when the sound goes off or the picture stops, and her feet didn't make any noise.

In fact, she couldn't feel the floor, just some kind of rubbery stuff that seemed to be holding her up. Same way with the arms of her chair. They weren't there, as far as her feeling them went.

Everything was dead still. She could hear her own breathing, and the gulp when she swallowed that last mouthful, and her heart beating if she listened close. That was all. When she got up and went out, she didn't step on anybody's feet—and she tried to.

Of course I asked her who was sitting next to her when it happened, but she doesn't remember. She didn't notice. It was like that with everybody.

Not to keep you in suspense, the Martian did it. We figured that out, later, and there still isn't any proof but it has to be that way. This Martian, the way it figures, looks just like anybody else. He could be the little guy with the derby hat and the sour expression, or the girl with the china-blue eyes, or the old gent with the chin spinach and glasses on a string—or anybody.

But he's a Martian. And being a Martian, he's got this power that people haven't got. If he feels like it, he just looks at you cockeyed, and zip—you're in some other dimension. I don't know what the scientists would call it, the Fourth or Fifth Dimension, or what, but I call it the next-door dimension because it seems it's right next door—you can see into it. In other words, it's a place where other people can see you, but they can't hear you or touch you, unless they're ghosts, too, and there's nothing but some kind of cloudy stuff to walk around on. I don't know if that sounds good or what. It stinks. It's just plain dull.

One more thing. He annoys easy. You crunch popcorn in his ear, he doesn't like that. You step on his toe, same thing. Say, "Hot enough for you?" or slap him on the back when he's got sunburn, serve him a plate of soup with your finger in it—zip.

The way we figured out it's a Martian, who else could it be? And nobody ever noticed him, so it must be he looks like anybody else. The way we know he annoys easy, there was eighteen "ghosts" wandering around when it first came to the attention of the public, during the early morning of September 6th. That was about eleven hours after he got Mrs. Economy.

Thirteen of them were up at Broadway and 49th, walking through traffic. They went right through the cars. By nine o'clock there were two wrecks on that corner and a busted hydrant gushing water all over. The ghost people walked through it and didn't get wet.

Three more showed up in front of a big delicatessen near 72nd Street and Amsterdam Avenue, just looking in the window. Every once in a while one of them would reach in through the glass and grab for something, but it was always no dice.

The other two were sailors. They were out in the harbor, walking on water and thumbing their noses at petty officers aboard the ships that were anchored there.

The first eight patrolmen who reported all this got told they would be fired if they ever came on duty drunk again. But by ten-thirty it was on the radio, and then WPIX sent a camera crew up, and by the time the afternoon papers came out there were so many people in Times Square that we had to put a cordon around the ghosts and divert traffic.

The delicatessen window up on Amsterdam got busted from the crowd leaning against it, or some guy trying to put his hand through the way the three ghosts did, we never figured out which. There were about sixty tugs, launches and rowboats in the harbor, trying to get close enough to the sailors—and three helicopters.

One thing we know, the Martian must have been in that crowd on Times Square, because between one and one-thirty P.M., seven more ghosts wandered through the barrier and joined the other ones. You could tell they were mad, but of course you couldn't tell what they were saying.

Then there were some more down by Macy's in the afternoon, and a few in Greenwich Village, and by evening we had lost count. The guesses in the papers that night ran from three hundred to a thousand. It was the *Times* that said three hundred.

The next day there was just nothing else at all in the papers, or on the radio or TV. Bars did an all-time record business. So did churches.

The Mayor appointed a committee to investigate. The Police Commissioner called out special reserves to handle the mobs. The Governor was understood to say he was thinking about declaring a statewide emergency, but all he got in most papers was half a column on page four. Later on he denied the whole thing.

Everybody had to be asked what he thought, from Einstein to Martin and Lewis. Some people said mass hysteria, some said the end of the world, some said the Russians.

Winchell was the first one to say in print that it was a Martian. I had the same idea myself, but by the time I got it all worked out, I was too late to get the credit.

I was handicapped, because all this time I still hadn't seen one of the ghosts yet. I was on Safe, Loft and Truck—just promoted last spring from a patrolman—and while I was on duty I never got near any of the places where they were congregating. In the evening I had to take care of my mother.

But my brain was working. I had this Martian idea, and I kept thinking, thinking, all the time.

I knew better than to mention this to Captain Rifkowicz. All I would have to do was mention to him that I was thinking, and he would say, "With what, Dunlop, with what?" or something sarcastic like that. As for asking him to get me transferred to Homicide or Missing Persons, where I might get assigned to the ghost case, that was out. Rifkowicz says I should have been kept on a beat long enough for my arches to fall, in order to leave more room on top for brains.

So I was on my own. And that evening, when they started announcing the rewards, I knew I had to get the Martians. There was fifteen hundred dollars, voted by the City Council that afternoon, for whoever would find out what was making the ghosts and stop it. Because if it didn't stop, there would be eighteen thousand ghosts in a month, and over two hundred thousand in a year.

Then there was a bunch of private rewards, running from twenty-five bucks to five hundred, offered by people that had relatives among the departed. There was a catch to those, though—you had to get the relatives back.

All together, they added up to nearly five thousand. With that dough, I could afford to hire somebody to take care of Ma and maybe have some private life of my own. There was a cute waitress down on Varick Street, where I had lunch every day, and for a long time I had been thinking if I asked her to go out, maybe she would say yes. But what was the use of me asking her, if all I could do was have her over to listen to Ma talk?

The first thing I did, I got together all the newspaper stuff about the ghosts. I spread it out on the living room table and sorted it and started pasting it into a scrapbook. Right away I saw I had to have more information. What was in the papers was mostly stories about the crowds and the accidents and traffic tieups, plus interviews with people that didn't know anything.

What I wanted to know was—what were all these people doing when the Martian got them? If I knew that, maybe I could figure out some kind of a pattern, like if the Martian's pet peeve was back-slappers, or people who make you jump a foot when they sneeze, or whatever.

Another thing. I wanted to know all the times and places. From that, I could figure out what the Martian's habits were, if he had any, and with all of it together I could maybe arrange to be on the spot whenever he got sore. Then anybody except me who was there every time would have to be him.

I explained all this to Ma, hoping she would make a sacrifice and let me get Mrs. Proctor from across the hall to sit with her a few evenings. She didn't seem to get the picture. Ma never believes anything she reads in the papers, anyway, except the astrology column. The way it struck her, the whole thing was some kind of a plot, and I would be better to stay away from it.

I made one try, emphasizing about the money I would get, but all she said was, "Well, then why don't you just *tell* that Captain Rifkowicz he's got to *let* you earn that reward?"

Ma has funny ideas about a lot of things. She came over here from England when she was a girl, and it looks like she never did get to understand America. I knew that if I kept after her, she would start crying and telling me about all the things she did for me when I was a baby. That breaks me down every time.

So what I did next, I took the bull by the horns. I waited till Ma went to sleep and then I just walked out and hopped an uptown bus on Seventh Avenue. If I couldn't get off during the daytime, I would cut down my sleep for a while, that was all.

I was heading for Times Square, but at 27th I saw a crowd on the sidewalk. I got out and ran over there. Sure enough, in the middle of the crowd was two of the ghosts, a fat man with a soupstrainer mustache and a skinny woman with cherries on her hat. You could tell they were ghosts because the people were waving their hands through them. Aside from that, there was no difference.

I took the lady first, to be polite. I flashed the badge, and then I hauled out my notebook and wrote, "Name and address please," and shoved it at her.

She got the idea and looked through her bag for a pencil and an envelope. She scribbled, "Mrs. Edgar F. Walters, Schenectady, N. Y."

I asked her, "When did this happen to you and where?"

She wrote it was about one P.M. the afternoon before, and she was in Schrafft's on Broadway near 37th, eating lunch with her husband. I asked her if the fat man was her husband, and she said he was.

I then asked her if she could remember exactly what the two of them were doing right at the moment when it happened. She thought a while and then said she was talking and her husband was dunking his doughnut in his coffee. I asked her if it was the kind with powdered sugar and she said yes.

I knew then that I was on the right track. She was one of those little women with big jaws that generally seem to have loud voices and like to use them; and I always hated people who dunk those kind of doughnuts, myself.

I thanked them and went on uptown. When I got home that night, about four A.M. the next morning, I had fifteen interviews in my book. The incidents had taken place all over the midtown area. Six got theirs for talking, four on crowded sidewalks—probably for jostling or stepping on corns—two for yelling on a quiet street at two in the morning, one for dunking, one for singing to himself on a subway, one, judging by the look of him, for not being washed, and one for coming in late to a Broadway play. The six talkers broke down to three in restaurants, two in a newsreel movie, and one in Carnegie Hall while a concert was going on.

Nobody remembered who they were next to at the time, but I was greatly encouraged. I had a hunch I was getting warm already.

I got through the next day, the eighth, in a kind of daze, and don't think Rifkowicz didn't call my attention to it. I suppose I wasn't worth more than a nickel to the City that day, but I promised myself I would make it up later. For the moment, I ignored Rifkowicz.

On the radio and TV, there were two new developments. In my head, there was one.

First, the radio and TV. I ate lunch in a saloon so as to catch the latest news, even though I had to give up my daily glimpse of the waitress in the beanery. Two things were new. One, people had started noticing that a few things had turned into ghosts— besides people, I mean. Things like a barrel organ, and an automobile that had its horn stuck, and like that.

That made things twice as bad, of course, because anybody was liable to try to touch one of these ghost things and jump to the conclusion they were a ghost, themselves.

Two, the TV reporters were interviewing the ghosts, the same way I did, with paper and pencil. I picked up four more sets of questions and answers just while I was eating lunch.

The ghosts came over fine on TV, by the way. Somehow it looked even creepier on the screen, when you saw somebody's hand disappear into them, than it did when you saw it with your own eyes.

The development in my head was like this. Out of the fifteen cases I already had, and the four I got from TV, there were eight that happened on the street or in subways or buses, five in restaurants, and six in places of entertainment. Four *different* places of entertainment. Now, at first glance, that may not look like it means much. But I said to myself, what does this Martian do? He travels around from one place to another—that's normal. He eats—that's normal. But he goes to four different shows that I know about in three days—and I know just nineteen cases out of maybe a thousand!

It all fitted together. Here is this Martian, he's never been here before —we know that because he just now started making trouble. The way I see it, these Martians look us over for a while from a distance, and then they decide to send one Martian down to New York to study us close up. Well, what's the first thing he does, being that he wants to find out all about us? He goes to the movies. And concerts and stage plays too, of course, because he wants to try everything once. But probably he sees two or three double features a day. It stands to reason.

So there he is in the movie, watching and listening so he shouldn't miss anything important, and some customer in the next seat starts making loud comments to her boy friend, rattling cellophane, and snapping her bag open and shut every five seconds to find a kleenex. So he flips her into the next dimension where she can make all the noise she wants without bothering him.

And that's the reason why there are so many ghosts that got theirs in the movies and places like that. On the streets of New York City you can walk for miles without running into more than two or three really obnoxious characters. But in any kind of theater there's *always* somebody talking, or coughing, or rattling paper. It stands to reason.

I went even further than that. I checked with my notes and then looked in a copy of *Cue* magazine to find out what was playing at each of these theaters when the Martian was there.

I found out that the play was a long-run musical—the concert was musical, naturally—and one of the two movies was a Hollywood remake of a musical comedy. The other was a newsreel.

There it was—I as good as had him. Then I got another idea and went back through my notes to find out where the theater victims had been sitting. The guy in Carnegie Hall had been in the balcony; that's where you hear best, I guess. But the other five had all been sitting down front, in the first four rows.

The little guy was nearsighted.

That's the way I was thinking about him now—a little nearsighted guy who liked music better than Westerns, and was used to some place where everybody's careful not to bother anybody else. It was hard not to feel sorry for him; after all, some people that come from places closer than Mars have a hard time in New York.

But it was me against him. That night the total rewards were up to almost twenty thousand dollars.

I thought of one thing I could do right away. I could write to the Mayor to make an announcement that if people didn't want to be ghosts, they should keep from making unnecessary noise or being pests, especially in theaters. But one, he probably wouldn't pay any attention to me, and two, if he did, twenty thousand other guys would be following my lead before I could turn around, and one of them would probably catch the Martian before I did.

That night, I did the same as before. I waited till Ma was sleeping, then went out to a movie on Broadway. It was a first-run house, they had a musical playing, and I sat down front.

But nothing happened. The Martian wasn't there.

I felt pretty discouraged when I got home. My time was running out and there are over three hundred theaters in Manhattan. I had to start working faster.

I lay awake for a long while, worrying about it in my head, and finally I came to one of the most important decisions in my life. The next morning I was going to do something I never did before—call in and pretend like I was sick. And I was going to stay sick until I found the Martian.

I felt bad about it and I felt even worse in the morning, when Rifkowicz told me to take it easy till I got well.

After breakfast, I got the papers and made a lists of shows on my way uptown. I went to one on 42nd Street first—it was a musical picture about some composer named Handle, and the second feature was a comedy, but it had Hoagy Carmichael in it, so I figured I should stay for that too. I sat in the fifth row. There was plenty of coughing going on, but nobody got turned into a ghost. I enjoyed both pictures.

Then I had lunch and went to another musical, on Broadway. I drew another blank.

My eyes were beginning to bother me a little from sitting so close to the screen, so I thought I would just go to a newsreel movie and then walk around a while before dinner. But when I got out of the newsreel I began to feel jittery, and I went straight to another double feature. The Martian wasn't there, either.

I had seen plenty of ghosts standing around on the streets, but they were all just standing there looking kind of lost and bewildered, the way they did after a while. You could tell a new victim because he would be rushing here and there, shoving his hands through things, trying to talk to people, and so on.

One thing I forgot to mention. Everybody was wondering now how these ghosts got along without eating. In this dimension where they were, there wasn't any food—there wasn't *anything*, just the stuff like rubbery clouds that they were standing on. But they all claimed they weren't hungry or thirsty, and they all seemed to be in good shape. Even the ones that had been ghosts now for four days.

When I got out of that last movie, it was about eight in the evening. I was feeling low in my mind, but I still had a healthy appetite. I started wandering around the side streets of Broadway, looking for a restaurant that wasn't too crowded or too expensive. I passed a theater that was on my list, except I knew I was too late to get a ticket for it. It was the premiere of the newest Rodgers and Hammerstein show, and the lobby and half the sidewalk were full of customers.

I went on past, feeling gloomier because of all the bright lights and excitement, and then I heard something funny. Without paying any attention, I had been listening to one of those raspy-voiced barkers inside the lobby going, "GETcha program here." Now, all of a sudden, he said, "GETch—" and stopped.

I turned around, with a funny prickling up the back of my spine. The voice didn't start up again. Just as I started back toward the lobby, a ghost came out of the crowd. There was no doubt about him being a ghost—he ran through people.

He had a bunch of big booklets with slick covers under his arm, and his mouth was wide open like he was shouting. Then he showed his teeth, and his face got all red, and he lifted the booklets in both hands and threw them away as hard as he could. *They* went through people, too.

The ghost walked away with his hands shoved into his pockets. I didn't try to stop him. I ran into that lobby, I shoved my badge at the ticket taker, and told him to find me the manager, quick.

When the manager came up, I grabbed him by the lapels and said, "I got reason to believe there's a dangerous criminal going to be in this audience tonight. With your cooperation, we'll get him." He looked worried, so I said, "There won't be any trouble. You just put me where I can see the front pews and leave the rest to me."

He said, "I can't give you a seat. The house is completely sold out."

I told him, "Okay, put me back in the wings, or whatever you call them."

He argued, but that's what he did. We went down the side aisle, through the orchestra pit and through a little door that went under the stage. Then we went up a little stairway to backstage, and he put me right at the edge of the stage, up front, where I could peek out at the audience.

There was a million people running back there behind the curtain, actors and chorus girls, guys in their shirt sleeves and guys in overalls. I could hear the hum out front—people were beginning to fill the seats —and I wanted that curtain to go up the worst way.

It took about a century, but finally the actors took their places, and the band suddenly started playing, and the curtain went up.

I understand that show is still playing to standing room only, even with all the trouble that's happened since then, but I didn't pay any attention to it and I couldn't even tell you what it was about. I was watching the front four rows, trying to memorize every face I saw.

Right in the middle there were three that I paid more attention to than the rest. One of them was a young blonde girl with blue eyes like the color of Ma's fancy china that she brought with her from the old country. Another was an old gent with chin spinach and glasses on a string. The third was a little guy with a sour expression and a derby hat.

I don't know why I picked out those three, except maybe it was a hunch. Maybe I was looking at the blonde girl just because she was pretty, but then again, I never saw eyes just that color before or since. It could be that Martians have china-blue eyes; how would I know? I might have had some wild idea that the old guy could be the Martian and was wearing the frizzy white whiskers because Martians don't have chins exactly like us. And I think I picked on the little guy because he fitted the picture I already had in my head. And the way he was clutching that derby in his lap, like it was made of gold—I was thinking to myself, maybe he's got some kind of ray gun built into that hat; maybe that's how he does it.

I admit that I wasn't thinking very logical—I was too excited—but I never took my eyes off that audience for a second.

I was waiting for somebody to start coughing or something and get turned into a ghost. When that happened, I would be watching the people, and if I was lucky I might see who was looking at the victim when it happened.

That's what I was waiting for. What I got was a sniff of smoke and then somebody screaming and yelling, "Fire!"

Half the audience was on their feet in a second. I looked up, and sure enough there was smoke pouring out at the back of the room. Some more women screamed and the stampede was on.

The girls on stage stopped dancing and the band stopped playing. Somebody—some actor—ran out on the stage and started saying, "Ladies and gentlemen, your attention please. *Walk*, do not run, to the nearest exit. There is no danger. *Walk*, do not run—"

I lost my head. Not on account of the fire—I knew the actor was right, and the only bad thing that could happen would be people trampling each other to death to get out of there. But the seats were emptying fast and it struck me all of a sudden that I didn't know my way through that tangle of scenery backstage—by the time I got down the stairs and out into the auditorium, the Martian might be gone.

I felt cold all over. I didn't even stop to remember that I didn't have to go back the way I came, because there were little steps right at the side of the stage. I ran out from behind the wings and started to jump over the musicians. At that, I would have made it if I hadn't caught my toe in that little trough where the footlights are.

I had worse luck than that, even. I landed smack in the middle of the bass drum.

You never heard such a sound in your life. It sounded like the ceiling caved in. Sitting there, with my legs and arms sticking out of that drum, I saw the people turn around and look at me like they had been shot. I saw them all, the girl with the china-blue eyes, the old gent with the whiskers, the little guy with the derby, and a lot more. And then, suddenly, all the sounds stopped like when you turn off a radio.

The guy who owned the drum leaned over and tried to pull me out of it. He couldn't.

His hands went right through me.

It's like I said, this Martian annoys easy. I don't know what he did about all those women screaming—maybe he figured there was a good reason for that and left them alone. But when I hit that bass drum, it must have burned him good. You know, when you're excited already, a loud noise will make you jump twice as far.

That's about the only satisfaction I got—that I probably annoyed him the worst of anybody in New York City.

That and being so close to catching him.

The company here is nothing brag about—women that will talk your arm off and half your shoulder, and guys that say, "Peaceful enough for you?" and back-slappers, and people that hum to themselves—

Besides that, the place is dull as dishwater. Clouds to stand on, nothing to eat even if you wanted to eat, and nothing to do except stand around and watch the new ones come through. We can't even see much of New York any more, because it keeps getting mistier all the time—fading away, kind of, like maybe this dimension is getting a little farther away from the ordinary one every day.

I asked Mr. Dauth yesterday how he thought the whole thing would wind up. Mr. Dauth isn't bad. He's a big, cheerful guy, about fifty. The kind that likes good food and good beer and a lot of it. But he doesn't complain. He admits that his habit of sucking his teeth is aggravating and says maybe he deserved what he got, which you'll admit is big of him. So I talk to him a lot, and the other day, when we were watching a new batch that had just come through, I asked him where he thought it would all end.

He pursed his lips and frowned like he was thinking it over, and then said that as far as he could see, there wasn't any human being that was perfect. Anybody is liable to do something aggravating sooner or later. That's the way people are.

"And this Martian of yours seems to be thorough," he said. "Very thorough. It might take him years to get through studying the Earth."

"And then what?" I asked him.

"Well," he said, "eventually, if he keeps it up long enough, we'll *all* be over here."

I hope he's right. Now that I come to think of it, that cute waitress I mentioned has a habit of setting down a coffee cup so half of it slops into the saucer. . . .

If he's right, all I've got to do is wait.

It stands to reason.

———

RICHARD MATHESON

SHIPSHAPE HOME

"THAT JANITOR GIVES me the creeps," Ruth said when she came in that afternoon.

I looked up from the typewriter as she put the bags on the table and faced me. I was killing a second draft of a story.

"The creeps," I repeated.

"Yes, he does," she said. "That way he has of slinking around, like Peter Lorre."

"Peter Lorre," I said, still concentrating on my plotting.

"*Babe,*" she implored, "I'm serious. The man is a creep."

I snapped out of the creative fog with a blink.

"Hon, what can the poor guy do about his face?" I said. "Heredity. Give him a break."

She plopped down in a chair by the table and started to take out groceries, stacking cans on the table.

"Listen," she said.

I could smell it coming, that dead serious tone of hers which she isn't even aware of any more, but which comes every time she's about to make one of her "revelations" to me.

"Yes, dear," I said. I leaned one elbow on the typewriter and gazed at her patiently.

"You get that expression off your face," she said. "You always look at me as if I were an idiot child."

I smiled. Wanly.

"You'll be sorry," she said, "some night when that man creeps in with an axe and dismembers us."

"He's just a poor guy earning a living. He mops the halls, he stokes the furnaces, he—"

"We have oil heat," she said.

"If we had furnaces, he would stoke them. Let us have charity. He labors like ourselves. I write stories; he mops floors. Who can say which is the greater contribution to civilization?"

"Okay," she said with a surrendering gesture. "Okay, if you don't want to face facts."

"Which are?" I prodded. I decided it was best to get it out of her before it burned a hole in her mind.

Her eyes narrowed. "You listen to me. That man has some reason for being here. He's no janitor. I wouldn't be surprised if . . ."

"If this apartment house were just a front for a gambling establishment. A hideout for public enemies numbered one through fifteen. An abortion mill. A counterfeiter's lair. A murderer's rendezvous."

She was already in the kitchen thumping cans and boxes into the cupboard.

"Okay," she said, "*okay*," in that patient if-you-get-murdered-don't-come-to-me-for-sympathy voice. "Don't say I didn't try. If I'm married to a wall, I can't help it."

I came in and slid arms around her waist. I kissed her neck.

"Stop that," she said, turning around. "You can't change the subject this easily. The janitor is . . ."

"You're *serious*," I interrupted, startled.

Her face darkened. "I am. The man looks at me in a funny way."

"What way?" I asked.

She searched. "In . . . in *anticipation*."

I chuckled. "Can't blame him. Who wouldn't?"

"I don't mean that way."

"Remember the time you thought the milkman was a knife killer for the Mafia?"

"I don't care."

I kissed her neck again. "Let's eat."

She groaned. "Why do I try to tell you anything?"

"Because you love me."

She closed her eyes. "I give up," she said quietly, with the patience of a saint under fire.

"Come on, hon. We have enough troubles."

She shrugged. "Oh, all right."

"Good," I said. "When are Phil and Marge coming?"

"Six," she said. "I got pork."

"Roast?"

"Mmmm."

"I'll buy that."

"You already did."

"I must get down to the typewriter again so we can afford it."

While I squeezed out another page, I heard her muttering to herself in the kitchen. All that came through was a grim: "Murdered in our beds or something."

"No, it's fluky," Ruth analyzed as we sat having dinner that night.

I grinned at Phil and he grinned back.

"I think so, too," Marge agreed. "Whoever heard of charging only sixty-five a month for a five-room apartment, furnished? Stove, refrigerator, washer—it's fantastic!"

"Girls," I said, "let's not quibble. Let's take advantage."

"Oh!" Ruth tossed her pretty blonde head. "If a man said, 'Here's a million dollars for you, old man,' you'd probably take it."

"I most definitely would take it," I admitted. "I would then run like hell."

"You're naive," she said. "You think everybody is Santa Claus."

"It *is* a little funny," Phil said, "Think about it, Rick."

I thought about it. A five-room apartment, brand-new, furnished in even better than good taste right down to a couple of sets of expensive dishes...

I pursed my lips. A guy can get lost writing about the bars on Mars. Maybe it was true. I could see their point. Of course, I wouldn't show it, though. And spoil Ruth's and my little game of war? Never.

"I think they charge too much," I said.

"Oh, Lord!" Ruth was taking it straight, as she usually did. "Too much? Five rooms yet! Furniture, dishes, linens, a television set! What do you want, a swimming pool?"

"A small one would be good enough."

She looked at Marge and Phil. "Let us discuss this thing quietly. Let us pretend that the fourth voice we hear is nothing but the wind in the eaves."

"I am the wind in the eaves," I said.

"Listen," Ruth restated her forebodings, "what if the place were a fluke? I mean, what if they just want people here for a coverup? That would explain the rent. You remember the rush on this place when they started renting?"

I remember as well as Phil and Ruth and Margie. The only reason we'd got apartments was we all happened to be walking past the place when the janitor put out the renting sign. The four of us had gone right in. I remember our amazement, our delight, at the rental. Why, we'd been paying more than double for half the size and ratty furniture, besides.

Phil and Marge and Ruth and I were the first tenants. The next day was like the Alamo under attack. It's a little hard to get an apartment these days.

"I say there's something funny about it," Ruth finished. "And did you ever notice that janitor?"

"He's a creep," I contributed.

"He *is*," Marge laughed. "My God, he's something out of a B picture. Those eyes! He looks like Peter Lorre."

"See!" Ruth was triumphant.

"Kids," I said, raising a hand of weary conciliation, "if there's something foul going on behind our backs, let's allow it to go on. We aren't being asked to help out or suffer by it. We are living in a nice spot for a nice rent. What are we going to do—look into it and maybe spoil it?"

"What if there are designs on us?" Ruth demanded.

"What designs, hon?" I asked.

"I don't know," she said. "But I sense something."

"Remember the time you sensed the bathroom was haunted? It was a mouse. I told you ghosts don't haunt bathrooms. Well, anybody who wants to make a career out of being sinister doesn't go in for janitoring. Limits his scope too much."

She started clearing off the dishes. "Are you married to a blind man too?" she asked Marge.

"Men are all blind," Marge said, accompanying my poor man's seer into the kitchen. "We must face it and be brave."

Phil and I lit cigarettes.

"No kidding now," I said, so the girls couldn't hear, "do you think there's anything wrong?"

He shrugged. "I don't know, Rick," he admitted. "I will say this—it's pretty strange to rent a furnished place for so little."

Yeah, I thought, awake at last.

Strange was the word.

I stopped for a chat with our strolling cop the next morning. Johnson walks around the neighborhood, afternoons. There are vicious gangs in the vicinity, he told me, traffic is heavy and, besides, the kids need watching after three in the afternoon.

He's a good Joe, lots of fun. I chat with him every day when I go out for anything.

"My wife suspects foul doings in our apartment house," I told him.

"This is my suspicion," Johnson said, dead sober. "It is my unwilling conclusion that, within those walls, six-year-olds are being forced to weave baskets by candle light."

"Under the whip hand of a gaunt old hag," I added.

He nodded sadly. Then he looked around, plotter-like.

"You won't tell anyone will you?" he begged. "I want to crack the case all by myself."

I patted his shoulder. "Johnson," I said, "your secret is locked behind these iron lips."

"I am grateful," he said.

We laughed.

"How's the wife?" he asked.

"Suspicious," I said. "Investigating. Curious."

"Everything is normal, then."

"Right. I guess I'll really start worrying when she stops acting like this."

"What is it she really suspects?"

I grinned. "She thinks the rent is too cheap. Everybody around here, she claims, pays a lot more for a lot less."

"Is that right?" Johnson said.

"Yeah," I said, punching his arm. "Don't *you* tell anybody. I don't want to lose a good deal."

Then I went to the store.

Ruth said, "I knew it. I *knew* it."

She gazed intently at me over a pan of soggy clothes.

"You knew what, hon?" I wanted to know, putting down the package of second sheets I'd gone out to buy.

"This place is a fluke." She raised her hand warningly. "Don't you say a word. You just listen to me."

I sat down. "Yes, dear. Not a word."

"I found engines in the basement," she said, and then waited for a reaction.

"What kind of engines, dear? Fire engines?"

Her lips tightened. "Come on, now," she said, getting a little burned up. "I saw the things."

She meant it.

"I've been down there too, hon," I said. "How come I never saw any engines?"

She looked around. I didn't like the way she did it. She nodded as if she really thought someone might be lurking at the window, listening.

"This is *under* the basement," she said.

I looked very dubious.

She stood up. "Damn it! You come on and I'll *show* you!"

She held my hand as we went through the hall and into the elevator. She stood grimly by me as we descended, my hand tight in her grip.

"When did you see them?" I asked, trying to make conversation.

"When I was washing in the laundry down there," she said. "In the hallway, I mean, when I was bringing the clothes back. I was coming to the elevator and I saw a doorway. It was a little open."

"Did you go in?" I asked.

She looked irritably at me.

"You went in," I said.

"I went down the steps there and it was light and . . ."

"And you saw engines."

"That's right."

"Big ones?"

The elevator stopped and the doors slid open. We went out.

"I'll show you how big," she said. It was a blank wall. "It's here."

I looked at her. I tapped the wall. "Honey," I said.

"Don't you dare say it!" she snapped. "Have you ever heard of doors in a wall?"

"Was this door in the wall?"

"The wall probably slides over it," she said, starting to tap. It sounded solid to me. "Darn it! I saw it, I tell you. I can just hear what you're going to say."

I didn't say it. I just stood there watching her.

"Lose something?"

The janitor's voice behind us *was* sort of like Lorre's, low and insinuating.

Ruth gasped, caught way off guard. I jumped a bit myself.

"My wife thinks there's a—"

"I was showing him the right way to hang a picture," Ruth interrupted hastily. "*That's* the way, babe." She turned toward me. "You put the nail in at an angle, not straight in. Now do you understand?"

The janitor smiled.

"See you," I said awkwardly. I felt his eyes on us as we walked back to the elevator.

When the doors shut, Ruth turned quickly.

"Good night!" she stormed. "What are you trying to do, get him on us?"

"What . . .?"

"Never mind," she said. "There are engines down there. Huge engines. I saw them. And he knows about them."

"Baby," I said, "why don't . . ."

"Look at me," she said quickly.

I looked.

"Do you think I'm crazy?" she asked. "Come on, now. Never mind the hesitation."

I sighed. "I think you're imaginative."

She looked disgusted. "You're as bad as . . ."

"You and Galileo," I added. "It's tough being ahead of your generation. Happens, though, to every genius."

"I'll show you those things," she said. "We're going down there again tonight, when that janitor is asleep. If he's *ever* asleep."

I got worried. "Honey, cut it out. You'll get me started, too."

"Good," she said. "*Good.* I thought it would take a hurricane."

I sat staring at my typewriter all afternoon, nothing coming out. But concern.

I didn't get it. Was she actually serious? All right, I thought, I'll take it seriously. She saw a door that was left open. Accidentally. That was obvious. If there really were huge engines under the apartment house. as she said, then the people who built them damn well wouldn't want anyone to know about them.

East 7th Street. An apartment house. And huge engines underneath it. Now where's the sense in that?

She was shaking. Her face was white. She stared at me like a kid who's read her first horror story.

"*The janitor has three eyes!*"

"Honey," I said. I put my arms around her. She was really scared. I felt sort of scared myself. And not about the janitor having an extra eye, either.

I didn't say anything at first. What can you say when your wife comes up with something like that?

She shook a long time. Then she spoke in a quiet voice, a timid voice. "You don't believe me."

I swallowed. "Baby," I said helplessly.

"We're going down tonight," she stated. "This is really important now. It's nothing to joke about."

"I don't think we should . . ." I started to say.

"I'm going down there." She sounded edgy now, a little hysterical. "I tell you there are engines down there. Goddamn it, there are *engines!*"

She started crying now. I patted her head, rested it against my shoulder.

"All right, baby," I said. "All right."

She tried to tell me through her tears, but it wouldn't work. Later, when she'd calmed down, I listened. I didn't want to get her upset. I figured the safest way was just to listen.

"I was walking through the hall downstairs," she said. "I thought maybe there was some afternoon mail. You know, once in a while our mailman will . . ."

"I know, hon," I soothed. "He comes around with another mail when the deliveries are heavy."

She stopped. "Never mind that. What matters is that I walked past the janitor."

"And?" I asked, afraid of what was coming.

"He smiled," she said. "You know the way he does. Sweet and murderous."

I didn't argue the point. I still didn't think the janitor was anything but a harmless guy who had the misfortune to be born with a face that was strictly from Charles Addams.

"So?" I said. "Then what?"

"I walked past him. I felt myself shivering, because he looked at me as if he knew something about me I didn't even know. I don't care what you say, that's the feeling I got. And then . . ."

She shuddered. I took her hand.

"Then?"

"I felt him looking at me."

I'd felt that, too, when he had found us in the basement. I knew what she meant. You actually felt the guy looking at you.

"All right," I said, "I'll buy that."

"You won't buy this," she went on grimly. "When I turned around to look, he was walking away from me."

"Oh, you both turned at the same time?"

She slapped the table. "I turned. He didn't."

"But you just said—"

"*He was looking at me.* He was walking away and his head was to the front and he was looking at me."

I sat there numbly. I patted her hand without even knowing I was doing it.

"How, hon?" I heard myself asking her.

"There was an eye in the back of his head."

"*Hon!*" I said.

She closed her eyes. She clasped her hands after drawing away the one I was holding. She pressed her lips together. I saw a tear wriggle out from under her left eyelid and roll down her cheek. She was white.

"I saw it," she said quietly. "So help me, I saw that eye."

I don't know why I went on with it. Self-torture, I guess. I really wanted to forget the whole thing, pretend it never even happened, but I couldn't leave it at that.

"Why haven't we noticed it before, Ruth?" I asked. "We've seen the back of the man's head before."

"Have we?" she said. "Have we?"

"Sweetheart, *somebody* must have seen it. Do you think there's never anybody behind him?"

"His hair parted, Rick, and before I ran away, I saw the hair going back over it. So you couldn't see it."

What could a guy possibly say to his wife when she talks to him like that? You're nuts? You're batty? Or the old, tired, "You've been working too hard"? She hadn't been working too hard. I make a living on my writing. Then, again, maybe she *had* been working overtime.

With her imagination.

"Are you going down with me tonight?" she asked.

"All right," I said quietly. "All right, sweetheart. Now will you go and lie down for a while?"

"But it's nothing like that."

"Sweetheart, go and lie down," I said firmly. "I'll go with you tonight, but I want you to lie down now."

She went into the bedroom and I heard the springs squeak as she sat down, then again when she drew up her legs and fell back on the pillow.

I went in a little later to put a comforter over her. She was looking at the ceiling. I didn't say anything to her. I don't think she wanted to talk to me.

"What can I do?" I said to Phil.

Ruth was asleep. I'd sneaked across the hall to Phil's apartment.

"Maybe she saw them," he said. "Isn't it possible?"

"Yeah, sure," I said. "And you know what else is possible."

"Look, you want to go down and see the janitor? You want to . . ."

"No," I said. "There's nothing we can do."

"You're going down to the basement with her?"

"If she keeps insisting," I said. "Otherwise, no."

"When you go, come and get us."

I frowned at him curiously. "You mean the thing is getting you, too?"

He looked at me in a funny way. I saw his throat move.

"Don't tell anyone," he said.

He glanced around. Then he turned back.

"Marge told me the same thing," he added. "She said the janitor has three eyes."

I went out after supper for some ice cream. Johnson was still walking around.

"They're working you overtime," I said as he started to walk beside me.

"They expect some trouble from the local gangs," he explained in that serious kidding way of his.

"I never saw any trouble," I said distractedly.

He shrugged. "They say to come here, I come."

"Mmmm."

"How's your wife?" he added.

"Fine," I lied.

"She still think the apartment is a front?"

I swallowed. "No," I said. "I've broken her of that. I think she was just needling me all the time."

He nodded and left me at the corner. For some reason, I couldn't keep my hands from shaking all the way home. I kept looking over my shoulder, too.

"Rick, it's time," Ruth said.

I grunted and rolled on my side. She nudged me. I woke up sort of hazy and looked automatically at the clock. The radium numbers told me it was almost four o'clock.

"You want to go *now*?" I asked, too sleepy to be tactful.

There was a silence. That woke me up.

"Do you?" I insisted.

"I'm going," she said quietly.

I looked at her in the half-darkness, my heart starting to do a drum beat too heavily. My mouth and throat felt dry.

"All right," I said, "wait till I get dressed."

She was dressed already. I heard her in the kitchen making some coffee while I put on my clothes. There was no noise. I mean it didn't sound as if her hands were shaking. She spoke lucidly, too. But when I stared into the bathroom cabinet mirror, I saw a worried husband. I washed my face with cold water and combed my hair.

"Thanks," I said as she handed me the cup of steaming coffee. I stood there, nervous before my own wife.

She didn't drink any coffee.

"Are you awake?" she asked. I nodded. I noticed the flashlight and the screwdriver on the kitchen table. I finished the coffee.

"I'm ready," I said. "Let's get it over with."

I felt her hand on my arm.

"I hope you'll . . ." she started. Then she turned her face.

"What?"

"Nothing," she said. "We'd better go."

The house was dead quiet as we went into the hall. We were halfway to the elevator when I remembered Phil and Marge. I told her.

"We can't wait," she said. "It'll be light soon."

"I'll just see if they're up," I said. "It won't take a minute."

She didn't say anything. She stood by the elevator door. I went down the hall and knocked quietly on the door of their apartment. There was no answer. I glanced up the hall.

She was gone.

I felt my heart lurch. Even though I was sure there was no danger in the basement, it scared me.

"Ruth!" I called out and headed for the stairs.

"Wait a second!" I heard Phil yell from his door.

"I can't!" I shouted back, charging down.

When I got to the basement, I saw the open elevator door and the light streaming out from the inside. Empty.

I looked around for a light switch, but there wasn't any. I started to move along the dark passage as fast as I could.

"Hon!" I whispered urgently. "Ruth, where are you?"

I found her standing before a doorway in the hall. It was open.

"Now stop acting as if I were insane," she said coldly.

I gaped and felt a hand pressing against my cheek. It was my own.

She was right. There were stairs. And it was lighted down there. I heard sounds—sounds of metallic clickings and strange buzzings.

I took her hand.

"I'm sorry, baby," I said. "I'm very sorry."

Her hand tightened in mine. "Never mind that now. There's something queer about all this."

I nodded. Then I said, "Yeah," realizing she couldn't see my nod in the darkness.

"Let's go down," she said.

"I don't think we better," I argued.

"We've got to know," she insisted as if the entire problem had been assigned to her.

"But there must be someone down there."

"We'll just peek."

She pulled me and I guess I felt too ashamed of myself to pull back. We started down. Then it came to me—if she was right about the doorway and the engines, she must be right about the janitor and he must really have . . .

I felt a little detached from reality. East 7th Street, I told myself again. An apartment house on East 7th Street. It's all real.

I couldn't quite convince myself.

We stopped at the bottom and just stared.

Engines, all right. Fantastic engines. And, as I looked at them, their structure, it occurred to me what kind of engines they were. I'd written some science articles and read a lot more.

I felt dizzy. You can't adapt quickly to something like that, to be plunged from a stone apartment house basement into this . . . this storehouse of energy.

It got me.

I don't know how much time passed, but I finally realized we had to get out of there and report it. We had to do something. First of all, get out, though.

"Come on," I said.

We moved up the steps, my mind working like an engine itself, fast and furious, spinning out ideas and theories. All of them crazy. All of them acceptable. Even the craziest one.

It was when we were moving down the basement hall.

We saw the janitor coming at us.

It was still dark, even with the little light that was coming from the early morning haze. I grabbed Ruth and we ducked behind a stone pillar. We stood there holding our breaths, listening to the sound of his approaching shoes.

He passed us. He was holding a flashlight, but he didn't play it around. He just moved straight for the open door.

As he came into the patch of light from the open doorway, he stopped. His head was turned away. The guy was facing the stairway.

But he was looking at us.

It knocked out what little breath I had left. I just stood there and stared at that eye in the back of his head. And, although there wasn't any face around it, that ghastly eye had a smile that went with it. A nasty, self-certain and frightening smile. He saw us and he was amused and didn't have to do a thing about it.

He went through the doorway and the door thudded closed behind him and the stone wall segment slid down and shut it from view.

We stood there shivering.

"You saw it," she finally said.

"Yes."

"He knows we saw those engines and still he didn't do anything."

We went on talking after we got in the elevator.

"Maybe there's nothing really wrong," I said, "Maybe . . ."

Then I stopped. I remembered those engines. I remembered what kind they were.

"What shall we do?" she asked, scared.

I put my arm around her for comfort. But I was scared, too.

"We'd better get out," I said. "Fast."

"Like this? Without packing?"

"We'll get our stuff together and leave before morning. I don't think they can do . . ."

"*They?*" she interrupted.

Why had I said that? But it had to be a group. The janitor couldn't have made or even assembled those engines all by himself.

I think it was the third eye that cemented my theory. And when we stopped in to see Phil and Marge and they asked us what happened, I told them what I thought. I don't think it surprised Ruth much. She probably had decided the same herself. What I said was:

"I think the house is a rocket ship."

Phil grinned, then stopped when he saw I wasn't trying to kid him.

"What?" Marge asked blankly, not getting it at all.

"I know it sounds crazy," I said, sounding more like my wife than she did, "but those engines are rocket engines. I don't know how they . . ." I shrugged helplessly at the whole idea. "All I know is that they're rocket engines."

"That doesn't mean it's a—a *ship?"* Phil finished weakly, switching from statement to question in mid-sentence.

"Yes," said Ruth.

And I shuddered. That seemed to settle it. She'd been right too often lately.

"What's the point?" Marge asked. "Why?"

"If you figure it out," said Ruth, "it makes sense."

We all turned toward her.

"How, baby?" I asked, afraid to be asking.

"That janitor," she said. "He's not a man. We know that. That third eye makes it a positive fact. I mean for sure."

"You telling me the guy actually *has* one?" Phil asked incredulously.

I nodded. "He has one," I said. "I saw it."

"Oh, my God," he said.

"He's not a man," Ruth repeated. "Humanoid, yes, but not from Earth. Except for the eye, he might look just about like us. But he might be completely different, so different that they'd change his form. Give him that extra eye just to keep track of us when we didn't know he was."

Phil ran a shaking hand through his hair. "This is crazy," he said.

He sank down into a chair. So did the girls.

I didn't. I felt uneasy about sticking around. I thought we should grab our hats and run. They didn't seem to feel in immediate danger. I finally decided it wouldn't hurt to wait until morning. Then I'd tell Johnson or somebody. Nothing could happen right now.

"This is crazy," Phil said again.

"I saw those engines," I stated. "They're really there. You can't get away from that fact."

"Listen," Ruth said, "they're probably extraterrestrials."

"What are you talking about?" Marge demanded irritably. She was good and afraid, I saw.

"Hon," I contributed weakly, "you've been reading too many science fiction magazines."

Her lips drew together. "You thought I was crazy when I suspected this

place. You thought so when I told you I saw those engines. You thought
so when I told you the janitor had three eyes. Well, I was right every
time. Now, lay off the imagination business. You need to do some guessing to explain all those things. Even you'll admit they don't happen every
day—as far as we know."

I shut up.

"What if they're from another planet?" she rephrased, for Marge's
benefit. "Suppose they want some Earth people to experiment on. To
observe . . ." she amended, though I don't know for whose benefit. But
the idea of being experimented on by three-eyed janitors from another
planet had something revolting about it.

"What better way," Ruth was saying, "of getting people than to build
a rocket ship that looks like an apartment house, rent it out cheap and
get it full of people fast?"

She looked at us without yielding an inch.

"And then," she said, "just wait until some morning, early, when
everybody is asleep and . . . goodby, Earth."

It was crazy, but I'd been shrewdly practical—and wrong—three times.
I couldn't afford to doubt now. It wasn't worth the risk. And I sort of felt
she was right.

"But the whole house?" Phil was saying. "How could they get it . . .
in the air?"

"If they're from another planet, they're probably centuries ahead of us
in space travel."

Phil started to answer. He faltered. Then he said, "But it doesn't *look*
like a ship."

"The house might be a shell over the ship," I said. "It probably is.
Maybe the ship just includes the bedrooms. That's all they'd need. That's
where everybody would be in the early morning hours if . . ."

"No," Ruth said. "They couldn't knock off the shell without attracting
too much attention."

We were all silent, laboring under a thick cloud of confusion and half-
formed fears. Half-formed because you can't shape your fears of something when you don't even know what it is.

"Suppose it *is* a building," Ruth said. "Suppose the ship is *outside*
of it."

Marge was practically lost. She got angry because she was lost.
"There's nothing outside the house. That's obvious!"

"Those people would be way ahead of us in science," Ruth said.
"Maybe they've mastered invisibility of matter."

We all squirmed at once, I think.

"Babe," I said.

"Is it possible?" Ruth challenged.

I sighed. "It's possible. I don't know what is or isn't any more."

We were quiet.

"Listen," Ruth said.

"No," I cut in. "You listen. I think maybe we're going overboard on this thing. But there *are* engines in the basement and the janitor *does* have three eyes. On the basis of that, I think we have enough reason to clear out. Tonight."

We all agreed on that anyway.

"We'd better tell everybody in the house," Ruth said. "We can't leave them here."

"It'll take too long," Marge argued.

"No, we have to," I said. "You pack, babe. I'll tell them."

I headed for the door and grabbed the knob.

It didn't turn.

A bout of panic drove through me. I grabbed at it and yanked hard. I thought for a second, fighting down fear, that it was locked on the inside. I checked.

It was locked on the outside.

Marge was ready to scream. You could sense it bubbling up in her.

"It's true," Ruth said, horrified. "Oh, my God, it's all true, then!"

I made a dash for the window.

The place began to vibrate, as if we were about to get hit by an earthquake. Dishes started to rattle and fall off their shelves. We heard a chair crash onto its side in the kitchen.

"What is it?" Marge cried.

Phil grabbed for her as she began to whimper. Ruth ran to me and we stood there, frozen, feeling the floor shake under our feet.

"The engines!" Ruth suddenly screamed. "They're going *now!*"

"They have to warm up!" was my wild guess. "We can still get out!"

I let go of Ruth and grabbed a chair. For some reason I felt that the windows would be automatically locked, too.

I hurled the chair through the glass. The vibrations were getting worse.

"Quick!" I shouted over the noise. "Out on the fire escape! Maybe we can make it!"

Impelled by panic and dread, Marge and Phil came running over the shaking floor. I almost shoved them out through the gaping window hole. Marge tore her skirt. Ruth cut her finger. I went last, dragged a glass dagger through my leg. I didn't even feel it, I was so keyed up.

I kept pushing them, hurrying them down the fire escape steps. Marge caught a heel in between two gratings and her shoe came off. She half limped, half fell down the orange-metal steps, her face white and twisted with fear. Ruth in her loafers clattered down behind Phil. I came last, shepherding them frantically.

We heard windows crashing above and below. We saw an older couple ahead of us crawl out hurriedly and start down. They held us up.

"Look out, will you!" Marge shouted at them in a fury.

They cast a frightened glance over their shoulders.

Ruth looked back at me. "Are you coming?" she asked quickly, her voice between a sob and a scream.

"I'm here," I said breathlessly. I felt as if I were going to collapse on the steps.

They seemed to go on forever.

At the bottom was a ladder. We saw the old lady drop from it and cry out in pain as her ankle twisted under her. Her husband climbed down and helped her up. The building was vibrating harshly now. We saw dust scaling out from between the bricks.

My voice joined the throng, all crying the same word: *"Hurry!"*

I saw Phil drop down. He caught Marge, who was sobbing in fright. I heard her half-articulate, "Oh, thank God!" as she landed. They started up the alleyway. Phil looked back over his shoulder at us, but Marge dragged him on.

"Let me go first!" I snapped quickly. Ruth stepped aside. I swung down the ladder and dropped, felt the sting in my insteps, a slight pain in my ankles. I looked up, extended my arms.

An old man behind Ruth was trying to shove her aside so he could jump down.

"Look out!" I yelled, like a raging animal, reduced suddenly by fear and concern. If I'd had a gun, I'd have shot him.

Ruth let the old man go by. He scrambled to his feet, breathing feverishly, and ran down the alley. The building was shaking and trembling. The air was filled with the roar of the engines now.

"Ruth!" I yelled.

She dropped and I caught her. We regained our balance and started up the alley. I could hardly breathe with that stitch in my side.

As we dashed into the street, we saw Johnson moving through the ranks of scattered people, trying to herd them together.

"Here now!" he was calling. "Take it easy!"

We ran up to him.

"Johnson!" I said. "The ship is . . ."

"Ship?" He looked blank.

"The house! It's a rocket ship! It's . . ." The ground shook wildly.

Johnson turned away to grab somebody running past.

My breath caught. Ruth gasped, then threw her hands over her face and shrieked in horror.

Johnson was still looking at us. With that third eye. The one that had a smile in it.

"No!" Ruth said. "No!"

And then the sky, which was growing light, grew dark. My head snapped around. Women were screaming their lungs out in terror. I looked in all directions.

Solid walls were blotting out the sky.

"We can't get out," she said. *"It's the whole block."*

And then the rockets started.

———

HOMO SOL

The seven thousand and fifty-fourth session of the Galactic Congress sat in solemn conclave in the vast semicircular hall on Eron, second planet of Arcturus.

Slowly, the president delegate rose to his feet. His broad Arcturian countenance flushed slightly with excitement, as he surveyed the surrounding delegates. His sense of the dramatic caused him to pause a moment or so before making the official announcement—for, after all, the entrance of a new planetary system into the great Galactic family is not a thing likely to happen twice in any one man's lifetime.

A dead silence prevailed during that pause. The two hundred and eighty-eight delegates—one from each of the two hundred and eighty-eight oxygen-atmosphere, water-chemistry worlds of the System—waited patiently for him to speak.

Beings of every manlike type and shape were there. Some were tall and polelike, some broad and burly, some short and stumpy. There were those with long, wiry hair, those with scanty gray fuzz covering head and face, others with thick, blond curls piled high, and still others entirely bald. Some possessed long, hair-covered trumpets of ears, others had tympanum membranes flush with their temples. There were those present with large gazellelike eyes of a deep-purple luminosity, others with tiny optics of a beady black. There was a delegate with green skin, one with an eight-inch proboscis and one with a vestigial tail. Internally, variation was almost infinite.

But all were alike in two things.

They were all Humanoid. They all possessed intelligence.

The president delegate's voice boomed out then: "Delegates! The system of Sol has discovered the secret of interstellar travel and by that act becomes eligible for entrance into the Galactic Federation."

A storm of approving shouts arose from those present and the Arcturian raised a hand for silence.

"I have here," he continued, "the official report from Alpha Centauri, on whose fifth planet the Humanoids of Sol have landed. The report is entirely satisfactory and so the ban upon travel into and communication with the Solarian System is lifted. Sol is free, and open to the ships of the Federation. Even now, there is in preparation an expedition to Sol, under the leadership of Joselin Arn of Alpha Centauri, to tender that System the formal invitation into the Federation."

He paused, and from two hundred and eighty-eight throats came the stentorian shout: "Hail, Homo Sol! Hail, Homo Sol! *Hail!*

It was the traditional welcome of the Federation for all new worlds.

Tan Porus raised himself to his full height of five feet two—he was tall for a Rigellian—and his sharp, green eyes snapped with annoyance.

"There it is, Lo-fan. For six months that damned freak squid from Beta Draconis IV has stumped me."

Lo-fan stroked his forehead gently with one long finger, and one hairy ear twitched several times. He had traveled eighty-five light years to be here on Arcturus II with the greatest psychologist of the Federation—and, more specifically, to see this strange mollusk whose reactions had stumped the great Rigellian.

He was seeing it now: a puffy, dull-purple mass of soft flesh that writhed its tentacular form in placid unconcern through the huge tank of water that held it. With unruffled serenity, it fed on the green fronds of an underwater fern.

"Seems ordinary enough," said Lo-fan.

"Ha!" snorted Tan Porus. "Watch this."

He drew the curtain and plunged the room into darkness. Only a dim blue light shone upon the tank, and in the murk the Draconian squid could barely be discerned.

"Here goes the stimulus," grunted Porus. The screen above his head burst into soft green light, focused directly upon the tank. It persisted a moment and gave way to a dull red and then almost at once to a brilliant yellow. For half a minute it shot raggedly through the spectrum and then, with a final glare of glowing white, a clear bell-like tone sounded.

And as the echoes of the note died away, a shudder passed over the squid's body. It relaxed and sank slowly to the bottom of the tank.

Porus pulled aside the curtain. "It's *sound* asleep," he growled. "Hasn't failed yet. Every specimen we've ever had drops as if shot the moment that note sounds."

"Asleep, eh? That's strange. Have you got the figures on the stimulus?"

"Certainly! Right here. The exact wave lengths of the lights required are listed, plus the length of duration of each light unit, plus the exact pitch of the sounded note at the end."

The other surveyed the figures dubiously. His forehead wrinkled and his ears rose in surprise. From an inner pocket, he drew forth a slide rule.

"What type nervous system has the animal?"

"Two-B. Plain, simple, ordinary Two-B. I've had the anatomists, physiologists, and ecologists check that until they were blue in the face. Two-B is all they get. Damn fools!"

Lo-fan said nothing, but pushed the center bar of the rule back and forth carefully. He stopped and peered closely, shrugged his shoulders, and reached for one of the huge volumes on the shelf above his head. He leafed through the pages and picked out numbers from among the close print. Again the slide rule.

Finally he stopped. "It doesn't make sense," he said helplessly.

"I know that! I've tried six times in six different ways to explain that reaction—and I failed each time. Even if I rig up a system that will explain its going to sleep, I can't get it to explain the specificity of the stimulus."

"It's highly specific?" questioned Lo-fan, his voice reaching the higher registers.

"That's the worst part of it," shouted Tan Porus. He leaned forward and tapped the other on the knee. "If you shift the wave length of any of the light units by fifty angstroms either way—any *one* of them—it doesn't sleep. Shift the length of duration of a light unit two seconds either way —it doesn't sleep. Shift the pitch of the tone at the end an eighth of an octave either way—it doesn't sleep. *But* get the right combination, and it goes straight into a coma."

Lo-fan's ears were two hairy trumpets, stiffly erect. "Galaxy!" he whispered. "How did you ever stumble on the combination?"

"I didn't. It happened at Beta Draconis. Some hick college was putting its freshmen through a lab period on light-sound reactions of molluscoids —been doing it for years. Some student runs through his light-sound combinations and his blasted specimen goes to sleep. Naturally, he's scared out of his wits and brings it to the instructor. The instructor tries it again on another squid—it goes to sleep. They shift the combination— nothing happens. They go back to the original—it goes to sleep. After they fooled around with it long enough to know they couldn't make head or tail of it, they sent it to Arcturus and wished it on me. It's six months since *I* had a real night's sleep."

A musical note sounded and Porus turned impatiently.

"What is it?"

"Messenger from the president delegate of Congress, sir," came in metallic tones from the telecaster on his desk.

"Send him up."

The messenger stayed only long enough to hand Porus an impressively sealed envelope and to say in hearty tone: "Great news, sir. The system of Sol has qualified for entrance."

"So what?" snorted Porus beneath his breath as the other left. "We all knew it was coming."

He ripped off the outer sheath of cello-fiber from the envelope and removed the sheaf of papers from within. He glanced through them and grimaced.

"Oh, *Rigel!*"

"What's wrong?" asked Lo-fan.

"Those politicians keep bothering me with the most inconsequential things. You'd think there wasn't another psychologist on Eron. Look! We've been expecting the Solarian System to solve the principle of the hyperatomo any century now. They've finally done it and an expedition of theirs landed on Alpha Centauri. At once, there's a politicians' holiday! We must send an expedition of our own to ask them to join the Federation. And, of course, we must have a psychologist along to ask them in a nice way so as to be sure of getting the right reaction, because, to be sure, there isn't a man in the army that ever gets proper training in psychology."

Lo-fan nodded seriously. "I know, I know. We have the same trouble out our way. They don't need psychology until they get into trouble and then they come running."

"Well, it's a cinch *I'm* not going to Sol. This sleeping squid is too important to neglect. It's a routine job, anyway—this business of raking in new worlds; a Type A reaction that any sophomore can handle."

"Whom will you send?"

"I don't know. I've got several good juniors under me that can do this sort of thing with their eyes closed. I'll send one of them. And meanwhile, I'll be seeing you at the faculty meeting tomorrow, won't I?"

"You will—and hearing me, too. I'm making a speech on the finger touch stimulus."

"Good! I've done work on it, so I'll be interested in hearing what you have to say. Till tomorrow, then."

Left alone, Porus turned once more to the official report on the Solarian System which the messenger had handed him. He leafed through it leisurely, without particular interest, and finally put it down with a sigh.

"Lor Haridin could do it," he muttered to himself. "He's a good kid—deserves a break."

He lifted his tiny bulk out of the chair and, with the report under his arm, left his office and trotted down the long corridor outside. As he stopped before a door at the far end, the automatic flash blazed up and a voice within called out to him to enter.

The Rigellian opened the door and poked his head inside. "Busy, Haridin?"

Lor Haridin looked up and sprang to his feet at once. "Great space, boss, no! I haven't had anything to do since I finished work on anger reactions. You've got something for me, maybe?"

"I have—if you think you're up to it. You've heard of the Solarian System, haven't you?"

"Sure! The visors are full of it. They've got interstellar travel, haven't they?"

"That's right. An expedition is leaving Alpha Centauri for Sol in a month. They'll need a psychologist to do the fine work, and I was thinking of sending you."

The young scientist reddened with delight to the very top of his hairless dome. "Do you mean it, boss?"

"Why not? That is—if you think you can do it."

"Of course I can." Haridin drew himself up in offended hauteur. "Type A reaction! I can't miss."

"You'll have to learn their language, you know, and administer the stimulus in the Solarian tongue. It's not always an easy job."

Haridin shrugged. "I still can't miss. In a case like this, translation need only be seventy-five percent effective to get ninety-nine and six tenths percent of the desired result. That was one of the problems I had to solve on my qualifying exam. So you can't trip me up that way."

Porus laughed. "All right, Haridin, I know you can do it. Clean up everything here at the university and sign up for indefinite leave. And if you can, Haridin, write some sort of paper on these Solarians. If it's any good, you might get senior status on the basis of it."

The junior psychologist frowned. "But, boss, that's old stuff. Humanoid reactions are as well known as . . . as— You *can't* write anything on them."

"There's always something if you look hard enough, Haridin. Nothing is well known; remember that. If you'll look at Sheet 25 of the report, for instance, you'll find an item concerning the care with which the Solarians armed themselves on leaving their ship."

The other turned to the proper page. "That's reasonable," said he. "An entirely normal reaction."

"Certainly. But they insisted on retaining their weapons throughout their stay, even when they were greeted and welcomed by fellow Humanoids. *That's* quite a perceptible deviation from the normal. Investigate it—it might be worth while."

"As you say, boss. Thanks a lot for the chance you're giving me. And say—how's the squid coming along?"

Porus wrinkled his nose. "My sixth try folded up and died yesterday. It's disgusting." And with that, he was gone.

Tan Porus of Rigel trembled with rage as he folded the handful of papers he held in two and tore them across. He plugged in the telecaster with a jerk.

"Get me Santins of the math department immediately," he snapped.

His green eyes shot fire at the placid figure that appeared on the visor almost at once. He shook his fist at the image.

"What on Eron's the idea of that analysis you sent me just now, you Betelguesian slime worm?"

The image's eyebrows shot up in mild surprise. "Don't blame me, Porus. They were your equations, not mine. Where did you get them?"

"Never mind where I got them. That's the business of the psychology department."

"All right! And solving them is the business of the mathematics department. That's the seventh set of the damnedest sort of screwy equations I've ever seen. It was the worst yet. You made at least seventeen assumptions which you had no right to make. It took us two weeks to straighten you out, and finally we boiled it down—"

Porus jumped as if stung. "I know what you boiled it down to. I just tore up the sheets. You take eighteen independent variables in twenty equations, representing two months of work, and solve them out at the bottom of the last, last page with that gem of oracular wisdom—'a' equals 'a.' All that work—and all I get is an identity."

"It's still not my fault, Porus. You argued in circles, and in mathematics that means an identity and there's nothing you can do about it." His lips twitched in a slow smile. "What are you kicking about, anyway? 'A' does equal 'a,' doesn't it?"

"Shut *up!*" The telecaster went dead, and the psychologist closed his lips tightly and boiled inwardly. The light signal above the telecaster flashed to life again.

"What do you want now?"

It was the calm, impersonal voice of the receptionist below that answered him. "A messenger from the government, sir."

"Damn the government! Tell them I'm dead."

"It's important, sir. Lor Haridin has returned from Sol and wants to see you."

Porus frowned. "Sol? What Sol? Oh, I remember. Send him up, but tell him to make it snappy."

"Come in, Haridin," he said a little later, voice calmer, as the young Arcturian, a bit thinner, a bit more weary than he had been six months earlier when he left the Arcturian System, entered.

"Well, young man? Did you write the paper?"

The Arcturian gazed intently upon his fingernails. "No, sir!"

"Why not?" Porus' green eyes peered narrowly at the other. "Don't tell me you've had trouble."

"Quite a bit, boss." The words came with an effort. "The psychological board itself has sent for you after hearing my report. The fact of the matter is that the Solarian System has . . . has refused to join the Federation."

Tan Porus shot out of his chair like a jack-in-the-box and landed, purely by chance, on his feet.

"What!"

Haridin nodded miserably and cleared his throat.

"Now, by the Great Dark Nebula," swore the Rigellian, distractedly, "if this isn't one sweet day! First, they tell me that 'a' equals 'a,' and then you come in and tell me you muffed a Type A reaction—*muffed it completely!*"

The junior psychologist fired up. "I didn't muff it. There's something wrong with the Solarians themselves. They're not normal. When I landed they went wild over us. There was a fantastic celebration—entirely unrestrained. Nothing was too good for us. I delivered the invitation before their parliament in their own language—a simple one which they call Esperanto. I'll stake my life that my translation was ninety-five percent effective."

"Well? And then?"

"I can't understand the rest, boss. First, there was a neutral reaction and I was a little surprised, and then"—he shuddered in retrospect—"in seven days—only seven days, boss—the entire planet had reversed itself completely. I couldn't follow their psychology, not by a hundred miles.

I've brought home copies of their newspapers of the time in which they objected to joining with 'alien monstrosities' and refused to be 'ruled by inhumans of worlds parsecs away.' I ask you, does that make sense?

"And that's only the beginning. It was light years worse than that. Why, good Galaxy, I went all the way into Type G reactions, trying to figure them out, and couldn't. In the end, we *had* to leave. We were in actual *physical* danger from those . . . those Earthmen, as they call themselves."

Tan Porus chewed his lip a while. "Interesting! Have you your report with you?"

"No. The psychological board has it. They've been going over it with a microscope all day."

"And what do they say?"

The young Arcturian winced. "They don't say it openly, but they leave a strong impression of thinking the report an inaccurate one."

"Well, I'll decide about that after I've read it. Meanwhile, come with me to Parliamentary Hall and you can answer a few questions on the way."

Joselin Arn of Alpha Centauri rubbed stubbled jaws with his huge, six-fingered hand and peered from under beetling brows at the semicircle of diversified faces that stared down upon him. The psychological board was composed of psychologists of a score of worlds, and their united gaze was not the easiest thing in the world to withstand.

"We have been informed," began Frian Obel, head of the board and native of Vega, home of the green-skinned men, "that those sections of the report dealing with Sol's military state are *your* work"

Joselin Arn inclined his head in silent agreement.

"And you are prepared to confirm what you have stated here, in spite of its inherent improbability? You are no psychologist, you know."

"No! But I'm a soldier!" The Centaurian's jaws set stubbornly as his bass voice rumbled through the hall. "I don't know equations and I don't know graphs—but I *do* know spaceships. I've seen theirs and I've seen ours, and theirs are better. I've seen their first interstellar ship. Give them a hundred years and they'll have better hyperatomos than we have. I've seen their weapons. They've got almost everything we have, at a stage in their history millennia before us. What they haven't got—they'll get, and soon. What they have got, they'll improve.

"I've seen their munitions plants. Ours are more advanced, but theirs are more efficient. I've seen their soldiers—and I'd rather fight with them than against them.

"I've said all that in the report. I say it again now."

His brusque sentences came to an end and Frian Obel waited for the murmur from the men about him to cease.

"And the rest of their science; medicine, chemistry, physics? What of them?"

"I'm not the best judge of those. You have the report there of those who know, however, and to the best of my knowledge I confirm them."

"And so these Solarians are true Humanoids?"

"By the circling worlds of Centauri, yes!"

The old scientist drew himself back in his chair with a peevish gesture and cast a rapid, frowning glance up and down the length of the table.

"Colleagues," he said, "we make little progress by rehashing this mess of impossibilties. We have a race of Humanoids of a superlatively technological turn; possessing at the same time an intrinsically unscientific belief in supernatural forces, an incredibly childish predilection toward individuality, singly and in groups, and, worst of all, lack of sufficient vision to embrace a galaxy-wide culture."

He glared down upon the lowering Centaurian before him. "Such a race must exist if we are to believe the report—and fundamental axioms of psychology must crumble. But I, for one, refuse to believe any such— to be vulgar about it—comet gas. This is plainly a case of mismanagement to be investigated by the proper authorities. I hope you all agree with me when I say that this report be consigned to the scrap heap and that a second expedition led by an expert in his line, not by an inexperienced junior psychologist or a soldier—"

The drone of the scientist's voice was buried suddenly in the crash of an iron fist against the table. Joselin Arn, his huge bulk writhing in anger, lost his temper and gave vent to martial wrath.

"Now, by the writhing spawn of Templis, by the worms that crawl and the gnats that fly, by the cesspools and the plague spots, and by the hooded death itself, *I won't allow this*. Are you to sit there with your theories and your long-range wisdom and deny what I have seen with my eyes? Are my eyes"—and they flashed fire as he spoke—"to deny themselves because of a few wriggling marks your palsied hands trace on paper?

"To the core of Centauri with these armchair wise men, say I—and the psychologists first of all. Blast these men who bury themselves in their books and their laboratories and are blind to what goes on in the living world outside. Psychology, is it? Rotten, putrid—"

A tap on his belt caused him to whirl, eyes staring, fists clenched. For a moment, he looked about vainly. Then, turning his gaze downward, he found himself looking into the enigmatic green eyes of a pygmy of a man, whose piercing stare seemed to drench his anger with ice water.

"I know you, Joselin Arn," said Tan Porus slowly, picking his words carefully. "You're a brave man and a good soldier, but you don't like psychologists, I see. That is wrong of you, for it is on psychology that the political success of the Federation rests. Take it away and our Union crumbles, our great Federation melts away, the Galactic System is shattered." His voice descended into a soft, liquid croon. "You have sworn an oath to defend the System against all its enemies, Joselin Arn—and you yourself have now become its greatest. You strike at its foundations. You dig at its roots. You poison it at its source. You are dishonored. You are disgraced. You are a traitor."

The Centaurian soldier shook his head helplessly. As Porus spoke, deep and bitter remorse filled him. Recollection of his words of a moment ago lay heavy on his conscience. When the psychologist finished, Arn bent his head and wept. Tears ran down those lined, war-scarred cheeks, to which for forty years now they had been a stranger.

Porus spoke again, and this time his voice boomed like a thunderclap: "Away with your mewling whine, you coward. Danger is at hand. *Man the guns!*"

Joselin Arn snapped to attention; the sorrow that had filled him a bare second before was gone as if it had never existed.

The room rocked with laughter and the soldier grasped the situation. It had been Porus' way of punishing him. With his complete knowledge of the devious ins and outs of the Humanoid mind, he had only to push the proper button, and—

The Centaurian bit his lip in embarrassment, but said nothing.

But Tan Porus, himself, did not laugh. To tease the soldier was one thing; to humiliate him, quite another. With a bound, he was on a chair and laid his small hand on the other's massive shoulder.

"No offense, my friend—a little lesson, that is all. Fight the sub-humanoids and the hostile environments of fifty worlds. Dare space in a leaky rattletrap of a ship. Defy whatever dangers you wish. But never, *never* offend a psychologist. He might get angry in *earnest* the next time."

Arn bent his head back and laughed—a gigantic roar of mirth that shook the room with its earthquakelike lustiness.

"Your advice is well taken, psychologist. Burn me with an atomo, if I don't think you're right." He strode from the room with his shoulders still heaving with suppressed laughter.

Porus hopped off the chair and turned to face the board.

"This is an interesting race of Humanoids we have stumbled upon, colleagues."

"Ah," said Obel, dryly, "the great Porus feels bound to come to his pupil's defense. Your digestion seems to have improved, since you feel yourself capable of swallowing Haridin's report."

Haridin, standing, head bowed, in the corner, reddened angrily, but did not move.

Porus frowned, but his voice kept to its even tone. "I do, and the report, if properly analyzed, will give rise to a revolution in the science. It is a psychological gold mine; and Homo Sol, the find of the millennium."

"Be specific, Tan Porus," drawled someone. "Your tricks are all very well for a Centaurian blockhead, but we remain unimpressed."

The fiery little Rigellian emitted a gurgle of anger. He shook one tiny fist in the direction of the last speaker.

"I'll be more specific, Inar Tubal, you hairy space bug." Prudence and anger waged a visible battle within him. "There is more to a Humanoid than you think—certainly far more than you mental cripples can understand. Just to show you what you don't know, you desiccated group of fossils, I'll undertake to show you a bit of psycho-technology that'll knock the guts right out of you. Panic, morons, panic! World-wide *panic!*"

There was an awful silence. "Did you say world-wide panic?" stuttered Frian Obel, his green skin turning gray. "Panic?"

"Yes, you parrot. Give me six months and fifty assistants and I'll show you a world of Humanoids in panic."

Obel attempted vainly to answer. His mouth worked in a heroic attempt to remain serious—and failed. As though by signal, the entire board dropped its dignity and leaned back in a single burst of laughter.

"I remember," gasped Inar Tubal of Sirius, his round face streaked with tears of pure joy, "a student of mine who once claimed to have discovered a stimulus that would induce world-wide panic. When I checked his results, I came across an exponent with a misplaced decimal point. He was only ten orders of magnitude out of the way. How many decimal points have you misplaced, Colleague Porus?"

"What of Kraut's Law, Porus, which says you can't panic more than five Humanoids at a time? Shall we pass a resolution repealing it? And maybe the atomic theory as well while we're about it?" and Semper Gor of Capella cackled gleefully.

Porus climbed onto the table and snatched Obel's gavel. "The next one who laughs is getting this over his empty head." There was sudden silence.

"I'm taking fifty assistants," shouted the green-eyed Rigellian, "and Joselin Arn is taking me to Sol. I want five of you to come with me—Inar Tubal, Semper Gor and any three others—so that I can watch their stupid faces when I've done what I said I would." He hefted the gavel, threateningly. "Well?"

Frian Obel gazed at the ceiling placidly. "All right, Porus. Tubal, Gor, Helvin, Prat, and Winson can go with you. At the end of the specified time, we'll witness world-wide panic which will be very gratifying—or we'll watch you eat your words, and how much more gratifying *that* would be." And with that, he chuckled very quietly to himself.

Tan Porus stared thoughtfully out the window. Terrapolis, capital city of Earth, sprawled beneath him to the very edge of the horizon. Its muted roar reached even to the half-mile height at which he stood.

There was something over that city, invisible and intangible but none the less real. Its presence was only too evident to the small psychologist. The choking cloak of dank fear that spread over the metropolis beneath was one of his own weaving—a horrible cloak of dark uncertainty, that clutched with clammy fingers at the hearts of Mankind and stopped short—just short—of actual panic.

The roar of the city had voices in it, and the voices were tiny ones of fear.

The Rigellian turned away in disgust. "Hey, Haridin," he roared.

The young Arcturian turned away from the televisor. "Calling me, boss?"

"What do you think I'm doing? Talking to myself? What's the latest from Asia?"

"Nothing new. The stimuli just aren't strong enough. The yellow men seem to be more stolid of disposition than the white dominants of America and Europe. I've sent out orders not to increase the stimuli, though."

"No, they mustn't," agreed Porus. "We can't risk *active* panic." He ruminated in silence. "Listen, we're about through. Tell them to hit a few of the big cities—they're more susceptible—and quit."

He turned to the window again. "Space, what a world—what a world! An entirely new branch of psychology has opened up—one we never dreamed of. Mob psychology, Haridin, mob psychology." He shook his head impressively.

"There's lot of suffering, though, boss," muttered the younger man. "This passive panic has completely paralyzed trade and commerce. The business life of the entire planet is stagnant. The poor government is helpless—they don't know what's wrong."

"They'll find out—when I'm ready. And, as for the suffering—well, I don't like it, either, but it's all a means to an end, a damned important end."

There followed a short silence, and then Porus' lips twitched into a nasty smile. "Those five nitwits returned from Europe yesterday, didn't they?"

Haridin smiled in turn and nodded vigorously. "And hopping sore! Your predictions have checked to the fifth decimal place. They're fit to be tied."

"Good! I'm only sorry I can't see Obel's face right now, after the last message I sent him. And, incidentally"—his voice dropped lower—"What's the latest on *them*?"

Haridin raised two fingers. "Two weeks, and they'll be here."

"Two weeks . . . two weeks," gurgled Porus jubilantly. He rose and made for the door. "I think I'll find my dear, dear colleagues and pass the time of day."

The five scientists of the board looked up from their notes and fell into an embarrassed silence as Porus entered.

The latter smiled impishly. "Notes satisfactory, gentlemen? Found some fifty or sixty fallacies in my fundamental assumptions, no doubt?"

Hybron Prat of Alpha Cepheus rumpled the gray fuzz he called hair. "I don't trust the unholy tricks this crazy mathematical notation of yours plays."

The Rigellian emitted a short bark of laughter. "Invent a better, then. So far, it's done a good job of handling reactions, hasn't it?"

There was an unmusical chorus of throat-clearings but no definite answer.

"Hasn't it?" thundered Porus.

"Well, what if it has," returned Kim Winson, desperately. "Where's your panic? All this is well and good. These Humanoids are cosmic freaks, but where's the big show you were going to put on. Until you break Kraut's Law, this entire exhibition of yours isn't worth a pinhead meteor."

"You're beaten, gentlemen, you're beaten," crowed the small master psychologist. "I've proven my point—this passive panic is as impossible according to classic psychology as the active form. You're trying to deny facts and save face now, by harping on a technicality. Go home; go home, gentlemen, and hide under the bed."

Psychologists are only human. They can analyze the motives that drive them, but they are the slave of those motives just as much as the commonest mortal of all. These galaxy-famous psychologists writhed under the lash of wounded pride and shattered vanity, and their blind stubbornness was the mechanical reaction due therefrom. They knew it was and they knew Porus knew it was—and that made it all the harder.

Inar Tubal stared angrily from red-rimmed eyes. "Active panic or nothing, Tan Porus. That's what you promised, and that's what we'll have. We want the letter of the bond or, by space and time, we'll balk at any technicality. Active panic or we report failure!"

Porus swelled ominously and, with a tremendous effort, spoke quietly. "Be reasonable, gentlemen. We haven't the equipment to handle active panic. We've never come up against this superform they have here on Earth. What if it gets beyond control?" He shook his head violently.

"Isolate it, then," snarled Semper Gor. "Start it up and put it out. Make all the preparations you want, but do it!"

"If you can," grunted Hybron Prat.

But Tan Porus had *his* weak point. His brittle temper lay in splintered shards about him. His agile tongue blistered the atmosphere and inundated the sullen psychologists with wave after wave of concentrated profanity.

"Have your way, vacuumheads! Have your way and to outer space with you!" He was breathless with passion. "We'll set it off right here in Terrapolis as soon as all the men are back home. Only you'd all better get from under!"

And with one last parting snarl, he stalked from the room.

Tan Porus parted the curtains with a sweep of his hand, and the five psychologists facing him averted their eyes. The streets of Earth's capital were deserted of civilian population. The ordered tramp of the military patrolling the highways of the city sounded like a dirge. The wintry sky hung low over a scene of strewn wreckage, scattered bodies—and silence; the silence that follows an orgy of wild destruction.

"It was touch and go for a few hours there, colleagues." Porus' voice was tired. "If it had passed the city limits, we could never have stopped it."

"Horrible, horrible!" muttered Hybron Prat. "It was a scene a psychologist would have given his right arm to witness—and his life to forget."

"And these are Humanoids!" groaned Kim Winson.

Semper Gor rose to his feet in sudden decision. "Do you see the significance of this, Porus? These Earthmen are sheer uncontrolled atomite. They can't be handled. Were they twice the technological geniuses they are, they would be useless. With their mob psychology, their mass panics, their superemotionalism, they simply won't fit into the Humanoid picture."

Porus raised an eyebrow. "Comet gas! Individually, we are as emotional as they are. They carry it into mass action and we don't; that's the only difference."

"And that's enough!" exclaimed Tubal. "We've made our decision, Porus. We made it last night, at the height of the . . . the . . . of *it*. The Solar System is to be left to itself. It is a plague spot and we want none of it. As far as the Galaxy is concerned, Homo Sol will be placed in strict quarantine. That is final!"

The Rigellian laughed softly. "For the Galaxy, it may be final. But for Homo Sol?"

Tubal shrugged. "They don't concern us."

Porus laughed again. "Say, Tubal. Just between the two of us, have you tried a time integration of Equation 128 followed by expansion with Karolean tensors?"

"No-o. I can't say I have."

"Well, then, just glance up and down these calculations and enjoy yourself."

The five scientists of the board grouped themselves about the sheets of paper Porus had handed them. Expressions changed from interest to bewilderment and then to something approaching panic.

Naru Helvin tore the sheets across with a spasmodic movement. "It's a lie," he screeched.

"We're a thousand years ahead of them now, and by that time we'll be advanced another two hundred years!" Tubal snapped. "They won't be able to do anything against the mass of the Galaxy's people."

Tan Porus laughed in a monotone, which is hard to do, but very unpleasant to hear. "You still don't believe mathematics. That's in your behavior pattern, of course. All right, let's see if experts convince you— as they should, unless contact with these off-normal Humanoids has twisted you. Joselin—Joselin Arn—come in here!"

The Centaurian commander came in, saluted automatically, and looked expectant.

"Can one of your ships defeat one of the Sol ships in battle, if necessary?"

Arn grinned sourly. "Not a chance, sir. These Humanoids break Kraut's Law in panic—and also in fighting. We have a corps of experts manning our ships; these people have a single crew that functions as a unit, without individuality. They manifest a form of fighting—panic, I imagine, is the best word. Every individual on a ship becomes an organ of the ship. With us, as you know, that's impossible.

"Furthermore, this world's a mass of mad geniuses. They have, to my certain knowledge, taken no less than twenty-two interesting but useless gadgets they saw in the Thalsoon Museum when they visited us, turned 'em inside out, and produced from them some of the most unpleasant military devices I've seen. You know of Julmun Thill's gravitational line tracer? Used—rather ineffectively—for spotting ore deposits before the modern electric potential method came in?

"They've turned it—somehow—into one of the deadliest automatic fire directors it's been my displeasure to see. It will automatically lay a gun or projector on a completely invisible target in space, air, water or rock, for that matter."

"We," said Tan Porus gleefully, "have far greater fleets than they. We could overwhelm them, could we not?"

Joselin Arn shook his head. "Defeat them now—probably. It wouldn't be any overwhelming, though, and I wouldn't bet on it too heavily. Certainly wouldn't invite it. The trouble is, in a military way, this collection of gadget maniacs invent things at a horrible rate. Technologically, they're as unstable as a wave of water; our civilization is more like a sanddune. I've seen their ground-car plants install a complete plant of machine tools for production of a new model of automobile—and rip it out in six months because it's completely obsolete!

"Now we've come in contact with their civilization briefly. We've learned the methods of one new civilization to add to our previous two hundred and eighty-odd—a small percentage advantage. They've added one new civilization to their previous one—a one-hundred-percent advance!"

"How about," Porus asked gently, "our military position if we simply ignore them completely for two hundred years?"

Joselin Arn gave an explosive little laugh. "*If* we could—which means *if* they'd let us—I'd answer offhand and with assurance. They're all I'd care to tackle right now. Two hundred years of exploring the new tracks suggested by their brief contact with us and they'd be doing things I can't imagine. Wait two hundred years, and there won't be a battle; there'll be an annexation."

Tan Porus bowed formally. "Thank you, Joselin Arn. That was the result of my mathematical work."

Joselin Arn saluted and left the room.

Turning to the five thoroughly paralyzed scientists, Porus went on: "And I hope these learned gentlemen still react in a vaguely Humanoid way. Are you convinced that it is not up to us to decide to end all intercourse with this race? We may—but they won't!

"Fools"—he spat out the word—"do you think I'm going to waste time arguing with you? I'm laying down the law, do you understand? Homo Sol *shall* enter the Federation. They are going to be trained into maturity in two hundred years. And I'm not asking you; *I'm telling you!*" The Rigellian stared up at them truculently.

"Come with me!" he growled brusquely.

They followed in tame submission and entered Tan Porus' sleeping quarters. The little psychologist drew aside a curtain and revealed a life-size painting.

"Make anything of that?"

It was the portrait of an Earthman, but of such an Earthman as none of the psychologists had yet seen. Dignified and sternly handsome, with one hand stroking a regal beard, and the other holding the single flowing garment that clothed him, he seemed personified majesty.

"That's Zeus," said Porus. "The primitive Earthmen created him as the personification of storm and lightning." He whirled upon the bewildered five. "Does it remind you of anybody?"

"Homo Canopus?" ventured Helvin uncertainly.

For a moment, Porus' face relaxed in momentary gratification and then it hardened again. "Of course," he snapped. "Why do you hesitate about it? That's Canopus to the life, down to the full yellow beard."

Then: "Here's something else." He drew another curtain.

The portrait was of a female this time. Full-bosomed and wide-hipped she was. An ineffable smile graced her face and her hands seemed to caress the stalks of grain that sprang thickly about her feet.

"Demeter!" said Porus. "The personification of agricultural fertility. The idealized mother. Whom does *that* remind you of?"

There was no hesitation this time. Five voices rang out as one: "Homo Betelguese!"

Tan Porus smiled in delight. "There you have it. Well?"

"Well?" said Tubal.

"Don't you see?" The smile faded. "Isn't it clear. Nitwit! If a hundred Zeuses and a hundred Demeters were to land on Earth as part of a 'trade mission,' and turned out to be trained psychologists—*Now* do you see?"

Semper Gor laughed suddenly. "Space, time, and little meteors. Of course! The Earthmen would be putty in the hands of their own personifications of storm and motherhood come to life. In two hundred years—why, in two hundred years, we could do anything."

"But this so-called trade mission of yours, Porus," interposed Prat. "How would you get Homo Sol to accept it in the first place?"

Porus cocked his head to one side. "Dear Colleague Prat," he murmured, "do you suppose that I created the passive panic just for the show —or just to gratify five woodenheads? This passive panic paralyzed industry, and the Terrestrial government is faced with revolution—another form of mob action that could use investigation. Offer them Galactic trade and eternal prosperity and do you think they'd jump at it? Has matter mass?"

The Rigellian cut short the excited babble that followed with an impatient gesture. "If you've nothing more to ask, gentlemen, let's begin our preparations to leave. Frankly, I'm tired of Earth, and, more than that, I'm blasted anxious to get back to that squid of mine."

He opened the door and shouted down the corridor: "Hey, Haridin! Tell Arn to have the ship ready in six hours. We're leaving."

"But . . . but—" The chorus of puzzled objections crystallized into sudden action as Semper Gor dashed at Porus and snatched him back as he was on the point of leaving. The little Rigellian struggled vainly in the other's powerful grasp.

"Let go!"

"We've endured enough, Porus," said Gor, "and now you'll just calm down and behave like a Humanoid. Whatever you say, we're not leaving until we're finished. We've got to arrange with the Terrestrial government concerning the trade mission. We've got to secure approval of the board. We've got to pick our psychologist. We've got to—"

Here Porus, with a sudden jerk, freed himself. "Do you suppose for one moment that I would wait for your precious board to start to begin to commence to consider doing something about the situation in two or three decades?

"Earth agreed to my terms unconditionally a month ago. The squad of Canopans and Betelguesans set sail five months ago, and landed day before yesterday. It was only with their help that we managed to stop yesterday's panic—though you never suspected it. You probably thought you did it yourself. Today, gentlemen, they have the situation in full control and your services are no longer needed. We're going home."

PART IV

Far Traveling

WILLIAM TENN

ALEXANDER THE BAIT

You AREN'T LIKELY to get a quick punch in the snoot these days by professing admiration for Alexander Parks. Time has softened even the families of the crews who rode the GA fleet into nowhere; and uncomfortable understanding of the great thing the man did has increased with the years.

Still, he is penalized by a hidebound agency in a manner that, to him at any rate, is especially horrible. I refer to the FLC. I hope they read this.

We wandered into each other a couple of years after the war to end isolationism. I had just landed a Toledo accordion on a freight runway and was now headed for a bar. There are some pilots who know just how much rye they need after towing an accordion; me, I just keep pouring it down until my heart floats back into place.

A cab came up to the flight building and a well-built man with a surprisingly small head got out. As I ran up to nail the cab, the man turned and stared at me. Something familiar about that shoe-button skull made me stop.

"Were you in the Army Air Forces?" he asked.

"Yeah," I answered slowly. "The so-called Swasticker Squadron. Forty— Alex Parks! The voice with a dial!"

He grinned. "That's right, Dave. For a minute I thought you were only talking to ex-flying officers. Ground control people carry a lot of inferiority complex around with them. You're looking well."

He looked better. The clothes he was wearing had been designed by a tailor with the salary of a movie executive. I remembered something from the newspapers. "Didn't you sell some invention or other to some corporation or other?"

"It was the Radar Corporation of America. Just been capitalized. I sold them my multi-level negative beam radar."

"Get much?"

He pursed his lips and let his eyes twinkle. "Oh, a million five hundred thousand dollars."

I flapped my lips and let my eyes bug. "L-lotta dough. What're you going to do with it?"

"A couple of unholy scientific projects I've always dreamed about. I might be able to use you." He motioned to the cab. "Can we go somewhere and talk?"

"I'm on my way to a bar," I told him as the cab got under way. "Just came in with an accordion."

"Accordion? Is that what you freight pilots call these glider trains?"

"Yeah. And if you want to know why, just think of what happens when you hit an airpocket. Or a sudden head-wind. Or a motor stall." I grunted. "We make music—heavenly music."

We sat in a back booth of the *Matched Penny Cafe*, Alex smiling admiringly as I consumed half the amber output out of a good-sized distillery. "You'd have to cut down on that guzzling if you came in with me," he said.

I finished the glass, licked my teeth, my lips, and sighed. "Where?"

"A mesa in Nevada I've purchased. Have to have someone I can trust to fly equipment in and help around the place with some moderately heavy construction. Someone I can trust to keep his mouth shut. A heavy drinker keeps his mouth open too much to suit me."

"I'll do that," I assured him. "I'd drink nothing but curded yak milk to get out of this aerial moving van business. Making an occasional trip will be nothing compared to my daily routine with collapsible coffins. It's the combination of monotonous grind with the angel of death that's making me bottle-happy."

He nodded. "And the lack of any long-range useful goal. You flew on almost as rigid a schedule during the war, but—well, that was war. If there were something fine for which you were risking your life, instead of the transportation of electrical harmonicas—"

"Like interplanetary travel? That was one of your bugs. Going to do some experimenting along that line?"

Alex slid his forefinger along the green marble table top. "I'd need much more money than that. It's a nice thought—the human race finds itself at the point today where a little research, a little refinement of existing techniques, would send it to the stars. But the people who could do it, the big manufacturing corporations, can't see enough incentive; the people who would do it, the universities and research foundations, can't see enough money. We sit on this planet like a shipwrecked sailor on a desert island who sees a pair of oars in one spot and a boat in another and can't quite make up his mind to bring the two together.

"No, not interplanetary travel. Not yet. But something along that line. That beam I discovered gave me the reputation of the world's greatest radar expert. I intend to build the largest installation ever on that mesa— and make a long-distance radar survey."

This wasn't the Alexander Parks I'd known. This idea, I decided, showed nothing of what I'd always thought he'd do if he had the money to indulge his sardonically soaring mind, his genius for subtlety. "A radar survey?" I asked weakly.

His little head grew wide with laughter. "A map, my dear Dave—a topographical map of the Moon!"

Nevada was nice. Plenty of landing space. Practically no one to ask questions. Sharp, fragrant air on the top of Big Bluff Mesa that affected me almost as strongly as hooch used to. Alex claimed atmospheric conditions here were perfect for maximum equipment efficiency.

The equipment was odd. Of course, I knew radar had developed enormously since the days of primitive gadgetry in the early forties. Parks' own MLN Beam had successfully fused communication and noncommunication radio into a fantastic set-up that required no transmitter and made it possible to tune in on any outdoor event in the world. (It was still in production then.)

Alex and I got the shacks built ourselves, but we ran into trouble with the huge horizontal antenna and the gyroscopically stabilized dipoles. In the end he hired a man named Judson from Las Vegas. Judson did odd jobs around the place and supplied an extra pair of hands in construction jobs. Mrs. Judson cooked our meals. Alex admitted the necessity for Judson, but seemed to regret it nonetheless. I suspected he sent me on sleeveless errands now and then, as if to keep me from having a coherent knowledge of his methods. I shrugged at that thought. If he thought I knew enough about modern radar, I was highly complimented.

When I flew in with a rattling glider train of impossible coils and surrealist tubes, he often insisted I stay put while he made some infinitesimal adjustment in the lab shack. I could climb out of the plane, then, but only if I went directly to the hut which was our living quarters.

Emmanuel Corliss, of the Radar Corporation of America, begged a ride from me once. All the way to Nevada he sang Alex's praises; he told me of the statue of Alex in the foyer of the corporation's skyscraper in Manhattan; he even had a copy of an unauthorized biography titled "Alexander Parks—Father of Global Communication." He said he wanted Alex to come back as chief research consultant. I thought atomhead would enjoy having his ego caressed.

I was wrong.

Fifty miles from Big Bluff, a deep voice rattled the reception panel. "Who's that you're talking to, Dave?"

Corliss piped up. "Thought I'd look in on you, boy. We might be able to use whatever you're working on now."

"Well, you can't. The moment you land, Dave, unhitch the gliders and fly Mr. Corliss back to the nearest airport. Got enough fuel?"

"Yep." I was embarrassed. Felt like a neighbor overhearing a newlywed couple's first quarrel.

"But, Parks," the executive wailed, "you don't know what an important figure you've become. The world wants to know what you're doing. Radar Corporation of America wants to know what you're doing."

Parks chuckled. "Not just yet. Don't get out of that plane, Corliss, or you'll get a load of buckshot in the most sensitive part of your upholstery. Remember, I can call you a trespasser."

Corliss sputtered angrily. "Now you listen to me—"

"No, you listen to me. *Don't get out of that plane* as you love your swivel chair. Believe it or not, old man, I'm doing you a favor."

That was sort of that. After I'd deposited the red-faced corporation president, I bumped down to the mesa pretty thoughtfully. Alex was waiting for me; he looked thoughtful, too.

"Don't do that again," he told me. "Nobody comes out here until I'm ready for, well, for publication. I don't want strangers, especially scientific strangers, poking around in my layout."

"Afraid they'd copy it?"

My question tickled him. "That's it . . . almost too exactly."

"Afraid I'll copy it?"

He threw a quick, shrewd glance at me. "Let's have supper and do some talking, Dave." He put his arm around my shoulders.

While Mrs. Judson dealt out the plain food very plainly prepared, Alex studied me in the hard, unwinking fashion he had. I thought again that he resembled nothing more than a miniature camera set on a massive, unwieldy tripod. Grease-stained blue jeans had long ago replaced the soft sartorial perfections in which I'd first seen him. The father of global communication!

He looked covertly at Judson, saw that the hired man was interested in nothing but his stew, and said in a low voice: "If you feel I distrust you, Dave, I'm sorry. There is a good reason for all this secrecy, believe me."

"That's your business," I told him shortly. "You don't pay me for asking questions. But I honestly wouldn't know an oscillator screen from an indicator rack. And if I did, I wouldn't tell anyone."

He shifted on the hard wooden bench and leaned against the metal wall behind him. "You know what I'm trying to do. I send a high-frequency beam at the Moon. Some of it is absorbed in the ionosphere, most of it gets through and bounces off the Moon's surface. I catch the reflection, amplify it, record the strength and minutest change in direction on a photographic plate and send another, slightly different, beam out immediately. On the basis of multiple beams, I build up a fairly detailed and accurate picture of the Moon from very close range. My multilevel negative radar provides a somewhat stronger beam than science has had at its disposal before, but essentially the principle is basic radar. It could have been done, with a little difficulty, ten years ago. Why wasn't it?"

Stew congealed into an unsavory jelly in my plate. I was interested in spite of myself.

"It wasn't done," he continued, "for the same reason we don't have interplanetary travel, suboceanic mining, grafting of complete limbs from corpses on amputation cases. Nobody can see any profit in it, any *immediate,* certain profit. Therefore, the small amount of research that is necessary to close the gap between the knowledge we already have and the knowledge we almost have goes unfinanced."

"But work goes on in those fields," I pointed out.

"Work goes on, all right. But at what a slow pace, under what heartbreaking conditions! Have you ever heard the legend of how my namesake, Alexander the Great, circled the world astride a giant bird? He hung a piece of meat from a long pole and dangled it in front of the bird's beak. A strong gust of wind blew the meat close enough for the creature to snatch, and the redoubtable Alexander immediately cut a piece of flesh from his side and attached it to the pole. Thus, he was able to complete his trip with the bird futilely trying to reach the meat by increasing his speed.

"The story occurs in several folklores with different heroes, but it shows how fundamental was the ancients' understanding of human motives. Incidentally, it is also a beautiful illustration of the laws of compensation. In every age, a man must offer himself up as bait so that progress will not be limited to the back pages of the dictionary. We can't be said to be moving forward if we touch none of our newer potentialities."

I stirred the stew with a heavy spoon, then pushed it away and reached for the coffee. "I see what you mean. But why tell me all this?"

Alex rose, stretched and moved towards the door. I smiled apologetically at my coffee and Mrs. Judson and followed him.

The cool Nevada night hung heavily as we walked outside. A myriad of stars blazed pinpoint mysteries. Was this black, inviting space man's natural medium, a domain waiting for the flashing tread of a master? Could it be that my puny species was the appointed ruler of these vastnesses? I wondered how it would feel to bank suddenly out there, to level out for a landing. My hands itched for an unmade, still nonexistent throttle.

"These are the maps I've made to date," my employer observed. We were standing in the lab shack with banked transformers, nightmares in spun glass and twisted wire weaving in and out of the huge display tubes around us.

I glanced carelessly at the maps; I was no astronomer. Then I glanced very carefully indeed at the maps.

The point is they weren't maps. They were pictures—over a thousand aerial photographs—taken from a uniform height of about five hundred feet. They had sharper detail than any aerial photographs I've ever seen. You could count the rocks on the surface; you could note pits and the narrowest fissures.

"They are pretty good," Alex said. He stroked one of the glossy sheets lovingly. "A section of the Tycho Brahë Crater."

"Why the Samuel Aloysius Hill don't you publish?"

"Couldn't till now." He seemed to be in the throes of a hard decision. "I had to check something first. And now I've got to trust you with my life's work by asking you to play a particularly dirty trick on yourself. I still can't afford to explain; my conversation tonight was sort of a song and dance to go with the request. But some day it will all fit."

"Go ahead. I'm a loyal employee; I love the firm."

The pinhead seemed to swell. "One week from today I want you to take a trip up to the Canadian North Woods with a couple of packages. You'll have a map with X's scattered over it; the co-ordinates of each X will be marked in the margin. Latitude and longitude in terms of degrees, minutes and seconds. Bury each package about two feet underground at X-designated spots, making certain that it is at the exact intersecting point of the co-ordinates. Then go away."

"Huh?"

"Go away and forget you ever saw those packages. Don't even dream about them. Don't see me except socially for at least three years. Forget you ever worked for me. You can keep the plane and I'll add a sizable check as a parting gift. Will you do it?"

I let my mind chew on it for a while. It didn't make sense, but I knew he'd told me all he intended to. "O.K., Alex, I'll take the high road and you'll take the dough road. I'll make out."

He seemed tremendously relieved. "You will make out—much better than you think. Just wait a few months. When the united savants of the world start flocking in here, there will be lectures and juicy magazine articles thrown at anyone who ever worked for me. Don't touch them with a transmitting antenna."

That made me laugh. "I wouldn't anyway. I don't play those games."

Alex shut off the light and we returned to the Judsons feeling pretty good about each other. That was the way a sweet guy called Alexander Parks climbed up on the altar of history. When I think of the fundamental ambition that drove him to that conversation, the action of the FLC seems cruel on a scale immeasurably picayune.

A week later I was flitting about the north woods laying little tarp covered eggs here and there by means of a chart so explicit as to be understandable by the littlest moron in one of his most difficult moments.

Newspapers caught my eye when I landed in Seattle. Full front-page spreads of the pictures Alex had showed me, smaller shots of Alex's small head surrounded by big-browed, white-maned profs from Oxford, Irkutsk and points east.

"Radar Genius Maps Moon," they screamed. "Sage of Nevada reveals work of two years. Scientists flock to mesa, claim telescopes now obsolete as checks. Alexander Parks announces he will make mineralogical survey of lunar surface."

So he had announced it. Good. I spent a portion of my last pay check investigating any new developments in the gentle art of making whiskey.

The liquor, I found, hadn't changed; unfortunately, *I* had. Laboring under a diminished capacity, I gamboled from binge to hangover, from bar to hotel room, until I woke up in a hospital surrounded by a straitjacket.

After the doctor had chased the six-headed snakes away, I sat up and chirruped at the nurses. One luscious little redhead took to reading me the newspapers in a pathetic attempt at self-defense. I was getting the news in jerky flashes, what with her dodging around night tables and behind screens, when I heard something that made me reach out and grab the newspaper. The girl, who had been preparing for a last, all-out effort, looked a little dazed.

I still have a hazy memory of that nurse standing in a corner and shaking her head while I got clearance. The doc didn't feel I was cured yet at all, but he decided that as long as I wasn't talking too loudly about ring-tailed octopi it would be just as well for his hypo house if I took up residence elsewhere.

Bascomb Rockets were the nearest and I was there a half hour after a starchy clerk had given me my clothes, money and a little white certificate, suitable for framing. I'd gone through every newspaper in reach by the time I arrived; so I was prepared for what I saw.

A two-by-three experimental house which had been operating on a frayed shoestring of a budget was expanding like a galaxy turned supernova. Far off into the distance, I could see shops and hangars going up, stock piles being built, equipment arriving by the cubic ton.

Tim Bascomb was checking blueprints in front of the half-finished Parthenon that was to be the company's main building. I'd met him at an ex-pilots' convention a year after the war, but I thought I might as well reintroduce myself—some insensitive people manage to forget me.

The moment he heard my voice, he dropped the blueprints and grabbed my hand. "Dave! You haven't signed any contracts yet?" he finished anxiously.

"Nary a clause," I told him. "Can you use a former B-29er and accordion player?"

"Can we use you? Mr. Hennessey—Mr. Hennessey, get me contractual form 16, no, better make that 18. You were in on the early jet and rocket jobs," he explained. "That puts you into an advanced category."

"Hiring a lot of the boys?"

"Are we? Every backyard gadgeteer in the country is forming a corporation these days and we're keeping up with the best of them. They say the airlines are using hostesses as co-pilots and candy butchers as radiomen. You'll find Steve Yancy and Lou Brock of the Canada-Mexico Line in that shack, over there; they'd like to see you."

Mr. Hennessey and a stenographer served as witnesses. I started scribbling my name on that contract as soon as I saw the numbers after the dollar sign under "salary." Bascomb laughed.

"I'll back our payroll against any in the world. Not that at least fifty other companies don't do as well. We've got the backing of Radioactive

Metals and the Ginnette Mining Corporation as well as a goverment subsidy of five million."

I wiped some blue-black ink off my fingers. "Since when is the government interested?"

He chuckled. "Since when?" We began walking to a huge structure labeled "Bascomb Rockets Experimental Pilots—No Admittance to Unauthorized Personnel." "Look, Dave boy, when Parks took those radar snapshots of the Moon, the astronomers were interested. When he worked out a spectroscopic table and found there were healthy hunks of gold under the surface, the banks and mines began to sit up. But when that Caltech prof turned Parks' gimmick along eighty miles of the Moon's Alpine valley and found alternate layers of radium and uranium, the nations of this planet looked up from atom bomb experiments long enough to harness everybody who knows the Moon is a quarter of a million miles from Earth. It's no longer a matter of the first extraterrestrial explorer becoming a trillionaire overnight, but of folks cooking atom bombs in their kitchens."

I looked at the tractors backing and filling around me; at the cement-sloppy wheelbarrows being trundled by an army of construction workers; at the bare scaffolding of shops rising on every bare foot of ground. This scene was being duplicated everywhere in every state, probably in every nation. Slap some sort of a ship together, solve the problems with any kind of jerry-built apparatus—*but get to the Moon first!*

"It isn't only a matter of national defense, either," Tim was explaining. "We almost have atomic power, in fact, we already have it but not in a commercial form. With the uranium that can be dredged out of the Moon, the old Sunday Supplement dream of crossing the Atlantic with a teaspoonful of sand for fuel will come true. General Atomics is devoting half their budget to spaceship research. They may not be the first outfit to set a job down on Tycho, but they sure will bust a gut trying."

He led me into the pilots' shack where a lecture on astrogation was in progress. And that day the only rockets on the Bascomb lot were still on drawing boards!

"The Mad Scramble"—isn't that the name of the definitive history of the period? It was mad. People still remember the first casualties to hit the front pages: Gunnar and Thorgersen getting blown to bits a half-mile up; those six Russian scientists flaming into an incandescence that registered on every astronomical camera pointed at the Moon. Then that wave of reaction sweeping the world toward the end of the decade and laws clamping down on irresponsible corporations and wildcat experimenters.

Even then, Steve Yancy and his kid brother got knocked off on a simple experimental flight outside Earth's atmosphere. No fundamental principle overlooked, we were just building carelessly.

When Parks finally dropped in on us on his way from the Leroy Propulsion Project, we seemed to be getting nowhere fast. That was the

Black April, the month of the GA Fleet. Bascomb had discovered I knew Parks personally and begged me to bring him into the firm. "He's just hopping about giving advice to anyone who wants it from him. With his reputation, if he ever went to work for one organization he could name his own price. Try to get him to name it for us."

"I'll try," I promised.

"Of course, I know his basic interest is in radar research. If his machine had stopped with mapping the Moon, every hick college would probably have had an appropriation for a radar telescope or whatever they call it. But since he found uranium in them thar craters, kids are being jerked into research projects as fast as they finish elementary physics. That guy from Caltech—what *was* his name?—who first detected radioactive stuff with Parks' equipment, they say he has to go up to the mesa every time he wants to survey some more moon. He can't get the university even vaguely interested in building a toy for him, and Alex P. won't let anyone near the layout unless he's on the scene holding their leash."

"Yeah." I grinned wryly, remembering the way Emmanuel Corliss had been sent back to his dictaphone. Even when some scientific journals had attacked the tight control he maintained over the world's only lunar-surveying radar, he had retorted angrily that the entire apparatus had been developed and built out of his own brain, time and funds and if anyone didn't like it they could build themselves another. Of course, with every research penny eventually finding its way into spaceship design, he had the only game in town.

Parks laughed when I gave him Bascomb's message. He clambered out of the new-smelling, black and silver job that I was to take on a shakedown in a week and sat on the curving metal runway.

"No, Dave, I like this being advisory expert to big business in rocket research. I get to travel and see all the different things we're trying. Did you know Garfinkel of Illinois is working on a Cosmoplane—sort of a sailboat sensitive to cosmic rays? I'd rather not get stuck in a job in one corner of this business. After all, anyone may hit it."

"But that isn't like you, Alex," I argued. "You were always the kind of guy who wanted to do things himself. This work isn't right up your alley, it *is* your alley. You're the one man Bascomb Rockets needs, not as a part-time unpaid specialist who hits us once a month on his look-see circuit, but as the director, the co-ordinator of our research. I'm just a stumblebum who can make with a joystick, but you are the guy who'll get us there."

"Ever mention our working together?"

"No." I sighed. He evidently didn't want in. I helped him change the subject. "Nasty—this GA business."

He was staring at the ground. He nodded slowly, then looked up. There were ridges of anguish on his face. "That was Corliss," he said in a low, earnest voice. "He became president of General Atomics six months ago. The idea of the Fleet probably seemed like a good publicity trick."

I disagreed with him. "After all," I pointed out, "the logic was good. Ten ships setting off for the Moon together. When one of them hit a snag, the others could come up and help. In case of an impending blowup, the crews of the threatened ship could be transferred to safety. It was just plain unfortunate that Fouquelles didn't discover the deep space Jura rays until a week after they left. From now on everything we build will be insulated against the stuff."

"Five hundred men," Alex brooded. "Five hundred men and women lost without a trace. Nothing in the papers today about a radio signal, about some debris coming down somewhere?"

"No. They probably got out of control and drifted into the sun. Or maybe the ships—those that are left—are scudding aimlessly out of the system."

He was himself again when I left him at the gate. "Maybe I'll have cracked it the next time I see you," I said. "We're moving pretty slowly, though."

"That doesn't mean anything." He shook my hand warmly. "Man has his heart set on getting off this planet. He'll do it—perhaps sooner than he thinks."

Two months later, Captain Ulrich Gall landed the Canadian *Flutterer III* in Plato Crater, using the double-flow drive. It's high-school history now how Gall lined his spacesuited crew behind him and prepared to move through the air lock. How he caught his foot on the ramp, and how his polynesian "boy," Charles Wau-Neil, hurrying to extricate him, tripped on the lock and shot out onto the lunar surface—thus being the first human to touch another world.

I was co-pilot of the fifth ship to reach the Moon—"The Ambassador of Albuquerque." I was also the first man to set insulated foot on the lunar Apennines. So I'll have a place in some six-volume detailed history of lunar exploration: "An interesting discovery is credited to a minor adventurer named—"

Well, you know what happened. Toehold, the colony Gall left on the Moon, continued the feverish examination of mineralogical samples. No go. In six months Toehold scientists radioed a complete confirmation of Gall's early suspicions.

There was no uranium on the Moon. No radium. And there was just enough gold to be detectable in the most delicate analyses.

Of course they did find some nice beds of iron ore. And someone discovered rocks beneath the surface from which oxygen and the lighter elements could be extracted with ease, making possible Toehold's present indigenousness. But no uranium!

I was on Earth when the storm of public opinion broke. Financed and encouraged by hysterical corporations, it broke first around the head of a certain California professor of astronomy and buried him. He, it was, who had first announced the presence of radioactive minerals on the Moon as a result of experiments with Parks' radar. Then it turned on Parks.

Remember the headlines that day? "Parks Admits Fraud" in letters as big as the end of the world. "Alexander Parks, Nevada charlatan, explained to the FBI today how he planted transmitters near pitchblende and gold deposits in Canada, co-ordinating his infernal machine with them to make it appear that the impulses were arriving from a given portion of the Moon. 'I never allowed anyone to investigate the machine too closely,' Parks leered, 'and this, with my international reputation as a radar expert, prevented discovery.'"

I scooted for his mesa. There were state police coming out of the woodwork, FBI men being trampled underfoot and what looked like a full infantry regiment marching back and forth. After I'd satisfied everybody that I was a reputable citizen, I was allowed to see Alex. He was evidently a *de facto* prisoner.

Alex was sitting at the plain table, his hands clasped easily in front of him. He turned and smiled with pleasure as I walked in. The man walking puffily up and down the small room turned too. With some difficulty I recognized the face above the purple neck as belonging to Emmanuel Corliss. He tore up to me and peering out of red-rimmed eyes began to grunt. After a while, I interpreted the grunts as *"You* ask him why. Ask him why he did it, why he ruined me!"

"I've told you that at least a dozen times," Parks said mildly. "There was nothing against you personally, nothing against anybody. I simply felt it was time we had interplanetary travel and that greed was a good incentive. I was right."

"Right!" Corliss screeched. "Right! Do you call it right to flimflam me out of three million dollars? I personally invested three million dollars to get what? Iron ore? If I want iron ore, isn't what we have on this planet good enough?"

"Your consolation, Mr. Corliss, in your financial bereavement, is that you have helped humanity to take a major historical step. You will recall that I went as far as using a shotgun in an attempt to keep you from getting involved in my . . . my plans. Beyond suggesting that you record it in your income tax under bad investments, I'm afraid I can't help you."

"Well, I can help you!" The president of General Atomics and the Radar Corporation of America shook a pudgy, quivering finger under Parks' nose. "I can help you into jail. I'll spend the rest of my life trying!" He slammed the door behind him so hard that the shack seemed to move three feet.

"Can he do anything, Alex?" I asked.

He shrugged. The pinhead looked tired. I suspected there had been a lot of this lately. "Not so far as I know. All the development on my lunar radar was out of my own funds. While I gave advice freely to those who wanted it, I never accepted a penny from any corporation or individual. I benefited in no material way from the fraud. My lawyers tell me it may be a tight squeeze, but there isn't anything that can be done in the way of punishment. I'm in the clear. Are . . . are you angry at me?"

"No!" I put my hand on his shoulder. "You've made life worth living for hundreds of us. Listen, Alex," I said softly, "I don't know what history will say, but there are a lot of sky-jockeys who will never forget you."

He grinned up. "Thanks, pal. I did try to keep you out of the mess. Name a precipice after me."

We can't go any further than the Moon right now, but I have a dandy little two-man ferrying job—secondhand of course—and as soon as I can scrounge up enough cash, I'm going to fit it with that new triple-flow drive. They say Venus should be in an early geological stage, and that means a lot of whole radium and uranium will be lying about. The first man to get there and stake out a claim would be kinda well-to-do the rest of his life. Yeah, that talk may be just some more sucker bait, but, just think, if it *is* so—

Whatever its original impulses, interplanetary transportation is here to stay. But what of the man responsible?

The Federal Lunar Commission (FLC) has issued a permanent injunction to all its offices against granting Alexander Parks terrestrial clearance. And unless he stows away on some supply ship, or time heals that particular wound, I'm afraid he'll be a wistful Earth-lubber to his dying day.

———————

Ray Bradbury

KALEIDOSCOPE

The first concussion cut the ship up the side like a giant can opener. The men were thrown into space like a dozen wriggling silverfish. They were scattered into a dark sea; and the ship, in a million pieces, went on like a meteor swarm seeking a lost sun.

"Barkley, Barkley, where are you?"

The sound of voices calling like lost children on a cold night.

"Woode, Woode!"

"Captain!"

"Hollis, Hollis, this is Stone."

"Stone, this is Hollis. Where are you?"

"I don't know, how can I? Which way is up? I'm falling. Good gosh, I'm falling."

They fell. They fell as pebbles fall in the long autumns of childhood, silver and thin. They were scattered as jackstones are scattered from a gigantic throw. And now instead of men there were only voices—all kinds of voices, disembodied and impassioned, in varying degrees of terror and resignation.

"We're going away from each other."

This was true. Hollis, swinging head over heels, knew this was true. He knew it with a vague acceptance. They were parting to go their separate ways, and nothing could bring them back. They were wearing their sealed-tight space suits with the glass tubes over their pale faces, but they hadn't had time to lock on their force units. With them, they could be small lifeboats in space, saving themselves, saving others, collecting together, finding each other until they were an island of men with some plan. But without the force units snapped to their shoulders they were meteors, senseless, each going to a separate and irrevocable fate.

A period of perhaps ten minutes elapsed while the first terror died and a metallic calm took its place. Space began to weave their strange voices in and out, on a great dark loom, crossing, recrossing, making a final pattern.

"Stone to Hollis. How long can we talk by phone?"

"It depends on how fast you're going your way and I'm going mine."

"An hour, I make it."

"That should do it," said Hollis, abstracted and quiet.

"What happened?" said Hollis, a minute later.

"The rocket blew up, that's all. Rockets do blow up."

"Which way are you going?"

"It looks like I'll hit the sun."

"It's Earth for me. Back to old Mother Earth at ten thousand miles per hour. I'll burn like a match." Hollis thought of it with a queer abstraction of mind. He seemed to be removed from his body, watching it fall down and down through space, as objective as he had been in regard to the first falling snowflakes of a winter season long gone.

The others were silent, thinking of the destiny that had brought them to this, falling, falling, and nothing they could do to change it. Even the captain was quiet, for there was no command or plan he knew that could put things back together again.

"Oh, it's a long way down, oh, it's a long way down, a long, long, long way down," said a voice. "I don't want to die, I don't want to die, it's a long way down."

"Who's that?"

"I don't know."

"Stimson, I think. Stimson, is that you?"

"It's a long way and I don't like it, oh God, I don't like it."

"Stimson, this is Hollis, Stimson, you hear me?"

A pause while they fell separate from one another.

"Stimson?"

"Yes." He replied at last.

"Stimson, take it easy, we're all in the same fix."

"I don't want to be here, I want to be somewhere else."

"There's a chance we'll be found."

"I must be, I must be," said Stimson. "I don't believe this, I don't believe any of this is happening."

"It's a bad dream," said someone.

"Shut up!" said Hollis.

"Come and make me," said the voice. It was Applegate. He laughed noisily, with a similar objectivity. "Come and shut me up."

Hollis for the first time felt the impossibility of his position. A great anger filled him, for he wanted more than anything in existence at this moment to be able to do something to Applegate. He had wanted for many years to do something and now it was too late. Applegate was only a telephonic voice.

Falling, falling, falling!

Now, as if they had discovered the horror, two of the men began to scream. In a nightmare, Hollis saw one of them float by, very near, screaming and screaming.

"Stop it!" The man was almost at his fingertips, screaming insanely. He would never stop. He would go on screaming for a million miles, as long as he was in radio range, disturbing all of them, making it impossible for them to talk to one another.

Hollis reached out. It was best this way. He made the extra effort and touched the man. He grasped the man's ankle and pulled himself up along the body until he reached the head. The man screamed and clawed frantically, like a drowning swimmer. The screaming filled the universe.

One way or the other, thought Hollis. The sun or Earth or meteors will kill him, so why not now?

He smashed the man's glass mask with his iron fist. The screaming stopped. He pushed off from the body and let it spin away on its own course, falling, falling.

Falling, falling down space went Hollis and the rest of them in the long, endless dropping and whirling of silent terror.

"Hollis, you still there?"

Hollis did not speak, but felt the rush of heat in his face.

"This is Applegate again."

"All right, Applegate."

"Let's talk. We haven't anything else to do."

The captain cut in. "That's enough of that. We've got to figure a way out of this."

"Captain, why don't you shut up?" said Applegate.

"What!"

"You heard me, Captain. Don't pull your rank on me, you're ten thousand miles away by now, and let's not kid ourselves. As Stimson puts it, it's a long way down."

"See here, Applegate!"

"Can it. This is a mutiny of one. I haven't a dang thing to lose. Your ship was a bad ship and you were a bad captain and I hope you roast when you hit the sun."

"I'm ordering you to stop!"

"Go on, order me again!" Applegate smiled across ten thousand miles. The captain was silent. Applegate continued, "Where were we, Hollis? Oh, yes, I remember. I hate you, too. But you know that. You've known it for a long time."

Hollis clenched his fists, hopelessly.

"I want to tell you something," said Applegate. "Make you happy I was the one who blackballed you with the Rocket Company five years ago."

A meteor flashed by. Hollis looked down and his left hand was gone. Blood spurted. Suddenly there was no air in his suit. He had enough air in his lungs to move his right hand over and twist a knob at his left elbow, tightening the joint and sealing the leak. It had happened so quickly that he was not surprised. Nothing surprised him any more. The air in the suit came back to normal in an instant now that the leak was sealed. And the blood that had flowed so swiftly was pressured as he fastened the knob yet tighter, until it made a tourniquet.

All of this took place in a terrible silence on his part. And the other men chatted. That one man, Lespere, went on and on with his talk about his wife on Mars, his wife on Venus, his wife on Jupiter, his money, his wondrous times, his drunkenness, his gambling, his happiness. On and on, while they all fell, fell. Lespere reminisced on the past, happy, while he fell to his death.

It was so very odd. Space, thousands of miles of space, and these voices vibrating in the center of it. No one visible at all, and only the radio waves quivering and trying to quicken other men into emotion.

"Are you angry, Hollis?"

"No." And he was not. The abstraction had returned and he was a thing of dull concrete, forever falling nowhere.

"You wanted to get to the top all your life, Hollis. And I ruined it for you. You always wondered what happened. I put the black mark on you just before I was tossed out myself."

"That isn't important," said Hollis. And it was not. It was gone. When life is over it is like a flicker of bright film, an instant on the screen, all of its prejudices and passions condensed and illumined for an instant on space, and before you could cry out. There was a happy day, there a bad one, there an evil face, there a good one, the film burned to a cinder, the screen was dark.

From this outer edge of his life, looking back, there was only one remorse, and that was only that he wished to go on living. Did all dying people feel this way, as if they had never lived? Does life seem that short, indeed, over and down before you took a breath? Did it seem this abrupt and impossible to everyone, or only to himself, here, now with a few hours left to him for thought and deliberation?

One of the other men was talking. "Well, I had me a good life. I had a wife on Mars and one on Venus and one on Earth and one on Jupiter. Each of them had money and they treated me swell. I had a wonderful time. I got drunk and once I gambled away twenty thousand dollars."

"But you're here now," thought Hollis. "I didn't have any of those things. When I was living I was jealous of you, Lespere, when I had another day ahead of me I envied you your women and your good times. Women frightened me and I went into space, always wanting them, and jealous of you for having them, and money, and as much happiness as you could have in your own wild way. But now, falling here, with everything over, I'm not jealous of you any more, because it's over for you as it is over for me, and right now it's like it never was." Hollis craned his face forward and shouted into the telephone.

"It's all over, Lespere!"

Silence.

"It's just as if it never was, Lespere!"

"Who's that?" Lespere's faltering voice.

"This is Hollis."

He was being mean. He felt the meanness, the senseless meanness of dying. Applegate had hurt him, now he wanted to hurt another. Applegate and space had both wounded him.

"You're out here, Lespere. It's all over. It's just as if it had never happened, isn't it?"

"No."

"When anything's over, it's just like it never happened. Where's your life any better than mine, now? While it was happening, yes, but now? Now is what counts. Is it any better, is it?"

"Yes, it's better!"

"How!"

"Because I got my thoughts; I remember!" cried Lespere, far away, indignant, holding his memories to his chest with both hands.

And he was right. With a feeling of cold water gushing through his head and his body, Hollis knew he was right. There were differences between memories and dreams. He had only dreams of things he had wanted to do, while Lespere had memories of things done and accomplished. And this knowledge began to pull Hollis apart, with a slow, quivering precision.

"What good does it do you?" he cried to Lespere. "Now? When a thing's over it's not good any more. You're no better off than me."

"I'm resting easy," said Lespere. "I've had my turn. I'm not getting mean at the end, like you."

"Mean?" Hollis turned the word on his tongue. He had never been mean, as long as he could remember, in his life. He had never dared to be mean. He must have saved it all of these years for such a time as this. "Mean." He rolled the word into the back of his mind. He felt tears start in his eyes and roll down his face. Someone must have heard his gasping voice.

"Take it easy, Hollis."

It was, of course, ridiculous. Only a minute before he had been giving advice to others, to Stimson, he had felt a braveness which he had thought to be the genuine thing, and now he knew that it had been nothing but shock and the objectivity possible in shock. Now he was trying to pack a lifetime of suppressed emotion into an interval of minutes.

"I know how you feel, Hollis," said Lespere, now twenty thousand miles away, his voice fading. "I don't take it personally."

But aren't we equal, his wild mind wondered. Lespere and I? Here, now? If a good thing's over it's done, and what good is it? You die anyway. But he knew he was rationalizing, for it was like trying to tell the difference between a live man and a corpse. There was a spark in one, and not in the other, an aura, a mysterious element.

So it was with Lespere and himself; Lespere had lived a good full life, and it made him a different man now, and he, Hollis, had been as good as dead for many years. They came to death by separate paths and, in all likelihood, if there were kinds of deaths, their kinds would be as different as night from day. The quality of death, like that of life, must be of infinite variety, and if one has already died once, then what is there to look for in dying for once and all, as he was now?

It was a second later that he discovered his right foot was cut sheer away. It almost made him laugh. The air was gone from his suit again, he bent quickly, and there was blood, and the meteor had taken flesh and suit away to the ankle. Oh, death in space was most humorous, it cut you away, piece by piece, like a black and invisible butcher. He tightened the valve at the knee, his head swirling into pain, fighting to remain aware, and with the valve tightened, the blood retained, the air kept, he straightened up and went on falling, falling, for that was all there was left to do.

"Hollis?"

Hollis nodded sleepily, tired of waiting for death.

"This is Applegate again," said the voice.

"Yes."

"I've had time to think. I listened to you. This isn't good. It makes us mean. This is a bad way to die. It brings all the bile out. You listening, Hollis?"

"Yes."

"I lied. A minute ago. I lied. I didn't blackball you. I don't know why I said that. Guess I wanted to hurt you. You seemed the one to hurt. We've always fought. Guess I'm getting old fast and repenting fast. I guess listening to you be mean made me ashamed. Whatever the reason, I want you to know I was an idiot, too. There's not an ounce of truth in what I said. To heck with you."

Hollis felt his heart began to work again. It seemed as if it hadn't worked for five minutes, but now all of his limbs began to take color and warmth. The shock was over, and the successive shocks of anger and terror and loneliness were passing. He felt like a man emerging from a cold shower in the morning, ready for breakfast and a new day.

"Thanks, Applegate."

"Don't mention it. Up your nose, you slob."

"Where's Stimson, how is he?"

"Stimson?"

They listened.

No answer.

"He must be gone."

"I don't think so. Stimson!"

They listened again.

They could hear a long, slow, hard breathing in their phones.

"That's him. Listen."

"Stimson!"

No reply.

Only the slow, hard breathing.

"He won't answer."

"He's gone insane, God help him."

"That's it. Listen."

The silent breathing, the quiet.

"He's closed up like a clam. He's in himself, making a pearl. Listen to the poet, will you. He's happier than us now, anyway."

They listened to Stimson float away.

"Hey," said Stone.

"What?" Hollis called across space, for Stone, of all of them, was a good friend.

"I've got myself into a meteor swarm, some little asteroids."

"Meteors?"

"I think it's the Myrmidone cluster that goes out past Mars and in toward Earth once every five years. I'm right in the middle. It's like a big kaleidoscope. You get all kinds of colors and shapes and sizes. God, it's beautiful, all the metal."

Silence.

"I'm going with them," said Stone. "They're taking me off with them. I'll be damned." He laughed tightly.

Hollis looked to see, but saw nothing. There were only the great jewelries of space, the diamonds and sapphires and emerald mists and velvet inks of space, with God's voice mingling among the crystal fires. There was a kind of wonder and imagination in the thought of Stone going off in the meteor swarm, out past Mars for years and coming in toward Earth every five years, passing in and out of the planet's ken for the next million years, Stone and the Myrmidone cluster eternal and unending, shifting and shaping like the kaleidoscope colors when you were a child and held the long tube to the sun and gave it a twirl.

"So long, Hollis." Stone's voice, very faint now. "So long."

"Good luck," shouted Hollis across thirty thousand miles.

"Don't be funny," said Stone, and was gone.

The stars closed in.

Now all the voices were fading, each on their own trajectories, some to the sun, others into farthest space. And Hollis himself. He looked down. He, of all the others, was going back to Earth alone.

"So long."

"Take it easy."

"So long, Hollis." That was Applegate.

The many good-bys. The short farewells. And now the great loose brain was disintegrating. The components of the brain, which had worked so beautifully and efficiently in the skull case of the rocket ship racing through space, were dying off one by one, the meaning of their life together was falling apart. And as a body dies when the brain ceases functioning, so the spirit of the ship and their long time together and what they meant to one another was dying. Applegate was now no more than a finger blown from the parent body, no longer to be despised and worked against. The brain was exploded, and the senseless, useless fragments of it were far-scattered. The voices faded and now all of space was silent. Hollis was alone, falling.

They were all alone. Their voices had died like echoes of the words of God spoken and vibrating in the starred space. There went the captain to the sun; there Stone with the meteor swarm; there Stimson, tightened and unto himself; there Applegate toward Pluto; there Smith and Turner and Underwood and all the rest, the shards of the kaleidoscope that had formed a thinking pattern for so long, now hurled apart.

And I? thought Hollis. What can I do? Is there anything I can do now to make up for a terrible and empty life? If I could do one good thing to make up for the meanness I collected all these years and didn't even know was in me? But there's no one here, but myself, and how can you do good all alone? You can't. Tomorrow night I'll hit Earth's atmosphere.

I'll burn, he thought, and be scattered in ashes all over the continental lands. I'll be put to use. Just a little bit, but ashes are ashes and they'll add to the land.

He fell swiftly, like a bullet, like a pebble, like an iron weight, objective, objective all of the time now, not sad or happy or anything, but only wishing he could do a good thing now that everyone was gone, a good thing for just himself to know about.

When I hit the atmosphere, I'll burn like a meteor.

"I wonder," he said. "If anyone'll see me?"

The small boy on the country road looked up and screamed. "Look, Mom, look! A falling star!"

The blazing white star fell down the sky of dusk in Illinois.

"Make a wish," said his mother. "Make a wish."

———————

"NOTHING HAPPENS ON THE MOON"

THE SHINING BALL of the full Earth floated like a smooth pearl between two vast, angular mountains. The full Earth. Another month had ticked by.

Clow Hartigan turned from the porthole beside the small air lock to the Bliss radio transmitter.

"RC3, RC3, RC3," he droned out.

There was no answer. Stacey, up in New York, always took his time about answering the RC3 signal, confound it! But then, why shouldn't he? There was never anything of importance to listen from Station RC3. Nothing of any significance ever happened on the Moon.

Hartigan stared unseeingly at the pink cover of a six-month-old *Radio Gazette*, pasted to the wall over the control board. A pulchritudinous brunette stared archly back at him over a plump shoulder that was only one of many large nude areas.

"RC3, RC3—"

Ah, there Stacey was, the pompous little busybody.

"Hartigan talking. Monthly report."

"Go ahead, Hartigan."

A hurried, fussy voice. Calls of real import waited for Stacey; calls from Venus and Jupiter and Mars. Hurry up, Moon, and report that nothing has happened, as usual.

Hartigan proceeded to do so.

"Lunar conditions the same. No ships have put in, or have reported themselves as being in distress. The hangar is in good shape, with no leaks. Nothing out of the way has occurred."

"Right," said Stacey pompously. "Supplies?"

"You might send up a blonde," said Hartigan.

"Be serious. Need anything?"

"No." Hartigan's eyes brooded. "How's everything in Little Old New York?"

Stacey's businesslike voice was a reproof. Also it was a pain in the neck.

"Sorry. Can't gossip. Things pretty busy around here. If you need anything, let me know."

The burr of power went dead. Hartigan cursed with monotony, and got up.

Clow Hartigan was a big young man with sand-red hair and slightly bitter blue eyes. He was representative of the type Spaceways sent to such isolated emergency landing stations as the Moon.

There were half a dozen such emergency landing domes, visited only by supply ships, exporting nothing, but ready in case some passenger liner was crippled by a meteor or by mechanical trouble. The two worst on the

249

Spaceways list were the insulated hell on Mercury, and this great, lonely hangar on the Moon. To them Spaceways sent the pick of their probation executives. Big men. Powerful men. Young men. (Also men who were unlucky enough not to have an old family friend or an uncle on the board of directors who could swing a soft berth for them.) Spaceways did not keep them there long. Men killed themselves, or went mad and began inconsiderately smashing expensive equipment, after too long a dose of such loneliness as that of the Moon.

Hartigan went back to the porthole beside the small air lock. As he went, he talked to himself, as men do when they have been too long away from their own kind.

"I wish I'd brought a dog up here, or a cat. I wish there'd be an attempted raid. Anything at all. If only something would *happen.*"

Resentfully he stared out at the photographic, black-and-white lunar landscape, lighted coldly by the full Earth. From that his eye went to the deep black of the heavens. Then his heart gave a jump. There was a faint light up there where no light was supposed to be.

He hurried to the telescope and studied it. A space liner, and a big one! Out of its course, no matter where it was bound, or it couldn't have been seen from the Moon with the naked eye. Was it limping in here to the emergency landing for repairs?

"I don't wish them any bad luck," muttered Hartigan, "but I hope they've burned out a rocket tube."

Soon his heart sank, however. The liner soared over the landing dome a hundred miles up, and went serenely on its way. In a short time its light faded in distance. Probably it was one of the luxurious around-the-solar-system ships, passing close to the Moon to give the sightseers an intimate glimpse of it, but not stopping because there was absolutely nothing of interest there.

"Nothing *ever* happens in this Godforsaken hole," Hartigan gritted.

Impatiently he took his space suit down from the rack. Impatiently he stepped into the bulky, flexible metal thing and clamped down the headpiece. Nothing else to do. He'd take a walk. The red beam of the radio control board would summon him back to the hangar if for any reason anyone tried to raise RC3.

He let himself out through the double wall of the small air lock and set out with easy, fifteen-foot strides toward a nearby cliff on the brink of which it was sometimes his habit to sit and think nasty thoughts of the men who ran Spaceways and maintained places like RC3.

Between the hangar and the cliff was a wide expanse of gray lava ash, a sort of small lake of the stuff, feathery fine. Hartigan did not know how deep it might be. He did know that a man could probably sink down in it so far that he would never be able to burrow out again.

He turned to skirt the lava ash, but paused a moment before proceeding.

Behind him loomed the enormous half globe of the hangar, like a phosphorescent mushroom in the blackness. One section of the half globe was flattened; and here were the gigantic inner and outer portals where a liner's rocket-propelled life shells could enter the dome. The great doors of this, the main air lock, reared halfway to the top of the hangar, and weighed several hundred tons apiece.

Before him was the face of the Moon: sharp angles of rock; jagged, tremendous mountains; sheer, deep craters; all picked out in black and white from the reflected light of Earth.

A desolate prospect. . . . Hartigan started on.

The ash beside him suddenly seemed to explode, soundlessly but with great violence. It spouted up like a geyser to a distance of a hundred feet, hung for an instant over him in a spreading cloud, then quickly began to settle.

A meteor! Must have been a fair-sized one to have made such a splash in the volcanic dust.

"Close call," muttered Hartigan, voice sepulchral in his helmet. "A little nearer and they'd be sending a new man to the lunar emergency dome."

But he only grimaced and went on. Meteors were like the lightning back on Earth. Either they hit you or they missed. There was no warning till after they struck; then it was too late to do anything about it.

Hartigan stumbled over something in the cloud of ash that was sifting down around him. Looking down, he saw a smooth, round object, black-hot, about as big as his head.

"The meteor," he observed. "Must have hit a slanting surface at the bottom of the ash heap and ricocheted up and out here. I wonder—"

He stooped clumsily toward it. His right "hand," which was a heavy pincer arrangement terminating the right sleeve of his suit, went out, then his left, and with some difficulty he picked the thing up. Now and then a meteor held splashes of precious metals. Sometimes one was picked up that yielded several hundred dollars' worth of platinum or iridium. A little occasional gravy with which the emergency-landing exiles could buy amusement when they got back home.

Through the annoying shower of ash he could see dimly the light of the hangar. He started back, to get out of his suit and analyze the meteor for possible value.

It was the oddest-looking thing he had ever seen come out of the heavens. In the first place, its shape was remarkable. It was perfectly round, instead of being irregular as were most meteors.

"Like an old-fashioned cannon ball," Hartigan mused, bending over it on a workbench. "Or an egg—"

Eyebrows raised whimsically, he played with the idea.

"Jupiter! What an egg it would be! A hundred and twenty pounds if it's an ounce, and it smacked the Moon like a bullet without even cracking! I wouldn't want it poached for breakfast."

The next thing to catch his attention was the projectile's odd color, or, rather, the odd way in which the color seemed to be changing. It had been dull, black-hot, when Hartigan brought it in. It was now a dark green, and was getting lighter swiftly as it cooled!

The big clock struck a mellow note. Time for the dome keeper to make his daily inspection of the main doors.

Reluctantly Hartigan left the odd meteor, which was now as green as grass and actually seemed to be growing transparent, and walked toward the big air lock.

He switched on the radio power unit. There was no power plant of any kind in the hangar; all power was broadcast by the Spaceways central station. He reached for the contact switch which poured the invisible Niagara of power into the motors that moved the ponderous doors.

Cr-r-rack!

Like a cannon shot the sound split the air in the huge metal dome, echoing from wall to wall, to die at last in a muffled rumbling.

White-faced, Hartigan was running long before the echoes died away. He ran toward the workbench he had recently quitted. The sound seemed to have come from near there. His thought was that the hangar had been crashed by a meteor larger than its cunningly braced beams, tough metal sheath, and artful angles of deflection would stand.

That would mean death, for the air supply in the dome would race out through a fissure almost before he could don his space suit.

However, his anxious eyes, scanning the vaulting roof, could find no crumpled bracing or ominous downward bulges. And he could hear no thin whine of air surging in the hangar to the almost nonexistent pressure outside.

Then he glanced at the workbench and uttered an exclamation. The meteor he had left there was gone.

"It must have rolled off the bench," he told himself. "But if it's on the floor, why can't I see it?"

He froze into movelessness. Had that been a sound behind him? A sound, here, where no sound could possibly be made save by himself?

He whirled—and saw nothing. Nothing whatever, save the familiar expanse of smooth rock floor lighted with the cold white illumination broadcast on the power band.

He turned back to the workbench where the meteor had been, and began feeling over it with his hands, disbelieving the evidence of his eyes.

Another exclamation burst from his lips as his fingers touched something hard and smooth and round. The meteor. Broken into two halves, but still here. Only, *now it was invisible!*

"This," said Hartigan, beginning to sweat a little, "is the craziest thing I ever heard of!"

He picked up one of the two invisible halves and held it close before his eyes. He could not see it at all, though it was solid to the touch. Moreover, he seemed able to see through it, for nothing on the other side was blotted out.

Fear increased within him as his fingers told him that the two halves were empty, hollow. Heavy as the ball had been, it consisted of nothing but a shell about two inches thick. Unless—

"Unless something really did crawl out of it when it split apart."

But that, of course, was ridiculous.

"It's just an ordinary metallic chunk," he told himself, "that split open with a loud bang when it cooled, due to contraction. The only thing unusual about it is its invisibility. That *is* strange."

He groped on the workbench for the other half of the thick round shell. With a half in each hand, he started toward the stock room, meaning to lock up this odd substance very carefully. He suspected he had something beyond price here. If he could go back to Earth with a substance that could produce invisibility, he could become one of the richest men in the universe.

He presented a curious picture as he walked over the brilliantly lighted floor. His shoulders sloped down with the weight of the two pieces of meteor. His bare arms rippled and knotted with muscular effort. Yet his hands seemed empty. So far as the eye could tell, he was carrying nothing whatever.

"What—"

He dropped the halves of the shell with a ringing clang, and began leaping toward the big doors. That time he *knew* he had heard a sound, a sound like scurrying steps! It had come from near the big doors.

When he got there, however, he could hear nothing. For a time the normal stillness, the ghastly, phenomenal stillness, was preserved. Then, from near the spot he had just vacated, he heard another noise. This time it was a gulping, voracious noise, accompanied by a sound that was like that of a rock crusher or a concrete mixer in action.

On the run, he returned, seeing nothing all this while; nothing but smooth rock floor and plain, metal-ribbed walls, and occasional racks of instruments.

He got to the spot where he had dropped the parts of the meteor. The parts were no longer there. This time it was more than a question of invisibility. They had disappeared actually as well as visually.

To make sure, Hartigan got down on hands and knees and searched every inch of a large circle. There was no trace of the thick shell.

"Either something brand-new to the known solar system is going on here," Hartigan declared, "or I'm getting as crazy as they insisted poor Stuyvesant was."

Increased perspiration glinted on his forehead. The fear of madness in the lonelier emergency fields was a very real fear. United Spaceways had been petitioned more than once to send two men instead of one to manage each outlying field; but Spaceways was an efficient corporation with no desire to pay two men where one could handle the job.

Again Hartigan could hear nothing at all. And in swift though un-admitted fear that perhaps the whole business had transpired only in his own brain, he sought refuge in routine. He returned to his task of testing the big doors, which was important even though dreary in its daily repetition.

The radio power unit was on, as he had left it. He closed the circuit.

Smoothly the enormous inner doors swung open on their broad tracks, to reveal the equally enormous outer portals. Hartigan stepped into the big air lock, and closed the inner doors. He shivered a little. It was near freezing out here in spite of the heating units.

There was a small control room in the lock, to save an operator the trouble of always getting into a space suit when the doors were opened. Hartigan entered this and pushed home the switch that moved the outer portals.

Smoothly, perfectly, their tremendous bulk opened outward. They always worked smoothly, perfectly. No doubt they always would. Nevertheless, rules said test them regularly. And it was best to live up to the rules. With characteristic trustfulness, Spaceways had recording dials in the home station that showed by power markings whether or not their planetary employees were doing what they were supposed to do.

Hartigan reversed the switch. The doors began to close. They got to the halfway mark; to the three-quarters—

Hartigan felt rather than heard the sharp, grinding jar. He felt rather than heard the high, shrill scream, a rasping shriek, almost above the limit of audibility, that was something to make a man's blood run cold.

Still, without faltering, the doors moved inward and their serrated edges met. Whatever one of them had ground across had not been large enough to shake it.

"Jupiter!" Hartigan breathed, once more inside the huge dome with both doors closed.

He sat down to try to think the thing out.

"A smooth, round meteor falls. It looks like an egg, though it seems to be of metallic rock. As it cools, it gets lighter in color, till finally it disappears. With a loud bang, it bursts apart, and afterward I hear a sound like scurrying feet. I drop the pieces of the shell to go toward the sound, and then I hear another sound, as if something were macerating and gulping down the pieces of shell, eating them. I come back and can't find the pieces. I go on with my test of opening and closing the main doors. As the outer door closes, I hear a crunching noise as if a rock were being pulverized, and a high scream like that of an animal in pain. All this would indicate that the meteor *was* a shell, and that some living thing *did* come out of it.

"But that is impossible.

"No form of life could live through the crash with which that thing struck the Moon, even though the lava ash did cushion the fall to some extent. No form of life could stand the heat of the meteor's fall and impact. No form of life could eat the rocky, metallic shell. It's utterly impossible!

"Or—is it impossible?"

He gnawed at his knuckles and thought of Stuyvesant.

Stuyvesant had been assigned to the emergency dome on Mercury. There was a place for you! An inferno! By miracles of insulation and supercooling systems the hangar there had been made livable. But the finest of space suits could not keep a man from frying to death outside. Nothing to do except stay cooped up inside the hangar, and pray for the six-month relief to come.

Stuyvesant had done that. And from Stuyvesant had begun to come queer reports. He thought he had seen something moving on Mercury near his landing field. Something like a rock!

Moving rocks! With the third report of that kind, the corporation had brought him home and turned him over to the board of science for examination. Poor Stuyvesant had barely escaped the lunatic asylum. He had been let out of Spaceways, of course. The corporation scrapped men suspected of being defective as quickly as they scrapped suspect material.

"When a man begins to see rocks moving, it's time to fire him," was the unofficial verdict.

The board of science had coldly said the same thing, though in more dignified language.

"No form of life as we know it could possibly exist in the high temperature and desert condition of Mercury. Therefore, in our judgment, Benjamin Stuyvesant suffered from hallucination when he reported some rocklike entity moving near Emergency Hangar RC10."

Hartigan glanced uneasily toward the workbench on which the odd meteor had rested.

"No form of life *as we know it.*"

There was the catch. After all, this interplanetary travel was less than seventy years old. Might there not be many things still unknown to Earth wisdom?

"Not to hear the board of science tell it," muttered Hartigan, thinking of Stuyvesant's blasted career.

He thought of the Forbidden Asteroids. There were over two dozen on the charts on which, even in direst emergency, no ship was supposed to land. That was because ships had landed there, and had vanished without trace. Again and again. With no man able to dream of their fate. Till they simply marked the little globes "Forbidden," and henceforth ignored them.

"No form of life as we know it!"

Suppose something savage, huge, invisible, lived on those grim asteroids? Something that developed from egg form? Something that spread its young through the universe by propelling eggs from one celestial body to another? Something that started growth by devouring its own metallic shell, and continued it on a mineral instead of vegetable diet? Something that could live in any atmosphere or temperature?

"I *am* going crazy," Hartigan breathed.

In something like panic he tried to forget the affair in a great stack of books and magazines brought by the last supply ship.

The slow hours of another month ticked by. The full Earth waned, died, grew again. Drearily Hartigan went through the monotony of his routine. Day after day, the term "day" being a strictly figurative one on this drear lunar lump.

He rose at six, New York time, and sponged off carefully in a bit of precious water. He ate breakfast. He read. He stretched his muscles in a stroll. He read. He inspected his equipment. He read. He exercised on a set of homemade flying rings. He read.

"No human being should be called on to live like this," he said once, voice too loud and brittle.

But human beings did have to live like this, if they aspired to one of the big posts on a main planet.

He had almost forgotten the strange meteor that had fallen into lava ash at his feet a month ago. It was to be recalled with terrible abruptness.

He went for a walk in a direction he did not usually take, and came upon a shallow pit half a mile from the dome.

Pits, of course, are myriad on the Moon. The whole surface is made up of craters within craters. But this pit was not typical in conformation. Most are smooth-walled and flat-bottomed. This pit was ragged, as if it had been dug out. Besides, Hartigan had thought he knew every hole for a mile around, and he did not remember ever seeing this one.

He stood on its edge looking down. There was loose rock in its un-craterlike bottom, and the loose rock had the appearance of being freshly dislodged. Even this was not unusual in a place where the vibration of a footstep could sometimes cause tons to crack and fall.

Nevertheless, Hartigan could feel the hair rise a bit on the back of his neck as some deep, instinctive fear crawled within him at sight of the small, shallow pit. And then he caught his lips between his teeth and stared with wide, unbelieving eyes.

On the bottom of the pit a rock was moving. It was moving, not as if it had volition of its own, but as if it were being handled by some unseen thing.

A fragment about as big as his body, it rolled over twice, then slid along in impatient jerks as though a big head or hoof nudged at it. Finally it raised up from the ground and hung poised about seven feet in the air!

Breathlessly, Hartigan watched, while all his former, almost superstitious fear flooded through him.

The rock fragment moved up and down in mid-space.

"Jupiter!" Clow Hartigan breathed hoarsely.

A large part of one end suddenly disappeared. A pointed projection from the main mass of rock, it broke off and vanished from sight.

Another large chunk followed, breaking off and disappearing as though by magic.

"Jupiter!"

There was no longer doubt in Hartigan's mind. A live thing had emerged from the egglike meteor twenty-seven days ago. A live thing, that now roamed loose over the face of the Moon.

But that section of rock, which was apparently being devoured, was held seven feet off the ground. What manner of creature could come from an egg no larger than his head and grow in one short month into a thing over seven feet tall? He thought of the Forbidden Asteroids, where no ships landed, though no man knew precisely what threat lurked there.

"It must be as big as a mastodon," Hartigan whispered. "What in the universe—"

The rock fragment was suddenly dropped, as if whatever invisible thing had held it had suddenly seen Hartigan at the rim of the pit. Then the rock was dashed to one side as if by a charging body. The next instant loose fragments of shale scattered right and left up one side of the pit as though a big body were climbing up and out.

The commotion in the shale was on the side of the pit nearest Hartigan. With a cry he ran toward the hangar.

With fantastic speed, sixty and seventy feet to a jump, he covered the ragged surface. But fast as he moved, he felt that the thing behind him moved faster. And that there *was* something behind him he did not doubt for an instant, though he could neither see nor hear it.

It was weird, this pygmy human form in its bulky space suit flying soundlessly over the lunar surface under the glowing ball of Earth, racing like mad for apparently no reason at all, running insanely when, so far as the eye could tell, nothing pursued.

But abysmal instinct told Hartigan that he was pursued, all right. And instinct told him that he could never reach the hangar in the lead. With desperate calmness he searched the ground still lying between him and the hangar.

A little ahead was a crack about a hundred feet wide and, as far as he knew, bottomless. With his oversized Earth muscles he could clear that in a gigantic leap. Could the ponderous, invisible thing behind him leap that far?

He was in mid-flight long enough to turn his head and look back, as he hurtled the chasm in a prodigious jump. He saw a flurry among the rocks at the edge he had just left as something jumped after him. Then he came down on the far side, lighting in full stride like a hurdler.

He risked slowing his speed by looking back again. A second time he saw a flurry of loose rock, this time on the near side of the deep crack. The thing had not quite cleared the edge, it seemed.

He raced on and came to the small air-lock door. He flung himself inside. He had hardly got the fastener in its groove when something banged against the outside of the door.

The thing pursuing him had hung on the chasm's edge long enough to let him reach safety, but had not fallen into the black depths as he had hoped it might.

"But that's all right," he said, drawing a great sigh of relief as he entered the hangar through the inner door. "I don't care what it does, now that I'm inside and it's out."

He got out of the space suit, planning as he moved.

The thing outside was over seven feet tall and made of some unfleshlike substance that must be practically indestructible. At its present rate of growth it would be as big as a small space liner in six months, if it weren't destroyed. But it would have to be destroyed. Either that, or Emergency Station RC3 would have to be abandoned, and his job with it, which concerned him more than the station.

"I'll call Stacey to send a destroyer," he said crisply.

He moved toward the Bliss transmitter, eyes glinting. Things were happening on the Moon, now, all right! And the thing that was happening was going to prove Stuyvesant as sane as any man, much saner than the graybearded goats on the board of science.

He would be confined to the hangar till Stacey could send a destroyer. No more strolls. He shuddered a little as he thought of how many times he must have missed death by an inch in his walks during the past month.

Hartigan got halfway to the Bliss transmitter, skirting along the wall near the small air lock.

A dull, hollow, booming sound filled the great hangar, ascending to the vaulted roof and seeming to shower down again like black water.

Hartigan stopped and stared at the wall beside him. It was bulging inward a little. Startled out of all movement, he stared at the ominous, slight bulge. And as he stared, the booming noise was repeated, and the bulge grew a bit larger.

"In the name of Heaven!"

The thing outside had managed to track him along the wall from the air lock, perhaps guided by the slight vibration of his steps. Now it was blindly charging the huge bulk of the hangar like a living, ferocious ram.

A third time the dull, terrible booming sound reverberated in the lofty hangar. The bulge in the tough metal wall spread again; and the two nearest supporting beams gave ever so little at the points of strain.

Hartigan moved back toward the air lock. While he moved, there was silence. The moment he stopped, there was another dull, booming crash and a second bulge appeared in the wall. The thing had followed him precisely, and was trying to get at him.

The color drained from Hartigan's face. This changed the entire scheme of things.

It was useless to radio for help now. Long before a destroyer could get here, the savage, insensate monster outside would have opened a rent in the wall. That would mean Hartigan's death from escaping air in the hangar.

Crash!

Who would have dreamed that there lived anywhere in the universe, on no matter how far or wild a globe, a creature actually able to damage the massive walls of a Spaceways hangar? He could see himself trying to tell about this.

"An animal big enough to crack a hangar wall? And invisible? Well!"

Crash!

The very light globes, so far overhead, seemed to quiver a bit with the impact of this thing of unguessable nature against the vast semisphere of the hangar. The second bulge was deep enough so that the white enamel which coated it began chipping off in little flakes at the bulge's apex.

"What the devil am I going to do?"

The only thing he could think of for the moment was to move along the wall. That unleashed giant outside must not concentrate too long on any one spot.

He walked a dozen steps. As before, the ramming stopped while he was in motion, to start again as he halted. As before, it started at the point nearest to him.

Once more a bulge appeared in the wall, this time bigger than either of the first two. The metal sheets sheathing the hangar varied a little in strength. The invisible terror outside had struck a soft spot.

Hartigan moved hastily to another place.

"The whole base of the hangar will be scalloped like a pie crust at this rate," he gritted. "What can I—"

Crash!

He had inadvertently stopped near a rack filled with spare power bulbs. With its ensuing attack the blind fury had knocked the rack down onto the floor.

Hartigan's jaw set hard. Whatever he did must be done quickly. And it must be done by himself alone. He could not stay at the Bliss transmitter long enough to get New York and tell what was wrong, without giving the gigantic thing outside a fatal number of minutes in which to concentrate on one section of wall.

He moved slowly around the hangar, striving to keep the invisible fury too occupied in following him to get in more than an occasional charge. As he walked, his eyes went from one heap of supplies to another in search of a possible means of defense.

There were ordinary weapons in plenty, in racks along the wall. But none of these, he knew, could do material harm to the attacking fury.

He got to the great inner doors of the main air lock in his slow march around the hangar. And here he stopped, eyes glowing thoughtfully.

The huge doors had threatened in the early days to be the weak points in the Spaceways hangars. So the designers, like good engineers, had made the doors so massive that in the end they were stronger than the walls around them.

Bang!

A bulge near the massive hinges told Hartigan that the thing outside was as relentless as ever in its effort to break through the wall and get at him. But he paid no attention to the new bulge. He was occupied with the doors.

If the invisible giant could be trapped in the main air lock between the outer and inner portals—

"Then what?" Hartigan wondered.

He could not answer his own question. But, anyway, it seemed like a step in the right direction to have the attacking fury penned between the doors rather than to have it loose and able to charge the more vulnerable walls.

"If I can coop it in the air lock, I might be able to think of some way to attack it," he went on.

He pushed home the control switch which set the broadcast power to opening the outer doors. And *that* gave him an idea that sent a wild thrill surging through him.

A heavy rumble told him that the motors were swinging open the outer doors.

"Will the thing come in?" he asked himself tensely. "Or has it sense enough to scent a trap?"

Bang!

The inner doors trembled a little on their broad tracks. The invisible monster had entered the trap.

"Trap?" Hartigan smiled mirthlessly. "Not much of a trap! Left to itself, it could probably break out in half an hour. But it won't be left to itself."

He reversed the switch to close the outer portals. Then, with the doors closed and the monster penned between, he got to work on the idea that had been born when he pushed the control switch.

Power, oceans of it, flooded from the power unit at the touch of a finger. A docile servant when properly channeled, it could be the deadliest thing on the Moon.

He ran back down the hangar to the stock room, and got out a drum of spare power cable. As quickly as was humanly possible, he rolled the drum back to the doors, unwinding the cable as he went.

It was with grim solemnity that he made his next move. He had to open the inner doors a few inches to go on with his frail plan of defense. And he had to complete that plan before the thing in the air lock could claw them open still more and charge through. For all their weight the doors rolled in perfect balance; and if the unseen terror could make dents in the solid wall, it certainly was strong enough to move the partly opened doors.

Speed! That was the thing that would make or break him. Speed, and hope that the power unit could stand a terrific overload without blowing a tube.

With a hand that inclined to tremble a bit, Hartigan moved the control switch operating the inner doors, and instantly cut the circuit again.

The big doors opened six inches or so, and stopped.

Hartigan cut off the power unit entirely, and dragged the end of the spare power cable to it. With flying fingers he disconnected the cable leading from the control switch to the motors that moved the portals, and connected the spare cable in its space.

He glanced anxiously at the doors, and saw that the opening between them had widened to more than a foot. The left door moved a little even as he watched.

"I'll never make it!"

But he went ahead.

Grabbing up the loose end of the cable, he threw it in a tangled coil as far as he could through the opening and into the air lock. Then he leaped for the power unit—and watched.

The cable lay unmoving on the air-lock floor. But the left door moved! It jerked, and rolled open another six inches.

Hartigan clenched his hands as he stared at the inert cable. He had counted on the blind ferocity of the invisible terror; had counted on its attacking, or at least touching, the cable immediately. Had it enough intelligence to realize dimly that it would be best to avoid the cable? Was it going to keep on working at those doors till—

The power cable straightened with a jerk. Straightened, and hung still, with the loose end suspended in midair about six feet off the air-lock floor.

Hartigan's hand slammed down. The broadcast power was turned on to the last notch.

With his heart hammering in his throat, Hartigan gazed through the two-foot opening between the doors. Gazed at the cable through which was coursing oceans, Niagaras of power. And out there in the air-lock a thing began to build up from thin air into a spectacle that made him cry out in wild horror.

He got a glimpse of a massive block of a head, eyeless and featureless, that joined with no neck whatever to a barrel of a body. He got a glimpse of five legs, like stone pillars, and of a sixth that was only a stump. ("That's what got caught in the doors a month ago—its leg," he heard himself babbling with insane calmness.) Over ten feet high and twenty feet long, the thing was, a living battering-ram, painted in the air in sputtering, shimmering blue sparks that streamed from its massive bulk in all directions.

Just a glimpse, he got, and then the monster began to scream as it had that first day when the door maimed it. Only now it was with a volume that tore at Hartigan's eardrums till he screamed himself in agony.

As he watched, he saw the huge carcass melt a little, like wax in flame, with the power cable also melting slowly and fusing into the cavernous, rocky jaws that had seized it. Then with a rush the whole bulk disintegrated into a heap of loose mineral matter.

Hartigan turned off the power unit and collapsed, with his face in his hands.

The shining ball of the full Earth floated like a smooth diamond between two vast, angular mountains. The full Earth.

Hartigan turned from the porthole beside the small air lock and strode to the Bliss radio transmitter.

"RC3, RC3, RC3," he droned out.

There was no answer. As usual, Stacey was taking his time about answering the Moon's signal.

"RC3, RC3—"

There he was.

"Hartigan talking. Monthly report."

"All right, Hartigan."

A hurried, fretful voice. Come on, Moon; report that, as always, nothing has happened.

"Lunar conditions the same," said Hartigan. "No ships have put in, or have reported themselves as being in distress. The hangar is in good shape, with no leaks."

"Right," said Stacey, in the voice of a busy man. "Supplies?"

"You might send up a blonde."

"Be serious, please. Supplies?"

"I need some new power bulbs."

"I'll send them on the next ship. Nothing irregular to report?"

Hartigan hesitated.

On the floor of the main air lock was a mound of burned, bluish mineral substance giving no indication whatever that it had once possessed outlandish, incredible life. In the walls of the hangar at the base were half a dozen new dents; but ricocheting meteors might have made those. The meteoric shell from which this bizarre animal had come had been devoured, so even that was not left for investigation.

He remembered the report of the board of science on Stuyvesant.

"Therefore, in our judgment, Benjamin Stuyvesant suffered from hallucination—"

He would have liked to help Stuyvesant. But on the other hand Stuyvesant had a job with a secondhand-space-suit store now, and was getting along pretty well in spite of Spaceways' dismissal.

"Nothing irregular to report?" repeated Stacey.

Hartigan stared, with one eyebrow sardonically raised, at the plump brunette on the pink *Radio Gazette* cover pasted to the wall. She stared coyly back over a bare shoulder.

"Nothing irregular to report," Hartigan said steadily.

TRIGGER TIDE

That first day and night I lay perfectly still. I was often conscious but there was no thought of moving. I breathed shallowly.

In midmorning of the second day I began to feel the ants and flies that swarmed in the cake of mud, blood and festering flesh I was wearing for clothes. Then, through the morning mists of its tiny sixth planet that giant white sun slammed down on me.

I had been able to see something of the surroundings before they began working me over. After they had taken the hood off my head and while they were stripping away my clothes and harness of power equipment, the first orbit moon—the little fast, pale green one—shot up out of the blue-black sea. I had been able to tell in its light that we were on a tide shelf, probably the third.

Now burnt, lashed and clubbed I lay face down in the quick growing weeds of the hot tide shelf. The weeds were beginning to crawl against my face in the breathless air and dimly I realized a moon must be rising.

It had been the predawn of the tenth day of period thirty-six when the two of them stepped out of an aircar on Quartz Street and the girl I was walking home to the Great Island Hotel turned me over to them. If it was true that I had been lying here that day and night and this was the next midmorning, and if this was the third shelf, there would soon be a tide washing over me.

That tide was not easy to calculate. That it could be figured out is a tribute to the way they drill information into you before you leave The Central on an assignment. But the most thorough textbook knowledge of a planet's conditions is thin stuff when you are actually there and have to *know* them better than the natives. I tried the calculation all over again with that great sun frying my skull and got the same answer.

In about an hour the big fifth orbit moon and the sun would be overhead. The equally big third orbit moon would be slightly behind. Together they would lift the sea onto the third shelf all through this latitude.

The kind of day it was these tides would come up smoothly and steadily. Through the buzzing of flies I could not hear the sea. That did not mean it was not a hundred feet away lapping rapidly higher on the third sea wall.

I lay perfectly still except for my shallow breathing and waited for the sea.

When the water came over me in a shallow rush I strangled. Quickly,

This story was originally published under the pseudonym of "Norman Menasco." The author's real name is here used by his request. *G. C.*

I refused to move. The water washed over me again and again softening the clotted mud that had kept me from oozing to death. Finally when the surf receded it was still about me and I had to try moving.

I got to my knees and set to work with my right hand to get some vision. With the sea now washing higher about me I finally got the clot from my right eye and achieved a blurred view of daylight.

You have to have at least some luck. When you run out of it altogether you are dead. The fourth sea wall was about fifty yards away and looked as though a normal man could make it quite easily. How I made it was another story. I could barely use my legs and the left arm was useless. All the time I was reopening my wounds on the quartzcar formations of the sea wall.

That quartzcar is not like the familiar coral that forms some of the islands of Earth. It is made up from quartz particles that are suspended in the ocean water. It is a concretion in an intricate lattice which small crustacea pile up in regular patterns. The animals build their quartzcar islands from the quartz dust that rises in tidal rhythms off the floor of the shallow planetary sea. Consequently the islands come in layers with tide shelves that correspond to the height of various lunar tides.

The only land on that planet is the countless archipelagoes of quartzcar. On the sea walls or when you dig it up it presents a fine rasplike face that opened my wounds and left me bleeding and gasping with pain when I reached the top.

That afternoon I was not unconscious. I slept. It was dark when I awakened. Then slowly, magnificently it was light again as the fifth orbit moon rose over the sea, a great ball of electric blue. Only a short time later the little chartreuse first moon came rocketing up to catch and finally, a shade to the south, to pass the larger body on its own quick trip to the zenith.

Back at The Central the "white haired boys," the psychostatisticians, can tell you all about why people get into wars. If they had not been right about every assignment they had plotted for me, I would never have lived to get beat up on this one. Sometimes their anthropoquations give very complex answers. Sometimes, as in the case of these people, the answer is simple. It was so simple in this case that it read like Twentieth Century newspaper propaganda. But lying there looking out into the glorious sky I didn't believe in wars. There never had been any. There never would be any. Surely they would close The Central and I could stay there forever watching the great moons roll across the galaxy.

I reawakened with a sharpened sense of urgency. I got to my feet. There was *going* to be a war if I didn't get on with the assignment. The fine part about this job was everyone wanted it "hush." The ideal performance for a Central Operator is, of course, to hit a planet, get the business over with and get out without anyone ever guessing you were doing anything but buying curios. Generally those you're up against try to throw you into public light—a bad light. These boys wanted it hush much worse than I did. It gave me a certain advantage tactically. I will not say the mess I had got myself into was part of my plan. But they were going to scramble at the sight of their mayhem walking back into the city.

I had to skirt half the city to reach my contact and a safe place to heal. To make it before morning I had to take advantage of every moment of moonlight.

After about half my journey I had a long wait in the dark before the fourth orbit moon came up and I was able to move ahead. I was skirting the city very close through the fern tree forest but, except for an occasional house and couples necking in aircars idling low over the fronds, I had little to worry about.

Toward morning the only light was the second brief flight of the tiny first moon and the going was much slower. But at least while it was up alone the vegetation did not move about so much. I finished the last lap to my Contact staggering and dangerously in broad daylight.

He didn't say anything when he opened the door of his cottage. He didn't show surprise or hesitate too long either. He led me in carefully and put me down on a bed.

Part of the time he was working on me I slept and part of the time I was wide awake gasping. It would have been just about as bad as when they worked me over except that he used some drugs and I knew he was trying to put me together instead of take me apart.

Then at last I slept undisturbed—that day and the next night. When I awoke he was still there staring down at me with no expression on his face.

It was the first time I had tried to form words with my mashed mouth. I finally got out, "How did you recognize me? You'd only seen me normal once."

I got two shocks in rapid succession. He said, "I'm awfully sorry about your eye."

It flashed over me that this man had gone sour as an Operator. No Central Operator is ever sorry for anything. Certainly no one ever says so when you've had "bad luck."

I got the second shock and pulled myself up from the bed. I searched the blurred room till I made out a mirror and went to it without his help. It was only then I realized they had put out one of my eyes.

I don't know whether it was just fury and determination to heal fast or whether he was right that there is some mysterious influence on that planet that accelerates healing. It took me only about three weeks to get back to the point where I felt I was in shape to tackle them again. The bones in my arm knitted very well and it was surprising how fast the burns healed.

He knew a lot about that planet, this Operator. He couldn't stop asking questions about it. What made the vegetation move when a moon was up? Why did the animal life, including men, slow its activity at the same time? The only question it seemed he hadn't asked was why he, an Operator for The Central, had adopted one of the major habits of the planet he had been assigned to. He wouldn't move while there was a cojunction of moons at zenith. Instead he criticized me for exercising my scarred legs while a moon was up. You'd think it would have reminded him that being inactive at such times was only a planetary habit.

It was impossible to question him along a consistent vein. He would start talking about their organization and end wondering about the possible influences on human behavior of subtle rhythms in gravity. He would open a conjecture about the daily habits of their Leader and it would end a theory on the psychology of island cultures. His long expressionless horseface would turn to me and he would conclude with something like, "You know, Herman Melville was right about the sea. It is not a vista but a background. People living on it experience mostly in a foreground."

Every Operator for The Central has at times to think profoundly about such things and be equipped better than average to do so. You can't deal effectively with the variegated human cultures now scattered far out into the galaxy without being neatly sensitive to the psychological influences of landscape, flora, climate, ancestry and planetary neighbors.

But at present I had a much blunter assignment. I had to reach a carefully protected man I had seen only in photographs. I had to reach him in the shortest possible time and kill him. Now, the worst luck of all, my only Contact had "taken root."

It happened every day of course. Psychostatistically it was inevitable. A fine Operator hit a planet where he began to take an emotional interest. He adopted quite seriously one or more of the major habits of the natives. This man had reached the next stage where his emotional interest in his new-found "home" dominated his finely drilled ties to The Central. In his case it had taken only a standard month and a half. In fact it had not been visible a month ago when the pilot of my tiny space shuttle dropped me off in the dark at his cottage. I finally realized the only thing I could get from him now was a rehearsal of the story he had told me that night before I walked alone into the strange city.

But I delayed asking him to retell his story. An odd thing happened. It happened just as I was about to ask him to go into town and buy me a set of the local power equipment. We were on our usual morning walk through the fern woods. Naturally he had refused to exercise until the passing of the second orbit moon. That had irritated me. I was on the verge of spitting out that I was wasting time and would be on my way as soon as he could run into town and buy me the local harness.

There in the middle of the path lay my own power equipment—the harness they had stripped off with my clothes down on the tide shelf three weeks before. If they had only left this harness on me, I would have been able to antigrav my way over the fourth sea wall instead of friction-ing my way up on peeling flesh. I knew the harness and helmet on sight. I picked it up and I was certain. The hair at the back of my neck stirred.

I didn't say anything and he was still enough of an Operator not to ask. We both knew it was no accident.

Back at the cottage I spent the rest of the day and most of the night checking that harness of power equipment. There was absolutely nothing wrong with it that I could find. The radio, sending and receiving, was in perfect order both on inspection and when I check-called to my ship waiting on the second orbit moon. The arms, both the microsplosive for killing single targets and the heavy 0.5 Kg. demolition pistol were as they had been when on my person. The antigravity mechanism and its neatly built-in turbojet, part by part, under Xray and on the fine balance he used for assaying quartzcar specimens, was an unblemished complexity. Again, when the equipment's own Xray was turned on its tiny "field-isolated" radioactive pile, no flaw could be seen. Naturally that was something of which I couldn't be sure. Something that I couldn't detect with these instruments might have been done to that tiny power pile at the subatomic level. The Xray defraction patterns were O.K. but—why did they want me to have my own harness? What reason outside the harness?

I had reduced to a simple question about its nuclear fission pile the highly multiple question, "Has this power equipment been tampered with?" I would have to gamble for the rest of the answer and it was worth the gamble. An Operator's power equipment is the best in the galaxy. From what I had seen of the equipment worn on this planet it was definitely second rate.

It was nearing morning but he was still sitting in a corner, his long melancholy face buried in the local books on quartzcar. One of them was titled in the native language, "The Planetary Evolution of Quartzcar." Well, it was not considered desertion to lose all interest in his assignment and all ties with The Central. It was just an occupational disease.

"You know," he said, suddenly standing up and walking to the greenish darkness of the window, "there are several piezoelectric substances."

"Yes," I answered. I was busy putting the intricate crystal plates back into the atomic fission pile.

"Quartz, of course, is one of them."

"Yes."

"You know how a piezoelectric substance behaves?"

I was annoyed. The job of slipping the countless delicate crystal plates back into the pile was exacting. "Well," I said without bothering to cover sarcasm, "why don't you tell me all about it. I got through physics on a fluke."

By the galaxy, he took me seriously. He stood there staring out at the fern forest and talked earnestly about electroelastic crystals like I was a first-year physics student.

"These substances convert electrical to mechanical energy and vice versa. You know how the old-fashioned phonograph pickup worked?"

I didn't pay any attention to him.

"The needle was activated by grooved impressions in a record by previous sounds. In the pickup device this needle pressed against a piezo-electric substance. Its mechanical movement against the crystal set up corresponding electrical discharges from it to the speaker." I was silent working on the pile. I decided that if he said, "You know" again I would get up and poke him. "You know," he continued, "every island on this planet is constructed from quartz—a piezoelectric substance."

I didn't get up and poke him. I continued to stare at the harness but I stopped working on it. He went right on without turning. "These constructions of quartz are subjected to rhythmic mechanical stress when the lunar tides pile up against them."

He was a capable man or he would not have been an Operator in the first place. That a man "took root" on some planet and became absolutely untrustworthy as an Operator did not mean he was not still a brilliant and sincere man. This one was obviously trying to solve a serious problem and doing well at it. I looked up with a new respect and he turned from the window.

He couldn't help smiling and I had to admit he had slipped one over on me. He said, "You see, it could be that these quartzcar islands generate an electrical field as the tides press on them. The strange blind movement of some of the vegetative forms could be a response stimulated by that electric field. The cessation of animal movement could be a safeguarding adaptation preventing disease which might develop when strenuous activity is pursued in the presence of such fields."

I couldn't help grinning. I had been blindly driving ahead because the assignment was urgent and I had missed all this.

"I realize," he continued, "that I have taken root but I think it is important that I was trying to solve the defeat of our first operation when I first took up the question of quartzcar."

"You know," I interrupted, "they treated me just as they treated your group—just as you described it to me that first night. They left me absolutely alone—no interference at all. I knew I was asking for it when I overplayed my hand. But I had to do something to get action. Up to then it was like working in a vacuum. You wouldn't have guessed there was a Party. There was no sign of them. It was only by boring in with the full intention of killing the Leader if I wasn't stopped that I finally forced them to show."

"Yes, that's how it was with us," he agreed. "Not one of the six of us met any interference until in a period of thirty seconds in various parts of the city two crashed from heights as though the antigravs had suddenly failed, two were blown to bits and one just simply died while walking through the rotunda of the Government Building where he was supposed to create a divergence in ten seconds.

"But why did they spare me? Was it because taking a shower was so innocent? If they could so neatly blow the whole plot wide open just at the moment it was climaxing they must have realized my part in it. They must have known I was innocently occupied taking a shower only because it was not my moment to be in action.

"Within seventy seconds their Leader would have been dead. Instead five of us were dead. It took me a long time to figure out that that was not due to a lot of concerted planning on their part. They had known it was going to happen at a certain time with no help from them. They knew *when* we were going into action and knew *therefore* that we would fail due to some calculable force. It wasn't necessary for them to interfere if we didn't plan to act before a certain time."

I nodded. "And I got what was coming to me because I went into action before they could calculate my defeat. Well, then the quicker I try again the better. I'm going in this morning." He almost volunteered to go with me.

Back in the city my mutilated face created attention. When I antigraved onto the sixth floor balconade of the Great Island Hotel people at nearby tables of the open-air restaurant turned to stare and turned quickly away. The table I had hoped for was unoccupied. I took it facing away from most of them so I could see the entertainment stage. Beyond the stage, as it was viewed from this point, were the antigrav tubes of the hotel. They were transparent and in them people rose to the upper floors or descended to the street without need of harness such as I was wearing.

The waiter came and took my order for a drink. He didn't recognize me, yet he and I had had a joke once about that drink.

My watch said it should be only a few minutes before she would be on the stage singing quiet little songs. It was on this stage that their Leader had first seen her. His only overt human quality was an interest in tall lanky women. He liked them at least eight inches taller than himself. This one he had promptly moved from the artists' and actors' quarters of the city to a penthouse atop the Great Island Hotel.

Presently the string trio she used for a background came out and lounged about the potted trees on the stage. They warmed up with a few dolorous little melodies. Beyond the stage the antigrav tubes were crowded. In one of them a tragic waterfall of humanity descended to the street level. In the other people drifted upward. Occasionally a person or couple in more casual ascent hesitated as they passed the restaurant and decided to come in for a drink.

The string trio started another number and she walked gracefully out onto the informal stage. She smiled on her audience with a possessive warmth that was half her popularity. Then she began singing in a husky, unmusical but dramatic voice. She was a beautiful girl all right but my attention was suddenly diverted.

I recognized the short scrawny one immediately—the big man when he spoke. "Say, I never thought we'd see you again. Mind if we sit down?" He waited politely.

I motioned to the chairs. "Say," he chuckled, closer to my face, "we sure did a beautiful job on you, didn't we?"

"Yes," I agreed, "I owe you both a great deal."

He had a big hearty laugh. "Well," he gasped between guffaws, "no hard feelings, I hope."

"I'm very objective. I understand it was all in a day's work."

"Sure," he said solemnly. "Let us buy you a drink." The waiter had come up.

I shrugged at my glass. "I'll have the same. There's no strychnine in it."

That set him off again. "Say," he burbled, "you're a card. You know when I first took a shine to you?"

I declared I couldn't imagine when it might have been.

"When I broke your arm. You really took it like a man. Didn't he take it well, Shorty?"

The little man wasn't saying anything. He was making his good-humored grin do as his contribution.

"Well, here's to your health." The big man raised his glass the minute the waiter set it down.

I drank with them and we sat in silence listening to her song until he called the waiter over for another round.

"Yes, sir," he exclaimed when it had arrived. "I sure never expected to see you again."

"Oh, you knew I got off the tide shelf. That's why you planted my power harness so I'd find it." That took the humor out of his eyes.

"I don't get you," he said in a level voice. The little guy had stopped grinning.

I explained about finding my power harness on our path in the fern forest.

"I think," he said with finality, "some animal dragged it up there. We left it on the tide shelf." There was ice in his eyes.

"That could be," I said, knowing it could not be.

"Waiter," he called, "bring us another drink."

Well, they had me and they weren't letting me go. I was going to have to sit quietly in the public restaurant of the Great Island Hotel and get drunk without making a scene.

It was getting on to noon and there was a big moon hitting its zenith. Activity in the restaurant was beginning to slow and there were fewer people in the antigrav tubes. She was singing her last number backing off stage with the trio.

I looked at the big man and his scrawny companion. There was one good solid reason why they had suddenly showed up and why they were gluing themselves to me. The Leader was up above in his Great Island Hotel penthouse waiting to spend the luncheon with his long lanky beauty.

How long would the siesta last? I wasn't very far into that thought when

I came up with a start and my hand stopped in the act of putting down my glass. They both glanced at me.

All five moons were going to be overhead at noon. They would lift the sea onto the fourth tide shelf. That was the biggest tide and it was rare. I calculated the last time it had happened was over a standard month and a half ago. If my sudden guess was right, the healthiest place for a Central Operator at that time would be in the shower.

"What's the matter?" the big man asked in a monotone. "You worried about something? You afraid you're stuck in bad company? Don't worry. We just want to have a couple more drinks with you and then we have to leave . . . in a hurry."

"Thanks. I'll sit the next one out. I want to have a little talk with that singer." I stood up and he grabbed my arm, the one he hadn't had any practice breaking.

"I wouldn't do that if I were you." He tightened down on the arm. But my advantage was the secrecy they needed.

"You wouldn't want a scene, would you?" I shook my arm loose. People were beginning to take notice and he sat quietly glaring at me.

I beat it through the stage door and back to her dressing room. I stepped in without knocking. She looked up startled from where she stood buckling a belt to her lounging shorts. She didn't recognize me and she didn't like me.

"Get out of here."

"You remember me," I soothed. "Three weeks ago you and I were regular pals. One night you went so far as to introduce me to a couple of special friends of yours in an aircar down there on the street."

She was genuinely horrified and began backing away. I walked toward her. "You thought they were going to kill me, didn't you?"

She nodded dumbly. Then, "For the Leader—" and automatically remembering another Party slogan, "for Planetary Security."

"You didn't know they were just going to torture me?"

She shook her head piteously almost imploringly—a little provincial girl caught in something bigger and uglier than she had dreamed.

"And leaving me alive to come back and ask you questions? Admitting the pleasure they took in how badly I would suffer when I regained consciousness how could they afford to take the chance of leaving me alive?"

"Because you will die anyway." There was an abrupt personal fright on her face. She raised her hands with the palms outthrust as though pushing the sight of me away.

I thought I saw something move at the open window and changed my position in the room backing from her. She was almost wailing, "You will die now . . . the tide . . . it's almost—"

One thing they weren't taking chances with was that I might radio her answer off the planet.

The scrawny devil popped up from where he had been antigraving at the window and the microsplosive he put in her chest made her dead throat shriek as the long beautiful legs crumpled to the floor. I blew his head off while her glaring face sank before me. His body spun but anti-graved where it was till I got to the window to haul it in.

From somewhere above the big guy fired at me as I yanked the body in and took the harness. I peeled out of my own power equipment and threw it in a corner and got out of the room. In a washroom down the hall I adjusted the little guy's harness to fit me. As I stepped out into the hall again there was a shattering explosion from her dressing room. I had got rid of that harness one hundred twenty seconds soon enough.

There was one spot the big hoodlum wouldn't be looking for me. I went right back to my table in the restaurant. There was, of course, no activity or conversation between the few who had stayed at their tables during the high tide. People sat in silence and seemingly asleep waiting for the moons to pass. I knew from experience that in that condition they would resist hearing my voice. I kept it low and held the radio pickup of the harness close to my lips.

After some hunting around due to the unfamiliar controls I made contact with my ship on the second moon. I told them where and when to pick me up. "Now," I said, "in case I don't make it get this down: Piezo-electric islands generate field in response to lunar tides. At highest tide this vibrates the field generating crystals of the fission pile in Operator's harness. Under interfering frequencies radioactives jar to critical mass and explode. Local harnesses do not react."

I was just leaving the table preparing to antigrav outside the building to where that penthouse hung in the mists fifty floors up when I saw my Contact racing toward me.

"I've come to help . . . I guess I still—"

"Get out of your harness. Throw it over the edge of the balcony."

He didn't ask questions. He hurried to the edge unfastening the harness. But from up in the mist they opened fire on him and he never took the harness off. He refastened it and antigraved swiftly up into the mist firing ahead of him with the heavy 0.5 Kg. demolition pistol set for proximity explosions.

That was quick thinking. Up there they might be antigraving alongside the building or they might be firing from windows and the unconfined proximity explosion was more likely to get both.

I followed him as fast as I could with the weaker harness I was wearing. I pulled out farther from the building to back his fire. We had both dropped the infrared viewers out of our helmets but in that mist they weren't much good. The mob above was having the same trouble and we were moving targets, hopeless for proximity fire. Our guns laid a sheet of flame high up on the building.

I believe he was hit but not killed on the way up. He seemed to stagger in his swerving ascent. But immediately their vantage came into view—a balcony surrounding the penthouse. Our fire had driven them back a few feet and he antigraved like a streak up over the edge.

There was a blinding flash and I reached the roof garden to find the mob of them dead in the explosion that had disintegrated him. One whole wall of the penthouse had been blown in. I leaped through this wreckage. The big man—the man I owed so much—was getting to his feet. Apparently he and two others with him had been guarding the door beyond. He looked surprised when he saw me. He must have thought till now it had been I who blew up out in the garden.

I slammed a target-set 0.5 Kg. demolition shell into them. It also blew the door apart. Across the room beyond their surprised Leader was sinking into the antigrav tube. He fired quickly and wildly and I fired a microsplosive from my left hand.

I thought I saw the shot get him but I dashed to the antigrav tube to make sure. Past shocked tenants who had rushed into the tube to escape the explosion-wracked upper floors his headless body lolled its way. The body, unmistakable in the distinctive white uniform he always wore, drifted down the tube stirring as it went a swelling murmur.

The psychostatisticians back at The Central get my vote as the "white haired boys." This was the first time in two hundred standard years that their anthropoquations had described one man and his lieutenant as the "cause" of a war movement. Generally the picture they turn up as "casualty" in a war is spiny with factors and it takes an army of Operators to cover all the angles. This time they had come out a little shamefacedly and said, "It looks like old-fashioned newspaper thinking but for once it's a fact. Get that one man and there will be no war."

As I leaned over the "down" antigrav in the Great Island Hotel his body drifted to oblivion. The murmur rising from the viewers had horror in it. But there was also an unmistakable note of relief. Finally, from far below, someone asked, "Did they get the rest of them?"

MURRAY LEINSTER

PLAGUE

". . . BY THE YEAR 2075—Earth Style—it was clear that merely the administration of intersolar and interplanetary affairs would soon absorb the entire attention of the Galactic Commission, so the formation of an administrative service was a necessity. It was not then realized that administrative services in the past had had the good fortune to be tested continually by emergencies and conflicts with other administrative services. (See WARS.) The Galactic Administrative Service had, however, a monopoly in its field, and had necessarily vast authority. Individuals, to whom authority *per se* is an ambition crowded into its ranks, fought bitterly among themselves for promotion, and unfortunately ultimately attained high posts. But individuals of this sort are unable to distinguish between authority and intelligence, subservience and subordination, or between protest and rebellion. After a hundred years with no emergencies or conflicts to reveal its faults, the Administrative Service was an ironclad, fossilized bureaucracy in which high place was an end in itself, pomposity a tradition, and red tape the breath of life. Red tape, alone, kept three solar systems from all contact with the rest of humanity for more than thirty years. Certain key documents had been misfiled, and without them no person had authority to give clearance to spaceships for those solar systems. Therefore, no ships could land on any planet of the three suns—not even Space-Navy ships! The accidental discovery of the situation by a member of the Galactic Commission led to the dismissal of the officials responsible, but the Service did not reform itself. The Electron Plague of 2194 (SEE (1) LORÉ. (2) LIFE-FORMS. (3) ENTITIES—*Immaterial.*) which threatened the entire human race came about because of bureaucratic stupidity alone. The Bazin Expedition had cleared from Pharona. After landing on Loré it was discovered that three out of more than six hundred documents then required to be filed by an exploring expedition had been improperly made out. The Expedition was ordered to return to Pharona to remedy its error. Scientists of the expedition, already at work, reported that strange life-forms on Loré made return inadvisable until they had been further studied. The sub-commissioner on Pharona took the protest as a defiance of his authority and ordered a naval spaceship to bring in the expedition under arrest. This was done and within two months more than ten million women, girls, and infants —half the population of Pharona—died of the plague unwillingly brought back by the Bazin Expedition. The scientists of the Expedition were under arrest for defiance of authority, and the plague had every chance of wiping out the entire human race throughout the Galaxy . . ."

(Article, "ADMINISTRATIVE SERVICE, *Reform of,*" in the Condensed Encyclopedia, Vol. 31, Edition of 2207, E.S.)

Ben Sholto was in the very act of getting up an extraordinary fine fix on a *sethee* bird in its elaborate nuptial dance, when the Reserve bracelet he was wearing nearly tore his arm off. It felt like that, at any rate. The electric shock tensed his muscles, threw the three-dimensional camera into an ungraceful wabble which wrecked the recording, and his sudden and violent movement revealed his presence. The *sethee* bird and her mate vanished with a thin whistling of wings to take up their matrimonial status, most likely, with a lack of ceremony their fellows might deplore.

Ben rubbed his arm vigorously and swore. He hastily dried the skin under the bracelet so that the order to follow would be less painful. It was sharp enough, at that—the series of long and short electric shocks which solemnly ordered him to get in touch with Reserve Headquarters for this sector at once.

"What do those brass hats think I'll do after an active-status warning?" Ben grumbled sourly.

He started through the jungle back toward his small space cruiser. He was a Reserve officer. He had been Space-Navy, and he had been ordered from on high to do something which was completely idiotic and would cost lives. He accomplished the mission in a simpler fashion, without losing any men at all. His report curtly stated that he had not followed instructions exactly because they seemed to have been issued through an error—and he was called up for court-martial, on the basis of his report that he had not obeyed his written orders. After his witnesses had testified, however, the court-martial was hastily dropped by order of the brass hat who had ordered it. If Ben had been convicted and had appealed, the magnificent imbecility of the orders he'd sidetracked would have become apparent to the local brass hat's superiors. So the brass hat ordered Ben transferred to the Reserve, which could not be appealed. There was a certain amount of pay attached to Reserve status, though, and it allowed Ben to knock about in his own cruiser wherever he pleased. In this particular section of space the privilege was valuable. So he roamed about, taking three-dimension pictures of flora and fauna for the feature-casts, and mourned his Space-Navy career and the romance that seemed to have gone glimmering with it. The romance had been named Sally, and it was her father who was the fatuous brass hat. But Ben missed her very much.

His cruiser rested in a leafy screen beside a particularly prismatic brook. He went in and to the GC—General Communication—phone. He stabbed the special Reserve Headquarters button and watched the screen without expression.

"Ben Sholto reporting for orders," he said curtly when it lighted.

A fat officer nodded uninterestedly.

"Acknowledged. Stand by."

The screen faded. Ben waited. And waited. Nothing happened. Half an hour later his Reserve bracelet nearly tore his arm off again. He seethed, and jabbed the button once more. The same officer appeared on the screen after a leisurely interval.

"Ben Sholto reporting for the second time," said Ben angrily. "I got a second set of shocks from my bracelet."

"Stand by," said the fat officer indifferently.

After almost half an hour, Ben opened the back of his bracelet and put his wrist in a basin of water. He felt a bare tingle when the third call came. He grinned. That would blow something at Headquarters.

The screen lighted. The fat officer scowled.

"Say, what are you trying to do?"

"Get my orders," said Ben. "What's the emergency? Simulated mobilization against mythical enemy force from another galaxy, or what? That's the standard, I think."

The fat officer said curtly:

"You Reserve men think you're smart! There's been a quarantine declared on Pharona, next System. Somebody's trying to break it. You'll be assigned guard duty. Plug in your writer and get written orders."

Ben threw the switch and prepared a meal. As he sat at the table, and before he threw his dishes in the fuel bin which would feed them to the converter as fuel—considerably more than a mere sports cruiser would ever need—the writer buzzed. He glanced at his orders.

You are to lie out in space and watch for a possible vessel breaking quarantine on Pharona trying to reach the planet on which you now are. Contact other Reserve watchers and divide the area surrounding your planet among you. If the vessel should be contacted by you, identify it, secure a list of crew and passengers, and destroy it. This order is not to be questioned.

Ben whistled, scowled, and then said furiously, "Pompous fatheads!" Then he shrugged philosophically.

He took off. There wasn't any other Reserve officer on this planet. It was uninhabited. The sports cruiser whistled up through thin air. Then there was empty space. Ben went out and established a casual orbit, set his detector screens, and settled down with a good book. He expected nothing at all to happen. Simply, he would draw active-status pay while on this so-called emergency duty, plus pay for the use of his ship. Since he had been robbed of a career—and a romance—by a brass hat, he felt no qualms at letting the same brass-hat mentality throw a few credits his way now and then.

He read until he was sleepy. Then he went to look at the instrument board before he turned in. The farthest screen of all was being nibbled at. The needle of its dial trembled almost imperceptibly. The alarm bell rang sharply.

He settled down in the pilot's chair and followed the detector-screen line on out. There was that odd, dizzying sensation at the beginning which always comes of a total-acceleration field taking hold. The little ship went hurtling through emptiness. As technical lieutenant, he knew atomic drive rather thoroughly. The Navy drive is in several essentials much above the commercial drive, though it requires more competent attention. Ben could give it, and he'd altered the drive of his small craft to Navy quality.

In ten minutes he'd sighted the craft of which his detectors had told him. It drove on for the very minor planet he had just left. He signaled by space-phone, but got no answer. The sharp, authoritative *"Identify yourself immediately"* dot-dash signal is known to all space craft. To fail to answer it is to confess illegality.

Ben pushed the Headquarters' button again. There was a long delay before the screen lighted. He had time to reverse his acceleration and match course with the unresponsive ship, at a distance of no more than ten miles. The fat officer looked annoyed.

"Ben Sholto reporting," said Ben. "I have located a vessel, on course apparently from Pharona. It refuses to reply to signals."

The fat officer said "Stand-by" and became officiously busy. A vast, bureaucratic dither went on behind the phone-screen focus. From time to time the fat officer answered some question put to him. At long last he turned to the screen again, pompously.

"No authorized vessel is in your locality. Destroy it."

"With what?" asked Ben mildly. "I've a positron-beam pistol, but that's all. This is a Reserve Auxiliary ship."

"Then . . . er . . . accompany the suspicious vessel," said the fat man, frowning portentously. "A destroyer will be sent to blast it."

Ben punched the cut-off button. He felt rather wry. There was no need to report his own position, of course. The same force that could make his Reserve bracelet give him senselessly severe electric shocks could cause it to radiate direction-waves by which he could be triangulated upon— even without his knowledge—from an incredible distance.

He regarded the hurtling ship some ten miles to one side. It was trimly streamlined, as if intended for at least occasional use as a yacht in atmosphere. It headed straight in for the planet now only a few thousand miles distant. It decelerated swiftly, and went into an orbit about the planet. Ben matched speed and course with the precision of long practice. Then he happened to glance at the phone board. There was a tiny bluish haze over to the left of the telltale tube, which reports the wave lengths of all broadcasters in operation, so that one may select. Curious, Ben tuned in that wave. It was a reflection-wave coming back from the planet's heaviside layer while most of the signal went through.

"*Ben!*" said a girl's voice desperately. "*Ben! If you're down there, signal me quickly! Please, Ben! Please!*"

Ben's heart leaped crazily and then seemed to cramp itself into knots. Because this was the girl who was the romance he'd been cheated of by a brass hat, and she was in the spaceship he'd been ordered to destroy, and there was a Navy ship coming now to blast it out of space—

"Sally!" he cried fiercely into the transmitter. "I'm here! I'm in the ship alongside!"

The visiphone screen lighted. And Sally Hale stared at him out of it, pale and hunted to look at. She tried to smile. Then she toppled from view. She had fainted.

Within this same hour, Galactic time, a sub-commissioner on Thallis II forbade the colonization of the planet's largest moon by arbitrary edict, which could not be gainsaid. The only reason ever discovered for the order was that the sub-commissioner enjoyed the hunting on that tiny planet, and it would be spoiled if the crowded population on Thallis II were admitted to colonists' rights. Simultaneously, four spacelines in the

Denib sector applied for permission to discontinue operations. They asserted, and offered to prove, that the cost of supplying required reports to the Administrative Service had grown to be the greatest single item of their operating costs, and made operation impossible save at a loss. (They were forbidden to discontinue operations.) And on the same Galactic day on Foorph—the solitary planet of Etamin—a crack express-liner from the Algol sector was refused landing and ordered to return to its port of departure. Of the more than eighteen hundred documents covering its voyage and cargo, exactly one lacked a sub-sub-clerk's indorsement. The Administrative Service was behaving exactly as usual.

But Ben Sholto was not behaving as a properly subordinate officer in the Naval Reserve. Half an hour after seeing Sally on the vision-screen, he cut loose the grapples and the tiny air lock hissed shut. The yacht seemed to swerve aside, but it was actually the little sports cruiser which abruptly altered course. Dead ahead, the blue-white sun of this minor solar system burned terribly in emptiness. The long, slim space yacht which had come so far sped on and on. The smaller ship curved away and drove hard to get orbital speed. Ben went to the GC phone. He stabbed at the Headquarters' button again. The fat officer thrust out an under lip.

"Well?" he demanded challengingly.

"Reporting," said Ben woodenly. "The ship from Pharona did not respond to repeated calls. It seemed to be heading straight for the sun, here. I have pulled away from it now, because on its present course it will either hit the sun or pass so close that nothing could possibly live on it. I suggest that the entire crew must be dead."

"Watch it," said the fat officer.

Ben clicked off the phone. He went back to the single stateroom in his sports cruiser. Sally Hale said faintly, "Really, Ben, I'm all right. Just . . . just you were the only person in the world I could appeal to. I'm . . . hunted."

"Not any more," said Ben. "You're safe now!"

"I . . . broke the quarantine on Pharona," said Sally. "It . . . it was terrible, Ben! They're . . . dying there by . . . by millions. Women. Only women. And girls. And nobody knows why. Their bodies give off cosmic rays, and they die. That's all. There's no real night on Pharona, you know, only twilight, so it was only the day before I left that they . . . discovered that women who have the plague glow, too. They get . . . phosphorescent. They don't feel badly, only oppressed. They get fever, and cosmic rays come from them, and in the dark they shine faintly, and they get weaker and weaker, and then they die. And men are immune, and they are going crazy! Their wives and sweethearts and daughters and mothers dying before their eyes. And they're not even in danger—"

"Don't tell me now if you don't want to," said Ben.

"I . . . think I'm all right. I must be!" said Sally. "I was twelve days on the way. If . . . if I'd had the plague I'd have died, wouldn't I? At least I'd be sick by now! But I'm not. Only . . . I couldn't sleep much, Ben. I was all alone on the yacht, and four days out I heard the alarm g-go out for me, and I've been hearing the GC phone organizing a hunt for me—"

"Maybe you'd better eat something, and take a nap," said Ben. "But how'd you come to pick this place to run to?"

Sally flushed a little.

"You were here." She looked at him pleadingly. "I . . . couldn't help it that my father . . . acted as he did. You know that after . . . well after my father got so angry with you, I felt badly. I went to Pharona to visit my uncle. And the Bazin Expedition came, and left for Loré, and the sub-commissioner ordered it back, and it came, protesting all the way, and . . . in four days the plague broke out. I was away over on the other side of the planet. The plague came back with the Bazin Expedition. We heard about it, and the quarantines that were clapped down, and finally the whole planet was quarantined. My uncle thought I would surely be safe, because his estate is so isolated. And then one of the maids got the plague. She'd been home visiting, and Uncle had put Geiger counters at the gates, so she didn't enter the grounds, but . . . it was time for me to get away. So he sent me off in the yacht. All by myself. He gave me my course. He stayed behind, with all his servants and staff. He . . . said he'd report I'd died. I couldn't have been exposed. Not possibly. I hadn't been within a mile of any woman who'd had the plague, or any man who'd been near any woman who had it. But if I stayed I'd die, so he sent me off. That was right, wasn't it?"

"Surely!" said Ben quietly. "Go on—"

"You see," she said pleadingly, "I hadn't been exposed, and . . . nobody was missing from the estate, because I was supposed to be dead. It seemed like it was perfect. But they . . . must have gone to seal the engines of the yacht so nobody could use it, and they found it gone, and thought somebody had stolen it—"

"So you're officially dead," said Ben. "All right. Go to sleep. You're safe. I've reported that the yacht didn't swerve from its course and dived into this sun. It's actually diving there now. Its not very probable that any spaceship coming out of interstellar space would hit a star by accident. It would take good piloting! But it may be just improbable enough not to seem like a made-up yarn."

Ben went out of the stateroom and forward to the control cabin. His face was set. In olden days, perhaps, a human being could move about freely. But in these days of the Galactic Commission and the brass hats under it, there was a vast amount of red tape about everything. The brass hats, of course, were the administrative officials under the Commission, and they climbed to authority by seniority and a pious avoidance of anything which could not be justified by written rules. They were a sort of galactic civil service, surrounded by pomp and power. Some of them were decent enough, but a deplorable lot were stuffed shirts and brass hats. Fortunately, they had no control over the surface of planets, but they supervised all traffic in space with a fussy particularity which was maddening. Any ship capable of space flight had to be registered and licensed, and all space-flights conducted under checks and double-checks which made spacemen utterly disrespectful.

"The question," said Ben wryly in the control room, "appears to be serious. Sally isn't legally alive. I have, in fact, official orders to kill her. I'm not going to do it. So, just how am I going to manage things?"

Every spaceship is inspected minutely at every spaceport it enters. He could not take Sally into any inhabited planet without questions he could not answer. He could not—

He pushed the GC button again. The screen lighted. The fat officer said boredly:

"What's the matter? A destroyer's on the way."

"The vessel I reported has vanished in the corona of this sun," said Ben smoothly. "This is a dwarf blue-white, as you may remember. The strange ship made an apparent grazing impact and is melted down to a blob of metal if it isn't vaporized by now. I was taking some pictures back yonder. May I be released from Reserve duty?"

"You will await orders—"

The fat officer began to speak with pompous indignation. Then there was a scream behind Ben. Sally came stumbling out of the stateroom, her face like chalk.

"Ben!" she choked. "I've . . . got the plague—"

Ben's left hand slammed off the GC phone, but it was too late. He knew it was too late. He'd seen the fat officer's eyes widen blankly. Sub-ether phone communication does not operate by ether waves, and no time-lag has ever been detected even between the two rims of the Galaxy. Already the fat officer at headquarters had seen Sally and heard her cry.

Ben was very white. Within minutes the whole Space-Navy of the Galaxy would have on their recorders the description of himself and his sports cruiser, with orders to hunt him down and blast him out of space on sight. Ten million dead on Pharona, and a case of the plague at large to start it up again— Of course!

He said hoarsely, in an effort to be reassuring:

"Don't be silly, Sally! You can't have it—"

Her teeth chattered.

"B-but I have! I t-turned out the light to try to sleep, and . . . and I saw my hand glowing. And I got up and looked in the mirror, and m-my face—"

She reached out and turned off the light switch in the control room. The instrument dials glowed faintly. But so did Sally. Her features and her throat and arms were faintly visible in an ethereal light which made her—rather than frightening—look like an angel. And from within the thin garments in which she had meant to sleep there came a faint effulgence, too.

Ben's throat made a queer sound.

"I . . . thought," gasped Sally pitifully, "that we . . . could be happy because . . . no one could ever forbid us to be together if I w-was supposed to be dead. But I didn't think I was going to die a-after I'd joined you—"

Ben took her in his arms, helplessly. For an instant she thrust away from him, but then she clung close.

"You c-can't catch it, anyway," she sobbed. "Please hold me close, Ben. I d-don't want to die, when I'd j-just run away so I could never l-leave you—"

At this time the members of the Galactic Commission, itself, were pressing the investigations which were later to make intergalactic exploration and colonization practical. They had set aside whole planets for research stations, and far out beyond the Galaxy's rim there were those infinitely hazardous laboratories where men extended the knowledge of stellar physics so that we who follow them have already circumnavigated the universe and some day may even understand it. The members of the Commission also directed the investigation of that endocrine balance which is youth, so that age is now a measure merely of time, and the word "senility" is now marked "obsolete" in the dictionaries. But on this same day the mines on Thotmes II had to be shut down despite their usefulness. An Administrative Service clerk had discovered a flaw in the charter of the space line which ran to Thotmes II. It was not authorized to carry mineral products. Therefore it had to be subjected to heavy fines, and it was driven into bankruptcy, and one hundred and twenty thousand miners were isolated from the rest of humanity by the breaking of their only transportation link.

And on this same day the Galaxy's greatest mind in medicine was refused space-transportation. He wanted to go to Pharona, but the sub-commissioner in residence on the planet on which he lived was a hypochondriac, and wished adequate medical attention to be available for his nervous stomach-aches.

And another sub-commissioner, on Pharona, diverted attention from his own stupidity—which had caused a plague with ten million victims—by pompously indignant demands for Ben Sholto's destruction.

Ben Sholto, however, paid no attention. The light was on in the control room again. His face was white and set. The Reserve bracelet was off his wrist, now. It had signaled violently for him to report to Headquarters. For answer, he'd hacked it in half and smashed its mechanism, and then thrust it down into the very tip of the fuel bin, pushing until he felt dizzy as the heavy metal of the bracelet turned into energy for the motors and the total-acceleration field. With metal for the converter to work on, the small craft surged ahead under an amount of power only armored cruisers normally developed.

Sally sat quietly in her chair, staring at Ben through eyes that were very steady now. He regarded a Geiger counter. It clicked busily. His face went gray.

"You're giving off cosmics," he said dry-throated. "That's the sign of the plague. There's nothing else known that will make the human body give off cosmics."

"I'll be dead in . . . two or three days," said Sally, unsteadily. "Sometimes women live a week. Sometimes ten days. M-mostly when the plague first starts, and there are a lot of women about. In the cities, at the beginning, the women lived even two weeks. But in small places they die quickly. And I'm the only woman here—"

"In two weeks," said Ben harshly, "doctors should have worked out some serum, some protection."

"They've . . . never seen the germ, Ben. Not even the electron microscope shows anything. Just . . . the women die—"

"But you're not going to!" said Ben fiercely. "Why couldn't I be a doctor or something useful!"

"You can be . . . comforting," said Sally bravely. "I . . . gave my whole life to you when I ran to you, Ben. There aren't but a few days, instead of . . . of years, but—"

He bent over her groaning. The clatter of the Geiger counter stopped abruptly. It had touched her arm. She shivered a little.

"Broken, I guess. But it was ticking my life away. Let's forget it."

Ben ground his teeth. He moved to thrust the instrument out of his way. It clattered briefly, and stopped again. It dangled from his hand by the cord to its electric connections. It clattered, and stopped, and clattered again. Ben stared down at it. It was not pointing at Sally. He swung it about. It clattered steadily when pointed at the instrument panel. It was mute when it pointed at Sally. It was mute when it pointed at anything else but the instrument panel. No. It was mute when it did not point to the GC phone. No. It clattered only when it pointed to the course-computer— It clattered only—

"Wait a minute!" said Ben harshly. "There's something funny here!"

He turned out the lights again. The instrument dials glowed as before. Sally did not! But there was a whitish luminosity at the top of the pilot's chair. It seemed spread along the metal frame. It was not phosphorescence. It was white, not bluish. Ben moved toward it. The Geiger counter chattered when Ben pointed it at the luminosity. Then, abruptly, the luminosity was not on the chair. A dial glowed whitely, as if a stronger light were behind it. The Geiger counter clattered when pointed at that dial. Ben swung the counter upon Sally. It was mute.

"Listen!" said Ben in a strained voice. "You say women with the plague give off cosmics. You're not giving them off, so you haven't it. But you did, so you did have it. My pilot's chair was giving off cosmics. Did it have the plague? Now the gravitometer is giving off cosmics. Has it got the plague?"

Sally drew in her breath quickly. There was silence in the cabin of the little sports cruiser of the void. The only sound anywhere was a tiny humming. That was the converter, turning Ben's Reserve bracelet and the refuse of his last meal into power—efficiency 99.9999 . . . 9 percent—to drive the little craft with an insanely mounting velocity away from its last known position.

The whitish glow reappeared suddenly. It was in the metal rim about the control ceiling light. It vanished, and reappeared on the handle of a metal door. It vanished yet again—

"The strange life-forms of Loré," said Ben, his voice rough in the darkness. "The Bazin Expedition didn't want to go back to Pharona. It said its return would be dangerous until it understood those life-forms. It was forced to go back, and it carried the plague. At a guess, this is one of the life-forms of Loré. It seems to stick to metal. It didn't move into the glass of the ceiling light, but stayed on the metal rim which holds it."

He swung the Geiger counter. Carefully. It clattered.

"It's somewhere in the stern. Engine room, most likely—"

Sally said unsteadily: "I . . . haven't got the plague, then—"

"No, you haven't got it." Ben's voice softened. "You're dead officially, my dear, but now it looks like you're going to stay actually alive for a long time. We'd better do some planning for ourselves. At the moment, I'm going to change course. We've got all the Fleet in this part of space hunting us right now. I was talking to Headquarters when you yelled—and we've got to hide. And I don't know for how long."

Sally said slowly, as if incredulous of hope: "I . . . don't care. I've gotten you into terrible trouble. The least I can do is . . . anything you tell me to."

He put his hand lightly on her shoulder.

"There's a meteor-stream," he said. "What we want is time and peace in which to make our plans. I'll dive into that stream and match up with it. We'll be one of several million small objects heading out to aphelion in the track of a comet nobody's ever seen. With our drive off and a little care, there's no faintest danger that we'll ever be picked up. I've supplies for a long enough time. We'll be beyond the outermost planets before we put the drive on again, and then we'll start for . . . where shall we go, Sally? Sirius? Rigel? I've heard there are some new colonies out beyond Rigel where things are rough and tough and the brass hats haven't yet been able to sit back with their tummies sticking out with dignity to regulate everything to justify their feeling of importance."

He moved to the pilot's seat, not bothering to turn on the lights again. He swung the little ship about. The converter was still working on the bracelet he had shoved into the feed. It was crushed and being extruded into the converter-chamber as an infinitesimally fine wire. The efficiency of the converter and the drive was high. In theory, with one hundred percent efficiency, the mass of fuel needed to give a spacecraft a given velocity in empty space is the mass the spaceship will gain because of that velocity. In practice, of course, much more is needed. To attain a speed of a hundred miles a second from rest, in space, the fuel consumption is actually about a milligram of disintegrated matter per ton mass of the ship. In anything like a sports cruiser, the fuel for merely interplanetary jaunts is supplied by the carbon remaining after the air-purifier has broken down the carbon dioxide from the breathed air. Ben used his dirty dishes—and the fuel pin periodically overflowed, though he drove the cruiser hard. His bracelet had weighed two ounces. Something like six thousand milligrams. The electrical mechanism of the bracelet was now smashed irreparably, but as waste it would more than accomplish an inter-planetary trip if he chose to coast.

He was not coasting. The position of the dwarf blue-white star of this solar system, and of its several planets, was accurately before him on the naviboard. There was a transparent map of the meteor-streams, with their inclination to the ecliptic. With such a map and a divider it was simple enough to navigate, especially when you used detector-screens to find out your results. He worked in the half-light of the instrument dials. He punched the computer and set the motor controls.

"Ben," said Sally's voice, shaken, behind him.

"Yes?"

He was thinking unhappily. He felt awkward. Sally could never return to civilization or her friends. He, himself, had to vanish completely. The brass hats would go into a monstrous pother of offended dignity, based upon the real fact that Sally had broken quarantine on a planet where ten million people had died of plague. Sally and Ben were outlaws, now. Forever. Unless they lived isolated for the rest of time, they would have to take new names and new identities—and new names and identities are not easy to acquire on civilized planets. They wanted to be married. The ceremony was somehow essential to the way Ben felt about Sally. And he was going to have to find some way to make a living, which did not in-volve space-navigation or the technical equipment of a technical lieutenant of the Space Navy, because all such persons were very rigorously checked.

"Ben," said Sally's voice in the darkness. It was strained. "The Thing is back! It's . . . it's on the leg of your chair."

He looked. But it was on the arm of his chair. He poked his finger ex-perimentally at it. There was no sensation. He touched it. It vanished. But his hand glowed. Both hands glowed. He gave off a faint, whitish luminosity. Just what Sally had had. But it contracted swiftly. He saw the reflection of his face and head in the glass of a dial. They shone brightly. The rest of him was dark. And he felt vague, formless pluckings at his brain. Something was probing hopefully. It was utterly alien, the Thing that probed for his thoughts. There could be no real contact of minds. He could never communicate with the Thing. But he felt its emotions. It was hopeful, and somehow terribly eager. But there was a dawning of dis-appointment. Somehow, he knew it was because it could not read his brain. Then he felt the formation of resolve; of a determined, restless patience.

His face ceased to glow. His hand shone brightly. He held it out and looked at it. The glow quivered, as if impatiently. He put his hand down on his navigating instruments. There was the impression of a flash of luminosity over all the instruments for the least possible part of a second. Then it was gone.

And then Sally made a queer sound. He looked at her. He saw her clearly, even though the control cabin of the cruiser was in darkness. Her face and throat and arms glowed whitely. Even through her clothing diffused faint light showed. The Geiger counter clattered—

"I've . . . got the Plague again," said Sally, her voice thin. "I . . . realize now. I've got the feeling I . . . had before. The feeling like there is something . . . inside me somehow . . . contented . . . and eager, and . . . waiting for something, but . . . almost purring while it waits."

Ben Sholto licked his lips. The fact that the luminous Thing had left Sally to rove inquisitively about the ship had made it seem merely one of the curious life-forms of Loré. But now, abruptly, he realized the truth. A plague doesn't go into the back of instrument-boards, or shine on the frame of a metal chair, or put probing tendrils of alien thoughts into one's brain. An ordinary plague doesn't. But this plague did. The plague on Pharona wasn't a disease whose lethal effects were the result of toxins secreted by multitudes of submicroscopic organisms or viruses. The plague on Pharona was—Things. They flowed into the tissues of women as they flowed through metal. But they fed, somehow, upon the life-force of women. And the women died.

Ten million women and girl-children had died on Pharona because of Things brought back from Loré. The things couldn't have come on one spaceship in numbers great enough to accomplish such slaughter—not if women lived from two days to two weeks after their bodies began to glow. No. The Things must multiply somehow. The patience, the resolution to wait for something, which both Ben and Sally had felt—that might be the Thing deciding that for some reason it must remain solitary for a while.

But Sally was the habitation of a Thing, one of those which had wiped out half the human race on Pharona. It interpenetrated her body. It waited eagerly for something. And it purred soundlessly while it waited.

The Universe rolled on. The Galaxy paid no attention. The Administrative Service Appeal Board, sitting on Arcturis II, denied a petition signed by more than three hundred million people inhabiting four planets of Algol. They asked permission to present their grievances directly to the Galactic Commission itself, since the Administrative Service was inextricably tied up in its own rulings and red tape. But the Board ruled that the petition asked action by the Board for which there was no precedent, and which, therefore, was automatically beyond the Board's discretion.

A sub-sub-commissioner on Phryne VII married the daughter of a subcommissioner, and traveled in state on a Rim-class battleship to his new post.

A clerk of the Administrative Service unearthed the fact that the charter of the Allioth Colonization Co-operative lacked two commas and a semi-colon, and that seven million people, therefore, lacked legal title to the cities, factories, and installations they had built, and that they could be displaced by anybody who filed a new application for colonists' rights on the planet. The clerk was regarded as a coming man in the Administrative Service.

A fleet captain in the Space-Navy resigned his commission rather than carry out orders commanding him to depopulate the planet Quenn "by any and all practical means," and was ordered under arrest. The order was carried out by subordinates, who affected to believe that the only practical means was to carry the inhabitants elsewhere. (It was later discovered that a clerical error had sent an order, intended for the Migration-Directive Bureau, to the Space-Navy Bureau. The order was meant to command the repopulation of Quenn by any and all practical means, because it had lost much of its population by emigration. The clerk responsible for the mistake was disciplined, but none of the higher officials who had countersigned it.)

And there was a plague on Pharona which was receiving very little attention, but an entire sub-sector battle fleet was being mobilized to capture a small sports cruiser of space which had defied official orders.

The GC phone muttered and muttered, its volume turned down low. The detectors clanged twice as the little ship hurtled on, but once it was the outermost screen which barely wavered into alarm-intensity, and the second time it was a Navy cruiser coming head-on along the sports-cruiser's course. It was coming fast, but Ben was going fast. He had kept the converter going at full capacity for days past, and the bracelet had been converted into kinetic energy—with other materials besides—of which a reasonable percentage had been imparted to Ben's little ship. Half an ounce of pure energy had been converted into speed. So the small ship smashed into the Navy cruiser's screens and through them. Had the passage been at a reasonable distance—say, five thousand miles or so—it might have been just barely possible for the automatic beam-pointers of the cruiser to range him, compute his course and speed in three dimensions, and fire ahead of him so a positron beam would hit squarely.

But the two craft actually passed within twenty miles. The passage would have been closer yet but for the flaring of energy into the Navy ship's meteor-diverters, which flung both Space-Navy cruiser and sports cruiser of the void aside from all danger of a collision. Such incomputable movements could not be anticipated by range finders. The giant projectors flared, and on the vision screen straight ahead they were visibly higher in the spectrum than was normal. The relative velocity of the two ships was an appreciable fraction of the speed of light itself.

Then the little ship was away, and once beyond screen-detection range, Ben began to decelerate at as violent a rate as he had before accelerated. The Navy now had the line of his flight, and it could compute his maximum acceleration. He would be expected to swerve aside, after his escape from the hunting ship, in any possible direction. But he would be expected to continue to flee.

A vast dragnet of the fleet would assemble, combing an expanding mushroom of space for the outlaws who carried with them the plague that had killed half of Pharona. The pomposity of a brass hat had caused the plague, but all the power of the Galactic Commission would be used pitilessly to stamp it out. Giant battleships of space would be entering sub-ether tubes for faster-than-light journeying to the scene of emergency. Monstrous motherships carrying destroyers and scouts would be vanishing in curiously wrinkled diminishment at spots parsecs away, and appearing nearby, reeling quaintly, to spout their brood of stingers to hunt for the sports cruiser which contained one sunken-eyed man and a white-faced girl. There were more than half a million men and thousands of space-craft engaged in the search for Ben and Sally within twenty-four hours after their narrow passing by the Navy ship. And brass hats had a field day, giving pompous, arbitrary orders and requiring acknowledgements in triplicate.

But the assumption was that Ben was running away. Actually, he was cutting down his velocity as fast as his converters could manage it. He reached the meteor-stream he had headed for at a bare crawl, and worked the little ship into it, and began to drift out and out toward the aphelion point of an unknown comet at a gradually diminishing rate, surrounded by pebbles and boulders and masses of inchoate matter ranging from pin-points to quasiasteroids in size. This, while the Navy hunted for a tiny ship in headlong flight.

"They'll have quite a time finding us now," said Ben tiredly, when he cut off the drive at last. "How do you feel?"

"I'm . . . all right, I guess," said Sally, thinly.

She was sitting in a chair Ben had insulated from the floor. At regular intervals, Ben took a Geiger counter reading. Always the counter clattered. The metabolism of the Thing involved the production of cosmic rays. Electric metabolism. The Thing was, in fact, an organization of electric charges. Since electric charges are essential to cellular life—such as human life—the Thing was not impossible. Electric charges in association with matter produce Terrestrial life, and the removal of the charges leaves merely dead matter. The first elucidation of ball lightning showed that energy alone can achieve organization and self-determined dimensions. So a creature which was merely an electrical pattern was not incredible.

Therefore the insulated chair. For hours after the first exploratory departure of the Thing from Sally's body, they had hoped it would repeat its excursion. It had seemed curious about apparatus. Ben insulated the chair and brought out piece after piece of apparatus—everything from his cameras to the hand positron-beam projector which was the only weapon on the ship. He had Sally go near them. He had her touch them. He hoped that curiosity would lure the Thing into a second journey of investigation. But there was no sign. The Geiger counter aimed at Sally's body clattered at the same rate, neither greater nor less. She said, her voice shaking a little, that she felt a sensation within her as of something which was eager, but very patient, and very contented despite its eagerness. Purring.

It was a disappointment. But the problem was not one of orthodox medicine, of ultra-microscopic organisms and the intricate interplay of enzymes, cells, and all the innumerable compounds of the body. This was a problem of a Thing. So Sally sat in an insulated chair. For three days.

"I don't know how intelligent it is," said Ben grimly, on the second day. "I doubt if its IQ could be estimated. But it has curiosity, it makes decisions, and it has emotion. Maybe some superorthodox scientist would say we still haven't proof that it's really alive, but I'll let it go at that. The Thing is a form of life which can exist apart from any specific bit of matter, but it is not independent of matter. It has to inhabit some bit or other. It prefers you to a bar of metal, or to me. You will die if it stays in your body long enough. Then it will doubtless hunt for another body. That must be what happened on Pharona. And it must reproduce, because it's alive. But on your journey from Pharona here it didn't. It doesn't seem to be now—because this is a long time. Maybe it realizes that you're the only woman here, and if you die— It looks like it somehow feeds on the vital energy of your body. It can't get that energy from me or from metal. It's . . . cannibalistic. It is life which feeds on other life. Your life. I wish it would try to take mine!"

Sally spoke very wearily from the insulated chair.

"I think it's hopeless," she said in a low voice. "There's only one of the Things, but it's going to kill me. We can't stop it. I could put on an insulated spacesuit—it can only move through a conductor—while I'm in this chair. It would be imprisoned, then. I could walk about, and it couldn't escape me. And I could go out the air lock and—the Thing could never harm anybody. But we . . . we couldn't ever land anywhere with this Thing alive. We couldn't loose a plague on another planet like the one which was loosed on Pharona! I . . . was there, Ben!"

Ben said fiercely:

"Do you think I'd let you walk out of the lock? Do you think I'd leave you in space?"

"I'd like it," she said humbly, "if you'd turn a positron beam on me instead."

"I'm waiting to use the positron beam on that Thing," said Ben grimly. "How do you feel?"

"All right, I guess. But I'm not comfortable. The Thing isn't quite as contented."

He nodded. His jaw set.

"Maybe we're getting somewhere. It must be a pattern of free electrons, bound into an organization which is alive. It can't be anything else! But its metabolism involves the production of cosmics rays. Making cosmic rays involves the production of positive charges. Insulated as you are, you're accumulating a positive charge that sooner or later is going to try to bind some of the free but organized electrons this Thing is made of. Maybe it'll die without knowing what is happening. It acts as a disease to humans. Maybe we've concocted a disease or a poison for it."

Ben could not touch Sally, lest he discharge the positive potential they were building up—or allowing the Thing to build up for its own destruction. They were trying to kill it by the product of its own metabolism; to suffocate it by the positive electricity it created, just as a human being will suffocate in the carbon dioxide he must exhale.

But Sally seemed to shrink into herself. She spoke rarely, and then in a strained voice. At last, on the third day, she spoke in a sudden gasp.

"I'm . . . sorry, Ben, but I can't stand it any longer. The Thing is suffering and it's making me suffer. I can't stand any more!"

Ben reached out to touch her wrist. On the instant her wrist glowed. The Thing gathered itself together, it concentrated itself to escape. It was visible even in the lighted cabin. At the touch of Ben's finger a tiny spark jumped. That was all. But Sally almost fainted with relief. She tried to smile a wabbly smile.

"It's . . . gone," she said unsteadily. "We drove it out. We . . . exorcised it, Ben."

Ben turned off the light. Sally vanished into the blessed darkness. He heard her sigh with relief so sharp that it was almost a sob.

"For the second time," she said, valiantly trying to be flippant, "I haven't got the plague. How quaint!"

"Sit still," said Ben savagely. "We'll watch for it. Positive electricity is poison to it. We know that, anyhow! And I've got my positron pistol here. Watch for it!"

There was silence. The GC phone muttered, and muttered. There was one voice which was much louder than the rest. The muttering died away. The sound of Sally's breathing grew steady and even. Presently she sighed deeply, and went on breathing evenly.

Then the bronze doorsill of the control-room door glowed whitely. The Thing, driven out of Sally's body, was suddenly there. It was a patch of whitish luminosity which almost but not quite filled the whole length of the sill. In case of accident, an air-tight door would snap shut across the opening, sealing the ship into separate compartments. Ben raised the positron pistol. Tiny radium dots marked the sights, but his hand trembled with hatred. He took both of them to steady his weapon. He pulled the trigger.

There was a reddish glow from the pistol. No noise. Nothing else. That was all.

But the white luminescence on the doorsill flared unbearably. Ben had an extraordinary sensation, as if he had heard a soundless scream. And the Thing went mad. It was here and there and everywhere. Every particle of bare metal in the control room seemed to flash as the Thing raced with incredible speed in a crazy, frenzied rush over every metallic path it had

traversed before. It could not be seen as an area of light, but it seemed
as if all bare metal in sight emitted a wavy, lunatic glow.

Ben started suddenly. He raised the pistol. And abruptly there was no
glow anywhere. The control room was normal. The dials of the instruments were visible, of course, but Sally could not be seen.

"If I'd pointed this beam anywhere at all and held it on," said Ben
bitterly, "the Thing might have run into it. But I didn't think of it in
time."

He turned on the light again. Sally was asleep in the insulated chair
in which she had endured for three days and nights. She was utterly
relaxed. She looked unspeakably weary and pathetic, sleeping in the abandoned confidence of a child.

Ben looked down at her, and his face softened.

"Maybe it's dead," he told her quietly, "and maybe it's not. But it'll
never get to you again!"

He went into the stateroom. He carefully and elaborately insulated the
bunk there from any possible electrical connection with floor or side walls.
He put on insulating shoes. He picked Sally up in his arms and carried
her, still sleeping, and laid her on the bunk. He covered her. He kissed
her very gently.

In the control-room a pale white glow appeared on the metal of the
pilot's chair. It rose to the top and stayed there. It was motionless, but it
wavered in intensity. It seemed to throb a little. If Ben had been in the
room—why just as he had felt a little while since that he felt a soundless
scream of agony, now he would have felt hatred so terrible that the
hackles at the back of his neck would have stirred.

He started back into the control room. The glow slid alertly down the
metal parts of the chair. It was gone when he came through the door.
Then it appeared suddenly in the stateroom. It went restlessly, ragingly,
back and forth upon the metal walls. And the stateroom seemed to be
filled with hatred also.

A space cruiser resignedly took up post in an orbit about the dark star
Lamda Boötes. It would circle that star for six months and be relieved.
Forty years before, a sub-commissioner had intended to change cruisers at
that place, and commanded that one be here to meet him. He had later
changed his plan of travel, but there was no order to withdraw the cruiser
posted at the rendezvous. The first cruiser asked for relief after six months
of utterly useless waiting. It was relieved by a cruiser under orders to take
its place. Seventy-eight cruisers, in turn, had uselessly swung about the
dark star for six months each because of an order given forty years before
and never rescinded.

Highly unofficial gossip, told behind official palms, informed the sub-
commissioner of the Formalhaut sector that the sub-commissioner of the
Markhab sector had said he was a fool. The sub-commissioner of the
Formalhaut sector, in indignation, ordered that no clearances be issued to

spaceships to Markhab or from it. All space lanes in that part of the Galaxy passed through the two sectors. In consequence, the economic system by which eight hundred millions of people lived was brought to a standstill.

The small sun Mu Aquila showed definite signs of instability—signs which by the McPherson-Adair formula indicated an imminent internal explosion. There was no office of the Administrative Service on any of its planets, which altogether had a bare five million inhabitants. Notification of the impending nova-flare was sent to the nearest sector office, with the usual request for evacuation of all the planets which would be destroyed or made uninhabitable. A clerk, recently transferred to that sector and desirous of distinguishing himself, observed an error in the drafting of the request. He returned it for re-preparation before forwarding it for action. He failed to mark it "Urgent Official," which meant that it went by ordinary mail and would not reach its destination for two months. Of course, the McPherson-Adair formula indicated that the explosion would take place in six to seven weeks.

There was a plague on Pharona, and a quarantine prohibited any private or commercial ship to land on or leave it. But an Administrative Service vessel landed, bringing dispatches, and left again after taking all normal sanitary precautions. It landed on Galata, and cases of the plague were observed there within twelve hours.

And Ben Sholto still defied the Space Navy, the Administrative Service, and presumably the Galactic Commission itself by remaining alive.

Great, jagged, rocky fragments floated in space between the stars. In between the greater pieces were innumerable smaller bits. The little spacecraft wallowed in a stream of cosmic flotsam, sharing its motion. The blue-white sun of this solar system was far away, now, and very faint. But even with the naked eye, from a port on the little sports cruiser, one could see half a dozen huge and irregularly-shaped masses within a matter of miles. This was the thickest part of the meteor-stream. This was, perhaps, the remnant of what had been the nucleus of a comet. Some of these great stones were half a mile by three-quarters. One needlelike mass was at least a mile and a half in length, but nowhere more than four hundred yards through.

Ben surveyed his surroundings carefully. A tiny electron telescope amplified even starlight upon cold stone to any desired degree. The GC phone muttered and muttered and muttered. Someone, somewhere, had fired a positron beam. A Space-Navy receiver had picked up the radiation involved—and positron-beam bursts do not occur in nature. Naval craft were concentrating to hunt for the source of the blast. It had been, of course, the shot Ben had fired at the Thing on the doorsill, and the coordinates on it were not as close as they might have been, because nobody had expected a fugitive to be so foolish. Even so, however, the hunt would have been much more deadly if spacemen had been conducting it, instead of being completely fettered by pompous orders issued by one brass hat, altered by another, and changed by a third in strict order of seniority.

Ben turned on a low trace of his space drive. Its force could almost have been measured in dynes, rather than in the milpos—millions of foot-pounds—commonly spoken of in engine rooms. The little spaceship swam slowly among the crowded bits of cometary debris. It came to rest close beside the flank of the largest of all the masses of matter in sight. He maneuvered until no more than fifty feet separated the small vessel from the great mass of metal and rock. There would be mutual gravitation between them, of course. They would tend to fall together. But the acceleration of that gravity was so slight that it might take a month or more for the sports cruiser to fall just fifty feet.

For two days, now, Sally had remained on the insulated bunk, except when she donned an insulated spacesuit with the helmet left off, to move about the little ship. The Thing could not reach her. She was recovering from the terrific ordeal she had endured—and now Ben swore at himself for what he considered stupidity. Instead of allowing the Thing itself to build up a positive potential, he could have made one artificially. If by any chance the Thing found a way to return to Sally, he felt confident that he could drive it out again, now, in minutes rather than days.

He knew that the Thing still existed. The Geiger counter revealed its presence from time to time. Sally had seen it, glowing balefully in the darkness of the stateroom, when she woke after infinitely restful sleep.

The little sports cruiser lay close beside a monstrous and misshapen hunk of stone and metal. It went drifting out and out from the blue-white sun. Destroyers and cruisers and even battleships hunted for it, bedeviled by authoritative brass hats in swivel chairs. The GC phone muttered and muttered. Without detector-screens, which were useless anyhow because of the meteor-stream all about, Ben could not even estimate the nearness of his pursuers, but he felt safe. They could not examine every one of the countless millions of objects in a cometary orbit. Not possibly.

He made a careful visual examination with the electron telescope, and grinned at Sally.

"Picking us out at even a thousand miles would be a miracle," he told her. "We can go in for conversation and such things until the Navy decides that somebody was mistaken or we are dead. Meanwhile I'm going to see if I can make that Thing a little more uncomfortable still."

The Thing was in the metal fabric of the ship. It could move anywhere that a conductor existed. But it was not, apparently, possible for it to extract subsistence from metal. It was cannibalistic—life which lived by devouring life. For some reason the life force in a male body—a man's body—was not suitable for it. It could only derive nourishment from the vital force in the cells of a woman's tissues. Yet its metabolism continued. It gave off cosmic rays in metal, as in human flesh. It must be that it lost energy while in nonliving matter, and regained energy—fed—in living stuff. If it could be kept from any access to Sally for a long enough time, it might starve, simply because it had radiated away in cosmic rays all the energy it possessed.

Sally smiled at Ben. They were bound to each other not only by feeling, but by the fact that they stood together literally against the universe. All the power of all the nations upon all the planets of all the suns of the Galaxy was opposed to them. They defied the pomposity of the brass hats of the universe simply by remaining alive. All authority demanded their death. Thousands of ships, with their number constantly increasing, and hundreds of thousands of men were devoting their every effort to the discovery of a sixty-foot space cruiser designed for sport, in which Ben Sholto and Sally Hale carried a plague which had wiped out ten million people. And fat men in swivel chairs grew purple with rage as stinging rebukes passed from higher to lower officialdom.

"Conversation?" said Sally, smiling. "We've been together—how long, Ben? We'll be together all the rest of our lives. Maybe only we two, hiding through all the years to come!"

"Maybe," admitted Ben, grinning, "in that case we'll hold hands."

She put her hand in its insulating glove upon his shoulder. She bent down. He kissed her. And then he started, as if startled by a flash of light.

She straightened up, her face stricken and pale.

"It's . . . back!" she said in a queer, racked voice. "Oh, Ben! It's back! I can . . . feel it! And it's raging! It's crazy with hatred! It's . . . it's . . . oh, it's terrible!"

Ben swung the Geiger counter. Pointed at Sally, it clattered. No, it did not clatter. It roared. The cosmic rays created by the Thing, as shown by the counter, were many, many times more than any previous amount. It seemed as if the Thing were starved, and tore at the life force of Sally's body with a terrible voracity.

"I'm going to pack you full of positive charges," and Ben, frantically, "and get that Thing out again, and I'm going to kill it."

He worked savagely. Sally sat down. In the insulated spacesuit the Thing could not leave her, though that was what they most desperately desired. Ben swiftly put together a static generator. It was old-fashioned. It was archaic, but it was what the only possible theory called for. He worked it by hand and touched its electrode to Sally's cheek. The existence of a high potential was instantly evidenced. Sally's hair stirred and tried to stand out from her head.

"How does it like that?" demanded Ben fiercely.

Sally babbled. And Ben had worked so swiftly and so concentratedly that he had hardly looked at her. Her face was flushed. Her eyes were bright but vague. She showed every sign of fever; high fever; fever producing delirium. But the Thing had fled, before, when the positive charge was vastly less than this.

Ben touched her cheek. A spark leaped, and she quivered a little.

"W-water, please." she babbled. "I'd like a drink of water with lots of ice and pink roses in it—"

But the Thing should be out, now. Ben turned off the lights to look at her. And she still glowed. The Thing had not come out.

A battered space-tramp was ordered blasted out of space as a "dangerous object" by a sub-commissioner when in defiance of orders not to land in the Beta Cetacia solar system it dived toward the surface of an uninhabited planet. It had reported desperately that its crew was nearly out of food and the air-supply would last for only four more days. But it could show no proper clearance from its last port-of-landing, and was suspected of smuggling. The Navy ship which trailed it did not destroy it until it had landed and its crew had escaped, and was ordered to return to port for arrest and disciplinary action.

Three thousand colonists were refused landing-permits on Thetis IX, because of missing papers they swore they had turned over on the day of their arrival. (The papers were found months later in an under-clerk's desk drawer. He had forgotten to forward them. For the credit of the Service they were destroyed and the affair hushed up.)

The sub-commissioner on Arcturis V issued an order forbidding criticism of the Administrative Service until criticized conditions had been reported to and passed upon by the Administrative Service Board of Appeals. On the same day he denied four requests for appeals to the Administrative Service Board of Appeals.

On Sirius II, one Arthur Matheson was ordered arrested for making scientific experiments endangering the authority of the Galactic Commission. The experiments were those which led ultimately to the Matheson Matter-transmitter.

And it was reported to Reserve Headquarters that Ben Sholto's position had been approximately determined and his capture was a matter of hours.

But Ben was frantically fighting the intangible Thing which occupied Sally's body. Three times he charged Sally, in the insulated spacesuit, with the highest potential the static generator could produce. Three times he drove the Thing to frenzy. And three times he released the charge. The number of Things which roved triumphantly about the metalwork of the small ship increased visibly. There were at least a dozen. But Sally's body continued to glow. The Geiger counter continued to make a roaring noise rather than a clattering. The Thing—somehow Ben assumed that it was the original one—remained, tearing at the life which remained in Sally, consuming it and raking revenge for the hurt it had suffered.

The GC phone muttered and muttered. Once or twice it spoke loudly and distinctly. Some one of the searching ships was very near. Then there came the blasting tone-signal of a General Order, and Ben automatically touched the volume-control, half-crazed as he was by the urgency of the problem the Thing presented.

He had fired a single positron-blast at the Thing. The radiation from that blast had been picked up. The co-ordinates on it were not accurate but now someone used that very inaccuracy in a statistical method of making it impossible for Ben to escape from a closing-in mass of ships. It had to be assumed that Ben would listen in on Navy orders, and he had dodged past one Space-Navy cruiser by passing too close to it, too fast for its ranging devices to operate. This order forestalled any chance of his doing such a thing again. The order commanded every Navy ship within certain fixed classifications—at least two thousand ships in all—to assume the co-ordinates of the positron-beam blast to be no better than approximate, and to use random mathematics to alter them within certain fixed limits. Each ship was then to head for its arbitrarily chosen—but nearby— destination at maximum acceleration.

The Space-Navy would close in on the section of space in which Ben's little ship was, of course. But it would not come in in any pattern. The courses of the ships would be unpredictable. They would come together, but in a manner and at intervals and speeds none could compute. If Ben had been planning flight, he would have recognized its hopelessness. He might have dodged or crashed through any orderly arrangement of en-globing ships, but this plan made evasion mathematically impossible. And, moreover, the General Order commanded the moving up of other thousands of ships behind the globe. Ben's positron-beam blast had been within or near the orbit of a meteor-stream. With all the might of the Galactic Commission behind the search for him, that meteor-stream would be examined. Every stony mass would be inspected. The task, of course, would be quite the most gigantic task ever undertaken even by the Galactic Fleet, but it ended, absolutely, any trace of hope for Ben and Sally.

But Ben had other, grimmer, more immediate reason for despair. Sally burned with fever. She had been rested, and she had been relatively strong. But now the Thing devoured her life.

Bitterly, he saw the flaw in the process which had driven the Thing out the first time. He had made Sally's body painful for it to inhabit. The first time, the Thing had fled at its first opportunity. But it had fled. It had not been forced out—it had been frightened out. And the Thing was intelligent. Now it realized that Ben would have to release the positive potential which caused it suffering, and that then it would cease to suffer. It endured the discomfort he created in order to work its revenge.

"I need," said Ben desperately, while the Galactic Navy moved to destroy him and Sally babbled in delirium, "to make something that will drag the Thing around! Drag it! Physically! And it isn't matter! It's just a pack of negative charges bound together. It's a bound charge. A bound charge—"

Electrons. A complex of electrons. It was energy on the verge of be-coming matter, or matter past the verge of becoming energy. What can you do to an electric charge? How can you make it move, save by its own tension? What can you do to a bound charge?

"Bound charge . . . bound charge—" muttered Ben, with sweat beading his forehead. "Sally's dying, and I'm thinking about bound charges— the stuff kids learn in kindergarten! What's a bound—Ah-h-h-h-h!"

He plunged at his instrument board. He dragged ruthlessly at the GC phone. He pulled off the front panel by main strength and jerked fiercely at certain wires within it. He wanted plate-current and condensers and a tiny rectifier capsule. The condensers and rectifier went into a unit hastily built up on an insulated handle. The device terminated in a ball-contact. There was a single, long, flexible lead to the plate-current terminal of the last of the amplifying tubes of the GC phone. He worked madly, and when it was done he set the originating circuit in the phone to oscillating, and pushed the oscillation frequency up to a hundred million per second. But his take-off was from the plate of the last tube, which did not yield oscillating current, but merely pulsating. It was current which varied in voltage—but not in direction of flow—a hundred million times a second. And the variations in voltage were a thousand volts or more. He checked his device, sweating, and went over to Sally. He was shaking with hope and hatred and terror. He turned off the ceiling light. Sally glowed terribly. The multiplied metabolism of the Thing made her seem almost white-hot. Ben touched the ball-contact to Sally's cheek. He pressed the contact which let the pulsating plate-current flow into his condenser. The glow of Sally's flesh vanished.

It was just as simple as that.

Ben raged at himself for not having done it earlier. It is taught almost in kindergartens that when one plate of a condenser is charged with positive electricity, and the second plate connected to an insulated body, that free—negative—electrons in the insulated body will be drawn into the condenser. If the condenser is taken away, it will carry those electrons with it. If its capacity and applied voltage are high enough, it will leave no free electrons in the insulated body. And the Thing was a complex of free electrons.

But it had will. It was alive. It had intelligence, and it could hate. And such an entity could resist, could figuratively dig in, could symbolically sink its teeth and claws into the body it inhabited and resist the drawing power of applied voltage, even the maximum that Ben could apply. But one can resist a steady pull where an intermittent one is irresistible. The pulsations of the plate-current, as Ben had now arranged it, caused no steady pull, but instead a series of fierce and wrenching jerks at the resistance of the Thing. The current now shook the Thing. It tore at it like a dog at the throat of a rat. The Thing was brutally torn at, and brutally released, one hundred million times in every second. Nothing, material or immaterial, could withstand such a mauling. The Thing's grip was broken, its will shattered, its resistance made impossible—perhaps it was rendered unconscious! It flowed into the condenser, and the rectifier capsule prevented its return. It was imprisoned in the small device in Ben's hand—and an unholy triumph filled him.

He turned on the lights and put the condenser-device very carefully down. He made sure to put it on an insolantite surface—an insulator of practically infinite resistance. He put on insulating boots. He stood before the Geiger counter, and it gave no sign. He picked up Sally and carried her for the second time to the bunk he had insulated from the floor. He laid her there. She still babbled, and her eyes were fever-bright, but the cause of that fever was gone. She would return to normal—but probably terribly weak—within a very little time.

Ben returned to the control room. His eyes burned more brightly with hatred than Sally's had burned with fever. He regarded his device with a vengeful satisfaction. He cut off the switch and discharged the positive plate. The knob he had touched to Sally's cheek began to glow fiercely, even though the lights were shining. There was more than one Thing in the condenser. Freed from the electric bondage Ben had contrived, but with no path by which to escape to the metal skin of the ship, there was a fierce glowing of the compressed, intolerably crowded Things.

He turned the Geiger counter upon the knob. It clattered furiously. He turned it away.

"Ah-h-h-h!" he said thickly. "You're there, eh? And you know you're caught!"

He seemed to feel waves of pure hate enveloping him. He grinned savagely.

"You'd kill Sally, eh? You're smart! Maybe you can understand me, and maybe you can't, but you know what's going to happen, don't you?"

He took out the little positron-beam pistol. He put it within inches of the knob of metal which glowed with pulsating, hating light. He pulled the trigger. There was a reddish glow from the pistol. There was a searing, intolerable light from the knob. There was an unhearable, unbearable shriek—the feeling of anguish and rage and insupportable hatred.

Then the knob was merely a bit of metal attached to a condenser and an electric cord. It did not affect the Geiger counter. Ben licked his lips, his rage unappeased. He turned out the lights once more. There was a glow on the pilot's chair. He stalked it, and touched the knob to it with the plate-current on. The glow vanished. He turned off the switch and discharged the positive plate. The knob glowed. More faintly, to be sure. There was but one Thing trapped this time. Ben laughed without mirth. He gave the Thing a blast of the positron beam. It screamed soundlessly and died.

Sally's babbling ceased. She called faintly. Ben went to her, all savagery and hate. He gave her water.

"I'm killing them!" he said thickly. "I'll get all of them! I'll kill every one! They made you suffer. They'd have killed you! I'll get every one—"

Sally smiled tiredly at him. She was utterly exhausted, and she was very weak indeed.

"We'll have to send word somehow, so they'll know what to do if the plague ever shows up anywhere else—"

Ben remembered. Sally was thinking in terms of hope, but there was no hope. He was killing the Things because they had harmed Sally. But the orders he'd overheard a little while back made anything he could do a mere futility. And worse, the plague had already spread from Pharona. A newscast, hours since—he'd hardly noticed it at the time—reported that a Galactic Commission cruiser had landed on Pharona with dispatches for the local sub-commissioner. He could not be cut off from his regular flow of documents to sign! It observed all sanitary precautions. But it did not think to prevent any possibility of bound electric charges entering its metal fabric. So when it went on to Galata it carried the plague, and women were now dying by thousands, and other women by more thousands glowed faintly with cosmic rays coming from their bodies.

Ben told her, his face savagely stern.

"We must tell," she insisted. "Even if we die, Ben—"

"My dear," said Ben bitterly, "you know the brass hat mind. The instant we open communication, every ship that's hunting us will come bouncing here to blast us out of space. And they'll find us. *If* we can get our information to them and on their recorders before we're killed . . . why . . . sooner or later, after maybe millions more lives have been lost, the information we've given will be passed on as the result of brilliant investigation under the supervision of brass hat so-and-so. But we'll be dead and disreputable. And we'll stay disreputable after we're dead, so that some pompous ass can claim credit for what we've found out and get a few more decorations to hang on his fat tummy."

"Maybe hers," said Sally. She lay there in the bunk, looking up at Ben with soft eyes. "Some brass hats are women, and a woman brass hat is even worse than a man. You can't blame them, Ben. They're important people. They have important posts. So they get dignified and pompous and stupid. If they could only feel that its their work instead of them that's important—"

"But they never will," said Ben grimly. "So we die. I pulled down the GC phone to get rid of the Things. I'll kill off the rest and put the phone back together. Then I'll broadcast my stuff, and we'll sit down and hold hands until we're killed."

"Darling!" said Sally wistfully. "Would you mind kissing me? You haven't kissed me but twice since we've been together—"

He bent down. He kissed her. And then they clung, suddenly. The little sports cruiser had reeled. Something had hold of it. With a tractor-beam. Ben fought against a savage acceleration, applied from without, and then there was a violent impact. They had been drawn violently against the hull of a much larger vessel. Tools worked instantly on the air lock, and before Ben could do more than reach the door of the stateroom with his positron-pistol in his hand, he found himself looking into the muzzles of other positron-guns. Navy men faced him.

"You're under arrest, Sholto," said a voice crisply. "We were ordered to burn you down on sight, but since the plague's hit Galata, we've got instructions to do it before a visiphone screen as a warning to anybody else who has the idea of breaking a planetary quarantine. Come along!"

Brass hat: an idiom accepted as Auxiliary Basic since Circa 2126 Earth Style. It originally referred to the headgear used to distinguish "staff officers" in an army (See ARMY) who gave orders without responsibility for their result, and which they were required to justify only by precedent, "political necessity" or "strategic reasons,"—terms which have no discoverable exact meaning. Costly blunders by officers of the mental pattern AF-IQ-R.37 and its derivatives—(to whom the career of a "staff officer" was irresistibly attractive in time of war)— led to the use of the term "brass hat" to indicate persons of those now-recognized mental patterns. It is an interesting case of instinctive popular recognition of mental patterning before personality analysis emerged from charlatanry.

(*Dictionary of Auxiliary Basic Words and Idioms.* Cephus, Antres VII. 2215 Earth Style.)

Ben grinned. There was no particular mirth in it, but it was the only possible expression of the way he felt.

"Ah-h-h!" he said softly. "The brass-hat mind in action! The order undoubtedly ended, 'this order is not to be questioned.' But try and carry it out! You can kill me, of course. But I've a pistol in my hand, too. Try and drag me to a visiphone! And you've got a boarding-mike with you, haven't you? Ah, yes! Everything I say will be recorded and goes through all the ranks of brass hats up to the Galactic Commission, if necessary. Very well! This is a plague ship. I have a girl here who has had the plague and has been cured of it. I know how to cure the plague. But the ship is infected—and so is yours, now! If there are as many as a dozen women on board it, you've got a dozen cases of plague in your ship's company, and you've only to set a Geiger counter in front of any one of them—or stand them in the dark—to find it out! What I've said is recorded! Now kill me and go and land on any planet in the universe!"

The boarding officer said uncertainly:

"I have orders to take you to a visiphone screen and blast you before it."

"Try it!" said Ben savagely.

He shook with fury. Because it seemed that every hope was gone, not only of his own life and Sally's, but of being able to get past the wall of pompous stupidity brass-hattism had erected. The Space-Navy and all interstellar traffic suffered intolerably from a policy which assumed that infinite wisdom lay in any person with authority to issue an order, and that only blind obedience should be practiced by inferiors.

He raged at himself, too. It was his use of the positron pistol to kill the Things which had led this Navy cruiser directly to him. Pulling out the GC phone to get its condenser had left him unaware of demands for surrender. His screens had been off. And now he would be killed, and the plague would go all through the galaxy. Because, of course, brass hats would refuse to believe anything they did not already know, and they would solemnly remove themselves from infected planets—with all sanitary precautions, of course—to exercise their authority elsewhere, and they would spread the plague themselves.

The boarding-officer's helmet phone hummed. His uncertainty vanished.

"Very good, sir," he said to the air. To Ben he said, "Your first statements have been checked. Four cases of plague have been found already. You say you can cure them. They will be brought here. The order for your execution is suspended for the time being."

"I'll do it," said Ben curtly, "in the control room."

People crowded through the air lock and into the control room. There were four women and a stout and pompous individual with the brass tabs of an under-commissioner. Of brass hat rating—and brass hat mentality.

"You are incredibly insolent!" he puffed. "You have defied the authority of the Galactic Commission! It is unheard of!"

"Also," said Ben grimly, "I've found out how to cure the plague. If you can't think of anything but my defiance of authority, you're a fool!"

The brass hat purpled and gasped. But Ben turned out the lights. The four women, in Space-Navy Auxiliary uniform, stood out starkly in the darkness. Their faces and throats and hands glowed with a pale white light. Ben picked up his condenser. He touched it to the cheek of the first woman, whose features were working convulsively. The glow vanished from her. The little knob glowed instead. Ben held it out and gave it a momentary positron blast. There was the feeling of a soundless scream. He touched the second woman. She no longer glowed. A second blast. A second unheard shriek. The third. When he had drawn the Thing from the fourth woman he did not use the blast upon it. Instead, he turned on the lights.

"Those four cases of plague are cured," he said shortly.

The brass hat puffed.

"In that case," he said querulously, "there is nothing more to be done. Regulations have to be obeyed. You will carry out your orders, lieutenant."

The boarding-officer's jaw dropped.

"You mean, sir—"

"He's been ordered to be executed," said the brass hat, indignantly. "Hasn't the Navy learned yet that orders are to be obeyed first and questions asked afterwards?"

Ben released the last Thing into the fabric of the ship.

"But the plague isn't finished," he said, his eyes burning. "I inform you—and all my words are recorded—that if you land on any planet with-

out my having cleaned your ship of the plague, you will start the plague
again wherever you land."

"But—that's blackmail!" cried the brass hat.

There were sounds. Three more people came through the air lock.
Two were the ranking officers of a Space-Navy cruiser. The third was a
white-haired woman in a gray cloak. She had alert, intelligent eyes.

"Ma'am," bellowed the brass hat. "This man has insulted and tried to
blackmail the Galactic Commission! I have ordered him blasted!"

It would be unthinkable, of course, to carry out a death sentence in
the presence of a member of the Galactic Commission itself. The white-
haired woman said gently:

"More immediately important, I am afraid, is the fact that he called
you a fool." She looked at Ben. "I am Myra Thorn. I am one of the
Galactic Commission. I was on my way to Galata, where the plague has
broken out, to try to press its investigation. Within the past five minutes
it appears that I have developed the plague myself. I feel that there is
something within me, but separate from me, which gloats in triumphant
hate. A Geiger counter verifies my diagnosis. And . . . I glow in darkness.
The plague is a form of life, is it not? An entity which is not quite
matter?"

"Yes, ma'am," said Ben. He regarded her from beneath frowning
brows. "It is an organized form of electron gas."

"I wish," said the white-haired woman, "that you would broadcast—
through the cruiser's GC phone, since your own is dismantled—all the
information you have on these entities, and the method you have devised
for destroying them."

"Yes, ma'am," said Ben. He still regarded her steadily.

"Then, at your convenience," she said quietly, "you may clean the
cruiser alongside, and last of all—but I must be last—you may cure me of
the plague."

"Easy enough," said Ben grimly.

"Very well—"

The brass hat bleated:

"But ma'am, there is an official order that he shall be blasted immediately upon his capture if not on sight! It is irregular! It is unheard of!
A Commission order—And he has defied the Commission! He tried to
blackmail it!"

The white-haired woman said meditatively:

"To be sure. Formalities must be observed. So I formally annul his
sentence. And, by the way, I order you under arrest for courtmartial. The
charge will be stupidity, incompetence, and arrogance. I have to make a
charge," she added mildly, "so we can have a psychometrist make a complete chart of your personality. Really, we must make regulations to keep
your sort from having authority, hereafter. You do too much damage."
She turned again to Ben. "Now, what will you need?"

"Five minutes with your technical officer," said Ben briefly. "Then he can do anything I could. But ma'am, I have a girl on board. She's been officially reported dead, and sentenced to death afterward. I would like—"

"A pardon? Of course!"

"No, ma'am, a wedding," said Ben. He grinned.

(*Formal announcement by the Galactic Commission, Sitting in Executive Session, January 16, 2195.*)

"The Galactic Commission makes it known that it recognizes that the plague upon Pharona, and its very great threat to the entire human race, cannot be blamed upon anything but certain ill-advised actions of members of the Administrative Service. Members of the Commission, having discovered this fact, have discovered other and further evidences of extraordinary incapacity and stupidity among high officials of the Administrative Service, and have determined that such persons fall into certain mental patterns which from now on are to be forbidden. Persons falling within patterns . . ." (Here follows a list of sixteen mental patterns) "are forbidden hereafter to hold any office under the Commission, or any office of authority in any enterprise under the Commission's guidance. The Commission recommends to planetary governments that such patterns be forbidden planetary positions of authority also, but since politics has enormous attraction for persons of these types, it cannot expect that they can successfully be excluded from legislative bodies until genetics supplies a means of breeding these strains out of the human race."

———

Jack Vance

WINNER LOSE ALL

Chief Officer Avery came up the tube into the bridge sucking a bulb of coffee. Second Mate Dart rose stiffly from the seat where he had spent his watch. "She's all yours."

Avery was thin, hawk-nosed. His complexion was sallow leather color, his hair lank and sparse. He had black eyes between narrow lids and the angle at which they crossed his cheeks gave his face a look of clownish melancholy. Dart was stocky, stub-featured. His hair was Airedale-red; he was abrupt and positive in his movements. Stretching with a quick wide sweep of short arms, he joined Avery by the forward cupola.

Avery leaned forward, looked up, down, right, left, tracing the veins of rose and electric blue across the black of macroid space. He said over his shoulder, "She's dim. Turn her up. Can't see twenty feet at this level."

Dart, blinking, half-asleep, adjusted a rheostat, increasing the flood of polarized light from the bow projectors, and the gristle-like lines of force out in macroid space shone with greater brilliance and detail.

Avery grunted, "That's a lot different. And there's a focus coming up, where those two stringers dent in toward each other."

Dart came to watch as the lines trembled, bulged toward each other. Films of color began to flow from the area: wan yellow, pink, green. Suddenly a hot spark of red appeared.

"There's the focus," said Avery sourly. "Three feet from your nose, the center of a sun."

Dart ruefully rubbed his chin, thankful that Avery rather than Captain Badt had caught him dozing.

"Yeah, I guess so."

"Small to medium, from the kink to that inner blue line," and Avery. "Well, let's check for planets; that's what we're out here for."

Inch by inch they searched the cupola, up, down, right, left. Dart said, "By golly, here it is. Just like the illustration in the text. Maybe we'll slice that bonus yet."

The hot red spark faded to yellow; the twist of colored veins which signified a planet started to uncoil. Avery sprang back, snapped the drift switch, and the lines became static.

For a moment he studied the pattern in the hemispherical cupola. "The sun's right about here." He indicated a point between himself and Dart. "The planet's just inside the cupola."

"We're big men," said Dart.

Avery twisted his mouth in a saturnine grimace. "Either big, or a long way off in a freak direction."

"With all these guys running loose claiming to be geniuses," said Dart, "it's funny one of them hasn't figured it out."

Avery had been searching the cupola for further kinks. "Figure what out?"

"What happens when we go into macroid space."

"You're a dreamer," said Avery. "The universe shrinks, or we and the ship get cosmically big. The main thing is, we get there. Talk to Bascomb, he'll give you ten answers, all different. That's genius for you." Bascomb was the ship's biologist, who had gained himself the reputation of a tireless polemist and theoretician.

Avery took one more look at the kink. "Call the captain, ring general quarters. We're going into normal space."

The unigen was an intelligent organism, though its characteristics included neither form nor structure. Its components were mobile nodes of a luminous substance which was neither matter nor yet energy. There were millions of nodes and each was connected with every other node by ten-drils similar to the lines of force in macroid space.

The unigen might be compared to a great brain, the nodes correspond-ing to the gray cells, the lines of force to the nerve tissue. It might appear as a bright sphere, or it might disperse its nodes at light speed to all cor-ners of the universe.

Like every other aspect of reality, the unigen was a victim of entropy; to survive, it processed energy down the scale of availability, acquiring the energy from radioactive matter. The unigen's business of living in-cluded a constant search for energy.

There were periods of plenitude when the unigen would wax heavy with energy and might expand the number of its nodes by a kind of parthenogenetic fission. Other times the nodes would wane, glowing only feebly, and the unigen would seek energy stuff like a wolf, stalking the planets, satellites, meteors and dark stars for crumbs of even low-grade energy material. During a lean time, one of the nodes, approaching the planet of a small sun, became aware of quanta suggesting the presence of radioactivity: a spangle of distinctive color against a mottled background.

Hope, an emotion compounded of desire and imagination, was not alien to the unigen. It speeded the node forward and the radiation came hard and sharp. The node flitted down through a high scud of cloud. The glow of colored light stretched, elongated, and near its middle shone a markedly bright spot, like a diamond on a band of silver, evidently where the radioactive material broke surface. Toward this spot the unigen di-rected the node.

As it dropped, the unigen sought evidences of danger: the spoor of energy-eaters, sources of static electricity, such as clouds, which might disrupt the tight coils of a node with a spark.

The air was clear and the planet seemed free of dangerous life-forms. The node fell like a bright snowflake toward the central concentration of radioactivity.

The ship circled the planet in a reconnaissance orbit. Captain Badt, taciturn and something of a martinet, stood by the bridge telescreen, receiving reports from the technicians and keeping his opinions to himself.

Dart muttered to Avery in a disgruntled voice, "I'd hardly call the place a tourist planet."

"Looks pretty grim in spots, but it looks like a bonus."

Dart sighed, shook his round red head. "There never yet was a world so tough that colonists wouldn't flock out to it. If it's not cold enough to freeze air and not hot enough to boil water, and if you can breathe with-out popping your eyes, then it's land, and men seem to want it."

"I was born on a planet a hell of a lot worse than this," said Avery shortly.

Dart was silent a moment; then, with the air of a man who refuses to admit discouragement, went on. "Well, it's livable. Breathable atmosphere, temperature and gravity inside the critical area, and—so far—no signs of life." He went to the cupola, which now overlooked the world below. "At home the ocean's blue. It's yellow on Alexander, red on Coralasan. Here it's green. Grass by-Jesus green."

"Different proposition altogether," said Avery. "The red and yellow come from plankton. This green is algae or moss or seaweed. No telling how thick it is. Might be a man could walk out on it and pasture his cows."

"Lots of good grazing," admitted Dart. "About four million square miles in sight from here. Probably the source of the planet's oxygen. According to Bascomb, there's no surface vegetation. Maybe lichens, a few shrubs and such. . . . That sea-bed must be thick with humus. . . ."

The speaker from the laboratory click-clicked. On the other wing of the bridge Captain Badt snapped, "Report!"

The code-sono opened the circuit; the voice of Jason the geologist said, "Here's a full report on the atmosphere. Thirty-one per cent oxygen, eleven per cent helium, forty per cent nitrogen, ten per cent argon, four per cent CO_2, the other four per cent inert. Substantially an Earth-type atmosphere."

"Thank you," said Captain Badt formally. "Off."

He paced up and down the bridge frowning, his hands clasped behind his back.

"The old man's in a hurry," Avery said quietly to Dart. "I can read his mind. He doesn't like survey duty, and he's figuring that if he finds a good Class A planet, he can use it as an excuse to take off for Earth."

Captain Badt marched stiffly back and forth, paused, went to the speaker. "Jason."

"Yes, sir?"

"What's the story on the geology so far?"

"I can't tell much from this high, but the relief seems generally a product of igneous action rather than erosion. Naturally, that's a guess."

"A good ore planet, possibly?"

"At a guess, yes. There's plenty of folding, lots of faults, not too much sediment. Where those mountains break up through the coastal strip, I'd expect schists, gneiss, broken rocks cemented with quartz and calcite."

"Thank you." Captain Badt went to the magniscreen, watched the landscape drift past. He turned to Avery. "I think we'll dispense with further investigation and set down."

The speaker click-clicked. "Report!" said Captain Badt.

It was Jason again. "I've located an extensive outcrop of radioactive ore, probably pitchblende or possibly carnotite. It shines like a searchlight when I drop the X-screen across the scope. It runs along the shore just south of the long inlet."

"Thank you." To Avery. "We'll set down there."

The reconnaissance party, consisting of Avery and Jason, walked along the black gravel pebbles of the shore. To their left, the ocean spread out to the horizon, a green velvety flat like a tremendous billiard table. To the right, black-shadowed gulleys led back into the mountains—crag-crested barrens of rock. The sun was smaller and yellower than Sol; the light was wan, like Earth sunlight through a pall of smoke. Although the air had been certified breathable, the men wore head-domes, precautions against possibly dangerous bacteria or spores.

Through a pick-up TV eye mounted above Avery's dome, Captain Badt watched from the ship. "Any insects, animal life of any sort?" he asked.

"Haven't noticed any so far . . . That upholstered ocean should make a good home for bugs. Jason threw a stone out and it's still sitting high and dry. I believe a man could walk out there with a pair of snowshoes."

"What is that vegetation to your right?"

Avery paused, inspected the shrub. "Nothing very different from those around the ship. Just one of those paint-brush plants a little larger than the others. Country seems rather arid, in spite of this ocean. Takes rain to make good soil. Right, Jason?"

"Right."

Captain Badt said, "After a while, we'll check into the ocean. Right now I'm interested in that uranium reef. You should be almost on top of it."

"I think it's about a hundred yards ahead, a ledge of black rock. Yep, Jason's detector is buzzing like mad . . . Jason says it's pitchblende—uranium oxide." He stopped short in his tracks.

"What's the trouble?"

"There's a swarm of lights over it. Flickering up and down like mosquitoes."

Captain Badt focused the image on the screen. "Yes, I see them."

"Might be some sort of fireflies," hazarded Jason.

Avery took a few cautious steps forward, halted. One of the luminous spots darted up, sped toward him, swung around his head, circled Jason, returned to the uranium ledge.

Avery said uncertainly, "I guess they're not dangerous. Some kind of bug, apparently."

Captain Badt said, "Peculiar how they're concentrated along that ledge. As if they're feeding on the uranium, or like the feel of the radiation."

"There's nothing else nearby. No vegetation of any sort, so it must be the uranium."

"I'll send Bascomb out," said Captain Badt. "He can investigate more closely."

The node which originally discovered the planet settled on an outcrop of the uranium oxide and was presently joined by other nodes, fleeting in from less rewarding areas. The absorption of energy began; pressing against the massive blue-black rock, a node would generate sufficient heat to vaporize a quantity of the ore. Enveloping the gas, the node worked a complicated alchemy which released the latent energy. The node absorbed this energy, compacting and augmenting its structure, kinking its whorls of force into harder knots. At the same time it discharged a flood of energy into the lines to the rest of the unigen, and everywhere in the universe nodes shone with a new golden-green luster.

Insofar as surprise may be equated to witnessing events which have previously been dismissed as improbable, the unigen felt surprise when it sensed the approach of two creatures along the shore.

The unigen had observed living creatures on other worlds. Some of these were dangerous, like the mirror-metal energy-eaters swimming in the thick atmosphere of another uranium-rich planet. Others were unimportant as competition for food. These particular slow-moving creatures appeared harmless.

To investigate at close hand, the unigen sent out a node, and received a report of infra-red radiation, fluctuating electromagnetic fields.

"Harmless autochthones," was the unigen's summation. "Creatures living by chemical reaction at a low energy level, like the land-worms of Planet 11432. Useless as energy sources, incapable of damage to the hard energy of a node."

Dismissing further consideration of the two creatures, the unigen absorbed itself with the uranium bank . . . Odd. On the surface of the ore had appeared what seemed to be a vegetable growth, a peppering of tiny spines rising from little flat collars. They had not been evident previously.

And here came another of the slow-moving creatures. This one, like the others, emitted infra-red radiation, several different weaker waves.

The creature halted, then slowly approached the ledge.

The unigen watched with mild curiosity. Precise visual definition was beyond its powers, so the land-worm's movements came as blurs of shifting radiation.

It seemed to manipulate a metal object which glinted and reflected sunlight—evidently a bit of pitchblende which had attracted its attention.

The land-worm moved closer. It made a few blurred motions, and suddenly appeared to have extended one of its members. It moved once more, and a mesh of carbonaceous material fell around one of the nodes.

Interesting, thought the unigen. The land-worm evidently had been attracted by the glitter and motion. The action implied curiosity; was the creature more highly evolved than its structure indicated? Or possibly it sustained life by trapping small bright animals, such as phosphorescent jellyfish from the sea.

The land-worm drew the net close. To resolve the problem, the unigen permitted the node to be carried along.

A brittle shell of another carbon compound was cupped over the node and an enclosure effected.

Was this perhaps the land-worm's organ of digestion? There appeared to be no digestive juice, no grinding or crushing action.

The land-worm moved slightly away from the ledge and performed a series of mysterious gyrations. The unigen was puzzled.

Two metal needles entered the brittle cage. In sudden consternation the unigen sought to snap the node free.

Avery and Jason continued along the pitchblende ledge. Presently it dipped from sight, and the shore of black-gray pebbles slanted up from the green velvet ocean to the heavy shoulder of the mountain.

"Nothing out here, Captain," said Avery. "Just looks like more shore and more mountains for ten or twenty miles."

"Very well, you can return." He added in a grumbling voice, "Bascomb's on his way out to check on those flickering lights. He thinks they're emanations, like will o' the wisps."

Avery winked at Jason, and cutting off the band to the ship said, "Bascomb won't be satisfied till he has one of 'em pinned to a board like a butterfly."

Jason held up a hand, signed Avery to listen. Avery switched back on the communication band, heard Bascomb's precise voice.

"—From a distance of thirty feet, the spectroscope shows a uniform band, radiating at apparently equal intensity in all frequencies. This is curious. Normal phosphors emit in discrete bands. Perhaps some such occurrence like St. Elmo's Fire is involved, though I confess I don't quite understand—"

Captain Badt growled impatiently, "Are they alive or aren't they?"

Bascomb's voice was petulant. "I've no idea, I'm sure. After all, this is a strange planet. The word 'life' has a thousand interpretations. Incidentally, I note a very odd type of vegetation growing on the pitchblende itself."

"Avery mentioned no vegetation," said Captain Badt. "I questioned him specifically."

Bascomb sniffed. "He could hardly have missed it. It's a line of shoots about six inches tall. They're like spikes, apparently stiff and crisp, rising from suckers clamped to the surface. Very similar to something I saw once on Martius Juvenal where a pitchblende vein breaks surface. . . . It's very peculiar. The roots seem to have drilled into the solid rock."

"You're the biologist," said Captain Badt. "You ought to know."

Bascomb's voice took on a note of cheery assurance. "Well, we'll see. I've read of emanations being observed near pitchblende deposits, but I have never observed them. Possibly the concentrated radioactivity might be acting on minute condensations of moisture. . . ."

Captain Badt cleared his throat. Very well, handle it your own way. Be careful and don't stir them up; they might be dangerous in some way."

Bascomb said, "I've brought along a net and specimen bottle. I planned to capture one of the motes and examine it under the microscope."

"I suppose you know what you're doing," said Captain Badt in a tired voice.

"I've devoted my life to the study of extraterrestrial life," replied Bascomb stiffly. "I rather imagine that these motes are analogous to the sparkleticks of Procyon B. . . . Now, if I just adjust my net. There! I've got one. Into the specimen jar. My, how it shines! Can you see it, Captain?"

"Yes, I can see it. What's it like under the microscope?"

"Hm . . ." Bascomb brought his pocket magnifier to bear. "There's no resolution. I see a central concentration of fire; undoubtedly that's where the insect is. I think I'll pass an electric spark through the creature and kill it, and perhaps I can examine it under higher power."

"Don't stir 'em up—" began Captain Badt. The screen flared white in his face, went dark. "Bascomb! Bascomb!"

Captain Badt received no reply.

Destruction of a node sent a restless shiver through the unigen. A node represented an integral fraction of the unigen's brain; it had been conditioned to modify a definite class of thoughts. When the node was destroyed, the thinking in the class was curtailed until another node could be produced and endowed with the same precise channels.

The implications of the event were further cause for anxiety. The metal energy-eaters on another planet used the same technique—a stream of electrons smashing across the center of the node, to upset the equilibrium. The flash was a flash of released energy, which the metal ovoids were able to absorb. Apparently the land-worm had been surprised by the explosion and destroyed—possibly mistaking the node for some less energetic type of creature.

It might be wise, thought the unigen, to destroy the land-worms as soon as they appeared, and thus prevent further accidents.

Still another vexation: the spike-vegetation was spreading its collars across the surface of the ledge, sinking deep roots into the energy-stuff. Apparently it built the displaced material into the spike. When the unigen sent a node to absorb the leached uranium, it found a hard shell of inert substance, proof against the node's kernel of heat.

Nodes flickered and quivered all over the universe as the unigen marshaled its computative abilities. Rigorous steps would have to be taken.

Far down the beach, Avery and Jason saw the white flash of the explosion, saw the black gullies light up in a ghastly swift glare. Then came a rolling sound and a jar of concussion.

Avery cut anxiously into the communication band. "Captain Badt, Avery calling. What's happened?"

Captain Badt said harshly, "That fool Bascomb s just blown himself up."

"We're up the beach about a mile, I think, from where the explosion came," said Avery hurriedly. "Should we—"

Captain Badt interrupted. "Don't do anything. Don't touch anything. This is a strange planet, and it's dangerous. Bascomb's just proved that."

"What did he do?"

"He apparently ran an electric current through one of those bright spots of light, and it went off in his face."

Avery stopped short, looked warily up the shore. "We went past pretty closely and they didn't bother us. It must be the electricity."

"You be careful on your way back. I can't afford to lose any more men. Keep out of the way of those lights."

"Yes, sir," said Avery. He motioned to Jason. "Let's go. We'd better skirt the water as close as possible."

Crowding the soggy verge of the ocean, they rounded the bend in the shoreline, approached the scene of the explosion.

"Doesn't seem to be much left of Bascomb," said Jason in a hushed voice.

"Not much crater either," said Avery. "It's a funny deal."

"Look, now there's thousands of those light-bugs. Like bees around a hive. And look at that stuff growing out of the ledge! That wasn't there when we went past! Talk about mushrooms . . ."

Avery turned his binoculars along the ledge. "Probably it's got something to do with the light-flecks. The lights could be spores or pollen or something of the sort."

"Anything's possible," said Jason. "I've seen vines thirty miles long, as thick around as a house, and if you jab them with a stick they quiver their whole length. They're on Antaeus. The kids in the Earth colony tap out Morse code back and forth to each other. The vine doesn't like it, but there's nothing it can do."

Avery had been watching the dancing lights over his shoulder. "They're like eyes watching us. . . . Before a colony's sent out here, these damn things will have to be destroyed. They'd be dangerous flying loose around electricity."

Jason said, "Duck! Here comes a couple of them after us!"

Avery said in a nervous voice, "Don't get excited, kid. They're just drifting on the breeze."

"Drifting, hell," said Jason, and started to run for the ship.

The unigen observed the land-worms returning along the shore, evidently seeking the sea-matter on which they fed. To guard against the accidental destruction of any more nodes, it would be wise to destroy the creatures as they appeared, and clean them from this particular section of the planet.

It dispatched two nodes toward the land-worms. They seemed to sense danger and broke into lumbering motion. The unigen accelerated the nodes; they darted forward at half-light speed, punctured the land-worms, reversed, shuttled back and forth a score of times, each time leaving a small steaming hole. The land-worms collapsed to the black pebbles, lay limp.

The unigen brought the nodes back to the uranium bank. Now to a more serious matter; the vegetation which was choking off the face of the uranium with its collars and roots.

The unigen concentrated the heat of twenty nodes on one of the spikes. A hole appeared, weakening the entire shoot. It sagged and shriveled, collapsed.

Pleasure was a quality which the structure of the unigen was incapable of expressing, the nearest approach being a calm coasting sense, an awareness of control and mastery of movement. In this state the unigen began a systematic attack on the spikes.

A second member fell over, became pale brown and a third . . .

Overhead appeared a flying object, similar to a land-worm except that it radiated more strongly in the infra-red.

Were the creatures everywhere?

Second Officer Dart had made the original suggestion, diffidently at first, half-expecting Captain Badt to freeze him with a stare the color of zinc. But Captain Badt stood like a statue looking into the blank magni-screen, still tuned to Avery's band.

Dart said with somewhat more boldness, "So far we have no conclusive report to make. Is the planet habitable or not? If we leave now we haven't proved anything."

Captain Badt answered in a voice without resonance, "I can't risk any more men."

Dart rubbed at his bristling red hair. It occurred to him that Captain Badt was getting old.

"Those little lights are vicious," Dart said emphatically. "We know that. They've killed three of our men. But we can handle them. An electric current blows 'em apart. Another thing, they're like bees around a hive; they mind their own business unless they're bothered. Bascomb, Avery, Jason—they got it because they approached that pitchblende ledge too closely. Here's my idea, and I'll take the risk of carrying it through. We knock together a light frame, string it with wire, and charge the strands alternately positive and negative. Then I'll go up in the service 'copter and drift it across the ledge. They're so thick now that we can't help but knock out two-three hundred at a swipe."

Captain Badt clenched and unclenched his hands. "Very well. Go ahead." He turned his back, stared into the blank magni-screen. This would be his last voyage.

With the help of Henry, the ship's electrician, Dart built the frame, strung it with wire, equipped it with a high-potential battery. Strapping himself into the 'copter harness, he rose straight up, dangling a mile of light cable. He became a speck on the gray-blue sky.

"That's it," said Henry into the communication mike. "Now I'll make fast this fly trap affair, and then—I've got another idea. We want the thing to move flatside forward, so I'll tie on a bridle with a bit of drag at the end."

He arranged the drag, snapped the switch on the battery. "She's ready to go."

A mile above, Dart moved across the sky toward the ledge of pitch-blende.

Captain Badt maintained an iron grip on the hand rail in the bridge, watching Dart's progress on the magni-screen.

"Up, Dart," he said. "Up four feet . . . There . . . Steady. That's about right. Take it slow . . ."

The unigen's range of perception included the lowest radio waves as well as the hottest ultra-cosmics, a spectrum of a million colors. Stereoscopic vision was implicit in the fact that each node served as an organ of sight. Resolution of images was achieved by accepting only radiation normal to the surface of the node. In this manner a coarse spherical picture was received by each node, although detail as fine as the frame strung with wire was nearly invisible.

The unigen's first warning was a pressure from the approaching electrostatic fields; then the frame swept across the ledge, full through the heaviest concentration of nodes.

The blast seared the ground, melted it into a flaming molten basin for a radius of fifty feet. The nodes which escaped the screen were flung pell-mell by the explosion out across the ocean.

Directly under the explosion, the spike-vegetation was scorched; elsewhere, little affected.

The structure of the unigen was no more capable of anger than pleasure; however, its will to survive was intense. Overhead flew the land-worm. One like it had destroyed a node through electricity; perhaps this one was somehow associated with the last catastrophic explosion. Four nodes slanted up at light speed, snapped back and forth through the land-worm like sewing-machine needles hemming a sheet. The creature fell to the ground.

The unigen assembled its nodes a hundred feet over the bank of uranium. Ninety-six nodes destroyed.

The unigen weighed the situation. The planet was rich with uranium, but it was also the home of lethal land-worms.

The unigen decided. There was uranium elsewhere in the universe, on thousands of worlds that were silent and dark and free of any kind of life. A lesson had been learned: avoid worlds inhabited by life-forms, no matter how primitive.

The nodes flashed off into the sky, dispersed into space.

Captain Badt relaxed his grip on the table. "That's it," he said in a flat voice. "Any world where we lose four good men in four hours—any world inhabited by swarms of crazy atomic bees—that's no world for human beings. Four good men . . ."

He stood silent a moment, limp and dejected.

The cadet wandered into the bridge, stared wide-eyed. Life-long habit reasserted itself. Captain Badt filled out, became erect, rigid. His tunic and trousers hung crisp, his eyes once more shone with authority.

"Ensign, you will act as chief officer until further notice. We're leaving the planet, returning to Earth. Please attend to all exterior ports."

"Yes, sir," said the new Chief Mate.

The planet was quiet. The ocean spread bright and green, the mountains rolled back into the badlands: crags, ravines, plateaus—black rock, gray rock, pockets of drifted ash.

On the pitchblende ledge the vegetation waxed tall, five, ten, twenty feet, gray spines mottled with white, ivory, silver. In each a central vein opened; the spike became a tube straight and stiff as a cannon barrel.

At the bottom of the tube, the fruit of the plant began to develop. There was a spore-case, enclosed by a jacket into which water percolated. Below the spore-case opened another compartment, globe-shaped, communicating with the base of the spike by four splayed channels.

A nub of uranium 235 accumulated in this chamber—one ounce, two ounces, three ounces, more and more diffused through the membranes of the plant by some evolutionary freak of a metabolism.

The fruit was ripe. One by one, the spikes reached a culmination. A tension within the water-jacket increased past the breaking strain. The jacket split, flooded the compartment below the spore-case, surrounded the knob of uranium.

Explosion. Steam bursting through the stern-pointing channels, back into the tube. Thrust, straight up. Sharp whipping blasts as the cases left the spikes. Up, up, up, at furious acceleration, into space. . . .

The water dissipated, the last puff of steam left the tubes. The spore-cases floated free on momentum. The gravitational field of the planet faded to a wisp, a film. The spore-cases drifted on. Now they cooled, cracked wide. From each a thousand capsules spilled into space, and the tiny jerk of the splitting case sent them in courses slightly divergent, enough to scatter them off toward different stars.

Endless seeping of life across space.

Smite into planet, the sift of spores, the search for the hot element, the growth, the culmination, the blast, the impulse.

Then space, years of drift. Out beyond, and past beyond. . . .

Eric Frank Russell

TEST PIECE

A SHINING BLUE-GREEN globe, approximately Earth-size, Earth-mass, the new planet was exactly as described in the report. It lay fourth from a type

G7 sun and unmistakably was the one they were seeking. The unknown and long-dead scout who had first found it certainly had picked a sphere that looked like home.

Pilot Harry Benton swung his superfast navy cruiser into a wide orbit while his two companions gave their destination a pre-landing survey. They found the largest city in the northern hemisphere, some seven degrees above the equatorial line and near to the shores of a great lake. Obviously it had not moved, or been replaced in greatness by some other city, as might well have happened in the three hundred years since the report was written. Time brings many wide and sometimes unexpected changes.

"Shaksembender," pronounced Navigator Steve Randle. "What a heck of a name to give a planet." He was looking at an official resume of the oldtime space-prober's message which—after all these years—had brought them on this hunt. "And to make it worse, their sun is dignified by the name of Gwilp."

"I've heard tell of a world in the Bottes sector called Plub," commented Engineer Joe Hibbert. "And furthermore, it's pronounced like you were blowing your nose. Give me Shaksembender—it's a speakable word."

"Then try your teeth on its capital city," Randle invited. He spelled it slowly. "Tschflodrithashaksembender." He grinned at the other's expression. "Meaning, literally, the biggest burg on the little green world. For your comfort, the report says a native takes the strain off his epiglottis by referring to it in the shortened form of Taflo."

Benton chipped in with, "Hold tight. We're going down." He wrestled his controls, trying to watch six meters at once. The cruiser blew out of its orbit, spiralled earthward, hit atmosphere and went through it. Soon it roared on its last circle low over the city, leaving behind it a four-mile trail of fire and superheated air. The landing took the form of a prolonged and bumpy bellyslide across meadows to the east. Twisting round in his seat, Benton spoke with irritating self-satisfaction. "See, no corpses. Am I good!"

"Sheer luck," grunted Hibbert disdainfully. "I saw you let go everything and madly stroke a rabbit's foot. It has always worked, but some day it won't."

"We pilots being far above the primitive practices of the engineering profession—if one can call it a profession," began Benton with manifest superiority, "it is not our habit in moments of crisis to toy with any part of a coney's anatomy. Therefore I would have you understand—"

"Here they come," interrupted Randle, who was looking through a sideport. "A dozen or more, on the run."

Hibbert joined him, gazed through the armorglass. "How nice to be cheered in by friendly humanoids. It's a welcome change from what we seem to meet almost everywhere else: suspicious or hostile things resembling figments of the mind after a ten-course Venusian supper."

"They're right outside now," continued Randle. He counted. "Twenty of them." His hand went out as he switched the automatic lock. "We'll let them in."

He had no hesitation about doing that despite rough and tough experiences on many other worlds. After centuries of exploration this was only the third humanoid-inhabited planet to be discovered, and when one has had more than one's fill of life-forms surpassing anything conceived in dreams there is something heartening about a familiar human shape and form. It gives confidence. Any bunch of humanoids in the outlandish cosmos was like a colony of nationals established in foreign parts.

They poured into the ship, a dozen of them, with a smaller group content to wait outside. It was good to look upon them; one head, two eyes, one nose, two arms, two legs, ten fingers, all the old familiar fixings. No especial difference from the ship's crew except that they were a little smaller, a little lighter in build, and had skins of a deep, rich copper color. Yes, that was the greatest contrast: the dark glow of copper skins and gleam of jet black eyes.

Their leader spoke in archaic cosmoparla, forming his words like things learned painstakingly from tutors who had passed them down generation to generation.

"You are Earthlings?"

Benton said happily, "You're dead right. I'm Benton, the pilot. You can ignore these two cretins with me—they're just ballast."

The other received this assurance with uncertainty and a touch of embarrassment. He studied the two cretins doubtfully, returned his attention to Benton.

"I am Dorka the Scholar, one of those deputed to preserve your language against this day. We have been expecting you. Fraser assured us that eventually you would come. We thought you would be here long before now." His black eyes remained upon Benton, watching him, examining him, trying to peer into his mind. No joy of meeting shone within them; rather did they show a strange and wistful uneasiness, a mixture of hope and fear that somehow was communicated to his fellows and gradually grew stronger. "Yes, we expected you long ago."

"Maybe we should have been here long ago," admitted Benton, sobered by the unanticipated touch of ice in the reception. Casually, he pressed a wall-stud, listened for the almost unhearable response of apparatus hidden behind. "But we navy boys go where we're told when we're told, and we got no instructions about Shaksembender until recently. Who's this Fraser?—the scout who discovered you?"

"Of course."

"H'm! I guess his report got buried in bureaucratic files where a lot of other valuable reports may still be resting. Those oldtime daredevil spacesnoopers like Frazer ran far beyond the official limits of their day, risking their necks and hides until they had a casualty list five yards long. An aged and bespectacled bureaucrat was about the only form of life that could frustrate them. That's the way to take the zip out of anyone troubled with excess of enthusiasm: file his report and forget it."

"Perhaps it is just as well," ventured Dorka, his peculiar air of uncertainty growing stronger. He glanced at the wall-stud but refrained from asking its purpose. "Fraser told us that the longer the time the better the hopes."

"He did, eh?" Mystified, Benton tried to analyze the other's deep copper features, but they revealed nothing. "What did he mean by that?"

Dorka fidgeted, licked his lips, behaved as if to say more was to say too much. Finally he evaded, "Which one of us can say what Earthlings mean? They are like us, yet not like us, for our thought-processes are not necessarily the same."

This was unsatisfactory. To gain a common understanding, a genuine basis on which an alliance might be founded, the matter was worth pursuing to the bitter end. But Benton did not bother. He had a special reason for that. It had to do with the apparatus still hissing faintly behind the wall. Centuries of space-roving inevitably compelled mankind to produce all the tools best fitted for the job.

So in a kindly and disarming manner, he said to Dorka, "I guess this Fraser was banking on closer accord based on ships lots bigger and faster than any known in his day. He slipped up slightly there. They're bigger all right, but hardly any faster."

"No?" Dorka's manner revealed that spaceship velocities had little or no bearing on whatever was bedevilling his mind. It was a polite, "No?" lacking surprise, lacking interest.

"They could be a whole lot swifter," Benton went on, "if we were content with the exceedingly low safety-margins of Fraser's time. But the era of death-or-glory has passed away. We build no suicide-bottles these days. We get from sun to sun in one piece and with clean underwear."

It was evident to all three that Dorka could not care less. He was preoccupied with something else, something elusive, unmentioned, some queer obsession to which there was no clue. In lesser degree it showed on the darkly colored faces of his companions crowding behind him. Amity chained by vague fear. Would-be friendliness concealed beneath a black shroud of doubt, of apprehension. They were like children who yearn to pat a strange animal but cannot be sure whether one end bites.

So obvious was their common attitude, and so contrary to expectations, that Benton could not help but try mentally to find a reason for it. His mind moiled and toiled until it became suddenly struck with the notion that possibly Fraser—their only Terrestrial contact to date—had fallen foul of his hosts sometime after transmitting his report. Perhaps there had been differences, words, threats and eventually a clash between these copper-skins and the tough Earthling. Perhaps Fraser had tried to fight his way out, impressing them for three hundred years with the efficiency of Terrestrial weapons and their tremendous power to kill.

The same or a similar process of reasoning must have operated within

Steve Randle's mind, because before Benton could speak again he shot a fast and pointed question at Dorka.

"How did Fraser die?"

The result was disappointing in its negativity. No guilt, no alarm came into the other's face. It merely showed retrospection as he answered.

"Samuel Fraser was no longer young when he found us. He said that we were his last venture, for the time had come to take root. So he stayed and lived among us until he grew old and weary and could no longer hold the breath of life. We burned his body as he had asked us to do."

"Ah!" said Randle, feeling defeated. His mind did not inquire why Fraser had not sought retirement on Earth, his home planet. It was notorious that the defunct Corps of Space Scouts had been composed entirely of very lone wolves.

"We had already melted down and made use of the metal of his ship, at his own suggestion," Dorka went on. "After his passing we placed the contents of his vessel in a shrine, along with his death-mask, and a bust of him made by our best sculptor, and a life-size portrait by our most talented painter. They are all here, those relics, still preserved and revered in Taflo." His eyes went inquiringly to each in turn as he added in quiet tones, *"Would you like to come and look at them?"*

It was idiotic and unreasonably and completely without justification, yet little alarm-bells rang faintly in Benton's mind. No question could have been more innocent or put more mildly; nevertheless it gave him a queer feeling that somewhere a trap-door had opened in readiness for him to drop through. The feeling was enhanced by the insufficiently concealed eagerness with which the copper-skins hung on his reply.

Would you like to come and look at them?

Will you walk into my parlor? said the spider to the fly.

That weird warning instinct, or intuition, or whatever it was, impelled Benton to yawn, stretch his arms wide and say, tiredly, "There is nothing we'd like more, but we're right at the end of a long, long trip and somewhat tuckered out. One good night's sleep will set us up like new men. How about first thing in the morning?"

Dorka became hurriedly apologetic. "I am so sorry. We should have known better than to impose ourselves upon you immediately you arrived. Please forgive us. We have waited so long for you and did not realize—"

"There is nothing to be regretted," assured Benton, trying in vain to reconcile his inward leeriness with the other's genuine and almost pathetic concern. "We could not have rested without first making contact. It would have been impossible. So your arrival saved us much trouble, for which we are truly grateful."

A little relieved, but still obviously bothered over what he chose to view as his own lack of consideration, Dorka backed out through the lock, taking his companions with him.

"We will leave you alone to your rest and sleep and I will see to it that you are not bothered by others. In the morning we will call again and show you around our city." Once more his gaze went penetratingly over all three. *"And we will show you Fraser's shrine."*

He departed. The lock closed. The mental alarm-bells were still ringing.

Sitting on the rim of the control-desk, Joe Hibbert massaged his ears and complained, "What I don't like about these whizz-bang receptions is that the thunderous cheers and the blare of massed bands leave me half deaf. Why can't people behave with more restraint, speak quietly, and invite us to a mausoleum or something?"

Frowning at him, Steve Randle said seriously, "There is something fishy about this business. They acted as if they were hopefully welcoming rich uncles rumored to have smallpox. They yearn to be remembered in the will but hanker after no spots." He glanced at Benton. "What do you think, Frowsy? Did you smell icicles?"

"I'll shave when some no-good thief returns my depilator, and my nose isn't good enough to smell the unsmellable, and I'm not bothering to do any more thinking until I've got data to think upon." Opening a recess just below the wall-stud, Benton took from it a platinum-mesh headpiece on the end of a length of thin cable. "Which data I am about to absorb."

He fixed the platinum on his own head, adjusted it carefully, set a couple of dials within the recess, lay back and appeared to go into a semi-trance. The others watched with interest. He sat there, saying nothing, eyes half-closed, while all sorts of expressions chased across his lean face. Finally he removed the cap, stowed it back in its hiding-place.

"Well?" prompted Randle, impatiently.

"His neural band coincides with ours, and the receiver picked up his thought-waves all right," said Benton. "It recorded them faithfully, but . . . I dunno."

"Most enlightening," commented Hibbert. "He doesn't know."

Ignoring him, Benton continued. "What all his thoughts boil down to is that they've not yet decided whether to kiss us or kill us."

"Huh?" Steve Randle stiffened aggressively. "Why the blazes should they contemplate the latter? We've done them no harm."

"Dorka's mind told a lot but it didn't tell enough. It said that reverence of Fraser has developed through the years until it has become almost a religion. Almost, but not quite. Being their only visitor from another world he's the most outstanding figure in their history, see?"

"That's understandable," agreed Randle. "But what of it?"

"Three hundred years have cast an aura of near-holiness around everything Fraser did and said. All the information he gave is preserved verbatim, the advice is treasured, the warnings remembered." Benton mused a moment. "And he warned them against Earth—*as it was in his day.*"

"Telling them to skin us alive first chance they get?" inquired Hibbert.

"No, definitely not. He warned them that Earth-psychology—as he knew it—would operate gravely to their disadvantage, even to their pain and sorrow, so that they might everlastingly regret the contact unless they had the wit and strength to break it by force."

"Growing old and on his last venture and ready to take root," remarked Randle. "I know the type. Doddering around, armed to the gums, thinking they're hot even while they're getting cold. He was too long in the void and went queer with it. Ten to one he'd been space-happy for years."

"Maybe," conceded Benton doubtfully. "But I am not so sure. Pity we've no information about this Fraser. So far as I'm concerned, he's just a forgotten name dragged out of some bureaucrat's pigeonhole."

"As I will be in due time," offered Hibbert morbidly.

"Anyway, he followed up that warning with a second one, namely, that it would be wise not to be impetuous in the matter of beating us off—because they might be beating their best friends. Human nature *does* change, he told them, and Earth-psychology changes with it. Any such change might be for the better, so much so that at some distant date Shaksembender would have nothing to fear. The longer it took us to make this contact, he asserted, the further into the future we'd be and the greater the likelihood of change." Benton looked vaguely worried. "Bear in mind that, as I told you, these views have become tantamount to heavenly commandments."

"This is one heck of a note," grumbled Hibbert. "By what this Dorka fondly imagines to be his secret thoughts—and probably they represent what all his fellows are thinking—we are going to be given the rah-rah or the rub-out according to whether in their opinion we've improved on some ephemeral standard laid down by a long-dead crackpot. Who the deuce was he to decide whether or not we're fit to associate with them? On what cockeyed basis are they going to determine the same thing today? How can they possibly *know* whether we've changed, and *how* we've changed, in the last three centuries? I don't see—"

Benton interrupted with, "You're planting your unwashed finger right on the sore spot. They think they can find out. In fact, they're sure of it."

"How?"

"If we speak two given words in a given set of circumstances we thereby betray ourselves. If we don't speak them, we're okay."

Hibbert laughed with relief. "Ships weren't fitted with thought-recorders in Fraser's time. They weren't even invented. He couldn't forsee those, could he?"

"No."

"So," continued Hibbert, amused by the futility of the situation, "you just tell us what circumstances were shown in Dorka's mind, and the fateful words, and we prove we're good guys by keeping our lips buttoned."

"All that is recorded of the circumstances is a shadowy mind-picture showing that they surround this shrine to which we've been invited," Benton told him. "Definitely, the shrine is the testing-place."

"And the two words?"

"Were not recorded."

Paling a little, Hibbert said, "Why not? Doesn't he know them?"

"That I can't say." Benton was openly moody about it. "The mind operates with thought-forms, with meanings, and not with pictorial words visible as such. The meanings become translated into words when speech is employed. Therefore he may not know the words at all or, alternatively, he cannot think of them in recordable manner because he doesn't know their meanings."

"Jeepers, they could be anything! There are millions of words."

"That would put the odds hugely in our favor," Benton pointed out grimly, "but for one thing."

"Such as what?"

"Fraser was a native Earthling who knew his own kind. Naturally he'd chose the two revealing words he considered *likeliest* to be used—then hope and pray he'd prove wrong."

Hibbert smacked his forehead in despair. "So early in the morning we amble to this museum like steers to a slaughterhouse. Then I open my big mouth and find myself holding a harp. All because these copper-faces place faith in a trap laid by an obscure space-nut." He stared irritably at Benton. "Do we blow free while the going is good, and report back to base? Or do we stay here and chance it?"

"Since when did the navy fail to see it through?" Benton inquired.

"I knew you would ask that." Sitting down, Hibbert resigned himself to what the morrow might hold. "Lend me your bit of rabbit, will you? I could use it right now."

The morning proved clear and cold. All three were ready when Dorka reappeared accompanied by a score who may or may not have been the same individuals as before. It was hard to tell; their features looked so much alike.

Entering the ship, he said with restrained cordiality, "I trust you are rested? We do not again disturb you?"

"Not the way you mean," muttered Hibbert under his breath. He kept watch on the natives while his hands hung casually near the butts of two heavy belt-guns.

"We slept like the dead," assured Benton, unconsciously sinister. "Now we're ready for anything."

"That is good. I am happy for you." Dorka's dark gaze found their belts. "Weapons?" He blinked but did not change expression. "Surely those are not thought necessary here? Did not your Fraser live with us in peace? Besides, as you can see, we are unarmed. There is not so much as a fishing-stick between us."

"No mistrust is implied," Benton declared. "In the space-navy we are the poor slaves of multitudinous regulations. One such ruling orders that weapons will be worn during all first official contacts. Therefore we wear them." He put on a disarming smile. "If an order required us to wear grass skirts, high hats and false noses, you would now be confronted by such a spectacle."

If Dorka disbelieved this preposterous tale of slavery at such a distance from base, he did not show it. He accepted the fact that the Earthlings were armed and intended to stay that way no matter whether the impression created thereby was good or bad.

He was on safe ground in this respect—his own ground, his own territory. Small arms, dexterously used, could avail nothing against great numbers if he chose to give the thumbs-down sign surreptitiously, without warning. They could only make the gesture costly, at best. There are occasions when results come cheap regardless of cost.

"Leman, the Keeper of the Shrine, awaits you there," Dorka informed. "He, too, is an able speaker of your cosmoparla. He is very learned. Shall we visit him first and the city afterward? Or have you other ideas?"

Benton hesitated. Pity this Leman had not attended with the others yesterday. It was extremely likely that *he* knew the two significant words. The thought-recorder could have picked them out of his brain and served them up on a platter after he had gone, thus springing the trap and making it harmless. There would be no way of examining Leman's mind at the shrine, since no pocket-sized version of the thought-recorder existed, and neither race was telepathic.

The shrine. The center-point of the circumstances laid down by Fraser. The spot marked X.

There, natives would crowd around them, strong in numbers, fired by unknown fear of unknown things, tensed for action, watching their every move, keyed to every word they uttered, waiting, waiting, until one of them innocently mouthed the syllables that would be the signal.

In conditions like that the most they could hope for was the doubtful pleasure of taking a few with them. Two words—and a concerted jump as first and only evidence that unwittingly one of them had blundered. Blows, struggles, sweat, curses, choking sounds, perhaps a futile shot or two before oblivion.

Two words.

Death!

Afterward, a compounding with consciences as a quasi-religious service was held over their bodies. Coppery features suffused with sorrow but filled with faith as a chant sounded through the shrine.

"They were tried according to thy rulings and dealt with according to thy wisdom. They were weighed in the balance and found wanting. We thank thee, Fraser, for deliverance from those who were not our friends."

The same fate for the crew of the next vessel, and the next, and the next—until Earth either cut this world away from the main-stream of inter-galactic civilization or subdued it with terrible retribution.

"Well, what do you wish?" persisted Dorka, eyeing him curiously.

Benton emerged from his mental ramblings with a start, conscious that all the others were looking at him. Hibbert and Randle were anxious.

Dorka's face showed only polite concern, in no way bloodthirsty or aggressive. That, of course, meant nothing. The Chinese of a thousand years ago could operate the communal strangling-post with total lack of visible emotion.

A voice which he recognized as his own came whispering out of nowhere, "Since when did the navy fail to see it through?"

Loudly and firmly, Benton said. "We'll go first to the shrine."

Neither in appearance nor bearing did Leman resemble the high priest of some strange other-star cult. Tall above the average for his race, gentle, solemn and very old, he looked like an aged and harmless librarian long escaped from ordinary life into a world of dusty books.

"These," he said to Benton, "are snapshots of the Earthly home that Fraser knew only in his boyhood. There is his mother, there is his father, and that peculiar hairy creature is what he called his dog."

Benton looked, nodded, said nothing. It was all very ordinary, very humdrum. Every guy had a home at some time or other. Every one had a father and mother, and many of them had owned dogs. He pretended a deep interest he did not feel while surreptitiously he tried to estimate the number of copper-faces in the room. Sixty to seventy of them—and another crowd outside. Too many.

With pedantic curiosity, Leman continued, "We have no creatures like that and there is no mention of them in Fraser's notes. What is a dog?"

A question! It had to be answered. His mouth must open and speak. Sixty or more pairs of eyes watching his lip. Sixty or more pairs of ears listening, waiting, waiting. Was this the fateful moment?

Involuntarily his muscles strained against a stab in the back as he replied, with poorly simulated carelessness, "A lesser animal, intelligent and domesticated."

Nothing happened.

Did the tenseness go down a little, or had it never been up except in his own apprehensive imagination? There was no way of telling.

Producing an object for their inspection, handling it like a precious relic, Leman said, "This article is what Fraser called his pal. It gave him great comfort, though we do not understand in what manner."

The thing was an old, battered and well-used pipe, its bowl burned partway down one side. There was nothing about it other than evidence of how pathetic are personal treasures when their owner has gone. Benton felt that he ought to say something but didn't know what. Hibbert and Randle determinedly played dumb.

To their relief, Leman put the pipe away, asked no prying questions about it. His next exhibit was the dead scout's beam-transmitter, its outer casing polished with loving care, its insides corroded beyond repair. It was this piece of antiquated apparatus which had boosted Fraser's report to the nearest inhabited sector whence planet after planet had relayed it back to Earthbase.

Next came a jack-knife, a rhodium-plated chronometer, wallet, automatic lighter, a whole host of old and petty things. Fourteen times Benton went cold as he was forced to answer questions or respond to remarks. Fourteen times the general strain—real or imagined—appeared to shoot up to peak then gradually relax.

"What is this?" inquired Leman, handing over a folded document.

Benton opened it carefully. An officially issued form of last will and testament. There were a few words upon it, hurriedly written, but neat, decisive.

"I, Samuel Fraser, Number 727 of the Terran Corps of Space Scouts, have nothing to leave but my good name."

Refolding it, he handed it back, explaining it and translating its script into cosmoparla.

"He was right," remarked Leman. "But what man can leave more?" Turning to Dorka, he spoke briefly in the liquid syllables of the local language which the three Earthlings did not understand. Then to Benton, "We will show you Fraser's likeness. You will then know him as we saw him."

Hibbert gave a nudge. "Why did he switch to that alien gabble?" he asked, doing substantially the same by speaking in English. "I'll tell you —because he didn't want us to know what he was saying. Get ready, brother, we're coming to it. I can feel it in my bones."

Benton shrugged, turned, the natives pressing close around him, too closely for the fast action that at any moment might be required. There was a peculiar fervor on the faces of the audience as they looked toward the end wall, an intensity as of people about to be favored once in a lifetime. The surge of emotion could be felt, a mass-emotion that could lead to anything, be directed anywhere, to everlasting brotherhood or to raging death.

A tremendous sigh came from this crowd as the aged Leman pulled aside high drapes and revealed the Man from Outside. There was a life-size bust on a glittering pedestal, also an oil painting between six and seven feet high. Both had those confident but indefinable touches that mark superb talent. So far as could be judged, both were excellent studies of their subject.

Silence for a long time. Everyone seemed to be waiting for some remark from the Earthlings. There was a deep, expectant hush like that in court when the foreman of the jury is about to pronounce the verdict. But here, in this crazily contrived and menacing situation, the defendants were saddled with the onus of mouthing their own verdict upon themselves. It was for those secretly on trial to pronounce themselves guilty or not guilty of an unknown crime committed in an unknown way.

The three had no illusions; they knew that this was indeed the crisis. They could sense it intuitively, could read it in surrounding coppery features. Benton posed grave-faced with firmly closed lips. Randle was fidgety, like one unable to decide which way to jump when the time came.

Belligerently fatalistic, Hibbert stood with legs braced wide apart, hands poised in readiness above his belt, in the manner of a man determined not to go down without exacting payment for it.

"Well," invited Leman, his voice suddenly hard, "what do you think of him?"

No response. They stood together, in a tight little group, wary, prepared, and stared at the picture of a scout three hundred years dead. None spoke.

Leman frowned. His tones sharpened. "Surely you have not lost the faculty of speech?"

He was forcing the issue, pushing it along to a conclusion. It was too much for the irritable Hibbert. Grasping his guns, Hibbert spoke fiercely, resentfully.

"I don't know what you expect us to say and it's got so I don't care a darn, either. But I'll tell you this, whether you enjoy it or not: Fraser is no god. Anyone can see that. He's just a plain, ordinary space-scout from pioneering days, and that's about as near as any man can get to being a god."

If he anticipated a violent reaction he was disappointed. Everyone hung on his words, but none viewed the speech as tantamount to insulting an idol in its own temple.

On the contrary, one or two listeners nodded in mild approval.

"Space breeds a certain type just as the great oceans breed a type," Benton put in by way of explanation. "That holds true for Terrestrials, Martians or any other cosmos-roaming form of life. You get so that you can recognize them at a glance." He licked dry lips, finished, "Therefore Fraser, being true to type, looks pretty ordinary to us. There's not much one can say about him."

"Guys like him are ten a penny in the space-navy today," added Hibbert. "Always have been, always will be. They're no more than men with an incurable itch. Sometimes they do wonderful things, sometimes they don't. They've all got guts but not all have the luck. This Fraser struck lucky, mighty lucky. He could have sniffed around fifty sterile planets— but he hit on one loaded with humanoids. That's the sort of bonanza every spaceman prays for even today. It is what makes history."

Hibbert ended, a little bemused because all his spouting had produced no adverse effect. It made him feel sort of triumphant. There is satisfaction in getting away with talk in circumstances where one's tongue might precipitate a sudden and violent end. Two words. Two commonplace and likely-to-be-used words, and somehow he had successfully dodged both of them without knowing what they were.

"You have nothing more to say?" asked Leman, watching them.

Benton offered amiably, "I guess not, except that it's nice to have seen what Fraser looked like. Pity he's not still alive. He would have been happy to find Earth at last responding to his call."

A slow smile came into Leman's dark features. He made a swift, pe-

culiar gesture to his audience, pulled the drapes together and hid the
picture.

"Now that you have finished here, Dorka will conduct you to the city
center. Persons high in our government are anxious to talk with you. Let
me say how glad I am to have met you. I hope it will not be long before
more of your people—"

"There is one thing before we go," Benton interjected hurriedly. "We'd
like an interview with you in private."

Faintly surprised, Leman signed toward a nearby door. "Very well.
Please come this way."

Benton pulled Dorka's sleeve. "You, too. This concerns you and you
might as well be in on it."

In the seclusion of his room Leman gave them chairs, seated himself.
"Now, my friends, what is it?"

"Among the latest instruments in our ship," explained Benton, "is a
kind of robot guardian which reads the minds of any life-forms utilizing
thought-processes similar to ours. Maybe it is a bit unethical, but it's a
necessary and valuable protection. Forewarned is forearmed, see?" He gave
a sly smile. "It read Dorka's mind."

"What?" exclaimed Dorka, standing up. He gazed around in bewilderment, became sheepish, sat down again.

"It told us that we were in some vague but definite peril," Benton went
on. "It said that inherently you were our friends, wanted to be and hoped
to be friends—but two words would reveal us as enemies, fit to be treated
as such. If we spoke those words we were through! We know now, of
course, that we have not uttered those words, else the situation would not
be as it is right now. We have passed muster. All the same, I want to
know something." He leaned forward, his gaze penetrating. "*What were
those two words?*"

Thoughtfully rubbing his chin, and in no way fazed by what he had
been told, Leman said, "Fraser's advice was based on knowledge we did
not and could not share. We accepted it without question, knowing
neither his reasons nor his motives, but recognizing that he drew from a
well of other-worldly wisdom unavailable to us. He advised us to show
you his shrine, his possessions, his picture. And if you spoke two words—"

"What were they?" Benton persisted.

Closing his eyes, Leman pronounced them clearly, painstakingly, like
part of a long-preserved creed.

Benton rocked back. He stared dumfoundedly at Randle and Hibbert,
caught them staring similarly at him. All three were puzzled, defeated.

At last Benton inquired, "What language is that?"

"Terrestrial of some sort," assured Leman. "Fraser's own natural speech."

"What do those two words mean?"

"That, I cannot tell you," said Leman, becoming equally puzzled. "I
have not the remotest notion of their significance. Fraser never told their
meaning and none asked him for an explanation. We have memorized and

practiced the sound of them, as the words of warning which he gave us, and that is all."

"It beats me," confessed Benton, scratching his head. "In all my sinful life I've never heard them."

"If those words are of Earthly origin it may be they're too ancient for anyone but some long-haired professor of dead languages," suggested Randle. He mused a moment, added, "I once heard that in Fraser's time they referred to the cosmos as the 'void' despite that it is filled with many forms of matter and anything but void."

"They might not be even an ancient Earth-language," Hibbert offered. "Those words could come out of oldtime space-lingo or archaic cosmoparla."

"Say them again," Benton invited.

Obligingly, Leman said them again. Two simple words of two syllables each, and none had heard the like.

Benton shook his head. "Three hundred years is a heck of a long time. Doubtless those were common words in Fraser's day. But now they're discarded, buried, forgotten—forgotten so long and completely that I couldn't hazard a guess at what they meant."

"Me, neither," agreed Hibbert. "Good job none of us got over-educated. It's a hell of a note when a spaceman can have his stone put up early just because he remembers a couple of out-of-date noises."

Benton came to his feet. "Oh, well, no use pursuing what has disappeared forever. Let's go see how the local bureaucrats compare with our own." He eyed Dorka. "Ready to take us along?"

Hesitating a moment, Dorka registered embarrassment as he asked, "Have you still got this thought-reading contraption with you?"

"It is firmly fixed in the ship." Benton laughed as he patted the other reassuringly. "Much too big to carry around. You think your own thoughts and be happy, because we won't know what they're about."

As they went out, the three men looked up at the drapes that covered the life-sized painting of the gray-haired, black-skinned Space Scout Samuel Fraser. ". . . . . .!" said Benton, repeating the forbidden words. "I don't get it. One might as well say *pfornid akshum*, since it's just as meaningless."

"It is so much clutter," indorsed Hibbert.

"Clutter," echoed Randle. "Now I come to think of it, they had a deuce of a funny word for that in olden days. I found it in a book once." He thought awhile, ended, "Yes, I remember it. They called it gabbledegook."

ENVIRONMENT

The sun was rising above the towers and spires of the city to the west. It sent questing fingers of brightness through the maze of streets and avenues, wiping away the last, pale shadows of night. But in the ageless splendor of the dawn, the city dreamed on.

The ship came with the dawn, riding down out of the sky on wings of flame, proclaiming its arrival in a voice of muted thunder. It came out of the west, dropping lower and lower, to cruise finally in great, slow circles. It moved over the city like a vast, silver-gray hunting hawk, searching for prey. There was something of eagerness in the leashed thunder of its voice.

Still the city dreamed on. Nothing, it seemed, could disturb its dreaming. Nothing could. It was not a sentient dreaming. It was a part of the city itself, something woven into every flowing line and graceful curve. As long as the city endured, the dream would go on.

The voice of the ship had grown plaintive, filled with an aching disappointment. Its circling was aimless, dispirited. It rose high in the sky, hesitated, then glided down and down. It landed on an expanse of green in what had once been a large and beautiful park.

It rested now on the sward, a great, silver-gray ovoid that had a certain harsh, utilitarian beauty. There was a pause of motionlessness, then a circular lock door opened in its side. Jon Gaynor appeared in the lock and jumped to the ground. He gazed across the park to where the nearest towers of the city leaped and soared, and his gray eyes were narrowed in a frown of mystification.

"Deserted!" he whispered. "Deserted— But why?"

Jon Gaynor turned as Wade Harlan emerged from the lock. The two glanced at each other, then, in mutual perplexity, their eyes turned to the dreaming city. After a long moment, Wade Harlan spoke.

"Jon, I was thinking— Perhaps this isn't the right planet. Perhaps . . . perhaps old Mark Gaynor and the Purists never landed here at all—"

Jon Gaynor shook his brown head slowly. He was a tall, lean figure in a tight-fitting, slate-gray overall. "I've considered that possibility, Wade. No—this is the place, all right. Everything checks against the data given in that old Bureau of Expeditions report. Seven planets in the system— this the second planet. And this world fits perfectly the description given in the report—almost a second Earth. Then there's the sun. Its type, density, rate of radiation, spectrum—all the rest—they check, too."

Gaynor shook his head again. "Granted there could exist another system of seven planets, with the second habitable. But it's too much to suppose that the description of that second planet, as well as the description of its sun, would exactly fit the expedition report. And the report mentioned a deserted city. We're standing in the middle of it now. The only thing that doesn't check is that it's still deserted."

327

Harlan gave a slight shrug. "That may not mean anything, Jon. How can you be certain that Mark Gaynor and the Purists came back here at all? The only clue you have is that old Bureau of Expeditions report, describing this city and planet, which you found among the personal effects Mark Gaynor left behind. It may not have meant anything."

"Perhaps— But I'm pretty sure it did. You see, old Mark and the Purists wanted to live far from all others, somewhere where there would be none to laugh at them for their faith in the ancient religious beliefs. The only habitable planets which answered their purposes were a tremendously remote few. Of them all, this was the only one possessing a city—and a deserted city at that."

"So you think they must have come here because of the benefits offered by the city?"

"That's one reason. The other . . . well, old Mark had a pile of Bureau of Expedition reports dating back for two hundred years. The report relating to this planetary system was marked in red, as being of special interest. It was the only report so marked—"

Harlan smiled in a friendly derision. "Add that to a misplaced hero-worship for a crackpot ancestor—and the answer is that we've come on a goose chase. Lord, Jon, even with the Hyperspacial Drive to carry us back over the immense distance, it's going to be a terrific job getting back to Earth. You know what a time we had, finding this planet. The Hyperspacial Drive is a wonderful thing—but it has its drawbacks. You go in here, and you come out there—millions of miles away. If you're lucky, you're only within a few million miles or so of your destination. If not— and that's most of the time— you simply try again. And again—"

"That's a small worry," Gaynor replied. "And as for old Mark, he was hardly a crackpot. It took one hundred and twenty years for the world to realize that. His ideas on how people should live and think were fine —but they just didn't fit in with the general scheme of things. On a small group, they could have been applied beautifully. And such a group, living and thinking that way, might have risen to limitless heights of greatness. Hero-worship? No—I never had such feelings for my great-great-uncle, Mark Gaynor. I just had a feverish desire to see how far the Purists had risen—to see if their way of life had given them an advantage over others."

Harlan was sober. "Maybe we'll never learn what happened to them, Jon. The city is deserted. Either the Purists came here and left—or they never came here at all."

Gaynor straightened with purpose. "We'll learn which is the answer. I'm not leaving until we do. We'll—" Gaynor broke off, his eyes jerking toward the sky. High up and far away in the blue, something moved, a vast swarm of objects too tiny for identification. They soared and circled, dipped and swooped like birds. And as the two men from another planet watched, sounds drifted down to them—sweet, crystalline tinklings and chimings, so infinitely faint that they seemed to be sensed rather than heard.

"Life—" Harlan murmured. "There's life here of sorts, Jon."

Gaynor nodded thoughtfully. "And that may mean danger. We're going to examine the city—and I think we'd better be armed."

While Harlan watched the graceful, aimless maneuvers of the aerial creatures, Gaynor went back into the ship. In a moment, he returned with laden arms. He and Harlan strapped the antigravity flight units to their backs, buckled the positron blasters about their waists. Then they lifted into the air, soared with easy speed toward a cluster of glowing towers.

As they flew, a small cloud of the aerial creatures flashed past. The things seemed to be intelligent, for, as though catching sight of the two men, they suddenly changed course, circling with a clearly evident display of excited curiosity. The crystalline chimings and tinklings which they emitted held an elfin note of astonishment.

If astonishment it actually was, Gaynor and Harlan were equally amazed at close view of the creatures. For they were great, faceted crystals whose interiors flamed with glorious color—exquisite shades that pulsed and changed with the throb of life. Like a carillon of crystal bells, their chimings and tinklings rang out—so infinitely sweet and clear and plaintive that it was both a pain and a pleasure to hear.

"Crystalline life!" Harlan exclaimed. His voice became thoughtful. "Wonder if it's the only kind of life here."

Gaynor said nothing. He watched the circling crystal creatures with wary eyes, the positron blaster gripped in his hand. But the things gave no evidence of being inimical—or at least no evidence of being immediately so. With a last exquisite burst of chimings, they coalesced into a small cloud and soared away, glittering, flashing, with prismatic splendor in the sunlight.

On the invisible wings of their antigravity flight units, Gaynor and Harlan had approached quite close to the cluster of towers which was their goal. Gliding finally through the space between two, they found themselves within a snug, circular inclosure, about the circumference of which the towers were spaced. The floor of the inclosure was in effect a tiny park, for grass and trees grew here, and there were shaded walks built of the same palely glowing substance as the towers. In the exact center of the place was a fountain, wrought of some lustrous, silvery metal. Only a thin trickle of water came from it now.

Gaynor dipped down, landed gently beside the fountain. He bent, peering, then gestured excitedly to Harlan, who was hovering close.

"Wade—there's a bas-relief around this thing! Figures—"

Harlan touched ground, joined Gaynor in a tense scrutiny of the design. A procession of strange, lithe beings was pictured in bas-relief around the curving base of the fountain. Their forms were essentially humanoid, possessed of two arms, two legs, and large, well-formed head. Except for an exotic, fawnlike quality about the graceful, parading figures,

Gaynor and Harlan might have been gazing at a depiction of garlanded, Terrestrial youths and maidens.

"The builders of the city," Gaynor said softly. "They looked a lot like us. Parallel evolution, maybe. This planet and sun are almost twins of ours. Wade—I wonder what happened to them?"

Harlan shook his shock of red hair slowly, saying nothing. His blue eyes were dark with somber speculation.

Gaynor's voice whispered on. "The city was already deserted when that government expedition discovered it some one hundred and thirty years ago. The city couldn't always have been that way. Once there were people on this planet—beings who thought and moved and dreamed, who built in material things an edifice symbolic of their dreaming. Why did they disappear? What could have been responsible? War, disease—or simply the dying out of a race?"

Harlan shrugged his great shoulders uncomfortably. His voice was gruff. "Maybe the answer is here somewhere. Maybe not. If it isn't, maybe we'll be better off, not knowing. When an entire race disappears for no apparent reason, as the people of this city seem to have done, the answer usually isn't a nice one."

The two men took to one of the paths radiating away from the fountain, followed it to a great, arching entranceway at the base of a tower-building. Slowly they entered—the sunlight dimmed and they moved through a soft gloom. Presently they found themselves in a vast foyer—if such it was. In the middle of the place was a circular dais, with steps leading to a small platform at the top.

They mounted the steps, gained the platform. Of a sudden, a faint whispering grew, and without any other warning, they began to rise slowly into the air. Harlan released a cry of surprise and shock. Gaynor ripped his positron blaster free, sought desperately to writhe from the influence of the force that had gripped him.

And then Gaynor quieted. His eyes were bright with a realization. "An elevator!" he gasped. "Wade—we stepped into some kind of elevating force."

They ceased struggling and were borne gently up and up. They passed through an opening in the ceiling of the foyer, found themselves within a circular shaft, the top of which was lost in the dimness above. Vertical handrails lined the shaft. It was only after passing two floors that they divined the purpose of these. Then, reaching the third floor, each gripped a handrail, and they stepped from the force.

They found themselves within a vast, well-lighted apartment. The source of illumination was not apparent, seeming to emanate from the very walls. Room opened after spacious room—and each was as utterly barren of furnishings as the last. Barren, that is, except for two things. The first was that the walls were covered with murals or paintings—life-sized, rich with glowing color, and almost photographic in detail. The second was that one wall of each room contained a tiny niche. Gaynor and Harlan investigated a niche in one room they entered. Within it was a solitary object—a large jewel, or at least what seemed to be a jewel.

"This is screwy," Harlan muttered. "It doesn't make sense. How could anyone have lived in a place like this?"

Gaynor's eyes were dark with thought. He answered slowly, "Don't make the mistake of judging things here according to our standard of culture. To the builders of the city, Wade, these rooms might have been thoroughly cozy and comfortable, containing every essential necessary to their daily lives."

"Maybe," Harlan grunted. "But I certainly don't see those essentials."

"This thing—" Gaynor lifted the jewel from its niche. "Maybe this thing holds an answer of some kind." Gaynor balanced the jewel in his palm, gazing down at it frowningly. His thoughts were wondering, speculative. Then the speculation faded—he found himself concentrating on the thing, as though by sheer force of will he could fathom its purpose.

And then it happened—the jewel grew cold in his hand—a faint, rose-colored glow surrounded it like an aura. A musical tinkling sounded. Harlan jumped, a yell bursting full-throated from his lungs. Gaynor spun about, surprised, uncomprehending.

"I . . . I saw things!" Harlan husked. "Objects, Jon— The room was full of them—angular ghosts!"

Gaynor stared at the other without speaking. His features were lax with a dawning awe.

Harlan said suddenly, "Try it again, Jon. Look at that thing. Maybe—"

Gaynor returned his gaze to the jewel. He forced his mind quiet, concentrated. Again the jewel grew cold, and again the tinkling sounded. Harlan was tense, rigid, his narrowed eyes probing the room. Within the room, outlines wavered mistily—outlines of things which might have been strange furniture, or queer, angular machines.

"Harder, Jon! Harder!" Harlan prompted.

Gaynor was sweating. He could feel the perspiration roll down his temples. His eyes seemed to be popping from their sockets.

Harlan strained with his peering. The outlines grew stronger, darkened—but only for a moment. The next they wavered mistily again, thinned, and were gone.

Gaynor drew a sobbing breath, straightened up. He asked, "Wade— what did you see?"

"I don't know for sure. Things—or the ghosts of things. Here—give me that. I'm going to see what I can do."

Gaynor relinquished the jewel. Holding it in his palm, Harlan gathered his thoughts, poised them, focused them. And, watching, Gaynor saw the ghostly outlines for the first time—misty suggestions of angles and curves, hints of forms whose purpose he could not guess. Alien ghosts of alien objects, summoned by will from some alien limbo.

Abruptly, the outlines faded and were gone. The tinkling of the jewel thinned and died.

Harlan drew a shuddering breath. "Jon—you saw them?"

"Yes. Dimly."

"We . . . we haven't got the strength, Jon. We haven't got the power necessary to materialize the objects—whatever they are."

"Maybe that's the drawback. Or—maybe we've got the strength, but simply can't materialize things—objects—whose size, shape, and purpose we do not know and cannot guess."

"That might be it." Harlan's voice grew sharp. "But, great space, Jon, what possibly could be the idea behind it? Why did they—that other race—construct buildings in which the rooms were left unfurnished, or which could be furnished merely by concentrating on . . . on these jewels? What could have been the reason behind it?"

Gaynor shook his head. "We'll never know that, perhaps. At least, we'll never know if we persist in thinking in terms of our own culture. The builders of this city were humanoid, Wade—but mentally they were alien. Don't forget that. These rooms may not have been living quarters at all. They may have been repositories for valuable things, of which the jewels were the means of materializing. Only those who knew how could materialize them. Thus, perhaps, those things were kept safe."

"That might be it," Harlan muttered. "It makes sense."

"These pictures"—Gaynor gestured at the paintings on the walls— "might contain the answer. If we knew how to read them, they might tell us the purpose of these empty rooms—why the furnishings or machines had to be materialized. I wonder, Wade . . . I wonder if each of these pictures is complete in itself, or if each is part of a greater series. You know—like a book. You read one page, and it doesn't make sense. You read the whole thing—and it does."

"The beginning, Jon," Harlan whispered. "We'd have to start at the beginning."

"Yes—the beginning."

Harlan replaced the jewel in its niche, and on the invisible wings of their antigravity flight units, they glided back to the force shaft. Here they switched off their units, allowed the force to carry them up. But the apartments on the upper floors contained nothing new or illuminating. Like the first they had visited, these were empty, save for the wall paintings and the jewels in their niches. They returned to the shaft again, this time to meet a complication.

"Say—how do we get down?" Harlan puzzled. "This thing has been carrying us up all the time, and there doesn't seem to be another one for descending."

"Why, you simply *will* yourself to go down," Gaynor said. Then he looked blankly surprised.

Harlan nodded gravely. "Of course," he said. "That's the answer. I should have thought of it myself."

They descended. Outside, the sun was bright and warm. Under its light the city dreamed on.

Gaynor and Harlan soared through the warmth. The city was very bright and still. Far away and high in the blue, glittering swarms of the crystal creatures darted. Their tinkling and chiming drifted down to the two men.

Gaynor and Harlan descended several times to investigate tower buildings, but these were very much like the first they had visited. The spacious apartments seemed to echo in their strange emptiness, each one seemingly louder than the last. Twice they took turns, attempted to materialize the unguessable furnishings of the rooms. Each time they failed. And afterward they did not disturb the jewels in their niches. They merely gazed at the flaming wall paintings, and came away.

Again they glided through the air, though slowly and thoughtfully, now. They were silent. Beneath them, the city dreamed. Once a cloud of crystal creatures flashed past, sparkling, chiming, but the two did not seem to notice.

"Jon—?" Harlan's voice was hesitant.

"Yes?"

"I don't know how to put it into words, but—well, don't you feel that you are beginning to *know?*"

"Yes—there's the ghost of something in my mind. Those pictures, Wade—"

"Yes, Jon, the pictures."

Again they were silent. Gaynor broke the silence.

"Wade—all my life I've been reading primers. Someone just gave me a college textbook, and I glanced through several pages. Naturally, I did not understand, but here and there I found words familiar to me. They left a ghost in my mind—"

"You've got to go back to the beginning, Jon. You've got to read all the books which will help you to understand that college textbook."

"Yes, Wade, the beginning—"

They drifted on while the city dreamed beneath them. The sun was a swaddling blanket of brightness. Like memory-sounds, faint chimings and tinklings wafted on the air.

And then Gaynor was grasping Harlan's arm. "Wade—down there. Look!" He pointed tensely.

Harlan stiffened as he saw it. The ship was a tiny thing, almost lost amid the greenery of the park. Almost in unison, the two touched the controls of their antigravity flight units, arrowed down in a swift, gentle arc.

The ship was very big, like no ship they had ever seen before. It was a thing of harsh angles, built of some strange red metal or alloy that gleamed in the sunlight with the hue of blood. A square opening gaped in its side. Slowly, Gaynor and Harlan entered it.

It was as though they entered the gloom of another world. Little of what they saw was familiar to them, and they had to guess the purpose of the rest. There were passageways and corridors, and rooms opened from these. A few they were able to identify, but the rest, filled with queer, angular furniture and sprawling machines, escaped classification. They left the ship—and the sunlight felt good.

Gaynor's voice rustled dryly. "They were humanoid, Wade, the people who built that ship. If nothing else made sense, the things we saw showed that. But the people who made that ship were not of the city. They were spawned on some planet circling another sun."

"They came here," Harlan rasped. "They came—and they left that ship behind—Jon . . . they came . . . and they never left this world—"

"Wade—I'm thinking. There might have been other ships—"

Harlan touched the butt of his positron blaster, and his face was pale. "We've got to look, Jon. That's something we've got to know."

They lifted into the air. Circling and dipping, they searched. The sun was at zenith when they found the second ship. By mid-afternoon they had found a third and a fourth. The fourth was the *Ark*, the hyper-spacial cruiser in which old Mark Gaynor and his band of Purists had left the Earth some one hundred and twenty years before.

The four ships which Gaynor and Harlan had found had two things in common. Each had been built by a different humanoid people, and each was completely deserted. Other than this, there was no basis of comparison between them. Each was separate and distinct, unique in its alienness. Even the *Ark*, long outmoded, seemed strange.

In the *Ark*, Gaynor and Harlan found nothing to indicate what had happened to its passengers. Everything was orderly and neat—more, even in the most excellent condition. Nothing written had been left behind, not the slightest scrap of rotting paper.

Gaynor whispered, "They *did* come here, then. And the same thing happened to them that happened to all the rest of the people who landed here. The same thing, I'm sure, that happened to the builders of the city. Why did they leave these ships behind? Where did they go? What *could* have happened to them?"

Harlan shook his red head somberly. "We'd better not know that. If we stay and try to find out, the same thing will happen to us. The government expedition which discovered this planet encountered the same mystery—but they didn't try to find out. They returned to Earth. Jon—we'd better get back to the *Paragon*. We'd better leave while we can."

"And in time more people would come to settle here. And there would be more empty ships." Gaynor's lips tightened to a stubborn line. "Wade —I'm not leaving until I crack the mystery of this place. I'm going to find what happened to old Mark and the Purists. We've been warned—we'll be on the alert."

Harlan met Gaynor's determined gaze, and then he looked away. He moistened his lips. After a long moment he gave a stiff nod. His voice was very low.

"Then we've got to start at the beginning, Jon. Those pictures—"

"Yes, Wade, the pictures. I'm sure they hold the answer to the whole thing. We've got to find that beginning. You've noticed how the city is strung out. At one end is the beginning, at the other—"

"The end!" Harlan said abruptly.

"No. Wade. The answer."

They returned first to the *Paragon*, to satisfy pangs of hunger too intense to be ignored any longer. Then, donning their antigravity flight units once more, they took to the air. They circled several times, set out finally for a point on the horizon where the city thinned out and finally terminated.

Their flight ended at a single, slender tower set in the midst of a parklike expanse. That they had reached the end of the city, they knew, for ahead of them no other building was in sight. They floated to the ground, stared silently at the tower. It glowed with a chaste whiteness in the late afternoon light—serene, somewhat aloof, lovely in its simplicity and solitariness.

Harlan spoke softly. "The beginning? Or—the end?"

"That's what we have to find out," Gaynor responded. "We're going in there, Wade."

The interior of the tower was dark and cool, filled with the solemn hush of a cathedral. It consisted solely of one great room, its ceiling lost in sheerness of height. And except for the ever-present wall paintings, it was empty—utterly bare.

Gaynor and Harlan gazed at the paintings, and then they looked at each other, and slowly they nodded. Silently they left.

"That . . . that wasn't the beginning," Harlan stated slowly.

"No, Wade. That was—the end. The beginning lies on the opposite side of the city. But we'll have to postpone our investigation until morning. We wouldn't reach the other end of the city until dark."

They returned to the *Paragon*. The sun was setting behind the towers of the city to the east, sinking into a glory of rose and gold. Slowly the paling fingers of its radiance withdrew from the city. Night came in all its starry splendor.

Gaynor and Harlan were up with the dawn. Eagerness to be back at their investigations fired them. They hurried impatiently through breakfast. Then, attaching kits of emergency ration concentrates to their belts and donning their antigravity flight units, they took to the air.

As they flew, Gaynor and Harlan had to remind themselves that this was the second day of their visit and not the first, so closely did the new day resemble the one preceding. Nothing had changed. The city beneath them still dreamed on. And far away and high in the blue, glittering clouds of the crystal creatures darted and danced, their chimings and tinklings sounding like echoes of melody from an elfin world.

The sun was bright and warm when Gaynor and Harlan reached the end of the city opposite the one which they had investigated the day before. Here they found no slender tower. There was nothing to show that this part of the city was in any way different from the rest. The general plan of tower-encircled courts was the same as everywhere else. The city merely terminated—or looking at it the other way, merely began.

Gaynor and Harlan glided down into one of the very first of the tower-encircled courts. They touched ground, switched off their flight units, stood gazing slowly about them.

Gaynor muttered, "The beginning? Or— Maybe we were wrong, Wade. Maybe there is no beginning."

"Those towers should tell us," Harlan said. "Let's have a look inside them, Jon."

They entered an arching doorway, strode into a great foyer. Within this they had their first indication that this part of the city actually was different from the rest. For within the foyer was no dais and force shaft as they had found previously. Instead, a broad stairway led to the floors above.

They mounted the stairs. The walls of the first apartment they investigated were covered with paintings, as everywhere else, but this time the spacious rooms were not empty. They were furnished. Gaynor and Harlan gazed upon softly gleaming objects which very clearly were tables and chairs, deep, luxurious couches, and cabinets of various sizes and shapes. At first everything seemed strange to them, and as they glanced about, they found themselves comparing the furniture to that which they had seen in homes on Earth. And after a while things no longer seemed strange at all.

Gaynor blinked his eyes rapidly several times. He frowned puzzledly. "Wade—either I'm crazy, or this room has changed."

Harlan was gazing at the wall paintings. His voice came as from far away. "Changed? Why, yes. Things are as they should be—now."

Gaynor gazed at the walls. and then he nodded. "That's right, Wade. Of course."

Gaynor walked over to a low cabinet. Somewhere before he had seen a cabinet like this one. He felt that he should know its purpose, yet it eluded him. He stared at it musingly. And then he remembered something—his eyes lifted to the paintings on the wall. No. The other wall? Yes.

Gaynor looked at the cabinet again—and now a slow murmur of melody arose within the room. Hauntingly familiar, poignantly sweet, yet formless. Gaynor looked at the walls again. The melody shaped itself, grew stronger, and the lilting strains of a spaceman's song flooded richly through the room.

> I'm blasting the far trails,
> Following the star trails,
> Taking the home trails,
> Back, dear, to you—

"The Star Trails Home to You," Gaynor whispered. Sudden nostalgia washed over him in a wave. Home. The Earth— His eyes lifted to the walls, and he was comforted.

Gaynor looked around for Harlan. He found the other standing before a second cabinet across the room. Gaynor approached him, noting as he did so that Harlan stood strangely rigid and still. In alarm, Gaynor ran the remaining distance. Harlan did not seem to notice. His face was rapt, trance-like.

Gaynor grasped Harlan's arm, shook him. "Wade! Wade—what is it? Snap out of it?"

Harlan stirred. Expression came back into his features—his eyes sharped upon Gaynor's face. "What . . . what— Oh, it's you, Jon. She . . . she had red hair, and . . . and her arms were around me, and—" Harlan broke off, flushing.

Investigation of the cabinets in the other rooms produced still more interesting results. One had a spigot projecting from its front, with a catchbasin below, much like a drinking fountain. Gaynor looked at the wall paintings, and then he looked at the spigot, and suddenly liquid jetted from it. He tasted it cautiously, nodded approvingly, not at all surprised.

"Scotch," he said. "I'll have it with soda."

"Hurry up, then," Harlan prompted impatiently.

There was another cabinet that they found particularly interesting. This one had a foot-square opening in its front, and after Gaynor and Harlan had gotten their proper instructions from the paintings, they moved on—each munching at a delicious leg of roast chicken.

Not all the cabinets produced things which were edible or audible, but all opened up new vistas of thought and experience. Gaynor and Harlan learned the purpose of each, and already in their minds they were devising new methods of test and application. The wall paintings were very expensive, and they were learning rapidly.

That was the beginning—

After the cabinets, which supplied every possible physical or mental want, came the machines. Simple things at first, for Gaynor and Harlan were still in the equivalent of kindergarten. But they were humanoid— and, therefore, inquisitive. The machines were delightful and of absorbing interest. Once their purpose and function became known, however, their novelty died, and Gaynor and Harlan quested on for new fields to conquer. Thus, in a very few days, they moved to the next unit.

Here was the same plan of tower-encircled court, but the cabinets and machines had become more complicated, more difficult of operation. But Gaynor and Harlan had become quite adept at reading the wall paintings which were their primers. They learned—

Instruction followed application, and in a very few days again, Gaynor and Harlan moved on. Thus they went, from unit to unit, and always the wall paintings pointed out the way.

The sun rose and the sun set, and the city dreamed on. And always, high in the sky, the crystal creatures circled and soared, tinkling and chiming. The days passed gently, mere wraiths of sunlight.

The machines grew larger, more intricate, ever more difficult of solution. Each was a new test upon the growing knowledge of Gaynor and Harlan. And each test was harder than the last, for the wall paintings no longer pointed out the way, but merely hinted now.

Gaynor and Harlan progressed more slowly, though none the less steadily. They were not impatient. They had no sense of restless striving toward a future goal. They lived for the present. They were submerged heart and soul in the never-ending fascinations of their environment to the exclusion of all else.

The machines continued to grow larger. At one point they were so huge, that a single machine filled an entire apartment. But that was the climax, for afterward the machines grew smaller, ever smaller, until at last they came to a unit the apartments of which were empty. Empty, that is, except for the wall paintings and the jewels in their niches.

Harlan peered about him, frowning. "I seem to remember this place."

"It *is* familiar," Gaynor said. His brows drew together, and after a time he nodded. "We were here before, I think. But that was many toree ago, when we were children."

"Yes—when we were children. I recall it, now." Harlan smiled reminiscently. "It is strange we knew so little as children that it should be so easily forgotten."

"Yes, we have grown. The memories of childhood are very dim. I can recall some things, but they are not very clear. There was a purpose that brought us to the city. A purpose— But what else could it have been than to learn? And there was a mystery. But there is nothing mysterious about the city, nothing strange at all. Mere imaginings of childhood perhaps—meaningless trifles at best. We will not let them concern us now. We have grown."

Harlan nodded gravely, and his blue eyes, deep with an ocean of new knowledge, lifted to the painting-covered walls. "Events of the past should no longer concern us. We have entered upon the Third Stage. The tasks of this alone should occupy our thoughts."

"Yes—the past has been left behind." Gaynor was looking at the walls. "The Third Stage. The tasks will be very difficult, Wade—but interesting. We'll be putting our knowledge into practice—actually creating. This means we'll have to deal directly with the powers of the various soldani and varoo. As these are extradimensional, control will be solely by cholthening at the sixth level, through means of the taadron. We'll have to be careful, though—any slightest relaxation of the sorran will have a garreling effect—"

"I guessed that. But there must be some way to minimize the garreling effect, if it should occur."

"A field of interwoven argroni of the eighth order should prevent it from becoming overpowering."

"We can try it. You're working on the woratis patterns?"

"Yes. I've managed to cholthen them into the fifth stage of development."

"Mine's the vandari patterns. I've found them more interesting than those of the woratis. Fourth stage of development. I'm starting at once. I'll use the next room."

Harlan left, and Gaynor took the jewel from its niche—the taadron, that is—and set his cholthening power at the sixth level. The thing flamed gloriously in his hand—light pulsed out in great, soft waves, washed over the wall paintings, made them glow with exquisite richness. Unearthly melody filled the room, tuneless, silver-sweet. Gaynor was creating. And as he did so, things began to take on form and substance within the room—things which might have been machines, but weren't machines, because they were intelligent and alive in a way no machine can ever be. Finally, Gaynor and his creations communicated. It was somewhat difficult at first, but he was well along now, and took the difficulty in his stride.

Gaynor learned things—just as, in the other room, Harlan was learning, too. And then he took up the taadron again and cholthened. The things which he had created vanished. He began to develop the woratis patterns into the fifth stage—

Bright day blended into bright day, gently, unnoticeably. The city floated on the gentle, green swells of the planet, and floating, dreamed.

After a time, Gaynor and Harlan moved on to the next unit. Then the next—and the next. Soon it came to pass that they entered the Fourth Stage. This, they knew, was the last one, but what came afterward did not worry them. They had reached a level of mind which was beyond all worrying.

The Third Stage had changed them greatly, though they were not aware of it. They would not have been concerned even if they had. They no longer used their natural vocal apparatus, now, for they had come to think in terms which simply could not have been put into words. They had become telepathic, conversing in pure ideas of the highest order. And they no longer materialized their food from the atoms of the air. A simple rearrangement of their body cells—simple, when understood as they understood it—now enabled them to feed directly upon certain nourishing extradimensional subatomic energies. And the anti-gravity flight units, which they had reduced to the size of peas for convenience, were now discarded entirely. They had learned to fly without the aid of any device.

The Fourth Stage changed them still further. They created now— the word does not quite describe their activities—without the aid of the taadron, for they had learned to ennathen, which was as great an advancement over cholthening as telepathy is over speech. Thus it came about that Gaynor and Harlan—or the beings who once had been Gaynor and Harlan—found their bodies an annoying encumbrance. For arms and legs, heart and lungs, and the senses and nerves which use of these required, had become quite unnecessary to them. They had outgrown these impedimenta of their childhood.

They spoke of this now by a telepathic means that was not quite telepathy, and they wondered what to do. For though they had mastered well the wall paintings which were their college textbooks, there was no clear answer. Their discussion of the problem could not have been made understandable, however roughly it might have been put, but suffice it to say that at last they reached a decision.

They had progressed from one end of the city to the edge of the other. Not quite the edge, though—for there was one building in which they had not yet narleened. They had *examined* it before, of course, but that was when they had been children—in those dim, pale days when they did not understand.

They decided to vogelar to this very last building. Here, perhaps, every question would be answered.

It was dawn when they vogelared through the arching doorway. The first feeble rays of morning crept through the opening—the interior of the Temple was very dark and cool. All the dreaming of the city seemed to be concentrated here in one vast stillness.

The beings who once had been Gaynor and Harlan narleened the paintings on the walls of the Temple, gazed upon them with this new, all-embracing sense which went far beyond the limited realms of mere vision—so that almost the paintings spoke to them and they answered back. They narleened the paintings.

Their every question was answered—for all eternity.

And thus it came about, after a time, that two great, faceted crystals emerged from the doorway of the Temple, and lifted, pulsing with a vibrant new life, flashing in rainbow splendor, into the sky. Higher, they lifted, and higher, chiming and tinkling, soaring to join the others of their kind.

The sun shone brightly in the sky. High and far away in the blue, glittering clouds of crystal creatures darted and danced, sending wave after exquisite wave of crystalline melody upon the gentle shores of air. Among them now were two who had still to learn the intricacies of flight.

And the city dreamed on.

A perfect environment, the city. Ideal for the inquisitive humanoid.

PART V

Adventures in Dimension

Alan E. Nourse

HIGH THRESHOLD

THEY CUT THE current the instant he began, switched off the main pumps, and broke into the vault. Half dragging him from the chamber, they tried to slap him into silence as his piercing screams cut into the thick atmosphere and deadened against the heavy walls, but he stood cowering and shrieking, his white face twisted beyond recognition, his eyes bulging and fear-ridden. Finally a quarter of morphine quelled the original attack, and he sat blubbering in the chair, totally incoherent in a desperate attempt to communicate, until he suddenly choked and vomited, and fell forward on the floor. Five minutes later there was no pulse nor blood pressure. He was quite dead.

McEvoy twisted the small round object from his clenched fist and examined it under the arc light—an eight centimeter ball of rubber, smooth and slick on the outside. With a penknife he sliced through the outer layer to reveal the fuzzy down that lined the interior. He snorted and tossed the ball to Fritzer. "There's your tennis ball," he said.

Dr. Marks was examining the body, his balding head extra pink, his hands trembling.

"What's the word, Doc?" asked McEvoy.

"Aortic rupture. Possibly auricular collapse, but I doubt it. The man simply died of fear."

McEvoy clenched a heavy fist and scowled. "What I thought. Same wretched thing as all the rest. What about it, Fritzer?"

The small sharp-faced man across the room puffed his pipe absently and tossed the peculiar tennis ball into the air a time or two, staring at the body on the floor. "We can't go on like this, you know."

"I know we can't"—McEvoy ran a hand through his sandy hair—"but we've got to go on somehow. We can't let this thing slide by—it's right in front of us. Right at our fingertips. And we can't touch it! Can't even get near it, it seems. We *can't* quit now, Fritz, just because—"

"Just because everybody dies?" Fritzer's blue eyes flashed sharply at McEvoy. There was something ruthless in the man's tireless drive, he thought, something almost inhuman. "You're the one that talked 'em into

341

it, McEvoy. 'Nothing to worry about, lad, it's all fixed this time,' you said. Good old Mac, always the persuader. So now he's dead. How would you like to go in there next time, Mac?"

"Not I," said McEvoy, glancing quickly away from the body on the floor. "Not after that, not I."

"The simple fact remains, Dr. McEvoy, that you'll have to close it down." The director tamped his pipe and applied a careful match to the coal. "We just can't have any more accidents of the sort we had this afternoon. They're out. If the Institute doesn't close you down, the Federal authorities will."

McEvoy was silent for a moment. Finally he spread his hands persuasively. "Sir, a careful consideration of all points has brought us to several definite conclusions. We'd at least like to present them."

"Dr. McEvoy, the evidence in my hands indicates that since you started this work in November, 1973—that's just six months ago—no less than five of our top-rank investigators, the very best we have, have been killed working on your problem, and you have nothing, absolutely nothing, in the way of a solution to offer for it. Those men would better be alive. The only definite conclusion I can reach is that you're playing with something you can't manage, and I think it's time to call a halt."

McEvoy squirmed in his chair. "You're right—we've lost five men, and I frankly wouldn't care to be the next. But we do have something to offer for it, at any rate. Tell him what we figured this afternoon, Doc."

Dr. Marks shuffled his feet and cleared his throat. An odd sort of person for a psycho-physician, this little, pink, balding man, but a top man in his field—a broad field, and an exacting one, in such a place as the Institute. "I think I may have a solution at least to the investigation problem," he said. "We've been able to trace a definite pattern in this thing, and it makes sense. In each case a man has gone into the vault after the cube had materialized. In each case he was alone, and was instructed as well as possible in the technique of observation. Since we are not sure with just what we are dealing, we can't instruct any man, exactly, regarding what to look for—he's just told to investigate in any way possible the effect we have at hand. And in each of the five cases he's come out staring mad, and died within hours. I guess Thompson was even sedated quickly enough to last until he got home, but as soon as the sedation wore off he went like the others. Every one of them died of the same thing. There were no external marks, and no indication of injury. Ultimately, each of them died of shock. Or fear. Or both."

The doctor cleared his throat. "I believe we're dealing solely with a matter of adjustment. Apparently these men have been faced with something that they've never met before. Something completely foreign to their experience, and something with which their nervous systems cannot cope. They've run into something so startling, or frightening, or stupendous, that their minds saw no escape but total and immediate break-down. It was adjust or collapse, and being unable to adjust, they collapsed, and the shock was too much for their systems. So they died. Of fear, if you will—there's nothing else to blame."

The director toyed with his pipe. "And your recommendations, Dr. Marks? Shall we just keep feeding good men to this thing?"

"Not quite. As I said, it's a problem in adjustment. We need a man with a high adjustment threshold—a *very* high threshold. We need a man with a cast-iron nervous system, a nervous system that can adjust to *anything*, regardless of impact or excitation of any sort. Give us that man, and I'd agree to another stab at it."

The director knocked out his pipe and placed it in his pocket with finality. "Well, Mac?" he said gently.

McEvoy smiled. "Down in the recording vault," he said quietly, "we have a cross-index file. I think I'll spend a sleepless night or two down there."

Ned McEvoy took the ball from his briefcase and laid it on the desk before the thin man with his pincenez. "What does that look like to you, Dr. Bamford?"

The man examined it closely, and looked up smiling. "It looks like a tennis ball that someone has turned inside out," he replied.

McEvoy chuckled. "And how would you go about turning a tennis ball inside out, Dr. Bamford?"

"Can't say I know, offhand." He looked quizzically at McEvoy. "What can I do for you, doctor?"

"You've heard the old story of the goats that were carried across the Andes on muleback—and all died of fright?"

"Of course."

"Well, we have the same problem in my laboratory. Only we have men dying of fright."

Dr. Bamford's eyebrows went up. "Adjustment?" he ventured.

"We think so. About six months ago we ran into a peculiar snag in the work I was supervising. The Institute of Physics has been concerned for several years with problems involving extremely low temperatures—nearly absolute zero temperatures. The work we originally planned called theoretically for an approach within six decimals of complete cessation of molecular motion. That involves a temperature of one millionth of one degree Kelvin. And we reached it."

McEvoy fingered his collar nervously, and shifted his weight in the chair. "Matter of fact, we did even better. Our pumps began acting up as we approached a thousandth of a degree. What happened, we think, was a reversal of the Franklinson effect in the extremes of high temperature, where the temperature nearly doubles quite suddenly with a tremendous molecular expansion. Our temperature took a sudden startling drop."

"I'm not quite sure I follow you," said Dr. Bamford. "From one degree Kelvin, just where does the temperature drop?"

McEvoy scowled. "A good question," he said. "I don't know, to be quite frank. Zero Kelvin is a relative and hypothetical point at which all molecular motion ceases. Below zero Kelvin, if such were possible, one could reasonably expect negative molecular motion. That may have been what we obtained; we don't know. But we certainly observed a change. The tungsten block we were treating simply evaporated. Vanished. The temperature recording device vanished. All we could see in the vault was a small glowing hole in the corner of the room where the block had been. Nothing in it, Dr. Bamford—*nothing*. And the hole, seen at a distance, appeared very suspiciously like a—hypercube."

The doctor was silent for a long moment. "Shades of Satan," he murmured quietly. "You investigated—?"

"We surely did. We're still trying. It looks as if we have a four-dimensional projection in our three-dimensional space—a corner, or an edge, of four-dimensional space. We've tried everything, and we're getting nowhere. So far we've lost five crackerjack technicians investigating. We're no better off than when we started."

"What about this?" The doctor pointed to the tennis ball.

"One characteristic of this thing we *are* able to investigate. Pretty good evidence, I think, that we have a reverse Franklinson effect. A small area of really—not *temperature*, that implies positive molecular motion—you might say *un*temperature where molecular motion is present, but negative. That tennis ball was quite ordinary when it was placed in the area of this hypercube. It came out the way you see it. I have a pencil that I inserted halfway into the area—and it came out with a thin layer of graphite all around a solid wooden core. We dropped a mouse into it, and . . . well, it was something of a mess. And it was still alive—"

Dr. Bamford toyed with the odd tennis ball for a moment. "And your investigators can't look at it, or examine it—this little area of space," he said at length. "Or if they do look at it they can't adjust to what they see, or describe it. It frightens them, or shocks them, into physical and mental breakdown. Right?"

McEvoy sighed. "Right. Now it appears to us that it is just what you mentioned: adjustment. Our investigators have undergone a terrific overload, somehow—crossed their adjustment thresholds, and couldn't go on. We need a man with a high adjustment threshold—very high. We need a tough nervous system, tougher than any we've seen before. Such a man might be able to investigate, and at least come out alive."

The doctor walked over to a filing cabinet in the corner. "Do you know what we've been doing in this laboratory?" he asked.

"Vaguely."

"Patterns of adjustment. Given a new or altered environment, one man can adjust and survive while another breaks down and withdraws to avoid facing the new circumstances. Why? More important, just what *is* the mechanism of adjustment? How does an individual manage to change his thinking to cope with a new environmental situation? And why can one mind work the change when another can't? That's what we've been working on."

McElvoy touched a lighter to his cigarette. "And your results?"

The doctor shrugged his shoulders. "We have answers to the questions, all right. Evidence indicates that they are right. Consider a man in a situation where a portion of his environment is suddenly and consistently foreign to his experience. In his mind is data which he has used for survival in his old familiar environment. In the old environment that data used in computations gave the right answers. But in the new environment he gets the wrong answers. The data is no good, and the wrong answers noticeably hinder his survival.

"There are two things he can do. He can refuse to think out or understand the reason for the false data, continue to attempt survival on the wrong-answer data, and end up with anything from a mild neurosis to a paranoiac withdrawal, depending on the nonsurvival value of the wrong answers he is getting. Or he can take the wrong-answer data, recognize it as such, and simply chuck it in a dead file as 'no good under these circumstances' and proceed to search for new data. Relating the recognizable part of his environment to the unrecognizable part, he accumulates new data with which to compute; as soon as all the wrong-answer data is out of the way, and as soon as all necessary data is collected, that individual is adjusted. Physiological and endocrine adjustments follow on the heels of the mental adjustment, if the new environment requires it, or if the individual's physiology allows it. But wherever it is possible to relate an unknown quantity in environment to already known quantities, the mental adjustment is theoretically possible.

"Some people are able to make the necessary switch quickly and easily; others stumble, get wrong answers to begin with, end up with even more dangerously wrong answers and data than before, and become so confused and frightened that their analysis shuts down, and adjustment is impossible. The adjustment threshold is high or low according to the ability of the individual to relate the unknown to the known, to make some sort of computational sense out of the environment he is in."

"What you mention," said McEvoy, "is an environment only partly changed. What would happen if such a high-threshold person were suddenly faced with a completely foreign and totally incomprehensible environment? No relation of any sort to anything in his previous environment. No place to stand. What would he do then?"

Dr. Bamford took the tennis ball from the desk and examined it for several moments before answering. Then he looked up sharply at McEvoy and said, "I wouldn't care to be responsible, myself."

McEvoy's face fell. "No chance of success?"

"Oh, I didn't say that. Take a person with a very high threshold, with a keen analytical mind, and he might find something in the incomprehensible environment upon which to work. You'd be amazed at the overload the human nervous system can take without cracking. We've tried every type of laboratory-induced neurosis we could devise on our workers —ever try living on a forty-hour day? It's an experience. Varied temperatures, disorientation, persistent and irritating noise effects, distorted spatial environment, negative transfer, induced successive dilemmas—everything. We've weeded out dozens. When one worker cracks we treat him and send him home. And some don't crack—"

"We need such a person."

"We have such a person. Just about the most perfectly adjustable nervous setup we've worked with—fully co-operative, intelligent—just about what you might be looking for. But I wouldn't care to be responsible."

McEvoy nodded excitedly. "Would he be willing to try this with us?"

Dr. Bamford smiled. "She might. Why don't you ask her?"

Gail sat in the consulting room, composedly leafing through a fashion magazine when McEvoy was introduced. She was a pretty girl, well groomed, with an easy smile and a most captivating air of unconcern about her. "How old are you, Gail?" McEvoy inquired.

"Almost nineteen," she grinned. "Dr. Bamford says you might have another test for me." She leaned back in her chair, completely at ease, and watched McEvoy curiously as she lighted a cigarette.

McEvoy didn't grin. "Maybe we have. We want to warn you, it may be a hard one. We want you to realize what you may be getting into."

The girl yawned. "O.K. Let's have it."

"We have a small cube we want you to observe for us. It isn't like anything you've ever seen before, and you may have difficulty, for it may affect you in a totally unforeseen manner. We think this cube—it just hangs all by itself in space and glows a little—may be a three-dimensional slice through a four-dimensional space. It doesn't look like anything at all, and we haven't been able to look at it squarely; it seems to avoid us. Several men have been driven completely mad—just by looking at it. You'll find it a large order, I think, but you might make it. Of course we want your whole-hearted co-operation."

The girl stared at him in disbelief. "You mean you just want me to go into a room and look at a box or something? What's in it for me?"

McEvoy looked annoyed. "Why, whatever you think it's worth, of course—"

"Oh, I wouldn't have any idea," the girl interrupted innocently, her eyes wide.

McEvoy smiled. "How would ten thousand dollars suit you?"

Gail looked carefully at her red fingernails, and her indifferent eyes became suddenly shrewd. "For getting my mind jogged all over the place? No soap, mister. A hundred thousand might sound more like it."

McEvoy swallowed hard and looked helplessly at Dr. Bamford. The doctor merely smiled.

"All right," said McEvoy finally. "One hundred thousand, when you produce—"

"Before I go in," the girl interrupted placidly.

"All right, before you go in. But remember—this little 'box' you're going to look at is a rather dangerous thing. It might affect you most strangely—"

"So do shock treatments," she cut in dryly. "Mister, after all the garbage I've had thrown at me in the past five years, I think I could take anything. You name it."

"Yes," said McEvoy, sourly. "I think you could."

Dr. Marks fidgeted and wiped his hands nervously on his pants. "Looks all right to me, Mac. I only hope we have what we want."

McEvoy, his hair mussed and his pants rumpled, breathed a quiet sigh. "*You* hope so, huh? At that price, we'd better have. Doc, if this doesn't go across, I'm going in there next time. There must be some way—"

Fritzer scowled. "You just think you're going in there," he said. "You really aren't, you know. This girl is the last, and that's straight from the top. If she goes—" he spread his hands eloquently.

Gail stood up and fluffed her skirt. "Haven't you finished my coffin yet?" she asked sourly. "Honestly, you'd think this was an ordeal or something. Isn't it about time to start?"

McEvoy flipped the intercom switch impatiently. "How about it, Franky? Got it about down?"

"Take a look, Mac. It should be clear down."

McEvoy slipped open the vault and peered in. The room was dark except for a small glowing area about three feet from the floor on the far right-hand side of the chamber. "All right, Gail," he said quietly. "Ready? It's all yours. Keep us posted on the intercom regularly. Keep it on all the time."

She went into the room, and the latch clicked heavily behind her. McEvoy took a seat at the intercom, placed pad and pencil before him, and clenched his fists.

"Well, I'm in here," said the girl. "Now what? Just go over and look at it?"

"That's right. Just look. Approach it carefully."

"It's about six inches square—almost square—and it glows like phosphorous."

There was a forty-second silence. "How're you coming?" asked McEvoy.

"This is very odd . . . it's . . . I can't describe it. But I think . . . **wait a minute—**"

Long silence.

"Gail!"

No answer. "Gail! By all that's holy!" McEvoy slammed down the master switch and made frantically for the vault door, kicking a chair aside as he went. The latch on the door caught and held tight under his urgent attack, and he banged it ineffectually with his fists, the urgency of immediate action driving through his mind. "Gail! Hold on! We're coming!"

The last thing she heard was McEvoy's voice, and the banging on the door. Then suddenly she'd slipped—inside. The deathless stillness settled over her like a blanket. No sound. No possibility of any sound. She could barely breathe.

She wanted to scream, but she knew she couldn't, for no screaming was possible here. She could see about her, clearly, but with no comprehension. A foreign place, if it was a place—alien, incomprehensible. Her mind twisted, and fear began creeping up her legs and arms—but she had no legs and arms, really. There was nothing here, *nothing* to grasp, to anchor her against the whirling tide of hopeless revulsion and withdrawal.

But of course there was something. *She was alive!* What more did she need? She was here, her mind was working, her bodily functions were continuing. She was alive, she was here, obviously—

That was her anchor!

Her mind centered and narrowed along that single line. Throw out all other data, start fresh—not just some, not part, but *everything*. She was alive, she was here, and this unbelievable place was here, too. They were coexistent. File out all other data, dead-file it. The effort was stupendous, but she began, slowly, to understand.

There was substance here, matter, solidity. She was—different, somehow; her body was not right. Part of it was gone, and part was distorted and situated several feet away. The vault was gone, of course, and there was dead stillness, but she could see the corner around which she had come to get here. Mustn't go back the way she came. Any other way? Of course! Anywhere she wanted to she could turn the—corner—and be back.

The twists and angles were not right, the way they should be. Three perfectly parallel lines which met each other at ninety-degree angles to form a perfect square with seven triangular sides—

It couldn't be!

"Why not? It is. I'm here. It's here. *Adjust to it!*"

The data, the new data, cleared in her mind. This would make no sense to anyone when she went back. Her own practiced mind was reeling to maintain control; she knew that no one else could adjust to this. McEvoy? She laughed to herself. No wonder his workers went mad. She would remember, she could report, but her report would make no sense to McEvoy or anyone else. She alone could investigate, but even she would never be able to correlate the universe outside that little glowing cube, where McEvoy was, and the one—inside, where she was. They had the minds, the analytical power, but the data in their minds could never be attenuated as she had attenuated hers, and even she couldn't do anything with what she observed. The only human mind that could actually investigate this place and correlate it with the universe outside would have to be a perfect analytical mind *without any data!*

Where in the universe could she find a human being with a perfect analytical mind, sharp, unhindered, high in computational potential, with absolutely no conscious data contained in it? The answer came to her with blinding clarity, and she knew the answer to the investigation problem. And the solution to the threshold.

A new-born baby!

Start him from birth, first on one side, then on the other. Let him grow up, first inside, then outside. Two sets of survival data. Two mutually incomprehensible worlds. He would live in either with equal ease. And he would learn to relate them one to the other.

Then the investigation could begin.

Gail collected herself and looked for an entrance back to the outside. McEvoy must never know now, he must be carefully and fully educated to the idea. Authorities would have to be won over. She knew that this was McEvoy's last chance. If she could prevent him from finding out, for a while, his investigation of the cube would have to be dropped. Until she could prepare the way.

Paranoiac withdrawal would appear logical, to McEvoy. Infuriating, but logical. It would block him, for the time being. And if he tried to force her—she could simply turn the corner and come back here. Inside. She wouldn't need an entrance any more, for *any place* could provide an entrance, and she knew now where to look.

She chose an entrance near the place where she had come through. As she turned the corner, she heard the banging on the door, and McEvoy's frantic voice shouting, "Gail! Hold on! We're coming!"

McEvoy saw her standing in the far right-hand corner of the room, staring at the glowing space which had faded as he watched it and blinked out.

"Gail, are you all right?"

She didn't answer him. She didn't even see him. Her eyes were fixed on a point in space in the center of the room, and she merely stood and breathed quietly.

They carried her into the control room, and finally bent her legs to sit her on a chair. Dr. Marks snapped on his pocket flashlight. After a few moments of examination he sighed disgustedly. "Typical," he muttered. "Complete, absolute paranoiac withdrawal."

He lifted her arm and released it; it remained suspended in midair as she gazed expressionlessly ahead. "Cataleptic trance. Call it what you will. She's out."

"You mean she'll go like the rest?"

"Oh, no. She won't die. She'll just be like this for weeks, maybe months, maybe until she dies. She's just withdrawn from our world entirely."

McEvoy stared at her, unbelievingly, his ruddy face turning purple. "You mean you think she has the solution?"

"Of course she has the solution!" Marks snapped. "Her mind has apparently just decided that what she saw she isn't going to tell—"

"Why, you cheat!" McEvoy snarled, whirling on the girl. "You sneaky little cheat!" He slapped her sharply across the face.

For a brief instant anger flooded her blank face; her eyes darkened, and the suspended hand tightened and clawed viciously at McEvoy's face. Then just as suddenly she regained her fixed stare.

McEvoy groaned in pain and grated his teeth. "Better get her into a strait jacket," he growled. "She's like a mad cat."

"Good idea," agreed Dr. Marks. "We can put her down in number three cubicle until we decide what to do."

Down in the cubicle the girl sat on the bunk, staring at nothing, motionless, barely breathing. "What can we do?" asked McEvoy.

"We can try to break the catalepsy, somehow. She undoubtedly has the answer—the whole solution to our problem, locked up in that brain of hers. She got it, all right, and decided to withdraw. Tomorrow we'll start some shock on her and see—we might just possibly jolt her out of the catalepsy and still retain her memory. Just possibly—"

They left her sitting on the bed, and walked out in the hall. As he was about to close and lock the cubicle door McEvoy took a last glance inside, and let out a strangled shout.

The cubicle was empty.

John D. MacDonald

SPECTATOR SPORT

Dr. Rufus Maddon was not generally considered to be an impatient man —or addicted to physical violence.

But when the tenth man he tried to stop on the street brushed by him with a mutter of annoyance Rufus Maddon grabbed the eleventh man, swung him around and held him with his shoulders against a crumbling wall.

He said, "You will listen to me, sir! I am the first man to travel into the future and I will not stand—"

The man pushed him away, turned around and said, "You got this dust on my suit. Now brush it off."

Rufus Maddon brushed mechanically. He said, with a faint uncontrollable tremble in his voice, "But nobody seems to care."

The man peered back over his shoulder. "Good enough, chum. Better go get yourself lobed. The first time I saw the one on time travel it didn't get to me at all. Too hammy for me. Give me those murder jobs. Every time I have one of those I twitch for twenty hours."

Rufus made another try. "Sir, I am physical living proof that the future is predetermined. I can explain the energy equations, redesign the warp projector, send myself from your day further into the future—"

The man walked away. "Go get a lobe job," he said.

"But don't I look different to you?" Rufus called after him, a plaintive note in his voice.

The man, twenty feet away, turned and grinned at him. "How?"

When the man had gone Rufus Maddon looked down at his neat grey suit, stared at the men and women in the street. It was not fair of the future to be so—so dismally normal.

Four hundred years of progress? The others had resented the experience that was to be his. In those last few weeks there had been many discussions of how the people four hundred years in the future would look on Rufus Maddon as a barbarian.

Once again he continued his aimless walk down the streets of the familiar city. There was a general air of disrepair. Shops were boarded up. The pavement was broken and potholed. A few automobiles traveled on the broken streets. They, at least, appeared to be of a slightly advanced design but they were dented, dirty and noisy.

The man who had spoken to him had made no sense. "Lobe job?" And what was "the one on time travel?"

He stopped in consternation as he reached the familiar park. His consternation arose from the fact that the park was all too familiar. Though it was a tangle of weeds the equestrian statue of General Murdy was still there in deathless bronze, liberally decorated by pigeons.

Clothes had not changed nor had common speech. He wondered if the transfer had gone awry, if this world were something he was dreaming.

He pushed through the knee-high tangle of grass to a wrought-iron bench. Four hundred years before he had sat on that same bench. He sat down again. The metal powdered and collapsed under his weight, one end of the bench dropping with a painful thump.

Dr. Rufus Maddon was not generally considered to be a man subject to fits of rage. He stood up rubbing his bruised elbow, and heartily kicked the offending bench. The part he kicked was all too solid.

He limped out of the park, muttering, wondering why the park wasn't used, why everyone seemed to be in a hurry.

It appeared that in four hundred years nothing at all had been accomplished. Many familiar buildings had collapsed. Others still stood. He looked in vain for a newspaper or a magazine.

One new element of this world of the future bothered him considerably. That was the number of low-slung white-panel delivery trucks. They seemed to be in better condition than the other vehicles. Each bore in fairly large gilt letters the legend WORLD SENSEWAYS. But he noticed that the smaller print underneath the large inscription varied. Some read, *Feeder Division*—others, *Hookup Division*.

The one that stopped at the curb beside him read, *Lobotomy Division*. Two husky men got out and smiled at him and one said, "You've been taking too much of that stuff, Doc."

"How did you know my title?" Rufus asked, thoroughly puzzled.

The other man smiled wolfishly, patted the side of truck. "Nice truck, pretty truck. Climb in, bud. We'll take you down and make you feel wonderful, hey?"

Dr. Rufus Maddon suddenly had a horrid suspicion that he knew what a lobe job might be. He started to back away. They grabbed him quickly and expertly and dumped him into the truck.

The sign on the front of the building said WORLD SENSEWAYS. The most luxurious office inside was lettered, *Regional Director—Roger K. Handriss.*

Roger K. Handriss sat behind his handsome desk. He was a florid grey-haired man with keen grey eyes. He was examining his bank book thinking that in another year he'd have enough money with which to retire and buy a permanent hookup. Permanent was so much better than the Temp stuff you could get on the home sets. The nerve ends was what did it, of course.

The girl came in and placed several objects on the desk in front of him. She said, "Mr. Handriss, these just came up from LD. They took them out of the pockets of a man reported as wandering in the street in need of a lobe job."

She had left the office door open. Cramer, deputy chief of LD, sauntered in and said, "The guy was really off. He was yammering about being from the past and not to destroy his mind."

Roger Handriss poked the objects with a manicured finger. He said, "Small pocket change from the twentieth century, Cramer. Membership cards in professional organizations of that era. Ah, here's a letter."

As Cramer and the girl waited, Roger Handriss read the letter through twice. He gave Cramer an uncomfortable smile and said, "This appears to be a letter from a technical publishing house telling Mr.—ah—Maddon that they intend to reprint his book, Suggestions on Time Focus in February of nineteen hundred and fifty. Miss Hart, get on the phone and see if you can raise anyone at the library who can look this up for us. I want to know if such a book was published."

Miss Hart hastened out of the office.

As they waited, Handriss motioned to a chair. Cramer sat down. Handriss said, "Imagine what it must have been like in those days, Al. They had the secrets but they didn't begin to use them until—let me see—four years later. Aldous Huxley had already given them their clue with his literary invention of the Feelies. But they ignored them.

"All their energies went into wars and rumors of wars and random scientific advancement and sociological disruptions. Of course, with Video on the march at that time, they were beginning to get a little preview. Millions of people were beginning to sit in front of the Video screens, content even with that crude excuse for entertainment."

Cramer suppressed a yawn. Handriss was known to go on like that for hours.

"Now," Handriss continued, "all the efforts of a world society are channeled into World Senseways. There is no waste of effort changing a perfectly acceptable status quo. Every man can have Temp and if you save your money you can have Permanent, which they say, is as close to heaven as man can get. Uh—what was that, Miss Hart?"

"There is such a book, Mr. Handriss, and it was published at that time. A Dr. Rufus Maddon wrote it."

Handriss sighed and clucked. "Well," he said, "have Maddon brought up here."

Maddon was brought into the office by an attendant. He wore a wide foolish smile and a tiny bandage on his temple. He walked with the clumsiness of an overgrown child.

"Blast it. Al," Handriss said, "why couldn't your people have been more careful! He looks as if he might have been intelligent."

Al shrugged. "Do they come here from the past every couple of minutes? He didn't look any different than any other lobey to me."

"I suppose it couldn't be helped," Handriss said. "We've done this man a great wrong. We can wait and reeducate, I suppose. But that seems to be treating him rather shabbily."

"We can't send him back," Al Cramer said.

Handriss stood up, his eyes glowing. "But it is within my authority to grant him one of the Perm setups given me. World Senseways knows that Regional Directors make mistakes. This will rectify any mistake to an individual."

"Is it fair he should get it for free?" Cramer asked. "And besides, maybe the people who helped send him up here into the future would like to know what goes on."

Handriss smiled shrewdly. "And if they knew, what would stop them from flooding in on us? Have Hookup install him immediately."

The subterranean corridor had once been used for underground trains. But with the reduction in population it had ceased to pay its way and had been taken over by World Senseways to house the sixty-five thousand Perms.

Dr. Rufus Maddon was taken, in his new shambling walk, to the shining cubicle. His name and the date of installation were written on a card and inserted in the door slot. Handriss stood enviously aside and watched the process.

The bored technicians worked rapidly. They stripped the unprotesting Rufus Maddon, took him inside his cubicle, forced him down onto the foam couch. They rolled him over onto his side, made the usual incision at the back of his neck, carefully slit the main motor nerves, leaving the senses, the heart and lungs intact. They checked the air conditioning and plugged him into the feeding schedule for that bank of Perms.

Next they swung the handrods and the footplates into position, gave him injections of local anesthetic, expertly flayed the palms of his hands and the soles of his feet, painted the raw flesh with the sticky nerve graft and held his hands closed around the rods, his feet against the plates until they adhered in the proper position.

Handriss glanced at his watch.

"Guess that's all we can watch, Al. Come along."

The two men walked back down the long corridor. Handriss said, "The lucky so and so. We have to work for it. I get my Perm in another year —right down here beside him. In the meantime we'll have to content ourselves with the hand sets, holding onto those blasted knobs that don't let enough through to hardly raise the hair on the back of your neck."

Al sighed enviously. "Nothing to do for as long as he lives except twenty-four hours a day of being the hero of the most adventurous and glamorous and exciting stories that the race has been able to devise. No memories. I told them to dial him in on the Cowboy series. There's seven years of that now. It'll be more familiar to him. I'm electing Crime and Detection. Eleven years of that now, you know."

Roger Handriss chuckled and jabbed Al with his elbow. "Be smart, Al. Pick the Harem series."

Back in the cubicle the technicians were making the final adjustments. They inserted the sound buttons in Rufus Maddon's ears, deftly removed his eyelids, moved his head into just the right position and then pulled down the deeply concave shining screen so that Rufus Maddon's staring eyes looked directly into it.

The elder technician pulled the wall switch. He bent and peered into the screen. "Color okay, three dimensions okay. Come on, Joe, we got another to do before quitting."

They left, closed the metal door, locked it.

Inside the cubicle, Dr. Rufus Maddon was riding slowly down the steep trail from the mesa to the cattle town on the plains. He was trail-weary and sun-blackened. There was an old score to settle. Feeney was about to foreclose on Mary Ann's spread and Buck Hoskie, Mary Ann's crooked foreman, had threatened to shoot on sight.

Rufus Maddon wiped the sweat from his forehead on the back of a lean hard brown hero's hand.

A. E. van Vogt

RECRUITING STATION

SHE DIDN'T DARE! Suddenly, the night was a cold, enveloping thing. The edge of the broad, black river gurgled evilly at her feet as if, now that she had changed her mind—it hungered for her.

Her foot slipped on the wet, sloping ground; and her mind grew blurred with the terrible senseless fear that *things* were reaching out of the night, trying to drown her now against her will.

She fought up the bank—and slumped breathless onto the nearest park bench, coldly furious with her fear. Dully, she watched the gaunt man come along the pathway past the light standard. So sluggish was her brain that she was not aware of surprise when she realized he was coming straight toward her.

The purulent yellowish light made a crazy patch of his shadow across her where she sat. His voice, when he spoke, was vaguely foreign in tone, yet modulated, cultured. He said:

"Are you interested in the Calonian cause?"

Norma stared. There was no quickening in her brain, but suddenly she began to laugh. It was funny, horribly, hysterically *funny* funny. To be sitting here, trying to get up the nerve for another attempt at those deadly waters, and then to have some crackbrain come along and—

"You're deluding yourself, Miss Matheson," the man went on coolly. "You're not the suicide type."

"Nor the pickup type!" she answered automatically. "Beat it before—"

Abruptly, it penetrated that the man had called her by name. She looked up sharply at the dark blank that was his face. His head against the background of distant light nodded as if in reply to the question that quivered in her thought.

"Yes, I know your name. I also know your history and your *fear!*"

"What do you mean?"

"I mean that a young scientist named Garson arrived in the city tonight to deliver a series of lectures. Ten years ago, when you and he graduated from the same university, he asked you to marry him, but it was a career you wanted—and now you've been terrified that, in your extremity, you would go to him for assistance and—"

"Stop!"

The man seemed to watch her as she sat there breathing heavily. He said at last, quietly:

"I think I have proved that I am not simply a casual philanderer."

"What other kind of philanderer is there?" Norma asked, sluggish again. But she made no objection as he sank down on the far end of the bench. His back was still to the light, his features night-developed.

"Ah," he said, "you joke; you are bitter. But that *is* an improvement. You feel now, perhaps, that if somebody has taken an interest in you, all is not lost."

Norma said dully: "People who are acquainted with the basic laws of psychology are cursed with the memory of them even when disaster strikes into their lives. All I've done the last ten years is—"

She stopped; then: "You're very clever. Without more than arousing my instinctive suspicions, you've insinuated yourself into the company of an hysterical woman. What's your purpose?"

"I intend to offer you a job."

Norma's laugh sounded so harsh in her own ears that she thought, startled: "I am hysterical!"

Aloud, she said: "An apartment, jewels, a car of my own, I suppose?"

His reply was cool: "No! To put it frankly, you're not pretty enough. Too angular, mentally and physically. That's been one of your troubles the last ten years; a developing introversion of the mind which has in-fluenced the shape of your body unfavorably."

The words shivered through the suddenly stiffened muscles of her body. With an enormous effort, she forced herself to relax. She said: "I had that coming to me. Insults are good for hysteria; so now what?"

"Are you interested in the Calonian cause?"

"There you go again," she complained. "But yes, I'm for it. Birds of a feather, you know."

"I know very well indeed. In fact, in those words you named the reason why I am here tonight, hiring a young woman who is up against it. Calonia, too, is up against it and—" He stopped; in the darkness, he spread his shadow-like hands. "You see: good publicity for our recruiting centers."

Norma nodded. She did see, and, suddenly, she didn't trust herself to speak; her hand trembled as she took the key he held out.

"This key," he said, "will fit the lock of the front door of the recruiting station; it will also fit the lock of the door leading to the apartment above it. The apartment is yours while you have the job. You can go there to-night if you wish, or wait until morning if you fear this is merely a device —now, I must give you a warning."

"Warning?"

"Yes. The work we are doing is illegal. Actually, only the American government can enlist American citizens and operate recruiting stations.

We exist on sufferance and sympathy, but at any time someone may lay a charge; and the police will have to act."

Norma nodded rapidly. "That's no risk," she said. "No judge would ever—"

"The address is 322 Carlton Street," he cut in smoothly. "And for your information, my name is Dr. Lell."

Norma had the distinct sense of being pushed along too swiftly for caution. She hesitated, her mind on the street address. "Is that near Bessemer?"

It was his turn to hesitate. "I'm afraid," he confessed, "I don't know this city very well, at least not in its twentieth century . . . that is," he finished suavely, "I was here many years ago, before the turn of the century."

Norma wondered vaguely why he bothered to explain; she said, half-accusingly: "You're not a Calonian. You sound—French, maybe."

"You're not a Calonian, either!" he said, and stood up abruptly. She watched him walk off into the night, a great gloom-wrapped figure that vanished almost immediately.

She stopped short in the deserted night street. The sound that came was like a whisper touching her brain; a machine whirring somewhere with almost infinite softness. For the barest moment, her mind concentrated on the shadow vibrations; and then, somehow, they seemed to fade like figments of her imagination. Suddenly, there was only the street and the silent night.

The street was dimly lighted; and that brought doubt, sharp and tinged with a faint fear. She strained her eyes and traced the numbers in the shadow of the door: 322! That was it!

The place was dark. She peered at the signs that made up the window display:

"FIGHT FOR THE BRAVE CALONIANS" "THE CALONIANS ARE FIGHTING FREEDOM'S FIGHT—YOUR FIGHT!" "IF YOU CAN PAY YOUR OWN WAY, IT WOULD BE APPRECIATED; OTHERWISE WE'LL GET YOU OVER!"

There were other signs, but they were essentially the same, all terribly honest and appealing, if you really thought about the desperate things that made up their grim background.

Illegal, of course. But the man had admitted that, too. With sudden end of doubt, she took the key from her purse.

There were two doorways, one on either side of the window. The one to the right led into the recruiting room. The one on the left—

The stairs were dimly lighted, and the apartment at the top was quite empty of human beings. The door had a bolt; she clicked it home, and then, wearily, headed for the bedroom.

And it was as she lay in the bed that she grew aware again of the incredibly faint whirring of a machine. The shadow of a shadow sound; and, queerly, it seemed to reach into her brain: the very last second before she drifted into sleep, the pulse of the vibration, remote as the park bench, was a steady beat inside her.

All through the night that indescribably faint whirring was there. Only occasionally did it seem to be in her head; she was aware of turning, twisting, curling, straightening and, in the fractional awakedness that accompanied each move, the tiniest vibrational tremors would sweep down along her nerves like infinitesimal currents of energy.

Spears of sunlight piercing brilliantly through the window brought her awake at last. She lay taut and strained for a moment, then relaxed, puzzled. There was not a sound from the maddening machine, only the noises of the raucous, awakening street.

There was food in the refrigerator and in the little pantry. The weariness of the night vanished swiftly before the revivifying power of breakfast. She thought in gathering interest: what did he look like, this strange-voiced man of night?

Relieved surprise flooded her when the key unlocked the door to the recruiting room, for there had been in her mind a little edged fear that this was all quite mad.

She shuddered the queer darkness out of her system. What was the matter with her, anyway? The world was sunlit and cheerful, not the black and gloomy abode of people with angular introversion of the mind.

She flushed at the memory of the words. There was no pleasure in knowing that the man's enormously clever analysis of her was true. Still stinging, she examined the little room. There were four chairs, a bench, a long wooden counter and newspaper clippings of the Calonian War on the otherwise bare walls.

There was a back door to the place. Dimly curious, she tried the knob —once! It was locked, but there was something about the feel of it—

A tingling shock of surprise went through her. The door, in spite of its wooden appearance, was solid metal!

Momentarily, she felt chilled; finally she thought: "None of my business."

And then, before she could turn away, the door opened, and a gaunt man loomed on the threshold. He snapped harshly, almost into her face:

"Oh, yes, it is your business!"

It was not fear that made her back away. The deeps of her mind registered the cold hardness of his voice, so different from the previous night. Vaguely she was aware of the ugly sneer on his face. But there was no real emotion in her brain, nothing but a blurred blankness.

It was not fear; it couldn't be fear because all she had to do was run a few yards, and she'd be out on a busy street. And besides she had never been afraid of Negroes, and she wasn't now.

That first impression was so sharp, so immensely surprising that the fast-following second impression seemed like a trick of her eyes. For the man wasn't actually a Negro; he was—

She shook her head, trying to shake that trickiness out of her vision. But the picture wouldn't change. He wasn't a Negro, he wasn't white, he wasn't—anything!

Slowly her brain adjusted itself to his alienness. She saw that he had slant eyes like a Chinaman, his skin, though dark in texture, was dry with a white man's dryness. The nose was sheer chiseled beauty, the most handsome, most normal part of his face; his mouth was thin-lipped, commanding; his chin bold and giving strength and power to the insolence of his steel-gray eyes. His sneer deepened as her eyes grew wider and wider.

"Oh, no," he said softly, "you're not afraid of me, are you? Let me inform you that my purpose is to *make* you afraid. Last night I had the purpose of bringing you here. That required tact, understanding. My new purpose requires, among other things, the realization on your part that you are in my power beyond the control of your will or wish.

"I could have allowed you to discover gradually that this is not a Calonian recruiting station. But I prefer to get these early squirmings of the slaves over as soon as possible. The reaction to the power of the machine is always so similar and unutterably boring."

"I—don't—understand!"

He answered coldly: "Let me be brief. You have been vaguely aware of a machine. That machine has attuned the rhythm of your body to itself, and through its actions I can control you against your desire. Naturally, I don't expect you to believe me. Like the other women, you will test its mind-destroying power. Notice that I said *women!* We always hire women; for purely psychological reasons they are safer than men. You will discover what I mean if you should attempt to warn any applicant on the basis of what I have told you."

He finished swiftly: "Your duties are simple. There is a pad on the table made up of sheets with simple questions printed on them. Ask those questions, note the answers, then direct the applicants to me in the back room. I have—er—a medical examination to give them."

Out of all the things he had said, the one that briefly, searingly, dominated her whole mind had no connection with her personal fate: "But," she gasped, "if these men are not being sent to Calonia, where—"

He hissed her words short: "Here comes a man. Now, remember!"

He stepped back, to one side out of sight in the dimness of the back room. Behind her, there was the dismaying sound of the front door opening. A man's baritone voice blurred a greeting into her ears.

Her fingers shook as she wrote down the man's answers to the dozen questions. Name, address, next of kin— His face was a ruddy-cheeked blur against the shapeless shifting pattern of her racing thoughts.

"You can see," she heard herself mumbling, "that these questions are only a matter of identification. Now, if you'll go into that back room—"

The sentence shattered into silence. She'd said it! The uncertainty in her mind, the unwillingness to take a definite stand until she had thought of some way out, had made her say the very thing she had intended to avoid saying. The man said:

"What do I go in there for?"

She stared at him numbly. Her mind felt thick, useless. She needed time, calm. She said: "It's a simple medical exam, entirely for your own protection."

Sickly, Norma watched his stocky form head briskly toward the rear door. He knocked; and the door opened. Surprisingly, it stayed open—surprisingly, because it was then, as the man disappeared from her line of vision, that she saw the machine.

The end of it that she could see reared up immense and darkly gleaming halfway to the ceiling, partially hiding a door that seemed to be a rear exit from the building.

She forgot the door, forgot the men. Her mind fastened on the great engine with abrupt intensity as swift memory came that *this* was the machine—

Unconsciously her body, her ears, her mind, strained for the whirring sound that she had heard in the night. But there was nothing, not the tiniest of tiny noises, not the vaguest stir of vibration, not a rustle, not a whisper. The machine crouched there, hugging the floor with its solidness, its clinging metal strength; and it was utterly dead, utterly motionless.

The doctor's smooth, persuasive voice came to her: "I hope you don't mind going out the back door, Mr. Barton. We ask applicants to use it because—well, our recruiting station here is illegal. As you probably know, we exist on sufferance and sympathy, but we don't want to be too blatant about the success we're having in getting young men to fight for our cause."

Norma waited. As soon as the man was gone she would force a show-down on this whole fantastic affair. If this was some distorted scheme of Calonia's enemies, she would go to the police and—

The thought twisted into a curious swirling chaos of wonder. The machine—

Incredibly, the machine was coming alive, a monstrous, gorgeous, swift aliveness. It glowed with a soft, swelling white light; and then burst into enormous flame. A breaker of writhing tongues of fire, blue and red and green and yellow, stormed over that first glow, blotting it from view instantaneously. The fire sprayed and flashed like an intricately designed fountain, with a wild and violent beauty, a glittering blaze of unearthly glory.

And then—just like that—the flame faded. Briefly, grimly stubborn in its fight for life, the swarming, sparkling energy clung to the metal.

It was gone. The machine lay there, a dull, gleaming mass of metallic deadness, inert, motionless. The doctor appeared in the doorway.

"Sound chap!" he said, satisfaction in his tone. "Heart requires a bit of glandular adjustment to eradicate the effects of bad diet. Lungs will react swiftly to gas-immunization injections, and our surgeons should be able to patch that body up from almost anything except an atomic storm."

Norma licked dry lips. "What are you talking about?" she asked wildly. "W-what happened to that man?"

She was aware of him staring at her blandly. His voice was cool, faintly amused: "Why—he went out the back door."

"He did not. He—"

She realized the uselessness of words. Cold with the confusion of her thought, she emerged from behind the counter. She brushed past him, and then, as she reached the threshold of the door leading into the rear room, her knees wobbled. She grabbed at the door jamb for support, and knew that she didn't dare go near that machine. With an effort, she said:

"Will you go over there and open it?"

He did so, smiling. The door squealed slightly as it opened. When he closed it, it creaked audibly, and the automatic lock clicked loudly.

There had been no such sound. Norma felt the deepening whiteness in her cheeks. She asked, chilled:

"What is this machine?"

"Owned by the local electric company, I believe," he answered suavely, and his voice mocked her. "We just have permission to use the room, of course."

"That's not possible," she said thickly. "Electric companies don't have machines in the back rooms of shabby buildings."

He shrugged. "Really," he said indifferently, "this is beginning to bore me. I have already told you that this is a very special machine. You have seen some of its powers, yet your mind persists in being practical after a twentieth century fashion. I will repeat merely that you are a slave of the machine, and that it will do you no good to go to the police, entirely aside from the fact that I saved you from drowning yourself, and gratitude alone should make you realize that you owe everything to me; nothing to the world you were prepared to desert. However, that is too much to expect. You will learn by experience."

Quite calmly, Norma walked across the room. She opened the door, and then, startled that he had made no move to stop her, turned to stare at him. He was still standing where she had left him. He was smiling.

"You must be quite mad," she said after a moment. "Perhaps you had some idea that your little trick, whatever it was, would put the fear of the unknown into me. Let me dispel that right now. I'm going to the police—this very minute."

The picture that remained in her mind as she climbed aboard the bus was of him standing there, tall and casual and terrible in his contemptuous derision. The chill of that memory slowly mutilated the steady tenor of her forced calm.

The sense of nightmare vanished as she climbed off the streetcar in front of the imposing police building. Sunshine splashed vigorously on the pavement, cars honked; the life of the city swirled lustily around her, and brought wave on wave of returning confidence.

The answer, now that she thought of it, was simplicity itself. Hypnotism! That was what had made her see a great, black, unused engine burst into mysterious flames.

And no hypnotist could force his will on a determined, definitely opposed mind.

Burning inwardly with abrupt anger at the way she had been tricked, she lifted her foot to step on the curb—and amazed shock stung into her brain.

The foot, instead of lifting springily, dragged; her muscles almost refused to carry the weight. She grew aware of a man less than a dozen feet from her, staring at her with popping eyes.

"Good heavens!" he gasped audibly. "I must be seeing things."

He walked off rapidly; and the part of her thoughts that registered his odd actions simply tucked them away. She felt too dulled, mentally and physically, even for curiosity.

With faltering steps she moved across the sidewalk. It was as if something was tearing at her strength. holding her with invisible but immense forces. The machine!—she thought—and panic blazed through her.

Will power kept her going. She reached the top of the steps and approached the big doors. It was then the first sick fear came that she couldn't make it; and as she strained feebly against the stone-wall-like resistance of the door, a very fever of dismay grew hot and terrible inside her. What had happened to her? How could a machine reach over a distance, and strike unerringly at one particular individual with such enormous, vitality-draining power?

A shadow leaned over her. The booming voice of a policeman who had just come up the steps was the most glorious sound she had ever heard.

"Too much for you, eh, madam? Here, I'll push that door for you."

"Thank you," she said; and her voice sounded so harsh and dry and weak and unnatural in her own ears that a new terror flared: in a few minutes she wouldn't be able to speak above a whisper.

"*A slave of the machine,*" he had said; and she knew with a clear and burning logic that if she was ever to conquer, it was now. She must get into this building. She must see someone in authority, and she must tell him—must—must— Somehow, she pumped strength into her brain and courage into her heart, and forced her legs to carry her across the threshold into the big modern building with its mirrored anteroom and its fine marble corridors. Inside, she knew suddenly that she had reached her limit.

She stood there on the hard floor, and felt her whole body shaking from the enormous effort it took simply to stay erect. Her knees felt dissolved and cold, like ice turning to strengthless liquid. She grew aware that the big policeman was hovering uncertainly beside her.

"Anything I can do, mother?" he asked heartily.

"Mother!" she echoed mentally with a queer sense of insanity. Her mind skittered off after the word. Did he really say that, or had she dreamed it? Why, she wasn't a mother. She wasn't even married. She—

She fought the thought off. She'd have to pull herself together, or there was madness here. No chance now of getting to an inspector or an officer. This big constable must be her confidant, her hope to defeat the mighty power that was striking at her across miles of city, an incredibly evil, terrible power whose ultimate purpose she could not begin to imagine. She—

There it was again, her mind pushing off into obscure, action-destroying, defeating thoughts! She turned to the policeman, started to part her lips in speech; and it was then she saw the mirror.

She saw a tall, thin, old, old woman standing beside the fresh-cheeked bulk of a blue-garbed policeman. It was such an abnormal trick of vision that it fascinated her. In some way, the mirror was missing her image, and reflecting instead the form of an old woman who must be close behind and slightly to one side of her. Queerest thing she had ever seen.

She half-lifted her red-gloved hand toward the policeman, to draw his attention to the distortion. Simultaneously, the red-gloved hand of the old woman in the mirror reached toward the policeman. Her own raised hand stiffened in midair; so did the old woman's. Funny.

Puzzled, she drew her gaze from the mirror, and stared with briefly blank vision at that rigidly uplifted hand. A tiny, uneven bit of her wrist was visible between the end of the glove and the end of sleeve of her serge suit. Her skin wasn't really as dark as—that!

Two things happened then. A tall man came softly through the door— Dr. Lell—and the big policeman's hand touched her shoulder.

"Really, madam, at your age, you shouldn't come here. A phone call would serve—"

And Dr. Lell was saying: "My poor old grandmother—"

Their voices went on, but the sense of them jangled in her brain as she jerked frantically to pull the glove off a hand wrinkled and shriveled by incredible age— Blackness pierced with agonized splinters of light reached mercifully into her brain. Her very last thought was that it must have happened just before she stepped onto the curb, when the man had stared at her pop-eyed and thought himself crazy. He must have seen the change taking place.

The pain faded; the blackness turned gray, then white. She was conscious of a car engine purring, and of forward movement. She opened her eyes—and her brain reeled from a surge of awful memory.

"Don't be afraid!" said Dr. Lell, and his voice was as soothing and gentle as it had been hard and satirical at the recruiting station. "You are again yourself; in fact, approximately ten years younger."

He removed one hand from the steering wheel and flashed a mirror before her eyes. The brief glimpse she had of her image made her grab at the silvered glass as if it were the most precious thing in all the world.

One long, hungry look she took; and then her arm, holding the mirror, collapsed from sheer, stupendous relief. She lay back against the cushions, tears sticky on her cheeks, weak and sick from dreadful reaction. At last she said steadily:

"Thanks for telling me right away. Otherwise I should have gone mad."

"That, of course, was why I told you," he said; and his voice was still soft, still calm. And she felt soothed, in spite of the dark terror just past, in spite of the intellectual realization that this diabolical man used words and tones and human emotions as coldly as Pan himself piping his reed, sounding what stop he pleased. That quiet, deep voice went on:

"You see, you are now a valuable member of our twentieth-century staff, with a vested interest in the success of our purpose. You thoroughly understand the system of rewards and punishments for good or bad service. You will have food, a roof over your head, money to spend—and eternal youth! Woman, look at your face again, look hard, and rejoice for your good fortune! Weep for those who have nothing but old age and death as their future! Look hard, I say!"

It was like gazing at a marvelous photograph out of the past, except that she had been somewhat prettier in the actuality, her face more rounded, not so sharp, more girlish. She was twenty again, but different, more mature, leaner. She heard his voice go on dispassionately, a distant background to her own thoughts, feeding, feeding at the image in the mirror. He said:

"As you can see, you are not truly yourself as you were at twenty. This is because we could only manipulate the time tensions which influenced your thirty-year-old body according to the rigid mathematical laws governing the energies and forces involved. We could not undo the harm wrought these last rather prim, introvert years of your life because you have already lived them, and nothing can change that."

It came to her that he was talking to give her time to recover from the deadliest shock that had ever stabbed into a human brain. And for the first time she thought, not of herself, but of the incredible things implied by every action that had occurred, every word spoken.

"Who . . . are . . . you?"

He was silent; the car twisted in and out of the clamorous traffic; and she watched his face now, that lean, strange, dark, finely chiseled, *evil* face with its glittering dark eyes. For the moment she felt no repulsion, only a gathering storm of fascination at the way that strong chin tilted unconsciously as he said in a cold, proud, ringing voice:

"We are masters of time. We live at the farthest frontier of time itself, and all the ages belong to us. No words could begin to describe the vastness of our empire or the futility of opposing us. We—"

He stopped. Some of the fire faded from his dark eyes. His brows knit, his chin dropped, his lips clamped into a thin line, then parted as he snapped:

"I hope that any vague ideas you have had for further opposition will yield to the logic of events and of fact. Now you know why we hire women who have no friends."

"You—devil!" She half sobbed the words.

"Ah," he said softly, "I can see you understand a woman's psychology. Two final points should clinch the argument I am trying to make: First, I can read your mind, every thought that comes into it, every vaguest emotion that moves it. And second, before establishing the machine in that particular building, we explored the years to come; and during all the time investigated, found the machine unharmed, its presence unsuspected by those in authority. Therefore, the future record is that you did— nothing! I think you will agree with me that this is convincing."

Norma nodded dully, her mirror forgotten. "Yes," she said, "yes, I suppose it is."

Miss Norma Matheson,
Calonian Recruiting Station,
322 Carlton Street,

Dear Norma:

I made a point of addressing the *envelope* of this letter to you c/o General Delivery, instead of the above address. I would not care to put you in any danger, however imaginary. I use the word imaginary deliberately for I cannot even begin to describe how grieved and astounded I was to receive such a letter from the girl I once loved—it's eleven years since I proposed on graduation day, isn't it?—and how amazed I was by your questions and statements re time travel.

I might say that if you are not already mentally unbalanced, you will be shortly unless you take hold of yourself. The very fact that you were nerving yourself to commit suicide when this man—Dr. Lell—hired you from a park bench to be clerk in the recruiting station at the foregoing address, is evidence of hysteria. You could have gone on city relief.

I see that you have lost none of your powers of expression in various mediums. Your letter, mad though it is in subject matter, is eminently coherent and well thought out. Your drawing of the face of Dr. Lell is quite a remarkable piece of work.

If it is a true resemblance, then I agree that he is definitely not— shall I say—Western. His eyes are distinctly slanting, Chinese-style. His skin you say is, and shown as, dark in texture, indicating a faint Negro strain. His nose is very fine and sensitive, strong in character.

This effect is incremented by his firm mouth, though those thin lips are much too arrogant—the whole effect is of an extraordinarily intelligent-looking man, a super-mongrel in appearance. Such bodies could very easily be produced in the far-Eastern provinces of Asia.

I pass without comment over your description of the machine which swallows up the unsuspecting recruits. The superman has apparently not objected to answering your questions since the police station episode; and so we have a new theory of time and space:

Time—he states—is the all, the only reality. Every unfolding instant the Earth and its life, the universe and all its galaxies are re-created by the titanic energy that is time—and always it is essentially the same pattern that is re-formed, because that is the easiest course.

He makes a comparison. According to Einstein, and in this he is correct, the Earth goes around the Sun, not because there is such a force as gravitation, but because it is easier for it to go around the Sun in exactly the way it does than to hurtle off into space.

It is easier for time to re-form the same pattern of rock, the same man, the same tree, the same earth. That is all, that is the law.

The rate of reproduction is approximately ten billion a second. During the past minute, therefore, six hundred billion replicas of myself have been created; and all of them are still there, each a separate body occupying its own space, completely unaware of the others. Not one has been destroyed. There is no purpose; it is simply easier to let them stay there, than to destroy them.

If those bodies ever met in the same space, that is if I should go back to shake hands with my twenty-year-old self, there would be a clash of similar patterns, and the interloper would be distorted out of memory and shape.

I have no criticism to make of this theory other than that it is utterly fantastic. However, it is very interesting in the vivid picture it draws of an eternity of human beings, breeding and living and dying in the quiet eddies of the time stream, while the great current flares on ahead in a fury of incredible creation.

I am puzzled by the detailed information you are seeking—you make it almost real—but I give the answers for what they are worth:

1. Time travel would naturally be based on the most rigid mechanical laws.

2. It seems plausible that they would be able to investigate your future actions.

3. Dr. Lell used phrases such as "atomic storm" and "gas immunization injections." The implication is that they are recruiting for an unimaginably great war.

4. I cannot see how the machine could act on you over a distance—unless there was some sort of radio-controlled intermediate. In your position, I would ask myself one question: Was there anything, any metal, *anything*, upon my person that might have been placed there by the enemy?

5. Some thoughts are so dimly held that they could not possibly be transmitted. Presumably, sharp, clear thoughts might be receivable. If you could keep your mind calm, as you say you did while deciding to write the letter—the letter itself is proof that you succeeded.

6. It is unwise to assume that here is greater basic intelligence, but rather greater development of the potential forces of the mind. If men ever learn to read minds, it will be because they train their innate capacity for mind reading; they will be cleverer only when new knowledge adds new techniques of training.

To become personal, I regret immeasurably having heard from you. I had a memory of a rather brave spirit, rejecting my proposal of marriage, determined to remain independent, ambitious for advancement in the important field of social services. Instead, I find a sorry ending, a soul disintegrated, a mind feeding on fantasia and a sense of incredible persecution. My advice is: go to a psychiatrist before it is too late, and to that end I inclose a money order for $200.00, and extend you my best wishes.

Yours in memory,

Jack Garson.

At least, there was no interference with her private life. No footsteps but her own ever mounted the dark, narrow flight of stairs that led to her tiny apartment. At night, after the recruiting shop closed, she walked the crowded streets; sometimes, there was a movie that seemed to promise surcease from the deadly strain of living; sometimes a new book on her old love, the social sciences, held her for a brief hour.

But there was nothing, nothing, absolutely nothing, that could relax the burning pressure of the reality of the machine. It was there always like a steel band drawn tautly around her mind.

It was crazy funny to read about the war, and the victories and the defeats—when out there, somewhere, in the future another, greater war was being fought; a war so vast that all the ages were being ransacked for manpower.

And men came! Dark men, blond men, young men, grim men, hard men, and veterans of other wars—the stream of them made a steady flow into that dimly lighted back room. And one day she looked up from an intent, mindless study of the pattern of the stained, old counter—and there was Jack Garson!

It was as simple as that. There he stood, not much older-looking after ten years, a little leaner of face perhaps, and there were tired lines all around his dark-brown eyes. While she stared in dumb paralysis, he said:

"I had to come, of course. You were the first emotional tie I had, and also the last; when I wrote the letter, I didn't realize how strong that emotion still was. What's all this about?"

She thought with a flaming intensity: Often, in the past, Dr. Lell had vanished for brief periods during the day hours; once she had seen him disappear into the flamboyant embrace of the light shed by the machine. Twice, she had opened the door to speak to him, and found him gone!

All accidental observations! It meant he had stepped scores of times into his own world when she hadn't seen him and—

Please let this be one of the times when he was away!

A second thought came, so fierce, so sharply focused that it made a stabbing pain inside her head: She must be calm. She must hold her mind away from give-away thoughts, if it was not already ages too late.

Her voice came into the silence like a wounded, fluttering bird, briefly stricken by shock, then galvanized by agony:

"Quick! You must go—till after six! Hurry! Hurry!"

Her trembling hands struck at his chest, as if by those blows she would set him running for the door. But the thrust of her strength was lost on the muscles of his breast, defeated by the way he was leaning forward. His body did not even stagger.

Through a blur, she saw he was staring down at her with a grim, set smile. His voice was hard as chipped steel as he said:

"Somebody's certainly thrown a devil of a scare into you. But don't worry! I've got a revolver in my pocket. And don't think I'm alone in this. I wired the Calonian embassy at Washington, then notified the police here of their answer: no knowledge of this place. The police will arrive in minutes. I came in first to see that you didn't get hurt in the shuffle. Come on—outside with you, because—"

It was Norma's eyes that must have warned him, her eyes glaring past him. She was aware of him whirling to face the dozen men who were trooping out of the back room. The men came stolidly, and she had time to see that they were short, squat, ugly creatures, more roughly built than the lean, finely molded Dr. Lell; and their faces were not so much evil as half dead with unintelligence.

A dozen pair of eyes lighted with brief, animal-like curiosity, as they stared at the scene outside the window; then they glanced indifferently at herself and Jack Garson and the revolver he was holding so steadily; finally, their interest fading visibly, their gazes reverted expectantly to Dr. Lell, who stood smiling laconically on the threshold of the doorway.

"Ah, yes, Professor Garson, you have a gun, haven't you? And the police are coming. Fortunately, I have something here that may convince you of the uselessness of your puny plans."

His right hand came from behind his back, where he had been half hiding it. A gasp escaped from Norma as she saw that in it he held a blazing ball, a globe of furious flame, a veritable ball of fire.

The thing burned there in his palm, crude and terrible in the illusion of incredible, destroying incandescence. The mockery in Dr. Lell's voice was utterly convincing, as he said in measured tones *at her*:

"My dear Miss Matheson, I think you will agree that you will not offer further obstacles to our purpose, now that we have enlisted this valuable young man into the invincible armies of the Glorious—and, as for you, Garson, I suggest you drop that gun before it burns off your hand. It—"

His words were lost in the faint cry that came from Jack Garson. Amazed, Norma saw the gun fall to the floor, and lie there, burning with a white-hot, an abnormal violence.

"Good Heaven!" said Jack Garson; and Norma saw him stare at the weapon enthralled, mindless of danger, as it shrank visibly in that intense fire.

In seconds, there was no weapon, no metal; the fire blinked out—and where it had been the floor was not even singed.

From Dr. Lell came a barked command, oddly twisted, foreignish words that nevertheless sounded like: "Grab him!"

She looked up, abruptly sick; but there was no fight. Jack Garson did not even resist, as the wave of beast men flowed around him. Dr. Lell said:

"So far, professor, you haven't made a very good showing as a gallant rescuer. But I'm glad to see that you have already recognized the hopelessness of opposing us. It is possible that, if you remain reasonable, we will not have to destroy your personality. But now—"

Urgency sharpened his tone. "I had intended to wait and capture your burly policemen, but as they have not arrived at the proper moment—a tradition with them, I believe—I think we shall have to go without them. It's just as well, I suppose."

He waved the hand that held the ball of fire, and the men carrying Jack Garson literally ran into the back room. Almost instantly, they were out of sight. Norma had a brief glimpse of the machine blazing into wondrous life; and then there was only Dr. Lell striding forward, leaning over the bench, his eyes glaring pools of menace.

"Go upstairs instantly! I don't think the police will recognize you—but if you make one false move, *he* will pay. Go—quickly!"

As she hurried past the window on semiliquid legs, she saw his tall figure vanish through the door into the back room. Then she was climbing the stairs.

Halfway up, her movements slowed as if she had been struck. Her mirror told the story of her punishment. The lean face of a woman of fifty-five met her stunned gaze.

The disaster was complete. Cold, stiff, tearless, she waited for the police.

For Garson, the world of the future began as a long, dim corridor that kept blurring before his unsteady vision. Heavy hands held him erect as he walked and—a wave of blur blotted the uncertain picture—

When he could see again, the pressure of unpleasant hands was gone from him, and he was in a small room, sitting down. His first dim impression was that he was alone, yet when he shook himself, and his vision cleared, he saw the desk; and behind the desk, a man.

The sight of that lean, dark, saturnine figure shocked electrically along his nerves, instantly galvanized a measure of strength back into his body. He leaned forward, his attention gathered on the man; and that was like a signal. Dr. Lell said derisively:

"I know. You've decided to co-operate. It was in your mind even before we left the presence of . . . er . . . pardon the familiarity . . . of Norma, to whose rescue you came with such impetuous gallantry. Unfortunately, it isn't only a matter of making up *your* mind."

There was a quality of sneer in the man's voice that sent an uneasy current through Garson. He shook himself mentally, trying to clear the remnants of weakness out of his system.

He thought, not coherently, not even chronologically: Lucky he was here in this room. Damned lucky they hadn't sprung a complication of futuristic newness on him, and so disorganized his concentration. Now there was time to gather his thoughts, harden his mind to every conceivable development, discount surprises, *and stay alive*.

He said: "It's quite simple. You've got Norma. You've got me in your power, here in your own age. I'd be a fool to resist."

Dr. Lell regarded him almost pityingly for a moment. And then— there was no doubt of the sneer as he spoke:

"My dear Professor Garson, discussion at this point would be utterly futile. My purpose is merely to discover if you are the type we can use in our laboratories. If you are not, the only alternative is the depersonalizing chamber. I can say this much: men of your character type have not, on the average, been successful in passing our tests."

That was real; every word like a penetrating edged thing. Actually, in spite of his sneers and his amused contempt—actually this man was indifferent to him. There was only the test, whatever that was; and his own conscious life at stake. The important thing was to stay calm, and to stick leechlike to this one tremendous subject. Before he could speak, Dr. Lell said in a curiously flat voice:

"We have a machine that tests human beings for degree of recalcitrancy. The Observer Machine will speak to you now!"

"What is your name?" said a voice out of the thin air beside Garson.

Garson jumped; his brain staggered, literally; and there was a terrible moment of unbalance. The dim, dismayed thought came that, in spite of determination, he had been caught off guard; and there was the still vaguer thought that, without his being aware of it, he had actually been in a state of dangerous tension.

With a terrific effort he caught himself. He saw that Dr. Lell was smiling again, and that helped! Trembling, he leaned back in his chair; and, after a moment, he was sufficiently recovered to feel a surge of anger at the way the chill clung to his body, and at the tiny quaver in his voice, as he began to answer:

"My name is John Bellmore Garson—age thirty-three—professor of physics at the University of—research scientist—blood type number—"

There were too many questions, an exhaustive drain of detail out of his mind, the history of his life, his aspirations. In the end, the deadly truth was a cold weight inside him. His life, his conscious life, was at stake *now*—this minute! Here was not even the shadow of comedy, but a precise, thorough, machinelike grilling. He must pass this test or—

"Dr. Lell!" The insistent voice of the machine broke in. "What is the state of this man's mind at this moment?"

Dr. Lell said promptly, coolly: "A state of tremendous doubt. His subconscious is in a turmoil of uncertainty. I need hardly add that his subconscious knows his character."

Garson drew a deep breath. He felt utterly sick at the simple way he had been disintegrated. And by one *newness*! A machine that needed neither telephone nor radio—if it was a machine! His voice was a rasping thing in his own ears, as he snapped:

"My subconscious can go straight to hell! I'm a reasonable person. I've made up my mind. I play ball with your organization to the limit."

The silence that followed was unnaturally long; and when at last the machine spoke, his relief lasted only till its final words penetrated. The disembodied voice said coldly:

"I am pessimistic—but bring him over for the test after the usual preliminaries!"

Preliminaries! Was it possible that this mindshaking test had been but the preliminary to the preliminary of the real test?

Rigid with dismay, he stood up to follow the bleakly smiling Dr. Lell out of the room.

He began to feel better, as he walked behind Dr. Lell along the gray-blue hallway. In a small way, he had won. Whatever these other tests were, how *could* they possibly ignore his determined conviction that he must co-operate? As for himself—

For himself, there was this colossal world of the future. Surely, he could resign himself to his lot for the duration of this silly war and lose himself in the amazing immensity of a science that included time machines, fireballs, and Observer Machines that judged men with a cold, remorseless logic and spoke out of thin air.

He frowned. There must be some trick to that, some "telephone" in the nearby wall. Damned if he'd believe that any force could focus sound without intermediary instruments, just as Norma couldn't have been made older in the police station without—

The thought collapsed.

For a paralyzed moment, he stared down where the floor had been.

It wasn't there!

With a gasp, Garson grabbed at the opaque wall; and then, as a low laugh from the doctor, and the continued hardness beneath his feet, told the extent of the illusion, he controlled himself—and stared in utter fascination.

Below him was a section of a room, whose limits he could not see because the opaque walls barred his vision on either side. A milling pack of men filled every available foot of space that he could see. Men, oh— The ironic voice of Dr. Lell pierced his stunned senses, echoing his thoughts with brittle words:

"Men, yes, men! Recruits out of all times. Soldiers-to-be from the ages, and not yet do they know their destiny."

The voice ended, but the indescribable scene went on. Men squirmed, shoved, fought. Upturned faces showed stark puzzlement, anger, fear, amusement, and all the combinations of all the possible emotions. There were men in clothes that sparkled with every color of the rainbow; there were the drab-clothed, the in-betweens; there were—

Garson caught his flitting mind into an observant tightness. In spite of the radical difference in the dress styles of the men who floundered down there like sheep in a slaughterhouse pen, there was a sameness about them that could only mean one thing. They were all—

"You're right!" It was that cool, taunting voice again. "They're all Americans, all from this one city now called Delpa. From our several thousand machines located in the various ages of Delpa, we obtain about four thousand men an hour during the daylight hours. What you see below is the main receiving room.

"The recruits come sliding down the time chutes, and are promptly revived and shoved in there. Naturally at this stage there is a certain amount of confusion. But let us proceed further."

Garson scarcely noticed as the solid floor leaped into place beneath his feet. The vague thought did come that at no time had he seen Dr. Lell press a button or manipulate a control of any kind, neither when the Observer Machine spoke with ventriloquistic wizardry, nor when the floor was made invisible, nor now when it again became opaque. Possibly here was some form of mental control. His mind leaped to a personal danger:

What was the purpose of this—preliminary? Were they showing him horror, then watching his reactions? He felt abrupt rage. What did they expect from a man brought up in twentieth-century environment? Nothing here had anything to do with his intellectual conviction that he was caught and that therefore he must co-operate. But—four thousand men in one hour from one city! Why, it meant—

"And here," Dr. Lell said, and his voice was as calm as the placid waters of a pond, "we have one of several hundred smaller rooms that make a great circle around the primary time machine. You can see the confusion has diminished."

Truth, Garson thought, had never suffered greater understatement than those words. There was absolute absence of confusion. Men sat on chesterfields. Some were looking at books; others chatted like people in a silent movie; their lips moved, but no sound penetrated the illusive transparency of the floor.

"I didn't," came that calm, smooth, confident voice, "show you the intermediate stage that leads up to this clublike atmosphere. A thousand frightened men confronted with danger could make trouble. But we winnow them down psychologically and physically till we have one man going through that door at the end of the room—ah, there's one going now. Let us by all means follow him. You see, at this point we dispense with coddling and bring forth the naked reality."

The reality was a metal, boiler-shaped affair, with a furnacelike door; and four beast humans simply grabbed the startled newcomer and thrust him feet first into the door.

The man must have screamed; for, once, his face twisted upward, and the contorted fear, the almost idiotic gaping and working of the mouth came at Garson like some enormous physical blow. As from a great distance, he heard Dr. Lell say:

"It helps at this stage to disorganize the patient's mind, for the depersonalizing machine can then do a better job."

Abruptly, the impersonalness went out of his voice. In an icily curt tone, he said: "It is useless continuing this little lecture tour. To my mind, your reactions have fully justified the pessimism of the Observer. There will be no further delay."

The deadly words scarcely touched him. He was drained of emotion, of hope; and that first blaze of scientific eagerness was a dull, aching ember.

After that incredible succession of blows, he accepted the failure verdict as—merited!

It was consciousness of the sardonic profile of his captor that brought the first emergence from that dark defeatism. Damn it, there was still the fact that he was logistically committed to this world. He'd have to harden himself, narrow his emotions down to a channel that would include only Norma and himself. If these people and their machine condemned on the basis of feelings, then he'd have to show them how stony-cold his intellect could be.

He braced himself. Where the devil was this all-knowing machine?

The corridor ended abruptly in a plain, black door, exactly like all the other doors, that held not the faintest promise of anything important beyond.

Amazingly, it opened onto a street!

A street of the city of the future!

Garson stiffened. His brain soared beyond contemplation of his own danger in a burning anticipation; and then, almost instantly, began to sag.

Puzzled, he stared at a scene that was utterly different from his expectations. In a vague way, mindful of the effects of war, he had pictured devastated magnificence. Instead—

Before his gaze stretched a depressingly narrow, unsightly street. Dark, unwashed buildings towered up to hide the sun. A trickle of the squat, semihuman men and women, beastlike creatures, moved stolidly along narrow areas of pavement marked off by black lines, that constituted the only method of distinguishing the road from the sidewalk.

The street stretched away for miles; and it was all like that, as far as he could see clearly. Intensely disappointed, conscious even of disgust, Garson turned away—and grew aware that Dr. Lell was staring at him with a grim smile. The doctor said laconically:

"What you are looking for, Professor Garson, you will not find, not in this or similar cities of the 'Slaves,' but in the palace cities of the Glorious and the Planetarians—"

He stopped, as if his words had brought an incredibly unpleasant thought; to Garson's amazement, his face twisted with rage; his voice almost choked, as he spat: "Those damnable Planetarians! When I think what their so-called ideals are bringing the world to, I—"

The spasm of fury passed; he said quietly: "Several hundred years ago, a mixed commission of Glorious and Planetarians surveyed the entire physical resources of the Solar System. Men had made themselves practically immortal; theoretically, this body of mine will last a million years, barring major accidents. It was decided available resources would maintain ten million men on Earth, ten million on Venus, five million on Mars and ten million altogether on the moons of Jupiter for one million years at the then existing high standard of consumption, roughly amounting to about four million dollars a year per person at 1941 values.

"If in the meantime Man conquered the stars, all these figures were subject to revision, though then, as now, the latter possibility was considered as remote as the stars themselves. Under examination, the problem, so apparently simple, has shown itself intricate beyond the scope of our mathematics."

He paused, and Garson ventured: "We had versions of planned states in our time, too, but they always broke down because of human nature. That seems to have happened again."

Not for a second had Garson considered his statement dangerous. The effect of his words was startling. The lean, handsome face became like frozen marble. Harshly, Dr. Lell said:

"Do not dare to compare your Naziism or Communism to—us! We are the rulers of all future time, and who in the past could ever stand against us if we chose to dominate? We shall win this war, in spite of being on the verge of defeat, for we are building the greatest time-energy barrier that has ever existed. With it, we shall destroy—or no one will win! We'll teach those moralistic scum of the planets to prate about man's rights and the freedom of the spirit. Blast them all!"

It was stunning. There was a passion of pride here, a violence of emotion altogether outside any possible anticipation. And yet—the fact remained that his own opinions were what they were, and he could not actually hope to conceal them from either Dr. Lell or the Observer; so—

He said: "I see an aristocratic hierarchy and a swarm of beast-men slaves. How do *they* fit into the picture, anyway? What about the resources they require? There certainly seem to be hundreds of thousands in this city alone."

The man was staring at him in rigid hostility, that brought a sudden chill to Garson's spine. Genuinely, he hadn't expected that any reasonable statement he might make would be used against him. Dr. Lell said too quietly:

"Basically, they do not use any resources. They live in cities of stone and brick, and eat the produce of the indefatigable soil."

His voice was suddenly as sharp as steel. "And now, Professor Garson, I assure you that you have already condemned yourself. The Observer is located in that metal building across the street because the strain of energy from the great primary time machine would affect its sensitive parts if it was any nearer. I can think of no other explanation that you require, and I certainly have no desire to remain in the company of a man who will be an automaton in half an hour. *Come along!*"

Briefly, there was no impulse in him to argue, nothing but awareness of this monstrous city. Here it was again, the old, old story of the aristocrat justifying his black crime against his fellow man. Originally, there must have been deliberate physical degradation, deliberate misuse of psychology. The very name by which these people called themselves, the Glorious, seemed a heritage from days when dastardly and enormous efforts must have been made to arouse hysterical hero worship in the masses.

Dr. Lell's dry voice said: "Your disapproval of our slaves is shared by the Planetarians. They also oppose our methods of depersonalizing our recruits. It is easy to see that they and you have many things in common, and if only you could escape to their side—"

With an effort, Garson pulled himself out of his private world. He was being led on, not even skillfully; and it was only too apparent now that every word Dr. Lell spoke had the purpose of making him reveal himself. For a moment, he was conscious of genuine impatience; then puzzlement came.

"I don't get it," he said. "What you're doing cannot be bringing forth any new facts. I'm the product of my environment. You know what that environment is, and what type of normal human being it must inevitably produce. As I've said, my whole case rests on co-oper—"

It was the difference in the texture of the sky at the remote end of that street that snatched his attention. A faint, unnormal, scarlet tinge it was, like a mist, an unnatural, unearthly sunset, only it was hours yet before the sun would set.

Astoundingly, he felt himself taut, growing tauter. He said in a tense voice:

"What's that?"

"That," Dr. Lell's curt, amused voice came at him, "is the war."

Garson restrained a crazy impulse to burst out laughing. For weeks speculation about this gigantic war of the future had intertwined with his gathering anxiety about Norma. And now this—this red haze on the horizon of an otherwise undamaged city—the war!

The dark flash of inner laughter faded, as Dr. Lell said:

"It is not so funny as you think. Most of Delpa is intact because it is protected by a local time-energy barrier. Delpa is actually under siege, fifty miles inside enemy territory."

He must have caught the thought that came to Garson. He said good-humoredly: "You're right. All you have to do is get out of Delpa, and you'll be safe."

Garson said angrily: "It's a thought that would occur naturally to any intelligent person. Don't forget you have Miss Matheson."

Dr. Lell seemed not to have heard. "The red haze you see is the point where the enemy has neutralized our energy barrier. It is there that they attack us unceasingly day and night with an inexhaustible store of robot machines.

"We are unfortunate in not having the factory capacity in Delpa to build robot weapons, so we use a similar type manned by depersonalized humans. Unfortunately, again, the cost in lives is high: ninety-eight percent of recruits. Every day, too, we lose about forty feet of the city, and, of course, in the end, Delpa will fall."

He smiled, an almost gentle smile. Garson was amazed to notice that he seemed suddenly in high good humor. Dr. Lell said:

"You can see how effective even a small time-energy barrier is. When we complete the great barrier two years hence, our entire front line will be literally impregnable. And now, as for your co-operation argument, it's worthless. Men are braver than they think, braver than reason. But let's forget argument. In a minute, the machine will give us the truth of this matter—"

At first sight, the Observer Machine was a solid bank of flickering lights that steadied oddly, seemed almost to glare as they surveyed him. Garson stood quite still, scarcely breathing; a dim thought came that this— this wall of black metal machine and lights was utterly unimpressive.

He found himself analyzing the lack: It was too big and too stationary. If it had been small and possessed of shape, however ugly, and *movement*, there might have been a suggestion of abnormal personality.

But here was nothing, but a myriad of lights. As he watched, the lights began to wink again. Abruptly, they blinked out, all except a little colored design of them at the bottom right-hand corner.

Behind him, the door opened, and Dr. Lell came into the silent room. "I'm glad," he said quietly, "that the result was what it was. We are desperately in need of good assistants.

"To illustrate," he went on, as they emerged into the brightness of the unpleasant street, "I am, for instance, in charge of the recruiting station in 1941, but I'm there only when an intertime alarm system has warned me. In the interim, I am employed on scientific duties of the second order—first order being work that, by its very nature, must continue without interruption."

They were back in the same great building from which he had come; and ahead stretched the same gray-blue, familiar corridor, only this time Dr. Lell opened the first of several doors. He bowed politely.

"After you, professor!"

A fraction too late, Garson's fist flailed the air where that dark, strong face had been. They stared at each other, Garson tight-lipped, his brain like a steel bar. The superman said softly:

"You will always be that instant too slow, professor. It is a lack you cannot remedy. You know, of course, that my little speech was designed to keep you quiet during the trip back here, and that, actually, you failed the test. What you do not know is that you failed startlingly, with a recalcitrancy grading of 6, which is the very worst, and intelligence AA plus, almost the best. It is too bad because we genuinely need capable assistants. I regret—"

"Let me do the regretting!" Garson cut him off roughly. "If I remember rightly, it was just below here that your beast men were forcing a man into the depersonalizing machine. Perhaps, on the staircase going down, I can find some way of tripping you up, and knocking that little gun you're palming right out of your hand."

There was something in the smile of the other that should have warned him—a hint of sly amusement. Not that it would have made any difference. Only—

He stepped through the open doorway toward the gray-blue, plainly visible stairway. Behind him, the door clicked with an odd finality. Ahead there was—

Amazingly, the staircase was gone. Where it had been was a large boilerlike case with a furnace-shaped door. Half a dozen beast men came forward—a moment later, they were shoving him toward that black hole of a door—

The second day Norma took the risk. The windows of the recruiting station still showed the same blank interior; walls stripped by the police of Calonian slogans, and signs and newspaper clippings trampled all over the floor. The door to the back room was half closed—too dark to see the interior.

It was noon. With drummed-up courage, Norma walked swiftly to the front entrance. The lock clicked open smoothly, and she was inside— pushing at that back door.

The machine was not there. Great dents showed in the floor, where it had malignantly crouched for so many months. But it was gone, as completely as Dr. Lell, as completely as the creaturemen and Jack Garson.

Back in her rooms, she collapsed onto the bed, and lay quivering from the dreadful nervous reaction of that swift, illegal search.

On the afternoon of the fourth day, as she sat staring at the meaningless words of a book, there was an abrupt tingling in her body. Somewhere a machine—*the machine*—was vibrating softly.

She climbed to her feet, the book forgotten on the window sill, where, freakishly, it had fallen. But the sound was gone. Not a tremor touched her taut nerves. The thought came: imagination! The pressure was really beginning to get her.

As she stood there stiff, unable to relax, there came the thin squeal of a door opening downstairs. She recognized the sound instantly. It was the back door that led onto the vacant back lot, which her window overlooked. The back door opening and shutting!

She stared, fascinated, as Dr. Lell stalked into view. Her thought of awareness of him was so sharp that he must have caught it—but he did not turn. In half a minute he was gone, out of her line of vision.

On the fifth day, there was hammering downstairs, carpenters working. Several trucks came, and there was the mumbling sound of men talking. But it was evening before she dared venture downstairs. Through the window, then, she saw the beginning of the changes that were being wrought.

The old bench had been removed. The walls were being redone; there was no new furniture yet, but a rough, unfinished sign leaned against one wall. It read:

EMPLOYMENT BUREAU

MEN WANTED

Men wanted! So that was it. Another trap for men! Those ravenous armies of the Glorious must be kept glutted with fodder. The incredible war up there in that incredible future raged on. And she—

Quite dumbly, she watched as Dr. Lell came out of the back room. He walked toward the front door, and there was not even the impulse in her to run. She stood there, as he opened the door, came out, meticulously closed the door behind him, and then, after a moment, stood beside her, as silent as she, staring into the window. Finally:

"I see you've been admiring our new set-up!"

His voice was matter-of-fact, completely lacking in menace. She made no reply; he seemed to expect none, for he said almost immediately, in that same conversational tone:

"It's just as well that it all happened as it did. Nothing I ever told you has been disproved. I said that investigation had shown the machine to be here several years hence. Naturally, we could not examine every day or week of that time. This little episode accordingly escaped our notice, but did not change the situation.

"As for the fact that it will be an employment bureau henceforth, that seemed natural at the period of our investigation because this war of your time was over then."

He paused, and still there was no word that she could think of saying. In the gathering darkness, he seemed to stare at her.

"I'm telling you all this because it would be annoying to have to train someone else for your position, and because you must realize the impossibility of further opposition.

"Accept your situation. We have thousands of machines similar to this, and the millions of men flowing through them are gradually turning the tide of battle in our favor. We must win; our cause is overwhelmingly just; we are Earth against all the planets; Earth protecting herself against the aggression of a combination of enemies armed as no powers in all time have ever been armed. We have the highest moral right to draw on the men of Earth of every century to defend their planet.

"However"—his voice lost its objectivity, grew colder—"if this logic does not move you, the following rewards for your good behavior should prove efficacious. We have Professor Garson; unfortunately, I was unable to save his personality. Definite tests proved that he would be a recalcitrant, so—

"Then there is your youth. It will be returned to you on a salary basis. Every three weeks you will become a year younger. In short, it will require two years for you to return to your version of twenty."

He finished on a note of command: "A week from today, this bureau will open for business. You will report at nine o'clock. This is your last chance. Good-by."

In the darkness, she watched his shape turn; he vanished into the gloom of the building.

She had a purpose. At first it was a tiny mindgrowth that she wouldn't admit into her consciousness. But gradually embarrassment passed, and the whole world of her thought began to organize around it.

It began with the developing realization that resistance was useless. Not that she believed in the rightness of the cause of Dr. Lell and of this race that called itself the Glorious, although his story of Earth against the planets had put the first doubt into her brain. As—she knew—he had intended it should.

The whole affair was simpler than that. One woman had set herself against the men of the future—what a silly thing for one woman to do!

There remained Jack Garson!

If she could get him back, poor, broken, strange creature that he must be now with his personality destroyed—somehow she would make amends for having been responsible, but—

She thought: What madness to hope that they'd give him back to her, ever! She was the tiniest cog in a vast war machine. Nevertheless, the fact remained:

She must get him back!

The part of her brain that was educated, civilized, thought: What an elemental purpose, everything drained out of her but the basic of basics, one woman concentrating on the one man.

But the purpose was there, unquenchable!

The slow months dragged; and, once gone, seemed to have flashed by. Suddenly, the Great War was over—and swarms of returned soldiers made the streets both dangerous and alive.

One night she turned a corner and found herself on a street she hadn't visited for some time. She stopped short, her body stiffening. The street ahead was thick with men—but their presence scarcely touched her mind.

Above all that confusion of sound, above the catcalls, above the roar of streetcars and automobiles, above the totality of the cacophonous combination, there was another sound, an incredibly softer sound—the whisper of a time machine.

She was miles from the employment bureau with its machine, but the tiny tremor along her nerves was unmistakable.

She pressed forward, blind to everything but the brilliantly lighted building that was the center of the attention of the men. A man tried to put his arm through hers. She jerked free automatically. Another man simply caught her in an embrace, and for brief seconds she was subjected to a steel-hard hug and a steel-hard kiss.

Purpose gave her strength. With scarcely an effort, she freed one arm and struck at his face. The man laughed good-humoredly, released her, but walked beside her.

"Clear the way for the lady!" he shouted.

Almost magically, there was a lane; and she was at the window. There was a sign that read:

WANTED

RETURNED SOLDIERS FOR DANGEROUS ADVENTURE

GOOD PAY!

No emotion came to the realization that here was another trap for men. In her brain, she had space only for impression.

The impression was of a large square room, with a dozen men in it.

Only three of the men were recruits; of the other nine, one was an American soldier dressed in the uniform of World War I. He sat at a desk pounding a typewriter. Over him leaned a Roman legionnaire of the time of Julius Cæsar, complete with toga and short sword. Beside the door, holding back the pressing throng of men, were two Greek soldiers of the time of Pericles.

The men and the times they represented were unmistakable to her, who had taken four years of university Latin and Greek, and acted in plays of both periods in the original languages.

There was another man in an ancient costume, but she was unable to place him. At the moment, he was at a short counter interviewing one of the three recruits.

Of the four remaining men, two wore uniforms that could have been developments of the late twentieth century: the cloth was a light-yellow texture, and both men had two pips on their shoulders. The rank of lieutenant was obviously still in style when they were commissioned.

The remaining two men were simply strange, not in face, but in the cloth of their uniforms. Their faces were of sensitive, normal construction; their uniforms consisted of breeches and neatly fitting coats all in blue, a blue that sparkled as from a million needlelike diamond points. In a quiet, blue, intense way, they shone.

One of the recruits was led to the back door, as she watched, her first awareness that there was a back door. The door opened; she had the briefest glimpse of a towering machine and a flashing picture of a man who was tall and dark of face, and who might have been Dr. Lell. Only he wasn't. But the similarity of race was unmistakable.

The door closed, and one of the Greeks guarding the outer entrance said: "All right, two more of you fellows can come in!"

There was a struggle for position, brief but incredibly violent. And then the two victors, grinning and breathing heavily from their exertion, were inside. In the silence that followed, one of the Greeks turned to the other, and said in a tangy, almost incomprehensible version of ancient Greek:

"Sparta herself never had more willing fighters. This promises to be a good night's catch!"

It was the rhythm of the words, and the colloquial gusto with which they were spoken that almost destroyed the meaning for her. After a moment, however, she made the mental translation. And now the truth was unmistakable. The men of Time had gone back even to old Greece, probably much farther back, for their recruits. And always they had used every version of bait, based on all the weaknesses and urgencies in the natures of men.

"Fight For Calonia"—an appeal to idealism! "Men wanted"—the most basic of all appeals, work for food, happiness, security. And now, the appeal variation was for returned soldiers—adventure—with pay!

Diabolical! And yet so effective that they could even use men who had

formerly been caught on the same brand of fly paper as recruiting officers
— These men must be of the recalcitrant type, who fitted themselves
willingly into the war machine of the Glorious One.

Traitors!

Abruptly ablaze with hatred for all nonrecalcitrants, who still possessed
their personalities, she whirled away from the window.

She was thinking: Thousands of such machines. The figures had been
meaningless before, but now, with just one other machine as a tremendous example, the reality reared up into a monstrous thing.

To think that there was a time when she had actually set her slim
body and single, inadequate mind against *them!*

There remained the problem of getting Jack Garson out of the hell of
that titanic war of the future!

At night, she walked the streets, because there was always the fear that
in the apartment her thoughts, her driving deadly thoughts, would be—
tapped. And because to be inclosed in those narrow walls above the
machine that had devoured so many thousands of men was—intolerable!

She thought as she walked—over and over she thought of the letter
Jack Garson had written her before he came in person. Long destroyed,
that letter, but every word was emblazoned on her brain; and of all the
words of it, the one sentence that she always returned to was. "In your
position, I would ask myself one question: Was there anything, any metal,
anything, upon my person, that might have been placed there?"

One day, as she was wearily unlocking the door of her apartment, the
answer came. Perhaps it was the extra weariness that brought her briefly
closer to basic things. Perhaps her brain was simply tired of slipping over
the same blind spot. Or perhaps the months of concentration had finally
earned the long-delayed result.

Whatever the reason, she was putting the key back into her purse
when the hard, metallic feel of it against her fingers brought wild, piercing
realization.

The key, metal, the key, metal, the key—

Desperately, she stopped the mad repetition. The apartment door
slammed behind her, and like some terrorized creature she fled down the
dark stairs into the glare of the night streets.

Impossible to return till she had calmed the burning, raging chaos that
was in her mind. Until she had—made sure!

After half an hour, the first flash of coherence came. In a drugstore,
she bought a night bag and a few fill-ins to give it weight. A pair of
small pliers, a pair of tweezers—in case the pliers were too large—and a
small screwdriver completed her equipment. Then she went to a hotel.

The pliers and the tweezers were all she needed. The little bulbous cap
of the skeleton-type key yielded to the first hard pressure. Her trembling
fingers completed the unscrewing—and she found herself staring at a

tiny, glowing point, like a red-hot needle protruding from the very center of the tube that was the inside of the key.

The needle vanished into an intricate design of spiderlike wires, all visible in the glow that shed from them—

The vague thought came that there was probably terrific, communicable energies here. But somehow there came no sense of restraint from the idea. Only enough reality of danger struck her to make her wrap her flimsy lace handkerchief around the tweezers—and then she touched the shining, protruding needle point.

It yielded the slightest bit to her shaky touch. Nothing happened. It just glowed there.

Dissatisfied, she put the key down and stared at it. So tiny, so delicate a machine actually disturbed to the extent of one sixteenth of an inch displacement—and nothing happened. She—

A sudden thought sent her to the dresser mirror. A forty-year-old face stared back at her.

Months now since she had returned to twenty. And now, in a flash, she was forty. The little touch of the pin against the needle's end, pushing, had aged her twenty years.

That explained what had happened at the police station. It meant—if she could only pull it back— She fought to steady her fingers, then applied the tweezers.

She was twenty again!

Abruptly weak, she lay down on the bed. She thought:

Somewhere in the world of time and space was the still-living body of the man that had been Jack Garson. But for him she could throw this key *thing* into the river three blocks away, take the first train East or West or South—anywhere—and the power of the machine would be futile against her. Dr. Lell would not even think of searching for her once she had lost herself in the swarm of humankind.

How simple it all really was. For three long years, their power over her had been the key and its one devastating ability to age her.

Or was that all?

Startled, she sat up. Did they count, perhaps, on their victims believing themselves safe enough to keep the key and its magic powers of rejuvenation? She, of course, because of Jack Garson, was bound to the key as if *it* was still the controller and not she. But the other incentive, now that she had thought of *it*, was enormous. And—

Her fingers shook as she picked up the dully gleaming key with its glowing, intricate interior. Incredible that they could have allowed so precious an instrument to pass so easily into the hands of an alien, when they must have known that the probability of discovery was not—improbable!

An idea came; and, with it, abrupt calm. With suddenly steady fingers, she picked up the tweezers, caught the protruding glow point of the key between the metal jaws, and, making no attempt to pull or push, twisted screw-wise.

There was a tiny, almost inaudible click. Her body twanged like a taut violin string, and she was falling—falling into dark, immeasurable distance.

Out of the night, a vaguely shining body drifted toward her, a body human yet not human; there was something about the head and the shoulders, something physically different that somehow eluded her slow thought; and in that strange, superhuman head were eyes that blazed like jewels, seemed literally to pierce her. The voice that came couldn't have been sound, for it was inside her brain, and it said:

"With this great moment, you enter upon your power and your purpose. I say to you, the time-energy barrier must not be completed. It will destroy all the ages of the Solar System. The time-energy barrier must not, *not*, NOT be completed—"

The body faded, and was gone into remoteness. The very memory of it became a dim mind-shape. There remained the darkness, the jet, incredible darkness.

Abruptly, she was in a material world. She seemed to be half-slumped, half-kneeling, one leg folded under her in the exact position she had occupied on the bed. Only she must have drooped there unconscious for long moments; her knees ached and ached with the hard, pressing pain of position. And—beneath the silk of her stockings was, not the hotel bed, but—metal!

It was the combination of surprise, the aloneness, and the stark fact of the mind-destroying thing that was going to happen that unnerved Garson. Involuntarily, he started to squirm, then he was writhing, his face twisting in strange mental agony; and then the strength of those rough, stolid hands holding him seemed to flow somehow into his nerves.

Almost literally, he clenched his mind, and was safe from madness!

There were no hands touching him now. He lay, face downward on a flat, hard surface; and at first there was only the darkness and a slow return of the sense of aloneness.

Vague thoughts came, thoughts of Norma and of the coincidence that had molded his life, seemingly so free for so many years, yet destined to find its ending here in this black execution chamber—for he *was* being destroyed here, though his body might live on for a few brief mindless hours. Or days. Or weeks. It mattered not.

The thing was fantastic. This whole damned business was a nightmare, and in a minute he'd wake up and—

At first the sound was less than a whisper, a stealthy noise out of remoteness, that prodded with an odd insistence at Garson's hearing. It quivered toward him in the blackness, edging out of inaudibility, a rasping presence that grew louder, louder—voices!

It exploded into a monstrous existence, a billion voices clamoring at his brain, a massive blare that pressed at him, *pressed him!*

Abruptly, the ferocity of the voices dimmed. They faded into distance, still insistent, somehow reluctant to leave, as if there was something still left unsaid.

The end of sound came, and briefly there was utter silence. Then— there was a click. Light flooded at him from an opening a scant foot from his head.

Garson twisted and stared, fascinated. Daylight! From his vantage point, he could see the edge of a brick-and-stone building, a wretchedly old, worn building, a street of Delpa.

It was over. Incredibly it was over.

And nothing had happened. No, that wasn't it exactly. There were things in his mind, confusing things about the importance of loyalty to the Glorious, a sense of intimacy with his surroundings, pictures of machines and—nothing clear, except—

A harsh voice broke his amazed blur of thought. "Come on out of there, you damned slow poke!"

A square, heavy, brutal face was peering into the open door, a big, square-built young man with a thick neck, a boxer's flat nose, and unpleasant blue eyes.

Garson lay quite still. It was not that he intended to disobey. All his reason urged instant, automatic obedience until he could estimate the astounding things that had happened.

What held him there, every muscle stiff, was a new, tremendous fact that grew, not out of the meaning of the man's words, but out of the words themselves.

The language was not English. Yet he had understood—every word!

The sudden squint of impatient rage that flushed the coarse face peering in at him brought life to Garson's muscles. He scrambled forward, but it was the man's truck-driver hands that actually pulled him clear and deposited him with a jarring casualness face downward on the paved road.

He lay there for an electric instant, tense with an anger that congealed reluctantly before the thought: He dare not get mad. Or act the fool!

The terrific reality was that something had gone wrong. Somehow the machine hadn't worked all the way, and if he was crazy enough to wreck the great chance that offered—

He stood up slowly, wondering how an automaton, a depersonalized human being, should look and act.

"This way, damn you," said that bullying voice from behind him. "You're in the army now."

Satisfaction came into the voice: "Well, you're the last for me today. I'll get you fellows to the front, and then—"

"This way" led to a dispirited-looking group of men, about a hundred of them, who stood in two rows alongside a great, gloomy, dirty building.

He walked stolidly to the end of the rear line, and for the first time realized how surprisingly straight the formation of men were holding their lines, in spite of their dulled appearance.

"All right, all right," bellowed the square-jawed young man. "Let's get going. You've got some hard fighting ahead of you before this day and night are over—"

The contemptuous thought came to Garson, as he stared at the leader: this, then, was the type *they* picked for nonrecalcitrant training: the ignorant, blatant, amoral, sensual pigmen. No wonder he himself had been rejected by the Observer.

His eyes narrowed to slits as he watched the line of dead-alive men walk by him in perfect rhythm; he fell in step, his mind deliberately slow and ice-cold, cautiously exploring the strange knowledge in his brain that didn't fit with his—freedom!

That didn't fit with anything! A little group of sentences that kept repeating inside him:

"The great time-energy barrier is being built in Delpa. It must not be completed, for it will destroy the Universe. Prepare to do your part in its destruction; try to tell the Planetarians, but take no unnecessary risks. To stay alive, to tell the Planetarians: those are your immediate purposes. The time-energy barriers must not— NOT—

Funny, he thought, funny! He squeezed the crazy thing out of his consciousness.

No trucks came gliding up to transport them; no streetcar whispered along in some superdevelopment of street-railway service; there was simply no machinery, nothing but those narrow avenues with their gray, side-walkless length, like back alleys.

They walked to war; and it was like being in a dead, old, deserted city —deserted except for the straggle of short, thick, slow, stolid men and women who plodded heavily by, unsmiling, without so much as a side glance. As if they were but the pitiful, primitive remnant of a once-great race, and this city the proud monument to— No!

Garson smiled wryly. Of all the fools, getting romantic about this monstrosity of a city. All too evident it was, even without Dr. Lell's words as a reminder, that every narrow, dirty street, every squalid building had been erected—to be what it was.

And the sooner he got out of the place, and delivered to the Planetarians the queer, inexplicable message about the great time-energy barrier—

With a half shudder, with deliberate abruptness, he cut the thought. Damn it, he'd have to be careful. If one of the Glorious should happen to be around, and accidentally catch the free thought of what was supposed to be an automaton—next time there'd be no mistake.

Tramp, tramp, tramp! The pavement echoed with the strange lifeless hollowness of a ghost city; and the tremendous thought came that he was here centuries, perhaps millenniums, into the future. What an awful realization to think that Norma, poor, persecuted, enslaved Norma, whose despairing face he had seen little more than an hour ago, was actually dead and buried in the dim ages of the long ago.

And yet she was alive. Those six hundred billion bodies per minute of hers were somewhere in space and time, alive because the great time energy followed its casual, cosmic course of endless repetition, because life was but an accident as purposeless as the immeasurable energy that plunged grandly on into the unknown night that must be—somewhere!

Tramp, tramp— On and on, and his thought was a rhythm to the march— With an ugly start he came out of his reverie, and instantly grew abnormally aware of the nearness of the red haze in the sky ahead. Why, it wouldn't take ten minutes now, and they'd be *there!*

Machines glinted in the slanting rays of the warm, golden, sinking sun; machines that moved and—fought! A sick thrill struck Garson, the first shock of realization that this—this tiny segment of the battle of the ages was real, and near, and deadly.

Up there, every minute men were dying miserably for a cause their depersonalized minds did not even comprehend. Up there, too, was infinitesimal victory for the Planetarians, and a small, stinging measure of defeat for the Glorious. Forty feet a day, Dr. Lell had said.

Forty feet of city conquered every day. What a murderous war of attrition, what a bankruptcy of strategy. Or was it the ultimate nullification of the role of military genius, in that each side knew and practiced every rule of military science without error?—and the forty feet was simply the inevitable mathematical outcome of the difference in the potential in striking power of the two forces.

Forty feet a day. In a blaze of wonder, Garson stood finally with his troop a hundred yards from that unnatural battle front. Like a robot he stood stiffly among those robot men, but his eyes and mind fed in undiminished fascination at the deadly mechanical routine that was the offense and defense.

The Planetarians had seven major machines, and there were at least half a hundred tiny, swift, glittering craft as escort for each of the great— battleships! That was it: battleships and destroyers.

Against them, the Glorious had only destroyers, a host of darting, shining, torpedo-shaped craft that hugged the ground, and fought in an endlessly repeated, complicated maneuver.

Maneuver against maneuver! An intricate chess game—it *was* a game, an incredibly involved game whose purpose and method seemed to quiver just beyond the reach of his reason.

Everything revolved around the battleships. In some way they must be protected from energy guns, because no attempt was made to use anything like that. Somehow. too, cannon must be useless against them. There was none in sight, no attempt to hurtle great gobs of metal either at the machines or—by the Planetarians at the more than a hundred troops like his own, who stood at stiff attention so close to the front, so bunched that a few superexplosive shells of the future would have smashed them all.

Nothing but the battleships and the destroyers!

The battleships moved forward and backward and forward and backward and in and out, intertwining among themselves; and the destroyers of the Glorious darted in when the battleships came forward, and hung back when the battleships retreated; and always the destroyers of the Planetarians were gliding in to intercept the destroyers of the Glorious; and as the sun sank in a blaze of red beyond the green hills to the west, the battleships in their farthest forward thrust were feet closer than they had been at the beginning; and the sharply delineated red line of haze, that *must* be the point where the time-energy barrier was neutralized, was no longer lying athwart a shattered slab of rock—but on the ground feet nearer.

That was it. The battleships somehow forced the time-energy barrier to be withdrawn. Obviously, it would only be withdrawn to save it from a worse fate, perhaps from a complete neutralization over a wide front. And so a city was being won, inch by inch, foot by foot, street by street— only the intricate evolution of the battle, the why of that almost immeasurably slow victory, was as great a mystery as ever.

The grim thought came: If the odd, tremendous message that had come into his brain in that out-of-order depersonalizing machine was true, then the final victory would never come in time. Long before the forty-foot-a-day conquerors had gained the prize that was Delpa, the secret, super, time-energy barrier would be completed; and the devilish spirit of war would at last have won its senseless goal—complete elimination of the human race and all its works.

Night fell, but a glare of searchlights replaced the sun, and that fantastic battle raged on. No one aimed a gun or a weapon at the lights; each side concentrated with that strange, deadly intentness on its part of that intricate, murderous game; and troop after troop dissolved into the ravenous, incredible conflagration.

Death came simply to the automatons. Each in turn crowded into one of the torpedo-shaped destroyers; and knowing—as he did—from the depersonalizing machine, that the tiny, man-sized tank was operated by thought control, flashed out into battle line.

Sometimes the end came swiftly, sometimes it was delayed, but sooner or later there was metallic contact with the enemy; and that was all that was needed. Instantly, the machine would twist and race toward the line of waiting men; the next victim would drag out the corpse, crawl in himself and—

There were variations. Machines clashed with the enemy and died with their drivers; or darted with frantic aimlessness, out of control. Always, swift, metallic scavengers raced from both sides to capture the prize; and sometimes the Planetarians succeeded, sometimes the Glorious.

Garson counted: one, two, three—less than four hundred men ahead of him—and the realization of how close his turn was brought the perspiration coldly to his face. Minutes! Damn it, *damn it,* he had to solve the rules of this battle, or go in there, without plan, without hope.

Seven battleships, scores of destroyers to each battleship and all acting as one unit in one involved maneuver and—

And, by heaven, he had a part of the answer. *One* unit. Not seven battleships out there, but one in the form of seven. One superneutralizing machine in its seven-dimensional maneuver. No wonder he had been unable to follow the intertwinings of those monsters with each other, the retreats, the advances. Mathematicians of the twentieth century could only solve easily problems with four equations. Here was a problem with seven; and the general staff of the Glorious could never be anything but a step behind in their solution—and that step cost them forty feet a day—

His turn! He crept into the casing of the torpedo cycle; and it was smaller even than he had thought. The machine fitted him almost like a glove. Effortlessly, it glided forward, too smoothly, too willingly, into that dazzle of searchlights, into that maelstrom of machines.

One contact, he thought, one contact with an enemy meant death; and his plan of breaking through was as vague as his understanding of how a seven-dimensional maneuver actually worked.

Amazed wonder came that he was even letting himself hope.

Norma began to notice the difference, a strange, vibrant, flamelike quality within herself, a rich, warm aliveness, like an electric wire quiescent with latent force tremendous— It was utterly different, alien, as new as life returning to a dead body. Only it was added life to the life that had always existed within her.

Physically, she was still crouching there tautly, her legs twisted under her, vision still blinded; and the hard pain of the metal beneath her was an unchanged pressure against the bone and muscle of her knees. But—

Along every nerve that wonderful sense of well-being, of strange, abnormal power quivered and grew—and yielded abruptly to the violence of the thought that flashed into her mind:

Where was she? What had happened? What—

The thought snapped in the middle because, amazingly, an alienness— intruded into it, another thought, not out of her own mind, not even directed at her, not—human!

"—Tentacle 2731 reporting to the Observer. A warning light has flashed on the . . . (meaningless) . . . xxxxx time machine. Action!"

The answer came instantly, coldly:

"An intruder—on top of the primary time machine. Warning from, and to, Dr. Lell's section. Tentacle 2731, go at once—destroy intruder. Action!"

There were stunning immensities in those hard wisps of message and answering message, that echoed back along the dim corridors of her mind.

The stupefying fact that she had effortlessly intercepted thought waves momentarily blotted out the immediacy of the greater fact that every chilling word of that death threat was meant for her. But then—

Before that colossal menace, even the knowledge of where she was came with a quiet unobtrusiveness, like a minor harmony in a clash of major discord. Her present location was only too obvious. Twisting the key the way she had, had sent her hurtling through time to the age of the Glorious, to the primary-time machine, where fantastic things called tentacles and observers guarded—

If only she could see! She *must* see, or she was lost before she could begin to hope.

Frantically, she strained against the blackness that lay so tight against her eyes and—

She could see!

It was as simple as that. One instant, blindness! The next, the urge to see. And then, sight, complete, without preliminary blur, like opening her eyes after a quiet sleep.

The simplicity part of it was crowded out of her brain by a whirling confusion of impression. There were two swift thoughts that clung—the brief wonder at the way sight had come back to her, merely from the wish that it would—and a flashing memory of the face that had floated at her out of the blackness of time. *With this great moment you enter upon your power and your purpose*—

The picture, all connecting thoughts, fled. She saw that she was in a room, a vast, doomed room, and that she was on top of a gigantic machine. There were transparent walls! and beyond—

Her mind and vision leaped beyond the room, through the transparent walls. There was something out there, something tremendous! A shimmering, roseate fire, like a greater dome that covered the near sky and hid the night universe beyond.

The effort of staring tired her. Her gaze came down out of the sky; and, back in the room, she saw that all the transparent wall that faced her was broken into a senseless pattern of small balconies, each mounting glittering, strangely menacing machinery—weapons!

So many weapons—for what?

With a jar that shocked her brain, the thought disintegrated. She stared in blank horror at a long, thick, tube-shaped metal thing that floated up from below the rim of the time machine. A score of gleaming, insectlike facets seemed to glare at her.

"Tentacle 2731—destroy the intruder—"

"No!" It was her own desperate negation, product of pure devastating panic, product of newness, of a hideous, alien threat that wrecked on the instant all the bravery that had made her experiment with the key in the first place.

Her mind spun like a dizzily spinning wheel, her body shrank from the sudden, abnormal fear that this—metal—would spray her with some incredible flame weapon before she could think, before she could turn or run, or even move!

Of all her pride and accumulated courage, there remained only enough to bring a spasm of shame at the words that burst senselessly from her lips:

"No! No! You can't! Go away—go back—where you came from! Go—"

She stopped, blinked, and stared wildly. The thing was gone!

The reality of that had scarcely touched her when a crash sounded. It came from beyond and below the rim of the machine. Quite instinctively, Norma ran forward to peer down.

The hundred-foot, precipicelike slope of metal time machine that greeted her startled gaze made her draw back with a gasp, but instantly she was creeping forward again, more cautiously, but with utter fascination to see again what that first brief glimpse had revealed.

And there it was, on the distant floor, the tube-shaped thing. Even as she watched, hope building up in her, there came a weak impulse of alien thought:

"Tentacle 2731 reporting—difficulty. Female human using Insel mind rays—power 100—no further action possible by this unit—incapacitation 74 mechanical—"

Hope grew gigantic, and there was a wild burst of surmise and a desperate, wondering half belief in the miracle that was taking place. She was doing this; her wish had brought instant return of sight, her despairing thought had sent the tentacle thing crashing to mechanical ruin. Insel mind rays, power 100! Why, it meant—it could mean—

The leaping thought sagged. One of a series of doors in the wall facing her opened, and a tall man emerged hurriedly. Quite automatically, she pressed back, tried to lie flat on the metal, out of sight; but it seemed to her those familiar, sardonic eyes were staring straight up at her. Dr. Lell's hard, tight, superbly confident thought came then like a succession of battering blows against the crumbling structure of her hope:

"This is a repetition of the x time and space manipulation. Fortunately, the transformation center this seventeenth time is a Miss Norma Matheson, who is utterly incapable, mathematically, of using the power at her disposal. She must be kept confused, kept on the run. The solution to her swift destruction is a concentration of forces of the third order, nonmechanical, according to Plan A4. Action!"

"Action immediate!" came the cold, distinctive thought of the Observer.

That was like death itself. Hope abandoned her; she lay flat on that flat metal, her mind blank, and not a quiver of strength in her body.

A minute passed; and that seemed an immense time. So much that the swift form of her thought had time to change, to harden. Fear faded like a dream; and then came returning awareness of that curious, wonderful sense of power.

She stood up, and the way her legs trembled with the effort brought the automatic memory of the way she had regained her vision. She thought tensely, consciously:

"No more physical weakness. Every muscle, every nerve, every organ of my body must function perfectly from now on and—"

A queer thrill cut the thought. It seemed to start at her toes, and sweep up, a delicious sense of warmth, like an all-over blush.

And the weakness was gone.

She stood for a moment, fascinated, utterly absorbed by this—toy! And hesitated to try it too far. Yet—

She thought: "No more mental weakness, no confusion; my brain must function with all the logic of which I am capable!"

It was strange, and not altogether satisfactory, what happened then. Her mind seemed to come to a dead stop. For an instant the blankness was complete; and then, a single, simple idea came into it:

Danger! For her there was nothing but danger and the getting out of that danger. Find the key. Go back to 1944. Get out of this world of Dr. Lell, and gain time to solve the secrets of the mighty power centralized in her.

She jerked, as a lean, yard-long flame struck the metal beside her, and caromed away toward the ceiling. She watched it bounce from the ceiling, out of sight beyond the precipicelike edge of the machine. It must have struck the floor, but instantly it was in sight again, leaping toward the ceiling with undiminished ardor.

Up, down, up, down, up, it went as she watched; then abruptly it lost momentum, and collapsed like an empty flaming sack toward the floor, out of her line of vision.

A second streamer of flame soared up from where Dr. Lell had been heading when last she saw him. It struck the ceiling, and like an elongated billiard ball, darted down—and this time she was ready for it. Her brain reached out: *Stop! Whatever the energy that drives you, it is powerless against me. Stop!*

The flame missed her right hand by inches, and soared on up to the ceiling; and from below, strong and clear and satirical, came the voice, or was it the thought of Dr. Lell:

"My dear Miss Matheson, that's the first of the third-order energies, quite beyond your control. And have you noticed that your mind isn't quite so cool as you ordered it to be. The truth is that, though you have power unlimited, you can only use it when you understand the forces involved, either consciously or unconsciously. Most people have a reasonably clear picture of their bodily processes, which is why your body reacted so favorably, but your brain—its secrets are largely beyond your understanding.

"As for the key"—there was laughter in the words—"you seem to have forgotten it is geared to the time machine. The Observer's first act was to switch it back to 1944. Accordingly, I can promise you death—"

Her brain remained calm; her body steady, unaffected. No blood surged to her head; there was the barest quickening of her heartbeat; her hands clenched with the tense knowledge that she must act faster, think faster—

If only Jack Garson were here, with his science, his swift, logical brain—

Strangely, then, she could feel her mind slipping out of her control, like sand between her fingers. Her body remained untroubled, untouched, but her mind was suddenly gliding down, down, into dark depths.

Terror came abruptly, as a score of flame streamers leaped into sight toward the ceiling, bounced and—

"Jack, Jack, help me! I need you! Oh, Jack, come—" The slow seconds brought no answer; and the urgency of her need brought no answer; and the urgency of her need could brook no waiting. "Back home," she thought. "I've got to get back home, back to 1944, back—"

Her body twanged. There was blackness, and a horrible sensation of falling.

The blow of the fall was not hard; and that unaffected, almost indestructible body of hers took the shock in a flash of pain-absorbing power. Awareness came of a floor with a rug on it. A vague light directly in front of her lost its distortion and became—a window!

Her own apartment! Like a young tigress she scrambled to her feet; and then poised motionless with dismay as the old, familiar, subtle vibration thrilled its intimate way along her nerves. The machine! The machine was in the room below and working!

Her will to safety had sent her back to her own time, but her call to Jack Garson had passed unheeded, unheard; and here she was, alone with only a strange unwieldy power to help her against the gathering might of the enemy.

And that was her hope, that it was only gathering! Even Dr. Lell must have time to transport his forces. If she could get out of this building, use her power to carry her, as it had already borne her from the time and space of the future—

Carry her where? There was only one other place she could think of: To the hotel! To the hotel room from where she had launched herself with the key.

It wasn't death that came then, but a blow so hard that she was sobbing bitterly with the pain even as her mind yielded reluctantly to unconsciousness; even as she was realizing in stark dismay that she had struck the wall of her apartment and this power she possessed had been betrayed once again by her inability to handle it. And now Dr. Lell would have time to do everything necessary—

Blackness came—

There was a memory in Garson of the night, and of the rushing machine that had carried him, the wonderful little metal thing that darted and twisted far to the left, as close to the red haze of the time-energy barrier as he dared to go—and not a machine had followed him. In seconds he was through the blazing gap, out of Delpa, safe from Dr. Lell —only something had struck at him then, a crushing blow—

He came out of sleep without pain, and with no sense of urgency. Drowsily, he lay, parading before his mind the things that had happened; and the comfortable realization came that he must be safe or he wouldn't be—like this!

There were things to do, of course. He must transmit the information to the Planetarians that they must conquer Delpa more swiftly, that final victory waited nowhere but in Delpa. And then, somehow, he must persuade them to let him return to 1941, to Norma and—

For a while he lay peacefully, his eyes open, gazing thoughtfully at a gray ceiling. From nearby, a man's voice said:

"There's no use expecting it."

Garson turned his head, his first alert movement. A row of hospital-like cots stretched there, other rows beyond. From the nearest bed, a pair of fine, bright, cheerful eyes stared at him. The man lay with his head crotched in a bunched, badly rumpled pillow. He said:

"Expecting to feel surprised, I mean. You won't. You've been conditioned into recovering on a gradual scale, no excitement, no hysteria, nothing that will upset you. The doctors, though Planetarian trained, are all men of the past; and up to a day ago, they pronounced you—"

Quite amazingly, the man paused; his brown eyes darkened in frown, then he smiled with an equally amazing grimness:

"I nearly said too much there. Actually you may be strong enough to stand any shock now, conditioning or no. But the fact is you'll learn the hard truths of your predicament soon enough, without getting yourself into a nervous state now. Here's a preliminary warning: Toughen your mind for bad news."

Strangely, he felt only the dimmest curiosity, and no sense of alarm at all. After what Dr. Lell had said directly and by implication of the Planetarians, no danger here could surpass what he had already been through. The only emotion he could sense within himself had to do with his double purpose of rescuing Norma from the recruiting station and—

He said aloud: "If I should be asleep the next time a doctor or Planetarian comes in, will you waken me? I've got something to tell them."

The odd, mirthless smile of the other made Garson frown. His voice was almost sharp, as he asked:

"What's the matter?"

The stranger shook his head half pityingly: "I've been twenty-seven days in this stage, and I've never seen a Planetarian. As for telling anyone on the Planetarian side anything, I've already told you to expect bad news. I know you have a message to deliver. I even know from Dra Derrel what it is, but don't ask me how he found out. All I can say is, you'll have to forget about delivering any message to anyone. Incidentally, my name is Mairphy—Edard Mairphy."

Garson lay quite still. For the moment he wasn't interested in names or the mystery of how they knew his message. There was a vague thrill of worry in the back of his mind. Every word this gentle-faced, gentle-voiced young man had spoken was packed with dark, tremendous implications.

He stared at Mairphy, but there was only the frank, open face, the friendly, half-grim smile, the careless wisp of bright, brown hair coming down over one temple—nothing at all of danger.

Besides, where could any danger be coming from? From the Planetarians?

That was ridiculous. Regardless of their shortcomings, the Planetarians were the one race of this "time" that must be supported. They might have curious, even difficult habits, but the other side was evil almost beyond imagination. Between them, there was no question of choice.

His course was simple. As soon as he was allowed to get up—and he felt perfectly well now—he would set out to make contact with a Planetarian in a reasonable persistent manner. The whole affair was beginning to show unpleasant, puzzling aspects, but—

He grew aware of Mairphy's voice: "The warning is all I'll say on that subject for the time being. There's something else, though. Do you think you'll be able to get up in about an hour? I mean, do you feel all right?"

Garson nodded, puzzled: "I think so. Why?"

"We'll be passing the Moon about then, and I understand it's a sight worth—"

"*What?*"

Mairphy was staring at him. He said slowly: "I forgot. I was so busy not telling you about our main danger, it didn't occur to me that you were unconscious when we started."

He shrugged. "Well, we're on our way to Venus; and even if there was nothing else, the cards would be stacked against you by that fact alone. There are no Planetarians aboard this ship, only human beings out of the past and tentacles of the Observer. There's not a chance in the world of you speaking to any of them because—"

He stopped; then: "There I nearly went again, damn it! I'll let out the devilish truth yet, before you ought to hear it."

Garson scarcely heard. The shock wouldn't go away. He lay in a daze of wonder, overwhelmed by the incredible fact that he was in space. *In space!*

He felt suddenly outmaneuvered. Even the events he knew about were abruptly a million miles ahead of his plans.

At first, the very idea was incredibly shocking. Pain pulsed in his temples from the wave of blood that charged there. He sat, rigidly, awkwardly, in the bed; and, finally, in a chocked voice he said:

"How long will it take to get to Venus?"

"Ten days, I believe!"

Very cautiously, Garson allowed the figures to penetrate. Hope surged through him. It wasn't so bad as his first despairing thought had pictured it. Ten days to get there, ten days to persuade someone to let a Planetarian have a glimpse of his mind, ten days to get back to Earth.

A month! He frowned. Actually, that wasn't so good. Wars had been lost, great empires collapsed in less time than that. Yet, how could he deliver his message—on a spaceship. Venus-bound? Courses of initial action suggested themselves, but—

He said in a troubled tone. "If I was back in 1941, at this point I would try to see the captain of the ship. But you've made me doubt that normal procedures apply on a Planetarian space liner. Frankly, what are my chances?"

He saw that the young man was grim. "Exactly none!" Mairphy replied. "This is no joke, Garson. As I said before, Derrel knows and is interested in your message, don't ask me how or what or when. He was a political leader in his own age, and he's a marvel at mechanics, but, according to him, he knows only the normal, everyday things of his life. You'll have to get used to the idea of being in with a bunch of men from past ages, some queer ducks among them, Derrel the queerest of them all.

"But forget that! Just remember that you're on a spaceship in an age so far ahead of your own that there's not even a record of your time in the history books and—"

Abruptly, that was what got him. Garson lay back, breathlessly still, dazzled once again by his strange, tremendous environment, straining for impression. But there was no sense of movement, no abnormality at all. The world was quiet; the room seemed like an unusually large dormitory in a hospital.

After a moment of tenseness, he allowed his body to relax, and the full, rich flood of thought to flow in. In that eager tide, the danger to which Mairphy had referred was like a figment of imagination, a dim, darkling shadow in remoteness.

There was only the wonder, only Venus and—this silent, swift-plunging spaceship.

Venus! He let the word roll around in his mind, and it was like rich, intellectual food, luscious beyond reason to a mind shaped and trained as was his.

Venus— For ages the dreams of men had reached longingly into the skies, immeasurably fascinated by the mind-staggering fact of other worlds as vast as their own; continents, seas, rivers, treasure beyond estimate.

And now for him there was to be glittering reality. Before that fact, other urgencies faded. Norma must be rescued, of course; the strange message delivered; but if it was to be his destiny to remain in this world till the end of war, then he could ask nothing more of those years than this glowing sense of adventure, this shining opportunity to learn and see and know in a scientist's heaven.

He grew aware that Mairphy was speaking: "You know"—the young man's voice was thoughtful—"it's just possible that it might be a good idea if you did try to see the captain. I'll have to speak to Derrel before any further action is taken and—"

Garson sighed wearily. He felt suddenly genuinely exhausted, mentally and physically, by the twisting courses of events.

"Look," he said, "a minute ago you stated it was absolutely impossible for me to see the captain; now it seems it might be a good idea and so the impossible becomes poss—"

A sound interrupted his words, a curious hissing sound that seemed to press at him. With a start he saw that men were climbing out of bed, groups that had been standing in quiet conversation were breaking up. In a minute, except for some three dozen who had not stirred from their beds, the manpower of that great room had emptied through a far door. As the door closed, Mairphy's tense voice stabbed at him:

"Quick! Help me out of bed and into my wheel chair. Damn this game leg of mine, but I've got to see Derrel. The attack must not take place until you've tried to see the captain. Quick, man!"

"Attack!" Garson began, then with an effort, caught himself. Forcing coolness through the shock that was gathering in his system, he lay back; he said in a voice that teetered on the edge of tremble:

"I'll help you when you tell me what all this is about. Start talking! Fast!"

Mairphy sighed: "The whole thing's really very simple. They herded together a bunch of skeptics—that's us; it means simply men who know they are in another age, and aren't superstitious about it, always potential explosive, as the Planetarians well understood. But what they didn't realize was that Derrel was what he was.

"The mutiny was only partially successful. We got the control room, the engine room, but only one of the arsenals. The worst thing was that one of the tentacles escaped out trap, which means that the Observer Machine has been informed, and that battleships have already been dispatched after us.

"Unless we can gain full control fast, we'll be crushed; and the whole bunch of us will be executed out of hand."

Mairphy finished with a bleak smile: "That includes you and every person in this room, lame, sick or innocent. The Planetarians leave the details of running their world in the hands of a monster machine called the Observer; and the Observer is mercilessly logical.

"That's what I meant by bad news. All of us are committed to victory or to death—and now, quick, let me get to Derrel, and stop this attack!"

His mind felt a swollen, painful thing with the questions that quivered there: skeptics—tentacles—mutiny— Good heavens!

It was not until after Mairphy's power-driven wheel chair had vanished through the door that had swallowed the men that he realized how weary he was. He lay down on the bed, and there didn't seem to be a drop of emotion in him. He was thinking, a slow, flat, gray thought, of the part of the message that had come to him in the depersonalizing machine, the solemn admonishment: "—Take no unnecessary risks—*stay alive!*"

What a chance!

The Moon floated majestically against the backdrop of black space, a great globe of light that grew and grew. For a solid hour it clung to size, but at last it began to retreat into distance.

It was the gathering immensity of that distance that brought to Garson a sudden empty sense, a dark consciousness that he was again a tiny pawn in this gigantic struggle of gigantic forces.

He watched until the glowing sphere of Moon was a shadowy, pea-sized light half hidden by the dominating ball of fire that was the Earth. His immediate purpose was already a waxing shape in his mind, as he turned to stare down at Mairphy in his wheel chair; it struck him there were lines of fatigue around the other's eyes; he said:

"And now that the attack has been called off, I'd like to meet this mysterious Derrel. After which you'd better go straight to sleep."

The younger man drooped. "Help me to my bed, will you?"

From the bed, Mairphy smiled wanly. "Apparently, I'm the invalid, not you. The paralyzer certainly did you no real harm, but the energy chopper made a pretty job of my right leg. By the way, I'll introduce you to Derrel when I wake up."

His slow, deep breathing came as a distinct shock to Garson. He felt deserted, at a loss for action, and finally annoyed at the way he had come to depend on the company of another man.

For a while, he wandered around the room, half aimlessly, half in search of the extraordinary Derrel. But gradually his mind was drawn from that undetermined purpose, as the men, the incredible men, grew into his consciousness.

They swaggered, these chaps. When they stood, they leaned with casual grace, thumbs nonchalantly tucked into belts or into the the armpits of strangely designed vests. Not more than half a dozen of that bold, vigorous-looking crew seemed to be the introvert, studious type.

Here were men of the past, adventurers, soldiers of fortune, who had mutinied as easily as, under slightly different circumstances, they might have decided to fight for, instead of against, their captors.

Bad psychology on the part of the Planetarians?

Impossible because they were perfectionists in the art.

The explanation, of course, was that an intelligence and ability as great as their own, or nearly as great, had entered the scene unknown to them, and easily duped the men of the past who operated the spaceship.

Derrel!

The whole thing was strangely, breathlessly exciting, a glittering facet of the full, violent aliveness of the life that had raged over the Earth through the ages; here were men come full grown out of their own times, loving life, yet by their casual, desperate attempt at mutiny proving that they were not remotely afraid of death.

One man was the responsible, the activating force and—

Three times Garson was sure that he had picked out Derrel, but each time he changed his mind before actually approaching the stranger.

It was only gradually that he grew aware of a lank man. The first coherent picture he had was of a tall, gawky man with a long face that was hollow-cheeked. The fellow was dressed casually in a gray shirt and gray trousers. Except for the cleanness of the clothes, he could have stepped out of a 1936 dust-bowl farmhouse.

The man half stood, half leaned, awkwardly against the side of one of the hospital-type beds, and he said nothing. Yet, somehow, he was the center of the group that surrounded him. The leader!

After a moment Garson saw that the other was surreptitiously studying him; and that was all he needed. Quite frankly, quite boldly, he surveyed the man. Before that searching gaze, the deceptive, farmerish appearance of the other dissolved like dark fog in a bright sun.

The hollow cheeks showed suddenly as a natural strength that distorted the almost abnormal strength of that face. The line of jaw ceased to be merely framework supporting the chin, showed instead in all its grim hardness, like the blunt edge of an anvil, not too prominently thrust forward. The nose—

At that point somebody addressed the man as Mr. Derrel; and it was as if Derrel had been waiting for the words as for a signal.

He stepped forward; he said in the calmest voice Garson had ever heard:

"Professor Garson, do you mind if I speak to you"—he motioned forcefully yet vaguely—"over there?"

Garson was amazed to find himself hesitating. For nearly an hour he had had the purpose of finding this man, but now—it was simply not in his nature to yield readily to the leadership of others. It struck him sharply that even to agree to Derrel's simple request was to place himself, somehow, subtly under the man's domination.

Their eyes met, his own hard with thought, Derrel's at first expressionless, then smiling. The smile touched his face and lighted it in astounding fashion. His entire countenance seemed to change; briefly, his personality was like a flame that burned away opposition.

Garson was startled to hear himself say: "Why, yes, what is it you wish?"

The answer was cool and tremendous: "You have received a warning message, but you need look no further for its source. I am Dra Derrel of the Wizard race of Lin. My people are fighting under great difficulties to save a universe threatened by a war whose weapons are based on the time energy itself."

"Just a minute!" Garson's voice was harsh in his own ears. "Are you trying to tell me you . . . your people sent that message?"

"I am!" The man's face was almost gray-steel in color. "And to explain that our position is now so dangerous that your own suggestion that you see Captain Gurradin has become the most important necessity and the best plan—"

Strangely, it was that on which his mind fastened, not the revelation, but the mind picture of himself leaving the placid security of this room, delivering himself into the ruthless clutches of men of some other, more merciless past than his own—and to tentacles—

Like a monstrous shadow overhanging every other emotion, the dark realization came that the law of averages would not permit him to face death again without—death!

Slowly, the other thought—Derrel's revelation—began to intrude. He examined it, at first half puzzled that it continued to exist in his mind; somehow, it wasn't really adequate, and certainly far from satisfactory as an explanation of all that had happened.

—A message delivered into the black narrowness of a Glorious depersonalizing machine, hurtled across distance, through a web of Glorious defenses from—

Derrel!

Garson frowned, his dissatisfaction growing by the second. He stared at the man from slitted eyes; and saw that the other was standing in that peculiar easy-awkward posture of his, gazing at him coolly as if—the impression was a distinct one—as if waiting patiently for his considered reaction. That was oddly reassuring, but it was far, far from being enough. Garson said:

"I can see I've got to be frank, or this thing's going to be all wrong. My angle goes like this: I've been building a picture in my mind, an impossible picture I can see now, of beings with tremendous powers. I thought of them as possibly acting from the future of this future, but, whatever their origin, I had the uttermost confidence that they were super-human, super-Glorious and—"

He stopped because the long-faced man was smiling in twisted fashion. "And now," Derrel said wryly, "the reality does not come up to your expectations. An ordinary man stands before you, and your dreams of god-power interfering in the affairs of men becomes what it always was basically: wishful hallucination!"

"And in its place—what?" Garson questioned coolly.

Derrel took up the words steadily: "In its place is a man who failed to take over a spaceship, and now faces a sordid death himself."

Garson parted his lips to speak, then closed them again, puzzled. There was nothing so far but honesty almost excessive. Still—confession was far from being satisfactory explanation.

Derrel's voice, rich with the first hint of passion the man had shown, beat at him: "Are you sure it was such a great failure? One man manipulating strangers who had no reason to fight—many of them invalids —and winning a partial success against the highly trained crew of a completely mechanized space cruiser, a crew supported by no less than four tentacles of the omniscient Observer."

Stripped as the account was, it brought a vivid fascinating flash of what the reality of that fight must have been. Flesh-and-blood men charging forward in the face of—energy—weapons, dealing and receiving desperate wounds, overwhelming the alert and abundant staff of an armored ship, and four tentacles, whatever they were. Tentacle—a potent, ugly word, inhuman— Nevertheless—

"If you're going to use logic on this," Garson said slowly, "you'll have to put up with my brand for another minute. Why did you go in for mutiny in the first place under such difficult conditions?"

Amazingly, the man's eyes flashed with contemptuous fire. When he spoke, his voice was thick with passion: "Can you reasonably ask for more than the reality, which is that our position is desperate because we took risks? We took risks because"—he paused, as if gathering himself; then his words flamed on—"because I am of the race of Wizards; and we were masters of the Earth of our time because we were bold. As was ever the way with the Wizards, I chose the difficult, the dangerous path; and I tell you that victory with all that it means is not yet beyond our grasp. I—"

In the queerest fashion, the glowing voice died. An intent expression crept into the man's eyes; he tilted his head, as if listening for a remote sound. Garson shook the odd impression out of his mind, and returned to the thoughts that had been gathering while the other was speaking; he said coolly:

"Unfortunately, for all that emotion, I was trained to be a scientist; and I was never taught to accept justification as a substitute for explanation. I—"

It was his turn to fall silent. With startled gaze, he watched the tall, gawky figure stride at top speed along the wall. The Wizard man halted as swiftly as he had started, but now his fingers were working with a strangely frantic speed at a section of the wall.

As Garson came up, the wall slid free; and Derrel, half lowered, half dropped it to the floor. In the hollow space revealed, wires gleamed; and a silver, shining glow point showed. Unhesitatingly, Derrel grasped at the white-hot-looking thing, and jerked. There was a faint flash of fire; and when his hand came away the glow was gone.

Derrel stared at Garson grimly: "Those seeming wires are not wires at all, but a pure energy web, an electron mold that, over a period of about an hour, can mold a weapon where nothing existed before. Tentacles can focus that type of mold anywhere; and the mold itself is indestructible, but up to a certain stage the molded thing can be destroyed."

Garson braced himself instinctively, as the other faced him squarely. Derrel said:

"You can see that, without my special ability to sense energy formations, there would have been surprise tragedy."

"Without you," Garson interjected, "there would have been no mutiny. I'm sorry, but I've got the kind of mind that worries about explanations. So—"

The man gazed at him without hostility; he said finally earnestly: "I know your doubts, but you can see yourself that I must go around examining our rather large territory for further electron-mold manifestations. Briefly, we Wizards are a race of the past who developed a science that enabled us to tap the time ways of the Glorious, though we cannot yet build a time machine. In many ways, we are the superiors of either Planetarians or Glorious. Our mathematics showed us that the time energy could not stand strains beyond a certain point; accordingly we have taken and are taking every possible action to save the Universe, the first and most important necessity being that of establishing a base of operations, preferably a spaceship."

He finished quietly: "For the rest, for the time being you must have faith. Regardless of your doubts, you must go to see the captain; we must win this ship before we are overwhelmed. I leave you now to think it over."

He whirled and strode off; and behind him he left half conviction, half confidence, but—Garson thought wryly—no facts!

What a vague, unsatisfactory basis on which to risk the only life he had!

He found himself straining for sounds, but there was no movement, nothing but a straggle of words that came at him from the other men. The ship itself, the wondrous ship, was quiet. It seemed to be suspended in this remote coign of the Universe; and it at least was not restless. It flashed on in tireless, stupendous flight, but basically it was unhurried, isolated from mechanical necessities, knowing neither doubt nor hope, nor fear nor courage.

Doubt! His brain was a dark opaque mass flecked with the moving lights of thoughts, heavy with the gathering pall of his doubt, knowing finally only one certainty:

With so much at stake, he must find out more about the so-called Wizard of Lin. It would be utterly ridiculous to make some move against the Planetarians, the hope of this war, on the glib say-so of—anyone! But what to do? Where to find out?

The urgent minutes fled. There was the black, incredible vista of space —but no answers offered there. There was lying in bed and staring at the gray ceiling; that was worse. Finally, there was the discovery of the library in a room adjoining the long dormitory; and that held such an immense promise that, for a brief hour, even the sense of urgency faded out of him.

Only gradually did awareness come that the books were a carefully selected collection. At any other time, every word of every page would have held him in thrall, but now now. For a while, with grim good humor, he examined volume after volume to verify his discovery. At last, weary with frustration, he returned to his bed—and saw that Mairphy was awake.

His mind leaped; then he hesitated. It was possible he would have to approach the subject of Derrel warily. He said finally:

"I suppose you've been through the library."

Mairphy shook his head, brown eyes slightly sardonic. "Not that one. But on the basis of the two I have seen, I'll venture to guess they're elementary scientific books, travel books about the planets, but no histories, and nowhere is there a reference to what year this is. They're not even letting us skeptics know that."

Garson cut in almost harshly: "These Planetarians are not such good angels as I thought. In an entirely different, perhaps cleverer way, this ship is organized to press us into their mold just as the Glorious used the deperson—"

He stopped, startled by the hard tenor of his thoughts. Good heavens! At this rate he'd soon work himself into an anti-Planetary fury. Deliberately, he tightened his mind. His job was not to hate, but to ask careful questions about Derrel—and stay alive!

He parted his lips, but before he could speak, Mairphy said: "Oh, the Planetarians are all right. If we hadn't gone in for this damned mutiny, we'd have been treated all right in the long run, provided we kept our mouths shut and conformed."

Garson's mind literally wrenched itself from thought of Derrel. "Mouths shut!" he said. "What do you mean?"

Mairphy laughed mirthlessly: "We're the skeptics who, in a general way, know where we are. The great majority of recruits *don't* know anything except that it's a strange place. For psychological reasons, they've got to feel that they're in perfectly rational surroundings. Their own superstitions provide the solutions.

"A slew of ancient Greeks think they're fighting on the side of Jupiter in the battle of the gods. Religious folks from about four hundred different ignorant ages think for reasons of their own that everything is as it should be. The Lerdite Moralists from the thirtieth century believe this is the war of the Great Machine to control its dissident elements. And the Nelorian Dissenter of the year 7643 to 7699 who— What's the matter?"

Garson couldn't help it. The shock was physical rather than mental. He hadn't, somehow, thought of it when Derrel talked of the Wizards of Lin, but now— His nerves shivered from that casual, stunning array of words. He said finally, shakily:

"Don't mind me. It's those damned dates you've been handing out. I suppose it's really silly to think of time as being a past and a future. It's all there, spread out, six hundred billion earths and universes created every minute."

He drew a deep breath. Damn it, he'd stalled long enough. Any minute, Derrel would be coming back and—

He said stiffly: "What about the Wizards of Lin? I heard somebody use the phrase, and it intrigued me."

"Interesting race," Mairphy commented; and Garson sighed with relief. The man suspected no ulterior motive. He waited tensely, as Mairphy went on: "The Wizards discovered some connection between sex and the mind, which gave them superintellect including mental telepathy. Ruled the Earth for about three hundred years, just before the age of Endless Peace set in. Power politics and all that, violence, great on mechanics, built the first spaceship which, according to description, was as good as any that has ever existed since. Most of their secrets were lost. Those that weren't became the property of a special priest clique whose final destruction is a long story and—"

He paused, frowning thoughtfully, while Garson wondered bleakly how he ought to be taking all this. So far, Derrel's story was substantiated practically word for word. Mairphy's voice cut into his indecision:

"There's a pretty story about how the spaceship was invented. In their final struggle for power, a defeated leader, mad with anxiety about his beautiful wife who had been taken as a mistress by the conqueror, disappeared, returned with the ship, got his wife and his power back; and the Derrel dynasty ruled for a hundred years after that—"

"Derrel!" Garson said. "The Derrel dynasty!"

And that, simply yet devastatingly, was that.

The echo of the shock yielded to time and familiarity, and died— They talked about it in low tones; and their hushed baritones formed a queer, deep-throated background to the measured beat of Garson's thoughts.

He stepped back, finally, as Mairphy eagerly called other men. With bleak detachment, he listened while Mairphy's voice recast itself over and over into the same shape, the same story, though the words and even the tone varied with each telling. Always, however, the reaction of the men was the same—joy! Joy at the certainty of victory! And what did it matter what age they went to afterward?

Garson grew abruptly aware that Mairphy was staring at him sharply. Mairphy said: "What's the matter?"

He felt the weight of other gazes on him, as he shrugged and said:

"All this offers little hope for me. History records that we won this ship. But I have still to confront the captain; and history is silent as to whether I lived or died— Frankly, I consider the message that I received in the Glorious depersonalizing machine more important than ever, and accordingly my life is of more importance than that of anyone else on this ship.

"I repeat, our only certainty is that Derrel escaped with the spaceship. Who else lived, we don't know. Derrel—"

"Yes!" said the calm voice of Derrel behind him. "Yes, Professor Garson."

Garson turned slowly. He had no fixed plan; there was the vaguest intention to undermine Derrel's position; and that had made him stress the uncertainty of any of the men escaping. But it wasn't a plan because— there was the unalterable fact that the ship had gotten away; Derrel had won.

No plan— The only factors in his situation were his own tremendous necessities and the inimical environment in which they existed.

For a long moment, he stared at the gangling body, studied the faint triumph that gleamed in the abnormally long yet distinctive face of the Wizard man. Garson said:

"You can read minds. So it's unnecessary to tell you what's going on. What are your intentions?"

Derrel smiled, the glowing, magnetic smile that Garson had already seen. His agate eyes shone, as he surveyed the circle of men; then he began to speak in a strong, resonant voice. There was command in that voice, and a rich, powerful personality behind it, the voice of a man who had won:

"My first intention is to tell everyone here that we are going to an age that is a treasure house of spoils for bold men. Women, palaces, wealth, power for every man who follows me to the death. You know yourself what a damned, barren world we're in now. No women, never anything for us but the prospect of facing death fighting the Glorious still entrenched on Venus or Earth! And a damned bunch of moralists fighting a war to the finish over some queer idea that men ought or ought not to have birth control. Are you with me?"

It was a stirring, a ringing appeal to basic impulses; and the answer could not have been more satisfactory. A roar of voices, cheers; and finally: "What are we waiting for? Let's get going!"

The faint triumph deepened on Derrel's face as he turned back to Garson. He said softly:

"I'm sorry I lied to you, professor, but it never occurred to me that Mairphy or anybody aboard would know my history. I told you what I did because I had read in your mind some of the purposes that moved your actions. Naturally, I applied the first law of persuasion, and encouraged your hopes and desires."

Garson smiled grimly. The little speech Derrel had just given to the men was a supreme example of the encouragement of hopes and desires, obviously opportunistic, insincere and—reliable only if it served the other's future purposes.

He saw that Derrel was staring at him, and he said:

"You know what's in my mind. Perhaps you can give me some of that easy encouragement you dispense. But, remember, it's got to be based on logic. That includes convincing me that, if I go to the captain, it is to your self-interest to set me down near a Planetarian stronghold, and that furthermore—"

The words, all the air in his lungs, hissed out of his body. There was a hideous sense of pressure. He was jerked off his feet; and he had the flashing, incomprehending vision of two beds passing by beneath him. Then he was falling.

Instinctively, he put out his hand—and took the desperate blow of the crash onto a third bed. He sprawled there, stunned, dismayed, but unhurt and safe.

Safe from what?

He clawed himself erect, and stood swaying, watching other men pick themselves up, becoming aware for the first time of groans, cries of pain and—

A voice exploded into the room from some unseen source: "Control room speaking! Derrel—the damnedest thing has happened. A minute ago, we were thirty million miles from Venus. Now, the planet's just ahead, less than two million miles, plainly visible. What's happened?"

Garson saw Derrel then. The man was lying on his back on the floor, his eyes open, an intent expression on his face. The Wizard man waved aside his extended hands.

"Wait!" Derrel said sharply. "The tentacle aboard this ship has just reported to the Observer on Venus; and is receiving a reply, an explanation of what happened. I'm trying to get it."

His voice changed, became a monotone: "—the seventeenth x space and time manipulations . . . taking place somewhere in the future . . . several years from now. Your spaceship either by accident or design caught in the eddying current in the resulting time storm— Still not the faintest clue to the origin of the mighty powers being exercised. That is all . . . except that battleships are on the way from Venus to help you—"

Derrel stood up; he said quietly: "About what you were saying, Garson, there is no method by which I can prove that I will do anything for you. History records that I lived out my full span of life. Therefore, no self-interest, no danger to the Universe can affect my existence in the past. You'll have to act on the chance that the opportunity offers for us to give you assistance later, and there's no other guarantee I can give."

That at least was straightforward. Only—to the opportunist, even truth was but a means to an end, a means of lulling suspicion. There remained the hard fact that *he* must take the risks.

He said: "Give me five minutes to think it over. You believe, I can see, that I will go."

Derrel nodded: "Both your conscious and subconscious minds are beginning to accept the idea."

There was utterly no premonition in him of the fantastic thing that was going to happen. He thought, a gray, cold thought:

So he was going! In five minutes.

He stood finally at the wall visiplate, staring out at the burnished silver immensity of Venus. The planet, already cast, was expanding visibly, like a balloon being blown up. Only it didn't stop expanding and, unlike an overgrown baloon, it didn't explode.

The tight silence was broken by the tallest of the three handsome Ganellians. The man's words echoed, not Garson's thoughts, but the tenor, the dark mood of them:

"So much beauty proves once again that war is the most completely futile act of man. And the worst of it is that, somewhere in the future of this 'future' there are people who know who won this war; and they're doing nothing—damn them!"

His impulse was to say something, to add once more his own few facts to that fascinating subject. But instead he held his thought hard on the reality of what he must do—in a minute!

Besides, Mairphy had described the Ganellians as emotional weaklings, who had concentrated on beauty, and with whom it was useless to discuss anything. True, he himself had given quite a few passable displays of emotionalism. Nevertheless—

The thought ended, as Mairphy said almost impatiently: "We've discussed all that before, and we're agreed that either the people of the future do not exist at all—which means the Universe was blown up in due course by the Glorious time-energy barrier—or, on the other hand, if the people of the future exist, they're simply older versions of the million-year-old bodies of the Planetarians or Glorious. If they exist, then the Universe was not destroyed, so why should they interfere in the war?

"Finally, we're agreed that it's impossible that the people of the future, whatever their form, are responsible for the message that came through to Professor Garson. If they can get through a message at all, why pick Garson? Why not contact the Planetarians direct? Or even warn the Glorious of the danger!"

Garson said: "Derrel, what is your plan of attack?"

The reply was cool: "I'm not going to tell you that. Reason: at close range a tentacle can read an unwary mind. I want you to concentrate on the thought that your purpose is aboveboard, don't even think of an attack in connection with it. Wait—don't reply! I'm going to speak to Captain Gurradin!"

"Eh!" Garson began, and stopped.

The Wizard man's eyes were closed, his body rigid. He said, half to Garson, half to the others: "A lot of this stuff here works by mind control—" His voice changed: "Captain Gurradin!"

There was a tense silence; then a steel-hard voice literally spat into the room: "Yes!"

Derrel said: "We have an important communication to make. Professor Garson, one of the men who was unconscious when—"

"I know whom you mean!" interrupted that curt voice. "For God's sake, get on with your communication!"

"Not later than the twenty-fourth century," Mairphy whispered to Garson. "Note his reference to God. God was expunged from the dictionary in the 2300s. And is he boiling at this mutiny and what it's done to his prestige!"

It wasn't funny. For all this was going to be real to him. The thought drained; Mairphy became a vague background figure. There was only Derrel and Captain Gurradin; Derrel saying:

"Professor Garson has just become conscious; and he has the answer to the phenomena that carried this spaceship thirty million miles in thirty seconds. He feels that he must see you immediately and communicate his message to the Planetarians at once."

There was a wave of chill laughter: "What fools we'd be to let any of you come here until after the battleships arrive! And that's my answer: He'll have to wait till the battleships arrive."

"His message," said Derrel, "cannot wait. He's coming down now, alone."

"He will be shot on sight."

"I can well imagine," Derrel said scathingly, "what the Planetarians would do to you if he is shot. This has nothing to do with the rest of us. He's coming because he must deliver that message. That is all."

Before Garson could speak, Mairphy said in a distinct voice: "I'm opposed to it. I admit it was my idea in the first place, but I couldn't favor it under such circumstances."

The Wizard man whirled on him. His vibrant voice was a drumming thing as he raged:

"That was a stab in the back to all of us. Here is a man trying to make up his mind on a dangerous mission, and you project a weakening thought. You have said that you come from the stormy period following the 13000 years of Endless Peace. That was after my time, and I know nothing about the age, but it is evident that the softness of the peace period still corroded your people. As a cripple, a weakling, who is not going to do any of the fighting, you will kindly refrain from further advice—to men!"

It could have been devastating, but Mairphy simply shrugged, smiled gently, unaffectedly, at Garson, and said: "I withdraw from the conversation." He finished: "Good luck, friend!"

Derrel, steely-eyed and cold-voiced, said to Garson: "I want to point out one thing. History says we conquered this ship. The only plan we have left revolves around you. Therefore you went to see the captain."

To Garson, to whom logic was the great prime mover, that thought had already come. Besides, his mind had been made up for five minutes.

The second corridor was empty, too; and that strained his tightening nerves to the breaking point. Garson paused stiffly, and wiped the thin line of perspiration from his brow.

And still there was no premonition in him of the incredible ending that was coming—for him; nothing but the deadly actuality of his penetration into the depths of a ship that seemed of endless length, and grew vaster with each step that he took.

A door yielded to his touch; and he peered into a great storeroom, piled with freight, thousands of tons, silent and lifeless as the corridors ahead— He walked on, his mind blanker now, held steady far from the thought of Derrel's intended attack.

He thought vaguely: If Norma could keep from Dr. Lell her action of writing a letter to him, then he could keep any thought from *anything* and—

He was so intent that he didn't see the side corridor till the men burst from it—and had him before he could think of fighting. Not that he intended to fight—

"Bring him in here!" said a hard, familiar voice; and after a moment of peering into the shadows of the receding corridor, he saw a slender man in uniform standing beside—

A tentacle!

That thick, pipe-shaped thing could be nothing else— It rolled forward, as if wheels held it up, and its faceted eyes glared at him. It spoke abruptly in a clear, passionless voice:

"I can catch no thoughts, which is unusual. It presupposes schooling, preparation for mindreading attempts. The Observer advises execution—"

The hard, young man's voice said impatiently: "To hell with the Observer. We can always execute. Bring him in here!"

A door opened; and light splashed out. The door closed behind him; and he saw that the room was no more than a small anteroom to some vaster, darkened room beyond.

But he scarcely noticed that. He was thinking with a stinging shock of fury: The logical Observer advising executions without a hearing. Why, that wasn't reasonable. Damn the stupid Observer!

His fury faded into vast surprise, as he stared at the captain. His first impression had been that the other was a young man, but at this closer view, he looked years older, immeasurably more mature. And, somehow, in his keyed-up state, that observation brought immense astonishment. Amazement ended, as his mind registered the blazing question in Captain Gurradin's eyes. Quite automatically, he launched into his story.

When he had finished, the commander turned has hard face to the tentacle: "Well?" he said.

The tentacle's voice came instantly, coldly: "The Observer recalls to your memory its earlier analysis of this entire situation: The destruction of Tentacles 1601, 2 and 3 and the neutralization of electron molds could only have been accomplished with the assistance of a mind reader. Accordingly, unknown to us, a mind reader was aboard.

"Four races in history solved the secret of the training essential to mental telepathy. Of these, only the Wizards of Lin possessed surpassing mechanical ability—"

It was the eeriness that held his whole mind—at first—the fantastic reality of this *thing* talking and reasoning like a human being. The Observer Machine of the Glorious that he had seen was simply a vast machine, too big to grasp mentally; like some gigantic number, it was there, and that was all. But this—this long, tubular monstrosity with its human voice and—

Eeriness ended in hard, dismaying realization that a creature that could analyze Derrel's identity might actually prove that death was his own logical lot, and that all else was illusion— The dispassionate voice went on:

"Wizard men are bold, cunning and remorseless, and they take no action in an emergency that is not related to their purpose. Therefore, this man's appearance is part of a plot. Therefore destroy him and withdraw from the ship. The battleships will take all further action necessary, without further loss of life."

That was stunning. With a sudden, desperate fear, Garson saw that Captain Gurradin was hesitating. The commander said unhappily: "Damn it, I hate to admit defeat."

"Don't be tedious!" said the tentacle. "Your forces might win, but the battleships *will* win."

Decision came abruptly. "Very well," said the captain curtly, "Willant, de-energize this prisoner and—"

Garson said in a voice that he scarcely recognized, an abnormally steady voice: "What about my story?"

Strangely, there was a moment of silence.

"Your story," the tentacle said finally—and Garson's mind jumped at the realization that it was the tentacle, and not the captain who answered —"your story is rejected by the Observer as illogical. It is impossible that anything went wrong with a Glorious depersonalizing machine. The fact that you were repersonalized after the usual manner on reaching our lines is evidence of your condition, because the repersonalizing machine reported nothing unusual in your case.

"Furthermore, even if it was true, the message you received was stupid, because no known power or military knowledge could force the surrender of Delpa one minute sooner. It is impossible to neutralize a time-energy barrier at more than one point at one time without destroying the neutralizing machine. Consequently, the attack can only be made at one point; the military maneuver being used is the ultimate development of dimensional warfare in a given area of space. And so—"

The words scarcely penetrated, though all the sense strained through, somehow. His mind was like an enormous weight, dragging at one thought, one hope. He said, fighting for calmness now:

"Commander, by your manner to this tentacle and its master, I can see that you have long ago ceased to follow its conclusions literally. Why: because it's inhuman; the Observer is a great reservoir of facts that can be co-ordinated on any subject, *but it is limited by the facts it knows*. It's a machine, and, while it may be logical to destroy me before you leave the ship, you know and I know that it is neither necessary nor just, and what is overwhelmingly more important, it can do no harm to hold me prisoner, and make arrangements for a Planetarian to examine the origin of the message that came to me."

He finished in a quiet, confident tone: "Captain, from what one of the men told me, you're from the 2000s A. D. I'll wager they still had horse races in your day. I'll wager furthermore that no machine could ever understand a man getting a hunch and betting his bottom dollar on a dark horse. You've already been illogical in not shooting me at sight, as you threatened on the communicator; in not leaving the ship as the Observer advised; in letting me talk on here even as the attack on your enemies is beginning—for there is an attack of some kind, and it's got the best brain on this ship behind it. But that's unimportant because you're going to abandon ship.

"What is important is this: You must carry your illogic to its logical conclusion. Retrieve your prestige, depend for once in this barren life here on luck and luck alone—"

The hard eyes did not weaken by a single gleam, but the hard voice spoke words that sounded like purest music:

"Willant, take this prisoner into the lifeboat and—"

It was at that moment it happened. With victory in his hands, the knowledge that more than two years remained before the time-energy barrier would be threatening the Universe, the whole, rich, tremendous joy that he had won—everything. All of that, and unutterable relief, and more, was in his brain when—

A voice came into his mind, strong and clear and as irresistible as living fire, a woman's voice—Norma's!

"Jack! Jack! Help me! I need you! Oh, Jack, come—"

The Universe spun. Abruptly, there was no ship; and he was pitching into a gulf of blackness. Inconceivable distance fell behind him and—just like that—the fall ended.

There was no ship, no earth, no light—

Time must have passed; for slow thought was in him; and the night remained.

No, not night. He could realize that now, for there was time to realize. It was not night; it was—emptiness. Nothingness!

Briefly, the scientist part of his brain grasped at the idea; the possibility of exploring, of examining this nonspace. But there was nothing to examine, nothing in him to examine *with,* no senses that could record or comprehend—nothingness!

Dismay came, a black tidal wave that surged in wild confusion through his being; his brain shrank from the sheer, terrible strain of impression. But, somehow, time passed; the flood of despair streamed out of him. There remained *nothingness!*

Change came abruptly. One instant there was that complete isolation; the next—

A man's voice said matter-of-factly: "This one is a problem. How the devil did he get into the configuration of the upper arc? You'd think he fell in."

"No report of any planes passing over Delpa!" said a second voice. "Better ask the Observer if there's any way of getting him out."

Figuratively, gravely, his mind nodded in agreement to that. He'd have to get out, of course, and—

His brain paused. *Out* of where? Nothingness?

For a long, tense moment, his thought poised over that tremendous question, striving to penetrate the obscure depths of it, that seemed to waver just beyond the reach of his reason. There had been familiar words spoken—

Delpa! An ugly thrill chased through his mind. He wasn't in Delpa, or —he felt abruptly, horribly, sick—*or was he?*

The sickness faded into a hopeless weariness, almost a chaotic dissolution: what did it matter where he was? Once more, he was a complete prisoner of a powerful, dominating environment, prey to forces beyond his lightest control, unable to help Norma, unable to help himself and—

Norma! He frowned mentally, empty of any emotion, unresponsive even to the thought that what had happened implied some enormous and deadly danger—for Norma! There was only the curious, almost incredible way that she had called him; and nightmarishly he had fallen—toward Delpa! Fallen into an insane region called the configuration of the upper arc—

With a start, he realized that the Observer's voice had been speaking for some seconds:

"—it can be finally stated that no plane, no machine of any kind, has flown over Delpa since the seventeenth time and space manipulation four weeks ago. Therefore the man you have discovered in the upper arc is an enigma, whose identity must be solved without delay. Call your commander."

He waited, for there was nothing to think about—at least not at first. Memory came finally that the spaceship had been pulled a million miles a second by the mysterious seventeenth manipulation of time and space; only Derrel had distinctly described it as a repercussion from several years in the future. Now, the Observer talked as if it had happened four weeks ago. Funny!

"Nothing funny about it!" said a fourth voice, a voice so finely pitched, so directed into the stream of his thought that he wondered briefly, blankly, whether he had thought the words, or spoken them himself; then:

"Professor Garson, you are identified. The voice you are hearing is that of a Planetarian who can read your mind."

A Planetarian! Wave on wave of relief made a chaos of his brain. With a dreadful effort, he tried to speak, but there was not even a sense of tongue, or lips, or body, nothing but his mind there in that—emptiness; his mind revolving swiftly, ever more swiftly around the host of things he simply had to know. It was the voice, the cool, sane voice, and the stupendous things it was saying, that gradually quieted the turmoil that racked him:

"The answer to what worries you most is that Miss Matheson was the center of the seventeenth space and time manipulation, the first time a human being has been used.

"The manipulation consisted of withdrawing one unit of the entire Solar System from the main stream without affecting the continuity of the main system; one out of the ten billion a second was swung clear in such a fashion that the time energy with its senseless, limitless power began to recreate it, carrying on two with the same superlative ease as formerly with only one.

"Actually, there are now eighteen solar systems existing roughly parallel to each other—seventeen manipulated creations and the original. My body, however, exists in only two of these because none of the previous sixteen manipulations occurred in my lifetime. Naturally, these two bodies of mine exist in separate worlds and will never again have contact with each other.

"Because she was the center of activity, Norma Matheson has her being in the main solar system only. The reason your physical elements responded to her call is that she now possesses the Insel mind power. Her call merely drew you toward her and not to her, because she lacks both the intelligence and the knowledge necessary to a competent employment of her power. As she did not protect you from intermediate dangers, you fell straight into the local time energy barrier surrounding the city of Delpa, which promptly precipitated you into the time emptiness where you now exist.

"Because of the angle of your fall, it will require an indefinite period for the machines to solve the equation that will release you. Until then, have patience!"

"Wait!" Garson thought urgently. "The great time-energy barrier! It should be completed about now!"

"In two weeks at most," came the cool reply. "We received your story, all right, and transmitted the startling extent of the danger to the Glorious. In their pride and awful determination, they see it merely as a threat to make us surrender—or else! To us, however, the rigidly controlled world they envision means another form of death—a worse form. No blackmail will make us yield, and we have the knowledge that people of the future sent the warning. Therefore—we won!"

There was no time to think that over carefully. Garson projected his next question hurriedly: "Suppose they're not of the future, not of this seventeenth, or is it eighteenth, solar system? What will happen to me if this solar system explodes out of existence?"

The answer was cooler still: "Your position is as unique as that of Miss Matheson. You fell out of the past into the future; you *missed* the manipulation. Therefore you exist, not in two solar systems, but only where you are, attached in a general way to us. Miss Matheson exists only in the main system. There is no way in my knowledge that you two can ever come together again. Accustom yourself to that idea."

That was all. His next thought remained unanswered. Time passed; and his restless spirit drooped. Life grew dim within him. He lay without thought on the great, black deep.

Immense, immeasurable time passed; and he waited, but no voices came to disturb his cosmic grave. Twice, forces tugged at him. The first time he thought painfully:

The time-energy barrier of the Glorious had been completed, and the pressure, the tugging was all he felt of the resulting destruction.

If that had happened, nothing, no one would ever come to save him!

That first tugging, and the thought that went with it, faded into remoteness, succumbed to the weight of the centuries, was lost in the trackless waste of the æons that slid by. And finally, when it was completely forgotten, when every thought had been repeated uncountable times, when every plan of action, every theory, every hope and despair—everything—had been explored to the nth degree—the second tug of pressure came.

A probing sensation it was, as if he was being examined; and finally a flaming, devastatingly powerful thought came at him from—outside!

"I judge it an extrusion from a previous universe, a very low form of life, intelligence .007, unworthy of our attention. It must be registered for its infinitesimal influence and interference with energy flowage—and cast adrift."

Returning consciousness stirred in her body. She felt the sigh that breathed from her lips, as dim awareness came that she must leave this place. But there was not yet enough life in her nerves, no quickening of the co-ordination, the concentration, so necessary to the strange, masochistic power she had been given.

She thought drearily: If only she had gone to a window instead of projecting her weak flesh against an impenetrable wall.

She must get to the breakfast-nook window that overlooked the roof.

She stood at the window, weary with pain, vaguely startled by the swift reaction to her thought. Hope came violently, and the thought that she had been briefly crushed by the hard reality of the wall revived— "Pain— No pain can touch me—"

Behind her, footsteps and other—stranger—sounds crashed on the stairway; behind her, the outer door blinked into ravenous flame; ahead— was the dark, lonely night.

She scrambled to the sill— In her ears was the sound of the things that were swarming into her apartment, forcing her to swift *will*. From the edge of the roof she could see the milling beast men on the sidewalk below, and she could see the street corner a hundred yards away.

Instantly, she was at the corner, standing lightly, painlessly, on the pavement. But there were too many cars for further "power" travel, cars that would make devastatingly hard walls.

As she stood in a passion of uncertainty, one of the cars slowed to a stop; and it was the simplest thing to run forward, open the door and climb in, just as it started forward again. There was a small man crouching in the dimness behind the steering wheel. To him, she said, almost matter-of-factly:

"Those men! They're chasing me!"

A swarm of the beast men wallowed awkwardly into the revealing glow of the corner light, squat, apelike, frightening things. Her driver yelped shrilly: "Good God!" The car accelerated.

Almost instantly, the man was babbling: "Get out! Get out! I can't afford to get mixed up in a thing like this! I've got a family—wife— children—waiting for me this instant at home. Get out!"

He shoved at her with one hand, as if he would somehow push her through the closed door. And, because her brain was utterly pliant, utterly geared to flight, she felt scarcely a quiver of resistance. A neon light a block away caught her gaze, her attention, and fitted completely into her automatic yielding to this man's desire. She said:

"There's a taxi stand. Let me off there—"

By the time she climbed out, tentacles were glittering shapes in the air above the dim street behind her. She struck at them with her mind, but they only sagged back, like recoiling snakes, still under control, obviously prepared now for her power.

In the taxi, her mind reverted briefly in astounded thought: That mouse of a man! Had she actually let him control her, instead of forcing the little pipsqueak of a human to her mighty will—

Will! She must use her will. No tentacle can come within—within— She'd have to be practical. How far had they retreated from her power— half a mile? No tentacle can come within half a mile of this car—

Eagerly, she stared out of the rear window, and her eyes widened as she saw they were a hundred yards away and coming closer. *What was wrong?* In brief, shrinking expectation she waited for the devastating fire of third-order energies; and when it did not come, she thought: This car, it must be made to go faster!

There were other cars ahead, and some passing, but altogether not many. There was room for terrible speeds if she had courage, didn't lose control and if the power would work.

"*Through there,*" she directed, "*and through there and around that corner—*"

She heard shrill yells from the driver, but for a time the very extent of his dismay brought encouragement—that faded bleakly as the tentacles continued their glittering course behind her, sometimes close, sometimes far away, but always relentlessly on her trail, unshakably astute in frustrating every twist of her thought, every turn of the car, every hope, only—

Why didn't they attack?

There was no answer to that, as the long night of flight dragged on, minute by slow minute. Finally, pity touched her for the almost mad driver, who half sat, half swooned behind the steering wheel, held to consciousness and to sanity—she could see in his mind—only by the desperate knowledge that this car was his sole means of livelihood, and nothing else mattered besides that, not even death.

Let him go, she thought. It was sheer cruelty to include him in the fate that was gathering out of the night for her. Let him go, but not yet.

At first, she couldn't have told what the purpose was that quivered in her mind. But it was there, deep and chill and like death itself, and she kept directing the car without knowing exactly where she was going.

Conscious understanding of her unconscious will to death came finally, as she climbed to the ground and saw the glint of river through the trees of a park. She thought then, quite simply:

Here in this park, beside this river, where nearly four years before she had come starving and hopeless to commit suicide—here she would make her last stand!

She watched the tentacles floating toward her through the trees, catching little flashing glimpses of them, as the dim, electric lights of the park shimmered against their metallic bodies; and the vast wonder came, untainted by fear:

Was this real? Was it possible that these living, miasmaticlike emanations from the most dreadful nightmare conceivable were actually surrounding her, and that in all this great world of 1944 there was no one, no weapon, no combination of air, land and sea forces, nothing that could offer her even a husk of protection?

In a sudden, wild exasperation, she thrust her power at the nearest glint—and laughed a curt, futile laugh when the thing did not even quiver. So far as the tentacles were concerned, her power had been nullified. The implications were ultimate: when Dr. Lell arrived, he would bring swift death with him, unless—

She scrambled down the steep bank to the dark edge of the sullen river; and the intellectual mood that had brought her here to this park where once she had wanted death filled her being. She stood taut, striving for a return of the emotion, for the thought of it was not enough.

If only she could recapture the black, *emotional* mood of that other dark night!

A cool, damp breeze whisked her cheeks—but there was not a fraction of real desire to taste those ugly waters. She wanted, not death, nor power, nor the devastation of third-order energies, but marriage, a home with green grass and a flower garden; she wanted life, contentment, Garson!

Garson!

It was more of a prayer than a command that rose from her lips in that second call for help, an appeal from the depths of her need to the only man who in all these long, deadly years had been in her thoughts:

"Jack, wherever you are, come to me here on Earth, come through the emptiness of time, come safely without pain, without body hurt or damage, and with mind clear. Come now!"

With a dreadful start, she jerked back. For a man stood beside her there by the dark waters!

The breeze came stronger. It brought a richer, more tangy smell of river stingingly into her nostrils. But it wasn't physical revival she needed. It was her mind again that was slow to move, her mind that had never yet reacted favorably to her power, her mind lying now like a cold weight inside her.

For the figure stood with stonelike stolidity, like a lump of dark, roughly shaped clay given a gruesome half-life; she thought in a ghastly dismay: Had she recalled from the dead into dreadful existence a body that may have been lying in its grave for generations?

The thing stirred and became a man. Garson said in a voice that sounded hesitant and huskily unnatural in his own ears:

"I've come—but my mind is only clearing now. And speech comes hard after a quadrillion years." He shuddered with the thought of the countless ages he had spent in eternity; then: "I don't know what happened, I don't know what danger made you call me a second time or whether any exists; but, whatever the situation, I've thought it all out.

"You and I are being used by the mysterious universe manipulators because, according to their history, we *were* used. They would not have allowed us to get into such desperate straits if they could come to us physically, and yet it is obvious that everything will fail for them, for us, unless they can make some direct physical contact and show us how to use the vast power you have been endowed with.

"They must be able to come only through some outside force; and only yours exists in our lives. Therefore, call them, call them in any words, for they must need only the slightest assistance. Call them, and afterward we can talk and plan and hope."

Thought began to come to her, and questions, all the questions that had ever puzzled her: Why had Dr. Lell kept repeating that she had made no trouble, according to the Glorious historical record of her, when trouble was all she had ever given? Why had she been able to defeat the first tentacle, and yet now her power that had called *the* man from some remote time was futile against them? And where was Dr. Lell?

With an effort she finally roused her brain from its slough of pondering over paradox. What words she used then, she could not have repeated, for no memory of them remained a moment after they were spoken. In her mind was only a fascinated horror of expectation that grew *and grew,* as a sound came from the water near her feet.

The water stirred; it sighed as if yielding to some body that pressed its dark elements; it gurgled with a queer, obscene horror; and a body blacker than itself, and bigger than any man made a glinting, ugly rill of foam—

It was Jack Garson's fingers, strong and unflinching, grasping her, and his hard, determined voice that prevented her from uttering the panicky words of demon exorcise that quivered at the verge of her mind.

"Wait!" he said. "It's victory, not defeat. Wait!"

"Thank you, Professor Garson!" The voice that came out of the darkness held a strange, inhuman quality that kept her taut and uneasy. It went on: "For your sakes, I could approach in no other way. We of the four hundred and ninetieth century A. D. are human in name only. There is a dreadful irony in the thought that war, the destroyer of men, finally changed man into a beastlike creature. One solace remains: We saved our minds and our souls at the expense of our bodies.

"Your analysis was right, Professor Garson, as far as it went. The reason we cannot use so much as a single time machine from our age is that our whole period will be in a state of abnormal unbalance for hundreds of thousands of years; even the tiniest misuse of energy could cause unforeseeable changes in the fabric of time energy, which is so utterly indifferent to the fate of men. Our method could only be the indirect and partially successful one of isolating the explosion on one of eighteen solar systems, and drawing all the others together to withstand the shock. This was not so difficult as it sounds, for time yields easily to simple pressures.

"Miss Matheson, the reason the tentacles could trail you is that you were being subjected to psychological terrors. The tentacles that have been following you through the night were not real but third-order light projections of tentacles, designed to keep you occupied till Dr. Lell could bring his destroyer machines to bear. Actually, you have escaped all their designs. How? I have said time yields easily to proper pressures. Such a pressure existed as you stood by the river's edge trying to recall the black mood of suicide. It was easier for you who have power to slip through time to that period nearly four years ago than for you to recapture an unwanted lust for self-inflicted death."

"Good heavens!" Garson gasped. "Are you trying to tell us that this is the night of 1941, and that a few minutes from now Dr. Lell will come along and hire a desperate girl sitting on a park bench to be a front for a fake Calonian recruiting station?"

"And this time," said that inhuman voice, "the history of the Glorious will be fulfilled. She will make no trouble."

Garson had the sudden desperate sensation of being beyond his depth. He literally fought for words. "What . . . what about our bodies that existed then? I thought two bodies of the same person couldn't exist in the same time and space."

"They can't!"

"But—"

The firm, alien voice cut him off, cut off, too, Norma's sudden, startled intention to speak. "There are no paradoxes in time. I have said that, in order to resist the destruction of the isolated eighteenth solar system, the other seventeen *were brought together* into one—this one! The only one that now exists! But the others *were*, and in some form you were in them, but now you are here; and this is the real and only world.

"I leave you to think that over, for now you must act. History says that you two took out a marriage license—tomorrow. History says Norma Garson had no difficulty leading the double life of wife of Professor Garson and slave of Dr. Lell; and that, under my direction, she learned to use her power until the day came to destroy the great energy barrier of Delpa and help the Planetarians to their rightful victory."

Garson was himself again. "Rightful?" he said. "I'm not so convinced of that. They were the ones who precipitated the war by breaking the agreement for population curtailment."

"Rightful," said the voice firmly, "because they first denounced the agreement on the grounds that it would atrophy the human spirit and mind; they fought the war on a noble plane, and offered compromise until the last moment. No automatons on their side; and all the men they directly recruited from the past were plainly told they were wanted for dangerous work. Most of them were unemployed veterans of past wars."

Norma found her voice: "That second recruiting station I saw, with the Greeks and the Romans—"

"Exactly. But now you must receive your first lesson in the intricate process of mind and thought control, enough to fool Dr. Lell—"

The odd part of it was that, in spite of all the words that had been spoken, the warm glow of genuine belief in—everything—didn't come to her until she sat in the dim light on the bench, and watched the gaunt body of Dr. Lell stalking out of the shadowed path. Poor, unsuspecting superman!

RAYMOND F. JONES

A STONE AND A SPEAR

FROM FREDERICK TO Baltimore, the rolling Maryland countryside lay under a fresh blanket of green. Wholly unaware of the summer glory, Dr. Curtis Johnson drove swiftly on the undulating highway, stirring clouds of dust and dried grasses.

Beside him, his wife, Louise, held her blowing hair away from her face and laughed into the warm air. "Dr. Dell isn't going to run away. Besides, you said we could call this a weekend vacation as well as a business trip."

Curt glanced at the speedometer and eased the pressure on the pedal. He grinned. "Wool-gathering again."

"What about?"

"I was just wondering who said it first—one of the fellows at Detrick, or that lieutenant at Bikini, or—"

"Said *what*? What are you talking about?"

"That crack about the weapons after the next war. He—whoever it was —said there may be some doubt about what the weapons of the next war will be like, but there is absolutely no doubt about the weapons of World War IV. It will be fought with stones and spears. I guess any one of us could have said it."

Louise's smile grew tight and thin. "Don't any of you ever think of anything but the next war—*any* of you?"

"How can we? We're fighting it right now."

"You make it sound so hopeless."

"That's what Dell said in the days just before he quit. He said we didn't *have* to stay at Detrick producing the toxins and aerosols that will destroy millions of lives. But he never showed us how we could quit— and be sure of staying alive. His own walking out was no more than a futile gesture."

"I just can't understand him, Curt. I think he's right in a way, but what brought *him* to that viewpoint?"

"Hard to tell," Curt said, unconsciously speeding up again. "After the war, when the atomic scientists were publicly examining their consciences, Dell told them to examine their own guts first. That was typical of him then, but soon after, he swung just as strongly pacifist and walked out of Detrick."

"It still seems strange that he abandoned his whole career. The world's foremost biochemist giving up the laboratory for a *truck farm!*" Louise glanced down at the lunch basket between them. In it were tomatoes that Dr. Hamon Dell had sent along with his invitation to visit him.

For nearly a year Dr. Dell had been sending packages of choice fruit

420

and vegetables to his former colleagues, not only at the biological warfare center at Camp Detrick but at the universities and other research centers throughout the country.

"I wish we knew exactly why he asked us to come out," said Louise.

"Nobody claims to have figured him out. They laugh a little at him now. They eat his gifts willingly enough, but consider him slightly off his rocker. He still has all his biological talents, though. I've never seen or tasted vegetables like the ones he grows."

"And the brass at Detrick doesn't think he's gone soft in the head, either," she added much too innocently. "So they ordered you to take advantage of his invitation and try to persuade him to come back."

Curt turned his head so sharply that Louise laughed.

"No, I didn't read any secret, hush-hush papers," she said. "But it's pretty obvious, isn't it, the way you rushed right over to General Hansen after you got the invitation?"

"It *is* hush-hush, top-secret stuff," said Curt, his eyes once more on the road. "The Army doesn't want it to leak, but they need Dell, need him badly. Anyone knowing bio-war developments would understand. They wanted to send me before. Dell's invitation was the break we needed. I may be the one with sufficient influence to bring him back. I hope so. But keep it under your permanent and forget your guessing games. There's more to it than you know."

The car passed through a cool, wooded section and Louise leaned back and drank in the beauty of it.

"Hush-hush, top secret stuff," she said. "Grown men playing children's games."

"Pretty deadly games for children, darling."

In the late afternoon they by-passed the central part of Baltimore and headed north beyond the suburb of Towson toward Dell's truck farm.

His sign was visible for a half mile:

YOU ARE WHAT YOU EAT
Eat the Best
EAT   DELL'S   VEGETABLES

"Dr. Hamon Dell, world's foremost biochemist—and truck farmer," Curt muttered as he swung the car off the highway.

Louise stepped out when the tires ceased crunching on the gravel lane. She scanned the fields and old woods beyond the ancient but preserved farmhouse. "It's so unearthly."

Curt followed. The song of birds, which had been so noticeable before, seemed strangely muted. The land itself was an alien, faintly greenish hue, a color repulsive to more than just the eyes.

"It must be something in this particular soil," said Curt, "something that gives it that color and produces such wonderful crops. I'll have to remember to ask Dell about it."

"You want Dr. Dell?"

They whirled at the sound of an unfamiliar voice. Louise uttered a startled cry.

The gaunt figure behind them coughed asthmatically and pointed with an arm that seemed composed only of bones and brownish skin, so thin as to be almost translucent.

"Yes," said Curt shakenly. "We're friends of his."

"Dell's in back. I'll tell him you're here."

The figure shambled away and Louise shook herself as if to rid her mind of the vision. "If our grandchildren ever ask about zombies, I can tell them. Who in the world do you suppose he is?"

"Hired man, I suppose. Sounds as if he should be in a lung sanatorium. Funny that Dell would keep him around in that condition."

From somewhere behind the house came the sound of a truck engine. Curt took Louise's arm and led her around the trim, graveled path.

The old farmhouse had been very carefully renovated. Everywhere was evidence of exquisite care, yet the cumulative atmosphere remained uninviting, almost oppressive. Curt told himself it was the utter silence, made even more tense by the lonely chugging of the engine in back, and the incredible harsh color of the soil beneath their feet.

Rounding the corner, they came in sight of a massive tank truck. From it a hose led to an underground storage tank and pulsed slowly under the force of the liquid gushing through it. No one was in sight.

"What could that be for?" asked Louise.

"You've got me. Could be gasoline, but Dell hasn't any reason for storing that much here."

They advanced slowly and amazement crept over Curt as he comprehended the massiveness of the machine. The tank was of elliptical cross section, over ten feet on its major axis. Six double wheels supported the rear; even the front ones were double. In spite of such wide weight distribution, the tires were pressing down the utterly dry ground to a depth of an inch or more.

"They must haul liquid lead in that thing," said Curt.

"It's getting cool. I wish Dell would show up." Louise glanced out over the twenty-acre expanse of truck farm. Thick rows of robust plants covered the area. Tomatoes, carrots, beets, lettuce, and other vegetables—a hundred or so fruit trees were at the far end. Between them ran the road over which the massive truck had apparently entered the farm from the rear.

A heavy step sounded abruptly and Dell's shaggy head appeared from around the end of the truck. His face lighted with pleasure.

"Curt, my boy! And Louise! I thought you weren't going to show up at all."

Curt's hand was almost lost in Dell's enormous grip, but it wasn't because of that that his grip was passive. It was his shocked reaction to Dell's haggard appearance. The fierce eyes looked merely old and tired now. The ageless, leathery hide of Dell's face seemed to have collapsed before some overpowering decay, its bronze smoothness shattered by deep lines that were like tool marks of pain.

Curt spoke in a subdued voice. "It's hard to get away from Detrick. Always one more experiment to try—"

"—And the brass riding you as if they expected you to win another war for them tomorrow afternoon," said Dell. "I remember."

"We wondered about this truck," Louise commented brightly, trying to change the subject. "We finally gave up on it."

"Oh, that. It brings liquid fertilizer to pump into my irrigation water, that's all. No mystery. Let's go on to the house. After you're settled we can catch up on everything and I'll tell you about the things I'm doing here."

"Who's the man we saw?" asked Curt. "He looks as if his health is pretty precarious."

"That's Brown. He came with the place—farmed it for years for my uncle before I inherited it. He could grow a garden on a granite slab. In spite of appearances, he's well enough physically."

"How has your own health been? You have—changed—since you were at Detrick."

Dell raised a lock of steel-gray hair in his fingers and dismissed the question with a wan smile. "We all wear out sometime," he said. "My turn had to come."

Inside, some of the oppressiveness vanished as the evening passed. It was cool enough for lighting the fireplace, and they settled before it after dinner. While they watched the flickering light that whipped the beamed ceiling, Dell entertained them with stories of his neighbors, whose histories he knew clear back to Revolutionary times.

Early, however, Louise excused herself. She knew they would want privacy to thresh out the purposes behind Dell's invitation—and Curt's acceptance.

When she was gone, there was a moment's silence. The logs crackled with shocking pistol shots in the fireplace. The scientist moved to stir the coals and then turned abruptly to Curt.

"When are you going to leave Detrick?"

"When are *you* coming back?" Curt demanded instead of answering.

"So they still want me, even after the things I said when I left."

"You're needed badly. When I told Hansen I was coming down, he said it would be worth five years of my own work to bring you back."

"They want me to produce even deadlier toxins than those I gave them," Dell said viciously. "They want some that can kill ten million people in four minutes instead of only one million—"

"Any man would go insane if he looked at it that way. It would be the same as gun-makers being tormented by the vision of torn men destroyed by their bullets, the sorrowing families—"

"And why shouldn't the gunmakers be tormented?" Dell's voice was low with controlled hate. "They are men like you and me who give the war-makers new tools for their trade."

"Oh, Dell, it's not as simple as that." Curt raised a hand and let it fall wearily. They had been over this so many times before. "Weapon designers are no more responsible than any other agents of society. It's pure neurosis to absorb the whole guilt of wars yet unfought merely because you happened to have developed a potential weapon."

Dell touched the massive dome of his skull. "Here within this brain of mine has been conceived a thing which will probably destroy a billion human lives in the coming years. D. triconus toxin in a suitable aerosol requires only a countable number of molecules in the lungs of a man to kill him. My brain and mine alone is responsible for that vicious, murderous discovery."

"Egotism! Any scientist's work is built upon the pyramid of past knowledge."

"The weapon I have described exists. If I had not created it, it would not exist. It is as simple as that. No one shares my guilt and my responsibility. And what more do they want of me now? What greater dream of mass slaughter and destruction have they dreamed?"

"They want you," said Curt quietly, "because they believe we are not the only ones possessing the toxin. They need you to come back and help find the antitoxin for D. triconus."

Dell shook his head. "That's a blind hope. The action of D. triconus is like a match set to a powder train. The instant its molecules contact protoplasm, they start a chain reaction that rips apart the cell structure. It spreads like fire from one cell to the next, and nothing can stop it once it's started operating within a given organism."

"But doesn't this sense of guilt—unwarranted as it is—make you *want* to find an antitoxin?"

"Suppose I succeeded? I would have canceled the weapon of an enemy. The military would know he could nullify ours in time. Then they would command me to work out still another toxin. It's a vicious and insane circle, which must be broken somewhere. The purpose of the entire remainder of my life is to break it."

"When you are fighting for your life and the enemy already has his hands about your throat," Curt argued, "you reach for the biggest rock you can get your hands on and beat his brains in. You don't try to persuade him that killing is unethical."

For an instant it seemed to Curt that a flicker of humor touched the corners of Dell's mouth. Then the lines tightened down again.

"Exactly," he said. "You reach for a rock and beat his brains in. You don't wipe human life off the face of the Earth in order to reach that enemy. I asked you to come down here to help me break this circle of which I spoke. There has to be someone here—after I'm gone—"

Dell's eyes shifted to the depths of shadows beyond the firelight and remained fixed on unseen images.

"Me? Help you?" Curt asked incredulously. "What could I do? Give up science and become a truck gardener, too?"

"You might say that we would be in the rock business," replied Dell. "Fighting is no longer on the level of one man with his hands about another's throat, but it *should* be. Those who want power and domination should have to fight for it personally. But it has been a long time since they had to.

"Even in the old days, kings and emperors hired mercenaries to fight their wars. The militarists don't buy swords now. They buy brains. We're the mercenaries of the new day, Curt, you and I. Once there was honor in our profession. We searched for truth for its own sake, and because it was our way of life. Once we were the hope of the world because science was a universal language.

"What a horrible joke that turned out to be! Today we are the terror of the world. The warmakers built us fine laboratories. shining palaces, and granted every whim—for a price. They took us up to the hills and showed us the whole world and we sold our souls for it.

"Look what happened after the last war. Invading armies carried off prize Nazi brains like so much loot, set the scientists up in big new laboratories, and these new mercenaries keep right on pouring out knowledge for other kings and emperors.

"Their loyalty is only to their science. But they can't experiment for knowledge any more, only weapons and counter-weapons. You'll say I'm anti-war, even, perhaps, anti-American or pro-Russian. I am not against just wars, but I am against unjust slaughter. And I love America too much to let her destroy herself along with the enemy."

"Then what are we to do?" Curt demanded fiercely. "What are we to do while enemy scientists prepare these same weapons to exterminate *us*? Sure, it's one hell of a mess. Science is already dead. The kind you talk about has been dead for twenty years. All our fine ideals are worthless until the politicians find a solution to their quarrels."

"Politicians? Since when did men of science have to wait upon politicians for solutions of human problems?" Dell passed a hand over his brow, and suddenly his face contorted in pain.

"What is it?" Curt exclaimed, rising.

"Nothing—nothing, my boy. Some minor trouble I've had lately. It will pass in a moment."

With effort, he went on. "I wanted to say that already you have come to think of science being divided into armored camps by the artificial boundaries of the politicians. Has it been so long ago that it was not even in your lifetime, when scientists regarded themselves as one international brotherhood?"

"I can't quarrel with your ideals," said Curt softly. "But national boundary lines do, actually, divide the scientists of the world into armed camps."

"Your premises are still incorrect. They do not deliberately war on each other. It is only that they have blindly sold themselves as mercenaries. And they can be called upon to redeem themselves. They can break their unholy contracts."

"There would have to be simultaneous agreement among the scientists of all nations. And they are men, influenced by national ideals. They are not merely ivory-tower dabblers and searchers after truth."

"Do you remember me five years ago?" Dell's face became more haggard, as if the memory shamed him. "Do you remember when I told the atomic scientists to examine their guts instead of their consciences?"

"Yes. You certainly *have* changed."

"And so can other men. There is a way. I need your help desperately, Curt—"

The face of the aging biochemist contorted again with unbearable pain. His forehead beaded with sweat as he clenched his skull between his vein-knotted hands.

"Dell! What is it?"

"It will pass," Dr. Dell breathed through clenched teeth. "I have some medicine—in my bedroom. I'm afraid I'll have to excuse myself tonight. There's so much more I have to say to you, but we'll continue our talk in the morning, Curt. I'm sorry—"

He stumbled out, refusing Curt's offer of aid with a grim headshake. The fire crackled loudly within the otherwise silent room. Curt felt cold at the descending chill of the night, his mind bewildered at Dell's barrage, some of it so reasonable, some of it so utterly confused. And there was no clue to the identity of the powerful force that had made so great a change in the once militant scientist.

Slowly Curt mounted the staircase of the old house and went to the room Dell had assigned them. Louise was in bed reading a murder mystery.

"Secret mission completed?" she asked.

Curt sat down on the edge of the bed. "I'm afraid something terrible is wrong with Dell. Besides the neurotic guilt complex because of his war work, he showed signs of a terrific and apparently habitual pain in his head. If that should be brain tumor, it might explain his erratic notions, his abandonment of his career."

"Oh, I hope it's not that!"

It seemed to Curt that he had slept only minutes before he was roused by sounds in the night. He rolled over and switched on the light. His watch said two o'clock. Louise raised up in sharp alarm.

"What is it?" she whispered.

"I thought I heard something. There it is again!"

"It sounds like someone in pain. It must be Dell!"

Curt leaped from the bed and wrestled into his bathrobe. As he hurried toward Dell's room, there was another deep groan that ended in a shuddering sob of unbearable agony.

He burst into the scientist's room and switched on the light. Dell looked up, eyes glazed with pain.

"Dr. Dell!"

"Curt— I thought I had time left, but this is as far as I can go— Just remember all I said tonight. Don't forget a word of it." He sat up rigidly, hardly breathing in the effort of control. "The responsibility for the coming destruction of civilization lies at the doors of the scientist mercenaries. Don't allow it, Curt. Get them to abandon the laboratories of the warriors. Get them to reclaim their honor—"

He fell back upon the pillow, his face white with pain and shining with sweat. "Brown—see Brown. He can tell you the—the rest."

"I'll go for a doctor," said Curt. "Who have you had? Louise will stay with you."

"Don't bring a doctor. There's no escaping this. I've known it for months. Wait here with me, Curt. I'll be gone soon."

Curt stared with pity at the great scientist whose mind had so disintegrated. "You need a doctor. I'll call a hospital, Johns Hopkins, if you want."

"Wait, maybe you're right. I have no phone here. Get Dr. Wilson—the Judge Building, Towson—find his home address in a phone book."

"Fine. I'll only be a little while."

He stepped to the door.

"Curt! Take the lane down to the new road—behind the farm. Quicker —it cuts off a mile or so—go down through the orchard—"

"All right. Take it easy now. I'll be right back."

Curt frantically got dressed, ran down the stairs and out to the car. He wondered absently what had become of the cadaverous Brown, who seemed to have vanished from the premises.

The wheels spun gravel as he started the car and whipped it out of the driveway. Then he was on the stretch of lane leading through the grove. The moonless night was utterly dark, and the stream of light ahead of the car seemed the only living thing upon the whole landscape. He almost wished he had taken the more familiar road. To get lost now might mean death for Dell.

No traffic flowed past him in either direction. There were no buildings showing lights. Overwhelming desolation seemed to possess the countryside and seep into his soul. It seemed impossible that this lay close to the other highway with which he was familiar.

He strained his eyes into the darkness for signs of an all-night gas station or store from which he could phone. Finally, he resigned himself to going all the way to Towson. At that moment he glimpsed a spark of light far ahead.

Encouraged, Curt stepped on the gas. In less than ten minutes he was at the spot. He braked the car to a stop, and surveyed the building as he got out. It seemed more like a power substation than anything else. But there should be a telephone, at least.

He knocked on the door. Almost instantly, footsteps sounded within.

The door swung wide.

"I wonder if I could use your—" Curt began. He gasped. "Brown! Dell's dying—we've got to get a doctor for him—"

As if unable to comprehend, the hired man stared dumbly for a long moment. His hollow-cheeked face was almost skeletal in the light that flooded out from behind him.

Then from somewhere within the building came a voice, sharp with tension. "Brown! What the devil are you doing? Shut that door!"

That brought the figure to life. He whipped out a gun and motioned Curt inward. "Step inside. We'll have to decide what to do with you when Carlson finds you're here."

"What's the matter with you?" Curt asked, stupefied. "Dell's dying. He needs help."

"Get in here!"

Curt moved slowly forward. Brown closed the door behind him and motioned toward a closed door at the other end of a short hall. They opened it and stepped into a dimly lighted room.

Curt's eyes slowly adjusted and he saw what seemed to be a laboratory. It was so packed with equipment that there was scarcely room for the group of twelve or fifteen men jammed closely about some object with their backs to Curt and Brown.

Brown shambled forward like an agitated skeleton, breaking the circle. Then Curt saw that the object of the men's attention was a large cathode ray screen occupied by a single green line. There was a pip on it rising sharply near one side of the two-foot tube. The pip moved almost imperceptibly toward a vertical red marker over the face of the screen. The men stared as if hypnotized by it.

The newcomers' arrival, however, disturbed their attention. One man turned with an irritable growl. "Brown, for heaven's sake—"

He was a bony creature, even more cadaverous than Brown. He caught sight of Curt's almost indecently robust face. He gasped and swore.

"Who is this? What's he doing here?"

The entire montage of skull faces turned upon Curt. He heard a sharp collective intake of breath, as if his presence were some unforeseen calamity that had shaken the course of their incomprehensible lives.

"This is Curtis Johnson," said Brown. "He got lost looking for a doctor for Dell."

A mummylike figure rose from a seat before the instrument. "Your coming is tremendously unfortunate, but for the moment we can do nothing about it. Sit here beside me. My name is Tarron Sark."

The man indicated a chair.

"My friend, Dr. Dell, is dying," Curt snapped out, refusing to sit down. "I've got to get help. I saw your light and hoped you'd allow me to use your phone. I don't know who you are nor what Dell's hired man is doing here with you. But you've got to let me go for help!"

"No." The man, Sark, shook his head. "Dell is reconciled. He has to go. We are awaiting precisely the event you would halt—his death."

He had known it, Curt thought, from the moment he entered that room. Like vultures sitting on cliffs waiting for the death of their prey, these fantastic men let their glance slip back to the screen. The green line was a third of the way toward the red marker now, and moving more rapidly.

It was nightmare—meaningless—

"I'm not staying," Curt insisted. "You can't prevent me from helping Dell without assuming responsibility for his death. I demand you let me call."

"You're not going to call," said Sark wearily. "And we assumed responsibility for Dell's death long ago. Sit down!"

Slowly Curt sank down upon the chair beside the stranger. There was nothing else to do. He was powerless against Brown's gun. But he'd bring them to justice somehow, he swore.

He didn't understand the meaning of the slowly moving pattern on the 'scope face, yet, as his eyes followed that pip, he sensed tension in the watching men that seemed sinister, almost murderous. How?

What did the inexorably advancing pip signify?

No one spoke. The room was stifling hot and the breathing of the circle of men was a dull, rattling sound in Curt's ears.

Quickly then, gathering sudden momentum, the pip accelerated. The circle of men grew taut.

The pip crossed the red line—and vanished.

Only the smooth green trace remained, motionless and without meaning.

With hesitant shuffling of feet, the circle expanded. The men glanced uncertainly at one another.

One said, "Well, that's the end of Dell. We'll soon know now if we're on the right track, or if we've botched it. Carlson will call when he's computed it."

"The end of Dell?" Curt repeated slowly, as if trying to convince himself of what he knew had happened. "The pip on the screen—that showed his life leaving him?"

"Yes," said Sark. "He knew he had to go. And there are perhaps hundreds more like him. But Dell couldn't have told you of that—"

"What will we do with him?" Brown asked abruptly.

"If Dell is dead, you murdered him!" Curt shouted.

A rising personal fear grew within him. They could not release him now, even though his story would make no sense to anybody. But they had somehow killed Dell, or thought they had, and they wouldn't hesitate to kill Curt. He thought of Louise in the great house with the corpse of Haman Dell—if, of course, he was actually dead. But that was nonsense.

"Dell must have sent you to us!" Sark said, as if a great mystery had suddenly been lifted from his mind. "He did not have time to tell you everything. Did he tell you to take the road behind the farm?"

Curt nodded bitterly. "He told me it was the quickest way to get to a doctor."

"He did? Then he knew even better than we did how rapidly he was slipping. Yes, this was the quickest way."

"What are you talking about?" Curt demanded.

"Did Dell say anything at all about what he wanted of you?"

"It was all wild. Something about helping with some crazy plans to retreat from the scientific world. He was going to finish talking in the morning, but I guess it wouldn't have mattered. I realize now that he was sick and irrational."

"Too sick to explain everything, but not irrational," Sark said thoughtfully. "He left it to us to tell you, since you are to succeed him."

"Succeed Dell? In what?"

Sark suddenly flipped a switch on a panel at his right. A screen lighted with some fuzzy image. It cleared with a slight dial adjustment, and Curt seemed to be looking at some oddly familiar moonlit ruin.

"An American city," said Sark, hurrying his words now. "Any city. They are all alike. Ruin. Death. This one died thirty years ago."

"I don't understand," Curt complained, bewildered. "Thirty years—"

"At another point in the Time Continuum," said Sark. "The future. Your future, you understand. Or, rather, *our* present, the one you created for us."

Curt recoiled at the sudden venom in Sark's voice. "The *future?*" That was what they had in common with Dell—psychosis, systematic delusions. He had suspected danger before; now it was imminent and terrifying.

"Perhaps you are one of those who regard your accomplishments with pride," Sark went on savagely, ignoring or unaware of Curt's fear and horror. "That the hydrogen bombs smashed the cities, and the aerosols destroyed the remnants of humanity seems insignificant to you beside the high technical achievement these things represent."

Curt's throat was dry with panic. Irrelevantly, he recalled the pain-fired eyes of Dell and the dying scientist's words: "The responsibility for the coming destruction of civilization lies at the doors of the scientist mercenaries—"

"Some of us *did* manage to survive," said Sark, glaring at the scene of gaunt rubble. Curt could see the veins pounding beneath the thin flesh of his forehead. "We lived for twenty years with the dream of rebuilding a world, the same dream that has followed all wars. But at last we knew that the dream was truly vain this time. We survivors lived in hermetically sealed caverns, trying to exist and recover our lost science and technology.

"We could not emerge into the Earth's atmosphere. Its pollution with virulent aerosols would persist for another hundred years. We could not bear a new race out of these famished and rickety bodies of ours. Unless Man was to vanish completely from the face of the Earth, we had only a single hope. That hope was to prevent the destruction from ever occurring!"

Sark's eyes were burning now. "Do you understand what that means? We had to go *back*, not forward. We had to arm to fight a new war, a war to prevent the final war that destroyed Mankind."

"Back? How could you go back?" Curt hesitated, grasping now the full insanity of the scene about him. "How have you *come* back?" He waited tautly for the answer. It would be gibberish, of course, like all the mad conversation before it.

"The undisturbed flow of time from the beginning to the end—neither of which we can experience—we call the Prime Continuum," Sark replied. "Mathematically speaking, it is composed of billions of separate bands of probability running side by side. For analogy, you may liken it to a great river, whose many insignificant tributaries merge into a roaring, turbulent whole. That is the flow of time, the Prime Continuum.

"You may change one of these tributaries, dam it up, turn it aside, let it reach the main stream at a different point. No matter how insignificant the tributary, the stream will not be the same after the change. That is what we are doing. We are controlling critical tributaries of the Prime Continuum, altering the hell that the scientists have so generously handed down to us.

"Dell was a critical tributary. You, Dr. Curtis Johnson, are another. Changing or destroying such key individuals snips off branches of knowledge before they come into fruit."

It was an ungraspable answer, but it had to be argued against because of its conclusion. "The scientists are not bringing about the war," Curt said, looking from one fleshless face to another. "Find the politicians responsible, those willing to turn loose any horror to gain power. *They* are the ones you want."

"That would mean destroying half the human race. In your day, nearly every man is literally a politician."

"Talk sense!" Curt said angrily.

"A politician, as we have come to define him, is simply one willing to sacrifice the common good for his own ends. It is a highly infectious disease in a day when altruism is taken for cowardice or mere stupidity. No, we have not mistaken our goal, Dr. Johnson. We cannot hasten the maturity of the race. We can only hope to take the matches away so the children cannot burn the house down. Whatever you doubt, do not doubt that we are from the future or that we caused Dell's death. He is only one of many."

Curt slumped. "I did doubt it. I still do, yet not with conviction. Why?"

"Because your own sense of guilt tells you that you and Dell and others like you are literally the matches which we have to remove. Because your knowledge of science has overcome your desire not to believe. Because you *know* the shape of the future."

"The war after the Third World War—" Curt murmured. "Someone said it would be fought with stones and spears, but your weapons are far from stones and spears."

"Perhaps not so far at that," said Sark, his face twisting wryly. He reached to a nearby table and picked up a tomato and a carrot. "These are our weapons. As humble and primitive as the stones and spears of cavemen."

"You're joking," Curt replied, almost ready to grin.

"No. This is the ultimate development of biological warfare. Man is what he eats—"

"That's what Dell's sign said."

"We operate hundreds of gardens and farms such as Dell's. We work through the fertilizing compounds we supply to these farms. These compounds contain chemicals that eventually lodge in the cells of those who eat the produce. They take up stations within the brain cells and change the man—or destroy him.

"Certain cells of the brain are responsible for specific characteristics. Ways of altering these cells were found by introducing minute quantities of specific radioactive materials which could be incorporated into vegetable foods. During the Third War wholesale insanity was produced in entire populations by similar methods. Here, we are using it to accomplish humane purposes.

"We are simply restraining the scientists responsible for the destroying weapons that produced our nightmare world. You saw the change that took place in Dell. There is a good example of what we do."

"But he *did* change," Curt pointed out. "He *was* carrying out your work. Wasn't that enough for you? Why did you decide he had to die?"

"Ordinarily, we don't want to kill if the change is produced. Sometimes the brain cells are refractory and the characteristics too ingrained. The cells develop tumorous activity as a result of the treatment. So it was with Dell. In his case, however, we would have been forced to kill him by other means if he had not died as he did. This, too, he understood very well. That was why he really wanted no doctor to help him."

"You must have driven him insane first!"

"Look at this and see if you still think so." Sark led the way to a small instrument and pointed to the eyepiece of it. "Look in there."

Curt bent over. Light sprang up at Sark's touch of a switch. Then a scene began to move before Curt's eyes.

"Dell!" he exclaimed.

The scene was of some vast and well-equipped biological laboratory, much like those of Camp Detrick. Silent mask-faced technicians moved with precision about their tasks. Dr. Dell was directing operations.

But there was something wrong. The figure was not the Dell that Curt knew.

As if Sark sensed Curt's comprehension of this, the scene advanced and swelled until the whole area of vision was filled with Dell's face. Curt gasped. The face was blank and hideous. The eyes stared. When the scene retreated once more, Curt saw now that Dell moved as an automaton, almost without volition of his own.

As he moved away from the bench like a sleepwalker, there came briefly into view the figure of an armed guard at the door. The figure of a corporal, grim in battle dress.

Curt looked up, sick as if some inner sense had divined the meaning of that scene which he could not yet put into words.

"Had enough?" asked Sark.

"What does it mean?"

"That is Dell as he would have been. That is what he was willing to die to avoid."

"But what *is* it?"

"A military research laboratory twelve years into your future. You are aware that in your own time a good deal of research has come to a standstill because many first-string scientists have revolted against military domination. Unfortunately, there are plenty of second-stringers available and they are enough for most tasks—the youngsters with new Ph. D.s who are awed by the glitter of golden laboratories. But, lacking experience or imagination, they can't see through the glitter or have the insight for great work. Some will eventually, too late, however, and they will be replaced by eager new youngsters."

"This scene of Dell—"

"Just twelve years from what you call now. Deadlier weapons will be needed and so a bill will be passed to draft the reluctant first-line men—against their will, if necessary."

"You can't force creative work," Curt objected.

Sark shrugged. "There are drugs that do wonderful and terrible things to men's minds. They can force creation or mindless destruction, confession or outrageous subterfuge. You saw your opponents make some use of them. A cardinal, for example, and an engineer, among others. Now you have seen your friend, Dell, as he would have been. Not the same drugs, of course, but the end result is the same."

Curt's horror turned to stubborn disbelief. "America wouldn't use such methods," he said flatly.

"Today? No," agreed Sark. "But when a country is committed to inhuman warfare—even though the goal may be honorable—where is the line to stop at? Each brutality prepares the way for the next. Even concentration camps and extermination centers become logical necessities. You have heard your opponents say that the end justifies the means. You have seen for yourself—the means become the end."

"But Dell could have escaped," Curt protested. "You could have helped him to your own time or another. He was still valuable. He needn't have died!"

"There is no such thing as actual travel in time," explained Sark. "Or at least in our day we have found none. There is possible only a bending back of a branch of the Prime Continuum so that we can witness, warn, instruct, gain aid in saving the future. And there can be meeting only in this narrow sector of unreality where the branch joins the main stream. Our farms adjoin such sectors, but farther than that we cannot go, nor can one of you become a citizen of the world you have created for us.

"But I wish it were so!" Sark bit out venomously. "We'd kidnap you by the millions, force you to look upon the ruin and the horror, let you breathe the atmosphere that no man can inhale and live, the only atmosphere there is in that world. Yes, I wish you could become our guests there. Our problem would be easier. But it can be done. This is the only way we can work.

"Dell had to go. There was no escape for him, no safety for us if he lived. He would have been tracked down, captured like a beast and set to work against his will. It was there in the Prime Continuum. Nothing could cancel it except death, the death that saves a billion lives because he will not produce a toxin deadlier than D. triconus."

The vengeance in Sark's voice was almost tangible. Involuntarily Curt retreated a step before it. And—almost—he thought he understood these men out of time.

"What is there—" he began hoarsely and had to stop. "What is there that I can do?"

"We need you to take over Dell's farm. It is of key importance. The list of men he was treating was an extremely vital one. That work cannot be interrupted now."

"How can you accomplish anything by operating only here?" Curt objected. "While you stifle our defenses, our enemies are arming to the teeth. When you've made us sufficiently helpless, they'll strike."

"Did I say we were so restricted?" answered Sark, smiling for the first time. "You cannot imagine what a fresh vegetable means on a professor's table in Moscow. In Atomgrad a ripe tomato is worth a pound of uranium. How do I know? Because I walked the streets of Atomgrad with my grandfather."

"Then you're a—"

Sark's face grew hard and bitter in the half light of the room.

"Was," he corrected. "Or might have been. There are no nationalities where there are no nations, no political parties where there are only hunger and death. The crime of the future is not any person's or country's. It is the whole of humanity's."

An alarm sounded abruptly.

"Carlson!" somebody tensely exclaimed.

Sark whirled to the panels and adjusted the controls. A small screen lighted, showing the image of a man with graying hair and imperious hair. His sharp eyes seemed to burn directly into Curt's.

"How did it go?" exclaimed Sark. "Was the Prime Continuum shift as expected?"

"No! It still doesn't compute out. Nothing's right. The war is still going on. The Continuum is absolute hell."

"I should have known so," said Sark in dismay. "I should have called you."

"What is it? Do you know what's wrong?"

"Johnson. Dr. Curtis Johnson. He's here."

Rage spread upon Carlson's face. An oath exploded from his lips. "No wonder the situation doesn't compute with him out of the Prime Continuum. Why did he come there?"

"Dell sent him. Dell died too quickly. He didn't have time to instruct Johnson. I have told him what we want of him."

"Do you understand?" Carlson demanded of Curt with abruptness that was almost anger.

Curt looked slowly about the room and back to the face of the questioner. Understand? If they sent him back, allowed him to go back, could he ever be sure that he had not witnessed a thing of nightmare in this shadowy dream world?

Yes, he could be sure. He had seen the blasted city, just the way he knew it could be—*would* be unless someone prevented it. He had seen the pattern on the scope, attuned to the tiny tributary of the Prime Continuum that was the life of Dr. Dell, had seen it run out, dying as Dell had died.

He could believe, too, that there was a little farm near Atomgrad, where a tomato on a scientist's table was more potent than the bombs building in the arsenal.

"I understand," he said. "Shall I go back now?"

Sark put a paper into his hands. "Here is a list of new names. You will find Dell's procedures and records in his desk at the farm. Do not underestimate the importance of your work. You have seen the failure of the Prime Continuum to compute properly with you out of it. You will correct that.

"Your only contact from now on will be through Brown, who will bring the tank truck once a year. You know what to do. You are on your own."

It was like a surrealist painting as he left. The moon had risen, and in all the barrenness there was nothing but the gray cement cube of the building. The light spilling through the open doorway touched the half dozen gaunt men who had followed him out to the car. Ahead was the narrow band of roadway leading through some infinite nothingness that would end in Dell's truck farm.

He started off. When he looked back a moment later, the building was no longer there.

He glanced at the list of names Sark gave him, chilled by the importance of those men. For some there would be death as there had been for Dell. For himself—

He had forgotten to ask. But perhaps they would not have told him. Not at this time, anyway. The chemically treated food produced tumors in refractory, unresponsive cells. He had eaten Dell's vegetables, would eat more.

It was too late to ask and it didn't matter. He had important things to do. First would be the writing of his resignation to the officials of Camp Detrick.

As of tomorrow, he would be Dr. Curtis Johnson, truck farmer, specialist in atomic-age produce, luscious table gifts for the innocent and not-so-innocent human matches that would, if he and his unknown colleagues succeeded, be prevented from cremating the hopes of Mankind.

Louise would help him hang the new sign:

YOU ARE WHAT YOU EAT
Eat the Best
EAT JOHNSON'S VEGETABLES

Only, of course, she wouldn't know why he had taken Dell's job, nor could he ever explain.

It would probably be the death of Curt Johnson, but that was cheap enough if humanity survived.

———

LEWIS PADGETT

WHAT YOU NEED

WE HAVE WHAT YOU NEED

THAT'S WHAT THE sign said. Tim Carmichael, who worked for a trade paper that specialized in economics, and eked out a meager salary by selling sensational and untrue articles to the tabloids, failed to sense a story in the reversed sign. He thought it was a cheap publicity gag, something one seldom encounters on Park Avenue, where the shop fronts are noted for their classic dignity. And he was irritated.

He growled silently, walked on, then suddenly turned and came back. He wasn't quite strong enough to resist the temptation to unscramble the sentence, though his annoyance grew. He stood before the window, staring up, and said to himself, "We Have What You Need. Yeah?"

The sign was in prim, small letters on a black painted ribbon that stretched across a narrow glass pane. Below it was one of those curved, invisible-glass windows. Through the window Carmichael could see an expanse of white velvet, with a few objects carefully arranged there. A rusty nail, a snowshoe, and a diamond tiara. It looked like a Dali decor for Cartier's or Tiffany.

"Jewelers?" Carmichael asked silently. "But why *what you need?*" He pictured millionaires miserably despondent for lack of a matched pearl necklace, heiresses weeping inconsolably because they needed a few star sapphires. The principle of luxury merchandising was to deal with the whipped cream of supply and demand; few people needed diamonds. They merely wanted them and could afford them.

"Or the place might sell jinniflasks," Carmichael decided. "Or magic wands. Same principle as a Coney carny, though. A sucker trap. Bill the Whatzit outside and people will pay their dimes and flock in. For two cents—"

He was dyspeptic this morning, and generally disliked the world. Prospect of a scapegoat was attractive, and his press card gave him a certain advantage. He opened the door and walked into the shop.

It was Park Avenue, all right. There were no showcases or counters. It might be an art gallery, for a few good oils were displayed on the walls. An air of overpowering luxury, with the bleakness of an unlived-in place, struck Carmichael.

Through a curtain at the back came a very tall man with carefully-combed white hair, a ruddy, healthy face, and sharp blue eyes. He might have been sixty. He wore expensive but careless tweeds, which somehow jarred with the decor.

"Good morning," the man said, with a quick glance at Carmichael's clothes. He seemed slightly surprised. "May I help you?"

"Maybe." Carmichael introduced himself and showed his press card.

"Oh? My name is Talley. Peter Talley."

"I saw your sign."

"Oh?"

"Our paper is always on the lookout for possible write-ups. I've never noticed your shop before—"

"I've been here for years," Talley said.

"This is an art gallery?"

"Well—no."

The door opened. A florid man came in and greeted Talley cordially. Carmichael, recognizing the client, felt his opinion of the shop swing rapidly upward. The florid man was a Name—a big one.

"It's a bit early, Mr. Talley," he said, "but I didn't want to delay. Have you had time to get . . . what I needed?"

"Oh, yes. I have it. One moment." Talley hurried through the draperies and returned with a small, neatly-wrapped parcel which he gave to the florid man. The latter forked over a check—Carmichael caught a glimpse of the amount and gulped—and departed. His town car was at the curb outside.

Carmichael moved toward the door where he could watch. The florid man seemed anxious. His chauffeur waited stolidly as the parcel was unwrapped with hurried fingers.

"I'm not sure I'd want publicity, Mr. Carmichael," Talley said. "I've a select clientele—carefully chosen."

"Perhaps our weekly economic bulletins might interest you—"

Talley tried not to laugh. "Oh, I don't think so. It really isn't in my line."

The florid man had finally unwrapped the parcel and taken out an egg. As far as Carmichael could see from his post near the door, it was merely an ordinary egg. But its possessor regarded it almost with awe. Had Earth's last hen died ten years before, he could have been no more pleased. Something like deep relief showed on the Florida-tanned face.

He said something to the chauffeur, and the car rolled smoothly forward and was gone.

"Are you in the dairy business?" Carmichael asked abruptly.

"No."

"Do you mind telling me what your business is?"

"I'm afraid I do, rather," Talley said.

Carmichael was beginning to scent a story. "Of course I could find out through the Better Business Bureau—"

"You couldn't."

"No? They might be interested in knowing why an egg is worth five thousand dollars to one of your customers."

Talley said, "My clientele is so small I must charge high fees. You . . . ah . . . know that a Chinese mandarin has been known to pay thousands of *taels* for eggs of proved antiquity."

"That guy wasn't a Chinese mandarin," Carmichael said.

"Oh, well. As I say, I don't welcome publicity—"

"I think you do. I was in the advertising game for a while. Spelling your sign backwards is an obvious baited hook."

"Then you're no psychologist," Talley said. "It's just that I can afford to indulge my whims. For five years I looked at that window every day and read the sign backward—from inside my shop. It annoyed me. You know how a word will begin to look funny if you keep staring on it? Any word. It turns into something in no human tongue. Well, I discovered I was getting a neurosis about that sign. It makes no sense backwards, but I kept finding myself trying to read sense into it. When I started to say 'Deen uoy tahw evah ew' to myself and looking for philological derivations, I called in a sign painter. People who are interested enough still drop in."

"Not many," Carmichael said shrewdly. "This is Park Avenue. And you've got the place fixed up too expensively. Nobody in the low-income brackets—or the middle brackets—would come in here. So you run an upper-bracket business."

"Well," Talley said, "yes, I do."

"And you won't tell me what it is?"

"I'd rather not."

"I can find out, you know. It might be dope, pornography, high-class fencing—"

"Very likely," Mr. Talley said smoothly. "I buy stolen jewels, conceal them in eggs, and sell them to my customers. Or perhaps that egg was loaded with microscopic French postcards. Good morning, Mr. Carmichael."

"Good morning," Carmichael said, and went out. He was overdue at the office, but annoyance was the stronger motivation. He played sleuth for a while, keeping an eye on Talley's shop, and the results were thoroughly satisfactory—to a certain extent. He learned everything but why.

Late in the afternoon, he sought out Mr. Talley again.

"Wait a minute," he said, at sight of the proprietor's discouraging face. "For all you know, I may be a customer."

Talley laughed.

"Well, why not?" Carmichael compressed his lips. "How do you know the size of my bank account? Or maybe you've got a restricted clientele?"

"No. But—"

Carmichael said quickly. "I've been doing some investigating. I've been noticing your customers. In fact, following them. And finding out what they buy from you."

Talley's face changed. "Indeed?"

"In-*deed*. They're all in a hurry to unwrap their little bundles. So that gave me my chance to find out. I missed a few, but—I saw enough to apply a couple of rules of logic, Mr. Talley. *Item*, your customers don't know what they're buying from you. It's a sort of grab bag. A couple of times they were plenty surprised. The man who opened his parcel and found an old newspaper clipping. What about the sunglasses? And the revolver? Probably illegal, by the way—no license. And the diamond—it must have been paste, it was so big."

"M-mm," Mr. Talley said.

"I'm no smart apple, but I can smell a screwy set-up. Most of your clients are big shots, in one way or another. And why didn't any of 'em pay you, like the first man—the guy who came in when I was here this morning."

"It's chiefly a credit business," Talley said. "I've my ethics. I have to —for my own conscience. It's responsibility. You see, I sell . . . my goods . . . with a guarantee. Payment is made only if the product proves satisfactory."

"So. An egg. Sunglasses. A pair of asbestos gloves—I think they were. A newspaper clipping. A gun and a diamond. How do you take inventory?"

Talley said nothing.

Carmichael grinned. "You've an errand boy. You send him out and he comes back with bundles. Maybe he goes to a grocery on Madison and buys an egg. Or a pawnshop on Sixth for a revolver. Or—well, anyhow, I told you I'd find out what your business it."

"And have you?" Talley asked.

" 'We have what you need,' " Carmichael said. "But how do you *know*?"

"You're jumping to conclusions."

"I've got a headache—I didn't have sunglasses!—and I don't believe in magic. Listen, Mr. Talley. I'm fed up to the eyebrows and 'way beyond on queer little shops that sell peculiar things. I know too much about 'em—I've written about 'em. A guy walks along the street and sees a funny sort of store and the proprietor won't serve him—he sells only to pixies—or else he *does* sell him a magic charm with a double edge. Well— *pfui!*"

"Mph," Talley said.

" 'Mph' as much as you like. But you can't get away from logic. Either you've got a sound, sensible racket here, or else it's one of those funny magic-shop set-ups—and I don't believe that. For it isn't logical."

"Why not?"

"Because of economics," Carmichael said flatly. "Grant the idea that you've got certain mysterious powers—let's say you can make telepathic gadgets. All right. Why the devil would you start a business so you could sell the gadgets so you could make money so you could live? You'd simply put on one of your gadgets, read a stockbroker's mind, and buy the right stocks. That's the intrinsic fallacy in these crazy-shop things—if you've got enough stuff on the ball to be able to stock and run such a shop, you wouldn't need a business in the first place. Why go round Robin Hood's barn?"

Talley said nothing.

Carmichael smiled crookedly. " 'I often wonder what the vintners buy one half so precious as the stuff they sell,' " he quoted. "Well—what do *you* buy? I know what you sell—eggs and sunglasses."

"You're an inquisitive man, Mr. Carmichael," Talley murmured. "Has it ever occurred to you that this is none of your business?"

"I may be a customer," Carmichael repeated. "How about that?"

Talley's cold blue eyes were intent. A new light dawned in them; Talley pursed his lips and scowled. "I hadn't thought of that," he admitted. "You might be. Under the circumstances. Will you excuse me for a moment?"

"Sure," Carmichael said. Talley went through the curtains.

Outside, traffic drifted idly along Park. As the sun slid down beyond the Hudson, the street lay in a blue shadow that crept imperceptibly up the barricades of the buildings. Carmichael stared at the sign—"We have what you need"—and smiled.

In a back room, Talley put his eye to a binocular plate and moved a calibrated dial. He did this several times. Then, biting his lip—for he was a gentle man—he called his errand boy and gave him directions. After that he returned to Carmichael.

"You're a customer," he said. "Under certain conditions."

"The condition of my bank account, you mean?"

"No," Talley said. "I'll give you reduced rates. Understand one thing. I really do have what you need. You don't *know* what you need, but I know. And as it happens—well, I'll sell you what you need for, let's say, five dollars."

Carmichael reached for his wallet. Talley held up a hand.

"Pay me after you're satisfied. And the money's the nominal part of the fee. There's another part. If you're satisfied, I want you to promise that you'll never come near this shop again and never mention it to anyone."

"I see," Carmichael said slowly. His theories had changed slightly.

"It won't be long before . . . ah, here it is now." A buzzing from the back indicated the return of the errand boy. Talley said "Excuse me," and vanished. Soon he returned with a neatly-wrapped parcel, which he thrust into Carmichael's hands.

"Keep this on your person," Talley said. "Good afternoon."

Carmichael nodded, pocketed the parcel, and went out. Feeling affluent, he hailed a taxi and went to a cocktail bar he knew. There, in the dim light of a booth, he unwrapped the bundle.

Protection money, he decided. Talley was paying him off to keep his mouth shut about the racket, whatever it was. O.K. live and let live. How much would be—

Ten thousand? Fifty thousand? How big was the racket?

He opened an oblong cardboard box. Within, nesting upon tissue paper, was a pair of shears, the blades protected by a sheath of folded, glued cardboard.

Carmichael said something softly. He drank his highball and ordered another, but left it untasted. Glancing at his wrist watch, he decided that the Park Avenue shop would be closed by now and Mr. Peter Talley gone.

" 'One half so precious as the stuff they sell,' " Carmichael said. "Maybe it's the scissors of Atropos. Blah." He unsheathed the blades and snipped experimentally at the air. Nothing happened. Slightly crimson around the cheekbones, Carmichael reholstered the shears and dropped them into the side pocket of his topcoat. Quite a gag!

He decided to call on Peter Talley tomorrow.

Meanwhile, what? He remembered he had a dinner date with one of the girls at the office, and hastily paid his bill and left. The streets were darkening, and a cold wind blew southward from the Park. Carmichael wound his scarf tighter around his throat and made gestures toward passing taxis.

He was considerably annoyed.

Half an hour later a thin man with sad eyes—Jerry Worth, one of the copy-writers from his office—greeted him at the bar where Carmichael was killing time. "Waiting for Betsy?" Worth said, nodding toward the restaurant annex. "She sent me to tell you she couldn't make it. A rush deadline. Apologies and stuff. Where were you today? Things got gummed up a bit. Have a drink with me."

They worked on rye. Carmichael was already slightly stiff. The dull crimson around his cheekbones had deepened, and his frown had become set. "What you need," he remarked. "Double-crossing little—"

"Huh?" Worth said.

"Nothing. Drink up. I've just decided to get a guy in trouble. If I can."

"You almost got in trouble yourself today. That trend analysis of ores—"

"Eggs. Sunglasses!"

"I got you out of a jam—"

"Shut up," Carmichael said and ordered another round. Every time he felt the weight of the shears in his pocket he found his lips moving.

Five shots later Worth said plaintively, "I don't mind doing good deeds but I do like to mention them. And you won't let me. All I want is a little gratitude."

"All right, mention them," Carmichael said. "Brag your head off. Who cares?"

Worth showed satisfaction. "That ore analysis—it was that. You weren't at the office today, but I caught it. I checked with our records and you had Trans-Steel all wrong. If I hadn't altered the figures, it would have gone down to the printer—"

"What?"

"The Trans-Steel. They—"

"Oh, you fool," Carmichael groaned. "I know it didn't check with the office figures. I meant to put in a notice to have them changed. I got my dope from the source. Why don't you mind your own business?"

Worth blinked. "I was trying to help."

"It would have been good for a five-buck raise," Carmichael said. "After all the research I did to uncover the real dope—listen. Has the stuff gone to bed yet?"

"I dunno. Maybe not. Croft was still checking the copy—"

"O.K.!" Carmichael said. "Next time—" He jerked at his scarf, jumped off the stool, and headed for the door, trailed by the protesting Worth. Ten minutes later he was at the office, listening to Croft's bland explanation that the copy had already been dispatched to the printer.

"Does it matter? Was there . . . incidentally, where were you today?"

"Dancing on the rainbow," Carmichael snapped, and departed. He had switched over from rye to whiskey sours, and the cold night air naturally did not sober him. Swaying slightly, watching the sidewalk move a little as he blinked at it, he stood on the curb and pondered.

"I'm sorry, Tim," Worth said. "It's too late now, though. There won't be any trouble. You've got a right to go by our office records."

"Stop me now," Carmichael said. "Lousy little—" He was angry and drunk. On impulse he got another taxi and sped to the printers, still trailing a somewhat confused Jerry Worth.

There was rhythmic thunder in the building. The swift movement of the taxi had given Carmichael a slight nausea; his head ached, and alcohol was in solution in his blood. The hot, inky air was unpleasant. The great Linotypes thumped and growled. Men were moving about. It was all slightly nightmarish, and Carmichael doggedly hunched his shoulders and lurched on until something jerked him back and began to strangle him.

Worth started yelling. His face showed drunken terror. He made ineffectual gestures.

But this was all part of the nightmare. Carmichael saw what had happened. The ends of his scarf had caught in moving gears somewhere and he was being drawn inexorably into meshing metal cogs. Men were running. The clanking, thumping, rolling sounds were deafening. He pulled at the scarf.

Worth screamed, ". . . knife! Cut it—"

The warping of relative values that intoxication gives saved Carmichael. Sober, he would have been helpless with panic. At it was, each thought was hard to capture, but clear and lucid when he finally got it. He remembered the shears, and he put his hand in his pocket—the blades slipped out of their cardboard sheath—and he snipped through the scarf with fumbling, hasty movements.

The white silk disappeared. Carmichael fingered the ragged edge at his throat and smiled stiffly.

Mr. Peter Talley had been hoping that Carmichael would not come back. The probability lines had shown two possible variants; in one, all was well; in the other—

Carmichael walked into the shop the next morning and held out a five-dollar bill. Talley took it.

"Thank you. But you could have mailed me a check."

"I could have. Only that wouldn't have told me what I wanted to know."

"No," Talley said, and sighed. "You've decided, haven't you?"

"Do you blame me?" Carmichael asked. "Last night—do you know what happened?"

"Yes."

"How?"

"I might as well tell you," Talley said. "You'd find out anyway. That's certain, anyhow."

Carmichael sat down, lit a cigarette, and nodded. "Logic. You couldn't have arranged that little accident, by any manner of means. Betsy Hoag decided to break our date early yesterday morning. Before I saw you. That was the beginning of the chain of incidents that led up to the accident. Ergo, you must have known what was going to happen."

"I did know."

"Prescience?"

"Mechanical. I saw that you would be crushed in the machine—"

"Which implies an alterable future."

"Certainly," Talley said, his shoulders slumping. "There are innumerable possible variants to the future. Different lines of probability. All depending on the outcome of various crises as they arise. I happen to be skilled in certain branches of electronics. Some years ago, almost by accident, I stumbled on the principle of seeing the future."

"How?"

"Chiefly it involves a personal focus on the individual. The moment you enter this place"—he gestured—"you're in the beam of my scanner. In my back room I have the machine itself. By turning a calibrated dial, I check the possible futures. Sometimes there are many. Sometimes only a few. As though at times certain stations weren't broadcasting. I look into my scanner and see what you need—and supply it."

Carmichael let smoke drift from his nostrils. He watched the blue coils through narrowed eyes.

"You follow a man's whole life—in triplicate or quadruplicate or whatever?"

"No," Talley said. "I've got my device focused so it's sensitive to crisis curves. When those occur, I follow them farther and see what probability paths involve the man's safe and happy survival."

"The sunglasses, the egg and the gloves—"

Talley said, "Mr. . . . uh . . . Smith is one of my regular clients. Whenever he passes a crisis successfully, with my aid, he comes back for another checkup. I locate his next crisis and supply him with what he needs to meet it. I gave him the asbestos gloves. In about a month, a situation will arise where he must—under the circumstances—move a red-hot bar of metal. He's an artist. His hands—"

"I see. So it isn't always saving a man's life."

"Of course not," Talley said. "Life isn't the only vital factor. An apparently minor crisis may lead to—well, a divorce, a neurosis, a wrong decision, and the loss of hundreds of lives indirectly. I insure life, health, and happiness."

"You're an altruist. Only why doesn't the world storm your doors? Why limit your trade to a few?"

"I haven't got the time or the equipment."

"More machines could be built."

"Well," Talley said, "most of my customers are wealthy. I must live."

"You could read tomorrow's stock-market reports if you wanted dough," Carmichael said. "We get back to that old question. If a guy has miraculous powers, why is he satisfied to run a hole-in-the-wall store?"

"Economic reasons. I . . . ah . . . I'm averse to gambling."

"It wouldn't be gambling," Carmichael pointed out. " 'I often wonder what the vintners buy—' Just what *do* you get out of this?"

"Satisfaction," Talley said, "Call it that."

But Carmichael wasn't satisfied. His mind veered from the question and turned to the possibilities. Insurance, eh? Life, health, and happiness.

"What about me? Won't there be another crisis in my life sometime?"

"Probably. Not necessarily one involving personal danger."

"Then I'm a permanent customer."

"I . . . don't—"

"Listen," Carmichael said, "I'm not trying to shake you down. I'll pay. I'll pay plenty. I'm not rich, but I know exactly what a service like this would be worth to me. No worries—"

"It wouldn't be—"

"Oh, come off it. I'm not a blackmailer or anything. I'm not threatening you with publicity, if that's what you're afraid of. I'm an ordinary guy. Not a melodramatic villain. Do I look dangerous? What are you afraid of?"

"You're an ordinary guy, yes," Talley admitted. "Only—"

"Why not?" Carmichael argued. "I won't bother you. I passed one crisis successfully, with your help. There'll be another one due sometime. Give me what I need for that. Charge me anything you like. I'll get the dough somehow. Borrow it if necessary. I won't disturb you at all. All I ask is that you let me come in whenever I've passed a crisis, and get ammunition for the next one. What's wrong with that?"

"Nothing," Talley said soberly.

"Well, then. I'm an ordinary guy. There's a girl—it's Betsy Hoag. I want to marry her. Settle down somewhere in the country, raise kids, and have security. There's nothing wrong with that either, is there?"

Talley said, "It was too late the moment you entered this shop today."

Carmichael looked up. "Why?" he asked sharply.

A buzzer rang in the back. Talley went through the curtains and came back almost immediately with a wrapped parcel. He gave it to Carmichael.

Carmichael smiled. "Thanks," he said. "Thanks a lot. Do you have any idea when my next crisis will come?"

"In a week."

"Mind if I—" Carmichael was unwrapping the package. He took out a pair of plastic-soled shoes and looked at Talley, bewildered.

"Like that, eh? I'll need—shoes?"

"Yes."

"I suppose—" Carmichael hesitated. "I guess you wouldn't tell me why?" ·

"No, I won't do that. But be sure to wear them whenever you go out."

"Don't worry about that. And—I'll mail you a check. It may take me a few days to scrape up the dough, but I'll do it. How much—?"

"Five hundred dollars."

"I'll mail a check today."

"I prefer not to accept a fee until the client has been satisfied," Talley said. He had grown more reserved, his blue eyes cool and withdrawn.

"Suit yourself," Carmichael said. "I'm going out and celebrate. You—don't drink?"

"I can't leave the shop."

"Well, good-by. And thanks again. I won't be any trouble to you, you know. I promise that!" He turned away.

Looking after him, Talley smiled a wry, unhappy smile. He did not answer Carmichael's good-by. Not then.

When the door had closed behind him, Talley turned to the back of his shop and went through the door where the scanner was.

The lapse of ten years can cover a multitude of changes. A man with the possibility of tremendous power almost within his grasp can alter, in that time, from a man who will not reach for it to a man who will—and moral values be damned.

The change did not come quickly to Carmichael. It speaks well for his integrity that it took ten years to work such an alteration in all he had been taught. On the day he first went into Talley's shop there was little evil in him. But the temptation grew stronger week by week, visit by visit. Talley, for reasons of his own, was content to sit idly by, waiting for customers, smothering the inconceivable potentialities of his machine under a blanket of trivial functions. But Carmichael was not content.

It took him ten years to reach the day, but the day came at last.

Talley sat in the inner room, his back to the door. He was slumped low in an ancient rocker, facing the machine. It had changed little in the space of a decade. It still covered most of two walls, and the eyepiece of its scanner glittered under amber fluorescents.

Carmichael looked covetously at the eyepiece. It was window and doorway to a power beyond any man's dreams. Wealth beyond imagining lay just within that tiny opening. The rights over the life and death of every man alive. And nothing between that fabulous future and himself except the man who sat looking at the machine.

Talley did not seem to hear the careful footsteps or the creak of the door behind him. He did not stir as Carmichael lifted the gun slowly. One might think that he never guessed what was coming, or why, or from whom, as Carmichael shot him through the head.

Talley sighed and shivered a little, and twisted the scanner dial. It was not the first time that the eyepiece had shown him his own lifeless body, glimpsed down some vista of probability, but he never saw the slumping of that familiar figure without feeling a breath of indescribable coolness blow backward upon him out of the future.

He straightened from the eyepiece and sat back in his chair, looking thoughtfully at a pair of rough-soled shoes lying beside him on a table. He sat quietly for awhile, his eyes upon the shoes, his mind following Carmichael down the street and into the evening, and the morrow, and on toward that coming crisis which would depend on his secure footing on a subway platform as a train thundered by the place where Carmichael would be standing one day next week.

Talley had sent his messenger boy out this time for two pairs of shoes. He had hesitated long, an hour ago, between the rough-soled pair and the smooth. For Talley was a humane man, and there were many times when his job was distasteful to him. But in the end, this time, it had been the smooth-soled pair he had wrapped for Carmichael.

Now he sighed and bent to the scanner again, twisting the dial to bring into view a scene he had watched before.

Carmichael, standing on a crowded subway platform, glittering with oily wetness from some overflow. Carmichael, in the slick-soled shoes Talley had chosen for him. A commotion in the crowd, a surge toward the platform edge. Carmichael's feet slipping frantically as the train roared by.

"Good-by, Mr. Carmichael," Talley murmured. It was the farewell he had not spoken when Carmichael left the shop. He spoke it regretfully, and the regret was for the Carmichael of today, who did not yet deserve that end. He was not now a melodramatic villain whose death one could watch unmoved. But the Tim Carmichael of today had atonement to make for the Carmichael of ten years ahead, and the payment must be exacted.

It is not a good thing to have the power of life and death over one's fellow humans. Peter Talley knew it was not a good thing—but the power had been put into his hands. He had not sought it. It seemed to him that the machine had grown almost by accident to its tremendous completion under his trained fingers and trained mind.

At first it had puzzled him. How ought such a device to be used? What dangers, what terrible potentialities, lay in that Eye that could see through the veil of tomorrow? His was the responsibility, and it had weighed heavily upon him until the answer came. And after he knew the answer—well, the weight was heavier still. For Talley was a mild man.

He could not have told anyone the real reason why he was a shopkeeper. Satisfaction, he had said to Carmichael. And sometimes, indeed, there was deep satisfaction. But at other times—at times like this—there was only dismay and humility. Especially humility.

We have what you need. Only Talley knew that message was not for the individuals who came to his shop. The pronoun was plural, not singular. It was a message for the world—the world whose future was being carefully, lovingly reshaped under Peter Talley's guidance.

The main line of the future was not easy to alter. The future is a pyramid shaping slowly, brick by brick, and brick by brick Talley had to change it. There were some men who were necessary—men who would create and build—men who should be saved.

Talley gave them what they needed.

But inevitably there were others whose ends were evil. Talley gave them, too, what the world needed—death.

Peter Talley had not asked for this terrible power. But the key had been put in his hands, and he dared not delegate such authority as this to any other man alive. Sometimes he made mistakes.

He had felt a little surer since the simile of the key had occurred to him. The key to the future. A key that had been laid in his hands.

Remembering that, he leaned back in his chair and reached for an old and well-worn book. It fell open easily at a familiar passage. Peter Talley's lips moved as he read the passage once again, in his room behind the shop on Park Avenue.

"And I say also unto thee. That thou art Peter— And I will give unto thee the keys of the kingdom of heaven—"

THE CHOICE

BEFORE WILLIAMS WENT into the future he bought a camera and a tape recording-machine and learned shorthand. That night, when all was ready, we made coffee and put out brandy and glasses against his return.

"Good-bye," I said. "Don't stay too long."

"I won't," he answered.

I watched him carefully, and he hardly flickered. He must have made a perfect landing on the very second he had taken off from. He seemed not a day older; we had expected he might spend several years away.

"Well?"

"Well," said he, "let's have some coffee."

I poured it out, hardly able to contain my impatience. As I gave it to him I said again, "Well?"

"Well, the thing is, I can't remember."

"Can't remember? Not a thing?"

He thought for a moment and answered sadly, "Not a thing."

"But your notes? The camera? The recording-machine?"

The notebook was empty, the indicator of the camera rested at "1" where we had set it, the tape was not even loaded into the recording-machine.

"But good heavens," I protested, "why? How did it happen? Can you remember nothing at all?"

"I can remember only one thing."

"What was that?"

"I was shown everything, and I was given the choice whether I should remember it or not after I got back."

"And you chose not to? But what an extraordinary thing to—"

"Isn't it?" he said. "One can't help wondering why."

This sketch was originally published anonymously in the British *Punch*. Special thanks are due to Matthew M. Cammen, of Corning, New York, for calling it to my attention. *G. C.*

PART VI

Worlds of Tomorrow

Andrè Maurois

THE WAR AGAINST THE MOON

*(Fragment of a Universal History, published
by the University of C—mb—e, 1992)*

CHAPTER CXVII

World Conditions in 1962

By 1962 the last traces of the havoc wrought by the World War of 1947 had at length disappeared. New York, London, Paris, Berlin, and even Peking had been rebuilt. The birth-rate had been such that—in spite of worldwide casualties exceeding thirty millions of men and women in 1947 —the globe as a whole had almost regained the pre-war population level, when the world-census of 1961 was taken. The industrial and financial crisis had quieted down, and once more the interest of mankind was turning to the arts and to sport. Every house had its wireless movie. The balloon-match between Tokyo and Oxford in 1962 attracted to Moscow more than three million spectators, who came from every corner of the globe, and was the occasion of a Worldwide Welcome Celebration.

The Dictators of Public Opinion

It must in fairness be admitted that this rapid recovery, this exceedingly prompt healing of the moral and material wounds of the War, was in large measure the handiwork of the five men to whom the world at that time gave the title, 'Dictators of Public Opinion.' After 1930, political theorists had begun to realize that every democracy—being a government of public opinion—is largely in the hands of those who make public opinion—that is to say, the newspaper-owners. In every country the big business men, the great financiers, were being compelled to purchase influential newspapers and had little by little succeeded in doing so. They had been very clever in respecting the external forms of democracy. The people continued to elect their deputies, who continued to go through the forms of choosing ministers and presidents; but the ministers, presidents, and deputies could hold on to their positions only so long as they did what the Masters of Public Opinion told them to do, and they were duly submissive.

This tyranny in disguise might well have become dangerous if the new Masters of the World had been unscrupulous, but, as events turned out, the world was actually fortunate. In 1940 the last independent French newspaper was purchased by Count Alain de Rouvray, who thus completed his chain of papers, 'Les Journaux Français Réunis.' The Rouvray family were steel men from Lorraine, bred in the austere tradition of the province. Alain de Rouvray was regarded as a tremendous worker and a kind of saint: in the Louvre you can see his portrait, painted when he was twenty, by Jacques-Emile Blanche. The thin face is that of an impassioned ascetic, and more than one feature recalls Maurice Barrès. In England, British Newspapers Ltd. had since 1942 belonged to Lord Frank Douglas, a young man who beneath a casual air concealed an abundance of good sense and a truly Etonian respectability. His tousled blonde hair and clear eyes gave Lord Frank the appearance of a poet rather than a man of action. The master of the American press was the aged Joseph C. Smack, an extraordinary individual, almost blind, who lived far out in the country surrounded by an army of readers and stenographers. Smack was celebrated for the blunt brutality of his radiograms, but commanded respect throughout the world. The owner of the German newspaper, Dr. Macht, and the Japanese proprietor, Baron Tokungawa, were the distinguished figures who completed the universal directorate.

From 1943 onwards these five men had adopted the habit of holding a weekly meeting by wireless telephotophony. The invention was at that time rather new, and the apparatus still cost several millions of dollars. Indeed, the public was amazed to learn that the Dictators of Public Opinion could hold their conferences, even though they were thousands of miles apart, and yet be assured of absolute secrecy in their deliberations by requiring the Universal Hertzian of Police to give rigid protection to a special wave length.

Nobody knows who first used the title 'Dictator of Public Opinion.' The brilliant monograph of James Bookish (*The Dictators of Opinion*, Oxford 1979) relies on letters and newspaper-clippings to show that the phrase was in current usage all over the planet after 1944, though it does not appear in an official document earlier than 1945. (*Chambre des Députés, Discours de Fabre-Luce, 4 Janvier, 1945*).

The War of 1947 and the Dictators of Public Opinion

Every source recently published and in particular the *Journals* of Rouvray and Lord Frank Douglas show that in 1947 all five of the Dictators had striven earnestly to head off the War. Rouvray wrote in his *Journal* under the date June 20, 1947: 'Infuriating to think that in spite of our

apparent strength we are powerless against the self-conceit of the nations.'
In Douglas's *Journal:* 'A World-War for Albania! The whole thing is too
stupid for words. . . . The crowd is stupid even though the individual be
divine.'

On the eve of the declaration of war, all the newspapers in the world
had published an appeal to common sense drawn up by Smack; but public
opinion, rebelling against its masters for once, expressed itself in spite of
the Press and in defiance of it. In several cities the newspaper offices were
ransacked. The pro-War sheets which suddenly began to issue from secret
printing-shops watched their circulation go up like wild fire; and, once war
was declared, of course everything had to be sacrificed to national safety.

After the treaty of peace had been signed at Peking in 1951, the Directorate was reconstructed, Dr. Kraft succeeding Dr. Macht in Germany.
The other four were still alive. The minutes of their first meeting by
telephotophone are now deposited in the world archives in Geneva. This
meeting was devoted to analysing the causes of war and discussing the
means for preventing future ones. The five agreed once more to undertake
the education of the public on this subject, to refuse to publish any news-
story that might create hatred or distrust between nations, and, in the
event—which was always possible—that international incidents should
occur, to have an investigation made by reporters of a nation which was
not involved: the results of this investigation to be published exclusively
by papers belonging to the 'World Newspaper Association.' As he came
out from this meeting, Rouvray remarked to Brun, his secretary: 'I am as
sure of their good faith as I am of my own. If we can't strangle war this
time, we must give up hope for the human race.' (*Mémoires de Brun*, II,
343).

The Wind Crisis, May 1962

One month after the Tokyo-Oxford match, which had attracted such a
fine representation of the entire world, Professor Ben Tabrit, of the University of Marrakech, invented the wind-accumulator, an apparatus which
has since become so familiar throughout the world that there is no need to
describe it. The principle is simple enough: by means of an accumulator,
which is at once thoroughly practical and very cheap and which is based
on the decomposition of water and the use of liquid hydrogen, it became
possible to store up the force of the winds, thus obtaining a form of
energy infinitely less expensive than that secured from gasoline or coal.
Several months passed before business-men grasped the far-reaching results of this discovery. It was clear enough, however, that industries concentrated in mining districts or near the water-power sites would move to
countries where the winds were strong and steady; and that certain districts hitherto uninhabited had suddenly attained an incredible value. It
was not long before the International Stock Exchange at Bagdad was list-

ing the stocks of the Gobi Desert and Wind Concern, the British Windmill Company, and the Société Française des Vents Alizés; and in December 1962 the struggle for sites suitable for accumulating plants burst out on land and sea.

Incidents of 1963

The year 1963 is marked by several serious incidents, the best known of which are the occupation of Mont-Ventoux and the seizure of the floating factory at Singapore. Mont-Ventoux, situated on the plain near Lyons, owes its name to the violent wind which is almost constantly roaring across its summit. At the beginning of the twentieth century a French scientist had estimated the capacity of windmills placed on top of Ventoux as equivalent in energy to Niagara Falls. A site of such value could not fail to stir the covetous instincts of big business. One should read Harwood's book, which has since become a classic (*The Mont-Ventoux Episode*, Boston 1988), the story of the incredible bickerings which broke out about this time between France and Italy. The affair of the floating factory of Singapore was still more difficult. An industrial privateer flying the flag of the Russo-Chinese Empire cut the towing-hawers, whereupon cruisers of the United Dominions, escorting the island on which the factory stood, opened fire and sank her. An extraordinary session of the Assembly of the League of Nations was immediately summoned.

The newspapers of the W. N. A. tried to calm public opinion, but unfortunately more powerful forces were working against them. The labouring masses began to understand that this scientific revolution would have the gravest possible consequences for them. The miners knew that within five years—or ten years at most—they would no longer be needed. The Trade Unions brought pressure to bear on the national governments to make sure they would gain possession of windy territories. The Assembly at Geneva in June 1963 was swept by violent storms, and, if it had not been for the tact of the Prince of Monaco, who presided, it is probable that the Assembly, which was intended to guarantee peace, would have been the scene and the occasion of a whole series of declarations of war. Thanks to the pacifying influence of Prince Rainbert, however, the delegates left Switzerland without making any irremediable decisions; but all the experts in international psychology warned their governments that a World War seemed inevitable. Smack directed his papers to run a scarehead:

RUSSO-CHINESE EMPIRE REJECTS FRANCO-GERMAN OFFER

Intervention of Lord Frank Douglas

On his return from Geneva, Lord Frank Douglas landed in Paris for a talk with Rouvray. We do not know the exact terms of this conversation, which was destined to have so far-reaching an influence upon the history not merely of the World but of the entire Solar System. The substance of what they said has been preserved by Brun (*Mémoires de Brun*, III, 159), but his text is not regarded as a word-for-word transcript. The author himself admits that he reconstructed it from memory several hours after the conversation. To catch its tone, one must read through the transcript— obviously honest, but rather dull—which was made by a young secretary, and also the *Journal* of Lord Frank, which is remarkable for the sturdy and paradoxical, yet cynical, spirit of the author.

The two men first exchanged opinions on the ground situation. They were agreed in believing that it was extremely serious. Rouvray was discouraged. Before the war of 1947 he had possessed an extraordinary confidence in the instrument he had himself created; but, after he had seen that catastrophe come without being able to avert it, he had become sad and sceptical. We may quote from Brun's text:

There was one thing in the world,' said M. de Rouvray, 'that people fear more than massacre, even more than death—and that is boredom. . . . They are getting bored with the era of understanding and international reasonableness that we have set up. . . . Our newspapers tell the truth and are reliable, but they are no longer exciting. Smack himself admits that his front pages are dull. . . . We have tried artistic remedies, not without success; sport and the great crimes saved us for twenty years, but look at the statistics! Police efficiency is getting to be so perfect that crime is becoming rarer and rarer. The World is tired of everything, tired even of boxing. The last two aerial balloon races didn't get more than a million spectators. . . . We have educated the crowds; we have taught them to respect order, to applaud the other side. They have nothing to hate any more. . . . Now, my dear Douglas, it is regrettable but true that hatred is the only thing that can unite mankind. . . . People say France used to be composed of provinces and those provinces ended by being collected into one country; and they ask why it shouldn't be the same way with the nations. My reply is: "The French provinces united against a neighbouring country, but what enemy is there against whom the nations of the whole world can unite?" Don't offer me any platitudes, my dear friend. Don't propose union against poverty, against disease. No, it is the popular imagination that is sick, and the popular imagination that must be taken care of. We need an enemy that we can see. Unfortunately, there isn't any.'

'Well,' said Lord Frank, 'we have got into almost the same predicament, Rouvray, in my country. Just now, as I was flying over Burgundy, I was thinking about the battles of the Kings of France and the Dukes of Burgundy, and I was saying to myself: "They united at last, but they united *against* somebody. Against whom can the world unite?" The only difference between you and me is that I think I have an answer.'

'There is no answer,' said M. de Rouvray. 'Against whom can we unite?'

'Well, why not against the Moon?' asked the Englishman, quietly.

M. de Rouvray shrugged his shoulders. 'You are a witty man, but I have no time for joking. In a few weeks, perhaps in a few days, a fleet of giant aeroplanes directed by a pitiless general staff in Bagdad or Canton will no doubt be at work above this city which to-day is so calm. These beautiful houses will be crashing down in a frightful mixture of concrete and human flesh. . . . And 1947 will begin again.'

'I am not joking, Rouvray, my dear fellow— I am serious as I can be. Listen! You know what our readers are like. You know how easy it is to make them believe anything. Haven't you seen them cured by remedies which had no merit at all—except that they were well advertised? Haven't you seen them go crazy over books of which they could not understand a word, over paintings which appealed to them simply because a clever publicity-campaign by publishers or art-dealers had prepared them to accept anything? Why should they be any more able to resist a campaign conducted by us? We ought to know all about that sort of thing—and we certainly control the most powerful instruments of publicity.'

'I don't know what you are driving at,' said Rouvray. 'What campaign do you want to undertake now?'

'Look here,' said Douglas; 'you have the same experience I had in 1947, and you have also read what happened in 1914. Each time the same thing happened in every country. Hatred of the enemy was created and then kept up by stories of crimes and atrocities, which were almost identical on each side. The critical spirit vanished completely, common sense became a crime, credulity became a duty. The most improbable yarn was immediately accepted by a public opinion which had gone mad. The people were so aroused that they were ready to believe anything about the enemy. Don't you agree?'

'Entirely,' said Rouvray. 'But I don't see anything in all this to help us out of our present predicament.'

'Wait,' said the Englishman. 'Just suppose that we could create this frenzied readiness to believe anything. Suppose we could get every country in the world into this frame of mind against an enemy who didn't exist at all—or who at least could never come into contact with us. Don't you suppose that we should then manage to infect these countries—this time without any danger at all—with a war-psychosis that would unite them? Don't you think that we should then at last succeed in creating a unity of the entire planet?'

'No doubt,' said the other newspaper-owner, somewhat irritated, 'but again I ask, "Against whom?"'

'I don't see any difficulty in your question. It doesn't in the least matter against whom we unite, because the chief characteristic of this enemy is precisely the fact that he does not exist at all. Against the inhabitants of the Moon—or Mars—or Venus—it is all the same to me. Look here, Rouvray! suppose tomorrow morning we should tell our readers throughout the entire word that some village had been mysteriously destroyed by powerful rays from any one of the three. Would they believe it?'

'They would believe it all right, but if they were to make an investigation—'

'But, my dear fellow, what do you care who makes an investigation or whether the investigation is published, since we control all sources of information—and consequently all public power. Only we mustn't be fools enough to have it happen in some place easy to get at. We shouldn't choose an avenue in London or New York or any place in Paris. Suppose we picked out a little village in Turkestan or Alaska. They wouldn't go there to check it up, would they?'

'No, you're right. They'll believe it. And then what?'

'The same kind of thing in China; the next day in Australia. Bigger and bigger headlines, of course: MYSTERIOUS FOE! WHO IS ATTACKING THE EARTH? General dismay. Already the squabble over windy territory is slipping over onto the second page. Do you get me?'

'I am beginning to be interested.'

'After eight days of this kind of thing, we could give them interviews with scientists. I know some men in England who won't refuse this little service when they understand it is the only way to save the world. You have some of them in France; Kraft has some in Germany. All the scientists will agree that by following up the path of the rays it can be proved that they converge in a common point of origin, which will be the Moon —or Mars, if you prefer.'

'No,' said Rouvray, 'I like the Moon better.'

'Ah?' said Douglas in surprise. 'On the whole, thinking it over, I should have liked Mars. They haven't been told very often that the Moon is inhabited.'

'I know,' said Rouvray; 'but all the same I am sure they'll believe it is. That's one thing we can rely on.'

'All right,' said Lord Frank. 'Then the Moon is the starting-place for this mysterious attack. After that begins our campaign against the men in the Moon, and if every youngster in the world is not convinced within three months that every inhabitant in the Moon is a monster, and that the first duty of every terrestrian is to hate and destroy the Moon, then I'll fire my editorial writers. But I am not worried about that. They know their business.'

I had been observing [writes Brun] the Chief's face during this conversation. He had begun by being somewhat annoyed. He had not liked what he thought was the daring wit of the Englishman, indulging in these paradoxes in view of the terrific tragedy which impended; but little by little he had taken on an air of interest and at length of satisfaction. When Douglas finished he got up and shook hands with him.

'I am with you. It is crazy, but it is probably our only chance to prevent war.'

He gave me orders to arrange a telephotophone conference of the
Council of Five and to warn the Hertzian Police. (Brun, III, 160, 164:
The Campaign against the Moon.) Even today, in spite of the progress
that has been made in applied psychology, it is hard to reread accounts of
the W. N. A.'s 1963 press-campaign against the Moon without admiring
their certainty of method and richness of invention. The campaign followed roughly the course mapped out by Douglas and Rouvray in the
conversation we have described. It included three main steps:

(*a*) The creation by fear of the belief in the mysterious and harmful
phenomena.

(*b*) Attribution of these phenomena to an unknown agent and the
search for that agent.

(*c*) Determination of the enemy and the great campaign, so-called,
against the Moon.

(See André Dubois, *La Campagne Anti-Lunaire*, Paris 1982).

The results were remarkable. One month after the campaign began, a
frenzied fury against the Moon burst out among all the peoples of the
world. The newspapers of the W. N. A. had been able, without any protest from any source, to adopt a standardized headline:

THE WORLD FIRST!

The squabble over windy territories had been adjusted as if by magic,
the whole agitation having been the work of jealous financiers who had
tried to drag their countries in the wake of their own interests. Terrified by
the movement of world-wide patriotism which transformed their struggles
into a crime, they suddenly discovered that nothing was simpler than to
establish a World-Wide Wind Company, which would absorb the Windmill Company and the United Mountain-Top Concern and would guarantee the administration of Mont-Ventoux by an international commission.
The general staffs—which in July were still busy getting ready their war
plans against one another—no longer thought of anything except col-
laboration and were busy with war plans for common defence. A Chinese
military commission had been cheered in Berlin and escorted down Unter
den Linden by a group singing the new *Hymn of Hate Against the Moon.*
In Japan a number of people had committed *hara-kiri* to avenge the insult
upon the honour of the world. In London the war-madness took a curious
form. In the music-halls, in the streets, and in their houses, men, women,
and children were singing the same refrain: *Oh, stop tickling me, Man
in the Moon; stop tickling, stop, ah! stop!* In the United States the sum of
$100,000,000, was voted by Congress—in spite of the opposition of two
pro-Moon Senators—for any scientist who could find a way of getting a
message through to the surface of the Moon, or, if not a message, any
missile which would be effective for reprisal.

Ben Tabrit's Attitude

Among the articles published at the beginning of this campaign by the W. N. A., one of the most remarkable was that of Ben Tabrit, Dean of the Faculty of Science of Marrakech University and inventor of the wind-accumulator. Most of the scientists who had collaborated in the campaign were among the personal friends of one or another of the five directors, and, realizing the desperate position of the planet, had consented—although with regret—to make themselves accomplices in this well-intended deception. But such was not the case with Ben Tabrit, a gloomy man living a retired life and seldom emerging from his laboratory, who nevertheless created a sensation by the vigour and originality of his ideas when he at length took a hand in the debate.

In this particular case he had written an article in reply to a pamphlet by Professor Baxley of Cambridge. Baxley had asserted that before fighting the Moon-men it was desirable to try to change their minds. Ben Tabrit in his reply raised the following question: 'Is it possible for living beings to exist on the surface of the Moon? Not if we understand by that term collections of cells similar to those which make up our bodies, breathing, building-up tissue, and breaking it down as we do. But why should we limit life to a single type? It may well be that these beings consist of stable groups of radiations, of volitional centres, which we cannot understand and never shall understand, but which, for some unknown and inconceivable reason, have at length made up their minds to destroy us. After all, if the Moon-men exist (and the phenomena which have for some weeks been observed by the earth seem to indicate that they do exist), they must necessarily be monsters—that is to say, creatures so different from ourselves that the idea of entering into relations with them and sending them messages of peace is simply madness. Between forms of life which have evolved in different ways during billions of years, there is no common point of contact for a common vocabulary. If the Moon-men exist, we must be in the same position towards them as the hunters of ancient days were in toward the tiger. They didn't argue with the tiger. They either killed him or were killed by him. Mankind has not civilized the tigers. It has simply wiped them out.

'Now, it would have been comparatively more easy to create a language common to mankind and the tiger than to build up a common philosophy for mankind and the Moon-men. A tiger was at least a mammal. Many of his physical functions resembled our own. We could understand a large part of his physiological reactions. But of the Moon-men we understand nothing at all. To attempt to explain them or to explain ourselves to them is to undertake to solve an equation consisting only of unknown quantities. The attempt to combat them has one meaning only—that is, to attempt to transmit to the surface of the Moon rays of such power that no combination can, in their presence, continue to exist.'

Conflict of Rouvray and Douglas

Lord Frank Douglas had read Ben Tabrit's article with amusement. He was delighted to see an idea which he had once thought so absurd stirring up the best brains on the planet. Rouvray, on the other hand, had for some time seemed curiously uneasy. More than once he had telephotophoned to Douglas and Smack asking if it wouldn't be better to give up the campaign. (*Journal de Brun*, III, 210.) The desired effect had been produced. The World-Wide Wind Company had been established. Why keep it up?

'There are three reasons,' replied Douglas. 'It is a bully good game. If we bring events to a sudden close, we shall make our campaign seem improbable. Moreover, the squabble over the winds was merely one incident explaining a state of mind which was, as you so aptly put it, a general condition of hostility. We have given them this craze about the Moon as a toy to keep them busy. Let us be careful how we take it from them. What are you afraid of, anyhow?'

'I may seem very naïve to you,' said Rouvray. 'What I am afraid of is that the Moon-men may exist after all.'

In the apparatus you could see Lord Frank's face dissolve into a hearty, boyish laugh.

'There you are! The greatest triumph of applied psychology yet! You have convinced yourself!'

'Don't laugh,' said Rouvray. 'I am genuinely upset. Yes, that's it, upset. What do you expect? I have just been reading over the scientific history of the war of 1914 and the war of 1947. Have you ever considered the almost incredible progress that has been brought about, under pressure of hatred and necessity, since those two periods? Consider what aviation was like in 1914 and what it had become in 1918. Consider what we knew about the energy within the atom in 1947 and what our knowledge had become in 1951. And suppose that if to-day—'

'But my dear Rouvray,' said Lord Frank, 'even if Ben Tabrit or somebody else should discover—by some miracle that I cannot imagine— apparatus for exploring the Moon or reaching some part of its surface, what earthly importance would that have, since it is certain nobody is there?'

'Who knows about that? You have read Ben Tabrit's article. There is no being there of the kind that we have hitherto understood by the phrase "living being," but may there not be, as he supposes, certain conglomerations of energy which are individuals in their own way and which may react, reason, or fight?' (Brun, 212, 213.)

About this date, according to Deline's *Life of Smack* (Leipzig, 1975), there was an exchange of radiograms between Rouvray and Smack. The latter's reply proves that Rouvray's arguments had not impressed him in the least. We give the exact wording, which is very characteristic: 'Must go ahead and let B. T. go to the devil. Hope you are well and happy. Ditto Madame Smack.'

At the next meeting of the Council of Five, Rouvray again advanced the same ideas, and was assailed by Douglas who easily got the upper hand. It was the general opinion that the passions they had aroused would be directed against some earthly object, if the hatred against the Moon-men was suddenly abated.

Ben Tabrit's Discovery

The entire autumn of 1963 was filled with the emotion aroused by new outrages, of which the newspapers gave more and more exact details, and by processions, meetings, and demonstrations in favour of World Unity. Countries which had heretofore been at swords' points exchanged delegations; in every school on the globe, planetary patriotism was taught. A cartoon of a Moon-man, created by an artist on the staff of *Punch*, became popular and could be seen on walls from Timbuktu to Benares.

In November, 1963, Ben Tabrit, who had been silently at work in his laboratory for several months, requested the W. N. A. to announce that he had at length discovered what he had been looking for, that is:

(*a*) a ray capable of destroying by its passage any combination of atoms, and

(*b*) a transmitting-apparatus powerful enough to send a ray thus produced to the surface of the Moon.

When this letter was communicated to the Council, Rouvray, in terror, proposed having Ben Tabrit come to Paris and there telling him the true situation. Douglas and Dr. Kraft were vigorously opposed. 'We all know Ben Tabrit. He is a scientific fanatic. If we tell him that some of his colleagues have consented, even for the benefit of Humanity, to publish inexact observations, he is quite capable of stirring up a public scandal. If he does that, all the authority of the W. N. A. will vanish in a couple of minutes—and our authority is all that stands between peace and a general massacre. What danger is there in letting Ben Tabrit go ahead with his investigations? Let him shoot his rays at the insensible matter in the Moon if he wants to! He will have to persuade the governments to put at his disposal the necessary funds for constructing his apparatus, and that will be a new and excellent food for public curiosity.'

All Rouvray could get was a decision that in the papers of the W. N. A. the outrages of the Moon-men should happen a little further apart. It was decided provisionally to have them about a month apart—at irregular intervals, of course, for probability's sake—and after several trials of Ben Tabrit's process, the press campaign was to come to a definite halt. It would then be possible to explain that the Moon-men—terrified, no doubt, by the Moroccan scientist's ray—had given up their crimes. The people of the world would have the joy of triumph, and it would probably be possible, thanks to this wave of feeling, to prolong World Unity for a certain period.

Next day Smack's newspapers announced in screaming headlines:

MOROCCAN SCIENTIST TO FIGHT THE MOON

The Catastrophe of February 1964

It had been easy enough to get from the governments funds sufficient to construct Ben Tabrit's apparatus, and by the end of January the distinguished scientist had collected at Marrakech all that he needed. The first experiment took place February 2nd. It was plainly a success. Through powerful telescopes it was possible to observe the ray's effect on the surface of the Moon. Craters of dizzying depth were hollowed out in a second. These attacks were made at three widely separated points on the flattest surface that could be found on the Moon, and next day all the newspapers of the W. N. A. published triumphant articles on the possible extent of destruction, with enlarged photographs: 'Condition of the Moon before the first attack. Condition of the Moon after the ray had passed.'

Who then imagined how soon there would be another opportunity to consider—on the surface of the Earth, itself—destructive attacks of the same kind?

The third and the fourth and the fifth days of February passed in the greatest calm. On the sixth, at five o'clock in the morning (Brun, IV, 17), Kraft called Rouvray on the telephotophone. Rouvray, who was half asleep, went to the apparatus and found Kraft's image rather vague.

'My dear friend,' said Kraft, 'I have terrible news for you. The city of Darmstadt was completely destroyed last night.'

'I can't hear you very well,' said Rouvray.

'I am talking from my aeroplane. The city of Darmstadt was destroyed last night in a way that can't be explained. I am flying over the ruins at this moment. My projectors show that in the place where the city stood, there is nothing left but glowing calcined rock. It is so hot that you cannot go down nearer than five hundred metres. Unfortunately, there's no doubt about it. The Moon is conducting reprisals.'

'Horrible, horrible!' said Rouvray. 'My fears were too well founded, and the men in the Moon—'

'Look out, Rouvray!' said Dr. Kraft. 'At this hour in the morning I cannot guarantee the secrecy of our wave. Be so kind as to call a secret meeting of the Council.'

'How will 8:15 do?' asked Rouvray. (Brun, IV, 19, 20.)

The Council of War on February 6

When the Council met, Dr. Kraft told his colleagues his story of the catastrophe. The village had been completely destroyed in the centre; in the suburbs a certain number of houses had been reduced to ashes. Others seemed to have escaped. There was no way of knowing whether the ruins sheltered any survivors, but it was scarcely to be hoped. The heat, which prevented aeroplanes from landing, must have finished off the injured. From villages outside of Darmstadt it was possible to learn a little. The Moon-men's attack must have been delivered a little after midnight. The sudden heat had awakened a good many people near the zone attacked. None of them had seen any light. The Moon-men were evidently using a dark ray. All day long the place where the city had been, when observed from the sky, looked like craters of an immense volcano.

Douglas opened the conference with a speech disclaiming responsibility for the catastrophe. All he had ever thought of was starting a harmless and even amusing delusion. The event showed that the idea of a planetary war could not be employed without danger to the world's domestic affairs. Rouvray, who seemed rather distracted, replied that they all shared the responsibility, that the whole Directorate had joined in this dangerous game with the best intentions, and that the question now was not to fix responsibility but to find remedies.

Dr. Kraft observed that, although within the secret circle of the Council it might be worth while to admit a common fault, their attitude, so far as public opinion was concerned, must not change. In fact, from that viewpoint, the situation had not changed at all. The outrages had become real instead of imaginary. That altered their physical importance, but not their metaphysical value. As for their value as propaganda, it had even been increased, and it was necessary to derive from them all possible advantage, for the safety of the world itself.

Smack, who spoke next, said that all the evening editions were discussing war-credits. Since Ben Tabrit was the only man who owned a weapon that was good for anything, he must be persuaded to reveal his process, and unlimited funds must be put at his disposal in order to finish up the Moon.

'May I be permitted to offer an opinion exactly opposed to Mr. Smack's?' asked Rouvray. 'It is extremely disagreeable to me to come here to triumph over the realization of a prophecy which I hardly believed when I made it. Nevertheless, it seems to me the unfortunate result of our efforts ought to be a warning to us. It seems clear enough to me that the more means we place at Ben Tabrit's disposal, the more we shall increase the force of the attacks and the vigorous reprisals that will result from them. Why not let the Moon-men alone? They never bothered us until we imprudently annoyed them. Isn't there reason for supposing that if we go ahead as we used to, paying no attention to them, they on their side will be glad enough of renewed quiet and escape from danger? It is impossible they should feel any lively hatred of us. Why, they hardly know us!'

'That, my dear Rouvray, is not clear reasoning,' said Douglas. 'One doesn't really hate anyone unless one has very little acquaintance with him. On the other hand, does the word "hatred" have any meaning on the Moon?'

'Well,' went on Rouvray, 'if we wish to give the most complete satisfaction that we can to public opinion and employ our credits in interplanetary undertakings, why not use these credits to get into communication with these beings? After all, in this undertaking our good faith would be complete. We thought we were striking a world in which there was no life. Is it possible to make the Moon-men understand that?'

'Quite impossible,' said Douglas. 'Remember Ben Tabrit's article. We have neither ideas nor vocabulary nor sense-organs in common with these creatures. How could we communicate with them?' [1]

In the end all of them, even Rouvray, admitted that he was right and that there was nothing left but to go to war. Again the dreadful word was pronounced. It was decided, however, to let the Moon alone and not to make any new attack if the Moon left the earth in peace (Brun, IV, 33).

Death of Rouvray

The events of the next two days are not very well known. The phono-photographic record of the Council meetings show that there was some question of having Ben Tabrit tuned in on the collective apparatus. Smack, who was well acquainted with the Moroccan scientist and had at one time collaborated with him, objected, urging that one member of the Council should go to Marrakech in person. Rouvray was naturally chosen, since it was he who had asked for temporary cessation of the attacks.

On the evening of the 6th it was learned that M. de Rouvray's aeroplane had not reached Marrakech. At 5 o'clock, the Central News-council of the W. N. A. was advised that the floating fragments of the plane had been discovered near the Balearic Islands. Rouvray was drowned. Many historians assert that the old Frenchman had committed suicide (see especially Jean Prevost's *Life of Rouvray*, Paris, 1970). It is obviously hard to prove the falsity of this theory. Rouvray always travelled alone, in a little monoplane which he drove himself. It is certain that since morning he had shown signs of unusual agitation, and then, too, the hypothesis of an accident is scarcely probable; for the aeroplane was of the general gyroscopic model, invented in 1962, and its stability was proof against any error of manipulation.

The suicide-theory was not accepted by Brun or Douglas, both of whom had had conversations with Rouvray before he left. He seemed so im-

[1] This phrase of Douglas's, so often quoted in our scholastic manuals as an example of false reasoning, is less absurd than is ordinarily supposed. It must be remembered that in 1964 there was no conception, even the vaguest sort, of the theory of sensory equivalents, and Douglas could not imagine the transpositions of language which to-day render interplanetary communication so easy. Consult *Sensory Equivalents*, published by the League of Planets, Venus, 1990.

pressed with the importance of his mission, had expressed so much hope of saving the world by immediate stopping of the attacks, that it is difficult to believe that he would have killed himself while he was engaged in what he believed to be his duty.

Brun (IV, 210-50) sets forth at length his own hypothesis, which is that Rouvray was assassinated by anti-Moon fanatics. It is certain that from 1964 onwards, the destruction of aeroplane-controls from a distance was very easy, but it must be admitted that in Rouvray's case there is no proof of any such crime. It is certain that anti-Moon fanaticism had attained tremendous violence in many minds; and it is impossible not to be impressed by the hatred with which a certain number of writers attacked Rouvray's memory with the epithet 'pro-moon.' On the other hand, however, his attitude at the Council on February 6 was unknown to the public at the time of his death. The meeting had been secret, and there is no way of determining who had decided on the crime, organized, and executed it. Suicide, accident, or assassination, Rouvray's death was a disaster for the planet.

The behaviour of Ben Tabrit was no less mysterious. Did he, as he claimed, fail to receive the radiogram directing him to suspend any new attack on the Moon, or was he unable to resist the temptation to make further tests of his apparatus? The question is highly controversial. (Consult *The Responsibilities for the Inter-Planetary War*, Jerusalem, 12 vols.) At any rate there is no doubt about the facts themselves. During the night of the 6th and 7th all astronomical observers on the earth observed that a new hole was being burned into the Moon by Ben Tabrit's ray. Retaliation was not long in coming. On February 7th, the cities of Elbeuf (France), Bristol, Rhode Island, and Upsala (Sweden) were burned to ashes by the Moon. The era of Inter-Planetary War had begun.

RALPH ROBIN

PLEASANT DREAMS

"YOUR WIFE IS beautiful and a charming hostess and very interesting," the visitor bubbled.

"Isn't she?" Gniss said. "I married her only last year. I was especially taken with her dark hair. That's extremely rare, you know."

They walked into Gniss's most private office, and soft lights came on. The visitor gazed around, surprised.

"I see you are looking for the desk or table. Men of my rank don't use any," Gniss said.

There were not even chairs, only the couches affected in late years by fashionable people. Gniss dropped onto one, grunting, and waved the visitor to another.

"Do you know what this divan I'm lying on is covered with?" Gniss did not wait for an answer. "Cloth made from the cocoons of moth larvae by an incredibly ancient and expensive method."

The visitor shook his head in wonderment. The couch he was on was upholstered more modestly in plastic—of the very best quality, of course.

"It must be convenient to live right where you work," the visitor said.

They had just dined in Gniss's apartment, the official residence of the Chief Watcher. The apartment was a grand affair; since the time that Gniss had risen to Chief Watcher, it had spread through a whole floor of the immense building.

"My wife says I might not work at night so much if I lived farther away," Gniss pointed out.

"Is there much to do at night?" the visitor asked.

"I don't have my title for nothing! Even while they sleep, we watch them."

"You mean you put microphones under suspects' beds and listen to them talk in their sleep?" The visitor smiled to show that he was joking.

Gniss bellowed and shook, surprising the visitor, who thought the response was more than his feeble joke deserved. But the good-natured laughter was something to remember, he noted for his mental scrapbook. At school, Gniss had been rather a dour boy.

"My dear fellow," Gniss said when he had control of his voice again, "they were doing that centuries before the first dispersal of man. Look at this!"

He shifted on his couch and began to play with a little jeweled wheel projecting from the wall. A section of the floor—at least a quarter of the large room—rose on slender pillars to make a platform. Under the platform, the purple floor appeared unchanged.

Gniss rolled his heavy body on one side and talked, it seemed to the visitor, to his pillow.

"Give me Blor," he said.

The visitor could see a faint hazy eddy above the platform. Nothing else happened.

"Oh, well," said Gniss. "He rarely sleeps in his own bed—that's what makes him useful. But he's only a double spy."

The visitor's eyes were wide. *Only* a double spy!

"I'll show you something really big," Gniss said. He spoke gently to the pillow: "Give me Stak."

"Not—" the visitor blurted.

"Correct," Gniss said. "The famous rebel."

"But I thought—"

"That we couldn't catch up with him? That's what we let out for the public, and, naturally, for him. But we ran him down, and now we are watching him in a hundred different ways. If we arrested him, he would undoubtedly kill himself. That's something that even my watchers can't stop a determined man from doing. But before he dies, we want to find out who the traitor was that kept him informed of the government's plans during the critical time last year."

The visitor hadn't known, of course, that Stak had made use of an agent in official circles, but he was discreet enough to say nothing. It frightened him a little to hear such portentous matters, yet it flattered him, too, that his old school friend would be so open with him.

The haze above the platform deepened, and shone with internal light. The platform itself began to glow and to vibrate on its delicate pillars. Or perhaps it did not move; perhaps it was an illusion from the shimmering light.

The visitor did not know what to expect, but he felt a warm ripple of excitement. He glanced at Gniss. His host was watching the platform with an indefinable expression, in which there was at least some official—or was it fashionable?—weariness.

He has seen so much, the visitor thought, turning back to the platform.

Vaporous waves of light were rolling straight up, to dissipate; the visitor did not know where. The waves split and were less like waves and then were not waves at all. They were vague forms, gray and colored: some suggested people; some suggested things. Continually, they changed in shape and in size and in color.

"They are dreams!" the visitor exclaimed.

"Stak's dreams," Gniss said. "Now we are getting some continuity. Look."

"Where is Stak?"

"Oh, you rarely see the dreamer. You see through his eyes. That woman —the old woman with the young face; it's an odd angle, and the water and the stream and the bare arms—he must be dreaming he's a child and she's giving him a bath. It's unfortunate she didn't drown him."

The woman melted, faded, and a green billow was a wood and was separating into trees, and there was a kind of park. A lamb with a very intelligent face walked around a tree. Suddenly the lamb opened its mouth and cried like a human baby.

The visitor was startled. It was the first sound from the dream projection.

"You mean you can hear the dreams too?" he asked naively.

"Of course, my friend. Our technical people are talented."

"I should say! Tell me, how is it all done?"

"Well, we were working along at a telepathic instrument, which isn't quite perfected yet. Thoughts, you know, are produced by electrical impulses in the brain and these induce weak electromagnetic fields. Our theory was to build up the patterns of visual and auditory thoughts from the electromagnetic fields. For some reason the instrument hasn't worked right as a general device, but we found out by accident that it worked perfectly for dreams. Dreams are a form of thought, but there is a subtle difference in the fields."

"Marvelous!" exclaimed the visitor. He had not noitced the metamorphosis of the technical people into "we."

Wait till I tell my children, the visitor thought. But maybe he had better not say anything at all about his call on Gniss. He smiled as he remembered how his children had tried to talk him out of visiting his old schoolmate.

"Visit the museums," they had told him. "The art galleries. Go inside that big statue of Kumat. See the insect zoo—it's a wonderful place and very educational." The youngsters had been to the capital twice, their father never, and they were very knowing. "There's plenty to do without looking for trouble," his boy Trenr had insisted.

"But Gniss and I were great friends at school, and I'm a respectable citizen. Why should Gniss cause me trouble?" he had asked, puzzled.

Images came into being on the stage, and vanished, in a bizarre panorama. Uniformed watchers, already taller than a dream roof, grew still taller until their heads were lost in the real ceiling. Their monstrous hands held hoop-shaped mind-rippers. A terrified voice cried, "No—no—no—" over and over. The word filled the room.

The visitor felt a surge of pity for the trapped outlaw, lost now in the nightmare of fear. Yet he said scornfully, as much to himself as to Gniss, "He's a coward after all, isn't he?"

"Everyone's a coward," Gniss replied. "But, awake, Stak is less a coward than most."

The nightmare dissolved into confused patterns; the terrified voice dropped to a thin, wordless babble. The dream projection focused to a sort of cellar. Twenty or thirty men and women were sitting on the floor. Their faces were turned toward Gniss and the visitor.

"He's dreaming about a meeting, and I think he's making a speech," Gniss said. "This is likely to be useful. Naturally it's being watched in the regular monitoring chambers. Our monitors will try to identify everybody at the meeting. There are difficulties. Sometimes several faces are blended into one in a dream.

"Look at those expressions! The sentimental fool thinks all his followers are noble souls. See that skinny fellow to the left? He positively drips nobility of soul. And that woman over there? She belongs in heaven. And will get there soon, no doubt," Gniss added with a laugh.

The visitor found himself saying, "But dreams are all pretty much mixed up. Isn't it possible he might put a chance acquaintance at one of those dream meetings? Or someone he saw on the street? Couldn't it happen to anybody?"

"We try to be as fair as we can. But you know the old saying: 'It is far better that ten innocent men be punished than that one guilty man go free.'"

"That's very true," the visitor said earnestly, "and everyone must be assumed to be guilty until he can prove his innocence."

Gniss motioned for him to be quiet. Stak's muttering voice was gaining strength. It sounded more like language, and soon the visitor could pick out words.

". . . choose . . . happy and free . . . man's will . . . life . . . sacrifice . . . era . . . Gniss . . ."

The word was unmistakable.

Gniss roared his laughter. "I'm even in their dreams. But I suppose this must be boring you. Shall I turn it off? I can always have it repeated by the recording system, if I need to see it later." His hand was at the little jeweled wheel.

"I'm enjoying it," the visitor protested.

"Would you rather take a walk through some of the installations? We work around the clock, you know. We could look in at the classification laboratory where we catalogue everybody by the positions of the atoms in their chromosomes. Give the technician a piece of your fingernail or a bit of hair or a scraping of skin—anything that contains at least one whole cell—and in five minutes he'll tell you your name. Or we could visit the mind-ripper range where we train recruits."

"I'd rather not see that," the visitor said. In the back of his mind was a rumor about the mind-ripper range that he had tried not to listen to.

"The targets for today didn't prove their innocence," Gniss explained drily. His hand was still at the wheel. "Well?"

"Let's watch it a little more," the visitor said. "It's changing to something new."

"H'mm, so it is. This looks interesting."

It was the park where the lamb had walked around the tree and cried. But there was no lamb: there was a young woman, walking, alone. She was wearing a long cloak of a kind out of fashion for several years, but, the visitor thought, more becoming than the short cloaks the women were wearing now. Her yellow hair was loosely tied with a filmy scarf. Her face was more beautiful than any real face the visitor had ever seen.

It was a face of delicate symmetry; of early love; of high intelligence.

Gniss raised himself and leaned on his elbow. "We know that Stak hasn't had a woman for some time, at least since we closed in. Watch, she'll be taking that cloak off pretty soon—and the rest of her clothes, too, no doubt. That's usual in dreams."

The visitor was shocked, but he tried to keep from showing it. "Be as good as the nakeds I used to go to when I was a young fellow," he said bravely.

As a matter of fact, he had always gone only to the half-nakeds and had taken his wife Naid, both before they were married and afterwards.

People had laughed at their being together so much, but they had had a fine life together. Then Naid had died while the children were still small. He wondered whether he ever dreamed of Naid. He never could remember his own dreams, probably because he generally jumped out of bed so quickly and went about the day's business.

On the dream stage, the image of a man was standing beside the girl. The man was young and was wearing the kind of clothes that students wore, and he was holding the girl's hand.

"It's Stak," Gniss said. "This is the less common kind of dream, though usual enough, where the dreamer seems to be watching himself from the outside. We get a full view of him then and we see his actions. It's the kind of dream that's clearest and gives us the best information. I recognize the girl now—Lell. She used to be Stak's sweetheart." He said the word contemptuously. "She was executed when he was first joining the revolt."

The dream couple embraced in pantomime. The scene was very real, and it was hard for the visitor to remember that these were only images from a dreaming brain. His knowledge that the girl was dead added a strange quality to the scene.

While he was thinking that this bright girl had been given to the sacred death birds—if indeed her body had been treated with such respect—Stak cried out: "It's you, Lell! But you're dead!"

Lell answered, "I've come back, darling. I've come back for your sake."

Now she did unfasten her cloak. Gniss chuckled and the visitor tried to chuckle as Stak was helping her to take off her clothes with frantic hands. But in a moment she was dressed again and beyond his reach.

"I'm dead, I'm dead, I'm dead," she was saying, and then she was not Lell at all, but another woman. The cloak she was wearing was short and her head was bare in the new style—and her hair was dark.

Gniss made a noise that could have been a breath, but sounded more like a growl or a cry.

It was a noise that made sweat extrude from the visitor's forehead, made his throat tighten as if he would never swallow again. He saw himself in the great statue of Kumat with other middle-aged tourists. He saw himself watching the fishes in the Luminous Pond. He saw himself at his desk in the criteria room, where he had worked for thirty years.

He saw the sacred death birds circle and lower.

The visitor made an effort to collect himself. He must decide whether it was better to speak or to be silent, to go on looking or to turn away. He did not know. The man on the couch of cocoon cloth was no longer his old schoolfellow; he was the Chief Watcher.

On the stage, the dark dream woman moved closer to Stak. "I love you too, Stak. I am not Lell. Lell is dead. I am Orv. But I love you, too."

Stak said, "To love me is to die. Even to know me is to die."

"What difference does that make? We are all going to die some day.

Why not die to bring a time when others can be free? Happy and free—unhappy and free—*free!*"

"My wife," Gniss said, in a terrible voice. "My wife Orv."

Now it was in the open, and the visitor knew he had to speak. He turned to Gniss. "It's a trick, of course. He got hold of a picture somehow. He knows his dreams are being watched, and rebels must have found some way of controlling their dreams. It can be done, you know. You consciously pick a subject or a person—"

"Be quiet," the Chief Watcher said, and the visitor regretted that he had spoken.

Gniss never took his eyes from the dream projection, but the visitor would not look. Already, he had seen too much.

He could not help hearing, though. Dream-Stak and dream-Orv spoke lovingly, eagerly. Their words grew more intense, were blurred, became rhythmic sobs.

Then there was silence. The visitor looked again. The images were gone. The lifeless platform was sinking into the floor.

Gniss said in a cold, faraway voice, "I will have to dispose of them. And of you, I am afraid. You may have heard the proverb of the North Tribes: 'Who sees what the gods want hidden had better been born blind.' I was at fault in bothering, childishly enough, to impress an old friend—but I have got where I am by making sure that other people expiate my faults."

"Surely, Gniss, you don't believe it. You must realize it's a trick." The visitor's voice was shrill with fear.

"It's not a trick. There were several reports, ambiguously phrased. I would not understand them; or, if I understood them, I would not believe them."

The visitor thought again of his children's advice. If only he had listened to them! He pictured them in his mind: his son, nineteen-year-old Trenr; his daughter, sixteen-year-old Zhom. They were so wise, yet so foolish in many ways, and so young. Knowing he would have to return to them, he grew calm.

He rose from the couch and, speaking slowly and steadily, said to the Chief Watcher: "You told me yourself that Stak's dreams were shown in the regular monitoring chambers, that they were recorded. And there are the reports you mention. How can this thing be kept a secret? A hundred people must know about it besides me. A hundred and one can't make it any worse.

"Do you really think that by killing me you can stop the story from reaching high men in the Government? I am only an ordinary citizen, but even I have heard of the rivalry among you powerful men.

"Gniss, you are destroyed. Destroying me won't save you. Nothing can save you. You may as well let me go home."

Gniss reacted in an astonishing way. He let loose his bellowing laugh.

"You have led too obscure a life," he said, choking. "You could have made a career for yourself here. You have just achieved something that calls for unusual talent—you've won a point simply by stating the obvious truth. I was only fooling myself, I see now. As you say, I am destroyed. I'll kill myself, of course."

Gniss put his hand to the jeweled wheel. The red and blue and green gems twinkled between his fat fingers.

"Go out that way," Gniss said, and the visitor turned and saw that the wall had opened to a small elevator. "It will take you to an unguarded door."

"Good-by," said the visitor. "An old friend's good-by. I know I will never see you again."

"Never," Gniss said gravely. "Good-by, old schoolfellow."

There were tears in the visitor's eyes as he walked into the elevator. As soon as he had entered, the door automatically closed, and the elevator automatically carried him to a lower floor, where it automatically and completely disposed of him.

Nothing was left for the sacred death birds.

"Little people, little minds," Gniss said. "As if killing oneself were all a man could do."

Then he spoke to his pillow quietly, giving orders for a hundred deaths. His wife's, first; then Stak's; then . . .

When he was through the list, he reconsidered and made it two hundred.

The hour was late and Gniss was tired when his mistress greeted him in her house, in an old quarter of the city.

They embraced.

"Dear girl, dear Jenj," Gniss said. "I have had to work late. It's been a difficult day and I'm exhausted."

"Poor darling," said Jenj. "Lie down right now and rest."

Gniss stretched out on a couch, grunting comfortably. The plastic felt a bit chilly, and he thought, *I'll have to find her some of that primitive larval stuff.*

A young man and a young woman walked in from another room. They were carrying small mind-rippers.

"Get out of the way," the man said to Jenj.

Jenj moved quickly.

Gniss jumped to his feet. He started to say something, but the full force of two mind-rippers stopped him. His body fell back on the couch.

Jenj began to cry.

"What's the matter, Jenj?" the man said. "Think of Stak. Think of Orv. I have never taken part in an execution that I regret less."

"You're not a woman," Jenj said, still crying. "After all, a woman can't simulate for so long without developing some emotional attachment, even for a monster like that."

But she made an effort to be stern.

"Who is going to take Stak's place?" she asked, as if nothing now remained to be said about Gniss.

The man answered, "It's not definite yet. Maybe Trenr. He's young, but Stak thought highly of him. He's very capable."

"And close-mouthed," the woman said. "Even his father, poor innocent, never knew Trenr was one of us. He was paying Gniss a social call. Imagine!"

H. B. Fyfe

MANNERS OF THE AGE

THE RED TENNIS robot scooted desperately across the court, its four wide-set wheels squealing. For a moment, Robert's hard-hit passing shot seemed to have scored. Then, at the last instant, the robot whipped around its single racket-equipped arm. Robert sprawled headlong in a futile lunge at the return.

"Game and set to Red Three," announced the referee box from its high station above the net.

"Ah, shut up!" growled Robert, and flung down his racket for one of the white serving robots to retrieve.

"Yes, Robert," agreed the voice. "Will Robert continue to play?" Interpreting the man's savage mumble as a negative, it told his opponent, "Return to your stall, Red Three!"

Robert strode off wordlessly toward the house. Reaching the hundred-foot-square swimming pool, he hesitated uncertainly.

"Weather's so damned hot," he muttered. "Why didn't the old-time scientists find out how to do something about that while there were still enough people on Earth to manage it?"

He stripped off his damp clothing and dropped it on the "beach" of white sand. Behind him sounded the steps of a humanoid serving robot, hastening to pick it up. Robert plunged deep into the cooling water and let himself float lazily to the surface.

Maybe they did, he thought. *I could send a robot over to the old city library for information. Still, actually doing anything would probably take the resources of a good many persons—and it isn't so easy to find people now that Earth is practically deserted.*

He rolled sideward for a breath and began to swim slowly for the opposite side of the pool, reflecting upon the curious culture of the planet.

Although he had accepted this all his life, it really was remarkable how the original home of the human race had been forsaken for fresher worlds among the stars. Or was it more remarkable that a few individuals had asserted their independence by remaining?

Robert was aware that the decision involved few difficulties, considering the wealth of robots and other automatic machines. He regretted knowing so few humans, though they were really not necessary. If not for his hobby of televising, he would probably not know any at all.

"Wonder how far past the old city I'd have to go to meet someone in person," he muttered as he pulled himself from the pool. "Maybe I ought to try accepting that televised invitation of the other night."

Several dark usuform robots were smoothing the sand on this beach under the direction of a blue humanoid supervisor. Watching them idly, Robert estimated that it must be ten years since he had seen another human face to face. His parents were dim memories. He got along very well, however, with robots to serve him or to obtain occasional information from the automatic scanners of the city library that had long ago been equipped to serve such a purpose.

"Much better than things were in the old days," he told himself as he crossed the lawn to his sprawling white mansion. "Must have been awful before the population declined. Imagine having people all around you, having to listen to them, see them, and argue to make them do what you wanted!"

The heel of his bare right foot came down heavily on a pebble, and he swore without awareness of the precise meaning of the ancient phrases. He limped into the baths and beckoned a waiting robot as he stretched out on a rubbing table.

"Call Blue One!" he ordered.

The red robot pushed a button on the wall before beginning the massage. In a few moments, the major-domo arrived.

"Did Robert enjoy the tennis?" it inquired politely.

"I did *not!*" snapped the man. "Red Three won—and by too big a score. Have it geared down a few feet per second."

"Yes, Robert."

"And have the lawn screened again for pebbles!"

As Blue One retired he relaxed, and turned his mind to ideas for filling the evening. He hoped Henry would televise; Robert had news for him.

After a short nap and dinner, he took the elevator to his three-story tower and turned on the television robot. Seating himself in a comfortable armchair, he directed the machine from one channel to another. For some time, there was no answer to his perfunctory call signals, but one of his few acquaintances finally came on.

"Jack here," said a quiet voice that Robert had long suspected of being disguised by a filter microphone.

"I haven't heard you for some weeks," he remarked, eying the swirling colors on the screen.

He disliked Jack for never showing his face, but curiosity as to what lay behind the mechanical image projected by the other's transmitter preserved the acquaintance.

"I was . . . busy," said the bodiless voice, with a discreet hint of a chuckle that Robert found chilling.

He wondered what Jack had been up to. He remembered once being favored with a televised view of Jack's favorite sport—a battle between companies of robots designed for the purpose, horribly reminiscent of human conflicts Robert had seen on historical films.

He soon made an excuse to break off and set the robot to scanning Henry's channel. He had something to tell the older man, who lived only about a hundred miles away and was as close to being his friend as was possible in this age of scattered, self-sufficient dwellings.

"I don't mind talking to *him*," Robert reflected. "At least he doesn't overdo this business of individual privacy."

He thought briefly of the disdainful face—seemingly on a distant station—which had merely examined him for several minutes one night without ever condescending to speak. Recalling his rage at this treatment, Robert wondered how the ancients had managed to get along together when there were so many of them. They must have had some strict code of behavior, he supposed, or they never would have bred so enormous a population.

"I must find out about that someday," he decided. "How did you act, for instance. if you wanted to play tennis but someone else just refused and went to eat dinner? Maybe that was why the ancients had so many murders."

He noticed that the robot was getting an answer from Henry's station, and was pleased. He could talk as long as he liked, knowing Henry would not resent his cutting off any time he became bored with the conversation.

The robot focused the image smoothly. Henry gave the impression of being a small man. He was gray and wrinkled compared with Robert, but his black eyes were alertly sharp. He smiled his greeting and immediately launched into a story of one of his youthful trips through the mountains, from the point at which it had been interrupted the last time they had talked.

Robert listened impatiently.

"Maybe I have some interesting news," he remarked as the other finished. "I picked up a new station the other night."

"That reminds me of a time when I was a boy and—"

Robert fidgeted while Henry described watching his father build a spare television set as a hobby, with only a minimum of robot help. He pounced upon the first pause.

"A new station!" he repeated. "Came in very well, too. I can't imagine why I never picked it up before."

"Distant, perhaps?" asked Henry resignedly.

"No, not very far from me, as a matter of fact."

"You can't always tell, especially with the oceans so close. Now that there are so few people, you'd think there'd be land enough for all of them; but a good many spend all their lives aboard ship-robots."

"Not this one," said Robert. "She even showed me an outside view of her home."

Henry's eyebrows rose. "She? A woman?"

"Her name is Marcia-Joan."

"Well, well," said Henry. "Imagine that. Women, as I recall, usually do have funny names."

He gazed thoughtfully at his well-kept hands.

"Did I ever tell you about the last woman I knew?" he asked. "About twenty years ago. We had a son, you know, but he grew up and wanted his own home and robots."

"Natural enough," Robert commented, somewhat briefly since Henry *had* told him the story before.

"I often wonder what became of him," mused the older man. "That's the trouble with what's left of Earth culture—no families any more."

Now he'll tell about the time he lived in a crowd of five, thought Robert. *He, his wife, their boy and the visiting couple with the fleet of robot helicopters.*

Deciding that Henry could reminisce just as well without a listener, Robert quietly ordered the robot to turn itself off.

Maybe I will make the trip, he pondered, on the way downstairs, *if only to see what it's like with another person about.*

At about noon of the second day after that, he remembered that thought with regret.

The ancient roads, seldom used and never repaired, were rough and bumpy. Having no flying robots, Robert was compelled to transport himself and a few mechanical servants in ground vehicles. He had—idiotically, he now realized—started with the dawn, and was already tired.

Consequently, he was perhaps unduly annoyed when two tiny spy-eyes flew down from the hills to hover above his caravan on whirring little propellors. He tried to glance up pleasantly while their lenses televised pictures to their base, but he feared that his smile was strained.

The spy-eyes retired after a few minutes. Robert's vehicle, at his voiced order, turned onto a road leading between two forested hills.

Right there, he thought four hours later, *was where I made my mistake. I should have turned back and gone home!*

He stood in the doorway of a small cottage of pale blue trimmed with yellow, watching his robots unload baggage. They were supervised by Blue Two, the spare for Blue One.

Also watching, as silently as Robert, was a pink-and-blue striped robot which had guided the caravan from the entrance gate to the cottage. After one confused protest in a curiously high voice, it had not spoken.

Maybe we shouldn't have driven through that flower bed, thought Robert. *Still, the thing ought to be versatile enough to say so. I wouldn't have such a gimcrack contraption!*

He looked up as another humanoid robot in similar colors approached along the line of shrubs separating the main lawns from that surrounding the cottage.

"Marcia-Joan has finished her nap. You may come to the house now."

Robert's jaw hung slack as he sought for a reply. His face flushed at the idea of a robot's offering *him* permission to enter the house.

Nevertheless, he followed it across the wide lawn and between banks of gaily blossoming flowers to the main house. Robert was not sure which color he disliked more, that of the robot or the unemphatic pastel tints of the house.

The robot led the way inside and along a hall. It pulled back a curtain near the other end, revealing a room with furniture for human use. Robert stared at the girl who sat in an armchair, clad in a long robe of soft, pink material.

She looked a few years younger than he. Her hair and eyes were also brown, though darker. In contrast to Robert's, her smooth skin was only lightly tanned, and she wore her hair much longer. He thought her oval face might have been pleasant if not for the analytical expression she wore.

"I am quite human," he said in annoyance. "Do you have a voice?"

She rose and walked over to him curiously. Robert saw that she was several inches shorter than he, about the height of one of his robots. He condescended to bear her scrutiny.

"You look just as you do on the telescreen," she marveled.

Robert began to wonder if the girl were feebleminded. How else should he look?

"I usually swim at this hour," he said to change the subject. "Where is the pool?"

Marcia-Joan stared at him.

"Pool of what?" she asked.

Sensing sarcasm, he scowled. "Pool of water, of course! To swim in. What do you think I meant—a pool of oil?"

"I am not acquainted with your habits," retorted the girl.

"None of that stupid wit!" he snapped. "Where is the pool?"

"Don't shout!" shouted the girl. Her voice was high and unpleasantly shrill compared with his. "I don't have a pool. Who wants a swimming pool, anyway?"

Robert felt his face flushing with rage.

So she won't tell me! he thought. *All right, I'll find it myself. Everybody has a pool. And if she comes in, I'll hold her head under for a while!*

Sneering, he turned toward the nearest exit from the house. The gaily striped robot hastened after him.

The door failed to swing back as it should have at Robert's approach. Impatiently, he seized the ornamental handle. He felt his shoulder grasped by a metal hand.

"Do not use the front door!" said the robot.

"Let go!" ordered Robert, incensed that any robot should presume to hinder him.

"Only Marcia-Joan uses this door," said the robot, ignoring Robert's displeasure.

"I'll use it if I like!" declared Robert, jerking the handle.

The next moment, he was lifted bodily into the air. By the time he realized what was happening, he was carried, face down, along the hall. Too astonished even to yell, he caught a glimpse of Marcia-Joan's tiny feet beneath the hem of her pink robe as his head passed the curtained doorway.

The robot clumped on to the door at the rear of the house and out into the sunshine. There, it released its grip.

When Robert regained the breath knocked out of him by the drop, and assured himself that no bones were broken, his anger returned.

"I'll find it, wherever it is!" he growled, and set out to search the grounds.

About twenty minutes later, he was forced to admit that there really was no swimming pool. Except for a brook fifty yards away, there was only the tiled bathroom of the cottage to bathe in.

"Primitive!" exclaimed Robert, eying this. "Manually operated water supply, too! I must have the robots fix something better for tomorrow."

Since none of his robots was equipped with a thermometer, he had to draw the bath himself. Meanwhile, he gave orders to Blue Two regarding the brook and a place to swim. He managed to fill the tub without scalding himself mainly because there was no hot water. His irritation, by the time he had dressed in fresh clothes and prepared for another talk with his hostess, was still lively.

"Ah, you return?" Marcia-Joan commented from a window above the back door.

"It is time to eat," said Robert frankly.

"You are mistaken."

He glanced at the sunset, which was already fading.

"It *is* time," he insisted. "I always eat at this hour."

"Well, I don't."

Robert leaned back to examine her expression more carefully. He felt very much the way he had the day the water-supply robot for his pool had broken down and, despite Robert's bellowed orders, had flooded a good part of the lawn before Blue One had disconnected it. Some instinct warned him, moreover, that bellowing now would be as useless as it had been then.

"What *do* you do now?" he asked.

"I dress for the evening."

"And when do you eat?"

"After I finish dressing."

"I'll wait for you," said Robert, feeling that that much tolerance could do no particular harm.

He encountered the pink-and-blue robot in the hall, superintending several plain yellow ones bearing dishes and covered platters. Robert followed them to a dining room.

"Marcia-Joan sits there," the major-domo informed him as he moved toward the only chair at the table.

Robert warily retreated to the opposite side of the table and looked for another chair. None was visible.

Of course, he thought, trying to be fair. *Why should anybody in this day have more than one chair? Robots don't sit.*

He waited for the major-domo to leave, but it did not. The serving robots finished laying out the dishes and retired to posts along the wall. Finally, Robert decided that he would have to make his status clear or risk going hungry.

If I sit down somewhere, he decided, *it may recognize me as human. What a stupid machine to have!*

He started around the end of the table again, but the striped robot moved to intercept him. Robert stopped.

"Oh, well," he sighed, sitting sidewise on a corner of the table.

The robot hesitated, made one or two false starts in different directions, then halted. The situation had apparently not been included among its memory tapes. Robert grinned and lifted the cover of the nearest platter.

He managed to eat, despite his ungraceful position and what he considered the scarcity of the food. Just as he finished the last dish, he heard footsteps in the hall.

Marcia-Joan had dressed in a fresh robe, of crimson. Its thinner material was gathered at the waist by clasps of gleaming gold. The arrangement emphasized bodily contours Robert had previously seen only in historical films.

He became aware that she was regarding him with much the same suggestion of helpless dismay as the major-domo.

"Why, you've eaten it all!" she exclaimed.

"All?" snorted Robert. "There was hardly any food!"

Marcia-Joan walked slowly around the table, staring at the empty dishes.

"A few bits of raw vegetables and the tiniest portion of protein-concentrate I ever saw!" Robert continued. "Do you call that a dinner to serve a guest?"

"And I especially ordered two portions—"

"Two?" Robert repeated in astonishment. "You must visit me sometime. I'll show you—"

"What's the matter with my food?" interrupted the girl. "I follow the best diet advice my robots could find in the city library."

"They should have looked for human diets, not song-birds'."

He lifted a cover in hopes of finding some overlooked morsel, but the platter was bare.

"No wonder you act so strangely," he said. "You must be suffering from malnutrition. I don't wonder with a skimpy diet like this."

"It's very healthful," insisted Marcia-Joan. "The old film said it was good for the figure, too."

"Not interested," grunted Robert. "I'm satisfied as I am."

"Oh, yes? You look gawky to me."

"*You* don't," retorted Robert, examining her disdainfully. "You are short and stubby and too plump."

"*Plump?*"

"Worse, you're actually fat in lots of places I'm not."

"At least not between the ears!"

Robert blinked.

"Wh-wh-WHAT?"

"And besides," she stormed on, "those robots you brought are painted the most repulsive colors!"

Robert closed his mouth and silently sought the connection.

Robots? he thought. *Not fat, but repulsive colors, she said. What has that to do with food? The woman seems incapable of logic.*

"And furthermore," Marcia-Joan was saying, "I'm not sure I care for the looks of you! Lulu, put him out!"

"Who's Lulu?" demanded Robert.

Then, as the major-domo moved forward, he understood.

"What a silly name for a robot!" he exclaimed.

"I suppose you'd call it Robert. Will you go now, or shall I call more robots?"

"I am not a fool," said Robert haughtily. "I shall go. Thank you for the disgusting dinner."

"Do not use the front door," said the robot. "Only Marcia-Joan uses that. All robots use other doors."

Robert growled, but walked down the hall to the back door. As this swung open to permit his passage, he halted.

"It's dark out there now," he complained over his shoulder. "Don't you have any lights on your grounds? Do you want me to trip over something?"

"Of course I have ground lights!" shrilled Marcia-Joan. "I'll show you— not that I care if you trip or not."

A moment later, lights concealed among the trees glowed into life. Robert walked outside and turned toward the cottage.

I should have asked her what the colors of my robots had to do with it, he thought, and turned back to re-enter.

He walked right into the closed door, which failed to open before him, though it had operated smoothly a moment ago.

"Robots not admitted after dark," a mechanical voice informed him. "Return to your stall in the shed."

"Whom do you think you're talking to?" demanded Robert. "I'm not one of your robots!"

There was a pause.

"Is it Marcia-Joan?" asked the voice-box, after considerable buzzing and whirring.

"No, I'm Robert."

There was another pause while the mechanism laboriously shifted back to its other speech tape. Then: "Robots not admitted after dark. Return to your stall in the shed."

Robert slowly raised both hands to his temples. Lingeringly he dragged them down over his cheeks and under his chin until at last the fingers interlaced over his tight lips. After a moment, he let out his breath between his fingers and dropped his hands to his sides.

He raised one foot to kick, but decided that the door looked too hard.

He walked away between the beds of flowers, grumbling.

Reaching the vicinity of the cottage, he parted the tall shrubs bordering its grounds and looked through carefully before proceeding. Pleased at the gleam of water, he called Blue Two.

"Good enough! Put the other robots away for the night. They can trim the edges tomorrow."

He started into the cottage, but his major-domo warned, "Someone comes."

Robert looked around. Through thin portions of the shrubbery, he caught a glimpse of Marcia-Joan's crimson robe, nearly black in the diffused glow of the lights illuminating the grounds.

"Robert!" called the girl angrily. "What are your robots doing? I saw them from my upstairs window—"

"Wait there!" exclaimed Robert as she reached the shrubs.

"What? Are you trying to tell me where I can go or not go? I—YI!"

The shriek was followed by a tremendous splash. Robert stepped forward in time to be spattered by part of the flying spray. It was cold.

Naturally, being drawn from the brook, he reflected. *Oh, well, the sun will warm it tomorrow.*

There was a frenzy of thrashing and splashing in the dimly lighted water at his feet, accompanied by coughs and spluttering demands that he "do something!"

Robert reached down with one hand, caught his hostess by the wrist, and heaved her up to solid ground.

"My robots are digging you a little swimming hole," he told her. "They brought the water from the brook by a trench. You can finish it with concrete or plastics later; it's only fifteen by thirty feet."

He expected some sort of acknowledgement of his efforts, and peered at her through the gloom when none was forthcoming. He thus caught a glimpse of the full-swinging slap aimed at his face. He tried to duck.

There was another splash, followed by more floundering about.

"Reach up," said Robert patiently, "and I'll pull you out again. I didn't expect you to like it this much."

Marcia-Joan scrambled up the bank, tugged viciously at her sodden robe, and headed for the nearest pathway without replying. Robert followed along.

As they passed under one of the lights, he noticed that the red reflections of the wet material, where it clung snugly to the girl's body, were almost the color of some of his robots.

The tennis robot, he thought, *and the moving targets for archery—in fact, all the sporting equipment.*

"You talk about food for the figure," he remarked lightly. "You should see yourself now! It's really funny, the way—"

He stopped. Some strange emotion stifled his impulse to laugh at the way the robe clung.

Instead, he lengthened his stride, but he was still a few feet behind when she charged through the front entrance of the house. The door, having opened automatically for her, started to swing closed. Robert sprang forward to catch it.

"Wait a minute!" he cried.

Marcia-Joan snapped something that sounded like "Get out!" over her shoulder, and squished off toward the stairs. As Robert started through the door to follow, the striped robot hastened toward him from its post in the hall.

"Do not use the front door!" it warned him.

"Out of my way!" growled Robert.

The robot reached out to enforce the command. Robert seized it by the forearm and put all his weight into a sudden tug. The machine tottered off balance. Releasing his grip, he sent it staggering out the door with a quick shove.

A hasty glanced showed Marcia-Joan flapping wetly up the last steps. Robert turned to face the robot.

"Do not use that door!" he quoted vindictively, and the robot halted its rush indecisively. "Only Marcia-Joan uses it."

The major-domo hesitated. After a moment, it strode off around the corner of the house. First darting one more look at the stairs, Robert thrust his head outside and shouted: "Blue Two!"

He held the door open while he waited. There was an answer from the shrubbery. Presently, his own supervisor hurried up.

"Fetch the emergency toolbox!" Robert ordered. "And bring a couple of others with you."

"Naturally, Robert. I would not carry it myself."

A moment after the robot had departed on the errand, heavy steps sounded at the rear of the hall. Marcia-Joan's robot had dealt with the mechanism of the back door.

Robert eyed the metal mask as the robot walked up to him. He found the color contrast less pleasant than ever.

"I am not using the door," he said hastily. "I am merely holding it open."

"Do you intend to use it?"

"I haven't decided."

"I shall carry you out back," the robot decided for him.

"No, you don't!" exclaimed Robert, leaping backward.

The door immediately began to swing shut as he passed through. Cursing, he lunged forward. The robot reached for him.

This time, Robert missed his grip. Before he could duck away, his wrist was trapped in a metal grasp.

The door will close, he despaired. *They'll be too late.*

Then, suddenly, he felt the portal drawn back and heard Blue Two speak.

"What does Robert wish?"

"Throw this heap out the door!" gasped Robert.

Amid a trampling of many feet, the major-domo was raised bodily by Blue Two and another pair of Robert's machines and hustled outside. Since the grip on Robert's wrist was not relaxed, he involuntarily accompanied the rush of metal bodies.

"Catch the door!" he called to Blue Two.

When the latter sprang to obey, the other two took the action as a signal to drop their burden. The pink-and-blue robot landed full length with a jingling crash. Robert was free.

With the robots, he made for the entrance. Hearing footsteps behind him as the major-domo regained its feet, he slipped hastily inside.

"Pick up that toolbox!" he snapped. "When that robot stops in the doorway, knock its head off!"

Turning, he held up a finger.

"Do not use the front door!"

The major-domo hesitated.

The heavy toolbox in the grip of Blue Two descended with a thud. The pink-and-blue robot landed on the ground a yard or two outside the door as if dropped from the second floor. It bounced once, emitted a few sparks and pungent wisps of smoke, lay still.

"Never mind, that's good enough," said Robert as Blue Two stepped forward. "One of the others can drag it off to the repair shop. Have the toolbox brought with us."

"What does Robert wish now?" inquired Blue Two, trailing the man toward the stairway.

"I'm going upstairs," said Robert. "And I intend to be prepared if any more doors are closed against me!"

He started up, the measured treads of his own robots sounding reassuringly behind him. . . .

It was about a week later that Robert sat relaxed in the armchair before his own telescreen, facing Henry's wizened visage.

The elder man clucked sympathetically as he re-examined the scratches on Robert's face and the bruise under his right eye.

"And so you left there in the morning?"

"I certainly did!" declared Robert. "We registered a marriage record at the city library by television, of course, but I don't care if I never see her again. She needn't even tell me about the child, if any. I simply can't stand that girl!"

"Now, now," Henry said.

"I mean it! Absolutely no consideration for my wishes. Everything in the house was run to suit her convenience."

"After all," Henry pointed out, "it *is* her house."

Robert glared. "What has that to do with it? I don't think I was as unreasonable as she said in smashing that robot. The thing just wouldn't let me alone!"

"I guess," Henry suggested, "it was conditioned to obey Marcia-Joan, not you."

"Well, that shows you! Whose orders are to count, anyway? When I tell a robot to do something, I expect it done. How would *you* like to find robots trying to boss you around?"

"Are you talking about robots," asked Henry, "or the girl?"

"Same thing, isn't it? Or it would be if I'd decided to bring her home with me."

"Conflict of desires," murmured Henry.

"Exactly! It's maddening to have a perfectly logical action interfered with because there's another person present to insist—*insist*, mind you—on having her way."

"And for twenty-odd years, you've had your own way in every tiny thing."

Somewhere in the back of Robert's mind lurked a feeling that Henry sounded slightly sarcastic.

"Well, why shouldn't I?" he demanded. "I noticed that in every disagreement, my view was the right one."

"It was?"

"Of course it was! What did you mean by that tone?"

"Nothing . . ." Henry seemed lost in thought. "I was just wondering how many 'right' views are left on this planet. There must be quite a few, all different, even if we have picked up only a few by television. An interesting facet of our peculiar culture—every individual omnipotent and omniscient, *within his own sphere.*"

Robert regarded him with indignant incredulity.

"You don't seem to understand my point," he began again. "I told her we ought to come to my house, where things are better arranged, and she simply refused. Contradicted me! It was most—"

He broke off.

"The *impudence* of him!" he exclaimed. "Signing off when *I* wanted to talk!"

Fredric Brown

THE WEAPON

The room was quiet in the dimness of early evening. Dr. James Graham, key scientist of a very important project, sat in his favorite chair, thinking. It was so still that he could hear the turning of pages in the next room as his son leafed through a picture book.

Often Graham did his best work, his most creative thinking, under these circumstances, sitting alone in an unlighted room in his own apartment after the day's regular work. But tonight his mind would not work constructively. Mostly he thought about his mentally arrested son—his only son—in the next room. The thoughts were loving thoughts, not the bitter anguish he had felt years ago when he had first learned of the boy's condition. The boy was happy; wasn't that the main thing? And to how many men is given a child who will always be a child, who will not grow up to leave him? Certainly that was rationalization, but what is wrong with rationalization when— The doorbell rang.

Graham rose and turned on lights in the almost-dark room before he went through the hallway to the door. He was not annoyed; tonight, at this moment, almost any interruption to his thoughts was welcome.

He opened the door. A stranger stood there; he said, "Dr. Graham? My name is Niemand; I'd like to talk to you. May I come in a moment?"

Graham looked at him. He was a small man, nondescript, obviously harmless—possibly a reporter or an insurance agent.

But it didn't matter what he was. Graham found himself saying, "Of course. Come in, Mr. Niemand." A few minutes of conversation, he justified himself by thinking, might divert his thoughts and clear his mind.

"Sit down," he said, in the living room. "Care for a drink?"

Niemand said, "No, thank you." He sat in the chair; Graham sat on the sofa.

The small man interlocked his fingers; he leaned forward. He said, "Dr. Graham, you are the man whose scientific work is more likely than that of any other man to end the human race's chance for survival."

A crackpot, Graham thought. Too late now he realized that he should have asked the man's business before admitting him. It would be an embarrassing interview; he disliked being rude, yet only rudeness was effective.

"Dr. Graham, the weapon on which you are working—"

The visitor stopped and turned his head as the door that led to a bedroom opened and a boy of fifteen came in. The boy didn't notice Niemand; he ran to Graham.

"Daddy, will you read to me now?" The boy of fifteen laughed the sweet laughter of a child of four.

Graham put an arm around the boy. He looked at his visitor, wondering whether he had known about the boy. From the lack of surprise on Niemand's face, Graham felt sure he had known.

"Harry"—Graham's voice was warm with affection—"Daddy's busy. Just for a little while. Go back to your room; I'll come and read to you soon."

"'Chicken Little?' You'll read me 'Chicken Little'?"

"If you wish. Now run along. Wait. Harry. This is Mr. Niemand."

The boy smiled bashfully at the visitor. Niemand said, "Hi, Harry," and smiled back at him, holding out his hand. Graham, watching, was sure now that Niemand had known; the smile and the gesture were for the boy's mental age, not his physical one.

The boy took Niemand's hand. For a moment it seemed that he was going to climb into Niemand's lap, and Graham pulled him back gently. He said, "Go to your room now, Harry."

The boy skipped back into his bedroom, not closing the door.

Niemand's eyes met Graham's and he said, "I like him," with obvious sincerity. He added, "I hope that what you're going to read to him will always be true."

Graham didn't understand. Niemand said, "'Chicken Little,' I mean. It's a fine story—but may 'Chicken Little' always be wrong about the sky falling down."

Graham suddenly had liked Niemand when Niemand had shown a liking for the boy. Now he remembered that he must close the interview quickly. He rose, in dismissal. He said, "I fear you're wasting your time and mine, Mr. Niemand. I know all the arguments, everything you can say I've heard a thousand times. Possibly there is truth in what you believe, but it does not concern me. I'm a scientist, and only a scientist. Yes, it is public knowledge that I am working on a weapon, a rather ultimate one. But, for me personally, that is only a by-product of the fact that I am advancing science. I have thought it through, and I have found that that is my only concern."

"But. Dr. Graham, is humanity *ready* for an ultimate weapon?"

Graham frowned. "I have told you my point of view, Mr. Niemand."

Niemand rose slowly from the chair. He said, "Very well, if you do not choose to discuss it, I'll say no more." He passed a hand across his forehead. "I'll leave, Dr. Graham. I wonder, though . . . may I change my mind about the drink you offered me?"

Graham's irritation faded. He said, "Certainly. Will whisky and water do?"

"Admirably."

Graham excused himself and went into the kitchen. He got the decanter of whisky, another of water, ice cubes, glasses.

When he returned to the living room, Niemand was just leaving the boy's bedroom. He heard Niemand's "Good night, Harry," and Harry's happy "'Night, Mr. Niemand."

Graham made drinks. A little later, Niemand declined a second one and started to leave.

Niemand said, "I took the liberty of bringing a small gift to your son, doctor. I gave it to him while you were getting the drinks for us. I hope you'll forgive me."

"Of course. Thank you. Good night."

Graham closed the door; he walked through the living room into Harry's room. He said, "All right, Harry. Now I'll read to—"

There was sudden sweat on his forehead, but he forced his face and his voice to be calm as he stepped to the side of the bed. "May I see that, Harry?" When he had it safely, his hands shook as he examined it.

He thought, *only a madman would give a loaded revolver to an idiot.*

JACK LONDON

THE SCARLET PLAGUE

THE WAY LED along upon what had once been the embankment of a railroad. But no train had run upon it for many years. The forest on either side swelled up the slopes of the embankment and crested across it in a green wave of trees and bushes. The trail was as narrow as a man's body, and was no more than a wild-animal runway. Occasionally, a piece of rusty iron, showing through the forest-mould, advertised that the rail and the ties still remained. In one place, a ten-inch tree, bursting through at a connection, had lifted the end of a rail clearly into view. The tie had evidently followed the rail, held to it by the spike long enough for its bed to be filled with gravel and rotten leaves, so that now the crumbling, rotten timber thrust itself up at a curious slant. Old as the road was, it was manifest that it had been the mono-rail type.

An old man and a boy travelled along this runway. They moved slowly, for the old man was very old, a touch of palsy made his movements tremulous, and he leaned heavily upon his staff. A rude skull-cap of goat-skin protected his head from the sun. From beneath this fell a scant fringe of stained and dirty-white hair. A visor, ingeniously made from a large leaf, shielded his eyes, and from under this he peered at the way of his feet on the trail.

His beard, which should have been snow-white but which showed the same weather-wear and camp-stain as his hair, fell nearly to his waist in a great tangled mass. About his chest and shoulders hung a single, mangy garment of goat-skin. His arms and legs, withered and skinny, betokened extreme age, as well as did their sunburn and scars and scratches betoken long years of exposure to the elements.

The boy, who led the way, checking the eagerness of his muscles to the slow progress of the elder, likewise wore a single garment—a ragged-edged piece of bear-skin, with a hole in the middle through which he had thrust his head. He could not have been more than twelve years old. Tucked coquettishly over one ear was the freshly severed tail of a pig. In one hand he carried a medium-sized bow and an arrow. On his back was a quiverful of arrows. From a sheath hanging about his neck on a thong, projected the battered handle of a hunting knife.

He was as brown as a berry, and walked softly, with almost a catlike tread. In marked contrast with his sunburned skin were his eyes—blue, deep blue, but keen and sharp as a pair of gimlets. They seemed to bore into all about him in a way that was habitual.

As he went along he smelled things, as well, his distended, quivering nostrils carrying to his brain an endless series of messages from the outside world. Also, his hearing was acute, and had been so trained that it operated automatically. Without conscious effort, he heard all the slight sounds in the apparent quiet—heard, and differentiated, and classified these sounds—whether they were of the wind rustling the leaves, of the humming of bees and gnats, of the distant rumble of the sea that drifted to him only in lulls, or of the gopher, just under his foot, shoving a pouchful of earth into the entrance of his hole.

Suddenly he became alertly tense. Sound, sight, and odor had given him a simultaneous warning. His hand went back to the old man, touching him, and the pair stood still. Ahead, at one side of the top of the embankment, arose a crackling sound, and the boy's gaze was fixed on the tops of the agitated bushes.

Then a large bear, a grizzly, crashed into view, and likewise stopped abruptly, at sight of the humans. He did not like them, and growled querulously. Slowly the boy fitted the arrow to the bow, and slowly he pulled the bowstring taut. But he never removed his eyes from the bear. The old man peered from under his green leaf at the danger, and stood as quietly as the boy.

For a few seconds this mutual scrutinizing went on; then, the bear betraying a growing irritability, the boy, with a movement of his head, indicated that the old man must step aside from the trail and go down the embankment. The boy followed, going backward, still holding the bow taut and ready. They waited till a crashing among the bushes from the opposite side of the embankment told them the bear had gone. The boy grinned as he led back to the trail.

"A big un, Granser," he chuckled.

The old man shook his head.

"They get thicker every day," he complained in a thin, undependable falsetto. "Who'd have thought I'd live to see the time when a man would be afraid of his life on the way to Cliff House? When I was a boy, Edwin, men and women and little babies used to come out here from San Francisco by tens of thousands on a nice day. And there weren't any bears then. No sir. They used to pay money to look at them in cages, they were that rare."

"What is money, Granser?"

Before the old man could answer, the boy recollected and triumphantly shoved his hand into a pouch under his bear-skin and pulled forth a battered and tarnished silver dollar. The old man's eyes glistened, as he held the coin close to them.

"I can't see," he muttered. "You look and see if you can make out the date, Edwin."

The boy laughed.

"You're a great Granser," he cried delightedly, "always making believe them little marks mean something."

The old man manifested an accustomed chagrin as he brought the coin back again close to his own eyes.

"2012," he shrilled, and then fell to cackling grotesquely. "That was the year Morgan the Fifth was appointed President of the United States by the Board of Magnates. It must have been one of the last coins minted, for the Scarlet Death came in 2013. Lord! Lord!—think of it! Sixty years ago, and I am the only person alive today that lived in those times. Where did you find it, Edwin?"

The boy, who had been regarding him with the tolerant curiousness one accords to the prattlings of the feeble-minded, answered promptly.

"I got it off of Hoo-Hoo. He found it when we was herdin' goats down near San José last spring. Hoo-Hoo said it was *money*. Ain't you hungry, Granser?"

The ancient caught his staff in a tighter grip and urged along the trail, his old eyes shining greedily.

"I hope Hare-Lip's found a crab . . . or two," he mumbled. "They're good eating, crabs, mighty good eating when you've no more teeth and you've got grandsons that love their old grandsire and make a point of catching crabs for him. When I was a boy—"

But Edwin, suddenly stopped by what he saw, was drawing the bow-string on a fitted arrow. He had paused on the brink of a crevasse in the embankment. An ancient culvert had here washed out, and the stream, no longer confined, had cut a passage through the fill.

On the opposite side the end of a rail projected and overhung. It showed rustily through the creeping vines which overran it. Beyond, crouching by a bush, a rabbit looked across at him in trembling hesitancy. Fully fifty feet was the distance, but the arrow flashed true; and the transfixed rabbit, crying out in sudden fright and hurt, struggled painfully into the brush.

The boy himself was a flash of brown skin and flying fur as he bounded down the steep wall of the gap and up the other side. His lean muscles were springs of steel that released into graceful and efficient action. A hundred feet beyond, in a tangle of bushes, he overtook the wounded creature, knocked its head on a convenient tree-trunk, and turned it over to Granser to carry.

"Rabbit is good, very good," the ancient quavered, "but when it comes to a toothsome delicacy I prefer crab. When I was a boy—"

"Why do you say so much that ain't got no sense?" Edwin impatiently interrupted the other's threatened garrulousness.

The boy did not exactly utter these words, but something that remotely resembled them and that was more guttural and explosive and economical of qualifying phrases. His speech showed distant kinship with that of the old man, and the latter's speech was approximately an English that had gone through a bath of corrupt usage.

"What I want to know," Edwin continued, "is why you call crab 'toothsome delicacy.' Crab is crab, ain't it? No one I ever heard calls it such funny things."

The old man sighed but did not answer, and they moved on in silence. The surf grew suddenly louder, as they emerged from the forest upon a stretch of sand dunes bordering the sea. A few goats were browsing among the sandy hillocks, and a skin-clad boy, aided by a wolfish-looking dog that was only faintly reminiscent of a collie, was watching them. Mingled with the roar of the surf was a continuous, deep-throated barking or bellowing, which came from a cluster of jagged rocks a hundred yards out from shore. Here huge sea-lions hauled themselves up to lie in the sun or battle with one another. In the immediate foreground arose the smoke of a fire, tended by a third savage-looking boy. Crouched near him were several wolfish dogs similar to the one that guarded the goats.

The old man accelerated his pace, sniffing eagerly as he neared the fire.

"Mussels!" he muttered ecstatically. "Mussels! And ain't that a crab, Hoo-Hoo? Ain't that a crab? My, my, you boys are good to your old grandsire."

Hoo-Hoo, who was apparently of the same age as Edwin, grinned.

"All you want, Granser. I got four."

The old man's palsied eagerness was pitiful. Sitting down in the sand as quickly as his stiff limbs would let him, he poked a large rock-mussel from out of the coals. The heat had forced its shells apart, and the meat, salmon-colored, was thoroughly cooked. Between thumb and forefinger, in trembling haste, he caught the morsel and carried it to his mouth. But it was too hot, and the next moment was violently ejected. The old man spluttered with the pain, and tears ran out of his eyes and down his cheeks.

The boys were true savages, possessing only the cruel humor of the savage. To them the incident was excruciatingly funny, and they burst into loud laughter. Hoo-Hoo danced up and down, while Edwin rolled gleefully on the ground. The boy with the goats came running to join in the fun.

"Set 'em to cool, Edwin, set 'em to cool," the old man besought, in the midst of his grief, making no attempt to wipe away the tears that still flowed from his eyes. "And cool a crab, Edwin, too. You know your grandsire likes crabs."

From the coals arose a great sizzling, which proceeded from the many mussels, bursting open their shells and exuding their moisture. They were large shellfish, running from three to six inches in length. The boys raked them out with sticks and placed them on a large piece of driftwood to cool.

"When I was a boy, we did not laugh at our elders; we respected them."

The boys took no notice, and Granser continued to babble an incoherent flow of complaint and censure. But this time he was more careful, and did not burn his mouth. All began to eat, using nothing but their hands and making loud mouth-noises and lip-smackings. The third boy, who was called Hare-Lip, slyly deposited a pinch of sand on a mussel the ancient was carrying to his mouth; and when the grit of it bit into the old fellow's mucous membrane and gums, the laughter was again uproarious. He was unaware that a joke had been played on him, and spluttered and spat until Edwin, relenting, gave him a gourd of fresh water with which to wash out his mouth.

"Where's them crabs, Hoo-Hoo?" Edwin demanded. "Granser's set upon having a snack."

Again Granser's eyes burned with greediness as a large crab was handed to him. It was a shell with legs and all complete, but the meat had long since departed. With shaky fingers and babblings of anticipation, the old man broke off a leg and found it filled with emptiness.

"The crabs, Hoo-Hoo?" he wailed. "The crabs?"

"I was foolin', Granser. They ain't no crabs. I never found none."

The boys were overwhelmed with delight at sight of the tears of senile disappointment that dribbled down the old man's cheeks. Then, unnoticed, Hoo-Hoo replaced the empty shell with a fresh-cooked crab. Already dismembered, from the cracked legs the white meat sent forth a small cloud of savory steam. This attracted the old man's nostrils, and he looked down in amazement. The change of his mood to one of joy was immediate. He snuffled and muttered and mumbled, making almost a croon of delight, as he began to eat. Of this the boys took little notice, for it was an accustomed spectacle. Nor did they notice his occasional exclamations and utterances of phrases which meant nothing to them, as, for instance, when he smacked his lips and champed his gums while muttering:

"Mayonnaise! Just think—mayonnaise! And it's sixty years since the last was made! Two generations and never a smell of it! Why, in those days it was served in every restaurant with crab."

When he could eat no more, the old man sighed, wiped his hands on his naked legs, and gazed out over the sea. With the content of a full stomach, he waxed reminiscent.

"To think of it! I've seen this beach alive with men, women, and children on a pleasant Sunday. And there weren't any bears to eat them up, either. And right up there on the cliff was a big restaurant where you could get anything you wanted to eat. Four million people lived in San Francisco, then. And now, in the whole city and country there aren't forty, all told. And out there on the sea were ships and ships always to be seen, going in for the Golden Gate or coming out. And airships in the air —dirigibles and flying machines. They could travel two hundred miles an hour.

"The mail contracts with the New York and San Francisco Limited demanded that for the minimum. There was a chap, a Frenchman, I forgot his name, who succeeded in making three hundred; but the thing was risky, too risky for conservative persons. But he was on the right clew, and he would have managed it if it hadn't been for the Great Plague. When I was a boy, there were men alive who remembered the coming of the first aeroplanes, and now I have lived to see the last of them, and that sixty years ago."

The old man babbled on, unheeded by the boys, who were long accustomed to his garrulousness, and whose vocabularies, besides, lacked the greater portion of the words he used. It was noticeable that in these rambling soliloquies his English seemed to recrudesce into better construction and phraseology. But when he talked directly with the boys it lapsed, largely into their own uncouth and simpler forms.

"But there weren't many crabs in those days," the old man wandered on.

"They were fished out, and they were great delicacies. The open season was only a month long, too. And now crabs are accessible the whole year around. Think of it—catching all the crabs you want, any time you want, in the surf of the Cliff House beach!"

A sudden commotion among the goats brought the boys to their feet. The dogs about the fire rushed to join their snarling fellow who guarded the goats, while the goats themselves stampeded in the direction of their human protectors. A half dozen forms, lean and gray, glided about on the sand hillocks or faced the bristling dogs. Edwin arched an arrow that fell short. But Hare-Lip, with a sling such as David carried into battle against Goliath, hurled a stone through the air that whistled from the speed of its flight. It fell squarely among the wolves and caused them to slink away toward the dark depths of the eucalyptus forest.

The boys laughed and lay down again in the sand, while Granser sighed ponderously. He had eaten too much, and, with hands clasped on his paunch, the fingers interlaced, he resumed his maunderings.

"'The fleeting systems lapse like foam,'" he mumbled what was evidently a quotation. "That's it—foam, and fleeting. All man's toil upon the planet was just so much foam. He domesticated the serviceable animals, destroyed the hostile ones, and cleared the land of its wild vegetation. And then he passed, and the flood of primordial life rolled back again, sweeping his handiwork away—the weeds and the forest inundated his fields, the beasts of prey swept over his flocks, and now there are wolves on the Cliff House beach." He was appalled by the thought. "Where four million people disported themselves, the wild wolves roam to-day, and our savage progeny, with prehistoric weapons, defend themselves against the fanged despoilers. Think of it! And all because of the Scarlet Death—"

The adjective had caught Hare-Lip's ear.

"He's always saying that," he said to Edwin. "What is scarlet?"

"'The scarlet of the maples can shake me like the cry of bugles going by,'" the old man quoted.

"It's red," Edwin answered the question. "And you don't know it because you come from the Chauffeur Tribe. They never did know nothing, none of them. Scarlet is red—I know that."

"Red is red, ain't it?" Hare-Lip grumbled. "Then what's the good of getting cocky and calling it scarlet?"

"Granser, what for do you always say so much what nobody knows?" he asked. "Scarlet ain't anything, but red is red. Why don't you say red, then?"

"Red is not the right word," was the reply. "The plague was scarlet. The whole face and body turned scarlet in an hour's time. Don't I know? Didn't I see enough of it? And I am telling you it was scarlet because—well, because it was scarlet. There is no other word for it."

"Red is good enough for me," Hare-Lip muttered obstinately. "My dad calls red red, and he ought to know. He says everything died of the Red Death."

"Your dad is a common fellow, descended from a common fellow," Granser retorted heatedly. "Don't I know the beginnings of the Chauffeurs? Your grandsire was a chauffeur, a servant, and without education. He worked for other persons. But your grandmother was of good stock, only the children did not take after her. Don't I remember when I first met them, catching fish at Lake Temescal?"

"What is *education?*" Edwin asked.

"Calling red scarlet," Hare-Lip sneered, then returned to the attack on Granser. "My dad told me, an' he got it from his dad afore he croaked, that your wife was a Santa Rosan, an' that she was no account. He said she was a *hash-slinger* before the Red Death, though I don't know what a *hash-slinger* is. You can tell me, Edwin."

But Edwin shook his head in token of ignorance.

"It is true, she was a waitress," Granser acknowledged. "But she was a good woman, and your mother was her daughter. Women were very scarce in the days after the Plague. She was the only wife I could find, even if she was a *hash-slinger,* as your father calls it. But it is not nice to talk about our progenitors that way."

"Dad says that the wife of the first Chauffeur was a *lady*—"

"What's a *lady?*" Hoo-Hoo demanded.

"A *lady's* a Chauffeur squaw," was the quick reply of Hare-Lip.

"The first Chauffeur was Bill, a common fellow, as I said before," the old man expounded; "but his wife was a lady, a great lady. Before the Scarlet Death she was the wife of Van Worden. He was President of the Board of Industrial Magnates, and was one of the dozen men who ruled America. He was worth one billion, eight hundred millions of dollars— coins like you have there in your pouch, Edwin. And then came the Scarlet Death, and his wife became the wife of Bill, the first Chauffeur. He used to beat her, too. I have seen it myself."

Hoo-Hoo, lying on his stomach and idly digging his toes in the sand, cried out and investigated, first, his toenail, and next, the small hole he had dug. The other two boys joined him, excavating the sand rapidly with their hands till there lay three skeletons exposed. Two were of adults, the third being that of a part-grown child. The old man hudged along the ground and peered at the find.

"Plague victims," he announced. "That's the way they died everywhere in the last days. This must have been a family, running away from the contagion and perishing here on the Cliff House beach. They—what are you doing, Edwin?"

This question was asked in sudden dismay, as Edwin, using the back of his hunting knife, began to knock out the teeth from the jaws of one of the skulls.

"Going to string 'em," was the response.

The three boys were now hard at it; and quite a knocking and hammering arose, in which Granser babbled on unnoticed.

"You are true savages. Already has begun the custom of wearing human teeth. In another generation you will be perforating your noses and ears and wearing ornaments of bone and shell. I know. The human race is doomed to sink back farther and farther into the primitive night ere again it begins its bloody climb upward to civilization. When we increase and feel the lack of room, we will proceed to kill one another. And then I suppose you will wear human scalp-locks at your waist, as well —as you, Edwin, who are the gentlest of my grandsons, have already begun with that vile pigtail. Throw it away, Edwin, boy; throw it away."

"What a gabble the old geezer makes," Hare-Lip remarked, when, the teeth all extracted, they began an attempt at equal division.

They were very quick and abrupt in their actions, and their speech, in moments of hot discussion over the allotments of the choicer teeth, was truly a gabble. They spoke in monosyllables and short jerky sentences that was more a gibberish than a language. And yet, through it ran hints of grammatical construction, and appeared vestiges of the conjugation of some superior culture. Even the speech of Granser was so corrupt that were it put down literally it would be almost so much nonsense to the reader. This, however, was when he talked with the boys. When he got the full swing of babbling to himself, it slowly purged itself into pure English. The sentences grew longer and were enunciated with a rhythm and ease that was reminiscent of the lecture platform.

"Tell us about the Red Death, Granser," Hare-Li demanded, when the teeth affair had been satisfactorily concluded.

"The Scarlet Death," Edwin corrected.

"An' don't work all that funny lingo on us," Hare-Lip went on. "Talk sensible, Granser, like a Santa Rosan ought to talk. Other Santa Rosans don't talk like you."

The old man showed pleasure in being thus called upon. He cleared his throat and began.

"Twenty or thirty years ago my story was in great demand. But in these days nobody seems interested—"

"There you go!" Hare-Lip cried hotly. "Cut out the funny stuff and talk sensible. What's *interested?* You talk like a baby that don't know how."

"Let him alone," Edwin urged, "or he'll get mad and won't talk at all. Skip the funny places. We'll catch on to some of what he tells us."

"Let her go, Granser," Hoo-Hoo encouraged; for the old man was already maundering about the disrespect for elders and the reversion to cruelty of all humans that fell from high culture to primitive conditions.

The tale began.

"There were very many people in the world in those days. San Francisco alone held four millions—"

"What is millions?" Edwin interrupted.

Granser looked at him kindly.

"I know you cannot count beyond ten, so I will tell you. Hold up your two hands. On both of them you have altogether ten fingers and thumbs. Very well. I now take this grain of sand—you hold it, Hoo-Hoo." He dropped the grain of sand into the lad's palm and went on. "Now that grain of sand stands for the ten fingers of Edwin. I add another grain. That's ten more fingers. And I add another, and another, and another, until I have added as many grains as Edwin has fingers and thumbs. That makes what I call one hundred.

"Remember that word—one hundred. Now I put this pebble in Hare-Lip's hand. It stands for ten grains of sand, or ten tens of fingers, or one hundred fingers. I put in ten pebbles. They stand for a thousand fingers. I take a mussel-shell, and it stands for ten pebbles, or one hundred grains of sand, or one thousand fingers. . . ."

And so on, laboriously, and with much reiteration, he strove to build up in their minds a crude conception of numbers. As the quantities increased, he had the boys holding different magnitudes in each of their hands. For still higher sums, he laid the symbols on the log of driftwood; and for symbols he was hard put, being compelled to use the teeth from the skulls for millions, and the crabshells for billions. It was here that he stopped, for the boys were showing signs of becoming tired.

"There were four million people in San Francisco—four teeth."

The boys' eyes ranged along from the teeth and from hand to hand, down through the pebbles and sand-grains to Edwin's fingers. And back again they ranged along the ascending series in the effort to grasp such inconceivable numbers.

"That was a lot of folks, Granser," Edwin at last hazarded.

"Like sand on the beach here, like sand on the beach, each grain of sand a man, or woman, or child. Yes, my boy, all those people lived right here in San Francisco. And at one time or another all those people came out on this very beach—more people than there are grains of sand. More— more—more. And San Francisco was a noble city. And across the bay— where we camped last year, even more people lived, clear from Point Richmond, on the level ground and on the hills, all the way around to San Leandro—one great city of seven million people. —Seven teeth . . . there, that's it, seven millions."

Again the boys' eyes ranged up and down from Edwin's fingers to the teeth on the log.

"The world was full of people. The census of 2010 gave eight billions for the whole world—eight crab-shells, yes, eight billions. It was not like to-day. Mankind knew a great deal more about getting food. And the more food there was, the more people there were. In the year 1800, there were one hundred and seventy millions in Europe alone. One hundred years later—a grain of sand, Hoo-Hoo—one hundred years later, at 1900, there were five hundred millions in Europe—five grains of sand, Hoo-Hoo, and this one tooth.

"This shows how easy was the getting of food, and how men increased. And in the year 2000, there were fifteen hundred millions in Europe. And it was the same all over the rest of the world. Eight crabshells there, yes, eight billion people were alive on the earth when the Scarlet Death began.

"I was a young man when the Plague came—twenty-seven years old; and I lived on the other side of San Francisco Bay, in Berkeley. You remember those great stone houses, Edwin, when we came down the hills from Contra Costa? That was where I lived, in those stone houses. I was a professor of English literature."

Much of this was over the heads of the boys, but they strove to comprehend dimly this tale of the past.

"What was them stone houses for?" Hare-Lip queried.

"You remember when your dad taught you to swim?" The boy nodded. "Well, in the University of California—that is the name we had for the houses—we taught young men and women how to think, just as I have taught you now, by sand and pebbles and shells, to know how many people lived in those days. There was very much to teach. The young men and women we taught were called students. We had large rooms in which we taught. I talked to them, forty or fifty at a time, just as I am talking to you now. I told them about the books other men had written before their time, and even, sometimes, in their time—"

"Was that all you did—just talk, talk, talk?" Hoo-Hoo demanded. "Who hunted your meat for you? And milked the goats? And caught the fish?"

"A sensible question, Hoo-Hoo, a sensible question. As I have told you, in those days food-getting was easy. We were very wise. A few men got the food for many men. The other men did other things. As you say, I talked. I talked all the time, and for this food was given me—much food, fine food, beautiful food, food that I have not tasted in sixty years and shall never taste again. I sometimes thing the most wonderful achievements of our tremendous civilization was food—its inconceivable abundance, its infinite variety, its marvelous delicacy. O my grandsons, life was life in those days, when we had such wonderful things to eat."

This was beyond the boys, and they let it slip by, words and thoughts, as a mere senile wandering in the narrative.

"Our food-getters were called *freemen*. This was a joke. We of the ruling classes owned all the land, all the machines, everything. These food-getters were our slaves. We took almost all the food they got, and left them a little so that they might eat, and work, and get us more food—"

"I'd have gone into the forest and got food for myself," Hare-Lip announced; "and if any man tried to take it away from me, I'd have killed him."

The old man laughed.

"Did I not tell you that we of the ruling class owned all the land, all the forest, everything? Any food-getter who would not get food for us, him we punished or compelled to starve to death. And very few did that. They preferred to get food for us, and make clothes for us, and prepare and administer to us a thousand—a mussel-shell, Hoo-Hoo—a thousand satisfactions and delights. And I was Professor Smith in those days—Professor James Howard Smith. And my lecture courses were very popular —that is, very many of the young men and women liked to hear me talk about the books other men had written.

"And I was very happy, and I had beautiful things to eat. And my hands were soft, because I did not work with them, and my body was clean all over and dressed in the softest garments—" He surveyed his mangy goat-skin with disgust. "We did not wear such things in those days. Even the slaves had better garments. And we were most clean. We washed our faces and hands often every day. You boys never wash unless you fall into the water or go in swimming."

"Neither do you, Granser," Hoo-Hoo retorted.

"I know, I know. I am a filthy old man. But times have changed. Nobody washes these days, and there are no conveniences. It is sixty years since I have seen a piece of soap. You do not know what soap is, and I shall not tell you, for I am telling the story of Scarlet Death. You know what sickness is. We called it a disease. Very many of the diseases came from what we called germs. Remember that word—germs. A germ is a very small thing. It is like a woodtick, such as you find on the dogs in the spring of the year when they run in the forest. Only the germ is very small. It is so small that you cannot see it—"

Hoo-Hoo began to laugh.

"You're a queer un, Granser, talking about things you can't see. If you can't see 'em, how do you know they are? That's what I want to know. How do you know anything you can't see?"

"A good question, a very good question, Hoo-Hoo. But we did see—some of them. We had what we called microscopes and ultramicroscopes, and we put them to our eyes and looked through them, so that we saw things larger than they really were, and many things we could not see without the microscopes at all. Our best ultramicroscopes could make a germ look forty thousand times larger. A mussel-shell is a thousand fingers like Edwin's. Take forty mussel-shells, and by as many times larger was the germ when we looked at it through a microscope. And after that, we had other ways, by using what we called moving pictures, of making the forty-thousand-times germ many, many thousand times larger still.

"And thus we saw these things which our eyes of themselves could not see. Take a grain of sand. Break it into ten pieces. Take one piece and break it into ten. Break one of those pieces into ten, and one of those into ten, and one of those into ten, and one of those into ten, and do it all day, and maybe, by sunset, you will have a piece as small as one of the germs."

The boys were openly incredulous. Hare-Lip sniffed and sneered and Hoo-Hoo snickered, until Edwin nudged them to be silent.

"The woodtick sucks the blood of the dog, but the germ, being so very small, goes right into the blood of the body, and there it has many children. In those days there would be as many as a billion—a crab-shell, please—as many as that crab-shell in one man's body. We called germs micro-organisms. When a few million, or a billion, of them were in a man, in all the blood of a man, he was sick. These germs were a disease.

"There were many different kinds of them—more different kinds than there are grains of sand on this beach. We knew only a few of the kinds. The micro-organic world was an invisible world, a world we could not see, and we knew very little about it. Yet we did know something. There was the *bacillus anthracis;* there was the *micrococcus;* there was the *Bacterium termo,* and the *Bacterium lactis*—that's what turns the goat milk sour even to this day, Hare-Lip; and there was *Schizomycetes* without end. And there were many others. . . ."

Here the old man launched into a disquisition on germs and their natures, using words and phrases of such extraordinary length and meaninglessness, that the boys grinned at one another and looked out over the deserted ocean till they forgot the old man was babbling on.

"But the Scarlet Death, Granser," Edwin at last suggested.

Granser recollected himself, and with a start tore himself away from the rostrum of the lecture-hall, where to another-world audience, he had been expounding the latest theory, sixty years gone, of germs and germ-diseases.

"Yes, yes, Edwin; I had forgotten. Sometimes the memory of the past is very strong upon me, and I forget that I am a dirty old man, clad in goat-skin, wandering with my savage grandsons who are goat-herds in the primeval wilderness. 'The fleeting systems lapse like foam,' and so lapsed our glorious, colossal civilization. I am Granser, a tired old man. I belong to the tribe of Santa Rosans. I married into that tribe. My sons and daughters married into the Chauffeurs, the Sacramentos, and the Palo-Altos. You, Hare-Lip, are of the Chauffeurs. You, Edwin, are of the Sacramentos. And you, Hoo-Hoo, are of the Palo-Altos. Your tribe takes its name from a town that was near the seat of another great institution of learning. It was called Stanford University. Yes, I remember now. It is perfectly clear. I was telling you of the Scarlet Death. Where was I in my story?"

"You was telling about germs, the things you can't see but which make men sick," Edwin prompted.

"Yes, that's where I was. A man did not notice at first when only a few of these germs got into his body. But each germ broke in half and became two germs, and they kept doing this very rapidly so that in a short time there were many millions of them in the body. Then the man was sick. He had a disease, and the disease was named after the kind of a germ that was in him. It might be measles, it might be influenza, it might be yellow fever; it might be any of thousands of kinds of diseases.

"Now this is the strange thing about these germs. There were always new ones coming to live in men's bodies. Long and long and long ago, when there were only a few men in the world, there were few diseases. But as men increased and lived closly together in great cities and civilizations, new diseases arose, new kinds of germs entered their bodies.

"Thus were countless millions and billions of human beings killed. And the more thickly men packed together, the more terrible were the new diseases that came to be. Long before my time, in the middle ages, there was the Black Plague that swept across Europe. It swept across Europe many times. There was tuberculosis, that entered into men wherever they were thickly packed. A hundred years before my time there was the bubonic plague. And in Africa was the sleeping sickness. The bacteriologists fought all these sicknesses and destroyed them, just as you boys fight the wolves away from your goats, or squash the mosquitoes that light on you. The bacteriologists—"

"But Granser, what is a what-you-call-it?" Edwin interrupted.

"You, Edwin, are a goat-herd. Your task is to watch the goats. You know a great deal about goats. A bacteriologist watches germs. That's his task, and he knows a great deal about them. So, as I was saying, the bacteriologists fought with the germs and destroyed them—sometimes. There was leprosy, a horrible disease. A hundred years before I was born, the bacteriologists discovered the germ of leprosy. They knew all about it. They made pictures of it. I have seen those pictures. But they never found a way to kill it.

"But in 1984, there was the Pantoblast Plague, a disease that broke out in a country called Brazil and that killed millions of people. But the bacteriologists found it out, and found the way to kill it, so that the Pantoblast Plague went no farther. They made what they called a serum, which they put into a man's body and which killed the Pantoblast germs without killing the man. And in 1910, there was Pellagra, and also the hook worm. These were easily killed by the bacteriologists. But in 1947 there arose a new disease that had never been seen before. It got into the bodies of babies of only ten months old or less, and it made them unable to move their hands and feet, or to eat, or anything; and the bacteriologists were eleven years in discovering how to kill that particular germ and save the babies.

"In spite of all these diseases, and of all the new ones that continued to arise, there were more and more men in the world. This was because it was easy to get food. The easier it was to get food, the more men there were, the more thickly were they packed together on the earth; and the more thickly they were packed, the more new kinds of germs became diseases. There were warnings. Soldervetzsky, as early as 1929, told the bacteriologists that they had no guaranty against some new disease, a thousand times more deadly than any they knew, arising and killing by the hundreds of millions and even by the billions.

"You see, the micro-organic world remained a mystery to the end. They knew there was such a world, and that from time to time armies of new germs emerged from it to kill men. And that was all they knew about it. For all they knew, in that invisible micro-organic world there might be as many different kinds of germs as there are grains of sand on this beach. And also, in that same invisible world it might well be that new kinds of germs came to be. It might be there that life originated—the 'abysmal fecundity,' Soldervetzsky called it, applying the words of other men who had written before him. . . ."

It was at this point that Hare-Lip rose to his feet, an expression of huge contempt on his face.

"Granser," he announced, "you make me sick with your gabble. Why don't you tell about the Red Death? If you ain't going to, say so, an' we'll start back for camp."

The old man looked at him and silently began to cry. The weak tears of age rolled down his cheeks, and all the feebleness of his eighty-seven years showed in his grief-stricken countenance.

"Sit down," Edwin counselled soothingly. "Granser's all right. He's just gettin' to the Scarlet Death, ain't you, Granser? He's just goin' to tell us about it right now. Sit down, Hare-Lip. Go ahead, Granser."

The old man wiped the tears away on his grimy knuckles and took up the tale in a tremulous, piping voice that soon strengthened as he got the swing of the narrative.

"It was in the summer of 2013 that the Plague came. I was twenty-seven years old, and well do I remember it. Wireless despatches—"

Hare-Lip spat loudly his disgust, and Granser hastened to make amends.

"We talked through the air in those days, thousands and thousands of miles. And the word came of a strange disease that had broken out in New York. There were seventeen millions of people living then in that noblest city of America. Nobody thought anything about the news. It was only a small thing. There had been only a few deaths. It seemed, though, that they had died very quickly, and that one of the first signs of the disease was the turning red of the face and all the body. Within twenty-four hours came the report of the first case in Chicago. And on the same day, it was made public that London, the greatest city in the world, next to Chicago, had been secretly fighting the plague for two weeks and censoring the news despatches—that is, not permitting the word to go forth to the rest of the world that London had the plague.

"It looked serious, but we in California, like everywhere else, were not alarmed. We were sure that the bacteriologists would find a way to overcome this new germ, just as they had overcome other germs in the past. But the trouble was the astonishing quickness with which this germ destroyed human beings, and the fact that it inevitably killed any human body it entered. No one ever recovered.

"There was the old Asiatic cholera, when you might eat dinner with a well man in the evening, and the next morning, if you got up early enough, you would see him being hauled by your window in the death-cart. But this new plague was quicker than that—much quicker. From the moment of the first signs of it, a man would be dead in an hour. Some lasted for several hours. Many died within ten or fifteen minutes of the appearance of the first signs.

"The heart began to beat faster and the heat of the body to increase. Then came the scarlet rash, spreading like wildfire over the face and body. Most persons never noticed the increase in heat and heart-beat, and the first they knew was when the scarlet rash came out. Usually, they had convulsions at the time of the appearance of the rash. But these convulsions did not last long and were not very severe. If one lived through them, he became perfectly quiet, and only did he feel a numbness swiftly creeping up his body from the feet.

"The heels became numb first, then the legs, and hips, and when the numbness reached as high as his heart he died. They did not rave or sleep. Their minds always remained cool and calm up to the moment their heart numbed and stopped. And another strange thing was the rapidity of decomposition. No sooner was a person dead than the body seemed to fall to pieces, to fly apart, to melt away even as you looked at it. That was one of the reasons the plague spread so rapidly. All the billions of germs in a corpse were so immediately released.

"And it was because of all this that the bacteriologists had so little chance in fighting the germs. They were killed in their laboratories even as they studied the germ of the Scarlet Death. They were heroes. As fast as they perished, others stepped forth and took their places. It was in London that they first isolated it. The news was telegraphed everywhere. Trask was the name of the man who succeeded in this, but within thirty hours he was dead. Then came the struggle in all the laboratories to find something that would kill the plague germs. All drugs failed. You see, the problem was to get a drug, or serum, that would kill the germs in the body and not kill the body. They tried to fight it with other germs, to put into the body of a sick man germs that were the enemies of the plague germs—"

"And you can't see these germ-things, Granser," Hare-Lip objected, "and here you gabble, gabble, gabble about them as if they was anything, when they're nothing at all. Anything you can't see, ain't, that's what. Fighting things that ain't with things that ain't! They must have been all fools in them days. That's why they croaked. I ain't goin' to believe in such rot, I tell you that."

Granser promptly began to weep, while Edwin hotly took up his defense.

"Look here, Hare-Lip, you believe in lots of things you can't see."

Hare-Lip shook his head.

"You believe in dead men walking about. You never seen one dead man walk about."

"I tell you I seen 'em, last winter, when I was wolf-hunting with dad."

"Well, you always spit when you cross running water," Edwin challenged.

"That's to keep off bad luck," was Hare-Lip's defense.

"You believe in bad luck? An' you ain't never seen bad luck," Edwin concluded triumphantly. "You're just as bad as Granser and his germs. You believe in what you don't see. Go on, Granser."

Hare-Lip, crushed by this metaphysical defeat, remained silent, and the old man went on. Often and often, though this narrative must not be clogged by the details, was Granser's tale interrupted while the boys squabbled among themselves. Also, among themselves they kept up a constant, low-voiced exchange of explanation and conjecture, as they strove to follow the old man into his unknown and vanished world.

"The Scarlet Death broke out in San Francisco. The first death came on a Monday morning. By Thursday they were dying like flies in Oakland and San Francisco. They died everywhere—in their beds, at their work, walking along the street. It was on Tuesday that I saw my first death—Miss Collbran, one of my students, sitting right there before my eyes, in my lecture-room. I noticed her face while I was talking. It had suddenly turned scarlet.

"I ceased speaking and could only look at her, for the first fear of the plague was already on all of us and we knew that it had come. The young women screamed and ran out of the room. So did the young men run out, all but two. Miss Collbran's convulsions were very mild and lasted less than a minute. One of the young men fetched her a glass of water. She drank only a little bit of it, and cried out:

" 'My feet! All sensation has left them.'

"After a minute she said, 'I have no feet. I am unaware that I have feet. And my knees are cold. I can scarcely feel that I have knees.'

"She lay on the floor, a bundle of notebooks under her head. And we could do nothing. The coldness and the numbness crept up past her hips to her heart, and when it reached her heart she was dead. In fifteen minutes, by the clock—I timed it—she was dead, there, in my own classroom, dead. And she was a very beautiful, strong, healthy young woman. And from the first sign of the plague to her death only fifteen minutes elapsed. That will show you how swift was the Scarlet Death.

"Yet in those few minutes I remained with the dying woman in my classroom, the alarm had spread over the university; and the students by thousands, all of them, had deserted the lecture-room and laboratories.

When I emerged, on my way to make report to the President of the Faculty, I found the university deserted. Across the campus were several stragglers hurrying for their homes. Two of them were running.

"President Hoag, I found in his office, all alone, looking very old and very gray, with a multitude of wrinkles in his face that I had never seen before. At sight of me, he pulled himself to his feet and tottered away to the inner office, banging the door after him and locking it. You see, he knew I had been exposed, and he was afraid. He shouted to me through the door to go away. I shall never forget my feelings as I walked down the silent corridors and out across that deserted campus. I was not afraid. I had been exposed and I looked upon myself as already dead. It was not that, but a feeling of awful depression that impressed me. Everything had stopped.

"It was like the end of the world to me—my world. I had been born within sight and sound of the university. It had been my predestined career. My father had been a professor there before me, and his father before him. For a century and a half had this university, like a splendid machine, been running steadily on. And now, in an instant, it had stopped. It was like seeing the sacred flame die down on some thrice-sacred altar. I was shocked, unutterably shocked.

"When I arrived, my housekeeper screamed as I entered and fled away. And when I rang, I found the housemaid had likewise fled. I investigated. In the kitchen I found the cook on the point of departure. But she screamed, too, and in her haste dropped a suitcase of her personal belongings and ran out of the house and across the grounds, still screaming. I can hear her scream to this day.

"You see, we did not act in this way when ordinary disease smote us. We were always calm over such things, and sent for the doctors and nurses who knew just what to do. But this was different. It struck so suddenly, and killed so swiftly, and never missed a stroke. When the scarlet rash appeared on a person's face, that person was marked by death. There was never a known case of a recovery.

"I was alone in my big house. As I have told you often before, in those days we could talk with one another over wires or through the air. The telephone bell rang, and I found my brother talking to me. He told me that he was not coming home for fear of catching the plague from me, and that he had taken our two sisters to stop at Professor Bacon's home. He advised me to remain where I was, and wait to find out whether or not I had caught the plague.

"To all of this I agreed, staying in my house and for the first time in my life attempting to cook. And the plague did not come out on me. By means of the telephone I could talk with whomsoever I pleased and get the news. Also, there were the newspapers, and I ordered all of them to be thrown up to my door so that I could know what was happening with the rest of the world.

"New York City and Chicago were in chaos. And what happened with them was happening in all the large cities. A third of the New York police were dead. Their chief was also dead, likewise the mayor. All law and order had ceased. The bodies were lying in the streets unburied. All railroads and vessels carrying food and such things into the great city had ceased running, and mobs of the hungry poor were pillaging the stores and warehouses. Murder and robbery and drunkenness were everywhere.

"Already the people had fled from the city by millions—at first the rich, in their private motor-cars and dirigibles, and then the great mass of the population, on foot, carrying the plague with them, themselves starving and pillaging the farmers and all the towns and villages on the way.

"The man who sent this news, the wireless operator, was alone with his instrument on the top of a loft building. The people remaining in the city—he estimated them at several hundred thousand—had gone mad from fear and drink, and on all sides of him great fires were raging. He was a hero, the man who staid by his post—an obscure newspaperman, most likely.

"For twenty-four hours, he said, no transatlantic airships had arrived, and no more messages were coming from England. He did state, though, that a message from Berlin—that's in Germany—announced that Hoffmeyer, a bacteriologist of the Metchnikoff School, had discovered the serum for the plague. That was the last word, to this day, that we of America ever received from Europe.

"If Hoffmeyer discovered the serum, it was too late, or otherwise, long ere this, explorers from Europe would have come looking for us. We can only conclude that what happened in America happened in Europe, and that, at the best, some several score may have survived that Scarlet Death on that whole continent.

"For one day longer the dispatches continued to come from New York. Then they, too, ceased. The man who had sent them, perched in his lofty building, had either died of the plague or been consumed in the great conflagrations he had described as raging around him. And what had occurred in New York had been duplicated in all the other cities. It was the same in San Francisco, and Oakland, and Berkeley. By Thursday the people were dying so rapidly that their corpses could not be handled, and dead bodies lay everywhere. Thursday night the panic outrush for the country began. Imagine, my grandsons, people, thicker than the salmon-run you have seen on the Sacramento River, pouring out of the cities by millions, madly over the country, in vain attempt to escape the ubiquitous death. You see, they carried the germs with them. Even the airships of the rich, fleeing for mountain and desert fastness, carried the germs.

"Hundreds of these airships escaped to Hawaii, and not only did they bring the plague with them, but they found the plague already there before them. This we learned, by the despatches, until all order in San

Francisco vanished, and there were no operators left at their posts to receive or send. It was amazing, astounding, this loss of communication with the world. It was exactly as if the world had ceased, been blotted out.

"For sixty years that world has no longer existed for me. I know there must be such places as New York, Europe, Asia, and Africa; but not one word has been heard of them—not in sixty years. With the coming of the Scarlet Death the world fell apart, absolutely, irretrievably. Ten thousand years of culture and civilization passed in the twinkling of an eye, 'lapsed like foam.'

"I was telling about the airships of the rich. They carried the plague with them and no matter where they fled, they died. I never encountered but one survivor of any of them—Mungerson. He was afterwards a Santa Rosan, and he married my eldest daughter. He came into the tribe eight years after the plague. He was then nineteen years old, and he was compelled to wait twelve years more before he could marry. You see, there were no unmarried women, and some of the older daughters of the Santa Rosans were already bespoken. So he was forced to wait until my Mary had grown to sixteen years. It was his son, Gimp-Leg, who was killed last year by the mountain lion.

"Mungerson was eleven years old at the time of the plague. His father was one of the Industrial Magnates, a very wealthy, powerful man. It was on his airship, the Condor, that they were fleeing, with all the family, for the wilds of British Columbia, which is far to the north of here. But there was some accident, and they were wrecked near Mount Shasta. You have heard of that mountain. It is far to the north. The plague broke out amongst them, and this boy of eleven was the only survivor. For eight years he was alone, wandering over a deserted land and looking vainly for his own kind. And at last, travelling south, he picked up with us, the Santa Rosans.

"But I am ahead of my story. When the great exodus from the cities around San Francisco Bay began, and while the telephones were still working, I talked with my brother. I told him this flight from the cities was insanity, that there were no symptoms of the plague in me, and that the thing for us to do was to isolate ourselves and our relatives in some safe place. We decided on the Chemistry Building, at the university, and we planned to lay in a supply of provisions, and by force of arms to prevent any other persons from forcing their presence upon us after we had retired to our refuge.

"All this being arranged, my brother begged me to stay in my own house for at least twenty-four hours more, on the chance of the plague developing in me. To this I agreed, and he promised to come for me next day. We talked on over the details of the provisioning and the defending of the Chemistry Building until the telephone died. It died in the midst of our conversation. That evening there were no electric lights, and I was alone in my house in the darkness.

"No more newspapers were being printed, so I had no knowledge of what was taking place outside. I heard sounds of rioting and of pistol shots, and from my windows I could see the glare of the sky of some conflagration in the direction of Oakland. It was a night of terror. I did not sleep a wink. A man—why and how I do not know—was killed on the sidewalk in front of the house. I heard the rapid reports of an automatic pistol, and a few minutes later the wounded wretch crawled up to my door, moaning and crying out for help.

"Arming myself with two automatics, I went to him. By the light of a match I ascertained that while he was dying of the bullet wounds, at the same time the plague was on him. I fled indoors, whence I heard him moan and cry out for half an hour longer.

"In the morning, my brother came to me. I had gathered into a hand-bag what things of value I purposed taking, but when I saw his face I knew that he would never accompany me to the Chemistry Building. The plague was on him. He intended shaking my hand, but I went back hurriedly before him.

"'Look at yourself in the mirror,'" I commanded.

"He did so, and at sight of his scarlet face, the color deepening as he looked at it, he sank down nervelessly in a chair.

"'My God!' he said. 'I've got it. Don't come near me. I am already a dead man.'

"Then the convulsions seized him. He was two hours in dying, and he was conscious to the last, complaining about the coldness and loss of sensation in his feet, his calves, his thighs, until at last it was his heart and he was dead.

"That was the way the Scarlet Death slew. I caught up my handbag and fled. The sights in the streets were terrible. One stumbled on bodies everywhere. Some were not yet dead. And even as you looked, you saw men sink down with the death fastened upon them. There were numerous fires burning in Berkeley, while Oakland and San Francisco were apparently swept by vast conflagrations. The smoke of the burning filled the heavens, so that the midday was a gloomy twilight, and, in the shifts of wind, sometimes the sun shone through dimly, a dull red orb. Truly, my grandsons, it was like the last days of the end of the world.

"There were numerous stalled motor cars, showing that the gasoline and the engine supplies of the garage had given out.

"I remember one such car. A man and a woman lay back dead in the seats, and on the pavement near it were two more women and a child. Strange and terrible sights there were on every hand. People slipped by silently, furtively, like ghosts—white-faced women carrying infants in their arms, fathers leading children by the hand; singly, and in couples. and in families—all fleeing out of the city of death. Some carried supplies of food, others blankets and valuables, and there were many who carried nothing.

"There was a grocery store—a place where food was sold. The man to whom it belonged—I knew him well—a quiet, sober, but stupid and obstinate fellow, was defending it. The windows and doors had been broken in, but he, inside, hiding behind a counter, was discharging his pistol at a number of men on the sidewalk who were breaking in. In the entrance were several bodies—of men, I decided, whom he had killed earlier in the day.

"Even as I looked on from a distance, I saw one of the robbers break the windows of the adjoining store, a place where shoes were sold, and deliberately set fire to it. I did not go to the grocery-man's assistance. The time for such acts had already passed.

"Civilization was crumbling, and it was each for himself.

"I went away hastily, down a cross-street, and at the first corner I saw another tragedy. Two men of the working class had caught a man and a woman with two children, and were robbing them. I knew the man by sight, though I had never been introduced to him. He was a poet whose verses I had long admired. Yet I did not go to his help, for at the moment I came upon the scene there was a pistol shot, and I saw him sinking to the ground. The woman screamed, and she was felled with a fist-blow by one of the brutes.

"I cried out threateningly, whereupon they discharged their pistols at me and I ran away around the corner. Here I was blocked by an advancing conflagration. The buildings on both sides were burning, and the street was filled with smoke and flame. From somewhere in that murk came a woman's voice calling shrilly for help. But I did not go to her. A man's heart turned to iron amid such scenes, and one heard all too many appeals for help.

"Returning to the corner. I found the two robbers were gone. The poet and his wife lay dead on the pavement. It was a shocking sight. The two children had vanished—whither I could not tell. And I knew, now, why it was that the fleeing persons I encountered slipped along so furtively and with such white faces. In the midst of our civilization, down in our slums we had bred a race of barbarians, of savages; and now, in the time of our calamity, they turned upon us like the wild beasts they were and destroyed us. And they destroyed themselves as well. They inflamed themselves with strong drink and committed a thousand atrocities, quarrelling and killing one another in the general madness.

"One group of workingmen I saw, of the better sort, who had banded together, and, with their women and children in their midst, the sick and aged in litters and being carried, and with a number of horses pulling a truck-load of provisions, they were fighting their way out of the city.

"They made a fine spectacle as they came down the street through the drifting smoke, though they nearly shot me when I first appeared in their path. As they went by, one of their leaders shouted out to me in apologetic explanation. He said they were killing the robbers and looters on sight, and that they had thus banded together as the only means by which to escape the prowlers.

"It was here that I saw for the first time what I was soon to see so often. One of the marching men had suddenly shown the unmistakable mark of the plague. Immediately those about him drew away, and he, without a remonstrance, stepped out of his place to let them pass on. A woman, most probably his wife, attempted to follow him. She was leading a little boy by the hand. But the husband commanded her sternly to go on, while others laid hands on her and restrained her from following him. This I saw, and I saw the man also, with his scarlet blaze of face, step into a doorway on the opposite side of the street. I heard the report of his pistol, and saw him sink lifeless to the ground.

"After being turned aside twice again by advancing fires, I succeeded in getting through to the university. On the edge of the campus I came upon a party of university folk who were going in the direction of the Chemistry Building. They were all family men, and their families were with them, including the nurses and the servants. Professor Badminton greeted me, and I had difficulty in recognizing him. Somewhere he had gone through flames, and his beard was singed off. About his head was a bloody bandage, and his clothes were filthy. He told me he had been cruelly beaten by prowlers, and that his brother had been killed the previous night, in the defence of their dwelling.

"Midway across the campus, he pointed suddenly to Mrs. Swinton's face. The unmistakable scarlet was there. Immediately all the other women set up a screaming and began to run away from her. Her two children were with a nurse, and these also ran with the women. But her husband, Doctor Swinton, remained with her.

"'Go on, Smith,' he told me. 'Keep an eye on the children. As for me, I shall stay with my wife. I know she is as already dead, but I can't leave her. Afterward, if I escape, I shall come to the Chemistry Building, and do you watch for me and let me in.'

"I left him bending over his wife and soothing her last moments, while I ran to overtake the party. We were the last to be admitted to the Chemistry Building. After that, with our automatic rifles we maintained our isolation. By our plans, we had arranged for a company of sixty to be in this refuge. Instead, every one of the number originally planned had added relatives and friends and whole families until there were over four hundred souls. But the Chemistry Building was large, and, standing by itself, was in no danger of being burned by the great fires that raged everywhere in the city.

"A large quantity of provisions had been gathered, and a food committee took charge of it, issuing rations daily to the various families and groups that arranged themselves into messes. A number of committees were appointed, and we developed a very efficient organization. I was on the committee of defence, though for the first day no prowlers came near. We could see them in the distance, however, and by the smoke of their fires knew that several camps of them were occupying the far edge of the campus.

"Drunkenness was rife, and often we heard them singing ribald songs or insanely shouting. While the world crashed to ruin about them and all the air was filled with the smoke of its burning, these low creatures gave rein to their bestiality and fought and drank and died. And after all, what did it matter? Everybody died anyway, the good and the bad, the efficient and the weaklings, those that loved to live and those that scorned to live. They passed. Everything passed.

"When the twenty-four hours had gone by and no signs of the plague were apparent, we congratulated ourselves and set about digging a well. You have seen the great iron pipes which in those days carried water to all the city-dwellers. We feared that the fires in the city would burst the pipes and empty the reservoirs. So we tore up the cement floor of the central court of the Chemistry Building and dug a well. There were many young men, undergraduates, with us, and we worked night and day on the well. And our fears were confirmed. Three hours before we reached water, the pipes went dry.

"A second twenty-four hours passed, and still the plague did not appear among us. We thought we were saved. But we did not know what I afterwards decided to be true, namely, that the period of the incubation of the plague germs in a human's body was a matter of a number of days. It slew so swiftly when once it manifested itself, that we were led to believe that the period of incubation was equally swift. So, when two days had left us unscathed, we were elated with the idea that we were free of the contagion.

"But the third day disillusioned us. I can never forget the night preceding it. I had charge of the night guards from eight to twelve, and from the roof of the building I watched the passing of all man's glorious works. So terrible were the local conflagrations that all the sky was lighted up. One could read the finest print in the red glare. All the world seemed wrapped in flames. San Francisco spouted smoke and fire from the score of vast conflagrations that were like so many active volcanoes. Oakland, San Leandro, Haywards—all were burning; and to the northward, clear to Point Richmond, other fires were at work.

"It was an awe-inspiring spectacle, civilization was passing in a sheet of flame and a breath of death. At ten o'clock that night, the great powder magazines at Point Pinole exploded in rapid succession. So terrific were the concussions that the strong building rocked as in an earthquake, while every pane of glass was broken. It was then that I left the roof and went down the long corridors, from room to room, quieting the alarmed women and telling them what had happened.

"An hour later, at a window on the ground floor, I heard pandemonium break out in the camps of the prowlers. There were cries and screams, and shots from many pistols. As we afterward conjectured, this fight had been precipitated by an attempt on the part of those that were well to drive out those that were sick. At any rate, a number of the plague-stricken prowlers escaped across the campus and drifted against our doors. We warned them back, but they cursed us and discharged a fusillade from their pistols.

"Professor Merryweather, at one of the windows, was instantly killed, the bullet striking him squarely between the eyes. We opened fire in turn, and all the prowlers fled with the exception of three. One was a woman. The plague was on them and they were reckless. Like foul fiends, there in the red glare from the skies, with faces blazing, they continued to curse us and fire at us. One of the men I shot with my own hand. After that the other man and the woman, still cursing us, lay down under our windows where we were compelled to watch them die of the plague.

"The situation was critical. The explosions of the powder magazines had broken all the windows of the Chemistry Building, so that we were exposed to the germs from the corpses. The sanitary committee was called upon to act, and it responded nobly. Two men were required to go out and remove the corpses, and that meant the probable sacrifice of their own lives, for, having performed the task, they were not to be permitted to re-enter the building.

"One of the professors, who was a bachelor, and one of the undergraduates volunteered. They bade goodbye to us and went forth. They were heroes. They gave up their lives that four hundred others might live. After they had performed their work, they stood for a moment, at a distance, looking at us wistfully. Then they waved their hands in farewell and went away slowly across the campus toward the burning city.

"And yet it was all useless. The next morning the first one of us was smitten with the plague—a little nurse-girl in the family of Professor Stout. It was no time for weak-kneed, sentimental policies. On the chance that she might be the only one, we thrust her forth from the building and commanded her to be gone. She went away slowly across the campus, wringing her hands and crying pitifully. We felt like brutes, but what were we to do? There were four hundred of us, and individuals had to be sacrificed.

"In one of the laboratories three families had domiciled themselves, and that afternoon we found among them no less than four corpses and seven cases of the plague in all its different stages.

"Then it was that the horror began. Leaving the dead lie, we forced the living ones to segregate themselves in another room. The plague began to break out among the rest of us, and as fast as the symptoms appeared, we sent the stricken ones to these segregated rooms. We compelled them to walk there by themselves, so as to avoid laying hands on them. It was heartrending. But still the plague raged among us, and room after room was filled with the dead and dying. And so we who were yet clean retreated to the next floor and to the next, before this sea of the dead, that, room by room and floor by floor, inundated the building.

"The place became a charnel house, and in the middle of the night the survivors fled forth, taking nothing with them except arms and ammunition and a heavy store of tinned foods. We camped on the opposite side of the campus from the prowlers, and, while some stood guard, others of us volunteered to scout into the city in quest of horses, motor cars, carts, and wagons, or anything that would carry our provisions and enable us to emulate the banded workingmen I had seen fighting their way out to open country.

"I was one of these scouts; and Doctor Hoyle, remembering that his motor car had been left behind in his home garage, told me to look for it. We scouted in pairs, and Dombey, a young undergraduate, accompanied me. We had to cross half a mile of the residence portion of the city to get to Doctor Hoyle's home. Here the buildings stood apart, in the midst of trees and grassy lawns and here the fires had played freaks, burning whole blocks, skipping blocks and often skipping a single house in a block. And here, too, the prowlers were still at their work.

"We carried our automatic pistols openly in our hands, and looked desperate enough, forsooth, to keep them from attacking us. But at Doctor Hoyle's house the thing happened. Untouched by fire, even as we came to it the smoke of flames burst forth.

"The miscreant who had set fire to it staggered down the steps and out along the driveway. Sticking out of his coat pockets were bottles of whiskey, and he was very drunk. My first impulse was to shoot him, and I have never ceased regretting that I did not. Staggering and maundering to himself, with bloodshot eyes, and a raw and bleeding slash down one side of his bewhiskered face, he was altogether the most nauseating specimen of degradation and filth I had ever encountered. I did not shoot him, and he leaned against a tree on the lawn to let us go by. It was the most absolute, wanton act. Just as we were opposite him, he suddenly drew a pistol and shot Dombey through the head. The next instant I shot him. But it was too late. Dombey expired without a groan, immediately. I doubt if he even knew what had happened to him.

"Leaving the two corpses, I hurried on past the burning house to the garage, and there found Doctor Hoyle's motor car. The tanks were filled with gasoline, and it was ready for use. And it was in this car that I threaded the streets of the ruined city and came back to the survivors on the campus. The other scouts returned, but none had been so fortunate. Professor Fairmead had found a Shetland pony, but the poor creature, tied in a stable and abandoned for days, was so weak from want of food and water that it could carry no burden at all. Some of the men were for turning it loose, but I insisted that we should lead it along with us, so that, if we got out of food, we would have it to eat.

"There were forty-seven of us when we started, many being women and children. The President of the Faculty, an old man to begin with, and now hopelessly broken by the awful happenings of the past week, rode in the motor car with several young children and the aged mother of Professor Fairmead. Wathope, a young professor of English, who had a grievous bullet-wound in his leg, drove the car. The rest of us walked, Professor Fairmead leading the pony.

"It was what should have been a bright summer day, but the smoke from the burning world filled the sky, through which the sun shone murkily, a dull and lifeless orb, blood-red and ominous. But we had grown accustomed to that blood-red sun. With the smoke it was different. It bit into our nostrils and eyes, and there was no one of us whose eyes were not bloodshot. We directed our course to the southeast through the endless miles of suburban residences, travelling along where the first swells of low hills rose from the flat of the central city. It was by this way, only, that we could expect to gain the country.

"Our progress was painfully slow. The women and children could not walk fast. They did not dream of walking, my grandsons, in the way all people walk to-day. In truth, none of us knew how to walk. It was not until after the plague that I learned really to walk. So it was that the pace of the slowest was the pace of all, for we dared not separate on account of the prowlers. There were not so many now of these human beasts of prey. The plague had already well diminished their numbers, but enough still lived to be a constant menace to us. Many of the beautiful residences were untouched by fire, yet smoking ruins were everywhere. The prowlers, too, seemed to have got over their insensate desire to burn, and it was more rarely that we saw houses freshly on fire.

"Several of us scouted among the private garages in search of motor cars and gasoline. But in this we were unsuccessful. The first great flight from the cities had swept all such utilities away. Galgan, a fine young man, was lost in this work. He was shot by prowlers while crossing a lawn. Yet this was our only casualty, though, once, a drunken brute deliberately opened fire on all of us. Luckily, he fired wildly, and we shot him before he had done any hurt.

"At Fruitvale, still in the heart of the magnificent resident section of the city, the plague again smote us. Professor Fairmead was the victim. Making signs to us that his mother was not to know, he turned aside into the grounds of a beautiful mansion. He sat down forlornly on the steps of the front veranda, and I, having lingered, waved him a last farewell.

"That night, several miles beyond Fruitvale and still in the city, we made camp. And that night we shifted camp twice to get away from our dead. In the morning there were thirty of us. I shall never forget the President of the Faculty. During the morning's march his wife, who was walking, betrayed the fatal symptoms, and when she drew aside to let us go on, he insisted on leaving the motor car and remaining with her. There was quite a discussion about this, but in the end we gave in. It was just as well, for we knew not which ones of us, if any, might ultimately escape.

"That night, the second of our march, we camped beyond Haywards in the first stretches of country. And in the morning there were eleven of us that lived. Also, during the night, Wathope, the professor with the wounded leg, deserted us in the motor car. He took with him his sister and his mother and most of our tinned provisions. It was that day, in the afternoon, while resting by the wayside, that I saw the last airship I shall ever see. The smoke was much thinner here in the country, and I first sighted the ship drifting and veering helplessly at an elevation of two thousand feet.

"What had happened I could not conjecture, but even as we looked we saw her bow dip down lower and lower. Then the bulkheads of the various gas-chambers must have burst, for, quite perpendicular, she fell like a plummet to the earth. And from that day to this I have not seen another airship. Often and often, during the next few years, I scanned the sky for them, hoping against hope that somewhere in the world civilization had survived. But it was not to be. What happened with us in California must have happened with everybody everywhere.

"Another day, and at Niles there were three of us. Beyond Niles, in the middle of the highway, we found Wathope. The motor car had broken down, and there, on the rugs which they had spread on the ground, lay the bodies of his sister, his mother, and himself.

"Wearied by the unusual exercise of continual walking, that night I slept heavily. In the morning I was alone in the world. Canfield and Parsons, my last companions, were dead of the plague. Of the four hundred that sought shelter in the Chemistry Building, and of the forty-seven that began the march, I alone remained—I and the Shetland pony. Why this should be so there is no explaining. I did not catch the plague, that is all. I was immune. I was merely the one lucky man in a million—just as every survivor was one in a million, or, rather, in several millions, for the proportion was at least that.

"For two days I sheltered in a pleasant grove where there had been no deaths. In those days, while badly depressed and believing that my turn would come at any moment, nevertheless I rested and recuperated. So did the pony. And on the third day, putting what small store of tinned provisions I possessed on the pony's back, I started on across a very lonely land. Not a live man, woman, or child, did I encounter, though the dead were everywhere. Food, however, was abundant. The land then was not as it is now. It was all cleared of trees and brush, and it was cultivated. The food for millions of mouths was growing, ripening, and going to waste. From the fields and orchards I gathered vegetables, fruits, and berries. Around the deserted farmhouses I got eggs and caught chickens. And frequently I found supplies of tinned provisions in the store-rooms.

"A strange thing was what was taking place with all the domestic animals. Everywhere they were going wild and preying on one another. The chickens and ducks were the first to be destroyed, while the pigs were the first to go wild, followed by the cats. Nor were the dogs long in adapting themselves to the changed conditions. There was a veritable plague of dogs. They devoured the corpses, barked and howled during the nights, and in the daytime slunk about in the distance. As the time went by, I noticed a change in their behavior. At first they were apart from one another, very suspicious and very prone to fight. But after a not very long while they began to come together and run in packs.

"The dog, you see, always was a social animal, and this was true before ever he came to be domesticated by man. In the last days of the world before the plague, there were many many very different kinds of dogs— dogs without hair and dogs with warm fur, dogs so small that they would make scarcely a mouthful for other dogs that were as large as mountain lions. Well, all the small dogs, and weak types, were killed by their fellows. Also, the very large ones were not adapted for the wild life and bred out. As a result, the many different kinds of dogs disappeared, and there remained, running in packs, the medium-sized wolfish dogs that you know to-day."

"But the cats don't run in packs, Granser," Hoo-Hoo objected.

"The cat was never a social animal. As one writer in the nineteenth century said, the cat walks by himself. He always walked by himself, from before the time he was tamed by man, down through the long ages of domestication, to to-day when once more he is wild.

"The horses also went wild, and all the fine breeds we had degenerated into the small mustang horse you know to-day. The cows likewise went wild, as did the pigeons and the sheep. And that a few of the chickens survived you know yourself. But the wild chicken of to-day is quite a different thing from the chickens we had in those days.

"But I must go on with my story. I traveled through a deserted land. As the time went by I began to yearn more and more for human beings. But I never found one, and I grew lonelier and lonelier.

"I crossed Livermore Valley and the mountains between it and the great valley of the San Joaquin. You have never seen that valley, but it is very large and it is the home of the wild horse. There are great droves there, thousands and tens of thousands. I revisited it thirty years after, so I know. You think there are lots of wild horses down here in the coast valleys, but they are as nothing compared with those of the San Joaquin. Strange to say, the cows, when they went wild, went back into the lower mountains. Evidently they were better able to protect themselves there.

"In the country districts the ghouls and prowlers had been less in evidence, for I found many villages and towns untouched by fire. But they were filled by the pestilential dead, and I passed by without exploring them. It was near Lathrop that, out of my loneliness, I picked up a pair of collie dogs that were so newly free that they were urgently willing to return to their allegiance to man. These collies accompanied me for many years, and the strains of them are in those very dogs there that you boys have today. But in sixty years the collie strain has worked out. These brutes are more like domesticated wolves than anything else."

Hare-Lip arose to his feet, glanced to see that the goats were safe, and looked at the sun's position, in the afternoon sky, advertising impatience at the prolixity of the old man's tale. Urged to hurry by Edwin, Granser went on.

"There is little more to tell. With my two dogs and my pony, and riding a horse I had managed to capture, I crossed the San Joaquin and went on to a wonderful valley in the Sierras called Yosemite. In the great hotel there I found a prodigious supply of tinned provisions. The pasture was abundant, as was the game, and the river that ran through the valley was full of trout. I remained there three years in an utter loneliness that none but a man who has once been highly civilized can understand. Then I could stand it no more. I felt that I was going crazy.

"Like the dog, I was a social animal and I needed my kind. I reasoned that since I had survived the plague, there was a possibility that others had survived. Also, I reasoned that after three years the plague germs must all be gone and the land be clean again.

"With my horse and dogs and pony, I set out. Again I crossed the San Joaquin Valley, the mountains beyond, and came down into Livermore Valley. The change in those three years was amazing. All the land had been splendidly tilled, and now I could scarcely recognize it, such was the sea of rank vegetation that had overrun the agricultural handiwork of man.

"You see, the wheat, the vegetables, and orchard trees had always been cared for and nursed by man, so that they were soft and tender. The weeds and wild bushes and such things, on the contrary, had always been fought by man, so that they were tough and resistant. As a result, when the hand of man was removed, the wild vegetation smothered and destroyed practically all the domesticated vegetation. The coyotes were greatly increased, and it was at this time that I first encountered wolves, straying in twos and threes and small packs down from the regions where they had always persisted.

"It was at Lake Temescal, not far from the one-time city of Oakland, that I came upon the first live human beings. Oh, my grandsons, how can I describe to you my emotion, when, astride my horse and dropping down the hillside to the lake, I saw the smoke of a campfire rising through the trees? Almost did my heart stop beating. I felt that I was going crazy. Then I heard the cry of a babe—a human babe. And dogs barked, and my dogs answered. I did not know but what I was the one human alive in the whole world. It could not be true that here were others—smoke, and the cry of a babe.

"Emerging on the lake, there, before my eyes, not a hundred yards away, I saw a man, a large man. He was standing on an outjutting rock and fishing. I was overcome. I stopped my horse. I tried to call out but could not. I waved my hand. It seemed to me that the man looked at me, but he did not appear to wave. I was afraid to look again, for I knew it was an hallucination, and I knew that if I looked the man would be gone. And so precious was the hallucination, that I wanted it to persist yet a little while. I knew, too, that as long as I did not look it would persist.

"Thus I remained, until I heard my dogs snarling, and a man's voice. What do you think the voice said? I will tell you. It said: *Where in hell did you come from?'*

"Those were the exact words, the exact words. That was what your other grandfather said to me, Hare-Lip, when he greeted me there on the shore of Lake Temescal fifty-seven years ago. And they were the most ineffable words I have ever heard. I opened my eyes, and there he stood before me, a large, dark, hairy man, heavy-jawed, slant-browed, fierce-eyed. How I got off my horse I do not know. But it seemed that the next I knew I was clasping his hand with both of mine and crying. I would have embraced him, but he was ever a narrow-minded, suspicious man, and he drew away from me. Yet did I cling to him and cry."

Granser's voice faltered and broke at the recollection, and the weak tears streamed down his cheeks while the boys looked on and giggled.

"Yet did I cry," he continued, "and desire to embrace him, though the Chauffeur was a brute, a perfect brute—the most abhorrent man I have ever known. His name was . . . strange, how I have forgotten his name. Everybody called him Chauffeur—it was the name of his occupation, and it stuck. That is how, to this day, the tribe he founded is called the Chauffeur Tribe.

"He was a violent, unjust man. Why the plague germs spared him I can never understand. It would seem, in spite of our old metaphysical notions about absolute justice, that there is no justice in the universe. Why did he live?—an iniquitous, moral monster, a blot on the face of nature, a cruel, relentless, bestial cheat as well. All he could talk about was motor cars, machinery, gasoline, and garages—and especially, and with huge delight, of his mean pilferings and sordid swindlings of the persons who had employed him in the days before the coming of the plague. And yet he was spared, while hundreds of millions, yea, billions, of better men were destroyed.

"I went on with him to his camp, and there I saw her, Vesta, the one woman. It was glorious, and . . . pitiful. There she was, Vesta Van Warden, clad in rags, with marred and scarred and toil-calloused hands, bending over the campfire and doing scullion work—she, Vesta, who had been born to the purple of the greatest baronage of wealth the world has ever known. John Van Warden, her husband, worth one billion, eight hundred millions and President of the Board of Industrial Magnates, had been the ruler of America. Also, sitting on the International Board of Control, he had been one of the seven men who ruled the world. And she herself had come of equally noble stock.

"Her father, Philip Saxon, had been President of the Board of Industrial Magnates up to the time of his death. This office was in process of becoming hereditary, and had Philip Saxon had a son that son would have succeeded him. But his only child was Vesta, the perfect flower of generations of the highest culture this planet has ever produced.

"It was not until the engagement between Vesta and Van Warden took place, that Saxon indicated the latter as his successor. It was, I am sure, a political marriage. I have reason to believe that Vesta never really loved her husband in the mad passionate way of which the poets used to sing. It was more like the marriages that obtained among crowned heads in the days before they were displaced by the Magnates.

"And there she was, boiling fish-chowder in a soot-covered pot, her glorious eyes inflamed by the acrid smoke of the open fire. Hers was a sad story. She was the one survivor in a million, as I had been, as the Chauffeur had been. On a crowning eminence of the Alameda Hills, overlooking San Francisco Bay, Van Warden had built a vast summer palace. It was surrounded by a park of a thousand acres. When the plague broke out, Van Warden sent her there. Armed guards patrolled the boundaries of the park, and nothing entered in the way of provisions or even mail matter that was not first fumigated. And yet did the plague enter, killing the guards at their posts, the servants at their tasks, sweeping away the whole army of retainers—or, at least, all of them who did not flee to die elsewhere. So it was that Vesta found herself the sole living person in the palace that had become a charnel house.

"Now the Chauffeur had been one of the servants that ran away. Returning, two months afterward, he discovered Vesta in a little summer pavilion where there had been no deaths and where she had established herself. He was a brute. She was afraid, and she ran away and hid among the trees. That night, on foot, she fled into the mountains—she, whose tender feet and delicate body had never known the bruise of stones nor the scratch of briars.

"He followed, and that night he caught her. He struck her. Do you understand? He beat her with those terrible fists of his and made her his slave. It was she who had to gather the firewood, build the fires, cook, and do all the degrading camp-labor—she, who had never performed a menial act in her life. These things he compelled her to do, while he, a proper savage, elected to lie around camp and look on. He did nothing, absolutely nothing, except on occasion to hunt meat or catch fish."

"Good for Chauffeur," Hare-Lip commented in an undertone to the other boys. "I remember him before he died. He was a corker. But he did things, and he made things go. You know, Dad married his daughter, an' you ought to see the way he knocked the spots outa Dad. The Chauffeur was a son-of-a-gun. He made us kids stand around. Even when he was croakin', he reached out for me, once, an' laid my head open with that long stick he kept always beside him."

Hare-Lip rubbed his bullet head reminiscently, and the boys returned to the old man, who was maundering ecstatically about Vesta, the squaw of the founder of the Chauffeur Tribe.

"And so I say to you that you cannot understand the awfulness of the situation. The Chauffeur was a servant, understand, a servant. And he cringed, with bowed head, to such as she. She was a lord of life, both by birth and by marriage. The destinies of millions, such as he, she carried in the hollow of her pink-white hand. And, in the days before the plague, the slightest contact with such as he would have been pollution. Oh, I have seen it. Once, I remember, there was Mrs. Goldwin, wife of one of the great magnates. It was on a landing stage, just as she was embarking in her private dirigible, that she dropped her parasol. A servant picked it up and made the mistake of handing it to her—to her, one of the greatest royal ladies of the land! She shrank back, as though he were a leper, and indicated her secretary to receive it. Also, she ordered her secretary to ascertain the creature's name and to see that he was immediately discharged from service. And such a woman was Vesta Van Warden. And her the Chauffeur beat and made his slave.

"—Bill—that was it; Bill, the Chauffeur. That was his name. He was a wretched, primitive man, wholly devoid of the finer instincts and chivalrous promptings of a cultured soul. No, there is no absolute justice, for to him fell that wonder of womanhood, Vesta Van Warden. The grievousness of this you will never understand, my grandsons; for you are yourselves primitive little savages, unaware of aught else but savagery. Why should Vesta not have been mine? I was a man of culture and refinement, a professor in a great university. Even so, in the time before the plague, such was her exalted position, she would not have deigned to know that I existed.

"Mark, then, the abysmal degradation to which she fell at the hands of the Chauffeur. Nothing less than the destruction of all mankind had made it possible that I should know her, look in her eyes, converse with her, touch her hand—ay, and love her and know that her feelings toward me were very kindly. I have reason to believe that she, even she, would have loved me, there being no man in the world except the Chauffeur. Why, when it destroyed eight billions of souls, did not the plague destroy just one more man, and that man the Chauffeur?

"Once, when the Chauffeur was away fishing, she begged me to kill him. With tears in her eyes she begged me to kill him. But he was a strong and violent man, and I was afraid. Afterwards, I talked with him. I offered him my horse, my pony, my dogs, all that I possessed, if he would give Vesta to me. And he grinned in my face and shook his head. He was very insulting.

"He said that in the old days he had been a servant, had been dirt under the feet of men like me and of women like Vesta, and that now he had the greatest lady in the land to be servant to him and cook his food and nurse his brats. 'You had your day before the plague,' he said, 'but this is my day, and a damned good day it is. I wouldn't trade back to the old times for anything.' Such words he spoke, but they are not his words. He was a vulgar, low-minded man, and vile oaths fell continually from his lips.

"Also, he told me that if he caught me making eyes at his wife, he'd wring my neck and give her a beating as well. What was I to do? I was afraid. He was a brute. That first night, when I discovered the camp, Vesta and I had a great talk about the things of our vanished world. We talked of art, and books, and poetry; and the Chauffeur listened and grinned and sneered. He was bored and angered by our way of speech which he did not comprehend, and finally he spoke up and said: 'And this is Vesta Van Warden, one time wife of Van Warden the Magnate—a high and stuck-up beauty, who is now my squaw. Eh, Professor Smith, times is changed. Here, you, woman, take off my moccasins, and lively about it. I want Professor Smith to see how well I have you trained.'

"I saw her clench her teeth, and the flame of revolt rise in her face. He drew back his gnarled fist to strike, and I was afraid, and sick at heart. I could do nothing to prevail against him. So I got up to go, and not be witness to such indignity. But the Chauffeur laughed and threatened me with a beating if I did not stay and behold. And I sat there, perforce, by the campfire on the shore of Lake Temescal, and saw Vesta, Vesta Van Warden, kneel and remove the moccasins of that grinning, ape-like human brute.

"—Oh, you do not understand, my grandsons. You have never known anything else, and you do not understand.

"'Halter-broke and bridle-wise,' the Chauffeur gloated, while she performed that dreadful menial task. 'A trifle balky at times, Professor, a trifle balky; but a clout alongside the jaw makes her as meek and gentle as a lamb.'

"And another time he said: 'We've got to start all over again and replenish the earth and multiply. You're handicapped, Professor. You ain't got no wife, and we're up against a regular Garden-of-Eden proposition. But I ain't proud. I'll tell you what, Professor.' He pointed at their little infant, barely a year old. 'There's your wife, though you'll have to wait till she grows up. It's rich, ain't it? We're all equals here, and I'm the biggest toad in the splash. But I ain't stuck up—not I. I do you the honor, Professor Smith, the very great honor of betrothing to you my and Vesta Van Warden's daughter. Ain't it cussed bad that Van Warden ain't here to see?'

"I lived three weeks of infinite torment there in the Chauffeur's camp. And then, one day, tiring of me, or of what to him was my bad effect on Vesta, he told me that the year before, wandering through the Contra

Costa Hills to the Straits of Carquinez, across the Straits he had seen smoke. This meant that there were still other human beings, and that for three weeks he had kept this inestimably precious information from me. I departed at once, with my dogs and horses, and journeyed across the Contra Hills to the Straits. I saw no smoke on the other side, but at Port Costa discovered a small steel barge on which I was able to embark my animals.

"Old canvas which I found served me for a sail, and a southerly breeze fanned me across the Straits and up to the ruins of Vallejo. Here, on the outskirts of the city, I found evidences of a recently occupied camp. Many clamshells showed me why these humans had come to the shores of the Bay. This was the Santa Rosa Tribe, and I followed its track along the old railroad right of way across the salt marshes to Sonoma Valley. Here, at the old brickyard at Glen Ellen, I came upon the camp. There were eighteen souls all told. Two were old men, one of whom was Jones, a banker. The other was Harrison, a retired pawnbroker, who had taken for wife the matron of the State Hospital for the Insane at Napa. Of all the persons of the city of Napa, and of all the other towns and villages in that rich and populous valley, she had been the only survivor. Next there were the three young men—Cardiff and Hale, who had been farmers, and Wainwright, a common day-laborer.

"All three had found wives. To Hale, a crude, illiterate farmer, had fallen Isadora, the greatest prize, next to Vesta, of the women who came through the plague. She was one of the world's most noted singers, and the plague had caught her at San Francisco. She has talked with me for hours at a time, telling me of her adventures, until at last, rescued by Hale in the Mendocino Forest Reserve, there had remained nothing for her to do but become his wife. But Hale was a good fellow, in spite of his illiteracy. He had a keen sense of justice and right-dealing, and she was far happier with him than was Vesta with the Chauffeur.

"The wives of Cardiff and Wainwright were ordinary women, accustomed to toil, with strong constitutions—just the type for the wild new life which they were compelled to live. In addition were two adult idiots from the feeble-minded home at Eldredge, and five or six young children and infants born after the formation of the Santa Rosa Tribe. Also, there was Bertha.

"She was a good woman, Hare-Lip, in spite of the sneers of your father. Her I took for wife. She was the mother of your father, Edwin, and of yours, Hoo-Hoo. And it was our daughter, Vera, who married your father, Hare-Lip—your father, Sandow, who was the oldest son of Vesta Van Warden and the Chauffeur.

"And so it was that I became the nineteenth member of the Santa Rosa Tribe. There were only two outsiders added after me. One was Mungerson, descended from the Magnates, who wandered alone in the wilds of Northern California for eight years before he came south and joined us.

He it was who waited twelve years more before he married my daughter, Mary. The other was Johnson, the man who founded the Utah Tribe. That was where he came from, Utah, a country that lies very far away from here, across the great deserts, to the east.

"It was not until twenty-seven years after the plague that Johnson reached California. In all that Utah region he reported but three survivors, himself one, and all men. For many years these three men lived and hunted together, until, at last, desperate, fearing that with them the human race would perish utterly from the planet, they headed westward on the possibility of finding women survivors in California.

"Johnson alone came through the great desert, where his two companions died. He was forty-six years old when he joined us, and he married the fourth daughter of Isadora and Hale, and his eldest son married your aunt, Hare-Lip, who was the third daughter of Vesta and the Chauffeur. Johnson was a strong man, with a will of his own. And it was because of this that he seceded from the Santa Rosans and formed the Utah Tribe at San José.

"It is a small tribe—there are only nine in it; but, though he is dead, such was his influence and the strength of his breed, that it will grow into a strong tribe and play a leading part in the recivilization of the planet.

"There are only two other tribes that we know of—the Los Angelitos and the Carmelitos. The latter started from one man and woman. He was called Lopez, and he was descended from the ancient Mexicans and was very black. He was a cow-herd in the ranges beyond Carmel, and his wife was a maid-servant in the great Del Monte Hotel. It was seven years before we first got in touch with the Los Angelitos. They have a good country down there, but it is too warm. I estimate the present population of the world at between three hundred and fifty and four hundred—provided, of course, that there are no scattered little tribes elsewhere in the world. If there be such, we have not heard from them.

"Since Johnson crossed the desert from Utah, no word nor sign has come from the East or anywhere else. The great world which I knew in my boyhood and early manhood is gone. It has ceased to be. I am the last man who was alive in the days of the plague and who knows the wonders of that far-off time. We, who mastered the planet—its earth, and sea, and sky—and who were as very gods, now live in primitive savagery along the water courses of this California country.

"But we are increasing rapidly—your sister, Hare-Lip, already has four children. We are increasing rapidly and making ready for a new climb toward civilization. In time, pressure of population will compel us to spread out, and a hundred generations from now we may expect our descendants to start across the Sierras, oozing slowly along, generation by generation, over the great continent to the colonization of the East—a new Aryan drift around the world.

"But it will be slow, very slow; we have so far to climb. We fell so hopelessly far. If only one physicist or one chemist had survived! But it was not to be, and we have forgotten everything. The Chauffeur started working in iron. He made the forge which we use to this day. But he was a lazy man, and when he died he took with him all that he knew of metals and machinery.

"What was I to know of such things? I was a classical scholar, not a chemist. The other men who survived were not educated. Only two things did the Chauffeur accomplish—the brewing of strong drink and the growing of tobacco. It was while he was drunk, once, that he killed Vesta. I firmly believe that he killed Vesta in a fit of drunken cruelty though he always maintained that she fell into the lake and was drowned.

"And, my grandsons, let me warn you against the medicine-men. They call themselves *doctors,* travestying what was once a noble profession, but in reality they are medicine-men, and they make for superstition and darkness. They are cheats and liars. But so debased and degraded are we, that we believe their lies. They, too, will increase in numbers as we increase, and they will strive to rule us. Yet are they liars and charlatans. Look at young Cross-Eyes, posing as a doctor, selling charms against sickness, giving good hunting, exchanging promises of fair weather for good meat and skins, sending the death-stick, performing a thousand abominations. Yet I say, to you, that when he says he can do all these things, he lies.

"I, Professor Smith, Professor James Howard Smith, say that he lies. I have told him so to his teeth. Why has he not sent me the death-stick? Because he knows that with me it is without avail. But you, Hare-Lip, so deeply are you sunk in black superstition that did you awake this night and find the death-stick beside you, you would surely die. And you would die, not because of any virtues in the stick, but because you are a savage with the dark and clouded mind of a savage.

"The doctors must be destroyed, and all that was lost must be discovered over again. Wherefore, earnestly, I repeat unto you certain things which you must remember and tell to your children after you. You must tell them that when water is made hot by fire, there resides in it a wonderful thing called steam, which is stronger than ten thousand men and which can do all man's work for him. There are other very useful things. In the lightning flash resides a similarly strong servant of man, which was of old his slave and which some day will be his slave again.

"Quite a different thing is the alphabet. It is what enables me to know the meaning of fine markings, whereas you boys know only rude picture-writing. In that dry cave on Telegraph Hill, where you see me often go when the tribe is down by the sea, I have stored many books. In them is great wisdom. Also, with them, I have placed a key to the alphabet, so that one who knows picture-writing may also know print. Some day men will read again; and then, if no accident has befallen my cave they will know that Professor James Howard Smith once lived and saved for them the knowledge of the ancients.

"There is another little device that men inevitably will rediscover. It is called gunpowder. It was what enabled us to kill surely and at long distances. Certain things which are found in the ground, when combined in the right proportions, will make this gunpowder. What these things are, I have forgotten, or else I never knew. But I wish I did know. Then would I make powder and then would I certainly kill Cross-Eyes and rid the land of superstition—"

"After I am man-grown I am going to give Cross-Eyes all the goats, and meat, and skins I can get, so that he'll teach me to be a doctor," Hoo-Hoo asserted. "And when I know, I'll make everybody else sit up and take notice. They'll get down in the dirt for me, you bet."

The old man nodded his head solemnly, and murmured:

"Strange it is to hear the vestiges and remnants of the complicated Aryan speech falling from the lips of a filthy little skin-clad savage. All the world is topsy-turvy, ever since the plague."

"You won't make me sit up," Hare-Lip boasted to the would-be medicine-man. "If I paid you for a sending of the death-stick and it didn't work, I'd bust in your head—understand, you Hoo-Hoo, you?"

"I'm going to get Granser to remember this here gunpowder stuff," Edwin said softly, "and then I'll have you all on the run. You, Hare-lip, will do my fighting for me and get my meat for me, and you, Hoo-Hoo, will send the death-stick for me and make everybody afraid. And if I catch Hare-Lip trying to bust your head, Hoo-Hoo, I'll fix him with that same gunpowder. Granser ain't such a fool as you think, and I'm going to listen to him and some day I'll be boss, ruling over the whole bunch of you."

The old man shook his head sadly, and said:

"The gunpowder will come. Nothing can stop it—the same old story over and over. Man will increase, and men will fight. The gunpowder will enable men to kill millions of men, and in this way only, by fire and blood, will a new civilization, in some remote day, be evolved. And of what profit will it be? Just as the old civilization passed, so will the new. It may take fifty thousand years to build, but nevertheless it will pass.

"All things pass. Only remain cosmic force and matter, ever in flux, ever acting and reacting and realizing the eternal types—the priest, the soldier, and the king. Out of the mouths of babes comes the wisdom of all the ages. Some will fight, some will rule, some will pray; and all the rest will toil and suffer sore while on their bleeding carcasses is reared again and yet again, without end, the amazing beauty and surpassing wonder of the civilized state.

"It were just as well that I destroyed those cave-stored books—whether they remain or perish, all their old truths will be discovered, their old lies lived and handed down. What is the profit—"

Hare-Lip leaped to his feet, giving a quick glance at the pasturing goats and the afternoon sun.

"Gee!" he muttered to Edwin. "The old geezer gets more long-winded every day. Let's pull for camp."

While the other two, aided by the dogs, assembled the goats and started them for the trail through the forest, Edwin stayed by the old man and guided him in the same direction. When they reached the old right of way, Edwin stopped suddenly and looked back.

Hare-Lip and Hoo-Hoo and the dogs and the goats passed on. Edwin was looking at a small herd of wild horses which had come down on the hard sand. There were at least twenty of them, young colts and yearlings and mares, led by a beautiful stallion which stood in the foam at the edge of the surf, with arched neck and bright wild eyes, sniffing the salt air from off the sea.

"What is it?" Granser queried.

"Horses," was the answer. "First time I ever seen 'em on the beach. It's the mountain lions getting thicker and thicker and driving 'em down."

The low sun shot red shafts of light, fan shaped, up from a cloud-tumbled horizon. And close at hand, in the white waste of shore-lashed waters, the sea-lions, bellowing their old primeval chant, hauled up out of the sea on the black rocks and fought and courted.

"Come on, Granser," Edwin prompted.

And old man and boy, skin-clad and barbaric, turned and went along the right of way into the forest in the wake of the goats.

ROBERT ABERNATHY

HERITAGE

IF EVERYONE WILL please keep his seat and refrain from mobbing the platform, I will make a very confidential admission. I am closely acquainted with the great time traveler, Nicholas Doody.

Now, I am not trying to add to the multitudes of pseudo-Doodyesque anecdotes which are perpetually being decanted into unoffending ears in Pullmans, clubs, cafés, and private drawing rooms, and which have undoubtedly driven countless persons into mental declines and padded cells. Neither am I endeavoring to verify either of the two prevailing opinions respecting the inventor of the time machine—one, that he is a half-cracked young genius whose invention's usefulness is rendered null and void by the immutable laws of time; the other, that he is an insanely selfish, misanthropic, antisocial wretch who is deliberately withholding from the human race a gift of incalculable value.

In sober reality, Nick Doody is a tall, dark-skinned, dark-haired young man of twenty-seven, who looks like a cross between a tennis champion and a naval officer. He is likable, friendly, and not at all standoffish, even regarding his remarkable invention—which he freely admits to be the result of sheer accident rather than of calculated research on his part. Almost anyone in twentieth-century America, he says, might have done it in the same way; the materials are within the grasp of practically everyone. The machine itself has all the simplicity of the first crude beginning of any new science; its very lack of complexity is what makes it such an enigma to your average Einsteinian physicist. But if it were taken apart or put together before you, your wife, or the man across the street, you would wonder why you didn't think of it yourselves.

As for the popular opinions of Doody—the first is hokum and the second is hogwash. The inventor labors under no mystical ideas about the immutability of the past or the inevitable predestination of the future; his machine affords just as much opportunity for control of the fourth dimension of time as ordinary tools offer for managing the usual three. However, neither is Doody subject to any illusions about his sacred duty to humanity being to reveal the secret of the time machine; he believes that humanity has made a quite adequate mess of its world in three spatial dimensions, and that to add a fourth would only complicate modern life to a point where nervous breakdowns would become as common as shiny seats on blue serge trousers.

Being a normal young fellow with a taste for adventure, he uses the time machine solely for minor exploring junkets into past or future ages, with no purpose save sheer amusement. In the process of these trips, as you might expect, he has seen and done many things which for sheer improbability outdo the wildest imaginings of the science-fiction writers.

It is possible that by making public the substance of a conversation which I had with Doody a few days ago—to be exact, on the evening of November 20, 1976—I may succeed in silencing a few of the macaw-voiced critics who have been loudly and raucously insisting that he turn the principle of time travel over to the American government.

"Johnny," remarked Doody, tête-à-tête with me over an excellent dinner served by the ménage of Elbert's Exquisite Eatery—or is the adjective Elegant? Perhaps you know the place—it's on Broadway, one of the most dignifiedly popular cafés of old New York, dating back to 1953. "Johnny, did you ever have any difficulty in proving that you are a man?"

"Not even when I went into the army," said I, leaning my elbows on the tablecloth and wondering at him frankly. "Why?"

Doody grinned, flashing two thirds of a perfect set of even white teeth. "I did, Johnny; once upon a time that hasn't happened yet. I stood trial on the question of whether I was or was not human, with my life as well as my reputation dangling in the balance. I conducted my own defense, such as it was—and I lost my case."

"Well!" I exclaimed, hoisting an eyebrow. "What did they prove you were—a throwback to the chimp?"

"No, not quite," replied Doody, smiling comfortably, though reflectively —in that curious manner which is his alone, of looking past a companion into far, dim vistas of time. "You know, I'm not sure that I lost that case, after all. Things were getting pretty hot, and I didn't delay my fade-out long enough to see. Maybe my final argument settled the prosecution's hash, although the jury had already brought in a verdict of guilty— guilty of impersonating a human being, a crime punishable in that far- off day by death. I'd like to go back to that era and find out; but my little gadget has practically no selectivity at such extreme ranges. I couldn't even be sure of hitting the right millennium. It would take a much more delicate and complex instrument, with a power source superior to my two dry cells, and a lot of other stuff I haven't bothered to work out and never will work out. Well, that's all beside the point, which is that this little experience of mine set me wondering."

"You wondering—along what line?" I wanted to know, understanding perfectly that I would get the story in Doody's own good time.

"Ah, that's a secret," he evaded amusedly. "Seriously, though, Johnny, I'll tell you the tale, and we'll see whether it doesn't evoke some speculation on your part—not overly pleasant, some of it. Push the signal for a waiter and order more champagne, Johnny, so they won't be considering giving us the respectfully firm send-off; and I'll give you the straight of it."

It seems that Doody, on his last safari into the dark hinterlands of the unexplored æons, had decided to try a longer jump across time than he ever had made before. It happened that on a previous excursion into one of the odd nooks and corners of chronology, he had had an intriguing little chat with a savant of the time, by name, I believe, Rudnuu Some- thing-or-Other—the surname being placed first—who belonged to a period which Doody estimated in the neighborhood of 13,000 A. D. (They had no system of dates reconcilable with ours, and their records of the elder civilizations of the Indo-European and Neo-European cycles were incomplete and unreliable.) This fellow, who was something of a philosopher and historical student as well as an important member of the technocratic government of his era, was frankly worried about the future of the human race.

In Rudnuu's day, eleven thousand years from our own, the civilization of the machine had advanced so far on Earth that there was no longer need for men to labor, with muscle or with mind. Briefly, the world- wide society of abundance had come at last into being; and, as the result of every culture which eliminates natural selection by permitting the survival of all, humanity was swiftly going to pot.

Of course, that was nothing new; it has never been new. It is the old,

old cycle of man—hardship, ingenuity, civilization, ease, degeneracy, hardship again.

But in the fourteenth millennium the mechanical refinement of life had risen to such a high that the unescapable collapse must be more than catastrophic. The scientist-leader believed that it would be final; that mankind would follow many another dominant breed into the long oblivion of extinction. Unchecked, morbid mutation, without selection, was precipitating the race into a bottomless slough of physical and mental decay.

Scientist Rudnuu had enough curiosity—a quality well-nigh unheard of in his day—to wonder, with a touch of wistfulness, what reasoning race would inherit the Earth when man was gone. Whatever that future breed might be, it must develop from one of two definite groups: either from among the few surviving wild species, which by tenacity and cunning had held their own on the outskirts of human civilization, or from among the tamed animals which man had continued to rear through all these ages for pets or servants, such as dogs and cats and some of the apes.

Even now the members of those groups were far better fitted to rule than decadent humanity. Fierce and quick and clever the wild things had grown, driven by the life struggle of existence in unnoticed crevices and hiding places of a world monopolized by man; strong and sharp-sighted and intelligent the beasts of man had become, bred through the hundreds of centuries for physical and mental perfection. Strong new races, lacking only the skillful hands and the tools of fire and metal to push man off the Earth and claim it for their own.

"So, then," said Rudnuu, with a shrug of defeat accepted sadly yet without bitterness, "the end is drawing near."

The upshot of the scientist's aeration of his views was that Nick Doody, in a hotel room in Brooklyn on a gray evening of 1976, set the simple adjustment of his absurd little instrument and closed its single switch. At once his three-dimensional being in space no longer existed; its four-dimensional counterpart, tenuous, fantastic, and unreal by human standards, was swept away along the world line of the Earth, rushing faster and yet faster, like a fleeting phantom, past the rise of empires and the fall of peoples, past the births and deaths of four hundred generations, to come to a final stop at a point twenty thousand years in our future— nine thousand years beyond the day of Doody's gloomily prophetic friend.

Though one is unconscious of the flight through time, the sensation, as the synthetic extension through the fourth dimension collapses once more into normal space, is one of inexpressible relief. Doody, gasping and dizzy, sank down upon a heavy carpet of moss and rested for a time, his breathing becoming more even and his eyes refocusing on this unknown future world.

What had been a blurred gold-and-green haze before then became the sunlit summer verdure of a great forest, a forest that was the work of ages.

Giant trees, with spreading limbs and twisted roots that clutched the earth protectively, rose on all sides to support the green, leafy ceiling overhead, shutting out vision; the hard, solid surface which supported his back, but which now was becoming painful to his spine and shoulder blades, was the rough bark of a massive trunk with the gnarled branches of an aged oak.

Somewhat giddily, Doody scrambled to his feet once more and stared around him. In all directions nothing was apparent but the primeval forest, hardly an insect song stirring the still, sultry air of the midsummer noonday. It had been autumn when he closed the switch; but that signified nothing. Nevertheless—unless the world lines had become unthinkably tangled—he should still be on Long Island. But if this was Long Island, real-estate values had evidently suffered a sharp decline since the late twentieth century—to say nothing of Rudnuu's nearer day, when from the Catskills to the Susquehanna had stretched the great world city.

"Well!" remarked Doody under his breath. "So the old boy was right, after all, and the human race has handed in its checks." It was easy to believe that, there in the virgin woodland, seeing no trace of human life and knowing what Doody knew. He shook his head to dispel disgust; he had preferred to think that mankind was made of sterner stuff.

Quickly and efficiently, he made certain that the equipment he always carried on such expeditions—a camera, flashlight, camp ax, and automatic pistol—was still with him and ready for use. Also, with a trace of gingerness, he felt the special inside pocket where, just in case of emergencies, he generally packed a pineapple—not the Hawaiian kind.

On consideration, he unfastened the little, sharp-edged ax, for use in blazing a trail as he explored these woods farther. If he could not find his initial location again for the return to his own time, he might find himself in any one of a number of awkward spots—under the wheels of a motor car, or in someone's boudoir.

Doody strolled away down the gentle, tree-covered slope, with the vague idea of eventually reaching the ocean shore which could not be far away. Dead leaves crackled, shockingly loud, beneath his feet at intervals, and birds twittered in fright and fluttered confusedly away from the branches where they had been drowsing in the shady heat; yet as he proceeded, perhaps because he himself was the child of a highly advanced civilization, he could not shake off the illusion that this whole pleasant woodland was merely an extensive municipal park, nor could he suppress a guilty feeling whenever he knocked a gleaming chip or two out of a tree trunk as he passed by. Objectively, he noted that the forest was entirely devoid of such common but galling annoyances as tangled and unlovely undergrowth, poison oak and ivy, and thorny trees and bushes; tall, graceful ferns and leafy shrubbery gave it an almost cared-for appearance. Of course, the whole Earth had been purified of such useless and troublesome flora many thousands of years ago, the planet turned by science into an Eden for the pleasure of a declining, luxurious race that—apparently—was gone.

Still, Doody glanced up hastily when, just as he was about to gash the straight, round trunk of a particularly fine Norway spruce, he heard a twig snap in the nearer bushes. His subconscious still half expected to behold a wrathful park policeman and be summarily pinched for trespassing, wanton vandalism, and wholesale destruction of public property; but the half a dozen warlike, seminaked figures advancing toward him at a swift trot looked like no policemen Doody had ever been arrested by.

They were short but well-proportioned and splendidly muscled figures, clad in clothing which even when new had been scanty, but which none the less informed Doody's alert eye that their people had invented—or retained—the knowledge of the loom and weaving. More immediately important, they brandished wicked-looking spears and knives, knowingly fashioned of gleaming bronze. And that, in turn, meant a tremendous past of evolution through the use of wood, of stone, of metal—or an equally long background of degeneration.

But these people did not look like degenerates; they resembled more an idealist's conception of the Noble Savage. That idea, of course, was fantastic; even nine thousand years could hardly have wiped out the corruption, the decadence, the utter decay of mind and body that had marked Rudnuu's machine civilization. This must be a new stock—but from where?

The leader of the little band, a powerful, stocky fellow with a mane of lank, uncombed red-brown hair that mingled with his great beard to fall to his heavily muscled shoulders, pressed forward before the rest to approach Doody, who stood erect, shoulders thrown back and head haughtily high, waiting with an immobility which he hoped was impressive—his right forefinger meantime crooked tensely about the trigger of his loaded automatic, where it rested in his pocket with the muzzle pointed toward the savage. The latter just might try to use the sharp, bronze-headed javelin in his hairy hand, which would prove that he thought Doody, as a visiting god, a failure; but a touch of the finger would send three .45-caliber explosive slugs at that formidable-looking head man, and Doody would at least make a name for himself as a very dangerous sort of devil!

The barbaric leader paused before the tall stranger, half crouching as he stared; he fidgeted for an uncomfortable moment, then sank slowly to his knees in the grass at his sandaled feet, bowing his shaggy head in sudden humility.

His next move startled even Doody, who had had previous experience in godhead far back in the icy Pleistocene. Carefully the kneeling savage laid his long-shafted spear crosswise on the earth before the unmoving Doody, and beside it his broad-bladed dagger of hammered bronze.

Evidently these people took their gods seriously; sullen yet awed, the six remaining hunters advanced one by one, similarly to do reverence and unburden themselves of their weapons. Some of them bore a quite inclusive equipment for war or the chase; when the impromptu disarmament program was finished, a sprawling heap of spears, daggers, and short, leaf-bladed bronze swords, as well as a couple of heavy stone-headed axes, lay on the ground at Doody's feet. He was uncertain of his part in this little ritual; if they expected him to carry all those away, he was afraid he wasn't equal to the job.

The leader arose, spread both calloused hands above his head, palms outward—the old, old gesture of peace—and spoke, in a voice which was gruffly tremulous, a gutturally monosyllabic tongue.

"It's all Sanskrit to me, old boy," said Doody, shaking his head half amusedly as he became aware of the incongruity of his position—the anachronistic traveler from the forgotten past, receiving deific worship from the uncultured children of the far future in that little, leaf-shaded forest clearing. But an instant later he was shocked and appalled as the savage, apparently misinterpreting his mere gesture of negation, flung himself frantically to the ground and pressed his bearded face into the soft leaf mold, his hands and body quivering in abject terror. It was quite plain that he conceived the mysterious avatar to have denied his homage, and believed himself in peril of instant destruction.

At that moment Doody thought of an article which he should have remembered before—the convenient little telepathic mechanism which Rudnuu, back in the fourteenth millennium, had called a "translator," and which even now nestled in Doody's inside coat pocket. Hastily fumbling for the flat little cylinder of the device, he unfolded its three thin, silvery aluminum grid plates, equivalent to the earphones of a radio headset, and slipped them over his head, sides and back; the vibration given off by the apparatus, which derived its feeble energy from the pulsation of the veins in the temples on which it pressed, hypersensitized the language centers of the human brain to such an extent that, with a little concentration, Doody could address the savages in their own idiom, and their words, coming to his ears, would be resolved by his brain into English terms and phrases.

At the moment he wished ardently for an all-purpose telepathor, which would enable him to read the thoughts of his new acquaintances—an achievement which could be very useful. However, one cannot have everything.

"*Ah-poonay*—rise," so commanded Doody in a deeply impressive voice. The rapport linking of his mind with the linguistic centers of his listeners' brains brought the alien words easily to his lips. "I will not harm any of you."

Tremblingly, abashedly, the seven kneeling warriors clambered to their feet and stood facing Doody in obvious unquiet—half a dozen fierce, mighty hunters of the woods, any one of whom, given a hold, could practically have torn the man of the twentieth century apart. Yet their glances were sidelong, and they fidgeted before him like small boys caught throwing spitballs in school. Doody was surprised, although gratified. Most primitive races have at least a modicum of healthy doubt respecting their gods—enough to make them somewhat wary of accepting too readily anyone representing himself as such.

"Take your weapons without fear," he said reassuringly; then added, as an inspired afterthought, "I do not need them; I have means of slaying my enemies far more potent."

The savage leader advanced a step hesitantly, his shoulders hunched as if to ward off a blow, and knelt again to fumble with jerky fingers at the pile of arms.

"That we know, O Man," he faltered fearfully, eyes on the ground. "We know that your lightning strikes dead whomever you will."

Doody himself was slightly thunderstruck at the moment; his jaw dropped as he stared at the seven sturdy, humbly bowed figures before him. "Man," the savage had called him! If they did not believe him a god, why did they submit to him?

He made his voice steady, confident, as he said, not daring to make any inquiries for fear of betraying a lack of divine omniscience—one of the great drawbacks to being a deity among primitive peoples—"You must take me to your village at once." Since the translator told him that they had a word for village, he knew they must have villages.

"At once, O Man." The leader repeated the mystifying term, which he pronounced as if it were a title of honor. "We will take you to Kuvurna, and you shall speak with him."

"Who is Kuvurna?" demanded Doody, unable to suppress the question this time. "Your chief—king?"

The eyes of the barbarian opened wide in obvious surprise, which he with equal obviousness endeavored to mask. Those eyes were large and brown in color, Doody noticed, with a curious wistful expression—hardly as fierce and bold as the eyes of an independent primitive man should be. "Do you not know who Kuvurna is? He is the Lord. He is our master, who rules over our village and over us all."

This was a shock, because it sounded very much like competition. But Kuvurna could be dealt with when the question of Kuvurna came up. "Lead on!" said Doody.

As he trudged northward through the parklike woods in the midst of his barbarically armed escort, which moved in a subdued, respectful silence, Doody found time to notice the curious uniformity displayed by these people. They were of even stature, about five feet six or seven; their hair and eyes were always reddish-brown; different, he thought, from any hair or eyes that he had ever seen before, yet somehow vaguely familiar. Their skin was quite white, though browned by the sun to which it was largely exposed. They were strangely different, less noisy and garrulous than any savages whom Doody had ever met before, utterly unlike the hairy Paleolithic brutes who had wanted to make living sacrifice to him forty thousand years before—yet for some odd reason he could not rid himself of the nagging conviction that somewhere he had seen these people before.

"Time traveling gets a man mixed up like the dickens," he growled to himself in English, passing a hand through his own curly black hair.

The village huddled about the base of a low, partially tree-clad hill; the ocean glinted, barely visible, beyond the slope on which it lay. It was about what you might expect of a backward bronze-age people—a squalid, degraded-looking assemblage of huts, built in this case of fairly substantial logs and timbers, in the manner of early American blockhouses, but with straw-thatched roofs, such as one still finds once in a while on European peasant cottages. The size of the dwellings clearly indicated that, like Dyak long houses, they were meant to hold several families.

The thatch, of course, meant an agricultural community rather than a hunting tribe; and, indeed, fields of tasseled maize were apparent beyond the village on the seaward slope of the island. For meat, however, they still depended on wild game, as was evidenced by the hunting party which Doody had encountered, and the fact that no livestock, or corrals or pens for livestock, were in evidence.

Another feature which Doody noted with mild surprise was the total absence of the usual canine riffraff of savagely barking, cowardly mongrel dogs which usually greet visitors to a savage kraal. In lieu thereof, innumerable naked and unbelievably dirty brats played and squabbled in the sun-baked mud of the crooked streets, while their fond mothers— clad quite as insufficiently as their mates in a single garment of coarse fabric which was draped from the waist to an undefined distance above the ground—stood about in chattering clusters, comparing extravagant notes on the spectacularly precocious attainments of their own particular offspring. A few males were in evidence, idling in doorways and conversing in rough voices, occasionally whittling lazily at sticks which might some day become spear shafts or ax handles; under the noontide heat, activity was at its daylight low.

The hamlet was laid out according to no humanly understandable plan; in fact, it had apparently never been laid out at all, having merely grown Topsy fashion. The little party consisting of Doody and his guard of honor stumbled through the tortuous lanes that twisted erratically among the hovels, and at last debouched unexpectedly, at least so far as the visitor was concerned, into a wide, grassless clearing in the midst of the village. This, though far from tetragonal, evidently passed for a town square.

Doody, who had until now remained wholly unimpressed by the sights of the village, drew in his breath in sharp surprise when he saw what occupied the middle of this naked, dusty space. He had been totally unprepared for a ten-foot stockade of sharpened stakes, sunk deep into the earth, which was heaped breastwork fashion around their bases; a hundred by fifty feet, it might be, laid out in a great rectangle. It looked like a palisaded fort, formidable to the primitive tribesmen; or perhaps—Doody's quick mind leaped over the possibilities—it was a barrier to prevent mere mortals from trespassing on sacred ground.

He did not need to inquire. "This, O Man of the forest, is the dwelling of Kuvurna, in which he remains always, hearing our every prayer, granting such as are right, refusing such as are evil. Kuvurna knows all, sees all, hears all, smells all."

Before Doody could even attempt to grasp the significance of the curious final clause of the formula, having references to Kuvurna's olfactory prowess—*phew*, thought Doody, I wouldn't care to be that sharp-scented—the chief hunter had detached himself from the escort and advanced toward a small gateway, closed by a heavy lattice of wood, which opened into the nearest face of the rampart.

Pausing, he knelt before the gate, laid his spear carefully on the bare earth, and dropped his knife beside it, even as he had upon prostrating himself before Doody. To the mind of the American, it became plain that whoever passed with these ignorant people as a god was not exactly carefree in his high office. He was evidently irked by the possibility of assassination.

The hunter rose and stooped to pick up a long-handled stone hammer which leaned against the stripped poles beside the entrance. Powerful muscles rippled under the brown hide of his back and shoulders as he raised it above his head and swung it in a deafening blow upon a great bronze gong which hung above the gateway. The dully musical booming echoed through the village, woke the sluggish afternoon echoes, penetrated into the secret interior of the forbidding fortress temple.

As Doody watched narrowly for signs of the reception awaiting him, a chain rattled audibly and the lattice swung slowly inward, the person performing the office of gatekeeper remaining invisible from outside. Doody, straining, caught a glimpse of dim green shadows beyond the gate; then the seeker of admittance, with one more profound genuflection, rose, straightened his shoulders, and with the resolute caution of one goose-stepping over a parade ground cobblestoned with rotten eggs, marched into the inner courtyard. The gate swung rapidly shut behind him.

Doody, still puzzled, turned on one of the savage warriors at his elbow. The fellow leaned heavily on his spear, his long red mane falling about a rugged, open face from which frank, undeceitful brown eyes turned questioningly toward the other.

Again Doody felt the overpowering sensation of having seen these people—those curious, worshipful eyes, in particular—somewhere, sometime, long ago. He put the ridiculous feeling from him and inquired brusquely:

"This Kuvurna of yours, friend. What is he like—what does he look like?"

The hunter's gaze was startled. "He is like you. He is like me," he illustrated correlatively. "He is a Man, and you are a Man; but I am not a Man. Because he is a Man we serve him, all of us, and give to him our best fruits and game, and make for him the drink of Men which is not permitted to us."

"Drink of the gods," muttered Doody quizzically to himself, trying to absorb one statement at a time. But—he wondered—was he going batty, or were his ears wronging him? "Listen," he said more loudly than was necessary. "If you aren't a man, then what the devil are you?" He was quite past worrying about suspicious queries; anyway, he ought to see Kuvurna, whoever Kuvurna was, right away, and then he might get straightened out. At the moment he felt a marked sensation of floundering—

The inquiring brown eyes were shocked at his question. "Are you not a Man, and do not Men know everything? But I am only a dog."

Doody felt faint, and somewhere a wholly primitive and probably unjustifiable fear crawled out of hiding and started up his back, beginning at his lowest spinal ganglion and squirming toward the base of his skull, to raise the short hairs there and pour ice water down his back with demoniac abandon. Abruptly everything around him seemed far away, alien, and unreal. The motionless, patiently waiting village hunters around him, the crowds which were timidly gathering against invisible barriers of apprehension in the freakish bystreets—the seeming women who stood watching the scene stolidly with babies parked on their ample hips, the seemingly human children who sprawled out into the square, noisily seeking new worlds to conquer in the making of mud pies—all were like creatures of an uncanny dream. For Doody knew now where he had seen those great appealing brown eyes, that particular quality of straight red-brown hair. Certainly he had known these people before. He had hunted with them, talked to their uncomprehending ears when he held their silky heads between his knees, on many an occasion in the past when they had gone on four feet instead of two—

It was only for the moment that the primitive fear held the fort in the region of Doody's medulla oblongata. Then he gave a snort of disgust and forced it back down into the realm of suppressed instincts, where it belonged. The statement which the creature who regarded him so worriedly had just made might be almost incredible, but it was not necessarily terrifying. The sense of strangeness persisted, though, as his conscious mind checked off one little-remembered item after another—tiny earmarks, unnoticed at the time, of the veiled unhuman.

Doody realized that his silence was growing awkward. He made himself speak again to the being that was not a man:

"Er—what does Kuvurna want of me?"

The warrior's gaze was that of a puzzled dog. "Does not a Man wish to speak to a Man? It is not for us to know what they will say." He paused, then added eagerly, "Perhaps now we will have two Men to rule over our village."

"If you think that, my boy," commented Doody in the private recesses of his own mind, "you don't know your men." He was framing a reply suitable for the other's ears, when its necessity was obviated by the return of the messenger who had vanished into Kuvurna's stronghold.

It was the sudden hushing of the subdued crowd murmur that caused Doody to wheel and behold the dogman who had entered emerge from the gate and stride swiftly toward the visitor and the hunting pack which had brought him, standing in an isolated huddle halfway between the edge of the wide, sun-drenched square and the high, bare palisade of Kuvurna's temple.

The silence was funereal by the time he reached the group. He knelt in the dust before Doody, and announced, his head bowed, but his voice raised to reach the breathlessly waiting hundreds about the southern side of the square:

"Kuvurna will see the Man of the forest!"

"This is well—for Kuvurna," replied Doody, in a voice that rang cold and just as clear. The silence was fractured by a swift, awed chorus of gasps which wheezed into an overwhelmed hush as Doody, tall, straight and impressive, stalked unattended toward the postern gate of Kuvurna's citadel.

Doody remarks that brass has carried him through many a narrow place in his career in which lead would only have totally wrecked his chances. He had a hunch—which grew stronger as he advanced on that ominous gateway—that bullets were no good here. So he was banking on a good front, plus, of course, the emergency getaway of the time machine in case things went cataclysmically wrong.

Before the gate he stopped and bent quickly to lift the long-handled stone hammer; twice and three times he swung it thunderously against the heavy lattice, shaking it almost from its wrought-bronze hinges. Then he tossed the implement scornfully aside and folded his arms in lofty disdain, controlling his breathing, however, with some effort. Swinging that Thor's hammer was no man's picnic.

After a scandalized pause the barrier wobbled slowly out of his way, and Doody, head up, marched in.

Inside, he halted for a moment only to orient himself, and to be impressed, after a fashion, under his assumed hauteur, by the fortress temple of the dogmen's god. In the shadows of the high palisade squatted a long, low building of hewn stone, built like an arsenal or fort, with the grim, high, narrow window slits of a medieval jail. The door was set far back behind a shadowed archway, from which the interior gloom seemed to spill almost into the sunlight outdoors, down the massive stone steps that ascended to the portral.

For the dog folk, with primitive tools and muscular power alone, the structure must represent long, back-breaking labor, which likewise must be employed in maintaining the garden which filled the inner court; in contrast to the dusty square outside, ivy clambered over the rough walls of the temple, roses tumbled about the stone stairway, and verdant, resilient grass underfoot defied the blazing power of the summer sun whose hot rays slanted over the jagged palisade. The water which brought forth all this greenery from the stubborn soil must be carried little by little, day after day, by the sweating slaves of the ruler.

None of the priesthood which is maintained by every god of means was in evidence, but Doody had that jittery, watched feeling, as of intent eyes fixed on the back of his neck. So strong was the sensation that he almost peered about the garden in search of concealed observers; but that would be to abandon his pose of nonchalance. He hesitated only momentarily, then advanced firmly to ascend toward the inset doorway.

The portal within the rough-hewn arch was massive and oaken, banded with strips of ornate bronzework. It stood a little ajar, opening on cool darkness within. It creaked only a little as Doody thrust it farther aside and slipped cautiously into the black interior—a hand in his coat pocket tense on the switch of his time machine, ready to snap it shut instantly if danger loomed near. He did not imagine that the fear-inspired reverence for the human overlord was all illusion on the part of the dogmen.

Inside the temple, to Doody's light-accustomed eyes, it seemed dark as the inside of a shark. He stumbled, banging his shins painfully against something that toppled with a most shocking crash; he thought that a rasping chuckle from the darkness mingled with the echoes, and became immobile, his eyes slowly beginning to adjust to the Stygian gloom which was unrelieved by the high, close-shuttered windows. Doody can see in the dark almost as well as a Negro; but it was only with great difficulty that he discerned vague, looming shapes in the obscurity, and thought he saw a flitting figure that could have been a man.

Then a voice came out of the shadows, a thick, greasy voice. "Make a light, Shahlnoo," it said heavily. "Let us see this one who calls himself Man."

A small flame flared suddenly in the darkness, illuminated dimly the interior of the temple—a flame of burning tinder, apparently, in the hand of a black figure which applied it quickly to a teakettle-shaped oil lamp, like those used by the ancient Greeks. The lamp blazed up with a smoky light, and the shadowy forms resolved themselves.

Doody first saw the aged, shriveled little dogman, clad in a single dirty garment that left his skinny figure almost naked, who crouched beside the pedestal of the lamp. Then his eyes flicked rapidly about the interior of the temple, taking in the barbaric luxury displayed in all its furnishings.

Great ornamental urns stood about the drapery-hung walls, and it was one of these which Doody had overturned in the dark; even now the light struggled feebly against the deep shades of the folded draperies. The chamber was like a somber courtroom of the Inquisition, or like some dim-lit crypt out of the tales of Poe—the product of a morbidly dismal imagination, utterly at variance with the healthy, outdoor cheerfulness of the dog-men.

At the other end of the long room the little wizened priest passed with noiseless tread from right to left to light another lamp. The illumination in the funereal chamber brightened, and for the first time Doody saw the fat man who lay in gross ease upon a draped and cushioned couch against the farther wall.

Kuvurna was fat, fat with the disgusting obesity of a long life of over-feeding and inaction. His piggish eyes peered out from between rolls of flesh that threatened to swamp them; his cheeks were blubbery, his chins multifarious. His face was that of the last of a long line of degenerate French Louises. His body was massive, effeminate in its corpulence.

The dog priest spoke, in a voice dry and cracked as a dead stick.

"Do not move, stranger. The lightning of Kuvurna strikes down whom he wishes to destroy!"

Doody stood obediently motionless, but his eyes were busy. There might be a portable atomic-blast rifle concealed among those curtains over the man-god's divan. Those weapons had been built to last forever; some might have endured nine thousand years and remained in the hands of this last decadent scion of a fallen humanity, enabling him to reinforce man's age-old lordship over the dog.

"My lightning," drooled Kuvurna lovingly, his plump fingers fumbling among the bed clothing while his small eyes blinked at the light. "Be careful, impostor, or it will slay you!"

Mentally, Doody placed Kuvurna as a low-grade imbecile, perhaps even an idiot. A rank odor hung in the air; Doody sniffed, and wrinkled his nose disgustedly at its familiarity. If ever he had smelled cheap corn whiskey, he smelled it now. Drink of the gods!

No doubt the priesthood controlled the alcohol supply and consequently Kuvurna. But the god's life was precious above all else, since without him the priests could not continue to impose on their credulous and loyal fellow villagers. Hence the fortresslike temple inclosure, the elaborate precautions and taboos.

"Kuvurna," remarked Doody loudly, "you are a great, swollen mass of corruption, and no Man worth the name!"

The deity winked stupidly; his blubbery face registered no expression. He heaved in vague displeasure at his visitor's frankness, though he was apparently incapable of rising. Doody felt a wave of revulsion in which he despised himself for being a man. If this was what civilization had done for the human race, thank God for barbarism, for blackest savagery!

The little priest was answering for his lord. "That is sacrilege, blasphemy," he spat in a voice like the snarl of an angry hound. "You are no Man or you would not speak thus of another Man."

Kuvurna reared angrily, like a great, unwieldy sea lion, among his gloomy cushions. His skin, under the flickering yellow light, was an unhealthy, pasty white which had seen too little of the sun; his eyes were muddy and befuddledly vicious.

"He is no Man," he repeated, his thick fingers twitching. Doody rose stealthily to the balls of his feet; he knew that, on guard, he could beat the degenerate's slow reflexes ten times out of ten. All the while, though, another part of his mind was struggling to piece out the answer to the wider question; but it was like arranging a tough puzzle with the key piece elsewhere. "He is no Man, but a lying dog; and for his lie he must be put to death!"

"Just a moment," said Doody, and was surprised at the suave smoothness of his own voice. "Has it occurred to you that the entire canine populace, now milling about outside your palisade, believes that I *am* a Man? They will require explanations, in all probability, if I fail to emerge after going in so bravely."

That made no difference to Kuvurna, armored in invulnerable stupidity. But the shrewd mind of the little priest was clearly disturbed. He turned with nervous haste to address his so-called "master":

"O Man of the village, he speaks the truth. The Pack believes his lie; and, having been once convinced, they will not readily disbelieve. What shall be done?" Then, almost without pause, as Kuvurna mumbled to himself, making the words register on the surface of the stagnant pool that was his mind: "If the master will hear his slave, I would suggest that the case of this impostor be tried according to the customs of the Pack; and, if he be proved what he is, let him be incontinently put to death. Thus will the law and the Pack be satisfied."

It sounded somewhat fishy to Doody; but Kuvurna seemed to find the solution gorgeously simple—as needs it must be for his dim mentality to grasp it. At least, he nodded his well-nigh hairless, oversized head, and continued to nod it in dreamy affirmation for some little time. But the priest turned swiftly on Doody, his face hideous with triumph:

"Do you hear, O dog who calls himself a Man? You are to be tried by the council and your abominable lie made plain. Tremble, then, and howl supplication to the spirits of your ancestors, for pardon that you ever denied them!" His tone was ferocious, a canine snarl. Doody found time to wonder what the fellow's background was; he had seen dogs before who had been kicked into viciousness.

Abruptly, no doubt at some prearranged signal, from behind the dark hangings which masked the stone walls emerged a dozen of the dogmen, spears thrusting menacingly as they surrounded Doody. The latter made no resistance, save to shake himself once as horny hands grasped insistently at his arms; his life seemed safe enough for the nonce. He went with them quietly, out through the creaking temple door and through the arch into suddenly blinding sunlight.

The high priest followed to stand at the summit of the stair and glare down at Doody and his guard—so different, this, from the innocently adoring escort of hunters who had led him out of the forest—with baleful eyes; the eyes of any priest who beholds a rival to the god that is his very bread and butter.

"Take the impostor forth before the people," his old voice crackled savagely. "Take him and hold him there, till Kuvurna comes forth and the council of the Pack sits in judgment over life and death!"

The gathering crowd out in the sunburned square had surged nearer and packed more densely as the grapevine telegraph carried the word of great doings to all quarters of the dog people's village.

The air was stifling with dust and the odor of many bodies pressed close together—an odor which differed subtly from that of humanity in the mass. Only a little space about the palisaded gate remained still invisibly roped off; in it, clustered closely and silently together, the little group of dogmen who had discovered Doody in their forest still waited bravely for the return of their marvelous heavenly messenger. But when they saw him emerge hemmed in by the armed acolytes of Kuvurna, a captive, threatened on all sides by sharp spears, yet failing to employ any homicidal magic for his liberation—hastily they shrank back, appalled, into the throng, slinking away fearful lest they should be involved in the consequences of their own error. But Doody, on the sharp-eyed alert, thought he saw more than one sinewy hand tighten convulsively on a spear haft before its owner thought better of his half-formed intentions.

The sun beat down uncomfortably, and Doody was sweating stickily under his clothes, while striving to preserve an airy nonchalance in the face of the heat and the indignity of his close, rather smelly cordon of priests. The watching crowd, most of its eyes and mouths wide, was hushedly silent, save for the intermittent shuffling of bare or sandaled feet as this or that shaded his eyes over his neighbor's shoulder, squinting into the sun, and for the shrill little yelping cries of the children—puppies—who played in the rear of the assemblage.

Dispassionately, Doody considered the dog people once more from his vantage point—this time for what they were, rather than as human beings. They were not an unhandsome breed, and were certainly well-made physically; and there was about them a gentleness, a humility, that the human animal lacks. Man had done a better job of domesticating them than he had ever succeeded in doing on himself.

There was a curious, wistful appeal in the great eyes of some of the young—well, female dogs. Doody broke off on that line of thought. Considering, he did not imagine that there had been any interbreeding. In the perfect uniformity of the dogmen there was no trace of the corruption which, even in Rudnuu's day, had been engulfing all humanity, and which seemed to have reached its nauseous fruition in the unwhisperable Kuvurna.

A stir went over the multitude, like the sigh of a single voice. Doody wheeled to stare over the heads of his guards, saw that the lattice gate had swung inward and that the canine high priest was issuing forth, strutting ceremonially and surrounded by his subordinates or accomplices in the priestly racket, as Doody mentally labeled them. The shriveled little dogman advanced to a point where he could command the attention of the whole great crescent of villagers ranged about the southern border of the square; then, flinging his two skinny arms on high, he cried in a loud and penetrating voice:

"Kneel, O Pack! The Man comes!"

With a combined rustle of ragged garments, the hundreds went down as one to their knees. Their eyes were turned upward eagerly to behold their deity; Doody was close enough to the front rank to see the look they held, rapt, worshipful, and it hit him with a queer nostalgia. He remembered a puppy that had been his when he had been a boy on an Ohio farm—only a spotted mongrel tyke, but a blue-ribbon winner so far as he was concerned.

Out of the court, as the throng still knelt expectant, was borne Kuvurna, a huge, degraded, pulpy hulk, lolling amid padded cushions, upon a swaying and luxurious litter carried aloft by six strong, sweating priests. A broad, fatuous smile covered his countenance as he fluttered his fat white hands languidly toward the worshiping dog folk, after the manner of a benediction. Doody averted his eyes and resolutely said "No" to his stomach.

The six priests eased the litter carefully to the bare, dusty ground, its barbarically ornate magnificence contrasting oddly with the naked square, the squalid rags of the onlookers.

"Arise, O dogs, and hear how justice is to be done! There has come among us a stranger, this person with the queer garments and the black hair, who says that he is a Man. He proclaimed himself as such to some of our hunters; and they, being of the ignorant ones, believed him. But for this they are to be excused on account of their ignorance of the law and the belief.

"This pretender must be tried according to our laws. The members of the Pack Council will now come forward and take their places at the foot of Kuvurna, in readiness to administer the high justice before all the people.

"But first I will remind the Council and the Pack that a Man, it is plain, should know a Man and welcome him as a brother; whereas from this who calls himself a Man our lord Kuvurna has turned away his face."

The fact that at that precise moment Kuvurna was gazing point-blank at Doody with a fixed and foolish grin, the while he blew small bubbles between his teeth, did not seem to disturb the speaker or his wide-eyed and attentive listeners. For some reason, Doody was reminded of the fact that most primitive idols wear bay windows and vacuous smirks.

From among the assembled dogmen, a round dozen individuals were wriggling and pushing their respective ways forward, and were beginning to form in a close huddle before Kuvurna's royal palanquin. This brow-beaten-looking handful must be the council—the rude beginning of a representative form of government, whose scanty influence was vastly overbalanced by that of the priests with their backing of divine omnipotence. They stood, shuffling their feet uneasily and eying Doody with some hostility—the high priest's statement of Kuvurna's position on the subject evidently carried much weight with them.

This Heliogabalus of the dogmen advanced swiftly to confront the "jury," as Doody's twentieth-century mind insisted on labeling them. His face was twisted, and his wasted old figure—clad only in a garment which resembled nothing more than a soiled towel wrapped around his waist with ends dangling—quivered with a fierce ecstasy compounded equally of religious fervor and burning hatred. His voice shook with the same feverish intensity, as, with one sidelong glance at Doody, he began in the singsong of one reciting from some ancient and holy record:

"Before you sit in righteous judgment, O Council of the Pack, I conjure you to remember the true belief, given to our ancestors of old, that the truth might be theirs and their children's:

"*For Man created the dog in His own image; in the image of Man created He him.*

"*And He said to him, be fruitful, and multiply, and cover the Earth, that in all the Earth may the aspect of My face be known, through all the ages of all the time to come.*

"*And for all his days shall the dog serve Man, because He created him, who was as the dust of the earth, and without understanding.*"

Doody did not hear the priest's voice grind on with the rasping indictment. He was lost in a blaze of sudden revelation that was like apotheosis; the lost piece of the great puzzle had been all at once supplied, and now he knew the answer to all his blind questioning.

His quick mind fitted the jigsaw together, constructed a picture of what had happened thousands of years in the past, when the dogmen had first come into being. Somewhere in the slough of rotting earthman civilization, a fine mind or minds had been born—rising, perhaps for the space of one lifetime only—above the sluggish apathy of degeneration, able to foresee but not to check the oncoming doom.

Perhaps they had been of the scientist rulers of that latter-day state, with its unlimited technical resources at their disposal. But more probably they had been rebels, daring, audacious. They had seen the extinction of humanity approaching; and for man they had made the last great gesture, the passing of the torch—the bestowal of man's erect form, his wonderful hands, and his immense stored knowledge upon a younger, stronger race.

What choice more logical for man's successor than that of man's age-old, trustworthy companion, the companion who had never forsaken him throughout a long, confused history of fifty thousand years? It had been no magic for the mighty science of that sunset age—to set the dog upon two feet, to alter body and brain to give him speech, to make him—by planned mutations, fine juggling of germ cells—outwardly a human creature. "That in all the Earth may the aspect of My face be known"—when man himself is dead and vanished from the universe.

Only a short time ago Doody had despised himself for belonging to a species which included such a creature as Kuvurna. But now he felt a brief, warm glow of pride—pride that his race, before it fell utterly, had risen high enough to make its last significant act one of exalted unselfishness and dedication to the hope of a future it would never know.

"—consider then the facts, O Council, and decide whether this one is not a liar and impostor worthy only of the meanest death!"

Doody came out of his cosmic reverie in time to hear the close of the high priest's hysterically vindictive speech. He glanced at the withered little dogman almost in pity, and, with a new understanding, over the jam-packed, breathless crowd which swayed back and forth, straining to catch a glimpse of their god and of the far more godlike prisoner.

"Prepare for death, stranger," snarled the priest, advancing to shake a knobby, clenched paw at the object of his hate. "Or perhaps in your ignorance you know no rites of preparation. But die you shall, and soon."

Doody ignored his fury in haughty silence, but his lips half formed the word, "Perhaps." He meant that to be a big perhaps.

His gaze fell once more on the dogmen's witless deity. His lips curled in a mirthless smile which brought shocked surprise into the faces of the watching priests. He was thinking—an activity which, in Doody's type, usually results in action—and his thought ran thus:

Humanity, being of sound mind and clear judgment—if only for a briefly lucid flash on the down path of its existence—had made its last will and testament. And the heir apparent of human civilization was *not* this loathsome last-born of the corrupt old race.

The council had gone into a deliberate huddle. Kuvurna drowsed in stupid torpor, lulled to a mindless serenity by the rhythm of the wide-headed fans with which his attendants kept the air above him moving. A gurgling snore bubbled in him. The rest of the assemblage sweltered uncomplainingly beneath the sinking but still blistering sun.

The high priest squatted like a deformed spider beside the litter of his man god, scrawling aimlessly in the dust and muttering to himself, but keeping an unwinking, murderous gaze on Doody. The latter scowled back, then affected a carefree, rakish grin, white teeth flashing in his dark face. It must have nettled the old hellhound considerably, for he bounded suddenly to his feet and whipped around to face the jury in high impatience.

"You have debated long enough, O Council of the Pack!" he snapped. "Let us hear your judgment upon the impostor!"

A dogman of more than usually heavy build, with a great red beard that tumbled fanwise over his massive chest, shuffled forward, nodding vigorous and jerky approval of the high priest's words, very like a child who knows he will be slapped if he does not say the right thing. He opened his mouth with diffidence to say the right thing, but Doody broke in.

"Hold on a minute!" he exploded, half enraged, half amused. "Am I to have no chance to speak in my own defense?"

The high priest whirled wrathfully, stood rigid for a moment, his skinny body vibrating like a tuning fork with the intensity of his passion. When he spoke, though, his voice had the quiet deadliness of a bushmaster's hiss. "Speak, then!"

"Very well, I will speak—and I have plenty to say," said Doody softly, and the amusement in his voice was genuine, if bitter. His hand had slipped unnoticed inside his coat and had closed on something there. He raised his voice, made it carry to the massed hundreds of the dogmen, silent and patient under the burning afternoon sun: "However, I first wish to state that the question of my human or canine nature is of small importance. There is another issue, though; one of great moment.

"What should be on trial, here and now—as man or dog may plainly see if he is not blinded by superstition or fear or sacerdotal dies—is the right of this bloated, depraved, hydrocephalic idiot who calls himself a Man, or any other like him, to rule over *you*, O strong young people!

"Look at him. What is he but a swollen parasite on the community, unable to feed or care for himself? Any of your young warriors, dog or not, is a better man. And I say to you in solemn truth that you are not dogs any longer, for I knew you when you were dogs, and I see that now you have become men!"

A murmur swept over the crowd and was followed by a rising babble of confusion that became a roar. The dog people surged to and fro, each trying to find room to gesture wildly and expound the revolutionary new idea to his neighbor. Some recoiled, shocked by the mad atheism of Doody's claims, horrified by the ruthless demolition of cherished tradition. But many of the younger ones grasped at it eagerly, for it went through the blood like a swift fever, a thrilling fever that urged instant action.

Doody watched, smiling still faintly—triumphantly. He wondered if the world had not lost an excellent firebrand political speaker when he had taken up time exploring. Even now shrill cries were raveling out from the tangle of chaotic hubbub; spears were lifted threateningly above the mob. Even Kuvurna had roused enough to blink incuriously and purse his lips as if in mild disapproval of such behavior.

But the man god's high priest was like one possessed as he saw his world rocking and crumbling around him, tottering on the verge of the final clash into oblivion. His face, as he fought his way toward Doody through the surging rabble, was terrible, unhuman. His eyes glared madly, his lips were drawn far back in a frightful snarl to display his long canine teeth. Over the surf roar of the crowd rose his piercing scream:

"Seize him! Seize the impostor! He is nothing but a dog—a dog who is not faithful! Kill him—*eeeyaaaah!*"

The last was a sheer animal shriek of unbearable rage as, with a bronze knife gleaming wickedly in his bony claw, the high priest hurled himself headlong upon Doody. The American wheeled half about to avoid the point and threw a lefthanded punch with muscle and weight behind it; the blow collided midway with the dogman's chin, and each of the two went staggering backward—Doody to make a lightning recovery, the high priest to roll over and over and lie sprawling, a limp bundle under the trampling feet of the crowd.

Through the milling mob, armed priests were thrusting toward the blasphemer of their faith, while their brethren ringed close about the divine litter, a dangerous cordon. But for the moment a space was clear about the stranger from time; he shook himself and took a deep breath, and then—

"Of course, I couldn't stay to see the rest of the show," said Doody regretfully. "But before I pulled out for the good old twentieth century, I took just time enough to jerk the pin from my emergency Mills bomb and let it fly with three seconds to go. If the old arm hasn't lost its knack since my baseball days, that hand grenade went squarely into the bulging paunch of the feeble-minded Kuvurna himself.

"That's the final argument I mentioned. I hope it did its bit to give the heirs of human civilization a fair start on the Earth. The world *is* going to the dogs, Johnny, and the sooner it arrives, the better. The dogmen were—are—will be—primitive, of course; but some day they will have progressed sufficiently to decipher the ancient records which the lost race has left behind. But I think they will really come into their heritage when they learn to call themselves men."

"You were right," I said, without preamble.

"Eh?" Doody's dark eyes opened drowsily; his thoughts might have been far away, down that long road he had journeyed to the dim and far-off time of the dogmen.

"It makes me—think," I confessed, studying the white tablecloth beneath the mellow, indirect lighting; but I fancied that I, too, could peer a little way into the mist of years. "You've followed the human race to its final end—you have yet to find its beginning. Perhaps it is another of the cycles—the beginning and end of the race are the same, and we are only the unknowing heirs of an elder culture—that of the beings men call gods. But somewhere there must be a true beginning—"

"Somewhere," said Doody softly, as if the word was sweet. "Some day. Perhaps I will seek it out—some day."

HISTORY LESSON

No ONE COULD remember when the tribe had begun its long journey. The land of great rolling plains that had been its first home was now no more than a half-forgotten dream.

For many years Shann and his people had been fleeing through a country of low hills and sparkling lakes, and now the mountains lay ahead. This summer they must cross them to the southern lands. There was little time to lose. The white terror that had come down from the Poles, grinding continents to dust and freezing the very air before it, was less than a day's march behind.

Shann wondered if the glaciers could climb the mountains ahead, and within his heart he dared to kindle a little flame of hope. This might prove a barrier against which even the remorseless ice would batter in vain. In the southern lands of which the legends spoke, his people might find refuge at last.

It took weeks to discover a pass through which the tribe and the animals could travel. When midsummer came, they had camped in a lonely valley where the air was thin and the stars shone with a brilliance no one had ever seen before.

The summer was waning when Shann took his two sons and went ahead to explore the way. For three days they climbed, and for three nights slept as best they could on the freezing rocks. And on the fourth morning there was nothing ahead but a gentle rise to a cairn of gray stones built by other travelers, centuries ago.

Shann felt himself trembling, and not with cold, as they walked toward the little pyramid of stones. His sons had fallen behind. No one spoke, for too much was at stake. In a little while they would know if all their hopes had been betrayed.

To east and west, the wall of mountains curved away as if embracing the land beneath. Below lay endless miles of undulating plain, with a great river swinging across it in tremendous loops. It was a fertile land; one in which the tribe could raise crops knowing that there would be no need to flee before the harvest came.

Then Shann lifted his eyes to the south, and saw the doom of all his
There was no way forward. Through all the years of flight, the glaciers
hopes. For there at the edge of the world glimmered that deadly light he
had seen so often to the north—the glint of ice below the horizon.
from the south had been advancing to meet them. Soon they would be
crushed beneath the moving walls of ice. . . .

Southern glaciers did not reach the mountains until a generation later.

545

In that last summer the sons of Shann carried the sacred treasures of the tribe to the lonely cairn overlooking the plain. The ice that had once gleamed below the horizon was now almost at their feet. By spring it would be splintering against the mountain walls.

No one understood the treasures now. They were from a past too distant for the understanding of any man alive. Their origins were lost in the mists that surrounded the Golden Age, and how they had come at last into the possession of this wandering tribe was a story that now would never be told. For it was the story of a civilization that had passed beyond recall.

Once, all these pitiful relics had been treasured for some good reason, and now they had become sacred though their meaning had long been lost. The print in the old books had faded centuries ago though much of the lettering was still visible—if there had been any to read it. But many generations had passed since anyone had had a use for a set of seven-figure logarithms, an atlas of the world, and the score of Sibelius' Seventh Symphony, printed, according to the flyleaf, by H. K. Chu and Sons, at the City of Pekin in the year 2371 A.D.

The old books were placed reverently in the little crypt that had been made to receive them. There followed a motley collection of fragments— gold and platinum coins, a broken telephoto lens, a watch, a cold-light lamp, a microphone, the cutter from an electric shaver, some midget radio tubes, the flotsam that had been left behind when the great tide of civilization had ebbed forever.

All these treasures were carefully stowed away in their resting place. Then came three more relics, the most sacred of all because the least understood.

The first was a strangely shaped piece of metal, showing the coloration of intense heat. It was, in its way, the most pathetic of all these symbols from the past, for it told of man's greatest achievement and of the future he might have known. The mahogany stand on which it was mounted bore a silver plate with the inscription.

> Auxiliary Igniter from Starboard Jet
> Spaceship "Morning Star"
> Earth-Moon, A.D. 1985

Next followed another miracle of the ancient science—a sphere of transparent plastic with strangely shaped pieces of metal embedded in it. At its centre was a tiny capsule of synthetic radio-element, surrounded by the converting screens that shifted its radiation far down the spectrum. As long as the material remained active, the sphere would be a tiny radio transmitter, broadcasting power in all directions. Only a few of these spheres had ever been made. They had been designed as perpetual beacons to mark the orbits of the asteroids. But man had never reached the asteroids and the beacons had never been used.

Last of all was a flat, circular tin, wide in comparison with its depth. It was heavily sealed, and rattled when shaken. The tribal lore predicted that disaster would follow if it were ever opened, and no one knew that it held one of the great works of art of nearly a thousand years before.

The work was finished. The two men rolled the stones back into place and slowly began to descend the mountainside. Even to the last, man had given some thought to the future and had tried to preserve something for posterity.

That winter the great waves of ice began their first assault on the mountains, attacking from north and south. The foothills were overwhelmed in the first onslaught, and the glaciers ground them into dust. But the mountains stood firm, and when the summer came the ice retreated for a while.

So, winter after winter, the battle continued, and the roar of the avalanches, the grinding of rock and the explosions of splintering ice filled the air with tumult. No war of man's had been fiercer than this, and even man's battles had not quite engulfed the globe as this had done.

At last the tidal waves of ice began to subside and to creep slowly down the flanks of the mountains they had never quite subdued. The valleys and passes were still firmly in their grip. It was stalemate. The glaciers had met their match, but their defeat was too late to be of any use to Man.

So the centuries passed, and presently there happened something that must occur once at least in the history of every world in the universe, no matter how remote and lonely it may be.

The ship from Venus came five thousand years too late, but its crew knew nothing of this. While still many millions of miles away, the telescopes had seen the great shroud of ice that made Earth the most brilliant object in the sky next to the sun itself.

Here and there the dazzling sheet was marred by black specks that revealed the presence of almost buried mountains. That was all. The rolling oceans, the plains and forests, the deserts and lakes—all that had been the world of man was sealed beneath the ice, perhaps forever.

The ship closed in to Earth and established an orbit less than a thousand miles away. For five days it circled the planet, while cameras recorded all that was left to see and a hundred instruments gathered information that would give the Venusian scientists many years of work.

An actual landing was not intended. There seemed little purpose in it. But on the sixth day the picture changed. A panoramic monitor, driven to the limit of its amplification, detected the dying radiation of the five-thousand-year-old-beacon. Through all the centuries, it had been sending out its signals with ever-failing strength as its radioactive heart steadily weakened.

The monitor locked on the beacon frequency. In the control room, a bell clamored for attention. A little later, the Venusian ship broke free from its orbit and slanted down toward Earth, toward a range of mountains that still towered proudly above the ice, and to a cairn of gray stones that the years had scarcely touched. . . .

The great disc of the sun blazed fiercely in a sky no longer veiled with mist, for the clouds that had once hidden Venus had now completely gone. Whatever force had caused the change in the sun's radiation had doomed one civilization, but had given birth to another. Less than five thousand years before, the half-savage people of Venus had seen Sun and stars for the first time. Just as the science of Earth had begun with astronomy, so had that of Venus, and on the warm, rich world that man had never seen progress had been incredibly rapid.

Perhaps the Venusians had been lucky. They never knew the Dark Age that held Man enchained for a thousand years. They missed the long detour into chemistry and mechanics but came at once to the more fundamental laws of radiation physics. In the time that man had taken to progress from the Pyramids to the rocket-propelled spaceship, the Venusians had passed from the discovery of agriculture to anti-gravity itself— the ultimate secret that Man had never learned.

The warm ocean that still bore most of the young planet's life rolled its breakers languidly against the sandy shore. So new was this continent that the very sands were coarse and gritty. There had not yet been time enough for the sea to wear them smooth.

The scientists lay half in the water, their beautiful reptilian bodies gleaming in the sunlight. The greatest minds of Venus had gathered on this shore from all the islands of the planet. What they were going to hear they did not yet know, except that it concerned the Third World and the mysterious race that had peopled it before the coming of the ice.

The Historian was standing on the land, for the instruments he wished to use had no love of water. By his side was a large machine which attracted many curious glances from his colleagues. It was clearly concerned with optics, for a lens system projected from it toward a screen of white material a dozen yards away.

The Historian began to speak. Briefly he recapitulated what little had been discovered concerning the third planet and its people.

He mentioned the centuries of fruitless research that had failed to interpret a single word of the writings of Earth. The planet had been inhabited by a race of great technical ability. That, at least, was proved by the few pieces of machinery that had been found in the cairn upon the mountain.

"We do not know why so advanced a civilization came to an end," he observed. "Almost certainly, it had sufficient knowledge to survive an Ice Age. There must have been some factor of which we know nothing. Possibly disease or racial degeneration may have been responsible. It has even been suggested that the tribal conflicts endemic to our own species in prehistoric times may have continued on the third planet after the coming of technology.

"Some philosophers maintain that knowledge of machinery does not necessarily imply a high degree of civilization, and it is theoretically possible to have wars in a society possessing mechanical power, flight, and even radio. Such a conception is alien to our thoughts, but we must admit its possibility. It would certainly account for the downfall of the lost race.

"It has always been assumed that we should never know anything of the physical form of the creatures who lived on Planet Three. For centuries our artists have been depicting scenes from the history of the dead world, peopling it with all manner of fantastic beings. Most of these creations have resembled us more or less closely, though it has often been pointed out that because *we* are reptiles it does not follow that all intelligent life must necessarily be reptilian.

"We now know the answer to one of the most baffling problems of history. At last, after a hundred years of research, we have discovered the exact form and nature of the ruling life on the Third Planet."

There was a murmur of astonishment from the assembled scientists. Some were so taken aback that they disappeared for a while into the comfort of the ocean, as all Venusians were apt to do in moments of stress. The Historian waited until his colleagues reemerged into the element they so disliked. He himself was quite comfortable, thanks to the tiny sprays that were continually playing over his body. With their help he could live on land for many hours before having to return to the ocean.

The excitement slowly subsided and the lecturer continued:

"One of the most puzzling of the objects found on Planet Three was a flat metal container holding a great length of transparent plastic material, perforated at the edges and wound tightly into a spool. This transparent tape at first seemed quite featureless, but an examination with the new subelectronic microscope has shown that this is not the case. Along the surface of the material, invisible to our eyes but perfectly clear under the correct radiation, are literally thousands of tiny pictures. It is believed that they were imprinted on the material by some chemical means, and have faded with the passage of time.

"These pictures apparently form a record of life as it was on the Third Planet at the height of its civilization. They are not independent. Consecutive pictures are almost identical, differing only in the detail of movement. The purpose of such a record is obvious. It is only necessary to project the scenes in rapid succession to give an illusion of continuous movement. We have made a machine to do this, and I have here an exact reproduction of the picture sequence.

"The scenes you are now going to witness take us back many thousands of years, to the great days of our sister planet. They show a complex civilization, many of whose activities we can only dimly understand. Life seems to have been very violent and energetic, and much that you will see is quite baffling.

"It is clear that the Third Planet was inhabited by a number of different species, none of them reptilian. That is a blow to our pride, but the conclusion is inescapable. The dominant type of life appears to have been a two-armed biped. It walked upright and covered its body with some flexible material, possibly for protection against the cold, since even before the Ice Age the planet was at a much lower temperature than our own world.

But I will not try your patience any further. You will now see the record of which I have been speaking."

A brilliant light flashed from the projector. There was a gentle whirring, and on the screen appeared hundreds of strange beings moving rather jerkily to and fro. The picture expanded to embrace one of the creatures, and the scientists could see that the Historian's description had been correct.

The creature possessed two eyes, set rather close together, but the other facial adornments were a little obscure. There was a large orifice in the lower portion of the head that was continually opening and closing. Possibly it had something to do with the creature's breathing.

The scientists watched spellbound as the strange being became involved in a series of fantastic adventures. There was an incredibly violent conflict with another, slightly different creature. It seemed certain that they must both be killed, but when it was all over neither seemed any the worse.

Then came a furious drive over miles of country in a four-wheeled mechanical device which was capable of extraordinary feats of locomotion. The ride ended in a city packed with other vehicles moving in all directions at breath-taking speeds. No one was surprised to see two of the machines meet headon with devastating results.

After that, events became even more complicated. It was now quite obvious that it would take many years of research to analyze and understand all that was happening. It was also clear that the record was a work of art, somewhat stylized, rather than an exact reproduction of life as it actually had been on the Third Planet.

Most of the scientists felt themselves completely dazed when the sequence of pictures came to an end. There was a final flurry of motion, in which the creature that had been the center of interest became involved in some tremendous but incomprehensible catastrophe. The picture contracted to a circle, centered on the creature's head.

The last scene of all was an expanded view of its face, obviously expressing some powerful emotion. But whether it was rage, grief, defiance, resignation or some other feeling could not be guessed. The picture vanished. For a moment some lettering appeared on the screen, then it was all over.

For several minutes there was complete silence, save the lapping of the waves upon the sand. The scientists were too stunned to speak. The fleeting glimpse of Earth's civilization had had a shattering effect on their minds. Then little groups began to start talking together, first in whispers and then more and more loudly as the implications of what they had seen became clearer. Presently the Historian called for attention and addressed the meeting again.

"We are now planning," he said, "a vast program of research to extract all available knowledge from this record. Thousands of copies are being made for distribution to all workers. You will appreciate the problems involved. The psychologists in particular have an immense task confronting them.

"But I do not doubt that we shall succeed. In another generation, who can say what we may not have learned of this wonderful race? Before we leave, let us look again at our remote cousins, whose wisdom may have surpassed our own but of whom so little has survived."

Once more the final picture flashed on the screen, motionless this time, for the projector had been stopped. With something like awe, the scientists gazed at the still figure from the past, while in turn the little biped stared back at them with its characteristic expression of arrogant bad temper.

For the rest of time it would symbolize the human race. The psychologists of Venus would analyze its actions and watch its every movement until they could reconstruct its mind. Thousands of books would be written about it. Intricate philosophies would be contrived to account for its behavior.

But all this labor, all this research, would be utterly in vain. Perhaps the proud and lonely figure on the screen was smiling sardonically at the scientists who were starting on their age-long fruitless quest.

Its secret would be safe as long as the universe endured, for no one now would ever read the lost language of Earth. Millions of times in the ages to come those last few words would flash across the screen, and none could ever guess their meaning:

A Walt Disney Production.

Lester del Rey

INSTINCT

SENTHREE WAVED ASIDE the slowing scooter and lengthened his stride down the sidewalk; he had walked all the way from the rocket port, and there was no point to a taxi now that he was only a few blocks from the biolabs. Besides, it was too fine a morning to waste in riding. He sniffed at the crisp, clean fumes of gasoline appreciatively and listened to the music of his hard heels slapping against the concrete.

It was good to have a new body again. He hadn't appreciated what life was like for the last hundred years or so. He let his eyes rove across the street toward the blue flame of a welding torch and realized how long it had been since his eyes had really appreciated the delicate beauty of such a flame. The wise old brain in his chest even seemed to think better now.

It was worth every stinking minute he'd spent on Venus. At times like this, one could realize how good it was to be alive and to be a robot.

Then he sobered as he came to the old biolabs. Once there had been plans for a fine new building instead of the old factory in which he had started it all four hundred years ago. But somehow, there'd never been time for that. It had taken almost a century before they could master the technique of building up genes and chromosomes into the zygote of a simple fish that would breed with the natural ones. Another century had gone by before they produced Oscar, the first artificially made pig. And there they seemed to have stuck. Sometimes it seemed to Senthree that they were no nearer recreating Man than they had been when they started.

He pushed the door open and went down the long hall, studying his reflection in the polished walls absently. It was a good body. The black enamel was perfect and every joint of the metal case spelled new techniques and luxurious fittings. But the old worries were beginning to settle. He grunted at Oscar LXXII, the lab mascot, and received an answering grunt. The pig came over to root at his feet, but he had no time for that. He turned into the main lab room, already taking on the worries of his job.

It wasn't hard to worry as he saw the other robots. They were clustered about some object on a table, dejection on every gleaming back. Senthree shoved Ceofor and Beswun aside and moved up. One look was enough. The female of the eleventh couple lay there in the strange stiffness of protoplasm that had died, a horrible grimace on her face.

"How long—and what happened to the male?" Senthree asked.

Ceofor swung to face him quickly. "Hi, Boss. You're late. Hey, new body!"

Senthree nodded, as they came grouping around, but his words were automatic as he explained about falling in the alkali pool on Venus and ruining his worn body completely. "Had to wait for a new one. And then the ship got held up while we waited for the Arcturus superlight ship to land. They'd found half a dozen new planets to colonize, and had to spread the word before they'd set down. Now, what about the creatures?"

"We finished educating about three days ago," Ceofor told him. Ceofor was the first robot trained in Senthree's technique of gene-building and the senior assistant. "Expected you back then, Boss. But . . . well, see for yourself. The man is still alive, but he won't be long."

Senthree followed them back to another room and looked through the window. He looked away quickly. It had been another failure. The man was crawling about the floor on hands and knees, falling half the time to his stomach, and drooling. His garbled mouthing made no sense.

"Keep the new robots out," he ordered. It would never do to let the public see this. There was already too much of a cry against homovivifying, and the crowds were beginning to mutter something about it being unwise to mess with vanished life forms. They seemed actually afraid of the legendary figure of Man.

"What luck on Venus?" one of them asked, as they began the job of carefully dissecting the body of the female failure to look for the reason behind the lack of success.

"None. Just another rumor. I don't think Man ever established self-sufficient colonies. If he did, they didn't survive. But I found something else—something the museum would give a fortune for. Did my stuff arrive?"

"You mean that box of tar? Sure, it's over there in the corner."

Senthree let the yielding plastic of his mouth smile at them as he strode toward it. They had already ripped off the packing, and now he reached up for a few fine wires in the tar. It came off as he pulled, loosely repacked over a thin layer of wax. At that, he'd been lucky to sneak it past Customs. This was the oldest, crudest, and biggest robot discovered so far—perhaps one of the fabulous Original Models. It stood there rigidly, staring out of its pitted, expressionless face. But the plate on its chest had been scraped carefully clean, and Senthree pointed it out to them.

"MAKEPEACE ROBOT, SER. 324MD2991. SURGEON."

"A mechanic for Man bodies," Beswun translated. "But that means—"

"Exactly." Senthree put it into words. "It must know how Man's body was built—if it has retained any memory. I found it in a tarpit by sheer accident, and it seems to be fairly well preserved. No telling whether there were any magnetic fields to erode memories, of course, and it's all matted inside. But if we can get it to working—"

Beswun took over. He had been trained as a physicist before the mysterious lure of the biolab had drawn him here. Now he began wheeling the crude robot away. If he could get it into operation, the museum could wait. The re-creation of Man came first!

Senthree pulled X-ray lenses out of a pouch and replaced the normal ones in his eyes before going over to join the robots who were beginning dissection. Then he switched them for the neutrino-detector lenses that had made this work possible. The neutrino was the only particle that could penetrate the delicate protoplasmic cells without ruining them and yet permit the necessary millions of times magnification. It was a fuzzy image, since the neutrino spin made such an insignificant field for the atomic nuclei to work on that few were deflected. But through them, he could see the vague outlines of the pattern within the cells. It was as they had designed the original cell—there had been no reshuffling of genes in handling. He switched to his micromike hands and began the delicate work of tracing down the neurone connections. There was only an occasional mutter as one of the robots beside him switched to some new investigation.

The female should have lived! But somewhere, in spite of all their care, she had died. And now the male was dying. Eleven couples—eleven failures. Senthree was no nearer finding the creators of his race than he had been centuries before.

Then the radio in his head buzzed its warning and he let it cut in, straightening from his work. "Senthree."

"The director is in your office. Will you report at once?"

"Damn!" The word had no meaning, but it was strangely satisfying at times. What did old Emptinine want . . . or wait again, there'd been a selection while he was on Venus investigating the rumors of Man. Some young administrator—Arpeten—had the job now.

Ceofor looked up guiltily, obviously having tuned in. "I should have warned you. We got word three days ago he was coming, but forgot it in reviving the couple. Trouble?"

Senthree shrugged, screwing his normal lenses back in and trading to the regular hands. They couldn't have found out about the antique robot. That had been seen by nobody else. It was probably just sheer curiosity over some rumor they were reviving the couple. If his appropriation hadn't been about exhausted, Senthree would have told him where to go; but now was hardly the time, with a failure on one hand and a low credit balance on the other. He polished his new head quickly with the aid of one of the walls for a mirror and headed toward his office.

But Arpeten was smiling. He got to his feet as the biolab chief entered, holding out a well-polished hand. "Dr. Senthree. Delighted. And you've got an interesting place here. I've already seen most of it. And that pig —they tell me it's a descendant of a boar out of your test tubes."

"Incubation wombs. But you're right—the seventy-second generation."

"Fascinating." Arpeten must have been reading too much of that book of "Proven Points to Popularity" they'd dug up in the ruins of Hudson ten years before, but it had worked. He was the director. "But tell me. Just what good are pigs?"

Senthree grinned, in spite of himself. "Nobody knows. Men apparently kept a lot of them, but so far as I can see they are completely useless. They're clever, in a way. But I don't think they were pets. Just another mystery."

"Um-m-m. Like men. Maybe you can tell me what good Man will be. I've been curious about that after seeing your appropriations since you opened here. But nobody can answer."

"It's in the records," Senthree told him sharply. Then he modified his voice carefully. "How well do you know your history? I mean about the beginning."

"Well—"

He probably knew some of it, Senthree thought. They all got part of it as legends. He leaned back in his seat now, though, as the biochemist began the old tale of the beginning as they knew it. They knew that there had been Man a million years before them. And somebody—Asimov or Asenion, the record wasn't quite clear—had apparently created the first robot. They had improved it up to about the present level. Then there had been some kind of a contest in which violent forces had ruined the factories, most of the robots, and nearly all of the Men. It was believed from the fragmentary records that a biological weapon had killed the rest of Man, leaving only the robots.

Those first robots, as they were now known, had had to start on a ruined world from scratch—a world where mines were exhausted, and factories were gone. They'd learned to get metals from the seas, and had spent years and centuries slowly rebuilding the machines to build new robots. There had been only two of them when the task was finished, and they had barely time enough to run one new robot off and educate him sketchily. Then they had discharged finally, and he had taken up rebuilding the race. It was almost like beginning with no history and no science. Twenty millennia had passed before they began to rebuild a civilization of their own.

"But why did Man die?" Senthree asked. "That's part of the question. And are we going to do the same? We know we are similar to Man. Did he change himself in some way that ruined him? Can we change ourselves safely? You know that there are a thousand ways we could improve ourselves. We could add antigravity, and get rid of our cumbersome vehicles. We could add more arms. We could eliminate our useless mouths and talk by radio. We could add new circuits to our brains. But we don't dare. One school says that nobody can build a better race than itself, so Man must have been better than we are—and if he made us this way, there was a reason. Even if the psychologists can't understand some of the circuits in our brains, they don't dare touch them.

"We're expanding through the universe—but we can't even change ourselves to fit the new planets? And until we can find the reasons for Man's disappearance, that makes good sense. We know he was planning to change himself. We have bits of evidence. And he's dead. To make it worse, we have whole reels of education tape that probably has all the answers—but it's keyed to Man's brain, and we can't respond to it. Give us a viable Man, and he can interpret that. Or we can find out by comparison what we can and cannot do. I maintain we can do a lot."

Arpeten shook his head doubtfully. "I suppose you think you know why he died!"

"I think so, yes. Instinct! That's a built-in reaction, an unlearned thought. Man had it. If a man heard a rattlesnake, he left the place in a hurry, even though he'd never heard it before. Response to that sound was built into him. No tape impressed it, and no experience was needed. We know the instincts of some of the animals, too—and one of them is to struggle and kill—like the ants who kill each other off. I think Man did just that. He couldn't get rid of his instincts when they were no longer needed, and they killed him. He *should* have changed—and we can change. But I can't tell that from animals. I need intelligent life, to see whether instinct or intelligence will dominate. And robots don't have instincts—I've looked for even one sign of something not learned individually, and can't find it. It's the one basic difference between us. Don't you see, Man is the whole key to our problem of whether we can change or not without risking extermination?"

"Um-m-m." The director sounded noncommittal. "Interesting theory. But how are you going to know you have Man?"

Senthree stared at the robot with more respect. He tried to explain, but he had never been as sure of that himself as he might. Theoretically, they had bones and bits of preserved tissue. They had examined the gene pattern of these, having learned that the cells of the individual contain the same pattern as that of the zygote. And they had other guides—man's achievements, bits of his literature. From these, some working theories could be made. But he couldn't be quite sure—they'd never really known whether man's pigment was dark brown, pinkish orange, white, or what; the records they had seemed to disagree on this.

"We'll know when we get an intelligent animal with instinct," he said at last. "It won't matter exactly whether he is completely like Man or not. At least it will give us a check on things we must know. Until then, we'll have to go on trying. You might as well know that the last experiment failed, though it was closer. But in another hundred years—"

"So." Arpeten's face became bland, but he avoided the look of Senthree. "I'm afraid not. At least for a while. That's what I came about, you know. We've just had word of several new planets around Arcturus, and it will take the major allocation of our funds to colonize these. New robots must be built, new ships . . . oh, you know. And we're retrenching a bit on other things. Of course, if you'd succeeded . . . but perhaps it's better you failed. You know how the sentiment against reviving Man has grown."

Senthree growled bitterly. He'd seen how it was carefully nurtured—though he had to admit it seemed to be easy to create. Apparently most of the robots were afraid of Man—felt he would again take over, or something. Superstitious fools.

"How much longer?" he asked.

"Oh, we won't cut back what you have, Dr. Senthree. But I'm afraid we simply can't allocate more funds. When this is finished, I was hoping to make you biological investigator, incidentally, on one of the planets. There'll be work enough . . . Well, it was a pleasure." He shook hands again, and walked out, his back a gleaming ramrod of efficiency and effectiveness.

Senthree turned back, his new body no longer moving easily. It could already feel the harsh sands and unknown chemical poisons of investigating a new planet—the futile, empty carding of new life that could have no real purpose to the robots. No more appropriations! And they had barely enough funds to meet the current bills.

Four hundred years—and a ship to Arcturus had ended it in three months. Instinct, he thought again—given life with intelligence and instinct together for one year, and he could settle half the problems of his race, perhaps. But robots could not have instincts. Fifty years of study had proven that.

Beswun threw up a hand in greeting as he returned, and he saw that the dissection was nearly complete, while the antique robot was activated.

A hinge on its ludicrous jaw was moving, and rough, grating words were coming out. Senthree turned to the dissecting bench, and then swung back as he heard them.

"Wrong . . . wrong," it was muttering. "Can not live. Is not good brain. No pineal. Medulla good, but not good cerebrum. Fissures wrong. Maybe pituitary disfunction? No. How can be?" It probed doubtfully and set the brain aside. "Mutation maybe. Very bad. Need Milliken mike. See nucleus of cells. Maybe just freak, maybe new disease."

Senthree's fingers were taut and stiff as he fished into his bag and came out with a set of lenses. Beswun shook his head and made a waiting sign. He went out at a run, to come back shortly with a few bits of metal and the shavings from machining still on his hands. "Won't fit—but these adapters should do it. There, 324MD2991. Now come over here where you can look at it over this table—that's where the . . . uh, rays are."

He turned back, and Senthree saw that a fine wire ran from one adapter. "He doesn't speak our bio-terminology, Senthree. We'll have to see the same things he does. There—we can watch it on the screen. Now, 324MD2991, you tell us what is wrong and point it out. Are your hands steady enough for that?"

"Hands one-billionth inch accurate," the robot creaked. It was a meaningless noise, though they had found the unit of measure mentioned. But whatever it meant, the hands were steady enough. The microprobe began touching shadowy bunches of atoms, droning and grating.

"Freak. Very bad freak. How he lived? Ketone—no ketone there. Not understand. How he live?"

Ceofor dashed for their chromosome blanks and began lettering in the complex symbols they used. For a second, Senthree hesitated, then he caught fire and began making notes along with his assistant. It seemed to take hours; it probably did. The old robot had his memory intact, but there were no quick ways for him to communicate. And at last, the antique grunted in disgust and turned his back on them. Beswun pulled a switch.

"He expects to be discharged when not in use. Crazy, isn't it?" the physicist explained. "Look, Boss, am I wrong, or isn't that close to what we did on the eleventh couple?"

"Only a few genes different in three chromosomes. We *were* close. But . . . um-m-m, that's ridiculous. Look at all the brain tissue he'd have—and a lot of it unconnected. And here—that would put an extra piece on where big and little intestines join—a perfect focal point for infection. It isn't efficient biological engineering. And yet most animals do have just that kind of engineering. I think the old robot was right—this would be Man!" He looked at their excited faces, and his shoulders slumped. "But there isn't time. Not even time to make a zygote and see what it would look like. Our appropriations won't come through."

It should have been a bombshell, but he saw at once that they had already guessed it. Ceofor stood up slowly.

"We can take a look, Boss. We've got the sperm from the male that failed—all we have to do is modify those three, instead of making up a whole cell. We might as well have some fun before we go out looking for sand fleas that secrete hydrofluoric acid and menace our colonies. Come on, even in your new body I'll beat you to a finished cell!"

Senthree grinned ruefully, but he moved toward the creation booth. His hands snapped on the little time field out of pure habit as he found a perfect cell. The little field would slow time almost to zero within its limits, and keep any damage from occurring while he worked. It made his own work difficult, since he had to force the probe against that, but it was insulated to some extent by other fields.

Then his hands took over. For a time he worked and thought, but the feeling of the protoplasm came into them, and his hands were almost one with the life-stuff, sensing its tiny responses, inserting another link onto a chain, supplanting an atom of hydrogen with one of the hydroxyl radicals, wielding all the delicate chemical manipulation. He removed the defective genes and gently inserted the correct ones. Four hundred years of this work lay behind him—work he had loved, work which had meant the possible evolution of his race into all it might be.

It had become instinct to him—instinct in only a colloquial sense, however; this was learned response, and real instinct lay deeper than that, so deep that no reason could overcome it and that it was automatic even the first time. Only Man had had instinct and intelligence—stored somehow in this tiny cell that lay within the time field.

He stepped out, just as Ceofor was drawing back in a dead heat. But the younger robot inspected Senthree's cell, and nodded. "Less disturbance and a neater job on the nucleus—I can't see where you pierced the wall. Well, if we had thirty years—even twenty—we could have Man again— or a race. Yours is male and mine female. But there's no time. Shall I leave the time field on?"

Senthree started to nod.

Then he swung to Beswun. "The time field! Can it be reversed?"

"You mean to speed time up within it? No, not with that model. Take a bigger one. I could build you one in half an hour. But who'd want to speed up time with all the troubles you'd get? How much?"

"Ten thousand—or at least seven thousand times! The period is up tomorrow when disbursements have to be made. I want twenty years in a day."

Beswun shook his head. "No. That's what I was afraid of. Figure it this way: you speed things up ten thousand times and that means the molecules in there speed up just that much, literally. Now, 273° times ten thousand—and you have more than two million degrees of temperature. And those molecules have energy! They come busting out of there. No, can't be done."

"How much can you do?" Senthree demanded.

Beswun considered. "Ten times—maybe no more than nine. That gives you all the refractories would handle, if we set it up down in the old pit under the building—you know, where they had the annealing oven."

It wasn't enough; it would still take two years. Senthree dropped onto a seat, vagrantly wondering again how this queer brain of his that the psychologists studied futilely could make him feel tired when his body could have no fatigue. It was probably one of those odd circuits they didn't dare touch.

"Of course, you could use four fields," Beswun stated slowly. "Big one outside, smaller one, still smaller, and smallest inside that. Fourth power of nine is about sixty-six hundred. That's close—raise that nine a little and you'd have your twenty years in a day. By the time it leaked from field to field, it wouldn't matter. Take a couple of hours."

"Not if you get your materials together and build each shell inside the other—you'll be operating faster each step then," Ceofor shouted. "Somebody'll have to go in and stay there a couple of our minutes toward the end to attach the educator tapes—and to revive the couple!"

"Take power," Beswun warned.

Senthree shrugged. Let it. If the funds they had wouldn't cover it, the directorate would have to make it up, once it was used. Besides, once Man was created, they couldn't fold up the biolabs. "I'll go in," he suggested.

"My job," Ceofor told him flatly. "You won the contest in putting the cells right."

Senthree gave in reluctantly, largely because the younger robot had more experience at reviving than he did. He watched Beswun assemble the complicated net of wires and become a blur as he seemed to toss the second net together almost instantly. The biochemist couldn't see the third go up—it was suddenly there, and Beswun was coming out as it flashed into existence. He held up four fingers, indicating all nets were working.

Ceofor dashed in with the precious cells for the prepared incubators that would nurture the bodies until maturity, when they would be ready for the educators. His body seemed to blur, jerk, and disappear. And almost at once he was back.

Senthree stood watching for a moment more, but there was nothing to see. He hesitated again, then turned and moved out of the building. Across the street lay his little lodging place, where he could relax with his precious two books—almost complete—that had once been printed by Man. Tonight he would study that strange bit of Man's history entitled "Gather, Darkness," with its odd indications of a science that Man had once had which had surpassed even that of the robots now. It was pleasanter than the incomprehensibility of the mysterious one titled "Mein Kampf." He'd let his power idle, and mull over it, and consider again the odd behavior of male and female who made such a complicated business of mating. That was probably more instinct—Man, it seemed, was filled with instincts.

For a long time, though, he sat quietly with the book on his lap, wondering what it would be like to have instincts. There must be many unpleasant things about it. But there were also suggestions that it could be pleasant. Well, he'd soon know by observation, even though he could never experience it. Man should have implanted one instinct in a robot's brain, at least, just to show what it was like.

He called the lab once, and Coefor reported that all was doing nicely, and that both children were looking quite well. Outside the window, Senthree heard a group go by, discussing the latest bits of news on the Arcturus expedition. At least in that, Man had failed to equal the robots. He had somehow died before he could find the trick of using identity exchange to overcome the limitation imposed by the speed of light.

Finally he fell to making up a speech that he could deliver to the director, Arpeten, when success was in his hands. It must be very short— something that would stick in the robot's mind for weeks, but carrying everything a scientist could feel on proving that those who opposed him were wrong. Let's see—

The buzzer on the telescreen cut through his thoughts, and he flipped it on to see Coefor's face looking out. Senthree's spirits dropped abruptly as he stared at the younger robot.

"Failure? No!"

The other shook his head. "No. At least, I don't know. I couldn't give them full education. Maybe the tape was uncomfortable. They took a lot of it, but the male tore his helmet off and took the girl's off. Now they just sit there, rubbing their heads and staring around."

He paused, and the little darkened ridges of plastic over his eyes tensed. "The time speed-up is off. But I didn't know what to do."

"Let them alone until I get there. If it hurts them, we can give them the rest of it later. How are they otherwise?"

"I don't know. They look all right, Boss." Coefor hesitated, and his voice dropped. "Boss, I don't like it. There's something wrong here. I can't quite figure out what it is, but it isn't the way I expected. Hey, the male just pushed the female off her seat. Do you think their destructive instinct— No, she's sitting down on the floor now, with her head against him, and holding one of his hands. Wasn't that part of the mating ritual in one of the books?"

Senthree started to agree, a bit of a smile coming onto his face. It looked as if instinct were already in operation.

But a strange voice cut him off. "Hey, you robots. When do we eat around here?"

They could talk! It must have been the male. And if it wasn't the polite thanks and gratitude Senthree had expected, that didn't matter. There had been all kinds of Men in the books, and some were polite while others were crude. Perhaps forced education from the tapes without fuller social experience was responsible for that. But it would all adjust in time.

He started to turn back to Ceofor, but the younger robot was no longer there, and the screen looked out on a blank wall. Senthree could hear the loud voice crying out again, rough and harsh, and there was a shrill, whining sound that might be the female. The two voices blended with the vague mutter of robot voices until he could not make out the words.

He wasted no time in trying. He was already out in the street and heading toward the labs. Instinct—the male had already shown instinct, and the female had responded. They would have to be slow with the couple at first, of course—but the whole answer to the robot problem lay at hand. It would only take a little time and patience now. Let Arpeten sneer, and let the world dote on the Arcturus explorers. Today, biochemistry had been crowned king with the magic of intelligence combined with instinct as its power.

Ceofor came out of the lab at a run with another robot behind him. The young robot looked dazed, and there was another emotion Senthree could not place. The older biochemist nodded, and the younger one waved quickly. "Can't stop now. They're hungry." He was gone at full speed.

Senthree realized suddenly that no adequate supply of fruit and vegetables had been provided, and he hadn't even known how often Man had to eat. Or exactly what. Luckily, Ceofor was taking care of that.

He went down the hall, hearing a tumult of voices, with robots apparently spread about on various kinds of hasty business. The main lab where the couple was seemed quiet. Senthree hesitated at the door, wondering how to address them. There must be no questioning now. Today he would not force himself on them, nor expect them to understand his purposes. He must welcome them and make them feel at ease in this world, so strange to them with their prehistoric tape education. It would be hard at first to adjust to a world of only robots, with no other Man people. The matter of instinct that had taken so long could wait a few days more.

The door opened in front of him and he stepped into the lab, his eyes turning to the low table where they sat. They looked healthy, and there was no sign of misery or uncertainty that he could see, though he could not be sure of that until he knew them better. He could not even be sure it was a scowl on the male's face as the Man turned and looked at him.

"Another one, eh? O.K., come up here. What you want?"

Then Senthree no longer wondered how to address the Man. He bowed low as he approached them, and instinct made his voice low and apologetic as he answered.

"Nothing, Master. Only to serve you."

He waited expectantly.